T [illegible]d

David McLean

The Wolf in the Blood by David McLean

Published by Swordsaint Press®

Email: publisher@swordsaintpress.co.uk

Swordsaint Press does not accept submissions.

First published in Great Britain 2018

ISBN (ebook): 978-1-9164366-0-2

ISBN (paperback): 978-1-9164366-1-9

Cover photo credit: andamanec/shutterstock.com. Used under licence.

Contents

Epigraph

起死回生

Wake from death, and return to life.

Japanese proverb

Prologue: 1981

In the August before her twelfth birthday Blix Summerland won a phone-in contest on her local radio station. The prize was a trip to London for the whole family, to visit the zoo in Regent's Park. The schools were out and Blix's parents were getting on, so the family made a trip of it.

It was the first time in London for Blix and her twin sister, Katy. London, from their perspective, was another world - a faraway place where things happened. Nothing ever happened in the North.

The day lived in her memory. They got the train down and stayed over in a hotel the night before. In the morning, they got up early and did some sightseeing - Buckingham Palace, Trafalgar Square, the Houses of Parliament - the usual landmarks, which Blix hadn't realised were within short walking distance of each other. Further downriver they saw Tower Bridge, then visited the Tower of London. They met some Beefeaters, saw the ravens and climbed the walls, because that's what you did at the Tower of London and they'd never been before.

They went into the jewel room, after standing forever in an enormously long queue. The crowns of state were pretty and seeing the Koh-i-Noor was cool, but the gold plate was underwhelming. It looked sad and cold and dull. Blix wasn't the kind of girl who played princesses and couldn't imagine herself using such things. There were a few jewels that the signs claimed had once been magical, but all that nonsense was in the distant past. Blix wasn't the kind of girl who played magicians either.

The zoo was much more Blix's thing. The prize included a personal tour guide for the whole afternoon. Just a student zookeeper, who seemed more interested in the fact that Blix and Katy were identical twins than in the animals she was showing them, but Blix learned a lot.

They had lions and bears, great apes and monkeys. They had African and Asian elephants, Bengal tigers and Hyrcanian tygers, and a pool of hippos which obligingly gaped their jaws wide as she stared at them, their yellow tusks giving ample evidence for the guide's claim that they were the most dangerous animal in Africa. There was a small herd of bonnacon which you were only allowed to see from a distance behind a tall glass screen. They could spray their dung for a dozen or more yards and it was like acid on human skin. They were in a big enclosure with the Indian rhinos, imperious militant unicorns for whom acid poo was a matter of no concern.

They had a Catalan drac, a species related to classical dragons. It turned out to be tiny, the size of her arm. It scudded back and forth in its bathing pool, singeing unwary fish. Much more interesting were the Komodo dragons, which stalked regally through their enclosure as though the glass was the only thing separating them from world domination. She'd also liked the meerkats, although it was a bit disconcerting the way they watched you and squeaked all the time. She thought they were talking about her. Her mother had told her not to be silly. Blix didn't see why that was silly and said so, so they had a row.

There was a special behind-the-scenes bit at the end of the tour, only for the competition winner. Katy, not at all jealous, disappeared with Dad to find an ice-cream. Blix and her mother were taken to the animal hospital. Mum decided to have a smoke; Blix went in by herself.

With Blix watching, the head vet sedated one of the gryphons, so he could extract a broken blood feather which had become infected. When the beast was asleep he allowed her to touch it. It was wonderful. She'd expected it to be majestic and terrible and gigantic, and it was. But she hadn't expected it to be so soft. From a distance the feathers looked a bit grubby. The gryphon was moulting and was getting on a bit. Up close though they were beautiful. Iridescent and almost dazzling as the afternoon sunlight coming through the window played across its chest.

Blix ran her fingers through them, brushing the vanes and sliding her fingers into the downy afterfeathers. She followed the line of rich blue amid the rusty brown from the gryphon's beak down to the tip of each wing. She traced the contour where the feathers gave way to fur as the eagle merged with the lion. She put her head on its chest and rose and fell with each breath.

'Beautiful, isn't she?' said the vet. He was an old man, maybe as old as sixty, with a bald head and a grey beard worn without a moustache. His hands were huge and covered with old scars and healed bite marks. He had a kind face and spoke in a light, reassuring Irish accent.

Blix nodded, her face buried in fur, lost in wonder.

'Isn't she just,' continued the vet, giving the sleeping animal an affectionate thump on its flank. 'I'll miss her when she's gone.'

Blix jerked upright. 'Gone? She's not ill, is she?'

'No,' said the vet, 'just old. Older than me. Her and the old boy, they're the last. The last two gryphons in the world. Got another few years in 'em maybe, but once they're gone, that's it. That'll be a sad day.'

This made Blix sad too, but it also made her think.

'I thought you could make more,' she said. 'Like, get a lion and an eagle and, um.' She stopped, not quite sure of the mechanics.

The vet shook his head. 'You could, but we won't.'

'Why not? Otherwise they'll be... extinct? Is that the word?'

The vet smiled. 'Yes, that's right. We won't because it's cruel.' He rubbed the gryphon again, and it stirred. 'This old girl, she's a proper gryphon. They look like half an eagle and half a lion but they're not. They're gryphons, *Gryphus gryphus*, a true liminal species. They evolved this way. The other kind, the griffins... You can make 'em, if you have the right animals, but they have problems. They aren't happy.'

Blix saw the look on his face and decided not to ask why griffins weren't happy or what their problems were. Instead she said, 'Why aren't there more real gryphons?'

The vet stroked his beard, thinking with his fingers. 'There weren't ever many. Hunted, until the ban. And all magical creatures are in severe decline now that there isn't magic anymore. My old grand-dad, he was born in eighteen seventy, he saw proper magic. He used to tell me stories about the great magical creatures. The ones that died.' His eyes went far away for a moment as he remembered. 'He was a good storyteller. That's why I became a vet, I suppose.' He patted the gryphon.

'It's a shame there's no more magic,' said Blix, examining the gryphon's beak as closely as she dared.

'Is it? I suppose so, in some ways. I would have liked to have seen a real unicorn. But mostly, it's for the best. Sixty-five years since it stopped working and we're only just beginning to trust each other. The old days weren't-'

There was a sharp rapping sound. Blix's mum peered around the door. She tapped on her watch.

'Amelia.'

Blix scowled. 'Blix. In a minute.'

'The train won't wait, Amelia.'

'*Blix.*'

Her mum sighed, and retreated.

The vet smiled, and raised an eyebrow. 'Blix?'

'*Yes.*'

'Mmm.' The vet teased a stray feather back into place. 'That doesn't sound like a girl's name.'

'It's not a girl's name. Or a boy's name. It's *my* name. One I chose for myself.'

'Mmm.' The vet stroked his beard again. 'Everyone should be who they are,' he said. 'Or someone, anyway. It's a good name. Names have power. Well. It's time to go, Blix.'

Blix didn't want to let go of the gryphon in case it died there and then. 'Are you sure these are the last?' she said. 'Maybe there are more we just haven't found, like in Africa or somewhere?'

The vet smiled his kind, sad smile. 'There might be,' he said. 'Not in Africa, but where they came from. The other world. But we can't go there anymore, so we'll never know.'

Blix's mother tapped on the door again.

'It's time to go,' said the vet again. He saw that Blix had her hand on the gryphon's talons. 'Do you know what they're made of?' he asked.

Blix looked down. She hadn't realised she was clutching the bird-like front feet. She shook her head.

'Keratin. Same as your fingernails, more or less.'

Blix looked down again. She touched the talons on the gryphon's front legs and the lion claws on its rear legs; they looked different, but felt the same. She stared at her fingernails, right up close. Then she looked back at the vet and said, 'How do I get to do what you do?'

Chapter One: The First of Wolves

The First of Wolves stood at the forest edge, waiting for the moon. Behind him his soldiers, naked and hairy, crowded together in the darkness, hungry for blood. They had run all day but still weren't tired. He could smell their eagerness, rising from them with the steam from their sweat, condensing in the winter air.

Ahead, the trees gave out to scrubland as the slope rose into the mountains. Snow covered the ground. Beneath that the hard earth turned to rock as the way steepened. Patches of ice and loose shale made each step treacherous. Huge boulders clustered on the high ground, tens and hundreds of feet high. Yet they were nothing compared to the sheer wall of rock that thrust out of the scree ahead of them, the heights invisible, dominating the land around it, threatening like the clenched fist of the earth.

Men called it the Anvil. It looked like one from a certain angle, a plateau narrowing to an overhanging point at one end. Men said that it was so-called because armies could hammer themselves against it and it would never break. A man at the top would never know that his enemies below cursed his name, for they would never reach him, and he would never hear them.

Two thirds of the way to the summit on the far side of the Anvil from where the First of Wolves stood, a clutch of buildings clung to the rock face. The First of Wolves had seen this. Dozens of buildings, constructed where the rock allowed. They snaked in a broken line across the south face of the escarpment. Bridges of rope and stone linked them, and steps cut into the rock, and tunnels cut through it. This was the Monastery. There were other places where monks dwelled but when men capitalized the word, this was where they meant.

The First of Wolves had heard men speak of the Monastery. All men agreed it was impregnable. Its ancient builders had climbed as high as they could, built into the living rock and pulled up the ladders behind them. The only way up was in a basket, a crude elevator which hung near the Anvil's point, lowered from there into the town at the base of the mountain.

Far beyond where the First of Wolves stood was a torch-lined road. It led from the lake villages far to the south to the small, fortified settlement at the foot of the Anvil's point. That guarded the Monastery's life-line to the outside world. The name of the town was Forge. Men had told the First of Wolves that this name was a joke.

Men had told him the way of things on the road. Ponderous yak-carts laden with tithed provisions creaked up to the town each day. They returned with prayer wheels, icons, blessings and banners made by the monks. Pilgrims walked the road, to pray at the shrines at the foot of the Anvil and convey their written supplication skyward. And every so often, so the men had told him, one who felt the call of faith came to the Anvil, climbed into a basket, and waited. They always had to wait; three days, to see if they were sure. Men called it 'climbing the Anvil' and that was a joke as well, because no one could climb the Anvil. And if they remained, then on the third day they ascended, never to return. As all men knew, no man who set foot in the Monastery was ever allowed to leave it, alive or dead - except just once, for one special task. There was one way up, and no way down.

The First of Wolves remembered the men who had told him these things, and what it had felt like when he'd killed them.

One way up, no way down. All men knew. *But I am not a man. I know another way.*

He stepped back into the trees. As he did so he brushed against a low branch, which snapped near the trunk. He knelt and examined the break. Reddish-brown flakes crusted the limb. As he touched them the wood beneath crumbled away.

It is here. Death precedes us, awaiting our arrival.

The First of Wolves wore a pouch around his neck. He kept small things in it which mattered to him. A stone from the first place of his pack. A tooth from his first kill. Hair from his dead mate. He often touched it when he felt unsure, or unhappy. He touched it now.

Wolves do not have keepsakes, he thought. *Wolves do not feel uncertain. Why am I different?*

'A question many men ask themselves,' said the man next to him. 'I am not sure there is a satisfactory answer. I have yet to discover one, certainly.'

'... I said that in my mind,' the First of Wolves replied, confusion evident on his face. 'How -'

'Don't give it a thought,' said the man warmly, and the First of Wolves did not give it a thought.

'I must say this is all rather pleasing,' said the man next to him. 'Do you know, I had never seen the lupine transformation before our association began? Of a pure blood Were that is, I have observed transmitted lycanthropy many times. Your species is no longer native to where I'm from. It has been most interesting. I may publish.'

The First of Wolves ignored him, turning the broken limb in his paw-like hands.

The man continued. 'One understands these things from an academic perspective, yet it's much more visceral in the flesh. So to speak. One forgets that genuine werewolves are not wolves or men, but rather something far more ancient and primal.'

He clapped his hands together and blew on them against the cold, then smoothed his moustache with the end of a finger. He took a pair of grey gloves from his pocket and pulled them on. Then he peered over the First of Wolves' shoulder at the broken branch.

'Have you an interest in matters arboreal, First of Wolves? I have seen some excellent specimens in my time. I lived in a kapok tree for a while, for research purposes you understand. The locals weren't happy about that for some reason, but I -'

'Save your words, magician,' growled the First of Wolves, irritated by the chatter. He discarded the branch and stood up. The man inclined his head in polite acquiescence.

The First of Wolves wasn't used to the company of humans who were not bleeding. Lately this had changed. He didn't like it. They talked without end, but only with their mouths. The wordless words of posture and scent that were the first language of werewolves meant nothing to them. They were unpredictable and bared their teeth when they were being pleasant in a way that made the First of Wolves want to attack them. And they smelled wrong. They smelled of the other animals they wore.

The man pulled his long black coat closer to him, and adjusted his tall hat into the wind. He smiled at the werewolf, who flexed his claws.

Behind him his soldiers grew restless. Or some of them did. The wolves of the Old Pack, the grey-pelt veterans who'd been born and grown with the First of Wolves, saved their energy. They knew what was coming. Wolves died, this was natural in life and in war and wolves did not mourn for long. But with each death the Old Pack diminished, and this was a sorrow beyond words.

Then there were the others. The New. Pelts as black as night without the moon. The coat of a cub, though most of them were not cubs. Some marked territory and squabbled among themselves like puppies. Some of them stared at the man at his side, hunger in their eyes. One or two made little surging half-steps toward him, working themselves up to attack. The First of Wolves snarled a warning, and they subsided.

They are an abomination. I am the only one who sees this. But they are necessary, thought the First of Wolves. *We must survive. We must Be.*

'Well, we must all do what we think we must, mustn't we?' said the man. 'Story of my life.'

'... what did you say?'

'Oh, I said nothing worth remembering,' said the man, and the First of Wolves did not remember it.

He found himself looking at the man, and considered him as he would any foe. The contrast between them was stark. The man was right. Werewolves of his kind were not one species which became another but a whole creature made in two halves. As men, their piercing amber eyes, muzzle-like jaws and pelt of hair were only the most visible aspects of their otherness. Humans found their man-shapes alien and terrifying to look at, even those they were not eviscerating at the time.

Most humans. This one viewed him with amiable curiosity, as though hell-born killing machines were a matter of no moment. His manner was that of a man with no cares, for whom everything came with ease, of a man used to being served by others. A soft man. The First of Wolves was not fooled by this pose. No one trifled with the magician and lived.

An arc of white light heralded moon-rise. The First of Wolves felt the beast stir within him and embraced it, let its power surge through him. He felt his bones pop and crack as they lengthened and deformed, the pain nothing compared to the fierce joy the change brought him. In moments, the mask of humanity sloughed off him, leaving the animal exposed. His pack howled as the change consumed them.

Their call echoed across the mountain. Villages barred their gates and men strapped on armour at the slightest wolf-sound, the First of Wolves knew. The town of Forge would summon all mendicants and traders within its great eye door, bar the way and imagine itself secure. But on the unscalable mountain, the monks would not even stir for something so far below. The First of Wolves joined the howling.

'Tremendous,' said the man, careless of the First of Wolves' warning. 'If I only had my heliogravure. Alas, it does not travel well.'

Clouds scudded across the moon. As it did the First of Wolves felt the wolf begin to leave him, his howl turning into a strangled shout. He was almost a man again before it reappeared. He felt the familiar surge and was wolfish again in seconds.

'Remarkable,' said the man, staring at him with genuine interest. 'Responsive to effulgence to an extraordinary degree. I did not know that. A novel experience! I am grateful.' He leaned forward. 'What does it feel like?'

'Like breathing.'

'I see. An autonomic process, then. A natural function. Intriguing. And the cycle of the moon? It is full this night, is that required?'

'We are the sons of the moon,' said the First of Wolves. 'The wolf walks in his sight, no matter how bright his eye. I feel him beyond the horizon. He pulls the wolf free. We wax and wane with him.'

He wondered why he was talking so much. Something about the man's interest in him made him want to talk. It seemed unnatural, somehow.

'Don't worry about that,' said the man, and the First of Wolves did not worry about it. 'You describe it with poetry, my dear First! I translate that to mean you change during any phase of the moon save full dark. Change for as long as moonlight is upon you. But you are less wolfy, perhaps, under the crescent or gibbous moons. Fascinating. It is different with created werewolves. They change only at full moon, and they remain transformed from moonrise to moonset, you know.'

The First of Wolves remained silent. The man mused on the subject for a moment. 'I am impressed beyond words by your transformation. It is, though, a little less, ah, full-bodied, perhaps, than that of lycanthropes-by-infection. I suppose the step from man-wolf to wolf-man is less dramatic than that from man to werewolf. Tell me, do you feel they have an advantage over you?'

'They are mindless,' said the First of Wolves. Human words were harder to speak now; his elongated jaw strangled the sounds. 'They are beasts. They are a disease we carry. We are a people.'

'There is that. And in transmitted lycanthropy the change is a catastrophic physical insult. Many don't survive the first.'

'Our blessing is their curse,' said the First of Wolves.

'Indeed. But those who do are healed and reborn! It is a matter of great interest to me. There is much to study. I may publish. But listen to me prattle on! We must prosecute our affairs!'

He turned to look at the mountainside. It loomed.

'Men can't climb the Anvil.'

'No.'

'But you can. Powerful leaps and bounds. Claws gripping hidden crevices and disguised footholds. Crannies, and the like.'

The First of Wolves nodded. 'Where you said.'

'Yes. Where I said. Where the moonflowers grow. There is a way.' The man sounded like he was saying another's words.

He pointed. The First of Wolves peered into the darkness. Here and there on the wall of rock he saw a twinkle of reflected light as the flowers unfurled to meet the moon. The twinkles were few and far apart.

'Yes,' the First of Wolves agreed. 'There is a way.'

'Hmm.' The man cocked an eye skyward. 'Windy tonight.'

'Yes.'

'Lots of cloud in the sky.'

'Yes.'

'So, you'll be men as you climb, I think. Some of the time.'

'Yes.'

'But men can't climb the Anvil.'

The First of Wolves turned to look at his soldiers. 'Some will fall.'

'I suppose so. Still, who wants to live forever, eh?' The man laughed a little, as though he had made a witticism. The First of Wolves did not see the joke but considered the remark nonetheless.

'Not I,' he allowed. 'But for my natural years, yes.'

'You are wise, First of Wolves. Wiser than you know.'

'Am I?' He looked again at the werewolves behind him, now as transformed as he. 'How many of these will I lead to their deaths this night?' he said, almost to himself.

Then he shook his head. *Why am I thinking like this?*

'Again, do not let it concern you,' said the man, and the First of Wolves was not concerned by it. 'But is there something in particular which moves you to emotion? Perhaps an undisclosed connection?'

The First of Wolves extended a finger, pointing toward a clutch of werewolves some distance into the trees. 'My cub is among these. My only seed. I would not see him die.'

'Ah!' The man clasped his hands together. 'The pathos! Who knew werewolves were capable of it?'

The First of Wolves looked the man squarely in the eye. 'We are not,' he said evenly. 'I am different.'

'Indeed you are, my dear First of Wolves. Remarkable. I may get a book out of it. Just point him out for me, would you?'

Wordlessly, the First of Wolves singled out a particularly boisterous werewolf. Black haired and barely out of adolescence, it was mock-fighting with another. The man nodded. 'A fine specimen. You can be proud, I assume. You can always leave him behind, if you wish your line to continue.'

The First of Wolves snarled. 'And shame him? The pack would cast him out. Then he would turn on me and try to kill me for it. Then I would kill him. Better he dies a wolf, if he must die. He is no coward.'

'How could he be, with such a sire?' said the man. 'Thank you, my dear First of Wolves, for this diverting conversation. You have taught me things I did not know. I live for such moments. Now, forget about all that,' he continued, and the First of Wolves forgot. 'You know your business?'

Anger surged through the werewolf. 'You come late to this to ask such questions. We have fought this war since before I was whelped. This is the Wolf Age. Our hour is now.'

The man smiled, a broad open grin. 'I do so admire men of purpose, First of Wolves. It is often the way with military men, I find.'

The First of Wolves snarled and looked away.

'But there is another matter?' the man prompted.

'Yes. You want the rock.'

'The bloodstone. You know what it looks like and where it is. You will not please me with some precious pebble you find on the mountain.'

'You will have it,' said the werewolf.

'Excellent. And you will remember to leave my little calling card?'

The First of Wolves nodded. 'The fire will go out. But we will take some bodies for our own purposes. Living ones.'

The man waved this away as though it were a trifle. 'Kill enough that the point is made. And the boy?'

'No promises,' said the First of Wolves. 'There will be hell. If the boy finds the end of a sword, or some teeth -'

'I understand. But you must understand the consequences if he does. It would be inconvenient. Vexing. I would be unhappy. You would share in my unhappiness.'

The First of Wolves snarled once more, contempt in his tone. 'And what would you do, magician? Kill me? I do not die so easily.'

The man smiled again, but there was no humour in it.

'I would exterminate your species,' he said.

The icy conviction in the man's voice struck the First of Wolves like a blow in the guts and he took an involuntary step backwards. He saw the certainty in the man's eyes. He knew he was telling the absolute truth, though he did not know how he knew. Sudden terror gripped him.

'We won't harm the boy,' he said after a time.

The man smiled again. 'Good dog.'

The rage rose like burning bile in the First of Wolves' throat, curling around his fear like a vast serpent and crushing it. He howled, and the pack howled with him. An outburst of anger and resentment and wrath rang through the mountains like the clarion of Death itself. The man covered his ears until the last echo faded.

The First of Wolves step in close to the man, until they were almost nose to nose. 'To hell with you, conjurer. I'd decorate these branches with your entrails if I had my way.'

The First of Wolves' hot breath billowed in the man's face. He looked discomfited, but unafraid.

'But you will not,' he said, his voice mild.

'The Wolfmaker commands that I obey you. I obey you. But your time will come.'

The man burst out laughing at the threat and for a moment the First of Wolves thought he had gone too far. But the man seemed amused. 'I hope so, First of Wolves,' he said. 'I do. That is rather the point of all this, after all. But it will not be this night.'

'No,' said the First of Wolves, stepping away. 'Tonight, we climb. Stay out of our way, Dragonville.'

Belmont Dragonville smiled again, and bowed. 'By all means, proceed,' he said.

In the deep forest, unseen by wolves or man, another watched.

'I can't help you,' he whispered. 'I'm sorry. Forgive me.'

Chapter Two: The Boy

Constant knelt on his prayer mat and shifted his weight until he was comfortable. He tried to clear his mind.

It had been a bad day. The news from the far south was bleak. The Bastion had fallen. Wolves roamed the southland, raping and slaughtering at will. None could stand against them. A few survivors had fled but there wasn't much for them to flee to. The land around the Bastion was hard country.

Constant wanted to do something, but there was nothing he could do. The worst thing was that everyone looked at him as if he had all the answers. He had ordered prayers said and bells struck for the people of the Bastion. The wheels turned and the monks chanted. Constant tried not to think about what the Bastion falling meant for humans, but he knew without thinking about it. There were no more cities to fall.

Prayers were always said.

On the floor in front of him there was a small metal bowl half-filled with water, a fire steel and tinder, and a thin yellow candle, tallow spitting as the flame danced around the wick.

Constant took a deep breath and steeled himself for what was to come. In his mind, he said his words.

I am myself

I am alone but not alone

I know my own mind.

Over and over he said them, until the familiar sense of calm flowed through him. He lowered himself into a half bow and held his arms out sideways in supplication. He counted in his head, eleven times to eleven, focusing on each number as he thought it, slowly emptying his head of all other thoughts. When he was ready he blew out the candle and began the prayer.

'Light in the darkness, he began. The chorus of voices rose in his head immediately, drowning out his own voice. The noise was painful.

Light in the darkness

possessed of infinite compassion

consumed by unimaginable wisdom

I honour you with my being.

Heart of existence

embodying indescribable nobility

exemplifying purity and virtue

I worship you with my existence.
Flame of the universe
eternal selfless benefactor
unflinching guardian visionary
I subsume myself into your completeness.

Constant struck the steel until sparks had caught in the tinder, then nursed the flame until he could re-light the candle.

I embrace the pure light of your perfection.

The voices ended with the prayer. Constant realised he'd been gritting his teeth. He touched his fingers in the water and then to his forehead. Then he tidied everything away and got ready for bed, the ringing in his ears subsiding.

Constant was not enjoying reincarnation this time around. He wondered sometimes whether any of his predecessors had.

Most of the time he wasn't aware of it. Most of the time he didn't feel like he'd ever been someone else. He wasn't some ancient monk looking out from inside a boy's skin, an image he still found creepy and wished he'd never thought of. Constant was Constant, and always had been.

Except sometimes he remembered being someone else. And quite often he found himself knowing things he didn't know, and feeling things he could not have felt. Like what it felt like to fight in a war, or to make love, or to be old, or to be woman.

That one had been fleeting, but alarming. No one had told him one of his predecessors had been female. The Great Record made no mention of it. Brother Simon had said that meant it was so long ago it was before the founding of the Faith. One of the Unnamed who did not know they were reincarnates, who were never Recognised.

Constant was twelve years old. His memory was four thousand years older.

Brother Simon had taught him the importance of maintaining composure and a detached perspective. It was a lesson he had come to appreciate. It was Simon who had taught him the words. Some words that calmed turbulent thoughts and distracted the user from their concerns. A tiny incantation, the only magic he was allowed to learn and the only magic which worked on the Anvil. One of the few bits of magic which still worked anywhere, according to Brother Simon. Not that Constant could go and check this for himself.

Ritual brought the old priests out. Whenever he did something which his predecessors had also done, he felt them. The Night Prayer was the worst. Most of them had said it every evening for their entire lives. When he spoke it the memory of their voices was so loud they might as well have been in the room, a chorus of intoners six dozen strong raising their voices as one. Brother Simon assured him it would get better as he grew older. Constant couldn't wait.

One of the side effects of reincarnation, he'd discovered, was a strong need to be alone and enclosed. There was a suite of rooms in the temple which belonged to him. There was a big bed and servants to look after his needs. Huge windows opened to the sky, looking south over the Path of Fire and the endless green of the great forest. Constant didn't like it. He felt exposed. Brother Simon had suggested he try one of the old novice cells deep in the mountain. They had no windows and no sky. That felt safe. He'd moved in as soon as he could.

He'd felt good about that decision. Then Brother Simon had told him that making the suggestion was one of the tasks appointed to him in the Tutor's Book. The book was almost four thousand years old and described in fine detail exactly what a reincarnate needed to learn. A desire to hide under a billion tons of rock was common among his predecessors, it seemed. That made Constant even less sure that he was thinking his own thoughts.

An advantage of the cells was that they were far away from any wide-eyed and adoring monks. Constant felt thankful for and guilty about this. He saw them often enough, in the rituals that marked his day. They treated him like he would shatter like egg shell if they got too close.

'You have to be who you are,' Brother Simon said often. 'You don't have to let it rule you.'

Constant hadn't read the Tutor's Book. He wasn't supposed to. He wondered sometimes whether it set out what kind of man the Tutor should be. He hoped so. He wanted to believe that one of his predecessors had thought about the qualities a Tutor needed and had decided that kindness, good humour and strength of character were high on the list. If it was just luck that Brother Simon was like that, then he might not be so lucky next time around.

'How much of me is me?' Constant had asked once, when he was much younger.

'You always say this,' Brother Simon had replied. His voice was reassuring. 'Each incarnation feels the same. It gets better. Each one of them was their own person. You know this. You can feel them. You are too. You have to be who you are. You don't have to let it rule you.'

You will not rule me. He stripped down to his breechcloth and rolled into his cot. He snuffed the candle, closed his eyes and tried to forget the past.

Constant dreamed.

In my dream, I am asleep by the seashore. I am dreaming I am a sparrow, darting from tree to tree, turning with the slightest wing beat, a thought of a bird in this dream within a dream. I throw my wings back, catch a branch in the curl of my claw, pause, and throw myself once more into the sky. I swoop through the forest, tumbling, rolling, a joyful staccato popping in my breast. Then I burst through the canopy and I am on the shore, the surf breaking hard against the rocks, the sea raging at the land. I alight on a rock and I wake up and I am boy again, no more than four years old. I wipe the sleep from my eyes and behind me I hear my father, that shining man, cry 'Dive little sparrow! Dive into the ocean!' And without turning to see him I dive deep, as deep as I can, because this is the game that we play together. The current pulls me down but I am a strong swimmer and I know that I am safe because my father is here. I touch the sand, push my fingers into the cold grit, turn and push up. As I reach the surface I see him through the water waiting for me, and as I breach he grabs me by the shoulders and pulls me to his chest in one motion. We are laughing and I am happy because he is my father and we are together and I love him.

Two men walk along the beach towards us. They wear shabby red robes and their heads are shaved. They are still some way off when they Recognise me. I start to cry, although I do not know why - but then I do know. I am crying because I have been found. I am crying because I have lost everything.

Now there is a boy here I do not recognise.

'Wake up right now,' *says the boy.* 'Wake up or we're going to die.'

Constant did not remember the boy when he woke up.

There was blood on Constant's face. He knew immediately it wasn't his.

Brother Simon stood over his cot. A deep gash had opened the left side of his face from scalp to chin. Blood seeped from the wound. He held a sword in his hand, wet and red. Beneath the blood, the edge shone silver.

'Wolves. Wolves in our house. They're at the Fourth Temple. You must go.' He thrust a long bundle into Constant's arms, rough cloth bound with rope, surrounding something hard. Constant felt the shape and knew what it was. The hilt of a sword protruded from one end.

'Come,' said Brother Simon. 'Come now.'

A strange separation occurred in Constant's mind. A corner of it started sobbing in fear. That part wanted Brother Simon to tell him everything would be okay. But the greater part, the part which took control of his body and propelled him out of his bed, was calm, collected, and older. But he still felt like himself. That was important.

He found some knee-breeches and pulled them on. Since moving into the mountain he'd taken to wearing a novice's short, red, hooded robe over a loose shirt, because they were warm. He shrugged into both.

'You're wounded?' he said, as he pulled the robe over his head.

'A few cuts,' said Simon. 'Nothing serious.'

Constant felt the lie more than he heard it. A blood flower bloomed at Brother Simon's side, soaking through his red robe. A wolf had stabbed or slashed him. It was bad. But he was upright, he was alive.

'What of the brothers?' Constant asked, pulling on his boots.

'Each brother now living stands between them and you. They fight. They're dying. We must go now.'

'Go where? If the wolves are in the fourth temple we're cut off. We can't reach the Sanctum or the Hall of Swords. We're cut off from the map room too. The novice cells aren't defensible. There's only the deep tunnels and the kitchens beyond here and they're dead ends.'

'You have to get off the Anvil.'

'We can't get to the basket either.'

'There's a way,' said Simon, his voice thick with pain. Constant noticed he was swaying and put out a hand to steady him, but Brother Simon brushed it away.

'There's no other way off the Anvil,' Constant objected.

'There's a way to the basket. Come with me.' Simon grabbed his arm and half-dragged Constant from his cell.

They stumbled down the ill-lit corridor further into the mountain. Constant could hear furious howls and the clang of steel echoing along the tunnels. A battle raged. It was close.

Simon led him deeper still into the mountain, until Constant was sure he was taking him to some hidden chamber or secret tunnel. But they turned and headed back upward. Before long they were in the kitchens. The doors were massive, Constant noticed, as Simon swung them closed and pulled a sturdy bar across them. Much thicker than a kitchen needed.

Simon caught his gaze. 'That won't hold for long,' he said.

Near the ceiling a deep shaft bored upwards at a sharp angle through the rock to the outside, letting in air and, in theory, light. A long ladder stood next to it. Constant thought he knew the plan then and headed toward it, but Brother Simon shook his head.

'No, that leads nowhere but sheer mountainside. This way.' He pointed to the chimney.

Constant peered up into the opening. Beyond the great spit and turning chains there was nothing but blackness.

Simon was filling a shoulder bag with food. Rummaging through drawers, he found some candles and a fire steel and shoved them in too.

'You can't show a light at first, they'll see it from below,' he said. 'You'll have to feel for the holds. They are uneven, could be on any wall. There's no time to show you. They are quite shallow. Test each before you move to the next. Brush out the dust. Brace yourself against the opposite wall when you change position.'

'Are you sure about this?'

'The first brothers were not fools,' said Simon. His breathing was becoming laboured. 'We have a Hall of Swords for a reason. We have an escape route for the same reason.'

'None of the brothers has ever spoken of this.'

'The brothers do not know. I know because it is my duty to know.'

'That makes no sense. What possible reason could there be for keeping this from... Oh.'

Simon nodded. 'This way is not meant for the brothers. It is for you. It is the reason we steer you to sleep in the novice cells. It is in the book.'

'Oh. Oh, of course it is,' said Constant, his voice bitter. He looked again into the hole, and sighed. 'How far must I climb?'

Simon tipped flour onto the table and began sketching in it.

'The chimney follows a natural crack in the rock. After a hundred cubits it turns to the right, almost horizontal. Go far along that tunnel. It rises toward the end. When you hit a wall, the next climb is above you. After another forty cubits, a tunnel branches off from the chimney on the opposite wall from the handholds. The air draws through it, feel for it, listen for it. If you climb past it you'll hit a dead end, so if you knock your head you've gone too far. it will be difficult to climb back down, so try not to miss it. Follow the tunnel until the end. It's low and narrow, you'll have to crawl. Rest and strike a light then, the wolves won't see it there. Don't rest long. The rest of the climb is straightforward.'

'How do you know all this?'

'I climbed it twenty years ago, when I began my training under the old Tutor. And again, last month, when the beasts burned New Amdo.'

'You're almost sixty!'

'It was a hard climb,' Brother Simon allowed.

Constant shook his head in disbelief. 'Where does it come out?'

'Almost at the plateau. There is a path of steps cut in the rock. Head for the point of the Anvil. To your left as the steps end. The way is dangerous and slippery. The basket winding mechanism is there, and steps leading down to the basket.'

'Then I have to lower myself down!' Constant almost screamed. 'It takes five men to wind the wheel! It's impossible!'

Simon shook his head. 'Not for you. Great Father, understand: this place is yours. Every stone and slate, every cut in the rock, the bridges and temples and paths, they all exist to keep you safe. For no other reason. The first brothers were not fools. Remember this, and live. There is old magic here, stored in the stone, which remains against need. The need is here.'

'I don't know anything about magic! You said the book said I wasn't allowed to learn magic. You said it never helps.'

'It will help you here.' Simon groaned suddenly, grabbed his stricken side, and went white. 'No, I yet live,' he said, as Constant moved to hold him. 'Listen. You can do magic here.'

Constant gaped stupidly. 'What? But… you said the stone only allowed the words!'

'That's what your words are, yes. But more, too.'

'How can -'

'The book says not to tell you. It is too dangerous. But the stone will respond to you. And you have been men who knew real magic. The Great Record says this.'

The revelation was like a blow. But Constant's mind moved quickly. 'They're all dead! *I* don't know spells, *I* don't know -'

Simon cut him off. 'There's no trick to magic. Spells are for frauds, mere show to fool the gullible. Say what you want to happen with the desire to make it so. That is magic. The rest is fakery. You know this. Remember.' He coughed suddenly and violently, and wiped away blood. 'On this mountain you do not need even that,' he continued. 'The magic here will know you. This was the First Father's gift. You just have to reach out with your mind. It will find you when you try. If you step into the basket, it will lower you down. Head to the Iris and away from here.'

'I just have to fight my way through an army of wolves to get there.'

'Yes.' Brother Simon smiled grimly at Constant's look of horror. 'I didn't say it was a great chance. It's just your only chance.'

'Where do I go then? I don't know anywhere but here!'

'There is one place you know.'

Constant swallowed hard. 'I don't... I mean, I was a baby, I've never... I don't know how!'

'You will.'

Constant scowled. 'You're asking me to take a lot on trust.'

'Yes. Do you trust me?'

'Yes,' said Constant immediately.

'And I you. You will survive. It is what you do best. And if not, your wheel will turn again.'

Constant steeled himself. 'Well then. I will go first, give me room before you start up. I will call where I find the holds.'

But Simon shook his head. 'You go,' he said. 'I will wait here a spell.'

Constant took a deep breath, and whatever was holding back his emotions gave way. He realised then that he was crying.

'You've got to come!' he said. 'I need you. You're my only friend. I love you.' He wrapped his arms around the old monk's chest, sobbing like a baby.

Simon pushed him away. 'Beloved son,' he said. 'Great Father. I will stay here. Werewolves can see in the dark. They can smell. They can climb. I will wait here, and discourage them.'

'They'll kill you!' Constant all but screamed.

Simon shrugged. 'I was a soldier before I was a monk. A good one. We'll see.'

He took Constant by the shoulders. 'Now listen. Wolves in the temple. Wolves everywhere. You know the Writing. This must be what it means. This is the start of it all. I am very sorry that this has fallen to you. You've done nothing to deserve it. But you must fulfil it. Or everything is lost. Everything.' His face twisted in agony and his weight pressed more heavily on Constant's shoulders. 'You can survive this,' he gasped.

'I can't!' Constant protested, tears beading in the corners of his eyes. 'I'm only twelve!'

'You are. And you must remember that. But you are older as well.' Brother Simon closed his eyes and Constant saw them moving rapidly under his lids as he searched his memory. He opened them again, or tried to; one eye stayed half closed.

'Look you. The Record tells us that seven hundred years ago, the fifty-eighth Great Father was not Recognised by the brethren until he was already a man. His name before then was Darcen Ysir. We have spoken of him. By then he was already a great warrior - one of the greatest ever, if you believe the histories. But not a good man. A bad man. It was a troubled time.'

He coughed up more blood, then continued.

'Think on him as you climb. Hear his voice. The warrior he was, not the monk he became. I know you don't like this but in some sense, you are him. Let his memories come forward. You have never learned to fight but it was meat and drink to him. Make his memory your own. You're going to need that when I am not there.'

Constant cried out as though he'd been struck. Simon placed his big calloused thumbs under Constant's eyes and wiped his tears away.

'Say the words, son,' he said. 'Feel this later, when you are safe. Say your words.'

Without thinking the incantation appeared in Constant's mind. He said the words, choking back his anguish. The familiar calm descended on him. The terrible hurt and grief he felt were still there. It seemed to him though that he had put it aside for a moment, safe and sound, to come back to after a time.

He gazed at Brother Simon, drinking in every detail of his face. Storing the sound of his voice, the way he moved and breathed, the light in his grey eyes. The blood on his hands. He tried to think of something to say, something which could convey the depth of his love for the only father he had ever known. He found himself saying the words of the Penance.

'For any hurt I have caused you, for any fault or sorrow, I ask forgiveness. My soul is yours.'

Simon closed his eyes and nodded a little. 'I forgive you, and your soul is your own. Go now, and know that you are loved.'

Both knew the meaning.

Constant strapped the long bundle across his back and threw the food bag over his shoulder. Then he kissed Simon hard on the cheek and ducked into the grate. Now that he knew they were there the first few footholds were visible, just, but they soon disappeared into darkness.

I hope one of you dead people was a mountaineer, he thought, and started to climb. He didn't look back.

Simon waited until he could no longer see the boy. He found a cask of spices and kicked it over, sending an earthily aromatic red powder into the air and masking Constant's scent. Then he dragged a heavy wooden chair across the room until it faced the doorway. He sat down hard, and as he did so tasted blood in his mouth again.

He knew death was beside him, waiting to take his hand. He'd spent his energy being strong for the boy. But perhaps there was a little left. Enough to give some werewolves pause.

There were noises in the corridor beyond. 'The wolf is at the door,' said Brother Simon, out loud. He felt light-headed. He laughed as the door split open. He raised his sword.

Chapter Three: 1986

Conversation stopped as Blix walked into the classroom. It was the Look, she told herself. The Look stopped them in their tracks. On the day 'Papa Don't Preach' came out Blix had walked into the hairdressers with the single cover and said, 'This.' She'd ditched her blazer for a high collared leather jacket and wore dark sunglasses even though it was November.

So, it was the Look. Partly it was the Look. It was the other thing too, of course. Partly the other thing.

'Dyke,' said a girl, under her breath. There was laughter from some kids nearby. The boy next to her snorted.

Blix stopped dead and turned on the girl. *Lisa Taylor, ugh.* She pushed her sunglasses down her nose and looked over them.

'Yes,' she said. 'What of it?'

The girl stuck her tongue in the V of her fingers and licked up and down. More laughter. She was braver than most. Blix was a known quantity in matters of violent retribution.

Showing off for the boy. What's his name? Mark something. Mark Unbearable. Don't bite. That's not who you are.

'Pfft,' she said, with a dismissive wave. 'That's not how it's done. You'll learn,' she added with a sly glance.

The girl looked angry. 'You dirty lezzer,' said the boy.

'Tell it to the finger,' said Blix, raising a middle one.

She ignored the expletives that followed and took her seat, reminded once again of her place in the school pecking order.

Her last essay paper was waiting for her. Mr Leicester had scrawled in the margin in bold red pen. *D minus. See me.*

'Bugger,' said Blix, slumping in her chair.

A ball of paper sailed over her shoulder and landed on her desk. She grabbed it before it skidded off and un-scrunched it, to reveal a crude drawing of something entirely obvious. Undertaken by circus-level contortionists, by the look of it. There were boyish giggles behind her.

'Well, that doesn't look like it would be any fun at all,' she said without looking around. 'And I'm blonde, dickhead.'

She crumpled it up again and hurled it toward the bin at the front of the room. It rolled around the rim and disappeared under the teacher's desk.

Before she could retrieve it, Mr Leicester arrived. Late and awkward, all knees and elbows, jerking like a mechanical spider. A distinct smell, like mothballs, wafted across the room ahead of him.

He screwed himself into his chair and called the class to order, without much success. Then he noticed the ball of paper, wrapped his long fingers around it and hoicked it up, and unfurled it. He regarded it for a moment then, to Blix's disgust, gave her a brief glance.

Blix was beginning to detest him.

Blix Summerland was just seventeen and bored, bored, bored.

The answer to the question "how do you get to do what a veterinarian of gryphons does" had turned out to involve a lot. Knowing things and passing exams and spending five years at university, for a start. You had to get A's all the way if you wanted to do anything more interesting in your career than pushing your arm up a cow's bum.

This was a problem. Exams weren't Blix's strong suit. She was clever and independent and forthright and lots of other things that didn't make her good at exams. She hadn't taken the eleven plus. No one seemed to be in doubt what the result would have been if she had. Which was offensive, to Blix's mind. Her sister has sailed through, and consequently now went to The Grammar, half an hour's drive away somewhere leafier. Blix didn't blame Katy for this.

The Comp wasn't a bad school for a comprehensive. It could be irritating. They didn't expect anything of her. Once, she'd told her year head what she wanted to be when she grew up. The old dear had tousled her hair and asked, wouldn't she prefer learning to type instead? Later she'd overheard the teacher sharing the joke with a colleague. They'd both laughed.

Blix wasn't stupid and didn't like it that they thought she was. She'd stomped off in a foul mood and had a cry in the toilets.

Katy was the smart girl. Blix was the other one. That was decided.

Blix had decided to undecide it. She couldn't imagine doing anything else with her life. She didn't want to end up sitting in a typing pool, or behind a till, or on the packing line at a factory, or on the dole, which seemed to exhaust the acceptable options for girls like her in a town like this. At least there was no chance of falling pregnant.

She'd read a lot in private, because doing it at school would have meant more abuse. She planned her O-level choices a year in advance. She did well enough in the pre-exams to get into the right sets for the subjects that mattered, while ignoring the rest. Natural Philosophy, and the other sciences, and some others to make up the numbers.

She'd loved Natural Philosophy. She'd learned lots of interesting things.

She'd learned that Persian chimeras were as dangerous as they were beautiful. The class had watched a documentary about them. The presenter had been bitten by the snake-headed tail of a new-born cub and his face had swollen up horribly. He'd laughed it off, somewhat unconvincingly to Blix's mind.

She'd learned far too much about the mating habits of the Russian common minotaur. That had been eye-opening in many alarming ways. There was a textbook you weren't allowed to read three chapters of if you were under sixteen, although she had anyway.

She'd learned the scientific name for the hydra, *Gigantophis lernaea.* Contrary to the general severe decline of liminal creatures, they were now endemic to the Florida everglades. Tourists were going on airboat excursions to hunt them, seven heads mounted on a wall being better than one. This often resulted in nature selecting against the tourists, which seemed only just to Blix.

She'd got an A. She'd got A's in all the important subjects, to everyone's astonishment. One of the boys had the gall to ask her how she'd cheated. Not if, but how. He'd got a punch for his trouble. It was clear that some of the teachers were of the same opinion. She didn't punch any of them. Her dad had bought her a new bike. Not for punching the boy, she'd thought at the time, but with her dad you never knew.

A-levels were the next step. Natural Philosophy, or Natural Philosophy and Anthropology as it was at A-level, was again top of the agenda, even though it had a reputation as the exam you did when you didn't know what exams you wanted to do. Not so for her. The university she wanted to get into required it. An easy A would help. The Physics and Chemistry syllabuses looked daunting.

But it was all going wrong.

The sciences were hard, but Blix was diligent and had an okay memory. She could understand enthalpy change and fractional distillation and atomic numbers without caring about them. But Natural Philosophy was turning into a disaster.

She had one hour of it on Tuesday morning and double on Friday afternoon, when everyone was sleepy and wanted to go home. The syllabus was tedious beyond belief. It was much wider than simply the insides of humans and animals, liminal or otherwise, and even when it did touch on magical creatures it sucked all the joy out of things she liked.

There was bone-dry statistical analysis of the migration patterns of sea-wyvern species. She had to work out what that implied about fish stocks and kraken population health. There was lots of politics of the post-magic era, and how the revolutions in the serf countries had changed the political map of Europe in the early 20th century.

It dwelt on the legal position of intelligent hemi-human species like Mermen and Harpies, and whether the Universal Declaration of Human Rights applied to them. Blix knew this was important but just didn't care. She wanted to learn about Harpy wings and what diseases they suffered from. She wasn't interested in whether they could march on Downing Street demanding equal pay.

Leicester droned on about something dull. Blix regarded the D minus sourly.

'What essay?' Katy asked.

'Stone circles. Placement of menhirs, to be exact. For tomorrow,' said Blix. 'I can't even start it, it's so deadly.' She gave a showy sigh, dripping with stage-school ennui. 'The whole subject's so dry it makes my lips crack just thinking about it.' She looked up hopefully. 'You like this sort of thing, don't you?'

Katy was doing Geography, Politics, Economics and History. She was doing very well. There was talk of Oxbridge. Blix did not resent this at all.

'I know lots about menhirs,' she said, sounding a bit smug in Blix's view. 'They rock. Really interesting.'

'For you maybe. What have they got do with Natural Philosophy, I ask you?'

'It's Natural Philosophy and Anthropology now isn't it? This would be the people part.'

'I don't like people,' said Blix moodily. 'I prefer animals.'

'People don't mind, animals don't care. Ask me a question.'

'Okay. Question: are menhirs the most boring things on the face of the earth, or is there something else equally as dull?'

Katy stuck her tongue out. 'Nah, you'll like them. Magicians and druids. The druids, anyway, no one likes magicians. It's all sex and drugs with druids, they were proper maniacs.'

'Tell me more, you have my undivided attention,' said Blix, trying to stifle a yawn.

In fact, what Katy knew about druids and stone circles was interesting. Or at least, the bits which involved gore-splattered drug orgies were. The girls acquired some gin from their parents' drinks cupboard and Katy shared the dirt. There was much ancient beardy-weirdness, enthusiastic virgin deflowering and bloody animal sacrifice. It was great stuff. After a particularly filthy anecdote Blix accused her sister of being a pornographer.

'Am not,' Katy said, giggling. 'It's in the textbooks.' She dragged a dog-eared hardback from her bookshelf and cracked it open. 'Look.'

'That's not a school book. Buy it from Paul Raymond, did you?'

'It's respectable I tell you. Academic. Serious-minded.'

'Respectable, academic, serious-minded smut.'

Katy threw the book at Blix. 'Of course, the real problem with circles is telling the druid ones from the real ones.'

'Real?'

'You know. Magic ones.'

'Pfft. There's no such thing anymore.' She picked up the book.

'Yeah. but there was once. Druids were wannabe gate-builders. They didn't know how, so they kind of pretended. Sympathetic magic, it's called. But not actually magic, just called that. A bit primitive, really.'

'Just as real as real magic, these days,' said Blix, yawning.

Which was fun, but didn't write an essay. Or could go in one, Blix realised, when the next morning arrived with a mild hangover and the paper still not done. Katy and their mum had left to drive to The Grammar. She found the textbook among Katy's things and, while her toast browned and her dad read his tabloid at the other end of the kitchen table, she copied out chunks of it on some lined paper, in her largest handwriting.

Menhirs are carved stones used in ancient religious and magical practices. They were first used in dolmens in the Neolithic period approximately seven thousand years ago. There are two kinds of dolmen; in Druidic practice, dolmens were raised over the burial sites of important people. The originals however were raised by magicians as gates to lock rifts. Rifts are magic holes in reality which lead to other worlds. The Greek and Roman civilisations regarded these as entrances to the underworld, 'mundus ceresis' and the menhirs, 'lapis manalis'. These were the precursors to more sophisticated earthworks such as circles and henges. With sufficient magic, you could open the gate and travel from one world to another. Most gates ceased working overnight in eighteen eighty-six while the remainder followed suit in nineteen sixteen. It is no longer

'Tick-tock, tick-tock,' said her dad, pointing at the clock without raising his eyes from page three. Blix realised she was going to be late.

'Great,' she muttered. 'Not even a page.' She scribbled the final words of the sentence.

It is no longer possible to travel between worlds.

Blix grabbed her satchel and the dry toast and ran, the fail-bomb fizzling in her hand.

Now it sat in front of her, ready to explode. Blix was certain that Leicester would humiliate her with it. He was that kind of person.

He was a supply teacher. Mr Henderson, who'd taught the O level and was due to take the A level class as well, hadn't come back after the October half term break. He was suffering from 'exhaustion,' which everyone knew meant he'd gone off his rocker.

'Retired to a nudist colony in the Languedoc,' Katy had said with certainty. How she had come by this intelligence Blix had no idea, given that she went to a different school. Blix wasn't sure where the Languedoc was, but she imagined it might be a bit chilly to be a nudist there in November.

Blix hadn't particularly liked or disliked Henderson. He'd been a good teacher for a pupil as committed to the bestiary as she was, and had been kind about the nightmare the class was turning into for her. But he was a candidate for sainthood compared to Mr Leicester.

He appeared to have come into teaching by mistake. He hated children and didn't try to hide it, although Blix had to concede that he was by no means unique among teachers in this respect. While he knew his subject backwards, he had no ability as a teacher and was poor at crowd control. This was a major flaw. He often asserted authority by picking on someone, which was always fun for everyone else.

His voice was grating, somewhere between a wheedle and a drone. It ranged in volume from a near-silent whisper to a high-pitched shriek when he felt threatened or ignored, which was often. Everyone thought he was a weirdo.

Then there were the hands. They were all over her, sort of. Leicester had never touched her, but the way he got close to her, the way his hands hovered over her like a mantis ready to strike, was creepy. She might have thought he was just another pervert waiting to try something. But he rarely looked straight at her and seemed to dislike her. Maybe he was just like that with everyone.

Now his teaching was competing with continuous background chatter; he was inaudible. He sat at his desk at the front of the class, face in the textbook, unconcerned about whether he held anyone's attention. Blix stared out of the window. The outside world looked inviting.

Blix thought about more important things. Such as: gryphons, which her brain tended to default to when there was nothing else going on. And whether she would ever see an Atlas Bear, her current animal of interest, in the wild. And whether Aisling O'Connell fancied her, or whether it was all part of some elaborate joke that Blix would later find she was the butt of.

Aisling had bullied her when they were growing up, on and off. Not as much as some, but enough that it felt real. But these days she was making doe eyes and smiling at her from across the room, and her old friends seemed to have dropped her.

Doe eyes was good. Most of her year either ignored her or tried to bully her. Verbal bullying only, these days. No one tried to pinch her or pull her hair. They weren't kids any more. Everyone knew words hurt more.

Blix didn't trust her motives. Then again, she was totally hot. Not a supermodel or anything but definitely a fox, so maybe -

Blix became aware that the class had fallen silent.

'Amelia Summerland.'

'My name is Blix,' she said automatically, before looking around. Leicester was right next to her.

'Is it. *Blix*,' he repeated, nastily, wielding her name as a weapon. 'What do you see, then, *Blix*, when you look for such a long time out of the window?' His tone was mild, but Blix wasn't a fool. She knew what was coming.

Play it with a straight bat. 'Nothing, Mr. Leicester.'

'How strange.' Leicester looked out of the window, shielding his eyes with his hand. The class tittered at the mockery, to Blix's disgust. 'I see the quadrangle, and beyond it some tarmac with a five-a-side pitch laid out on it, then the playing fields, and then the woods. To the left, the sports block, to the right Sycamore Road and the housing estate. Look, there are some cars on the road. Do you see those things, *Blix*?'

'Yes, Mr. Leicester.'

'Do you see any eminent educators giving of their immense wisdom to an ungrateful rabble of idiot children?'

The class stirred with resentment at that, but Blix knew better and kept her face blank. 'No, Mr. Leicester.'

'That is because I am in here,' Leicester snapped, giving her a nasty look before turning away again.

'Well, *Blix*, I was about to give you all a test, but as punishment for your inattention I will give it to you alone instead. I hear you are quite the little intellectual, in some respects. I do not see it in your work.'

That got the class back on his side. Blix groaned. *Annoy him by knowing the answers or don't know them and look stupid. Prepare for humiliation either way.*

'Your essay, brief thought it was, contained several interesting facts. We shall explore your understanding of them.'

He knows I just copied them out. Blix desperately hunted for anything she could remember from the night before. She remembered gin.

'A dolmen is… what?'

Katy had got that much into her head, at least. 'A collection of standing stones?'

'Don't ask questions when you mean to make statements. Describe, *in your own words,* what a gate is.'

Blix tried not to look exasperated at the exaggerated emphasis he put on the words. This was baby stuff. Everyone knew this.

'There were holes. Magic holes. Leading to different worlds. People used to fall through them. And, um, things came the other way.'

'Um is not a word. Resume.'

'Gates kept the holes closed. But they could open them again.'

'Yes. The term "gate" being an example of that subtle, rapier-like quality, the wit of magicians.'

Something from Katy's book finally scuttled across Blix's memory. 'The Druids thought human sacrifice caused the holes, they-'

'Blood feeds everything,' Leicester said. 'In the Druidic worldview,' he added. 'They were superstitious fools. Thousands of years late with the wrong answer to a question already answered.'

Leicester was at the back of the class now, where the wasters struggled to look alert under his unexpected scrutiny. His voice was a distant squeak. Blix didn't look at him.

'I am not concerned with Druids. Let us discuss civilised people. Back to Dolmens. The Romans called them *mundus ceresis*, you say. Which means…?'

Bugger. Blix had half-formed the words don't know, sir when she had a flash of inspiration.

'Pits of Ceres. Who was a Goddess. Sir.'

There was a slight catch in Leicester's breath, as if he'd been about to berate her but found he couldn't. 'And the stones? *Lapis manalis?'*

'Stones of the Manes. Chthonic deities of the underworld.'

Blix fought the urge to looked pleased with herself for the word 'chthonic'. She didn't know where she'd dragged either of those facts up from. She didn't remember Katy mentioning them. Maybe Bamber Gascoigne had asked them on *University Challenge* once.

'Thank you.' She heard the irritation in Leicester's voice. She was not supposed to have known those answers. He continued.

'The Romans thought they led to Hell. But they led to -

'Other worlds. I said.'

'You did. But what does that mean? Describe, please.'

'I don't know what you want,' said Blix, sulking.

'I am a teacher, *Blix*, I want you to understand. I want you to be accurate. Describe to the class the nature of these other worlds. What they are, how they came to be, and so forth.'

Bollocks to it. Let's just get to the telling off. 'Don't know, sir,' she muttered into her desk.

'Ah!' he said, and Blix could hear the pleasure in his voice. How small his life must be, she thought, if humiliating schoolgirls got him off. 'Allow me to enlighten you. No one knows.'

'That's not fair!' said Blix, scowling. There were chuckles from elsewhere in the room, which she silenced with a sweeping glare.

'Too bad,' said Leicester. 'You must think before you answer, or fail to answer in this case. You could have said: we don't know, but we know what they are not. We know they are not parallel earths in alternate realities. We know they are not heavens or hells. We know they are habitable to humans, but we don't know why. They are many and varied. Some different to the world we know. Larger or smaller. With different composition of rocks, minerals, flora and fauna. Although many of the same too, just to complicate things - am I boring you, *Blix*?'

Blix stifled a yawn, wondering how he'd seen it from behind her. 'No, Mr Leicester,' she said. This was in fact true. The yawn had been involuntary. Blix wasn't bored, she was fuming.

'Good. We might then think that they are worlds elsewhere in this universe, but we do not know that either. Any claims to recognise star positions from this world or that are tenuous at best. And end before modern radio astronomy. So, they might be in another universe altogether. We don't know.'

This is all bollocks, thought Blix. The world rolled around her mind, pleasing to hear in the privacy of her head.

'We do know some things,' Leicester continued. 'We know that they are worlds on which magical creatures are everyday fauna. Some intelligent, some merely beasts. Fauna which, you are correct, sometimes fell through the holes of their own accord before the gates existed.'

For a moment. Blix thought he might ask her about the creatures, but she wasn't that lucky. He bored on.

'For thousands of years particularly bold or reckless humans used the gates to colonise other worlds. Without incident, for the most part, but sometimes expiring in screaming agony. I think "intestinally dispersed" is the best description I have seen. Often a precursor to a gate locking itself for good, if you believe the modern literature. Name some of the other worlds, we are aware of, please.'

'Um. Well. Atlantis, and, um, Hy-brasil, and, um, Cockaigne?' - she waited for the tittering to die down - 'and, um. Um.'

'Um is not a place either, *Blix*, unless you are proposing it as one. It would be a tiresome place, or should that be tiresUM, ha ha. Ha. No, your ancient and medieval ancestors were more imaginative. They named the worlds they colonised after the places on their Earth maps which didn't exist, and the dead kingdoms of their ancestors. Hy-Brasil and Lyonesse, Luggnagg and Issedon, Ziklag, Rheged and Aeron. And so forth. We know of around four hundred. Please name the last discovered world.'

Blix shrugged, defeated. 'Don't know, sir,' she muttered.

'Something else you don't know, sir,' sneered Leicester. 'Pellucidar! Discovered in late nineteen fourteen via an unknown Toltec-era circle in New Mexico. Named by the popular press after one of Edgar Rice Burroughs' fictional lands. American Expeditionary Force sent in mid nineteen sixteen. Contact almost immediately lost. Why?'

Blix was back on firmer ground. This was at least a bit relevant to her interests.

'The end of magic,' she said.

'Do explain, *Blix*.'

'Well, there were two losses, one in the mid eighteen eighties, then another in nineteen sixteen.'

'Correct,' said Leicester, annoyed now she was answering the questions again. 'And please do tell us, *Blix*, what happened in those years?'

I swear, if he doesn't stop doing that I'll... She took a breath. 'Okay. On Christmas day eighteen eighty-six people stopped being able to do quite a lot of magic, and what they could still do got a lot harder. Lots of gates stopped working. I mean, gates had always stopped working, like you said, but not all at once.' She stopped, hoping that was enough.

'And what happened to magic?'

'Top level magic had always been hard and rare. Proper magician stuff. But everyday trivial magic, fire sparking and light shows, became top level. Everything above that became impossible. Then thirty years later all magic stopped working, overnight, everywhere. There was none left. Lots of magical species dropped dead immediately and the rest are almost all endangered. Which is why the O Level is all about shagging,' she added. It got a laugh, but not from Leicester.

'Thank you, *Blix*. And tell me, *Blix*, why did these disasters occur?'

Bollocks again. 'I don't know.' *But you don't get me twice.* 'Because no one knows. There are lots of theories, but no proof. Most people think it was something to do with the war, but no one knows what.'

'Something to do with the war. The greatest unexplained disaster in the history of the world and you wave it away thus. The event that turned humanity from casual puissance in the esoteric arts into the mundane plebeians I see before me. Something. Hmph.'

He was behind her again, as close as a breath. Blix's skin crawled. Then Blix felt something on her neck and was certain, *certain* that Leicester had brushed her skin with his finger. She cringed away in disgust and turned ready to accuse him. To her surprise, he was nowhere near her. He was on the other side of the classroom. So far that he couldn't have touched Blix and crossed the room in the fraction of a second it had taken her to spin in her chair.

'Well, well,' he said. 'A most unexpected event had occurred. You have passed the test. You have adequate knowledge. The b … I am impressed.' Now he was in front of her. He looked angry and frustrated, as if something he had planned had gone wrong. He picked up her paper and held it up for the class to seer, holding it between thumb and forefinger as if it was dirty or infected. 'I must ask you then, *Blix*, why none of this or anything like it appears in this worthless excrescence of an essay?'

That was the last straw; Blix saw red.

'Because it's bloody pointless bollocks!' she shouted. 'All this, this *rubbish*, it's completely meaningless! Why do we need to learn about bloody gates anyway? Do you know the most important thing I know about menhirs and dolmens and megaliths and all that crap? They're just bloody rocks! They don't work anymore! They don't work and they won't ever work again because there's no bloody magic anymore! Why the *fuck* do we have to waste our time on them, you perverted bullying bastard? *And stop saying my fucking name like that!*'

The words were out of her mouth before she could stop herself. Her classmates gasped. An excited thrill ran around the room. Blix Summerland was going to get *done.*

Leicester froze, struggling to control himself. His face turned waxy and mottled, as if his muscles were squirming under too tight skin. Blix thought he was going to hit her, but he took a deep breath and relaxed. Getting expelled for flattening a teacher, even in self-defence, would not look good on her CV.

Leicester smiled to himself then, and Blix had the strong sense that something unpleasant was coming her way.

'I believe you now have something to say, Miss Summerland.'

Anger was still bubbling through Blix, but common sense asserted itself.

'Yes sir. I'm sorry, sir.'

'Sorry. I suppose you are. Wretched, pitiful, a sorry excuse for a girl.'

Blix burned scarlet with suppressed anger, but said nothing.

'I must punish you for your outburst. Detention, that goes without saying. And I will write to your mother. But I think that punishment should fit the crime, don't you? Perhaps I can increase your appreciation of ancient constructions. Tell me, Miss Summerland, where is the nearest stone circle?'

Blix didn't know where this was going. 'Don’t know, sir.'

'At St. John Chrysostom. The stones they call the Conspirators. Noted for their well-preserved runic carvings. You will have seen them in books and on television, perhaps? No? Then let me open your mind, Miss Summerland. You will go there over the weekend - I hear the weather will be dreadful - and take a rubbing of the runes.'

'St John’s! That's miles away!' Blix complained. 'Up in bloody Durham!'

'Yes. A rubbing mind you - not that I think for a second that you would otherwise copy them out of a book! Heaven forfend. I suggest you go tomorrow. You will need Sunday to compose the five-page essay on the history of the Conspirators which you will present to me on Monday morning. Monday, not Tuesday, mark you. And then on Friday please bring the rubbings with you to class; as an exciting treat your little friends will translate them. And detention for anyone who fails.'

Blix took a moment to reflect on quite how unpopular she had just become.

'That's completely out of order,' she began, but Leicester interrupted her.

'Do all this and I will consider the matter closed and give your essay a fair mark. Fail or refuse and I'll throw you off the course and recommend expulsion to the Headmaster. And that will be that for your future plans. Your precious gryphons will have to live, hah, without you.'

Blix took a deep breath, then thought better of what she'd been about to say.

'Right, fine,' she said abruptly, hunching over her desk, scowling. By contrast, Leicester had a tiny look of triumph on his otherwise expressionless face.

'The right choice,' he said. 'I look forward to reading your thoughts. In the meantime...' he paused, and glanced at the clock. As he did the end of day bell rang in the hallway. Leicester looked back at Blix.

'... see me after class.'

Chapter Four: A Smart Girl

Blix hated the estate after dark, but didn't tell anyone because she didn't want to ruin her image. She walked briskly between the flickering yellow cones of safety falling from the streetlights, leather jacket zipped up to her chin, armour against the watchers her imagination hid in the dark doorways.

The lift wasn't working again. She contemplated the eight floor climb with distaste. The stairwell stank of urine and glue. A big dog growled at her from the third-floor corridor. A drunken voice yelled 'Ha'way, man!'

There was a skinhead on the fifth-floor landing. A couple of years older than Blix, she remembered him from school but not his name. He hadn't stayed for A-levels and had acquired a bad tattoo high on his neck since then. He wore a two-tone blue shell suit jacket, tracksuit bottoms and trainers which had once been white. He didn't live on the estate. He shuffled nervously, a strange, hunted look on his thin, slightly sunken face. He made eye contact and nodded sharply at her, but looked like he was thinking about something else. Something he was thinking about all the time.

You have problems, Blix thought. *You're a junkie.*

'Listen,' he started, 'I've lost me bus fare, lend us twenty pence so I can get home like? Help us out man, please.'

'I don't have any money,' said Blix, hurrying past him up the stairs. It looked like he would follow her. Instead he thrust his hands deep in his jacket pockets and subsided against the wall, thinking about something else. She was glad when she got to the flat. She bolted the door and put the chain on.

It was past six. Katy was watching the telly. Blix dumped her school bag on the floor and flopped onto the sofa beside her. She sighed in a rather high-blown manner. Katy ignored her. Flouncing was a Blix art form.

The news was on. The newsreader was reporting on an outbreak of centaurism in America. Police had arrested four men and some foals had been taken into care.

'Disgusting,' said Katy once the report had finished. 'I hope those perverts get life. Those poor horses!' Katy liked horses.

'It's worse than that,' said Blix, kicking off her shoes. 'You can make a centaur, if you have the right kind of horse and you're sick in the head, but you can't make them human. These freaks always think they're going to father the new Chiron or Hylonome and breed a race of noble horse lords. What they get is horses. With human bodies and faces. It's disturbing and cruel.'

Katy shuddered. 'I wish you hadn't told me that, that's awful. They should string them up.'

'It's America, they might. Interesting how attitudes have changed, isn't it? Before the tank the British Army lived on centaurs. No one thought it was creepy then. Mind you, there were wild centaurs then, lots of them. They didn't have to, um, make them.'

Katy glared at her sister. 'Stop talking about making centaurs.'

'Sorry. Where's mum?'

'Work. She left money for chips. Dad took it to the pub by mistake. There are tins in the cupboard if you're hungry. I had the ravioli, but there's beans and hoops and things.'

'I'll live. I might be sick if I eat anything, Remember I told you about that flathead Leicester? The one who's got a huge hard-on for me? He's been feeling me up all afternoon.'

'What, for real?'

'Well, no. But he wanted to, I could tell. Hot eyes all over me. He's a kiddy-fiddler.'

'We're seventeen. You're in sixth form, not the infants.'

'What, are you his mate then?'

Katy rolled her eyes. 'Ugh, no, he's vile. I saw him a couple of weeks ago, when mum picked you up on the way to my oboe lesson. He's got horrible waxy skin, have you noticed? It's like someone's melted him a bit. Anyway, even if he did try it on, you do kung-fu, you could fu him 'til he said he was sorry.'

'Karate. For the millionth time, I *did* karate. For, like, three weeks, two years ago.'

'Before they threw you out.'

'Yeah, well, the *sensei* was a bigot. Turns out I don't like bigots.'

'You hit him in the nuts. Men hate that.'

'He wasn't pleased, yeah. Honestly, you'd think someone who teaches people how to fight would be better at taking a punch.'

'You're lucky he didn't have you arrested.'

'Wouldn't be good advertising for him, would it? "Come and learn the Japanese art of self-defence at my famous Karate school, where I once got emasculated by a teenage girl." Nah.'

Katy laughed. 'You could punch Leicester in the nuts. There's so little to him, *I* could punch him in the nuts, and I've never punched anyone in the nuts in my life.' She uppercut the air. 'Bosh! Kung-fu! Like that.'

Blix gave her the thumbs up. 'Top fu-ing there, brutal. You wouldn't punch your way out of a paper bag like that. Always drive through.'

'What does that mean?'

Blix thrust her straight arm past Katy's head, leading with the heel of her hand. 'Aim for a spot three inches behind your target and hit that. That way you're still driving through when you connect.' She punched again, this time with her fist.

Katy wrinkled her nose. 'Duly noted. Are you going to report him then? Leicester, I mean.'

'Nah. He didn't do any *actual* fiddling, so I can't. Who'd believe me, anyway? You know what it's like. He wanted to though, I'd put money on it. And he did touch me. I think. I'm sure of it...'

'You don't sound sure.'

'No, I am. Sort of. It was weird.' Blix shook her head, irritated. 'It was an annoying day.'

Katy perked up. 'Ah-ha! You'll have bought chocolate then. Hand it over,' she demanded. 'Payment for putting up with your moaning.'

Blix smiled. 'There's half a bar in my satchel.'

'Excellent.' Katy upended Blix's satchel and dumped the contents on the floor. Books, papers and assorted educational detritus spread out over the carpet.

'Hey, that's my stuff!' Blix objected. 'Treat it with respect!'

'You don't care about this stuff. And I'll never find it otherwise. You have too much stuff.'

'This from the owner of the handbag of doom.'

'Do not mock the doombag,' said Katy severely. 'I love that bag more than you.'

'It's ridiculous. It's like, two Thatchers worth of handbag. No one needs two Thatchers. You look like a granny.'

'Shut up, it's practical. And gorgeous. And designer, that's Italian leather you know.'

'It's a bottomless pit of black Taiwanese plastic you got from the market. And it's not designer, what brand is it then?'

'Do not make me choose between you,' said Katy, ignoring the question. 'It will go badly for you.'

She glowered at her sister, then giggled. Then she noticed something in Blix's stuff. 'What's this?'

'No, don't touch that,' said Blix, as Katy picked up a brown envelope from the pile.

'What's yours is mine. It's addressed to mum.'

Blix sighed. 'Letter from the headmaster. She's got to come into school and be told about me again.'

'I think she already knows,' said Katy, around a mouthful of chocolate.

'Sod off. Anyway, I got detention. Two bloody hours of it. And more to come.'

'What was it this time?'

'I called Leicester a perverted bastard. To his face. In front of the class.'

'Excellent!'

'May also have effed him a bit. Or quite a lot.'

Katy mock-applauded. 'How'd the detention go?'

'As well as you'd expect. Writing out "I must not swear at teachers" so many times I started doubting they were really words.'

'I hate lines.'

'When have you ever done lines? Anyway, that wasn't the worst bit. Leicester spent the whole time staring at me in total silence. Looked at me like I was his next meal. Well creepy. Swear down, he's planning my murder. At least I wasn't alone, some third year gave a kid a Chinese burn and got held back.'

'The answer is obvious. Stop getting detention.'

'Yeah, thanks, hadn't thought of that. Like that's going to happen.' She sighed heavily. 'I thought it would be better in sixth form.'

'You know, you can just leave if you want to. You're seventeen. Nothing's keeping you there.'

'That's not going to happen either.'

'So,' Katy continued brightly, once it was clear Blix wasn't going to say any more, 'once they expel you, are you going to hang around on street corners committing petty crimes until they send you to borstal? Or are you to go straight to drug addiction, prostitution and homelessness? You know, like it says in the papers?'

'You're not funny,' said Blix. 'There was a skaghead on the stairs just now.'

'Yeah, I saw him. The sooner we get out of this town the better.'

'I don't think I'm ever getting out,' said Blix quietly.

Katy began to make another joke, then saw her sister's face. 'What's the matter?' she asked.

'It's all going wrong, isn't it? I'm no good at the thing I want to be good at. That I need to be good at to be who I want to be.'

'Don't panic just yet,' Katy said. 'It's only November. You've got almost two years to fix it.'

'I know, I just… I just don't want them to be right, you know? I don't want to live down to their expectations. I just want to be… someone, I don't know,' she finished lamely.

'You are someone,' said Katy firmly. 'You're me. And I'm awesome. Which means you are too. Scientific fact.' She crossed her arms and nodded decisively.

'Right on,' said Blix, trying not to smile.

'But you can't be awesome if you're expelled,' Katy continued with mock severity. 'Don't do that. You'll make me look bad.'

Now Blix did smile. 'Well I wouldn't want that. I'm not getting expelled, or even suspended. I think. Leicester likes creative punishment.'

Blix explained what she had to do. 'It's so unfair,' she finished. 'I don't even know how to do a bloody rubbing! Who does rubbings in this day and age, I ask you? Do I look like I wear socks with sandals? Do I have a chin beard? I don't even know where the sodding rocks are!'

'I know,' said Katy. 'We went there on a field trip.'

'Of course you did. Bloody Grammar. How the other half live.'

'Bugger off. Actually, wait on.'

Katy nipped out of the room. She returned a moment later with a sheaf of lined paper. It was a bit crumpled. 'Here.'

Blix squinted at the paper. Squiggles scratched across the page. 'Is this shorthand? Your handwriting is terrible.'

'Bugger off, slightly further. These are my notes on the Conspirators. So you can make it sound like you care about them to Leicester.'

'I still have to go though, don't I?' said Blix, aggrieved. 'I have no choice.'

'You'll like them, they're beautiful.'

'Great. You can go then, I'll stay in bed.' She fired the papers back to Katy.

'Ha, no. But I'll come with you. It'll be less tedious than going by yourself and I'm not doing anything tomorrow. Anyway, with a punishment that specific you've got to think Leicester might be waiting there to see if you do it. Or to jump on you. In which case I want to be there to see you punch him in the nuts.'

'You are disturbingly fixated on that.'

'It'd be brilliant! I'd call Jeremy Beadle and get *Game For A Laugh* out to film it. But failing that we can find a yokel pub where they don't care how old you are and get smashed.'

'That's a good idea.'

'I'm known for them. Speaking of good ideas, have you kissed that girl you like yet?'

'Ah, no, stop,' said Blix, her cheeks colouring.

'You have!' Katy gave a little excited clap. 'Was it good? Did she use tongues?'

'Actually stop.' Blix squirmed in her seat. She could feel her ears glowing. 'No, obviously I haven't kissed her. You know I'm no good at that stuff. Talking to people. Girls. I don't even know if she's a lez.'

'So much for Ms. Tough Girl. I could light a match an inch from your face right now, do you know?' Katy thought for a moment. 'Stand next to her. If she touches you for any reason, she likes you. Well-known fact.'

'That sounds made up. I can't stand next to her, that's like, doing something. I'll just die. Literally die. She probably doesn't like me anyway.'

'She probably doesn't. You're not very likable.'

Blix stuck out her tongue. 'Bite me.'

'No thanks, I know where you've been.' Katy thought some more. 'You go swimming at the same time, don't you?'

Blix's blush, which had been fading, returned to full crimson. 'Sort of. A couple of times.'

'You're stalking her you mean. My advice is, you should snog her in the pool.'

'Oh my actual God just *stop*. I'm putting my fingers in my ears. I would *actually* die.'

'Come off it. You come over all embarrassed, but I know better. I remember you going skinny-dipping up at Linhope Spout. All off for all the world to see.'

'I was eight! It's not rude when you're eight.'

The weather forecast came on. Black cloud symbols littered the map. Blue circles indicated minus temperatures. Raindrops covered the North. The weatherman, safe in a warm London television studio, looked terribly pleased.

Blix's already poor mood worsened a lot. 'Oh look, it's going to toss it down. That's just great.'

'Don't be such a sourpuss! We'll just have to wear our wellies. Come on, it'll be fun!'

Blix couldn't tell whether Katy was in fact excited or just mocking her. She decided it was both.

'Bollocks to it,' she sighed, and pushed herself off the sofa. 'I'll worry about tomorrow's shitty day tomorrow. Are you staying in here?'

'Yes. It's *Wogan* in a bit. You?'

'I'm going to the bedroom to listen to loud music and be angry.'

'Well, you are seventeen,' said Katy, sagely.

Lying on her bed with her headphones on, Blix thought about why she and her sister were so different. She thought about it a lot.

She took out the worn little black and white photo of them she kept in her wallet, taken when they were fourteen. It was her favourite picture. Standing together, arms around each other, beaming at the camera. It was the picture in which they looked most alike.

Identical. Both blonde, blue-eyed, good looking, middle height and athletic. Katy had long hair, Blix short, but otherwise, identical. Well put together, their dad said. Worth paying attention to, their mother said, which Blix chose to interpret in a way she cared about more than looks. Not that people paid attention to her.

Beyond those common points, they diverged. There was the whole 'being a lesbian' thing. Her parents had taken her coming out well. Not least, Blix suspected, because she'd never been 'in' in any noticeable way. Her mother had taken Blix ditching her given name much harder. Blix didn't see why. Amelia was a bit aspirational for where they lived.

Katy had asked Blix once why she was a lesbian. Blix thought for a long time before answering.

'I am because I am,' she said finally. 'I just am. That's what I am.'

That had seemed fair enough to Katy, but Blix herself wasn't quite satisfied with the answer. It seemed like a get-out-of-jail-free card. But she didn't know enough about herself to give a better one.

Blix was physical, tough, a non-sufferer of fools. A tomboy stereotype, as she was well aware and wasn't sure she liked. Prone to moods and theatrics. This last trait wasn't helped by her ostracism by every other girl in her class. Her world revolved around bestiary animals.

Katy was the happy-go-lucky one, the one who wore dresses and backcombed and had friends. Who dated boys. She was smart enough to get into the Grammar and smart enough that Blix expected to see the letters PhD after her name one day. She was also more than capable of looking after herself, as the occasional over-keen boy could attest.

Differences. They were superficial. Blix didn't understand what made them different, but she knew what made them the same. They were each other.

Much later Katy came in to go to bed to find that Blix had fallen asleep with her clothes on. Something tinny played through the headphones. As Katy slipped them over her sister's head, Blix muttered something, and rolled over.

'How did who know about what gryphons?' Katy asked.

No answer. Blix was sound asleep. She dreamed of eyes watching in the darkness.

Chapter Five: The Conspirators

Saturday came, bleak and miserable.

Katy wore a duffle coat, yellow sou'wester hat, pleated sports skirt and thick rainbow-stripe tights. It made her look like a sexually available rag doll, in Blix's opinion. Katy stuck the V's up at her when she said so.

Blix had her image to think of. She was wearing her black leather jacket, her CHOOSE LIFE t-shirt, which Blix swore down was a proper legit one not the cheap street market knock-off Katy suspected, and skinny faded jeans. She'd made few official concessions to the elements. A Russian ushanka hat with furry ear flaps which clipped together under her chin, and some fingerless gloves. She also had her thermal vest on and thick hiking socks, but she didn't tell Katy that. Blix had her satchel; Katy, the doombag. Both wore Wellington boots. Katy's had smiley faces on them.

They took a bus from the stand in the town centre. Up the A road, then into and out of a town, then down some lanes, to a bus stop by a farmer's field in the middle of nowhere, where the driver ejected them, an hour after they started.

'It is not the middle of nowhere,' said Katy. 'It's a picturesque example of unspoilt native pasture land, situated in the former industrial heart of the nation.'

'Is that Tourist Boardese for "desolate windscape only fit for growing cow flop?"'

'Yes. God, it's grim.' Katy pulled her coat tighter at the collar. A stiff breeze blew in from the north east. Blix mentally thanked Norway. A sheep ambled up to the fence, glared at her malevolently, then ambled off again. 'What do we do here?'

'We wait half an hour for the next bus to show up.'

Blix blew on her fingers and stamped her feet so hard that her toes tingled. Wet sludge splattered up her boots. 'Marvellous.'

The next bus arrived eventually, and eventually deposited them in front of the Exciseman pub. It was just opening. It looked warm and inviting and promised beer. After a long, heavy-lidded look from the barman in the face of Katy's disingenuous claim to be eighteen, it provided it.

'One pound eighty-four,' he said, putting two pints on the bar.

'Ninety-two pence for a pint of lager?' said Blix, outraged. 'That's robbery!'

'Shocking, isn't it?' the barman agreed. 'Price of things these days.' He curled his thick fingers around the glasses and made to take them back. 'If you don't want them...'

'We want them,' said Katy firmly, steering the beer back their way. 'And pies,' she added, as the smell of kidneys wafting from the kitchen hit her nose. 'Hot, hot pies. And chips. And peas.'

'We should stay in here,' said Blix, when both pint and pie were inside her. 'It's nasty out there.' On cue, thick raindrops started blatting against the glass. 'It'll ruin your hair. And after you put so many hours into it.'

Katy gave her a professorial look. 'My hair will be fine. I have hairspray. It's only down the road. We can go, rub whatever you need to rub, and be back in half an hour.' Katy vacuumed up the last of her mushy peas. 'Forty minutes, tops. Then you don't get expelled and have to stack shelves for a living.'

'There is that. Oh, okay then.' Cue more rain. 'But I'm not going out until that's blown over.'

'You'll feel better about it when you've got a beer jacket on. Same again please, and get the dessert menu.'

After another pint and a sticky toffee pudding Blix's mood had improved a lot. By two-thirty the weather had changed. There was even a suggestion of sun.

Katy stood up. 'Come on, we're going while it's dry.' She wobbled a bit, and shouldered her handbag. It had a definite heft to it.

'What on earth have you got in that thing?'

'Not much. Just the essentials. A scarf, two notebooks, couple of pens, cough drops, hair pins. A big book about stone circles by a hippie. My compact, earrings, lipstick, lip salve and my purse. Two bars of chocolate. A needle and thread, a first aid kit, tampons, condoms -'

'Condoms?'

'I'm responsible,' said Katy. 'Don't tell mum. Spare knickers, pencil torch with a compass on the end, some mints, the flat key, a nail file, nail clippers. A hair brush, hairspray, a comb, five fags I nicked from mum, some matches, an empty plastic water bottle, a can of cola and Dad's hip flask full of vodka.'

'And a partridge in a pear-tree,' Blix sang. 'Give me a cigarette. I can't believe you memorised all that. Or can carry it.'

'I made a list.' Katy lit a cigarette. 'And butcher's paper and crayons, for the rubbings. In case you forgot. Did you forget?'

'Ha! No!' Blix dived into her satchel and pulled out sheets of crumpled paper. 'See?'

'Well done. Anything else useful in there?'

'My cassette player. Although the batteries are almost gone. And my shades. And a big wad of tissues in case the facilities are a bit primitive.'

'Good grief, it's the British countryside not the rainforest. No, then. You should be more practical, like me.'

'You're right,' Blix agreed. 'If we're ever lost in the wilderness all that'll come in handy. We could burn it to signal for help.' She grabbed the cigarette from her sister's grasp and took a puff.

'Oi! Can't you read?' The barman pointed to a sign by the door. 'No smoking in the public bar. The saloon bar's open if you want a fag.'

'We're just heading out for a bit. You don't close in the afternoons, do you?'

'Yep. Law's the law. Three o'clock. Bar opens again at six-thirty.'

Katy tried her winsome smile again; it seemed more successful this time. The barman grinned.

'Where are you off then?'

'St John's.'

The barman gave them a look which said, rather you than me. 'You'll have it to yourself then, it's bitter out. Tell you what, knock us up when you get back and I'll let you in. If you hang around 'til doors open you'll freeze to death. It's no weather to be out in.'

Blix sighed. Katy beamed at the barman. 'Thanks! Can you fill my water bottle before we go please?'

The ruin of St. John Chrysostom sat high on a hill. It had once commanded the view for miles around, but wild woods had grown in over the centuries and the church was now hidden from the road.

Katy knew a lot about the abbey.

'It was a double monastery,' she said. 'For monks and nuns, like Whitby. St. Hrodgar Leofwine founded it in 703AD. He was a great man in the early English church. Guess what his name means,' she said, giggling.

'Go on then.'

'Roger the Agreeable.'

Blix perked up. 'I like that. I like that a lot.'

'I thought you would.' Katy giggled again.

Graves lined the gravel path from the churchyard gate, which led up the hill. The ruin was just visible through some trees.

'I like graves,' said Katy. 'They're interesting.'

'Only if Dracula is rising from one.'

'I like all the old names. The ones you don't see any more. Like that one.'

The girls stopped by the grave that had caught Katy's eye. It was a simple granite stone; its sight line from the path drew the attention. A life-like carving of a bovine head dominated the top half. Blix read the inscription out loud.

'"Montague R. Rhodes." That's about as Victorian a name as you can get, I expect. I can't make out the dates. Is that… something eighteen fifty-three, died something something eighty-six?'"

'"Trust the Soul"' Katy finished. 'What does that mean?'

'Search me. God-bothering doesn't have to make sense. Come on, I'm cold and I want to get back to the pub.'

The gravel path rose up the hill from the churchyard gates toward the ruin of St John's. As they got closer to the church the graves became grander. Simple stones gave way to imploring angels and life-size statues of the dead standing guard over their own tombs.

Blix climbed onto a plinth to get a closer look at one particularly lachrymose effigy. A seated woman, head lying on one shoulder, dolorous and heartsick, cradled a broken lyre on her lap.

'This is well Goth,' said Blix, putting her arm around the statue's shoulders and mimicking its pose.

'It's a copy of the statue on Chopin's grave,' said Katy. 'There's quite a few knock-offs like that around here. Copying famous tombs was a thing once. Look over there.'

She pointed beyond the weeping woman into an overgrown area set back from the path. A shoulder-high oblong of rough granite was almost consumed by ivy. The stone was broken and thrown back at one end as a life-size bronze man burst out of the grave.

Blix laughed. 'Zombies! I've seen this film, there'll be zombies in a second. Brought back from the grave by zombie radiation from Chernobyl, or something. I'm lots faster than you, you'll be brains on toast. Braaaiins on toooaaaaaast.' She stuck out her arms in a Frankenstein pose and let out a deep groan. Then she jumped down, laughing.

'You wish, slow coach. I am Zola Budd and Mary Decker put together compared to you. Anyway, that's a copy of some Belgian guy's grave. I read it in the guide book.'

'Research is fun! But not as much as drinking and being warm. Where's the circle?'

'Behind the abbey,' said Katy. 'We can walk through.'

All that remained of the front of the abbey was the arching lintel of the front door and part of the white marble surrounding it. The long floor plan of the chapel was still clear, and some of the vestry and side rooms were better preserved, but all the roof was long gone. Someone was caring for what remained, but was losing the battle against nature and time. Trees, grass, and ivy crowded the walls, outside and in.

Blix looked around with interest as they walked through. 'This is pretty cool. It must have been spectacular when it was new. Well done, Saint Rog! I hope I get a name like Roger the Agreeable after I'm gone. Like, Blix the Brilliant. Or, Blix the Billionaire!'

'Amelia the Annoying.'

'Harsh. Very harsh.'

'You meant to say fair, there,' said Katy, and hiccupped. They both giggled.

They walked across the boundary line that marked the missing back wall, then down a short slope and along a path through a stand of conifers to the clearing where the Conspirators stood.

Blix wasn't quite sure what she was expecting from a stone circle, but she wasn't expecting the colour.

'They're green!'

'Olivine. Olivine gabbro. It's a mafic igneous rock formed when -' Katy realised her sister wasn't listening. 'Yes, they're green. They have peridot in them.'

That got Blix's attention. 'That's a gemstone. Are we rich?'

'No. Peridot's called olivine when it's too coarse for gems. Anyway, you can't loot a national monument. The Queen would come around and tell mum.'

There were twelve monoliths in all, flat-faced and arranged in four groups of three in a rough circle, fifty feet across. They were big, each between fifteen and twenty feet high, but they lacked the gravitas of something like Stonehenge. Perhaps it was the location, surrounded by mature trees which hid them from the outside world. The Conspirators seemed almost intimate.

Now that she saw them, Blix understood how they'd got their name. Each stone leaned in toward the other two in its group. The slight twists and turns, bends and deformations in the rocks made them look like they were whispering in each other's ears, breathing together. The effect was subtle and, in the dull light of a northern winter made darker still by crowding trees, a little sinister.

There was also a strong sense of time. Blix felt that if she'd been there a thousand years ago, they would have looked just the same. And if she came again a thousand years hence, they would still be there, unchanged, waiting for her. Conspiring against someone.

'This is ancient,' said Blix, without quite knowing why she said it.

Katy had the stone circle book open. 'The circle predates the church. In fact, building the church here was a deliberate statement. It was Christianity taking over an important pagan site.'

'Why didn't they knock it down, then?'

'Dunno. The book doesn't say. Why don't you go back in time and ask them?'

'Yeah, cheers, I was just asking.'

The path continued around the outside of the circle. The grass in the middle was mown, ready for winter. A neat little sign ordered them to KEEP OFF THE GRASS, but the girls agreed that meant other people. They walked into the circle.

'What?' said Blix, stopping short.

'What what?'

'That was weird.'

'Zombie walk over your grave?'

'Yeah. Well, no. I had the strangest feeling. I felt that I was about to walk into a wall. And then I didn't. Because there isn't one.' She shook her head a little.

Katy gave her sister a Look. 'No more booze for you,' she said. 'Have the pop instead.' She cracked the can and handed it to Blix.

'Don't drop the ring-pull, they're bad for wildlife.'

'I know, you've told me that, like, a million billion times. At least.'

As she drank Blix put her hand on the nearest stone, felt the roughness, traced the grain of the rock. On one stone of each group there were runes. She could just make out columns of inch-high lines cut into the stone. The runes were shallow, some little more than suggestions of an incision in the rock.

'These are well preserved, are they?'

'Not to speak of, they've weathered a lot.'

'Leicester said... never mind what Leicester said. What's the deal with the runes?'

'The book says they're written in Futhorc, dated to around the late sixth century AD. So, much younger than the stone circle and only a bit older than the church. Druids did them, which is significant because the Romans suppressed Druidism in the second century AD. So there shouldn't have been Druids any more. They were, like, underground Druids, sneaking around. Stealth Druids.' She narrowed her eyes and looked stealthy. She looked quite silly.

Blix giggled again. 'You love all this stuff, don't you?'

'Yes! History is ace! Horrifying and stupid, sometimes, but well cool. You'd like it if you got into it.'

'I like living things.'

'History is a living thing! Think of the past as a big, sad-eyed, floppy-haired puppy. One that doesn't quite know why it pooed on the carpet and is quite sorry in hindsight but who will do poo again if you ignore it. Poo *everywhere.*'

'Charming. No, it's not for me. Too many dusty books by dead white males for my liking.'

'Right on, sister.' Katy gave a clenched fist salute and got a finger in return. 'In all seriousness, they're good too. Reading history is like listening to the dead without, you know, zombies.'

'It's going to be a zombie day, isn't it? I should keep my mouth shut. Back to the runes please, I can't feel my fingers anymore. What do they say? If Leicester's going to torture us by making us translate them in class, I'm bloody well going to memorise as much as I can. He hates it when I know stuff. It'll annoy the arse off him.'

'English translation, here you go. They're in verse.' Katy passed the book over, indicating a paragraph in italics next to a picture of the Conspirators. It numbered the stones to the verses. Blix oriented herself to the first stone and read out loud.

'Okay, first verse. You who travel, know this. Myrddin's heir set me here, carried me here from fair Hyperborea question mark in square brackets. I honour the she-wolf, born in terror, alive before birth, twice-born, risen from the dead.' She paused. 'What's all that guff about?'

'Myrddin's heirs means magicians. Myrddin is an old name for Merlin. It means the Druids didn't erect this circle. Magicians did. Druids just added the runes.'

'Okay, got it. And the rest?'

'Well, the question mark means the translator was guessing, that Hyperborea bit might not be right. There was a world called that, but the Greeks used that name for part of China so it might mean there. Or it could just be wrong. And I've no clue about the rest. There's a she-wolf in the Romulus and Remus story, but that's Roman not Druid.'

'Fair do's, incomprehensible mumbo-jumbo it is then. Next!' She swung around to the second group of rocks and continued reading.

'You who travel, know this; Myrddin's heir set me here, carried me here from fair - hey, this is the same.'

'That bit repeats on every stone.'

'Right. I honour the God-aurochs, born in lust, this is more like it, prisoner in darkness, secret-keeper, blood-drenched. Nice! Sex and violence, you can't beat it. There's a Channel 4 series in this. Right then, next verse, same as the first, blah Myrddin blah. Then: I honour the Lion-man, noble spirit, corrupted prophet, truth speaker, ever hungering. That's meaningless.'

'That's the most well understood one as it happens. It's referring to a sphinx.'

'Oh, right. I should have got that. An androsphinx, since it says man. Sphinxes are extinct, thousands of years ago. They have an almost complete skeleton in the Museum of Cairo. But what's this about truth-speaking? Sphinxes weren't intelligent. They were animals with humanish faces. They couldn't speak.'

'Everyone know the sphinx story,' said Katy. 'Answer the riddle or get eaten. It was important to whoever carved this, clearly. Do the last one.'

'Usual business, then: I am the traveller, unanchored, lost, yet found. Well. That was different.'

'Yeah, no one has a clue what that means. Doesn't stop them speculating, mind.'

'They should ask a magician. There's a bloke in the sheltered housing behind the estate that claims he was one. He's like, ninety-five or something. He showed me a card trick once. Nice old codger.'

'Wrong kind of magician, I think. The real kind didn't socialize. Power is a solitary pursuit.'

'Deep.' Blix looked around at the ancient stones. 'I don't think a magician of any kind has been around here for a long time. Even back when we still had magicians.'

'I think you're right. Magicians went where power was. This gate has been dead for centuries. I'm not sure it's ever been active. There's a folk story here dating back to Roman Britain which might suggest it was open then. But that's kind of weird, because by then Greco-Roman civilisation knew what the gates did. They were good at recording them too. So a folk tale is a bit passé. Herodotus in his Histories tells of -'

'Sounds fascinating, bore me with it later. Let's get this done and get back in the warm. Tell me, given your plentiful experience, how do you rub a rock-hard erection such as th- ow!' Blix concluded, as Katy punched her on the arm. 'But seriously, how?'

'It's like brass rubbing in reverse. First dry off the stone a bit. Take paper. Apply paper to runes. Take crayon. Rub crayon lengthways on paper, nice and softly. Build up the colour. The crayon is the raised area, anything which doesn't take colour is an indent in the rock. Meaning a rune. Easy peasy.' Katy demonstrated as she spoke, colouring in a large sheet of paper. She pulled it away and held it up for inspection. 'Et voila!'

Blix frowned. 'Which bits are the runes?'

Katy looked at her paper. 'Oh. It hasn't worked. I must have pressed too hard. Or maybe the runes are a bit crap on this one. Let's have a go at a couple of the others.'

The girls split up. Each took the other stone in the group; then they moved to the next group of stones and tried there. Then they each tried a new stone on the other side of the circle. Then another.

Eventually Blix threw down her remaining nub of crayon in disgust and sat on a dry bit of grass with her back to a stone. 'This is useless.'

Katy examined her efforts. 'I can't get a good impression. There's a few here and there, but nothing worth much.' She looked at her sister. 'I've run out of paper.'

Blix fumed. 'He must have known. It was a trick all along. Wasting my weekend and giving him something to humiliate me with next week. Bastard.' She thumped the base of the stone in frustration.

A sharp pain ran up her arm; it felt like she'd got a small electric shock. 'Ow! What the hell?' she cried, scrambling to her knees and away from the stone.

'What happened?'

'I got bitten!' She looked at her hand but there was no bite mark or blood. 'Or stung. Shocked, or something.'

'Zombie bite? Should I destroy your brain? Might take a while, cos, you know, small target... What's that?'

Blix followed her gaze. A yellow light flickered at the base of the megalith. 'I don't know.'

'Don't touch it.'

Blix crawled back toward the stone. A small group of lines and curves, cut into the rock just above the earth, pulsed with a strange light.

'Are those runes? They look a bit Chinese. Why are they doing that? Is it that thing you said? Is it, like, what's the word, fluorescent?'

'Olivine? I don't think so. There are lots of minerals that fluoresce, but - hey, don't get any closer, it might be dangerous.'

Katy looked around. From the base of each stone the same ominous yellow light pulsed. She looked back at her sister. 'Blix, I don't like this. Something's wrong. Let's get out of here.'

Blix was right down now, almost flat on her face a few inches from the strange characters. 'Pass me that book, would you? This is...'

'Blix,' said Katy urgently. 'I mean it.'

'No, look, this is strange.' She looked up at her sister. 'I can read this. I know what it says.'

Katy sat back on her knees. 'You can't read runes,' she said.

'I know. I can't. But I can read this. It's a sentence. Is it in your book?' She took the tome from her sister and started looking for the page on the Conspirators.

'What does it say?'

'"Shambhala. *Come and see.*"'

At once there was a terrible screeching sound, like the scream of grinding steel. The girls screamed as one and clutched their ears. The earth shook and buckled, knocking Katy onto her backside. A spear of yellow lightning crackled up the stone and arced across the circle. It licked the top of each stone and ran down its spine. The book leapt toward the stone Blix had examined, pulled by some strange force, and burst into flame. Then there was silence, and stillness.

'Look,' said Katy.

The runes on each stone were glowing red.

A burst of electricity exploded from the base of the stone. It threw Blix into the sky, flipping her over like a rag until she landed hard on her back in the centre of the circle. She cried out in shock and pain.

'Blix!' Katy screamed, scrambling to her sister's side.

'I'm okay,' said Blix, sitting up, blinking. 'Fuck, that hurt,' she added. 'Fucking run,' she concluded, jerking to her feet.

They ran toward the church. As they reached the circle's edge they slammed into nothing and fell to the ground. In a trice, Blix was on her feet again but slammed into nothing for a second time. A ripple of yellow energy ran through the air in front of her.

'We're trapped!'

'Trapped by what? There's nothing there!'

The ground rumbled. Spikes of power shot off each stone, fizzling and cracking around the circumference, faster and faster. A foul, acrid smell of melting rock bit into their nostrils and made them gag. The girls clung to each other, terrified and disoriented.

'What the hell's happening, Katy?' Blix shouted above the screeching.

Katy looked around. 'The gate's working! It's active! We're going somewhere!'

'That's impossible!'

'It's happening! Hold on to me and don't let go!'

The air above their heads blackened and curled like burnt paper, then exploded upward. A ragged hole split the sky and a sudden surge of power dragged the earth up into the howling vortex, taking the screaming girls with it. The hole snapped shut behind them.

For a moment, all was quiet. Then with an almighty crack one of the stones split in two at an angle halfway up its face. It slid sideways, collapsing into its companions and breaking them apart.

Chapter Six: Fingertips

I am Constant.

I am Darcen Ysir, Darcen of the blood-red hands, the head-taker, killer of wolves and men.

I am Constant.

The mountains had exhausted Constant. It was affecting whose eyes he looked out of. He was finding it difficult to keep himself separate from the memories.

The high forest surrounded him. He crouched beneath the bank of a frozen tarn and broke through the ice to find the trickle of running water beneath. He brought it to his lips, ignoring the bitter cold. He sat on a flat stone, back against the freezing earth, and wondered which would kill him first, the frost or the werewolves. He flipped up his hood and rubbed his ears with the thick wool. He could at least still feel them.

There were werewolves everywhere. He'd killed two on the Anvil, in the tunnel that led to the lowering basket. He struck them down in a terrified frenzy with a sword he'd never held before but somehow wielded like a war-leader in the heat of battle.

There were many more in the town below. He'd hidden from them, ducking from house to house as they rampaged, slaughtering the mountain men as they staggered from their beds. His luck held. He'd made it through the blood-wet streets, to the mighty gate that barred entry to the settlement. It was unbarred from the inside.

Down the great steps he ran, leaving the path, crossing the ice mountain to the great forest which lay beyond, his mind whirling with fear and shock as he left the Anvil for the first time in his life. Behind him smoke began to rise as the wolves put the town to the flame.

Was it luck, or fate? Is the Writing real? Who knows, if not I? What wolves are these, who use fire? Werewolves hate fire. I killed them! Everyone I know is dead. The world of men is dead. What do I do now? I don't know. I don't know. Live.

And here he was, still living. He'd been pushed further and further east, far out of his way, by the need to avoid werewolves. It should have taken him a day to reach his destination. It was now near the end of the third day since he'd left the Anvil and he'd only just managed to circle around to the south side of the mountain again. He'd spent the nights, cold and sleepless, tied to the high branches of the tallest trees he could find, saying his words over and over to calm his mind. A tree was no safer than the ground but did at least make it harder for the werewolves to attack as a group.

He'd managed to avoid them. He knew this was only by chance. Still, it was no bad thing. The part of Constant that was remembering Darcen Ysir knew that the best way to win a fight was not to fight it. The two in the tunnel were met by chance and killed by surprise. The memory of his past self guided his hand as it struck the blow, but the thought of Ysir felt wrong and strange when it rose within his mind. The words had quieted the voice, like all the others, but not silenced it. The memory of the young Ysir was something terrible he had tried to forget but only now realised had always been there, just below the surface, only a thought away, ready to be recalled.

Constant knew what the Great Record said about Ysir. Darcen Ysir had been an extremely bad man before he'd been a good one. A searching brother Recognised him by chance when he was well into his forties. The shock changed him in profound ways. He became deeply spiritual overnight, according to the Record. Spiritual and penitent. A great man of faith for almost sixty years, nigh on a hundred when he passed. The next Great Father was a baby when the monks found him.

Like me, Constant thought, without meaning to.

Across the river, deeper in the forest, there was movement.

Constant froze. He said his words and let the familiar calm slow his racing heart and shallow his breath. He watched carefully, trying to focus on the movement and the contrast between the shapes and the trees.

Two or three. Quite far away. I am downwind. My robe must look like the earth. Don't move. They might hear it if you draw your sword. You don't need it yet. Just wait, and watch. They are moving away. Wait. Just wait.

After a while Constant felt able to breath normally again. He carefully stretched his stiffening muscles.

That's the second time. He glanced at some scratches on his hands, mementoes of a headlong dive into some bushes the day before. *My luck is holding. Maybe you were right Simon. Maybe I can survive this.*

The thought of Brother Simon made Constant's eyes ache. It was too cold for tears. Even if it weren't, here was not the place for them. He rubbed his eyes, tired beyond anything he'd ever known.

I thought 'I' am downwind just now. Then I thought 'you'. Who is present and who is past?

He bent over to drink some more, and caught sight of his reflection in the clear ice. He was slightly shocked to see it was a boy's.

'That is my face,' he said out loud. 'I am Constant. I am twelve. I must remember that.'

His eyes hurt a lot. He closed them, and pushed the memory of Brother Simon as far away as possible.

Constant dreamed.

In my dream, I ride along the forest trail, brooding on my defeat. I am not used to defeat. Seven of my men ride behind me, in varying states of disrepair. One carries another over the neck of his horse. The other is dead. The rider weeps. He must have cared for the dead man in some way. I do not understand such things. I would have left the corpse where it fell and forgotten it. I will make another corpse if the one who lives does not stop sobbing soon.

In my dream, I think, if the sentries were still alive I'd kill them for their failure. The night before last we burned Golo's Staad and took spoils aplenty. By dawn the men were drunk or asleep or hilt deep in a woman. The sentries should have sworn off and kept their watch. But they were weak. The enemy overtook them.

The enemy. Keeper's men from the Bastion judging by the uniforms. They stole up in the grey hour before sunrise, disciplined and efficient. They slit the throats of the night-watchmen then stampeded our own horses through the camp, killing men under hoof and confusing the rest when they needed to be alert. I came awake to volleys of arrows falling from the sky, felling my soldiers as they rose naked from their blankets. Only a shield at my hand saved me from taking one in the eye. Then their own horsemen charged. Terrifying Bright Helms with steel-tipped lances and horse-swords that could cut a man in half. Finally, their infantry marched in, shields locked high and spears ready, to mop up. That was a formality.

In my dream, I think, I escaped, but only just. Clinging to a panicked horse, letting it drag me beyond sight of the invaders. I don't know if any others did. These seven, soon to be six if that fool doesn't stop bawling, may be all that remain. Half a thousand of the world's most feared killers, exterminated in minutes. Everything I have built over twenty years, lost.

'I'll have to start again,' I think, only to find that I have said it out loud.

The man next to me says something and I think he is responding to me, but he nods up the trail. We are passing between high banks, well covered with trees. A man sits against a trunk on the right side, long legs crossed in front of him. He wears a padded shirt with a high steel collar and mail sleeves over thick leather vambraces. Armour against werewolves. He is reading a small book and affects not to notice us.

I know what this means.

'Ho, friend,' I say, in a pleasant way. I have practiced this.

The man looks up. 'Ho yourself,' he says, in a broad rural voice, also friendly-like. We begin the dance. 'Where away?' says he.

'Passing through. From back there to up yonder. Is this your place?'

I pull out my smoking pipe as I speak and tamp the leaves into it. It's the sort of unthreatening thing a peaceful man might do.

'This is anyone's place,' he says. He has the measured tone of a confident killer. He is reading, so he is no peasant. Some lordling, then. He turns down the corner of his book to mark his place and sets it down.

'The Bastion's writ does not run here. The Anvil is thousands of miles away. Free men live here. All who come in peace are welcome.'

Meaning I am fucked. Well. I have a plan.

'What is your name, friend?' I continue. I think on a small trick I know and snap my fingers.

'Burn,' I say.

Fire appears in the pipe bowl. It draws the eye, this trick, and when they are watching the fire they are not watching my eyes. I scan the treeline and the nearby bushes. I can see where the ambush will be sprung. My men, who have heard me call this man "friend" and know I have marked him for death, stir a little in their saddles, and look for themselves, and see what I see.

'I am Colmm of the Karyv Bahn,' says he, naming a nearby hold. He touches his forehead with a finger in polite salute. 'And who are you, brother magician?'

Men in this age do not call each other "friend" and "brother" and expect to walk away. I assume this to be a similar signal to some hidden bowmen. In my dream, I think, I will give them some pause now.

'I'm no magician. My name is Darcen Ysir.'

The Karyv Bahnner considers this. I can see him turning the information over in his mind. He does not seem cowed. There must be a few of them.

'That's a famous name,' he says after a while.

'I've done some things,' I agree.

The man muses some more. 'I've heard him called the head-taker.'

'Stops them getting back up,' I say.

Another pause. Men must be creeping into position.

'Head-taking's become quite the pastime hereabouts,' the man says. 'The All-men are carrying around a head they say answered to that name. It's on a spear point.'

'They are mistaken.'

'Mayhap. Nonetheless, there is a head with a name. I saw it yestereve, a league or two south of here. Whatever his name, he seemed quite unhappy about the situation.'

His gaze flicks behind me and I see we are ready.

'Do you think I use another man's name?' I ask.

'No,' he says. 'I think you're you. I won't insult you by saying otherwise. Who would claim to be you who was not? You'd kill him.' He grins. I like this one, I realise. Shame.

An arrow whistles my death song, but I am already under my horse when it arrives to claim me. It takes the weeping fool in the throat instead. My sharp lads have already planned their moves and are away, swords screaming, laying about the camouflaged woodsmen who are finding that the surprise is on them.

I gain the high bank in three great leaps. My new friend has risen with a good longsword in hand. He crouches, hilt behind his head, mailed shield arm extended ahead of him ready to deflect my swing so he can leap and stab me in the heart, striking down through my neck into my breast. A good stance I think, one I might take, but I am inside his guard and have killed him before he realises I am there.

He clutches at me and I let him slide to the ground as I pull out my blade. His face is still friendly, even as he spews up blood.

'Not your fault,' I say, though I am not sure why. 'It's just chance. It could have gone the other way. As if it matters.'

He nods. He understands. Then he dies.

Now there is a boy here I do not recognise.

'I'm glad you survived, Constant,' *he says.* 'Not just for selfish reasons either. Although for them as well. You can be a bit of an oaf, but it could be a lot worse. This one was hard work. A very strange mind. Very persistent. I had to bear down on him. Gave him a real epiphany when he was Recognised. Didn't have to do that to you.'

The boy gives me a kindly look, one a boy might give a favourite pet.

'I'm expending a lot of energy to keep you alive, do you know that? Of course you don't. You should have died of exposure by now. It's a long time since I've had to do this, I'm not sure I can do it for much longer. I don't want to leave you, Constant. That would be terrible. WAKE UP.'

Constant did not remember the boy when he woke up.

Constant jerked back to consciousness, hitting the sword pommel on the under hang and showering himself with earth. He had no idea where he was, or who he was. He pushed the panic away and collected himself, breathing calmly and with focus as he had been taught to do. *I am Constant. There is no doubt.* He said his words until he felt better.

He rubbed his eyes and tried to work out how long he'd been asleep. Only a few minutes he guessed, not long enough for the sky to darken. Clouds like white bone knives serrated the sky.

Did I dream? I don't remember. Something about Ysir? He had a trick...

Constant stared at his fingers for several minutes. Then he found a twig, and stared at it instead. He rubbed his forehead irritably, trying to grasp a memory, trying to focus.

'Burn?' he suggested. He snapped his fingers.

'Ahh!' He stifled the exclamation and jerked back, showering himself with dirt again, as a sharp pain pierced his two fingertips. It felt like a snake bite. A wisp of smoke curled from the twig, gone as soon as it appeared. Constant shook his fingers as they tingled and numbed.

Well I won't try that again. Say what you want with the desire to make it happen? Great Fathers, Simon, I wish you had taught me magic. The words aren't enough.

His eyes ached again. Tiredness made his head buzz, a strange pulsing that felt like blood washing behind his eyes. He rubbed them again, his numb fingertips feeling like they belonged to a stranger. Patterns of light danced across the darkness.

Constant dreamed.

In my dream, I am walking through a forest. I am always walking through a fucking forest. The entire world is nothing but trees and mountains. The first men thought it was paradise. The place they came from must have been hell. There is nothing worth having here.

In my dream, it is winter, and snow is thick on the ground. The trees look like the ghosts of their summer selves. It is freezing, but I don't feel the cold like other people. I don't feel anything like other people.

In my dream, I have two hundred men at my back, strung out through the woods. Up ahead, somewhere, is a town. It is well defended. People like me have been trying to take it for generations, without much luck. Under the snow, under the earth, lie the bones of those people. That's where we'll all end up, sooner or later. When my time will come, I don't know. There have been many times I've lived when I should have died.

'I see steel,' whispers a man to my left, and we all stop and take a knee. The word ripples through the line without the word ever being spoken. I grip my sword and loosen it in its scabbard. My free hand goes to the stone strung around my neck.

I look where the man points and see what he sees. Metal glinting in the weak sunlight. Metal where it should not be. I watch for some time until I realise what I am seeing. Then I stand up again.

'There's no enemy there,' I say. 'None that can hurt us, anyway.'

We approach. It's a sword, stuck in a tree. No, stuck is the wrong word. The sword fell here years ago, when the tree was a sapling, struck from some unlucky hand. It cut into the wood and the tree grew around it, from sapling to full grown oak, longer ago that I have been alive. The sword is part of the tree now.

I look around. Now that I have eyes to see them, such relics are everywhere. Here, a pole grows through a rusted helmet, lifting it over generations from the ground to a man's height. There, a tree wears a mail vest, the flesh and ribs that it grew through long since consumed by the earth. It is quite beautiful, in a way. I am not a man who sees beauty in things.

One of my men says, 'It's as if the forest goes to war. It's an omen. What does it mean?'

'It means that life is as meaningless as it looks,' I say. 'Let me hear no more of that superstitious crap. People lived and died and now lie here under the soil and it doesn't matter. The town is ahead. Let's kill these people and take what they've got. As if that matters either.'

The word goes down the line. We walk on.

Now there is a boy here I do not recognise.

'This fellow's being quite assertive for a memory, isn't he? You've been saying the words for so long I'd forgotten it could be like this. It'll be easier to deal with once you've had some sleep. If you stay here, you'll sleep here. If you sleep here, you'll die. So, let's keep moving. It's not far now. In the meantime, there's something going on nearby you should investigate. A lot of magic in the air. A lot. That shouldn't be possible. I don't like it. Go and have a look, it's on your way. Stay well clear though, no point risking our lives after we went to all this effort to save them, is there?'

Constant did not remember the boy when he woke up.

Constant jerked awake again.

If I stay here I'll sleep here. If I sleep here, I'll die. The words appeared in his mind as though thought by someone else. He wasn't sure who. His memories of his former lives, though vague and fleeting, had shape and form, an anchor in the past which held them together. This thought was attached to Nothing.

I'm so tired I'm forgetting who I am. I'm right though. If I stay here I'll die. I must keep moving.

His route led down the mountain. He wasn't at all sure how he knew, but he did. There was a house at the end of it, with a bed and a fire and a woman he did not remember.

He slipped out of cover, stood up and stretched. He hoped there was food there too. He walked toward the treeline, going home. His fingertips were still numb.

Chapter Seven: Separation

The sky heaved and turned itself inside out and spat Blix and Katy out of nothingness and into the world. They hit the ground hard, tumbled, slid and skidded to a halt. The air sizzled and popped around them.

Blix lay still, staring at the sky, panting. Her whole body felt numb. When she tried to sit up the world turned unexpectedly, and she collapsed. She heard her sister throwing up. Her own stomach turned over.

'What happened?' she managed.

'God, Blix, are you there?' her sister cried.

'Yes,' she said. 'I can't stand up,' she said.

'I can't see! I can't see anything!'

With effort Blix rolled over. She cried out at the sudden agony which convulsed her body, as though all her muscles had cramped at once. She crawled across to her sister. There was a gash across Katy's hairline. It looked deep and ugly.

'There's blood in your eyes. Lie still.'

The doombag lay nearby. It looked undamaged. Blix reached for it, only to discover her hand was shaking uncontrollably. She took deep, ragged breaths, steadied herself, and dug through the bag until she found the water. She splashed it in her sister's eyes, wiping the blood away with the heel of her hand. She dug some tissues out of her satchel, wadded them and held them on Katy's wound. A bloom of blood turned the white paper crimson.

Blix's strength gave out and she collapsed next to her sister. They lay there for a little while, holding each other and sobbing as the terror receded.

'What in God's name happened?' said Blix, rolling over with difficulty.

Katy sat up, wincing. Blood trickled down her face. 'First aid kit,' she said absently, reaching for her bag. 'Always pack a first aid kit.'

'Katy. What the actual fuck just happened?'

'The gate opened!' Katy shouted. 'We went through! We're on the other side!'

'That's impossible!'

'I know! What the fuck did you do, *Amelia*?' Anger mottled Katy's face.

'It wasn't me! I didn't do anything!'

'You did something! You read the runes!'

'You asked me!'

'You should have kept your mouth shut! Aaah!' Katy winced and cradled her head. 'God, this hurts.'

'Let me see.' Blix moved her sister's hand away, and peeled back the matted wad of tissue. 'Okay, not as bad as I thought. It might need a stitch or two, but you won't look like Frankenstein's monster.'

She found the first aid kit. There was a sterile dressing and adhesive tape; she cleaned the wound again and taped the dressing over it. 'There. The good thing about wanting to be a vet is that people are animals too.'

'Thanks,' said Katy, testing the dressing. 'Sorry,' she added. 'I was upset.'

'Forget it. Where are we?'

'I don't know. Wherever the gate pointed.'

Blix could feel her toes again; they hurt. She struggled to her knees. The effort made her head swim.

They were in a stone circle, different to the Conspirators. A group of eight almost identical red basalt menhirs about ten feet high. Their prosaic uniformity nonetheless seemed ancient and strange.

On one side of the circle, mountains towered above them. On the other, a dense pine forest. Outside the ring deep snow pushed up to the edge the stones. Inside it had melted. The grass beneath had burned red-black. It crumbled into dust at Blix's touch.

'I still don't get it,' said Blix. 'The gate was dead. All gates are dead. The magic doesn't exist anymore. How did we get here?'

'Come now, Miss Summerland,' said a familiar voice behind her. 'I expect more of you than gaping stupidity. Not much more.'

'Leicester!' gasped Blix.

Her teacher was leaning against a menhir, arms folded across his chest, wide-eyed and staring.

'That's Mister Leicester to you, although I suppose we can dispense with that charade now. You may call me by my real name. The name I am described by. I am *Echmoth*.' He uncurled himself from the rock and moved toward her.

Without even thinking, Blix sprang to her feet to run, her pain forgotten, dragging her sister up with her. But as she turned to flee she immediately stumbled to a halt, horrified by what she saw.

Echmoth wasn't alone. Ranged around the circle were six men who were not men, their monstrous, alien nature uncanny and bestial and wrong. Blix's flesh crawled at the sight.

'Christ, Katy, they're werewolves! Real ones!'

'What do we do?'

'I don't know!'

The werewolves towered over them. Each had a sword strapped to its waist. Most were covered in pitch-black, lank, matted hair, some with a few scraps of rusted armour here and there. But there was one, larger by a head than the rest, whose fur was silver-grey.

The silver-grey werewolf loped across the circle and stopped beside Echmoth. The rest skulked at the edge, bored. They stank of wet fur and rotting meat, and blood. Blix wanted to run but she knew they'd kill her without a thought. She clung to her sister.

'Y-you did this?' she stammered.

Echmoth scowled. 'Really, what a stupid thing to say. I spend a dreary afternoon lecturing you on gate magic. I send you on a contrived errand to a gate. It comes to life after centuries of somnolence and drags you across space and time. Here I am at the other end. And you ask whether I did it. It is evident. Two and two is four indeed.'

'You opened the gate?' said Katy, her voice shaking.

Echmoth seemed to notice her for the first time. 'Ah, the other Miss Summerland. Do you know, I think this body would have rather preferred to have taught you? You care about the same things. I might not have come to despise you as I despise your sister. Alas, the magician saw her first. Still, it matters not in the long run. Or the short run, for you.'

His demeanour changed; he looked at once awestruck and hungry. 'You are so special...' He trailed off, rapt, and then grimaced.

'This body reminds me that I have not answered your question. It desires strict accuracy. Damn the man and his pedantry. I had to let far more of Leicester's personality survive than I normally would to do his blasted job. Well, *Blix* Summerland,' he continued nastily, making air quotes around her first name with his fingers, 'I hope you appreciate the pain and tedium I have suffered to be near you. To ensure you remained intact.'

Echmoth winced again. 'Damn you Leicester. When you die, I will laugh. Very well. In strictness, no, I did not open the gate. I caused it to occur. The credit goes to Dragonvi-'

He turned, expecting someone to be there who was not, and frowned. 'Dragonville? Where are you?'

There was no response. He raised his voice to the querulous squeak that Blix had come to hate.

'Dragonville! Come here at once!'

A man sauntered forth from the tree line. He was handsome, perhaps in his late forties, and wore a thick black moustache and side whiskers. He was well dressed in an old-fashioned style, like something out of a Charles Dickens novel. A long, double-breasted coat, buttoned to the collar against the cold, fell to his knees. He wore a top hat, set at a jaunty angle, and grey leather gloves. He was smiling as if on a pleasant walk in the country. He patted one of the werewolves on the shoulder as he entered the ring. It shied away and snarled in fury.

'My apologies, Echmoth old thing. I went somewhat further back than you.' His voice was rich and full of laughter. It made Blix think of ripe plums. He stopped next to Echmoth and looked at Blix and Katy with apparently genuine good humour. 'The pair! How wonderful. Just as I expected.' He turned to Echmoth. 'And you doubted me.'

'With good reason. I convey an apology, if that is necessary.'

'Not at all old thing, not at all.'

Echmoth regarded the man with ill-disguised disdain. 'Hiding in the trees, Dragonville?'

'I'm surprised you didn't too. Your new body looks somewhat fragile.'

Echmoth scowled, disgusted by the man's bonhomie.

'It is adequate. It has an annoying and persistent desire for exactness which I find tiresome. But it allowed me to gain proximity to the child, so it served its purpose. I do not think it will last. But did you think your magic would test its robustness, Dragonville? Do you lack faith in your own power? Is the bloodstone so uncontrollable?'

The man called Dragonville slipped a hand inside his coat. He pulled out what looked to Blix like a thick green disk about the size of a pocket watch. He flipped it like a coin and caught it between his index and middle fingers. He smiled easily.

'No,' he replied. 'Quite simple. A child could say the gate words and the power in the artefact is readily accessible, if you are exact enough. That's all there is to it. That and the desire to do it.'

He held the stone up to the fading light and watched the dim green and red glow as the sun's rays caught its edge. 'Although I must say, Echmoth, what an artefact! It is quite extraordinary. There are no words which adequately describe it. Even given what I have already done with it - magic, look you, of incalculable power - I could open gates daily for a century and not come close to draining it. It is exquisite. Even though *somebody* managed to damage it when they were acquiring it.' He glanced pointedly at the werewolf leader, who looked like he wanted to rip Dragonville's throat out.

'But you see, Echmoth, although the pieces are easy, the whole was really quite difficult, you know. Only prudent to be careful. Significant sorcery can come with unexpected side effects. Explosions and maimings and suchlike. Magic is practiced by the puissant, but survived by the cautious.'

He laughed in sudden delight, and span on his heels like a dancer, arms raised to take the appreciation of an imagined audience.

'And what magic! I tell you Echmoth, this experiment reminds me of the carefree days of my youth. It's all too marvellous. Take just today, the magic of this moment. Beyond-sight across the rift to see when the Misses Summerland arrived.' He touched the brim of his hat to Katy and Blix. 'Then synchronising through the gain and activating the runes. And, my apologies dear lady, a tiny shock to attract your attention, and a little spell so you could read the activation rune. All fine works of magic in themselves, but together! I have been subtle and exquisite in my craft.'

Echmoth looked unimpressed. 'You boast, Dragonville. You've dragged half the countryside through with them.'

'I do not. It is a matter of fact that the task required extraordinary magic. I am an extraordinary magician. As for the rest, the gate is old even by the standards of gates. I admit I wasn't certain it would pull across such a long distance, gave it a bit of umph to make sure, perhaps a bit much.' He touched one of the stones and looked into the middle distance. 'Yes, looks like the old girl couldn't take it. The other side's caved in.' He laughed, and then winked at Blix. 'Could have been worse, hey? Could have blown. Would've been raining menhirs and bits of the Summerland girls as far as the eye can see. But never fear, here you are safe and sound, for the time being. Don't need to use it again anyway. It's not like you're going home.'

His tone was so pleasant that Blix almost missed his last words. Her blood chilled as she realised what he'd said.

Something caught her eye. Katy was shaking her head. Blix recognized the look; she was trying to rationalise things.

'How can you do magic? There isn't magic anymore.'

Belmont Dragonville inclined his head. 'You are mistaken.'

'No, I'm not. There's no such thing as magic anymore. That's a fact.'

'I regret I must correct you, dear lady. Your statement requires qualification. There isn't magic in England in nineteen eighty-six. But we are not in England in nineteen eighty-six, are we? Which is a marvellous place by the way, just marvellous. But this world is more receptive to magic than dear old dead dull and boring Blighty. As for the year - how do you say the year here, my dear First of Wolves?' He turned to the monster.

'This is the Wolf Age,' the thing growled.

'Yes, that's not helpful. The late thirty-nine-hundreds I believe, dated from some local religious profundity.'

'We've travelled through time!' blurted Blix, astonished. The wizard smirked and shook his head.

'Ah, no. Not terribly so, anyway. That's just how they say nineteen eighty-six here. It's all quite different to Earth, I've found. Never been here before, you see. Never saw the need. A bit desolate and very uphill. Never gave it a thought. Ironic I suppose. Turns out to be *terribly* interesting. Scope for a monograph at least I'd say. I may publish.'

'Enough words,' growled the First of Wolves. 'You yelp like puppies. Take them.'

'I am in charge here,' said Echmoth sharply. 'But you are right. We waste time. It seems I have a choice, Dragonville. Two Misses Summerland, each as special as the other. I need only one.'

'You can't have her,' said the girls in unison. Everyone ignored them.

'Which?' said the werewolf.

Echmoth considered. 'They're both suitable. Identical twins are physiologically the same person, displaying virtually no chromosomal diff-'

'Which?' interrupted the werewolf, irritated. 'The Great Pack has made the crossing without me. We must return to the Wolfmaker. She is waiting for us. For *you.*'

'Indeed. My business will conclude shortly. The Narrow Way will open. And afterward, *Elpis.*'

'Say rather, *spes,*' said Dragonville. '*Spes vetus.* It is rather more exact, don't you think? Better to live in hope than expectation.' He chuckled as though he had made a small joke.

'Yes. *Spes vetus.*' Echmoth looked back to the First of Wolves. 'Then you will unleash your Great Pack across worlds. There will be blood such as will sate even your thirst.'

The werewolf looked at him with abject hatred in its eyes. 'I am not interested in blood,' it said.

'You are unique among wolves. You will get what you want too. I know what that is.'

The beast threw its head back and howled. The other werewolves joined it. It was the most terrifying thing Blix had ever heard. It set off something primal inside her and she couldn't think anymore. She fell to her knees, clutching her ears, begging for it to stop, sobbing in fear and panic, joined seconds later by her sister.

'Enough, First of Wolves,' said Dragonville, wincing. 'I have enough problems without adding deafness to them.'

The First of Wolves glared at him and stopped. His men followed suit. Blix gasped explosively as the terror abated.

The sound echoed around the mountains. In the far distance, other voices took up the howl. *They're everywhere*, Blix thought.

Echmoth had remained unmoved during the werewolves' display, considering his problem. He rested a thumb on his chin and tapped a long finger against one cheek.

'Hmm. Well. Choices, choices. A month on that poxy world, guarding *Blix* until the day I could bring her here. Living in this shell, suffering when salvation was so close at hand. I have observed her. Fixed her in my eye over all things. I've grown to dislike her. She is rude and stupid. I have no desire to be stupid. I'll take the other one instead. She is a little brighter and looks the part. More a rose than this little thorn.'

'No!' said Katy and Blix.

The First of Wolves strode over to the girls and pushed them apart. He grabbed Katy, lifting her bodily and wrapping her under his arm as if she weighed nothing. Katy screamed and beat her hands against him, to no effect.

'You bastard, leave her alone!' Blix yelled. She sprang at him and slammed her fists as hard as she could into his side. He grunted, then with a contemptuous sweep of his arm sent her flying. She landed heavily on her left shoulder and screamed sharply as pain daggered through her arm. Her head bounced off the bare earth and her vision swam. She struggled to get up, but the world revolved around her and she collapsed.

'Blix!' Katy wailed.

The First of Wolves was unmoved. 'This one is yours. And the other?'

Echmoth shrugged. 'She was rude to me. I should punish her. Give her to your wolves. Perhaps they are as efficient rapists as they are killers.'

He turned to the monsters, who were suddenly paying attention to him, and raised his voice. 'You have served well. This is my reward. Make her wish she was dead, then kill her. Make sure she is dead. Another like me may find her otherwise, and I am not sociable.'

Blix was barely conscious now. She heard Echmoth and the horror of his words dragged some last ounce of strength out of her terrified soul. She heaved herself to her feet, but managed no more than two or three steps before her legs gave way. She collapsed, helpless, at Dragonville's feet. She twisted until she faced the First of Wolves again.

'Let her go or I'll kill you,' she said, spitting up blood. 'I'll kill you!'

The First of Wolves considered her for a moment. 'You have spirit,' he said. He looked at the struggling girl under his arm. 'You too.' He cuffed Katy hard with the back of his paw. She went limp. He slung the unconscious girl over one shoulder and turned to Echmoth.

Dragonville stepped over Blix. He looked down at her, his smile almost kind. But Blix looked into his eyes, drawn to them somehow even through her daze. It seemed that the twinkling blue vanished, replaced by a strange silver streaked with corroded red, a rust of iron. They were dead and hollow, soulless.

A thought swam through her treacle-thick mind and surfaced in her consciousness. *This is not a man,* thought Blix.

'Oh, I'm a man right enough,' said Dragonville, though Blix was sure she had not spoken aloud. 'I have, however, made some *terrible* decisions in my life.'

Then the moment was gone and the colour returned to his eyes, as blue as sweet melancholy once more.

'Sorry, child,' he said. 'This is where it ends for you. Look on the bright side though. At least you get to die.'

Then clawed hands were on her body, dragging her roughly to her feet. One werewolf held her under her arms from behind. Four others approached her, panting with excitement, their eyes a burning, chemical yellow.

One spoke to the First of Wolves. 'We will be left behind.'

The First of Wolves shook his head. 'When the human is dead, howl the rest down from the mountains to gather here. In three days, the conjuror will open the air once more.'

'Will I?' said Dragonville, giving them the lazy eye. 'I suppose I will. I'll open it now, too. Stand back now, there's a good fellow.'

He took an object from an inside pocket. It looked like an old monocle, though somewhat larger, a blue glass lens surrounded by several layers of gold wire.

'Now then, 'ware magic! Shadrach, Meshach, Abednego, off we go!'

A red-gold light exploded from the lens with a thunderous crack. It seemed to Blix that it hit the air like light projected on a cinema screen. Then in the circle of light there was a picture of a large stone-built room set with long, heavy wooden bookcases, arranged as spokes in a wheel under a high stained-glass ceiling. Life size and lifelike, the image of the room appeared out of nowhere and hung there. Then it was real.

Dragonville walked through the image and leaned against one of the bookcases. 'Ta-da,' he said, executing a little flourish with his hands. 'The Bastion awaits.'

Echmoth looked unimpressed. 'Really, Dragonville. I have seen you do that a dozen times without the light show or the thunderclap or- magic words, Dragonville? Are we children? Who do you seek to impress?'

Dragonville laughed, and curled his moustache. 'Why, everyone! I am enjoying my new toys, Echmoth. A little smoke and mirrors hurts no one and gives pleasure to all. Well, most. You can't deny a man his theatrics, as Mr Maskelyne says. What is life if not show?'

'Pain,' said Echmoth, as grim as midwinter. 'But not for much longer.' He glanced at Blix. 'A little longer for you.'

He walked into the room, followed by the First of Wolves, carrying Katy. Dragonville adjusted the lens and the room vanished, as if it had never been there.

Blix was left on the mountain with five werewolves.

'Please, don't,' she said.

Chapter Eight: The Bitten Man

'I'm first,' said a werewolf, pushing forward. 'I'm going to fuck you 'til you're dead inside, bitch.'

'Let's see the meat,' said another. Blix screamed as it yanked back her jacket. It split and hung off her. The monster's claws sliced through her t-shirt and undershirt; her bra went the same way.

'Too smooth,' the wolf complained, pawing roughly at her breasts. 'Not a proper bitch.' It jerked her jeans open and pulled them down to her ankles, and tore away her knickers. 'Some fur at least.' The werewolves laughed, a vicious, guttural gurgle of hate.

The one holding her grabbed her throat. 'I'm going to eat those pretty eyes, little girl.'

The werewolves crowded around her, hard and eager. Blix shook violently. A low, primal wail of utter terror and despair erupted from her throat.

'Yes,' said the last werewolf. 'Sing to us. Sing that song as we tear you apart. Sing it as I break your teeth. It sounds so sweet. Sing louder.'

'Enough talk,' said the first. 'Bend her over.' It grabbed Blix and bent her double, twisting her so she could still see its face.

'I'm going to bite the flesh from your bones,' it said, its mouth gaping wide.

'Bite this,' said a voice, and the werewolf's head exploded in an arc of silver and blood.

Blix was flung sideways by the force of the blow. The shattered wolf corpse collapsed alongside her, fountaining blood from the pulp of its skull. A second wolf was dead before the first hit the ground. Its guts spilled out from the hole hacked through its torso, which burned and crumbled as though soused with acid. It looked surprised as its legs gave way.

The other three werewolves leapt away from the blows, then turned to see their attacker.

'It's a boy!' said one.

'I am the death of wolves,' said the boy. A long, bright sword flashed in his hand. 'I am vengeance for the dead. I will strike you down like the dogs you are.'

The werewolf who'd spoken shook his muzzle violently and roared in strangled, incoherent rage. It sprang high through the air, clawing for the boy's face. The boy stepped forward and turned under the creature, swinging the blade up into its chest and dragging it back hard. It bit deeply into the werewolf's flesh, twisting the beast under its own momentum further through the plane of the sword. When the werewolf landed it was almost in two pieces.

'Next,' said the boy.

The last two werewolves looked at each other, and drew their own swords.

'Sensible,' said the boy. 'You can't fight me with your hands, claws or no. Swords are better. As if it matters.'

The werewolves spread out until they were almost either side of the boy, then charged him as one, swords swinging for his head. The boy parried one strike behind his head then, lightning fast, turned and took the second on his blade as well. He ducked under the swords, grabbed the arm of the wolf to his left and pushed its own sword into its face. He sliced across its eyes, not deep but enough to make it howl and stagger backwards holding its face as blood welled up. He back-heeled the other wolf hard in the midriff and as it doubled over he thrust the point of his sword up though its chin and into its brain. He yanked it out, swung it in a high circle around his head, and decapitated the last wolf. The sword sliced through the neck and hands as though they were the stems of dead flowers. The wolf's head landed upright. It blinked and gaped as it watched its body fall. Then the orange flame in its eyes spluttered and went out.

'Of course, you can't fight me at all,' the boy continued, although there was only Blix left to hear him. He held the silver sword up for inspection, looking at it as if he'd never seen it before. He watched as thickening wolf blood slid down the blade toward the hilt. 'Sharp sword,' he said.

The whole battle had lasted less than a minute.

The boy pushed back his hood to reveal a round, serious-looking face, scratched and bruised, under a shock of black hair. He cleaned his sword on a dead werewolf. The sword was almost as long as he was tall. He walked over to Blix, who lay where she had fallen, too terrified to move.

'Hello. My name's Constant. You can get up now, they're all dead.'

Wild-eyed and shaking, Blix looked from the boy to the scene of carnage and back again.

'You killed them!'

'Yes.'

'Five men! You just killed them!'

'Not men. Wolves. Werewolves. They were trying to rape you, they deserved it. Are you bitten? There are scratches on your breast, but are you bitten?'

Blix remembered she was nearly naked. She scrambled away from him, turning and covering herself as well as she could with her tattered clothes.

'Don't worry,' said Constant, gently. 'I'm twelve. And I'm a monk. I'm not going to hurt you. Here, cover yourself with this.'

Constant unwound the string binding his bundle together. There was a scabbard for the big sword, plain and ancient-looking, and a large, thin cloth. He gave the sheet to Blix and sheathed the sword. 'Have my belt too, they've ruined yours.' He undid the rope at his waist and threw her that as well, letting his robe hang free. 'I'll turn away if you like. Let me know if I should kill anything behind me. And hurry up. We can't stay here.'

The werewolves had ripped Blix's jeans from the waist down. One seam and the button were burst, but with the boy's belt they held together and stayed up. They'd also torn her t-shirt, vest and bra, and sliced her leather jacket from top to bottom beside the zip.

Self-conscious, she slipped out of the jacket, keeping her back to the boy while also trying to watch him. The cloth turned out to be a cotton sheet, faded and a bit dirty, about the size of a double bedspread. There was strange writing in a script she didn't understand. She doubled it over and wrapped around her like a toga, tight against her skin, and put her jacket back on over the top. It felt strange and scratchy, but secure. She stuffed the ruined clothes into her satchel, which had miraculously survived the attack unscathed.

The carnage around her was horrifying. But with the horror came a profound relief. And guilt, and shame, anger, hatred, disgust, happiness. She didn't know what to think or how to react or what to do, and then suddenly she couldn't cope. She sat down hard, drew her knees up to her chest and held them tight, and cried so hard her whole body hurt with each bitter, convulsive sob.

Constant let her cry.

Constant dreamed.

In my dream, I stand before seven kneeling men. I am leaning on a huge horse sword I recently took from someone. The hilt reaches my chest and the blade is thicker than my thigh. It's a ridiculous weapon, which is why its former owner is dead. It looks impressive though. The men look terrified. This is the correct reaction to seeing me behind any kind of sword.

A few of my men guard them, not that they need guarding. Millet farmers who thought to take up the cudgels against the evil bandits. They didn't win. The rest of them are dead, or wish they were. These are the cowards. They surrendered when they saw that all was lost. I don't know what they thought they'd gain by that.

'Mercy,' says one very naive elder.

'Of course,' I say. 'I'm known for my mercy.' Chuckles from my men.

'I take no prisoners,' I say loudly. A moan rises from the kneeling farmers. Something primal from the pits of their stomachs. I see one of them look desperately at my sword, as though he might lunge for it and take it from me.

'I wouldn't,' I say. 'You'll die.'

The man subsides, and looks away. The one next to him is crying in impotent fear. As if it matters.

'Tell you what though. Let's play a game. First man to say my name gets to run away.'

Silence. The men look at each other.

'I don't know your name,' stutters the elder.

'That's a shame,' I say, and behead him.

The others cry out as the old man's head rolls across the ground. I watch it for a moment until it comes to a stop, eyes in the dirt. I wonder when death starts, whether he still hears my words.

I turn to the next man. 'Do you know my name?' I ask.

In my dream, I walk along the line, asking the question and taking the head from each man who gets it wrong. The fourth and fifth babble names desperately, but none of them are mine.

I see straight away that the sixth is not like others. He is the one who looked to take my sword. He is scared sure enough, crying with it in fact, but his fear is not the terror of the others. He has something inside which gives him strength.

'Do you know my name?' I ask.

'I don't,' he says. He bows his head. 'Let's get this over with.'

I raise the sword. Then I lower it again. Something isn't right. He is wearing a ragged shirt, suitable for field work. I see that it has been torn and mended several times. No, torn doesn't quite describe it. "Rent" would be a better word. I see something under his collar. I push it back. Then I tear it away, ripping the shirt until it hangs in rags at his waist.

'Bites.'

His shoulders are covered with tooth marks, semicircles of pierced flesh. The thing that attacked him was ferocious. I'm surprised he's alive.

'That must have hurt,' I say.

'Worst day of my life.' He looks up. 'So far.'

'And now you're a werewolf. A changer.' I hold the big sword up to his face. The steel glistens with the blood of his friends. 'This can't kill you.'

'Not so I can't come back.' There's a hint of smugness in his voice. 'You don't look rich enough to have silver. You wouldn't be here if you were.'

'No, I don't look rich. I'm not, in fact.'

I move on to the next man. 'Do you know my name?'

He is already rocking back and forth; as I speak he bursts into tears, bawling like a baby, and bends forward into a foetal position, hugging his knees. By the smell of him he's soiled himself too. His weakness is contemptible and irritating.

'Look at you,' I say. 'You bend like the bough before it breaks. Disgusting. You're a grown man. You should be more like your friend here.' I raise the sword, and then pause. 'Of course, he thinks he can't be killed. He has hope. Hope is a wonderful thing, I am told. As if it matters.'

I put the sword aside. I look at the bitten man. 'I'm not rich, you're right. The knight I took this sword from though, he was well off. He had this.'

I show him the poignard with the silver tip. He sees it for long enough to know what it is, then I plunge it through his eye and into his brain and twist. He's dead before I pull it free.

'Looks like you're last,' I tell the shitter. 'Oh well.'

The man now has his arms across the back of his neck, as though their flesh and bone will turn my steel.

'My name is Darcen Ysir. Do you think you'll remember?'

The shitter is too far gone to hear me. I kick him until he pays attention. 'Darcen Ysir. My name. Do you think you'll remember?'

'Yes,' he stammers. I kick him some more. 'Yes!' he screams.

'Good. Now fuck off, shit for brains. Tell everyone I was here.'

He doesn't pause to understand or thank me. He's up off his knees and running as hard as he can before I finish speaking, trailing shit and piss behind him.

Now there is a boy here I do not recognise.

'Why did you interfere?' *he says.* 'I specifically told you not to interfere. We could have been killed! You need to listen to me, Constant. You need to do what I tell you. I'm trying to keep you alive. I can't guide you if you're going to make spur of the moment decisions.

The boy looks upset and frustrated. It is the expression of a child whose toy is broken.

'It's done now,' *he continues.* 'You saved the girl, well done. She's *special.* That's unexpected. And useful. Take her with you while I think this through. Get a move on or you'll both freeze to death.'

Constant did not remember the boy when he woke up.

She bends like the bough before it breaks.

Constant came awake. He realised he'd fallen asleep on his feet. *For how long? A second? A minute? Not long enough to fall. Great Fathers, I need to rest.*

The girl was still crying. He looked around. No wolves were creeping up on him to avenge their brothers. Yet. The part of Constant that was Constant grew nervous. The sky was darkening. The evening was crisp and still and sound carried for a long way in the winter. The girl's cries seemed to ring through the mountains. His head was fogged with tiredness and thoughts he wasn't sure were his.

She bends like the bough before it breaks. I take no prisoners.

No. I am Constant.

Blix thought she had forgotten how to stop crying. Then the boy touched her on the shoulder and said something gentle that she didn't quite catch. Something comforting and calming. The waves of fear broke and the weight crushing her chest lifted. She drew deep, ragged breaths and uncurled herself, flexing her fingers as they unclenched. 'Who are you?' she managed.

'My name's Constant. I'm a monk. I lived nearby. What's your name?' He spoke in a kind tone. Blix felt better for listening to him.

'Blix.' She suppressed a gulping sob. 'Blix Summerland.'

'I'm sorry we had to meet like this, Blix.' He looked around at the stone circle, taking in the difference between the ground inside and snow beyond. He rubbed his forehead with the heel of his hand nervously, grimaced, then looked back at her. He looked exhausted. 'I think you are not from around here, Blix. Do you know what attacked you?'

Blix shuddered and was almost sick, but took another deep breath and the feeling subsided.

'Werewolves. They were werewolves. Real ones. Oh God.'

'Yes, that's right. But now they're dead so you don't have to be afraid of them anymore. Now, this is important, Blix. Did they bite you? Any bite at all, even if it just grazed the skin.'

'I don't think so. No. I'm in a lot of pain. I thought I'd dislocated my shoulder, but I don't think so now. I think one side of my body is all bruise. I was so frightened. But I wasn't bitten.'

As she spoke she began to feel detached from the whole thing, as if she'd stood outside herself and watched it happen to another her. Even the pain lessened a little - it still hurt, and she still felt it, held at a distance from her emotions. A bomb without a fuse. She felt more alert and clear-headed.

'Good,' said Constant. 'Now, we have to get off the mountain. Now. We have to leave now.' His voice became more urgent as he spoke.

'I can't leave! I have to find my... my... sister! I have to do whatever he did... I don't know how to,' she finished.

'That's your problem,' said Constant flatly. 'As if it matters.' He inhaled sharply, looking slightly shocked, closed his eyes, and let the breath out slowly. 'Sorry,' he continued. 'That wasn't me. I mean, all I meant to say was, we have a more pressing problem.' He rubbed his eyes. 'Sorry. I've had a bad few days.'

An emotion stormed the wall surrounding Blix's psyche; it was fury.

'Oh really? You've had a bad day? Let me tell you about my day. My teacher kidnapped us! By magic! Which is impossible! But it dragged us into the sky, then threw us out of the sky somewhere different. Monsters terrified us, assaulted and kidnapped my sister again and I was almost raped and fucking eaten! Why don't you tell me about how bad your day has been, and what exactly the fuck is more pressing than getting my sister back?'

Constant's stare drilled through her, puncturing her rage.

'The day before yesterday, wolves murdered everyone I've ever known and loved. They attacked the Monastery where I lived and killed everyone, and burned it to the ground judging by the smoke I saw. I escaped because the man I thought of as my father showed me a way out, then stayed behind to defend it. He's dead too, I expect. I've spent the time since then avoiding werewolves. I'm frightened and I haven't slept, and I am tired beyond anything I have ever felt. That was my bad few days.

'What's more pressing than finding your sister is staying alive. I would love nothing more than to track the rest of those wolves down and slaughter them. But that's suicide. We must find somewhere safe. I seem to be good at killing, but I can't take on a wolf pack by myself. That's dozens of wolves. I'm twelve. It is important I remember that.'

He spoke quietly and with determination and as he did, the anger drained out of Blix. When he'd finished she said, 'I'm sorry. I didn't know.'

'It's okay. How could you? And what happened to you is terrible. You should have vengeance. Terror for terror.' He shook his head again. 'No, that's wrong. I mean justice. Yes.'

He looked lost for a second, then his resolve returned. 'I promise you we'll talk more about this, but right now we need to get out of here. There's a house nearby. In the forest, somewhere south of here, at the base of the mountain.' He looked uncertain. 'I think there is. It has been a long time. Night's coming in. You won't help your sister by freezing to death. The woman who lives there will give you some clothes and food and a place to sleep.'

Blix wanted to argue, but she knew he was right. 'Okay. Okay then.'

Constant considered the corpses for a moment then approached the one he'd beheaded. It lay on its front, blood still oozing from its neck, seeping into the ground. It still held its sword.

'I wonder when death starts,' he said, absently.

'What?'

'Nothing.' He drew his sword once more and, to Blix's horror, stabbed the severed head through the skull. Then he pried the sword out of the werewolf's fingers, kicked the body over, and unbelted the scabbard. He handed them both to Blix.

'I've never-' she began.

'If it comes to it, swing it hard,' Constant said. 'Don't think about it. Just do it.'

He walked out of the circle. A path led into the woods. Hesitantly, Blix followed him, stowing the sword on her back as she went, the same way that he carried his. It felt awkward and wrong.

They'd only gone a few feet when Blix gasped and ran back across the circle. She appeared moments later lugging Katy's handbag.

'She'll want it back,' she explained.

The path wound through the trees for a few hundred yards. It disappeared at the lip of a shallow bank, which dropped twenty feet down to a narrow beck. Constant and Blix slid-jumped through the slush to the stream. It was little more than a trickle under a thin layer of ice. It cracked under foot as Constant led them downstream. Blix knew enough to keep quiet, but it was difficult. Every breath hurt. She wondered if she'd broken a rib. She struggled on, and said nothing. The bitter cold seeped into her flesh.

After a while they came across a well-worn cattle track fording the stream. They followed it downhill until they reached the edge of the trees. A long slope of snow-covered scree lay ahead. The forest continued in the distance below, covering the landscape to the far horizon.

Blix gasped, forgetting in that moment all the terror and horror she felt. 'It's so beautiful!' she breathed.

The last of the sun had set fire to the western sky. It bathed the mountains in shining gold, as radiant as the halo on an icon. It looked as if it might at any moment flow down the slopes and bury the forest in a glorious avalanche of light.

Constant did little more than glance at the amazing sight. 'We're exposed. The temperature is going to plummet. Come on.' He started down the slope. The snow was deeper here and uneven, and he hopped forward, here stepping on rock, there plunging to his knees in a drift.

Blix dragged her eyes from the vision in the heavens. She started to follow but something caught her attention. A wrong shape in the snow almost out of sight to her left, a shape that shouldn't be there.

'What's that?' she said, pointing.

Constant followed her finger, squinted a little, then drew the big sword. 'That's a dead man,' he said. 'Maybe. Wait here.' Something hard in his voice chilled Blix more than the air.

Constant made his way across the snow, walking crabwise to keep his balance. He slowed as he neared the shape, and stopped complete while still out of range of a sudden lunge, crouching down for a better look. Then he straightened and sheathed the sword. Blix realised then she'd forgotten to draw hers.

Constant bent over the body. A few minutes later he returned, carrying a large bundle.

'You looted a corpse!' said Blix.

'Whatever he had, he doesn't need it anymore. We do. Put this on.'

He held out a black fur cloak, crackling with frost. It was longer than Blix. There was a large tear in the back where claws had raked it. Thinking about that made Blix's flesh crawl.

'I don't want to.'

Constant shrugged. 'Be cold, then.' He dropped the fur and started down the slope again.

Blix watched him for a second, then looked at the cloak. Then she made a decision, wondering what it said about her.

'Wait for me!' She grabbed the fur and headed after the boy, struggling into it as she went. 'Hey! Don't just walk off! Tell me what's going on! Where are we?'

Constant stopped and looked back over his shoulder. 'I know you have questions. I'll do my best to answer them. But not now. I must pay attention and I'm asleep on my feet. When we're safe - safer - I'll tell you everything I can, I promise.'

Without waiting for a reply, he turned and continued down the slope. Having no other choice, Blix followed.

They made the tree line as night fell. Stars which Blix had never seen before dusted the sky, a ribbon of diamonds sparkling in a coal seam, crushed by the immensity above them. After a few steps the canopy hid the star-shine. Within moments Blix could no longer see her hand in front of her face. It was a total darkness of a kind that Blix had never experienced before, and it deeply unnerved her. She stepped backward until she saw stars again. There was no sound and only a breath of wind. Blix felt that the forest was watching her, waiting to see what she would do.

Constant dug something out of his bag. 'Our dead friend back there had a couple of these stuck in his belt.' He held up two thick black rods, about the same size and shape as rounders bats.

'What are they?'

'Lowlights. They burn hot and slow but without much light - enough to see the path by, but not so much that we'll announce our presence across the forest. They'll preserve our night vision a bit too. And we might not get frostbite.' He rooted in his bag for a moment. 'I left his fire steel behind. I thought I had one. But I don't. It's in a tunnel on the mountain.'

He raised a hand and looked about to say something, but instead frowned and lowered it again, rubbing his fingertips against each other. 'Maybe not.' He looked at Blix. 'Do you have one?'

'No. I have a box of matches though.' In the dim light she saw Constant's blank expression. 'You know, matches.'

Constant shook his head. 'What's a matches?'

'You don't have matches here?'

'I won't know unless you show me.'

Blix rooted through Katy's bag and found the matches by touch. They were still dry. She struck one on the box and nursed the flame behind her hand until it took. She held it up to illuminate Constant's mildly astonished face.

'You've really never seen a match before, have you,' said Blix. 'What kind of place is this?'

'A cold one,' said Constant. He held the end of the lowlight to the flame and turned it until it started glowing a dull red. Blix shook the match out as the fire reached her fingertips. Her eyes took a moment to adjust to the lowlight's dim glow. She touched the unburned portion; it felt like pencil lead.

'You have these, but you don't have matches. And you have magic.'

'I'd prefer to have matches,' said Constant. 'They look more useful than magic. Magic never helps. Come on, it's not too far now. I think.'

Even held high the light was negligible. After a few moments walking the boy was no more than a small black blob in front of her. She followed his shape, and hoped he could see more than she could.

They walked for a few minutes. The forest was still; the only sounds were the crunching of the snow and leaf litter underfoot, and their breath. Then suddenly there was a sound, a clank and a grunt, something alive, something close. 'What was that?' cried Blix. Her voice sounded shockingly loud.

Constant glared at her. 'Not a wolf. Come on, they already know we're here.'

They pushed through the branches into a small clearing, little more than a widening of the path. A knot of fear twisted in Blix's stomach. The darkness resolved into a huge mass of black fur squatting in their way, darkness made flesh. There was something horrific about it which made Blix want to scream. She tensed to run.

The darkness licked her hand, and grunted sleepily.

'Yaks!' Blix said, relief flooding through her. The osculating bovine ambled back to the safety of the herd, a cowbell around its neck clanking as it went. 'They're yaks!'

'Of course they're yaks. What did you think they were, werecows?'

Blix threw up her arms in exasperation. 'I couldn't see them. How could I know there'd be yaks? I've never been here before.'

Blix found that she could see the yaks a bit better now. There were perhaps a dozen of them. Huge, long-haired hillocks standing in the snow, huddled together for warmth. They stood so close together that they'd appeared as one beast in Blix's mind. They stirred a little at the noise, and there was a smattering of ruminant complaints.

'I love yaks,' said Blix. '*Bos grunniens.* They have some in the city farm at home. They're friendly. They're, like, the gentle but massive hippies of the cow world.'

She reached out to stroke the nearest flat, hairy face, but Constant stayed her hand.

'You should ask permission before you touch other people's property.'

'Who could I ask permission fr… oh.'

The man was old, so old that it was impossible to tell how old. He was much smaller than Blix. His face was heavily lined, ancient striations of worry and toil carved into dark, leathery skin. He was Asian, Blix thought, Chinese or Korean maybe. He wore a long robe of grey fur, belted at the waist, and a peaked fur cap with long tassels which swung freely as he turned his head. He had a sword in his belt and Blix saw his hand was on the hilt - not exactly threatening, but ready just the same.

'*Jyed machogpa,*' said Constant, bowing.

The man looked at them for some time, then nodded and said '*Tashi deleq.*' His voice was a spidery whisper.

Constant launched into a rapid speech in a language Blix didn't understand. The old man interjected now and then. Blix got the strong impression he didn't like what he was hearing. When Constant finished, the man sighed and said something which seemed to be 'thank you.' He turned and slapped a yak on its rump a few times until it got the message and shuffled forward a few steps.

There were four people in the midst of the herd. Two men, a woman and a small child had set up camp. They were dressed much like the old man and looked like a family. The woman crouched over a small copper fire bowl, nursing an ember and shielding the light. The child, a fat-faced toddler in a thick blue dress and bright red cap, smiled at Blix and wobbled toward her. One of the men, tall and lean-faced with a wispy moustache, put out a leg to guide the child back to her mother. He didn't take his eyes off Blix. Both men had their hands on their sword hilts.

Blix was about to say something friendly. Then she saw the body.

It was wrapped head to foot in a fur blanket and bound with rope. It was slung over the back of one of the yaks, which seemed unaware of its burden and stood chewing the cud.

The second man, shorter and older than the first, saw where she was looking. Blix saw the anguish on his face and guessed who lay in the shroud.

Without thinking she said, 'How did she die?'

Almost immediately she realised it was the wrong thing to say, but Constant said, 'I'll ask,' and did so before she could stop him.

The old man spoke, his pained whisper barely audible. He looked as if his world had ended. Constant translated.

'They met three werewolves on the road. They killed one with an arrow straight away. Silver tipped. The only silver they had. They fought the other two, killed one the hard way and drove one off to lick its wounds. The arrow served to end the wolf left behind too. Only silver kills werewolves permanently.' He nodded at the second man. 'They killed his wife.' He looked back at the old man. 'She was his daughter.'

Blix didn't know what to say, so she said, 'I'm sorry.' The words sounded even more inadequate out loud.

'You might be,' said Constant, looking even harder than usual. 'That means there's a wounded wolf nearby. It won't be wounded for long.'

'You just killed five.'

'I surprised them. They were young, and busy. That luck won't happen twice.'

The old man spoke to his family. Whatever he said affected them badly. The men looked even grimmer; the woman clutched her child to her breast.

'What's wrong?'

'They were going to seek refuge at the Anvil. I told him they're too late.'

'The what?'

'A mountain. Back where we came from. There's a town at the foot, small but fortified. They thought they'd be safe there. The wolves burned it three days ago.'

'Can they go somewhere else?'

'There is nowhere else.' Constant was beginning to look uneasy. 'We can't stay.'

'We can't just leave them,' Blix began, but Constant cut her off.

'Believe me, they're better off without us.' Constant said something to the old man, who nodded. To Blix's surprise the boy touched the old man behind his right ear, and said a word. One by one he did the same to the others. When he came to the little girl, he knelt and kissed her on the forehead. She giggled, and Constant smiled. Then he stood abruptly and headed out of the clearing, leaving Blix running to catch up before the darkness enfolded him.

'What was that?' she asked.

'A blessing,' said Constant, without looking around. 'I'm a monk. I blessed them.' He sounded uncomfortable.

'Oh.' Blix tried to think of any blessings she knew. Only the Lord's Prayer came to mind. 'What blessing?'

'I said I hoped they wouldn't die.'

Blix considered this. 'That's a *good* blessing. I hope someone's blessing us like that.'

'Me too.'

They walked on, always downhill, staying on the yak trail. At some point they crossed a mist line and the rest of the forest vanished completely. Blix's exhausted mind lost track of time; she concentrated on putting one foot in front of another. Constant took her hand and pulled her along.

Twice more they met herders on the path, noisier and less cautious than the first, still on the move, all heading the same way. As their paths crossed Constant moved among them, speaking softly. As he passed, women took up their children, bells were muffled, and men drew swords. Drivers whipped up the pace until the lumbering mountains of snow-peaked fur stirred themselves into a jog. They headed away up into the mist and were gone.

Tired as Blix was, curiosity got the better of her.

'What language was that?'

'Tibetan.'

'Tibetan? We're not in Tibet.'

'No. They're descendants of the first people to come here. The High Gate in the west used to point to somewhere near Gyangtse. That's a town, if you've never been.'

The boy's tone had changed, Blix noticed. He sounded like a professor giving a lecture. Something in his posture had changed too, which Blix couldn't quite put her finger on. She felt like she was on a field trip.

'There's another gate?'

'There *were* several. A few gates on this world point to the Tibetan plateau. I'm told it is very beautiful there. I've never been. The holes were active before they were gated, people just fell through. But the High Gate stopped working almost as soon as whoever it was raised the stones. None of them work now. Some magic can be controlled, some can't. That was thousands of years ago.'

His tone changed again, became harsher and contemptuous. 'They were fools, those first men. They thought they'd found the Hidden Kingdom.' He spat. 'They should have looked harder. They found out what this place is like. But the name stuck.'

'What name?'

'Shambhala.'

Chapter Nine: The Jug

Constant turned off the track and picked up the pace. A few minutes later the mists parted and in the bare light Blix saw the shape of a small house sitting in a clearing. It was built of rough stone and wood. A high peaked roof of wood shingles, warped and sunken, swept almost to the ground on two sides. It looked like it had stood there for generations, and in the way of old buildings had merged with the land. Moss and evergreen ivy made it look like the house had grown up from the soil. A thick crown of snow gave it a Christmas card prettiness.

But there was no light, no smoke, no movement or sound. No smell of cooking, no cattle lowing in the byre. No people asking who wandered in the night.

They were almost at the door before Blix could see it. As it resolved before them Constant stopped dead and drew his sword.

The door was hanging off its hinges, twisted in and down. It had been barred from the inside, but the bar had snapped in two and the bracket wrenched from the wall.

Constant pushed the door wider with the tip of his sword. 'Wait here,' he commanded, and edged into the house, scanning the room, lowlight held slightly behind him to save his eyes, trying to see everything at once.

Blix stared nervously into the pitch-black forest, imagining werewolves. Then she remembered she had a sword, and drew it. The dead weight of it on her arm dragged the point to the ground immediately. She struggled to find the balance, trying to hold it two-handed from the waist, ready to take the attack, like she'd seen in films. Then she stopped, feeling a bit ridiculous.

The only way I'm going to kill anyone with this lump of metal is if they stand still and wait for me to get up speed, she thought. 'Better to run,' she said out loud.

'Better to fight,' said Constant from directly behind her. Blix's heart leapt into her mouth. 'Running won't help,' he continued. 'They're faster and they like the chase. Always better to fight.'

'Jesus! You scared the life out of me!' said Blix, struggling to calm down.

'Sorry. You can come in now. There's no one here.' His voice was clipped and terse, as if he'd just choked on something sharp.

The house was devastated. Chairs had been dashed against the walls and broken. A long wooden table had been overturned and had snapped in the middle. Dark brown streaks and spatter on the walls, just visible in the lowlight's faint glimmer, told the end of the tale.

'Whoever lived here doesn't any more,' said Blix.

'My mother lived here,' said Constant absently. He traced the blood arc with his finger.

'Oh God, I'm so sorry! You must-'

'I didn't know her,' said Constant, turning away. 'The monks found me before I was one.' He rubbed his eyes as if they ached. 'I'm not sure how I knew how to get here.'

None of that made sense to Blix. She took in the ruined interior. There was something settled about it which made her think the monsters which had caused it were long gone.

'When do you think this happened?'

Constant turned over a chair; two legs were broken. 'A few days ago,' he said. 'A week at the most. Not much of a fight. A lot of rage. A couple of wolves, I'd say.' He knelt and examined the floor. 'Someone was dragged out. Dead, I think.' He nodded to himself. 'Dead.'

'Always better to fight,' said Blix under her breath, wondering at the boy's dispassion in the face of his mother's death.

'Always,' said Constant, although she hadn't meant him to hear. 'Make them kill you. This wasn't quick.'

He rubbed his eyes again. Blix thought he was going to cry, and instinctively put a hand in his shoulder, but he shrugged it off.

'She should have fought harder,' he said harshly. 'She was weak. She should have made them *bleed.*' He turned aside. 'As if it matters.'

Even after everything she'd seen that day, Blix was shocked at the coldness in his tone. But before she could say anything the boy inhaled sharply, as if he'd shocked himself. To Blix's amazement he suddenly punched himself on the forehead, quite hard, with the side of his fist. 'Bloody stop it,' he said.

'I didn't -'

'Not you.'

'I don't under-'

'Don't try. That's enough talk. We need to be practical. We need a fire or you'll freeze. It's a risk, but we don't have a choice. The wolves have probably moved on. If they haven't I'll kill them. You lay the fire, I'll fix the door.'

'I've never set a fire,' said Blix, wondering whether she'd fallen in with a crazy person.

'Have you ever fixed a door? Keep it small.'

The fireplace was iron-backed and looked ancient. Split logs were strewn to either side, white ashes lay in the grate. A spit was set in the mortar, from which a small cauldron hung on a chain.

A footstool had survived the carnage. Blix sat on it as she set the fire, piling it like she'd seen on TV. She used pages torn from one of Katy's notebooks as spills.

Constant, busy pressing nails back into boards, paused to watch her strike another match.

While she waited for the fire to take she did an inventory. Most of the contents of Katy's handbag had survived, although one of the pens had leaked all over the scarf. She tossed the pen away. The circle book was gone - Blix remembered with a start that it had gone up in flames.

She started on her own bag. 'Crap.'

'What's wrong?' said Constant immediately. His hand moved toward his sword.

'My tape player's smashed. I must have landed on it. It was a birthday present.'

Constant stared at the silver box in Blix's hand uncomprehendingly, then returned to his task. Blix took a big swig of the vodka and pulled a face, but felt a bit better as it defrosted her from the inside. She took another one, and then a third which emptied the flask.

The now ragged butcher's paper that she'd used to rub the runes at the Conspirators was crumpled decisively and thrown onto the fire, then abruptly snatched back. Blix unscrunched the papers, carefully folded them into neat squares and put them back in her satchel. The thought of stuffing them in Mr Leicester's gaping mouth and watching him choke was more appealing than incinerating them.

It felt good to focus on something. Emotion surged through her, like molten rock coiling under an old lava flow. The surface looked cool, but underneath she burned. But it was deep beneath the surface, and that seemed strange. She didn't understand why she felt so distant from it so quickly, but it was only distant, it wasn't absent. Part of her brain thought about nothing else. Sometimes it screamed.

This is shock. I'm in shock. Is this what it feels like?

Blix felt better once the fire was going. She hadn't realised how cold she was. Her left hand was still numb, however.

Constant braced the door with planks from the former table, pressing the ends into the gaps between the stone flags.

'That won't keep anyone out for long,' he said. 'But we'll get a moment to prepare.'

He turned to the two small windows set high in one wall, simple openings without glass. Constant closed the shutters and pulled the thick woollen curtains across.

Blix showed him her hand. 'Everything works. I just can't feel it.'

'Let me see.' He examined her fingers minutely, turning her hand gently as his did so. 'I don't think you have frostbite. The skin isn't discoloured, there's no cracking or blisters. Did you hurt this arm?'

'When the big werewolf knocked me over I landed heavily on it. But I think it was numb before then. My legs were completely numb when we first arrived. I think my hand was too.'

'It doesn't look injured, there's no bruise or break. I think it's gate shock.'

'What?'

'Gate shock. Travelling between worlds isn't easy. You did that, didn't you?'

Blix nodded uncertainly, knowing how crackers that sounded. The boy didn't seem phased.

'It can be a profound insult to the senses. Did you faint?'

'Yes. I was sick too.'

'Yes, that happens all the time.' He looked slightly unsure. 'I am told,' he continued. 'I've never experienced it myself.' He let go of her hand. 'I shouldn't worry. I think it'll wear off soon. If it was going to be a problem you'd know by now.' He looked critically at Blix's face. 'You know, you're quite dirty.'

'You're not the first boy that's told me that,' said Blix, smiling tiredly.

Constant's blank expression told her he didn't get it; monks didn't, she supposed. She tried again. 'Someone threw me at the world. I bounced.'

Constant nodded seriously. 'You should wash that off, your cuts will fester otherwise. I'll get some water from the stream. It's deep enough here that it should still be flowing.' He frowned. 'I should have done that before I braced the doors. Oh well.' He paused, and then said, 'There's something I need to do. Can I use one of your fire sticks?'

Blix gave him the box. 'Don't waste them,' she said. 'I think we're a long way from a tobacconist.'

'I don't know what that is. I'll be careful. I'll just be a moment.'

He took down the braces again. Then he found an earthenware jug which was only broken at the rim, and went outside. Blix stared into the fire and listened to the screaming in her mind get louder.

Constant broke through the iced over stream and filled the jug. He stood there for a while, inhaling deeply as he tried not to listen to the voices in his head. Other people's memories, brought forward by the turmoil he felt now.

- kill the dogs, hunt them down and hang their entrails from the trees so the others see what's coming to them -

- walked this trail a hundred times as a boy, my father knew the woodcutter well, he would tap a barrel of chhaang when we arrived and they would sip together and tell lies about women they'd known. My father cried like a baby when the monks Recognised me -

- my mother is dead and I never knew her and I don't know what to think about that -

- not seemly to display emotion. Serenity is my watchword, continuity is my task. My mother died birthing me, I believe -

- kill each wolf which dares show its face, wear their teeth on a necklace -

Constant pushed the voice of Darcen Ysir as far down as he dared. Thinking like Ysir was becoming more troubling the longer he did it. He remembered what Brother Simon had said about him. A great man of faith, later.

You were Great Father for almost sixty years. Let's hear that voice. Are those memories not important too?

With some effort, he banished the others completely. It was harder than he expected. Maybe it was tiredness. He put that aside for the time being. This left him alone with the thought that he didn't feel very much about his mother's death.

His father had died before he was born, he had been told. An accident in the forest. Among the centuries of memories that vied for his attention there were none of his mother that he recognised. Presumably they were there somewhere, wrapped in his one-year-old self's blurry sense of the world. He felt he should be frustrated by this, but he wasn't. There didn't seem much to feel. He wondered whether he should be more troubled by that than Ysir's resurgent blood-lust.

He turned the jug in his hands, feeling the rough-fired clay, tracing each line, imagining the turn of the potter's wheel and the hands that smoothed the jug to a peak, which pulled the lip forward, which set the clay to prove and fired it hard. Were they her hands? Had she put something of herself into it? When he touched this clay, did he touch her hands? *And why don't I cry?*

Constant closed his aching eyes, but tears did not come.

Constant dreamed.

In my dream, I am an old man. I am dying. I am lying in the big bed in the apartment I do not like. I am lost in it. I have grown so small.

In my dream, it is almost morning. Brothers surround me. My voice has gone and I cannot tell them to leave. My death is more than my death, for the brothers it is rebirth. I hope it will not happen this time. I do not want to join the memories. I want to remain myself.

In my dream, I think, it might be today. The fever relented in the night, and I slept for a while. Now it has returned. There is dish of soup by the bed. I can't eat it. I can't remember when last I ate anything. I caught sight of myself in the long mirror yesterday. I didn't recognise myself. I'm just skin and bones. A shadow of my former self. I feel thin – not just in body, but spiritually. As though I have been stretched out, pulled beyond my years against my will. It is a strange thought. I have only remained, after all.

In my dream, I think, Death can be cruel to some men. I think about death a lot. Sometimes when I close my eyes I see the dead I have made, those souls sent to hell or glory or their next turn on the wheel by my blade. Many died in their prime, such as it was. In those moments, I feel I can reach out to them, to brush their cheeks and hold their faces in my hands. They do not seem unhappy. I wonder whether that will be my hell, for the part of me that does not remain; to join the men I have killed and for them not to hate me. Would that be better or worse than another turn of the wheel, I wonder.

In my dream, I think, when you are very old, you die before you die. Warriors say, he died well. What they think they mean is that he died fighting, or in the arms of a woman, or at the height of fame or power. But what they mean is, he looked like himself. He died as the man we knew, the one that appears in our memory. That's not how it has gone for me. And that is well. For the man I was, the man they knew, was terrible.

I have fought hard, though. I have fought to the last breath. Fighting is what I am best at. As if it matters.

Now there is a boy here I do not recognise.

'I don't believe in coincidences,' *says the boy.* 'This special girl was with the wolves that destroyed our home. Let's find out why, shall we?'

Constant did not remember the boy when he woke up.

Constant woke with a jerk, shocked to find he'd fallen asleep on his feet again. He hadn't even dropped the jug. *I have to sleep,* he thought.

But that meant he had to do something else first. He'd barely slept in three days, and hadn't said the Night Prayer at all, scared to distract himself from the hunting werewolves. He felt guilty, although he supposed in the circumstances that the universe would forgive him.

The jug was fine. He still had the candles that Simon had given him. He spoke his words, relaxing a little as he said the familiar mantra. He knelt in the snow, counted eleven times to eleven, and emptied his thoughts. He found the striking end of a match by touch and, remembering how the girl had done it, scraped it along the box. He watched it for a moment, then set the flame it to the wick and watched it take. Once it was properly alight, he blew it out.

'Light in the darkness,' he began.

The torrent of sound that exploded in his mind poleaxed him to the ground, clutching his head in agony. Dozens upon dozens of voices forced their way into his consciousness, their words a cacophony of overlapping babble that turned the prayer into torment. More voices than he had ever been people; in one moment he heard the same voice start the prayer as a child, a grown man and an ancient. Constant almost screamed but the sound never came, drowned by the bellowing in his mind. And it would not stop; the prayer ended but new voices took it up instantly.

He tried to focus. *The words, the words, where are the words?* The prayer-noise smothered any other thought. Gritting his teeth, he forced himself to focus on the first word, finding the shape of it, fighting off the clamour. Then the next, and the next, until he had them fixed in his mind, defending them with strength of will. Then he said them.

I am myself
I am alone but not alone
I know my own mind.

Nothing happened. He said them again, and then again and again, grinding them through the mill-race of his thoughts, each time feeling the strength of them growing, and with it the bedlam in his head diminishing, until soon there were five voices, three, only one voice repeating the Night Prayer, and when that voice was finished, it was over.

Shaking, Constant got to his feet, drenched in icy sweat. His head ached terribly. It felt like someone had drilled into it to release evil spirits.

'What was *that?*' he said out loud.

I lost control, he thought. He was reasonably sure it was him thinking that.

Then he heard crying, deep heart-tearing sobs of pain. It took him a moment to realise it wasn't in his mind.

The girl didn't hear him come in; she was clutching herself tightly and rocking back and forth. She looked frightened and lost, and Constant felt generations of kindly old men reach out to her from deep inside him with a powerful, heartfelt compassion.

He did the only thing he knew how. He closed his eyes and said his words in his mind until they were fixed, until he could feel them, almost see them. Then he touched her, and let the magic flow out of him.

It was stronger than he had ever known.

Blix felt a hand on her shoulder and felt better immediately. Her body felt what her mind's eye saw, and that was hairy paws, clawing obscenely at her. But the touch she felt was a kindly one, and the knowledge that there was still kindness in the world seemed to push the dreadful things away, down into a cage in her mind.

Something else went with them.

I am myself

I am alone but not alone

I know my own mind.

Blix looked up at a boy. He had his eyes closed and was muttering under his breath. She smiled. *Who are you?* she almost said, but as the thought appeared it was instantly replaced.

'Constant! You startled me. Are you praying for me? I'm not very religious I'm afraid.'

Constant opened his eyes, and for a moment looked alarmed, then very relieved when Blix smiled at him. He suddenly looked very young.

'I will pray for you,' he said. 'I hope it will help. I'm not a very good monk. Brother Si- my Tutor said I think too much.'

'I wish I could stop thinking,' said Blix quietly.

'You'll feel better,' said Constant, so seriously that was almost an order. 'Think about something else.' He brandished a small sack. 'Pottage. The makings of it, anyway.'

'What's pottage?'

'Food.' He looked doubtful. 'Probably. I packed in a hurry. In this instance, lentils, chickpeas, looks like a couple of wizened onions, and some bacon I found earlier which doesn't look too bad.'

'Where's Keith Floyd when you need him? How do you cook that then?'

'Behold.' Constant threw everything into the cauldron, poured in some water, and swung it over the fire. 'Now we wait.' He handed her the jug. 'You can wash with the rest.'

'Marvellous. I have some chocolate for afters.'

'What's chocolate?'

'Bloody hell.'

While they waited for the stew to cook Blix washed her face and hands, and watched Constant. He was swaying where he sat, so tired he might collapse at any moment.

Should I be afraid of you?

On the one hand, she was seventeen and a girl and he was twelve and a boy, so they were practically different species anyway. And he was a monk. So the weird things he did and said might just be what twelve-year-olds and boys and monks did here. And he seemed to be kind. Kindness was important.

On the other hand, he was a merciless and single-minded killer who seemed prone to sudden mood swings. This was not a happy combination.

She thought about Mr Leicester, or Echmoth, if that was his real name. She thought about what he'd done and who he was, and about Dragonville, and what he'd done and who he was, and perhaps what he was. But it was no good; everything was all jumbled up in her mind, events falling over themselves to defy explanation, and too tied up with werewolves and violence and terror to be made sense of yet.

She thought about Katy, and how terribly she missed her. But as she did so a strange thing happened. It was if her memory skipped a beat, like a scratched record or a damaged video tape. Katy was there, but Blix couldn't quite take hold of precisely what she'd said or done. The terrible trauma of losing her sister seemed suddenly far away and... separate, somehow. It was weird.

God I'm tired, she thought, and forgot about it. Tired or not, some things couldn't wait.

'We need to talk,' she said.

Chapter Ten: A Long Conversation in The Night

'We need to eat, and we need sleep,' Constant said, as he spooned the pottage into a pair of wooden bowls. He did look almost grey with tiredness, but Blix wasn't going to be put off again.

'I'm tired too, but sleep can wait. You promised. You promised you'd answer my questions.'

The boy sighed. 'I did. I don't know if I'll be able to, but okay. We'll do that. I have questions too. Eat something, then we'll talk.' He sat down in front of the fire, crossed his legs under him, and tucked in with gusto. 'Eat, it's good,' he encouraged.

This turned out to be a lie, but Blix was grateful for the warmth and the taste of something other than blood and dirt in her mouth.

'I only really have one question,' she said after a couple of mouthfuls.

Constant looked up from his bowl, which was almost empty. 'Go on.'

'Where the hell are we and what the hell happened and who the hell are you?'

The boy laughed. 'That's a big question. "Where the hell are we," I already told you. This is Shambhala. New Amdo province. Does that mean anything to you?'

Blix shook her head.

'It's mostly mountains,' he continued. 'Named after where the first people came from.'

'The Tibetans. You don't look Tibetan.'

'Several peoples have found this world over the centuries. Tibetan, some Mongols, Khazars, Rus. There used to be quite a few gates. All before they used those names for themselves. My ancestors were called the All-men, I think. I'm not sure. The brothers discourage identification with tribes. We are One. Which world are you from?'

It was such a strange question that it took Blix a moment to answer. 'Why, Earth, of course.'

'Why do you say "of course?" There are lots of worlds with humans on them, you could have come from anywhere.'

'The gate opens to Earth. Obviously, I'm from there.'

I didn't know the gate pointed to Earth. I didn't know this particular gate existed until today.' He frowned, and looked confused. 'At least, I think I didn't... maybe I did... I know a lot about gates... I know everything about them...' He rubbed his forehead irritably. 'Anyway. That's why I didn't know you were an Earthman.'

'Fair enough, I suppose. That's weird, though.'

'What?'

'You calling us Earthmen. It's the sort of thing you hear in old science fiction films.' She did some robot moves with her arms. "'Greetings earthmen, we come in peace, prepare to die!" Like that. Don't give me that side-eye, I can see it you know.'

'Sorry. I don't understand you.'

'Many don't. A film. Don't you have them here? it's like - how do I explain this - a series of photographs put together to make it look like a moving image, with sound.'

'That didn't mean much to me I'm afraid. What's a photograph?'

'You don't have photos? How long has this world been cut off?

'From Earth? The last gate stopped working about six hundred years ago. I think a year here is about the same as a year on Earth.'

'Wow. That's, like, since the Dark Ages, or something. Forever.'

'Forever is longer. What's a photograph?'

'Oh, right. Here, I'll show you.'

She took out her wallet and showed him the picture of Katy and her together. Seeing it almost made her burst into tears, but she managed to hold them back.

'There are two of you,' said Constant. He turned the tiny photo over and over, examining it carefully.

'We're twins. You must have twins here. Two peas in a pod, Mum says. Except we're not. Not really.'

'Capturing images is interesting magic.'

'No, not magic, it's chemicals and light and, um, I don't know exactly, it wasn't on the chemistry syllabus. I can tell you lots about polymers and fractional distillation and the periodic table.'

'I didn't understand a lot of that. I may say this often as we converse.'

'Sorry.' A thought occurred to Blix. 'Hang on. You did understand *most* of that though, didn't you? If we're on another planet that's been cut off from Earth for six hundred years -

'Well, maybe a bit more than that in fact, because -'

' - *then how can I speak to you,'* continued Blix emphatically. 'Languages change, don't they? I mean, if I went back in time six hundred-odd years I wouldn't understand, um, one of the King Edward's I think, someone like that, the poker up the bum one. I don't do history. He'd be all thees and thous and ye oldes and stuff. How come you don't sound like that to me? How are you even speaking English? It was probably Norman or something back then.'

'Oh, gosh, I don't know,' said Constant. He massaged his forehead again. 'No, actually I do. It's something to do with the gate magic. It makes people understand the local language of their destination. I'm not speaking English. I think you are speaking Shambhalhai.'

'Really?' Blix mouthed a few words silently, testing the shape of her mouth. 'Nope, don't buy that,' she continued, frowning. 'My words haven't changed, and I don't just hear you speaking English, I can see you forming English words with your mouth.'

'And I can see you speaking in Shambhalhai. Which is not English with a different name, I think I know some English words, from long ago. You can't trust what you see. It's the magic.' He looked away, seeing something else behind his eyes. 'I haven't been taught much about it. It's in the Tutor's Book that I mustn't do magic.'

'I'm speaking like you and not realising it because of magic. I don't like that.'

'You shouldn't. It changes you.' He suddenly looked incredibly uncomfortable. 'I mean, sometimes magic is benign, you know, for little things...'

'So I talk like you,' Blix interrupted, still trying to get her head around it. 'Does that mean I'm going to start sounding like a really aggressive geography teacher? That was a joke,' she added, seeing Constant's hurt look.

'Oh. Okay. No, I don't think so. I think I'll sound a bit like you to you and you'll sound a bit like me to me. It's our brains that are doing the interpreting.' He drew his legs up under his chin. 'And that's not really me,' he muttered into his knees.

'I think we've moved on to "what the hell happened",' said Blix. 'What does Leicester want?'

'Leicester?'

'Leicester. Mr Leicester? My Natural Philosophy teacher? The one who brought me here? They called him Echmoth, is that his real name? It's not his first name. His first name is Frank.'

'I don't know. Was this man at the red circle? I only saw wolves.'

Now Blix was confused. 'You don't know? But you rescued me! I thought-'

'No, I understand,' he interrupted, and his tone was hard and sarcastic. 'You thought that because I saved your life I was there to save your life. Sorry child, I have my own problems, I know nothing of yours. I just happened along.'

'There's no need to take that tone. Really aggressive, see? And don't call me child, I'm older than you are.'

Constant was instantly apologetic. 'Sorry, it's, it's, lack of sleep. And everything that's happened to me. I'm not myself. Sorry. Look, why don't you tell me your story, and I'll tell you -'

- some of -

'- mine, perhaps we can meet in the middle.'

Blix shrugged. 'Okay. I do Natural Philosophy at school, right? My teacher, Mr Leicester, he was at the circle, he's a man, looks like he's made of greasy sticks, he was my teacher, he sent me to the Conspirators, that's a gate, on some bullshit pretence, I don't know why he just didn't kidnap me, and it came alive! The gate opened! Which is impossible because that's magic and there isn't magic anymore, but I said the words and it worked and we couldn't escape and it brought me here, brought us here, and he was called Echmoth and there was someone called Dragonville and he'd done it!

And there were werewolves! Real werewolves! And the big one hit me and, they took, and they took, they took my sister! Katy! And and, and -'

Constant saw she was trembling; in seconds, he was on his feet and by Blix's side. He took her hand gently. 'It's all right,' he said, and then the words came into his mind unbidden, and then it *was* all right and Blix wasn't trembling any more.

'Sorry,' she said, in a small voice. 'That got away from me.'

'It's going to be like that for a while. I'm here for you.' He said it with such utter sincerity that Blix blushed, but the boy seemed unaware of the effect of his words.

'What you said just now,' he continued. 'I think I can help you understand some of that.'

'Anything which makes this make sense.'

'Okay. Let's start with magic. You said there was no magic on your world.'

'Not since nineteen-sixteen.' She saw him about to ask the question and said, 'Seventy years ago. It all just stopped overnight.'

Constant nodded thoughtfully. 'It wasn't like that here. But something did happen around then. Magic became a lot harder to perform. And the world became colder. I doubt we've had a decent harvest in fifty years.'

'But you do still have magic?'

'I'd rather have bread. But yes, some still worked. Trivial things. Things that helped people. But no big stuff. No bad things. All the Gates had stopped working hundreds of years before.'

'We were always told that Earth had no magic left at all. You can't trust the Government, though. They might have lied.'

'So, there was no real magic on Earth and not much here for seventy years, and then there was again, right now as far as we know.'

'Yes, and used to drag me across the universe. Katy and me. Why? What possible reason could there be? I mean, at the circle Leicester made it pretty clear he specifically wanted me for something.' Her mind was still foggy for some reason. She shook her head slightly, and concentrated. 'Me, or Katy. We're identical twins. He took her instead of me. Either of us would do for it. Because we're the same person, he said. Something about me. Us. Not just anyone. He wanted us. He said we were special. He picked Katy because she "looked the part." What part?'

Blix realised that while she felt angry and guilty that her sister had been taken, she also felt relieved that she hadn't been. And, weirdly, angry that she hadn't been picked. This made her feel even more guilty.

'Are you special?' asked Constant earnestly.

'Many have wondered,' said Blix. 'You're not going to get my jokes, are you?' she continued, as Constant remained po-faced.

'Probably not,' the boy agreed, and this time he did smile. 'Whatever magic is letting us talk doesn't help with idiom, or references to your culture. I'll try not to make any to mine.'

'Thanks. I'll try to stop making jokes then, I guess.'

'Don't be someone you're not,' said Constant. 'I can tell it's a defence mechanism. I'll try not to be offended again.'

'Thank you, Doctor Freud. That was one. So no, I'm not special. I'm completely normal. I mean, I'm differently normal, but still bloody normal.' The defiance in her tone came from experience, but she realised Constant had no idea what she meant. 'I'm just a girl,' she finished. 'A woman,' she amended immediately.

'Not "just", it seems.'

'No. The whole thing is crazy and stupid. From the start, actually. I mean if Leicester wanted to kidnap me why didn't he, I don't know, force me into a car at gunpoint or something? Why send me off to do that stupid assignment?' She explained briefly about the rune rubbing. 'What if I'd stayed in bed? It's stupid!'

'Actually, I think it's quite clever.' Constant rubbed his head again. 'Do you know much about gates?'

'Um. Less than I should,' said Blix, managing to sound only slightly guilty. 'I had this book...'

'You can't be compelled to cross a live gate boundary. It must be an informed choice. You must want to. The ancient magicians who created the circles built that into the foundation magic that powered the gates.'

'That's convenient. Why?'

'The whole point of the megaliths was to focus and control the holes between the worlds, to stop people falling across accidentally. You must knowingly interact with a gate or it doesn't work. No one can be forced or tricked into entering a circle, or carried across unconscious or anything like that. I think magicians are quite paranoid. Comes from not being able to trust anyone, I expect.'

Blix raised a finger. 'I beg to differ. I was definitely tricked. We were, I mean. We definitely didn't choose to come here.'

Constant seemed quite energised again. 'No, you didn't listen. The restriction is crossing the boundary without knowing why you're there. Traveling is different. I'll come on to that. But let's stick to this for now.'

Blix flicked something unpleasant-looking from her bowl into the fireplace. 'You're the one giving the lecture, stick to whatever you want.'

'So, this Leicester has an active gate and wants you inside it, so he needs to find a way around the restriction - to make it your informed choice to enter, but still not tell you anything about it otherwise you won't go, right?'

'With you so far. I'll probably have to watch the Open University programme if it gets complicated though.'

Constant ignored that. 'The magic doesn't care what you do once you cross the boundary, you can walk out again if you want. Leicester told you enough about gates so that your choice to cross the boundary was informed. He sent you there to do something else than travel between worlds, but it was legitimate from the gate's point of view.'

Blix looked dubious. 'The gate's point of view? Come on now. Magic can't have a point of view. It's a force, I think. Like gravity. The force that changes other forces. We did that in physics. You're saying that a load of rocks looked in my brain and decided I knew enough about gates to enter one? It made a value judgment about me? You make it sound like magic is alive.'

'Do I?' said Constant. He suddenly sounded bone weary again. 'Could that be true? Not in the same way as us, but in some way. I wish I knew more about it. If it is, I don't think it likes us. It never helps.'

'Right, that's it. Mind. Officially. Blown.'

'Sorry. That's what I think, anyway. I know about gates. I'm not a magician.'

Blix thought about what she'd just learned, as Constant stifled a yawn. 'Okay, not sure about any of that, but let's say it's true. So why couldn't we run away then? We definitely didn't want to come here. We tried to leave, we couldn't. We ran into nothing.'

'That's the other side of the coin. You can't enter a circle without wanting too, but you can't leave once you've activated the gate. Otherwise you might cross the boundary as you transport. Which would be messy.'

Blix hmphed disapprovingly. 'Still sounds pretty stupid to me.'

'Humans obey authority figures. Trust me, I know. You say you might have stayed in bed, but you didn't, did you? You went. Grudgingly perhaps, but you still went of your own free will.'

'Yes. And took my sister,' said Blix morosely.

'You weren't to know. And yes, you might have stayed in bed, in which case we wouldn't be talking now. But I expect if this hadn't worked he'd have found some other way to get you to the gate on some other day. Someone who's gone to this much trouble to get you here isn't going to be put off.'

Blix thought about this for a while, staring into the fire as the logs popped and settled into ash.

'You know,' she said eventually, 'I've known Leicester for a few weeks. He has wire nerves. He's a screamer. But the other one, Dragonville… I looked into his eyes. He has no soul. Who is he?'

'If he opened the gate he's a powerful magician, incredibly powerful. I've never heard of him. I would have heard of him if he was from Shambhala.'

He trailed off again, rubbing his eyes. 'I don't know about these people. But it wasn't just them at the gate. Whatever they're doing, the wolves are involved. I do know about them. Whatever they're doing, it's bad, very, very bad.'

Blix caught her breath, but felt stronger now. 'Yes. Werewolves. We don't have them on Earth anymore.'

Constant raised his eyebrows. 'Really? You don't have people who change at full moon?'

'Oh yes, that kind of werewolf we have. Just not the original kind. *Lupus sapiens.'*

'Of wolf and woman born,' he said, in a voice that sounded like it was carving stone tablets.

'Delicately put. If there was any of that it was a long time ago. Real werewolves are a species, true liminals. This is what *I* know lots about,' she added, with a hint of pride. 'We don't have them anymore.'

'Why not? asked Constant, interested despite his crushing tiredness.

'We killed them,' said Blix simply. 'They were exterminated hundreds of years ago. Most European hemi-humans were, like the true centaurs. I'd have liked to meet a true centaur. One that thinks, you know? Some species survived, like merfolk and harpies, because it's really hard to find them. Even they are endangered. They were mad times. I'm told. I only really know the bits about the animals.'

'Shambhala is where true werewolves are from. I suppose some must have fallen through to your world in the distant past. They were born in the forests far to the south of here and that's mostly where they stayed. There weren't many of them. When humans came here we quickly learned to stay away from them and they didn't expand beyond their ranges. The world is large. We've co-existed for thousands of years.'

He stopped, deep in thought, but Blix could see he hadn't finished.

'Then?' she prompted.

'Then, about sixty years ago, they started moving. They moved into human lands and destroyed everything. Everyone. And at first people thought they were just moving ranges. But then a month later they did it again. Always at the full moon, when they are at their strongest. There are always more of them. And so it has gone for us, every month for those sixty years. We have been destroyed. They've slaughtered their way across the continent. Every city, every town, every village and hamlet - all destroyed. Every man killed and worse for the wom- ah, I mean, ah. Sorry. But this is how it is. They think of themselves as wolves, but they are as much man as beast. They act as men do to women in war.'

He saw Blix turning pale and hurriedly moved on. 'From the Bastion in the far south, now to the Anvil. Only the ice holds of the far north and the islands of the Atlas ocean are still untouched.'

'Didn't you fight?'

'Yes. Men did. But only silver kills werewolves, and silver is incredibly rare on this world. It doesn't occur naturally. Everything else they can recover from, eventually. You can rend a werewolf limb from limb, break the bones and shred the flesh, take the head from its shoulders and destroy the brain, and it will eventually rebuild itself. Only silver is fatal.'

'Did you miss the part when I said I knew about werewolves? Boys always want to explain. Can I see your sword?'

Constant hesitated, then with a sharp tug he unsheathed his sword about an inch, and then after another wary pause, fully. The silvered blade sparkled in the firelight. Blix looked at the sword properly for the first time. It was made for a much bigger man than the boy who wielded it now. It was almost oval, a single edged blade set into a wooden hilt made of a burnished red wood, about a third the length of the blade. The silver glittered in the firelight.

'What's it called?'

'Excuse me?'

'Magic swords always have names. Like, Storm-smiter or Elf-slicer, or something like that.'

'It's not magic. It's just sharp. Silver layered over saric iron.'

'It must have a name though,' Blix persisted.

'I don't know. I'd never seen it until three days ago. I think.' Constant considered the blade. '*Sahsą*,' he said.

'Sasha?'

'*Sahsą*,' Constant enunciated.

'Saw-sa. Sorcha! Brilliant! That's a great name. I knew a Sorcha once, she was fit as. That'll do. I presume it means something?'

'Cutter.' He slid the newly-named Sorcha into its scabbard.

'Brutal. Literal, but brutal.' Blix looked over her shoulder to where the werewolf's steel blade lay. 'Not silver. So completely useless.' She gave it a pretend scowl. 'No name for you.'

'Not completely useless. You can still badly injure a werewolf with a normal blade. A sharp edge is a sharp edge. Or a club or arrow, or anything for that matter. You can certainly slow it down. But it won't kill it, and it will quickly be whole again. There are a few swords like this, but not enough to make a difference. We're losing. We've lost.'

They were quiet for a while, listening to the crackle of the fire. Blix thought about Constant's story.

'Werewolves and men living peacefully, sort of. Then, suddenly, generations of mass murder. If you've lived together for thousands of years without war, what changed?'

'We don't understand why. We only know it's not random. They're not a horde, they're an army. An army with a leader.'

'He was there!' said Blix excitedly. 'At the gate! The big wolf, the one who hit me! The magician called him "First of Wolves". That must mean he's the boss!'

Constant looked grim. 'I wish I'd known. I was downwind and out of sight.' He rubbed his eyes again, until Blix thought they might burst.

'Why do your rub your head like that all the time?' she asked.

'Do I do that? I didn't know. I suppose it helps me remember. Think.'

'You look like you're punching yourself.'

'Don't tempt me.' He groaned, squeezing the bridge of his nose. 'This is all connected,' he said suddenly, startling her. 'It has to be. The magicians, the wolves with them, your sister and you. It's all about the same thing. You are special, you must be.'

'I'm not! I'm just me. He never said why he wanted me.'

'Tell me what they said.'

'I'm not sure I can remember exactly. I was being terrorised.'

'Try hard.' he leaned over and took her hand. 'Look past the terror. Put it aside. Tell me what you remember.'

Blix felt calm and collected as she remembered.

'Okay. First Leicester slagged me off for asking if he'd opened the gate, as impossible things should be obvious, apparently. Then he said something about his body wanting him to be more accurate which I didn't get. Then he said this guy Dragonville had done it, who was hiding in the forest in case everything went kablooey. So Dragonville pitched up and started calling Leicester "Echmoth" like it was his name. Then Dragonville said something about a bloody stone -'

Constant started. 'The bloodstone?'

'Yes, that was it. I saw it. It was green with red bits, so big.' She measured with her fingers.

'The bloodstone.'

'What's that when it's at home, then?'

'A powerful source of magic. It was in the Monastery. It protected it,' he continued, his voice suddenly bitter. 'These men were behind the attack on my home.' He gripped the pommel of his sword until his knuckles went white. 'Two more to kill,' he said, as if they were just marks on a tally. It made Blix incredibly nervous. He looked like he had forgotten she was there. Then he relaxed slightly and refocused on Blix. 'Go on.'

'Um. Um, yeah, okay. Well, Dragonville spent ages bashing on about how brilliant he was for doing the magic. Echmoth got a bit shirty about him boasting. I don't think they like each other. The big werewolf got annoyed with them and said they had to get back to the Bastion and the Wolfmaker. What's a Bastion and a Wolfmaker?'

'The Bastion is a fortress. The other I don't know. Nothing friendly, I expect.'

'Okay. What was next? Leicester told the First of Wolves to be cool because some narrow thing was going to open and something about Elvis that I didn't get but there'd be loads of blood. Then it got really noisy 'cos the werewolves started howling and - what's wrong?'

Constant had turned deathly white. 'Say that again.'

'Something about opening a n -'

'No!' Constant leaned forward and grabbed her wrist roughly. His voice sounded different, angry and afraid at the same time. 'The exact words he said! Repeat then exactly!'

It was a command. The change in him was so sudden and oppressive that Blix felt faint. She closed her eyes and realised she remembered everything.

'The First of Wolves said: The Great Pack has made the crossing without me. We must return to the Wolfmaker. She is waiting for us. For you. Echmoth said: Indeed. My business will conclude shortly. The Narrow Way will open. And afterward, *Elpis*. Dragonville said: Say rather, *spes. Spes vetus.* It is rather more exact, don't you think? Better to live in hope than expectation. He laughed. Echmoth said: Yes. *Spes vetus.* Then you will unleash your Great Pack across worlds. There will blood such as will sate even your thirst. The First of Wolves said: I am not interested in blood. Echmoth said: You are unique among wolves. You will get what you want too. I know what that is. The First of Wolves howled. The other werewolves howled. I do not speak werewolf. I said: Stop, please stop. I cried. Katy cried. Dragonville said: Enough, First of Wolves. I have enough problems without adding deafness to them. Echmoth said: Hmm. Well. Choices, choices. A month on that poxy world, guarding Blix until the day I could bring her here. Living in this shell, suffering when salvation was so close at hand. I have observed her. Fixed her in my eye over all things. I've grown to dislike her. She is rude and stupid. I have no desire to be stupid. I'll take the other one instead. She is a little brighter and looks the part. More a rose than this little thorn. I said: No. Katy said: No. Katy screamed. I said: You bastard, leave her alo-'

'Stop,' said Constant. Blix felt the compulsion to speak disappear. She felt dazed.

'What just happened?' she asked.

'They're...' he whispered, and trailed off. He looked terrified, then shook his head like someone waking from a dream. 'I'm sorry,' He said. 'I didn't mean to... what you said...' He covered his mouth with one hand, shock evident on his face. 'How did I do that?'

'Did you just do magic on me?' demanded Blix hotly.

'I didn't mean to. I'm sorry. I'm not myself.'

'Oh really? Not yourself? Well I'll tell you who you are. You're a bloody hypocrite is who you are! All that chat about how bad magic is and how wrong it is to change people without asking and what did you do?'

'I'm really sorry!' said Constant, so unhappily that he was suddenly childlike again. He was almost crying. 'I didn't mean to do that! I didn't know I could! I'm sorry!'

He looked so unhappy that Blix's indignation cooled a little.

'Well okay, then. Just don't do it again. But tell me what happened there, okay? You looked like you'd seen the dead rise from the grave.'

'Just the opposite. Look, will you trust me? I need to think about things before I have a coherent answer to your question, and I can't think any more. I'm so tired I think I might die if I don't sleep now. I promise I'll tell you when I've thought it through. Will you trust me?'

The question hung there while Blix glowered at him. Then, very reluctantly, she said, 'Okay. But I won't forget. As for trusting you, I'm not sure that I do. You're up and down like a yo-yo.'

'You know, I did save your life. And bring you somewhere safe. You could at least say thank you.'

'Thank you. I don't trust you. You have more swords that a twelve-year-old should have access to and you don't know you can do magic. You kill things. You're dangerous, even if you're a good guy.'

'Okay. I think that might be true. Okay.' Constant tried to think of something normal to say. 'You can have the bed. I checked it earlier, it looked more or less undamaged.' He rolled into a sleeping position in front of the fire, which was spluttering towards extinction.

Blix looked at him for a few moments trying to gauge what he would do when she was asleep. She decided he would probably just sleep.

She climbed the ladder, still wrapped in the winding sheet and wearing her tattered jacket and jeans, too tired to contemplate taking them off. There were thin blankets on the bed. She pulled the bearskin over the top and crawled underneath.

After a while she thought of something.

'Hey. *Hey.*'

'What.' The boy sounded like he'd been dragged back from unconsciousness very unwillingly.

'We never got to "who the hell are you?" Who the hell are you?'

Constant was shocked to realise he had to think for a second.

'I'm nobody,' he said. 'Go to sleep.'

Blix listened to his breathing in the stillness of the cottage. It quickly became a snore. She rolled over and thought about her sister. But not for very long.

When he was sure Blix was unconscious Constant stopped pretending to be asleep and sat up. He rubbed his forehead nervously.

They know about the Writing. These men, they know what they cannot know. How can they know? It was hidden. It was safe. No one can know. They know what it says.

I know. The Narrow Way. I know what I must do.

The rose and the thorn. The sun-crowned child. You're her. You're her. You must be her.

Chapter Eleven: Run

The werewolf paused to listen to the distant howl that told it another human was dead, then limped on.

It had a deep wound on one leg. Blood matted its fur and the wound made it limp badly, but it was nothing to worry about. Already it could feel the flesh knitting back together. Soon it would be as if the steel sword that cut it had never been swung.

The humans had fought bravely. This was important in the werewolf view of things. But few of them had silver and those that did were overwhelmed. They were prepared for assault from without their walls; they had not imagined that an enemy could descend from above.

When the slaughter was done, the werewolves spread out across the countryside, hunting. A few humans had escaped from the settlement during the battle; they were quickly overtaken. Now the pack sought the villages and herder families that dotted the mountain country, scratching a living through the snow and rock. They had no maps or charts showing where the humans lived. They followed the scent.

The werewolf had come across some humans and their beasts that day, and could still taste their blood and flesh in its mouth. But neither their blood nor his own concerned him now. There was wolf blood in the air, a lot of it. One of the pack was dead. Maybe more than one.

It was dawn when the werewolf, diminished to its most man-like without the moon, came upon the stone circle.

Without sentiment, it observed the scene. Wolves died. These had died in battle. A good death, as wolves saw it.

The werewolf was well versed in war and a shrewd judge of its triumphs and reversals. As it paced through the charnel field within the circle it constructed a picture of the fight in its mind. A bold killer had taken its brothers by surprise, seized the moment, and ended it quickly. It saw too that the dead wolves were New and, with that, barely more than cubs. This wolf was grey and silver-scarred, and would not have died so cheaply, it thought.

The warrior had taken one wolf's head clean off its shoulders. As he approached, that wolf's scent became distinct from the red smell of death and the wolf snorted in recognition. This wolf was not New. A glance at the face confirmed it.

The wolf raised its muzzle to the sky and howled, a long, high keen of sorrow, sorrow not for the wolf, but for the pack, for wolf-kind. The howl echoed across the mountains and was picked up by others, and those voices echoed by others still, as wolves across the forest heard the tidings and passed them on.

There were wolves everywhere. The message spread steadily southward, as fast as the wind could carry it.

The wolf could smell man scent, mingling with that of wolf and death. Two it recognised - the laughing magician had been here, with the man who smelled of rot and anger. There were three other scent trails it did not know. One disappeared. Two led off into the trees. One of those smelled of wolf blood and the icy-sweet tang of silver.

The wolf loped into the forest, following the scent.

Constant dreamed.

In my dream, I am in a large hall which smells of fresh plaster. It's a comforting smell, like clay on a potter's wheel. My grandfather was a potter and the smell reminds me of him. I remember him but do not miss him. This is a change. They said I would become serene as I grew older. It seems I have.

The window is not quite finished. We wait for the last few panes to be sent up from below. A fresh breeze blows through the gap, fluttering the cloth that covers it. It should be an icy blast, given how high in the mountains we are, but it feels merely cool. The magic sees to that. The magic has made life on the Anvil possible.

In my dream, the brothers are covering the floor with sheets, ready to paint the walls. I think they are being optimistic.

'Has the plaster gone off?' I ask.

'This wall has, Great Father,' says Brother Gautselin, pointing to the one facing the window. 'The others are still damp in places. Another day for them.'

'That is good progress. How is Brother Thancmar?'

'Well. He's a builder, he's had more lime burns than I've had hot dinners. Five minutes with his arm in the vinegar tun dealt with it.'

'I will remember him in my prayers. You have all done great work here.'

Brother Gautselin inclines his head. The brothers who build do not seek praise. 'We but carry on the work of those who came before.'

'I remember those men, sometimes. You are equal to them.' To spare his blushes I continue. 'Where is Brother Egino?'

'Hiding. He's still new. He doesn't know how to act around you.'

This makes me laugh. 'Am I so awe-inspiring?'

Brother Gautselin scratches his forehead. 'A bit. You are God, after all.'

He says this to bait a line for me. I know this, but I rise to it anyway. 'I am not God. I'm an incarnation... You know what I am, you told me. I am not God.'

'Eh, you are a bit.' He perks up. 'Do you know, I've just realised what my epitaph will be? "Gautselin of Dulebskathn, Tutor to the twenty-second Great Father. He wiped God's arse when God was a lad."'

His eyes seek the ceiling to avoid mine. The brothers laying down the sheets try hard not to react. Brother Gautselin was Tutor for many years, before he became Mason. He knows how to make me laugh.

'Fetch the boy, you irreligious rogue,' I command with a smile. He bows himself out, making many pious gestures.

In my dream, I contemplate the empty wall until the young artist is retrieved from his bolt hole. Gautselin accompanies him, for moral support.

'Your work on the map is magnificent,' I say, once he has finished genuflecting. 'The illusion of depth is incredible. I feel I could reach into the wall and out into space.'

'I but carry on the work of those who came before, Great Father,' he mumbles, looking at his shoes as though the words are written on his toes.

'You have a gift,' I say. 'Let us put it into practice. You know what I want?'

'Yes, Great Father.'

'Can you do it?'

'Yes, Great Father.'

'Tell me.'

He looks up then. I expect to see confusion, or fear, or awe. What I see is genius.

'I see it in my mind's eye,' he says. 'It seems to me that it is already on the wall. My brush will only reveal it.'

I believe him. 'And the stone?'

'The glint in its eye, Great Father.'

'Excellent,' I say. I dismiss him. He scurries away, looking profoundly grateful to have escaped. Gautselin and I share a smile.

'Have you thought about my requirement?' I ask.

The smile vanishes. He draws me aside, so the others cannot hear.

'I have,' he says. 'I still do not understand why.'

I try and put into words what I have felt these last months. The aching fear I have felt inside since I heard of the glass marvel at the Bastion and what it can do. The need to see for myself. To know all that can be known about the gates.

'The map... the map is not decorative,' I say. 'I must know this thing. I feel it very strongly. I don't know why. I think it's...'

I trail off awkwardly, but Gautselin knows my mind.

'You think you're telling yourself something. The part of you whose arse I didn't wipe.'

'Yes. I believe I am being told something. I feel they are a threat, these holes between worlds. To us. To everyone. I must see them. I must know which ones still work. How they are connected. How they are used. I can't go to the Bastion. That means doing magic here. And I can't. Unless you can tell me differently.'

'Ah.' Gautselin nods in a distracted way. I know his face better than the one I see in the mirror. I see he is arriving at a resolution. The path his mind walks must be a painful one. I do not interrupt him.

'There is a way,' he finally whispers. 'I suppose I am allowed. If there is a threat to you. I must keep you safe. We may do anything to keep you safe.'

'Allowed?' I ask.

'To tell you what is written in the book.'

'About?'

'About how the stone may be used.' His voice is barely audible.

This is not an answer I had imagined hearing. I asked him to think about how we might get around the restriction the stone places on us.

'You have done this before,' he continues. 'Do you remember? I see you don't.'

'No. I am at peace with the voices. The words keep them where they should be.' This is not wholly true, but it is true enough. There is no need to disturb Brother Gautselin with what it means to be me. 'I remember them when I pray.' That is true.

Brother Gautselin is still conflicted. He speaks as if the words are being dragged from him by wild horses.

'The book contains a warning. It is not a warning about using the stone. It is about using the stone again.'

I get the sense that the book contains words he is not willing to tell me. I guess at what their import may be.

'I do not wish to use magic,' I say.

'Now. Who is to say that the next you will feel the same?'

He hesitates. I wait patiently for him to come to terms with his actions.

'You will put it on the wall?' he says.

'Yes.'

'And never touch it again?'

'Yes.'

'That's ambiguous,' he says sharply. 'Say the word. I know you will not lie.'

'I will never touch it again,' I say.

Another silence. 'Very well,' he says at last. 'I will write it in the book.'

I begin to say more, but we are interrupted. The librarian approaches. It is not often he emerges from his domain. He carries a thick scroll wound tightly around a pin. He looks agitated.

'Great Father, may I speak?

'Certainly.'

'Word rises from below. I have received new books. Hymns from a new religion on Earth.'

'A new religion on Earth. How many is that today?' quips Gautselin. There is a little laughter from the brothers. It is not ill-meant. I have taught them that all faiths are expressions of the Faith. The flame burns for all.

The librarian does not laugh. 'Great Father, one speaks of Rakshasa.'

The brothers fall silent.

'Come,' I say.

In my dream, we walk through the halls until we reach the library. We pass through the stacks and into the room where the Writing is held. There is no reason to be here. I know the Writing as I know my name. It just seems right to be in its presence.

'Show me what it says,' I ask.

Now there is a boy here I do not recognise.

'What the hell happened?' *he says. He is agitated, as though he has had a terrible shock.* 'I almost left you! When you said the words, I almost went into her!' *He paces back and forth.* 'Was it because you gave her your words before? Or something else? Is that what happens when there are two of you together? I can just leave? Incredible. There have never been two of you before.'

He closes his eyes and flattens his palms in front of him, as though smoothing an imaginary bedspread. When he opens them again he has calmed himself a little.

'Hold on to her, Constant. I need to know more. Don't let her go. In the meantime, I am going to bury myself so deep in your mind that nothing will drag me out.'

In my dream the boy rubs his forehead with the heel of his hand in a way I know to be my own. He looks up at me.

Why don't you remember me when you're awake? *he says.* 'It's very inconvenient.'

He looks around him, taking in the great tomes and scrolls, and the Writing itself. 'Evidently I don't have to tell you the significance of what she said, you wouldn't be remembering the Writing if you didn't know. These men, who are they? Do they know what is written? They can't. Is Simon right? Is what is foretold coming to pass? Yes, she has sun-hair, it's not uncommon. You need a bit more than passing resemblances before you start getting excited.'

The boy seems to realise that he is the one getting excited.

'We'll deal with that later. I know you're looking for something, Constant. You could have dreamed of some other time. You won't find it here. You need to go deeper. In the meantime, you heard something in your sleep. A wolf howling. The same howl, over and over. I have a bad feeling. Something is coming. Get up, get out, get away from here. Take us somewhere safe. Take us... take us *home*.'

Constant did not remember the boy when he woke up.

Constant's left little finger itched. This, he decided sleepily, was the least of his problems.

It felt to Constant like he'd been punched back into consciousness. Every part of him ached, and while he was warm on the outside the core of him felt like old ice, calved from a glacier that was slowly grinding over him.

The fire was alight again, and something was bubbling in the cauldron. It smelled nice.

Constant thought: *Fire is like magic. It burns brightly but if you let it, it consumes you.*

Then he thought: *Whose thought was that! Not mine. Last night I gave chapter and verse on gate magic, a subject about which I know nothing. Who was thinking my thoughts? Why didn't the words work? For me...*

Constant realised he'd slept with his arms and legs wrapped around the silver sword. Which was now called Sorcha. *Swords should have names, according to this girl. And why not?* The part of him that was a twelve-year-old boy was rather taken with the idea.

There was another part of him. *She is her. She is her. Is she? How do I know? Can I ask her? No, keep this close.*

Stiff muscles protested as he uncurled himself. He groaned.

'Back with us then?' said Blix, looking down from the sleeping platform. She was lying down, arms folded under her chin, and Constant could only see her face. She grinned at him.

'You sleep like the dead,' she said. 'I've been up and down this ladder half a dozen times this morning. Very slowly, I must admit. I'm about ninety percent bruise. I had to step over you to light the fire and you still didn't notice.'

Constant sat up, prompting further complaints from various tendons. 'I'm as stiff as a board,' he said.

'You can talk. You weren't beaten up. You haven't got a toothbrush, have you?'

'What's a- never mind. No.'

'No toothbrushes? Lovely. This place is, like, East Germany or somewhere.'

Constant became aware that there was something over his head. A couple of items that Constant took a few moments to register as undergarments were hanging off the mantle. They were steaming gently. Blix saw him looking.

'I went outside and got some water, I needed to wash my things. I have a spare... I mean, Katy had a spare pair of knickers, but I've only the one bra, and it was slashed up. It got blood on it. Cold water for blood.'

'Bra? A breast-band? You've fixed it.'

'Breast-band, good grief, it really is the Dark Ages here, isn't it? Yeah, I fixed it. I have a needle and thread.' She frowned briefly. 'Katy. Katy had them. My t-shirt and vest are write-offs, but I fixed my jacket and jeans, sort of.'

She pointed behind him. Blix's leather jacket hung on the back of a chair, which itself had been reassembled from the debris. Broad stitches had brought the leather back together, but calling it fixed was pushing it.

'I've never really done sewing before,' she continued. 'I stitched a stuffed frog once in junior school. It took me three months.'

'The bearskin is more practical.'

'I'll wear the cloak on top. The leather's mine, I'm not going to leave it behind, not while there's a stitch holding it together.'

Constant shook his head, still feeling fuddled and heavy-lidded. 'You've been busy. How long was I asleep?'

'Ages. It's mid-morning. My watch has stopped.'

'Goodness. I was really tired.'

'Yeah, I had breakfast without you, you looked like you needed to sleep more than eat. I ate some of your cheese. I like goat's cheese.'

Constant rubbed the sleep out of his eyes. 'It's yak, I think.'

'Then I like yak cheese.'

'What's cooking?'

'Pottage mark two. This time with actual food value. There were some storage jars in the eaves, with pulses and dried veg and stuff.'

Constant regarded her curiously. She seemed normal, as far as he knew what normal was for seventeen-year-old girls from another planet. But still there was something not quite right with her.

'How do you feel?' he asked carefully.

'My entire left side is purple. It hurts when I think about moving.'

'I meant about... things.'

'Oh.' Her expression changed. She looked confused. 'It's strange. I should feel terrible. I know I should. And I kind of do. But I don't, too. It's like it happened to someone else and I just heard about on the news. I feel normal. It's strange.'

'It's probably delayed shock, or something,' Constant said, feeling guilty as he told the lie. 'If you start feeling upset, tell me. I know some breathing exercises which will help. I'm here for you.'

Blix smiled. 'That's the second time you've said that. You look so serious when you do.'

'Do I? I'll take your word for it. I don't know myself very well I'm afraid.'

'Don't have an existential crisis, one of us being a basket case is enough. Mum always says you cut your cloth from the bolt you have. Well, not always, you know what I mean. I think she means you are who you are and what you make of it is up to you. That's quite profound for my mum.'

'I think that's very wise,' said Constant. 'It's up to me.'

'God, my mum though. She'll have called the police by now. She'll be worried sick, wondering where I am. Where we are...' Blix's attention wandered; she looked like she was seeing something in her mind's eye which didn't quite make sense.

'Blix?'

'What? Sorry. Hey, speaking of cloth, yours is on the table. Thanks for letting me wear it. What's all the writing about? I can't read the lingo.'

'It's scripture, I suppose you'd call it,' said Constant. 'The core text of my religion. Revealed to be true by the Co... by the Ultimate.'

'That sounded like a capital U. Is that your God?'

'That's everyone's God.'

‘Yeah, okay, I’ve been to church, let’s not start a debate. Well, again, thanks for letting me wear it. Probably saved me from catching my death. I hope I didn't mess it up too much. It looks a bit elderly.'

'It's four thousand years old,' said Constant, and smiled as he saw the look of horror on Blix's face. 'Don't worry, it’s protected.’

‘More magic.’

‘Yes, but nothing to worry about. It just preserves it.’

‘I get that. If I had the Shroud of Turin with me, I’d want to look after it too. Even then I can’t imagine someone would let me wear it.’

‘People are more important than things,’ Constant said. ‘I didn't want you to die.’ He remembered Brother Simon. ‘Those who have faith believe unto death,’ he whispered, staring into space. He roused himself a second later. ‘I wouldn’t want to leave it behind,’ he continued in a more normal voice, ‘but it’s the Writing that is important, not the object. I’ve learned it by heart. Seventy times,’ he added to himself.

'Pardon me?'

'Nothing. Are you going to stay up there all day?'

'Is that an option?' Blix pushed herself up, wincing.

Constant raised his eyebrows. 'That's a lively shirt.'

Suddenly Blix was all smiles. 'I know. Isn't it brilliant?' She was wearing a crimson shield-fronted shirt with yellow stitching and eleven bright brass buttons. She wore it outside her ragged jeans. It was slightly too big for her, and the tails hung halfway down her thighs.

Constant smiled despite himself. 'Brilliant is definitely the word. It practically glows in the dark.'

'It was in the wardrobe. There are chaps, too. They're *awesome.* And then there are these.'

Blix held up a pair of bloomers for inspection. They were mainly silk with lots of lace, ending at the knee where they were drawn in with bows. ‘These are what you call 'lingerie'.'

Constant looked blank. 'What are what I call what?'

'Lingerie. Pants with malice aforethought. Whoever wears these, I bet they wear corsets. Like, in burlesque or something. I think I’d be into that. Mmm.’

Her eyes took on a slightly dreamy look which Constant didn’t understand. She looked back at him and turned slightly red.

‘Forget I said that. Your mother, adventurous woman, was she?'

'I don't know. I shouldn't think so. She was a peasant. Why?'

'Let's just say if the right woman was wearing these you wouldn't be a monk for very long.’

'I don't understand.'

'I should hope not, you're not old enough.'

Constant grimaced. 'No, actually I do. It's about intercourse, isn't it? Sorry, it's not the first thing that occurs to monks.'

'They must put something in your tea.' Blix considered the item critically. 'You know, these clothes don't look local, if you know what mean. All respect to your homeland, but anywhere which has sword-wielding monks, real werewolves and people referred to unironically as 'peasants' isn't the sort of place which also manufactures lacy derrière-wear.'

'Hmm.' Constant looked up at the sleeping platform. 'I wonder what else is up there?' He shinned up the ladder.

At first glance the bedroom seemed as broken and dishevelled as the room below. Simple, well-made furniture, upended in a struggle. A tall wardrobe had been tipped over and a blanket box broken open. Constant touched the wardrobe. He didn't know much about peasants - about anyone other than monks, really - but he didn't suppose their funds ran to buying furniture. Someone who lived here had built this, and the bed and blanket box, just as someone had built the house, stone and timber, with their own hands. Constant wondered what that would feel like. Everything had been handed down, one generation to the next, down a line that ended with him. The thought affected Constant quite a lot. He didn't like things coming to an end.

He returned his attention to the room. The fight had extended to the sleeping platform, it seemed. But something about the scene seemed off. It looked staged, somehow. Now that he thought about it, he realised the whole house made him feel like that.

A board creaked underfoot. Constant crouched down to have a look and saw something under the bed, right at the back against the wall. 'That's surprising.'

With some effort he heaved out an old canvas backpack with a bedroll tied at the top. A pair of leather saddle bags came next, strapped closed with big brass buckles. There were a few small sacks which looked like food bags, and some crumpled clothes which looked like they had been stuffed there in a hurry.

Constant unbuckled one of the saddlebags and looked inside. He pulled out a cylindrical bottle, a little longer than his thumb, made of thick green glass with a faded yellow label pasted on it. He showed Blix.

'I can't read this. It's squiggles.'

Blix looked at it. 'It's in English,' she said. 'I believe,' she added. 'After our conversation last night, I'm not sure any more. It says "Mexican Mustang Liniment. For the Outward Ailments of Man and Beast." And then that's been crossed out and underneath someone's written "snake oil."' She put it back in the bag. 'So. That's what it says. What does it mean?'

'It means someone's been living here,' Constant said, drumming his fingers nervously on the floorboards. 'Since the wolves left, I mean.'

'Someone from Earth, too. That's where Mexico is, if you don't know.'

'Maybe your teacher has a friend?'

Blix wafted the bloomers back and forth suggestively. 'Not one who wears these I wouldn't have thought. He doesn't seem the type.'

Constant suddenly realised he felt anxious, but didn't know why. He chewed his bottom lip pensively.

'Well, whoever they belong to, they aren't here now,' Blix continued, oblivious to Constant's concern. 'I wouldn't stay out all night around here. Maybe she was wolfed.'

'Maybe.'

'Anyway, they're mine now. Finders keepers. The chaps too, they're not the wafty kind, they should hold my jeans together.'

'We should see whether there's anything useful,' said Constant.

'We can get all that stuff out and see what's there in a minute. For the moment, bugger off downstairs so I can put these on.' She waggled the bloomers again, and giggled. 'In fact, go outside, I don't want you watching.'

'Still a monk,' Constant reminded her.

'Still a boy. Offski. Now.'

Constant took a bowl of the broth with him. He stood just outside the door, facing into the forest, sipped the food carefully, and tried to work out why he felt wrong.

The forest was different in the morning. Where the night had closed in and threatened, daylight opened it up. Just being able to see more than a few steps ahead of him was a great relief. To see that a looming mass was not a werewolf about to claw the skin from his bones but just a few moss-draped boulders made flesh and fur by his imagination.

At some point in their night walk they'd left the needle trees behind and crossed into old broad-leaf forest. He could see larch and alder, ash and oak, daractchi and budahen. Saplings in their first straight growth and grandfather trees, knotted and gnarled. Those held some of their leaves still; most were bare. He could see where the trees had been coppiced; broad stools of birch and oak, some with long poles of new growth, spoke of generations, centuries of careful management. That would end now. A well coppiced tree would never die. Now they would grow, and live, and age, and cease to be.

I am a coppice, he thought. *I have been well managed.*

Constant's knowledge of the forest felt good and normal. This was only slightly marred by the fact that he, Constant, had never seen trees like this before and didn't know how to tell one from the other. Someone else was bleeding into his mind, but for once he didn't mind. Whoever it was had a simple, pastoral way of thinking that made the horrors of the past few days seem quite distant. Darcen Ysir's constant anger was absent. A good night's sleep had pushed him back down inside where he belonged.

Constant wandered over to the edge of the clearing, brushed the snow from a tree stump and sat, ignoring the chill and slight dampness that seeped through his robes. He closed his eyes and breathed the forest in. He felt the bark and grass and the hard earth beneath his feet, and reached inside himself. He found the voice quite quickly. His memories were very close to the surface, as if the forest had summoned him forth. Comen sen-Hersa, a wildsman from the water margin of the great forest of Samatha, on the edge of the lake country, three thousand miles to the south and east. He'd lived and died almost five hundred years before but there he was, his memories as bright in Constant's mind as the image in a silvered mirror.

sen-Hersa had been a man who, by choice, had lived virtually without human contact for most his life, until he was Recognised. A mystic of sorts, and had felt a deep bond with the land. A man of the grain of the soil, who'd spent half a lifetime watching the seasons turn, thinking about the why of the world. A man who had never raised a hand to another.

He was another one who hadn't been Recognised until his forties, and alongside the serenity that all Constant's predecessors eventually felt, there was a deep sense of loss. Comen had been a poet without letters, crafting a life-long ode to nature through his manner of living. His new life had taken that voice and given him another, one that was only partly his.

Why did he feel stolen? Constant wondered. *He went willingly. We all go willingly, those who are old enough to know.*

The forest through sen-Hersa's eyes was a place of wonder and beauty. But something wasn't right.

He looked closely at a nearby birch. Something red-brown and scaly afflicted the bark near the ground, smothering the silver-grey as it rose from the snow. Constant found a stick and prodded the tree. A large chunk of wood crumbled into powder.

The tree was ill, probably dying. It was no disease Constant-as-sen-Hersa recognized. He looked around and, now that he had an eye for it, saw the same affliction on other trees - not every tree, but enough to surmise that it would be every tree, eventually. He sat back down on the stump and thought about it.

Something bad has happened. The forest sickens. I wasn't told about this.

A change in the wind stirred Constant from his thoughts. He wondered what chaps were, and how long it took to put them on.

Something wasn't right.

Constant chewed on his bottom lip, trying to pin down what he felt, the strange unease. Abruptly he pushed off from the stump and circled around the clearing, trying to make sense of what his mind was telling him.

As he turned the corner to the back of the house he saw something out of place. A rough pole had been thrust into the earth and a line strung between it and a wooden hook on the wall. Pegged on the line were six werewolf ears, three pairs neatly sliced at the root, drying in the weak morning sun.

'That's strange,' said Constant, out loud. *But just strange. There's something else. Something's not right.*

Constant opened his mind a little more to the memories of Comen sen-Hersa, and let him into his senses.

There was no sound. Constant bolted for the house.

Blix was standing on the upper platform with her back to the door as Constant burst in. 'Hey!' she exclaimed, hastily clutching the red shirt to her chest. 'I said wait outside! I'm not finished! I haven't got my bra on!'

She'd pulled a pair of close-fitting leather outers over her trousers, the lacing up of which had clearly taken some time, but Constant barely noticed.

'Get dressed,' he said urgently. 'Do it now. *Now.*'

'Not while you're watching!'

'I don't care! For goodness sake! Can't you hear it? Can't you hear the silence? The forest is terrified. Wolves are coming. *Now.* If they catch us inside we're dead meat. We've stayed here too long. I'm a fool. We need space to fight. *Move.*'

Blix stared at him uncomprehendingly for a moment. Then she span around and struggled into her bra, threw the shirt over her head and grabbed her satchel and the doombag.

'Leave those,' Constant ordered.

'I'm not leaving it!' said Blix, clutching at the doombag.

'We're not running. They'll still be there if we live.'

With great reluctance Blix put the bags back down. She took up the bearskin cloak instead, and pulled it on as though the stiff, thick leather was really armour.

'What about all the stuff up here?' she asked. 'There might be something useful -'

Constant shook his head. 'We haven't got time. Bring your sword.'

Blix slid down the ladder, grabbed the wolf sword and followed Constant through the door, only to crash into his back as he stopped in his tracks. Her cry of surprise was stifled immediately by Constant's hand. The silence of the forest shaped itself around something terrible, something savage, something *there.*

The urge to run was almost overpowering. From the corner of his eye Constant saw Blix let the bearskin slip away, seemingly without realising she had done so - the heavy fur now more like a dead weight on her shoulders than protection against attack.

Constant's sword whispered along the leather sheath as he drew it. His voice, when he spoke, was no louder. 'When it comes, get out of the way, stay well behind me. Let me deal with it. But if you must strike, strike as hard as you can, hard and low. Remember -'

Then the werewolf was there, stepping carefully through the trees, a continuous low growl rumbling across the wood. Constant felt it in his chest; Blix looked like the sound had turned her bones to rubber. It was big, much bigger than the ones who had attacked Blix at the circle. Even in the daytime the man-wolf was terrifyingly lupine - it's jaw more like a muzzle, fangs distorting its shape, wicked claws in place of fingernails, and a thick grey pelt covering its body. It wore a mail shirt taken from a human and split almost to the waist to fit the beast's torso. Its leading arm was covered by rusted plate, and it held a long sword lightly in its other hand.

Constant tensed and waited for it to spring at them but it paused at the edge of the grass, sizing them up. Everything about it, its stance and caution and armour, made him think it had fought men many times before and learned from the experience. There'd be no foolish clawing from this one, not while Constant held silver.

The werewolf's lips curled contemptuously. 'Whelps,' it rasped.

'I am the death of wolves,' Constant replied, raising the silver sword. Blix took several steps backwards.

The almost-muzzle curled again. 'A cub playing at heroes.' It transferred its cruel gaze to Blix. 'And a terrified bitch,' it continued. 'Poor sport.'

Then it was on them, the long blade cutting down hard and fast toward Constant's shoulder. Constant's mind reached for Darcen Ysir, but to his horror Ysir was not there. Instead the memory of Comen sen-Hersa fumbled with a weapon he had never held against a foe he had never fought. Constant instinctively swung his sword to push the werewolf's away, but there was no strength or technique in his action. The weight of the blow forced Constant down hard, twisting him awkwardly back and to his left and plunging the silver sword almost upright through the snow and six inches into the earth.

The werewolf was unbalanced by the failed defence and went down too, but wasted no time on a second strike. Instead it swung its plated arm around and up and took Constant full in the chest, lifting him up into the air and sending him flying across the clearing as if he weighed nothing. He landed badly, skidded in slush and mud, and lay still.

The werewolf got to its feet. It watched Constant for a few moments, until it was satisfied he wouldn't get up. Then it considered the silver sword, still quivering where it stood, and carefully, without touching the blade, pressed down on the pommel until the sword was in the hard ground up to the hilt.

Then it turned to look at Blix. 'Run from me,' it said.

Arms trembling, Blix raised her sword, holding it in both hands, out in front of her. 'Better to fight,' she said in a fragile voice.

The werewolf bark-laughed briefly. It wiped thick slaver from its mouth and slung the spittle into Blix's face. She cringed automatically and scraped it off and as she did, the werewolf was somehow there in front of her, clamping the blade of her sword with both hands. She tried to swing or pull or push the blade, but the sword might as well have been plunged into stone for all the good it did.

The werewolf leant forward over the blade until its face was nearly against Blix's. Its stinking breath plumed into her face and terror hit her like a blow to the heart.

'Fight and die now,' growled the man-wolf. 'Run and live longer.'

Its grey tongue curled obscenely long in its mouth, and the werewolf licked Blix's face from chin to scalp, wet and soft but with a rough surface that tore at her skin.

'I like to hunt,' it said. 'I'll give you a head start.' It suddenly threw its arms wide and barked frenziedly, its slashing fangs inches from Blix's face.

Something deep in the core of Blix's personality thought: *Look. Papillae on the tongue. For licking flesh from bone. Carnassial teeth. Specialised for slicing through meat.*

Blix dropped the sword and ran.

The treeline embraced her and swallowed her up. Immediately the ground became treacherous underfoot and she slipped, skidded and fell as she scrambled headlong over snow, rock, earth and root, up out of the valley where the little house sat. She ran, ran as hard as she could, ran like all hell was at her heels because it was. But as she fled she knew, knew it was futile, knew that it was a game with one end and one winner. Even through her panic Blix could sense the werewolf behind her. She knew it could easily overtake her. It was just toying with her. The realisation added despair to her terror. Every now and then she caught sight of it, loping lazily through the trees, swinging first left then right across her path, driving her onward for its own amusement.

As she reached the lip of the dell the werewolf was there, rearing up in front of her. It swung a hand, sweeping it around in a huge arc from high above its head, claws spread wide. Blix screamed and threw herself sideways. The claws caught her jacket, sending her spinning and sliding back down the slope. She crashed into a tree trunk but rolled around it and careened on without losing momentum. Behind her, the werewolf resumed the chase.

Blix ran even faster downhill and in moments was back in the clearing and stumbling toward her only hope; the silver sword Sorcha, sheathed in the earth. She dived on it, gripped the hilt and pulled with all her strength. Her arms screamed in agony and she screamed with them, but the sword did not move.

The werewolf appeared through the trees, and walked casually toward her. Blix braced herself directly above the sword and put everything she had into pulling it free. Suddenly it moved a fraction. Agonisingly slowly the earth began to give it up, inch by silver inch, but it was too late, too late.

The werewolf stood over her, blocking the weak winter sun, fury made flesh.

'Poor sport,' it repeated, pressing the sword back into the ground with its heel. Blix sobbed as she watched the blade disappear and sat back on the wet earth, all strength and hope exhausted, waiting to die. The werewolf raised its paw, claws glistening wetly. 'Goodbye,' it said.

A shot rang out, echoing whip-crack loud through the cold air. A flower of red blossomed on the beast's forehead, and a puzzled look spread across its face. Its jaw gaped as though it were trying to say something. Slowly it fell forward. It thudded into Blix's body and she scrambled backwards to escape it, scraping her way from underneath the dead werewolf, tearing her jeans and the fresh stitches in her haste to get free. She sat there for a moment, breathing heavily, shocked to the core. Then she looked around.

A young woman was leaning against a tree, a rifle braced against her shoulder. Older than Blix but not much, she had an impish look, with phoenix eyes and an open, smiling but strangely tough-looking face, as if hard living had worn away smooth edges. A short black bob of hair poked out from under a tan cowboy hat. She wore a short buckskin coat, long western style boots and a pair of tight canvas trousers. A pistol sat on one hip and a long coil of rope was hitched on the other. A bandolier crossed her chest from her left shoulder; white metal bullets gleamed strangely, like moonlight.

When it was clear that the werewolf would not move again she lowered the rifle and blew the smoke from the barrel. The tang of gunpowder filled the air. She sauntered over to Blix, extended her hand and dragged the terrified girl upright. Then she pushed back her hat and smiled so broadly it almost split her face.

'Seems there was a dog off the leash ma'am,' she said. 'Had to put it down I'm afraid.'

Blix had never heard a voice like it in real life, but a thousand movies and TV shows had burned it into her memory.

'You're American!' she said.

'Yes, I am!' said the stranger. 'From the great state of Nebraska! And most lately from Utah. Although technically I'm half Japanese. And daddy was really from Kentucky, though ain't no one ever held that against him much.' She gave Blix a confidential look. 'Don't tell those Nebraska boys though. They can be downright insular folks sometimes.' Words tumbled out of her at top speed, while her accent rolled around her mouth like a ripe peach.

'You have a gun!'

'Yes, I do!' said the woman, smiling even more broadly. 'You can tell 'cause I just shot a guy. Say, Fido there didn't catch you one in the head, did he?'

'Oh my God!' The terror was beginning to subside, but the adrenaline wasn't. She steadied herself against the house and tried to calm down. The woman strode over to the werewolf, who had landed face down, tutted, then gave him an experimental kick or two.

'Yup, he's dead,' she confirmed, sounding pleased. 'Dead as a dodo.' She hooked a foot under the corpse and rolled it over.

'My, my,' she breathed. 'He was a healthy fellow and no mistake. Shame to see a set like that go to waste.' She pulled out a knife, crouched by the dead monster and, to Blix's horror, lopped its ears off, first the left, then the right. She glanced up and saw the look on Blix's face. 'Hey, the bounty on these is seven bucks in Utah. The Mormons have got a thing about werewolves. Waste not, want not. I got a string of 'em out back.'

She put the ears in a soft leather pouch on her belt and pulled the drawstring closed. 'Salt,' she explained to the still open-mouthed Blix. 'It'll preserve 'em until I can cure 'em for real.'

Blix recovered herself a little. 'You hunt werewolves? But werewolves are people! Um. Most of the time.'

'Sure they are! Back home. Not here. Here they're the real deal. But sure, back home they're people. Law ain't got no problem with them when they're people. Or when they change, long as they don't hurt nobody. But, you know, if they do...' She mimed sighting down a rifle, then jerked the imaginary weapon back as if she'd fired it. 'Ka-blam! Frontier justice.' She kicked the werewolf again. 'Like old Sweetlips here got. He'd have been fine if he didn't try to kill no one. But he did, so he got what he deserved. I take it you didn't mind that so much.'

Blix took a deep breath. After waiting a moment to make sure the torrent of words had properly stopped she said, 'Whoever you are, thank you. You saved my life!'

'Shucks. All in a day's work,' said the woman. She thrust her hand out. Blix took it hesitantly and found her arm being pumped in an almighty shake.

'Kit McCoy!' said the woman.

'Excuse me?' said Blix, freeing her hand.

'My name. Kit McCoy! That's my name.' She grinned.

'Oh! Um. I'm Blix. Blix Summerland.'

'Well that's a right pretty name,' said Kit. 'Delighted make your acquaintance. Is there some special reason you're wearing my clothes?'

'Ah.' Blix fidgeted slightly. 'Well, you see, I was attacked, and my clothes got ripped, and so I, um, borrowed-'

'Well that's just fine!' the woman interrupted. 'Wear 'em all you want!' Her eyes narrowed. 'Waitaminute. Are you wearing my under things?'

'Um,' said Blix.

'Oh, that's all right! I bet you look cute as a button in them!'

Blix bit her lip.

'When you're quite ready, I'm still alive over here,' came a small voice from some distance away.

Blix clapped a hand to her mouth in horror. 'Oh God, Constant!' She ran toward his voice.

Constant was lying flat on his back in a thick patch of snowdrops. His robe was torn open at the front and a huge bruise was already darkening his chest. He was prodding gingerly at his ribs with his left hand. His eyes were unfocused and he looked confused.

'Are you all right?' said Blix.

'Bloody wolf damn near caved my chest in,' he complained. He looked at them slightly vacantly. 'I see four of you.' He closed his eyes and counted to three, then opened them again. 'That's a bit better, now there's only two. One of you looks like someone else though. That's weird, why's that happening?'

'Because I am someone else, kid,' said Kit McCoy. 'Say, did old Jip there knock your brains loose too?'

'Very possibly,' said Constant weakly. 'You killed the wolf? Properly?'

'Blew a hole in his head you could whistle through,' said Kit proudly. 'Silver bullets. Got 'em made special in Colorado. Guaranteed to bring stray dogs to heel or send 'em to the big kennel in the sky!'

'You have a charming way with words, miss.' Constant pressed a little harder, winced and went pale.

'Are your ribs broke?' Kit asked, squinting professorially at his chest. 'Got some medicine for that.' She looked sidelong at Blix and pursed her lips. 'If y'all didn't, mmm, borrow it. Are they broke or not?'

Constant continued his careful exploration. 'I don't think so,' he said. He took a deep breath, and coughed violently. 'No,' he croaked when he'd recovered.

'Well that's dandy!' said Kit slapping her thigh.

Constant looked at the woman, distrust clear in his eyes. 'Who are you and what do you want?' he said.

Kit beamed, and thrust out her hand again, downward this time. 'My name's Kit McCoy and I'm here to kill a man!' she announced. She glanced at the body behind her. 'A different man,' she qualified.

Constant sighed deeply and appeared to regret it almost immediately. 'I hope it's not me,' he said. 'That would be quite easy right now. Kit McCoy, my name is Constant. We should probably get to know each other.'

He reached up to take her hand and heave himself up. Instantly his face turned as white as the snow around him.

'That was a mistake,' he said. He fainted.

Constant dreamed.

In my dream, I am in the stone garden of the Monastery. It is made in a fissure in the mountain core, open to the sky. It is a place of contemplation filled with religiously precise swirls of stones, illustrating ideas about peace and serenity. The sun has moved around the Anvil and the air is beginning to cool. Scrolls and sheets of parchment are strewn on the ground before me, where I have thrown them. They tell of strange and wonderful things on other worlds. The intricate designs carefully raked into the gravel have been destroyed where I have paced back and forth.

In my dream, I am extremely angry.

'Because you can't,' says Brother Jamyang, my tutor. He sits on the contemplation seat, his legs crossed beneath him. His name means 'gentle voice'. He is well named. He has been very patient today.

I kick my toe into the gravel. A few small stones arc through the air and bounce off the hem of Brother Jamyang's robe. He raises an eyebrow at me. I am aware how petulant I must look. This makes me angrier.

'I am Great Father, thirty-second of my name! You must obey me! I command -'

'No,' says Jamyang.

This staggers me. No one has ever said no to me.

'What do you mean, no?' I say, sputtering. 'You can't say no!'

'In this, I can,' he says. 'The brothers are charged to keep you safe. The First Father commanded it. We obey you in all things, saving only if you try to leave the Anvil. You must remain. You must be kept safe. We may do anything to keep you safe. This is our way.' He makes a pious gesture. I am in no mood for it.

I glower at him, then transfer my glower to the stone garden. The elegant walls, alternating sheets of black granite and the columns of smooth white sandstone set into them, seem at this moment more like a prison that encircles me, with thick bars preventing my escape. 'This place mocks me,' I say.

'It does nothing,' says Jamyang. 'It's a rockery. It's supposed to give you a place to contemplate the universe. Perhaps you are not in the right mood today. The universe will wait, perhaps.'

'I'm trapped,' I say, not bothering to hide my bitterness. 'Condemned never to leave this rock.'

'You always feel like this,' Jamyang says. 'The book says so. It will pass. You bear a terrible burden. This is understood. This place, these good men, exist to make it easier for you. We follow the way without having walked it, knowing only that it has been walked. Eventually you will bear your burden with serenity. But however you feel, you must bear it. You have no choice.'

He rubs a hand back and forth across his carefully shaved head. I hear the slight rasp of dry skin against stubble.

'I am sorry,' he says, and I believe him. 'I chose to come here, to live this life, but you, the you here present with me now, you were just a baby. I am your tutor, it is given to me to say these things, but I take no pleasure in it. Trust me that you will feel different in time. It is always true.'

Once again, I am reminded that I am not wholly myself. I hate this.

'I could kill myself,' I say suddenly. 'Throw myself off the mountain. Then I would be free.'

Brother Jamyang seems unperturbed by my theatrics. 'I'd rather you didn't,' he says mildly. 'I'm just getting used to having you around.'

'Or I could order you to kill yourself,' I plough on. 'Then I could escape.'

I don't know why I say this. It is stupid and childish. I am almost sixteen, I should know better. This man is the only father I have ever known. I regret it even as the words leave my mouth.

Brother Jamyang seems to consider this prospect seriously.

'You could,' he says. 'And under other circumstances I would obey. After I had carefully requested several times that you reconsider. But now, knowing your mind, I would be remiss in my duty if I selfishly followed my earnest desire to obey you in all things without a care to the First Father's command. So, I would refuse. I'd feel guilty about it, if that helps.'

I know he is poking fun at me in his gentle way, but strangely it does help. I realise I have taken Jamyang's devotion for granted, and that of the other monks as well. This is an unusual thought for me. Perhaps this is the first step toward serenity, I think. This is also an unusual thought for me. Because I do think about throwing myself off the mountain, sometimes.

I sigh heavily and throw up my hands. Jamyang sees this for the apology it is. I turn over a sheet of paper with my toe. It is a map of a different world. The word 'AFRICA' catches my eye. It is written in Greek, a language from another world I know but have never learned.

I pick up a different scroll and hand it to Jamyang. He unrolls it carefully; he respects books. He holds it at arm's length and squints a little. Then he surprises me by reading it aloud.

'"Chronicles of the Newly-Discovered Worlds,"' he says. '"Being the work of Charon of Lampsacus, written in the reign of the first Artaxerxes, recording the accounts of those who travelled through the lands of the dead and returned to tell the tale. Copied by Apollonius of Cythera, this his hand."' He looks over the scroll at me. 'What about it?'

'Have you read it?'

'I've read everything you've read. In this life, at least.'

'It stays in my mind. What did you think of it?'

Jamyang sniffs disparagingly. 'I thought it was a pack of lies, to be honest. Rivers that aren't poison but just kill you if you touch them, rivers that steal your mind but leave the rest of you intact, rivers that set you on fire, not a river of molten rock mind you, just water. Nonsense to gull the credulous. There isn't enough magic on any world to make a river that steals your mind. How do you fix magic to water? It just flows away. That would kill the magician that tried it.'

'They could be natural phenomena. Some property of the water.'

Brother Jamyang shakes his head. 'The other worlds are much like here. Different beasts perhaps, different forests and mountains, but normally different. As different as one sees here travelling from one country to the next. Not impossibly different. Even the magic is the same kind of magic.'

Another resentment rears its head. 'I wouldn't know. I'm not allowed to learn magic.'

'It is our way.'

'It is stupid.' But I have no heart for another argument, because I am thinking. Thinking about one of the few things besides me that matters to anyone here. 'This world, Horkos. There is a line in the Writing...'

'"Drink of forgetting, and remember,"' says Jamyang immediately. Everyone knows the Writing by heart.

'Stealing your mind... It could mean something. I must know. I will send brothers,' I say, suddenly decisive. This is also unlike me. I feel older somehow in saying it.

'Brothers may not leave the Anvil,' says Jamyang firmly. 'Not for this. Only when a new Great Father appears.'

He means when I die. 'Then send word to those below. I will fund a party to go there and report back.'

The rasp of fingers on stubble once more. 'That is allowed,' he says, but he sounds reluctant. 'I will make it so. They will not know where to go.'

'The book says there are Greeks there, they can ask for assistance when they arrive. Plot a route on the great map.'

'I will.' For all his reluctance, Jamyang is good at planning. 'They'll need magic. An artefact. We only have one and it can't leave here.'

'I know that. There are still magicians on Shambhala, are there not? We'll buy one. The treasury spills over with useless gems.'

Jamyang turns his head and spits on the ground. I have never seen Brother Jamyang spit. I have never seen the look on his face before either. It is a look of contempt.

'Magicians. They can't be trusted on these matters. On anything.'

'How do you know? Have you ever travelled to another world?'

'Yes,' he says. This answer stuns me. Jamyang has never mentioned this. I had assumed he had always been a monk.

'Tell me,' I say, my anger suddenly forgotten. 'Tell me what it was like.'

Jamyang looks away for a moment, thinking back through the years.

'My father traced his ancestry to before the first crossing. He was very taken with it. When he knew he was dying, he asked me to take his ashes through the gate - the one near Kalsang's Town, where I was born - and scatter them in the land of our ancestors. I honoured this wish. A magician lived in Kalsang's Town at that time, a manipulator of magic rather than a real mage but a good one nonetheless. I paid him a lot of money for a stone with which to open the gate.'

'What was it like to go through the gate?' I ask. 'Was it as bad as the books say?'

He thinks carefully before answering. 'It was like being grabbed by the ankles by an angry cyclops and repeatedly slammed into the ground. While it was on fire.' He nods firmly. 'It hurt.'

'And between the gates? What did you see?'

More deep thought. This is Jamyang's real way. 'With gates, you are sucked in, you are spat out. That is all you know. Is there a between? I don't know. I have no memory of it.'

'That is what the books say.' I am disappointed. I was hoping for insight. 'What was it like? The land of our ancestors, I mean.'

Jamyang's eyes seek out the memory. 'There were a lot of very high mountains, and a great plain that went on for weeks unbroken by a tree. It was beautiful, in its way. I could have stayed there quite happily.'

'Why did you come back?'

'I intended to marry a girl. Unfortunately, when I returned three years had passed and she had married someone else. So I became a monk.'

'I am sorry,' I say.

'So was I.' He smiles at me. 'But not anymore. I am supposed to be here. That was merely my path. It always ended here.'

'As does mine, it seems.' I gesture vaguely to the rest of the papers. 'I've read these scrolls from end to end and a hundred more besides. I know the great map frontwise and backwards, I could trace it in my sleep. I can tell you how to get to any world from any other, and describe the great wonders and mysteries to be seen there. But I'll never see them. It's not fair.'

'No,' agrees Jamyang. 'It's not. Life isn't.'

I brood on this for some time while Jamyang waits patiently. A thought occurs to me about his story. 'Why did you stay three years on Earth?' I ask. 'Did the girl promise to wait and then betray you with another?' I have also read a number of romances.

'She thought I was dead,' he says, looking at his feet, and I see too late that he was lying when he said he was no longer sorry. I am picking at a wound which has not healed. 'I was supposed to be away for a month. I returned through the gate one month after I went. But three years had passed here. That is how the gate worked. The magician didn't tell me that,' he says bitterly.

I do not know what to say. I look away so I do not see the wetness in his eyes. And as I look anywhere but at Brother Jamyang, I see the stone garden as if for the first time. See it for what it really is. It is so obvious. I have sat in this place a thousand times. I can't think why I haven't realised before.

'Why is there a gate on the Anvil?'

Jamyang's head swings up.

'I mean, it's dead, obviously, but why is it here at all? One way up, the brothers say.'

His eyes are suddenly blazing. He speaks in a voice which is not his own. A broken whisper, crumbled into dust. 'You cannot know this. Do not remember. Only when you need it will you find it.'

I do not remember.

Now there is a boy here I do not recognise.

'Right then,' *says the boy,* 'I've worked out why you can't remember me when you're awake and it's really annoying. We'll have to improvise. I might not be able to tell you things, but I think I can make you feel them. We'll try that.'

The boy glances at Brother Jamyang. 'What was he saying? I wasn't paying attention for a moment there.' *He shakes his head as though a wasp has passed his ear.* 'No matter,' *he says.* 'Now, this fellow here is Palden Ngapoi, although he barely had two months of that name before the monks took it away from him. It took me a while to find him. I have a lot of memories. You're going to need him later. I'll make you feel that need when it's time. Because I think Simon was right. It has fallen to you. The girl is part of that. She must be.'

He looks at Jamyang almost tenderly. 'I miss this one. Of all of them, he cared the most, despite what it cost him. Anyway. For now, think on the angry one with the killing streak. You'll need him first.

'Now, you're going to wake up in a lot of pain. Once you're over that, we must go back. Safety first. Then, I am afraid, we must do something stupid and reckless. So be it. The Writing is real. We know this. By the way, *she's not human.*'

Constant did not remember the boy when he woke up.

Constant smelled something awful.

Kit McCoy was kneeling next to him, holding something under his nose. She pulled it away as he started to retch. 'Sorry about that, kid.'

Constant tried to speak but the words died as he dry-heaved again. Eventually he steadied himself enough to gasp out some words.

'What was that? It was *rank.*'

The woman grinned again. 'Essence of corpse flower. Picked it up on my travels. Makes a good werewolf repellent. An everything repellent, as a matter of fact.'

'It smelled like rotting vomit.'

'It's a bold fragrance, ain't it? You get it on your clothes, you might as well burn 'em.' She held up a thimble-sized glass phial between thumb and forefinger. 'The bottle's *real* tough. Lid screws down tight.'

Constant rubbed his palm down his face repeatedly, as if trying to scrape away the smell. 'Why did you stick that in my face?'

'You fainted,' said Blix, who was standing a bit further away. 'We were worried you had concussion. Or brain damage. Or had died. She said the stuff would wake you even if you were dead.'

'And I was right, too!'

Constant lifted his head. It was extraordinarily painful, but it worked and didn't seem to be broken.

'Thank you,' he croaked.

'Ain't nothing,' said Kit. 'Done it a dozen times.' She frowned slightly. 'They all died though. Y'all probably should watch out for that.'

'I will definitely do that,' Constant agreed. He got up very carefully, grimacing as pain shot through his body.

The American saw him hurting. 'I got some snake oil that'll make that go away right soon. It don't smell of nothin',' she added.

'Thank you,' said Constant. *Fighting werewolves is definitely a job for Darcen Ysir,* he thought as he sat up. *I'll keep you close.* The memory of the warrior rose from where he had pushed it. He could not feel Comen sen-Hersa at all.

The woman noticed the hilt of Constant's sword poking out of the ground. With what seemed like no effort at all she pulled it free. 'Fancy. Yours?'

'Yes.'

'It's called Sorcha,' Blix said perkily. 'I named it. Me.'

'Very fancy.' She offered it to Constant hilt first. 'Maybe use it as a walking stick for a while, kid.'

'That is good advice.' Gingerly Constant levered himself up. He went as white as a sheet and nearly collapsed. Kit and Blix caught him before he went down.

'Something's not right,' he said.

'Relax, kid, said the American. 'We'll carry you.'

'Who is going to carry me?' Blix grumbled. But she lifted Constant under one arm and, with Kit on the other, guided him back to the house.

Kit retrieved the bottle of "snake oil" and dripped a tiny bead of it in each of their mouths. It looked like water. As promised, there was no smell, nor taste. Yet the moment it touched Constant's tongue he felt it bloom in his mouth, and mere moments later he felt it throughout his body, not just taking away the pain but making him whole again. Soon he felt able to get to his feet once more, albeit very cautiously.

'That's incredible,' said Blix, feeling her bruises and finding them vanished. 'What on earth is it?'

'Ah-ah,' said Kit, wagging a finger. 'None of your beeswax, kiddo. It's patent. Pending. But it hits the spot, right? Right, kid? You know, you can say thanks any time you like.'

Constant was looking somewhere else.

'Blix?

'Yes?'

'Was your leg bleeding?'

Blix looked down. Her trousers and the leather chaps were torn open below her knee. A smear of red glistened on the skin.

'Oh, yes. I must have caught it in the chase. I can feel the snake oil healing it, amazing. I'll put a plaster on it just in case. I've got some.'

Constant chose his words carefully. 'Did you catch it? Or was it something else?'

'Oh my,' said Kit.

'I don't understand,' said Blix. 'What-'

'Let me see,' Kit interrupted. 'I know wounds.'

She knelt by Blix's leg and pulled her boot off. With a sharp jerk, she tore the trouser leg open a little further, and examined the blood. She sat back on her haunches and exhaled sharply.

'That,' she said, 'is a tooth mark.'

There was a moment's pause.

'No, it can't be,' Blix said.

'The werewolf landed on you as it died,' said Kit.

'Yes, I remember, but-'

'Its mouth must have been open.'

'Yes, but -'

'You've been bitten. By a werewolf. And lived,' said Constant.

Blix said, '*Fuck*.'

Chapter Thirteen: A Walk in The Woods

'You're going to turn into a werewolf,' said Constant bluntly.

'I *know,'* said Blix miserably. 'Christ on a bike, how's *that* going to feel?'

'Terrible,' said the boy. The harsh tone was back in his voice, the fragile, polite invalid vanished. 'First your mind will change, then your senses. It's already started. You're going to feel strange soon. You'll feel the wolf in your mind, in your bones, in your blood. You'll lose control. Then when the light of a full moon first hits you, you'll change. It will be the worst thing you've ever experienced. Agony that you cannot imagine. Catastrophic trauma to your body.'

'Hey now,' Kit began, but Constant interrupted her.

'She needs to know.' He turned back to Blix. 'You're turning into a different species, one with different bones and blood, organs and nerves, different sight and senses. Come the full moon your body is going to destroy itself and make itself anew in the image of the wolf. It's going to slough off your skin and grow a pelt. It's going to do it very quickly. The you that you know will cease to exist. You'll be a mindless killing machine. And then, if you survive that, you'll do it all again at daybreak, in reverse. It'll be hell. You might not live. You're quite likely not to live.'

'Oh, for fuck's sake,' said Blix, putting her head in her hands. 'It was a rhetorical question! I know all that, okay? I know about lycanthropy. I know all about magical creatures, I told you. Jesus.' Her voice trembled.

Kit gave Constant a Look. 'Don't ever go into the medicine trade, kid,' she said. 'Your bedside manner sucks.' Kit gently touched Blix's chin with a fingertip, lifting her face. 'Hey, kiddo, don't you listen to that boy. He's an asshole.'

'He isn't wrong. I know he isn't.'

'No. But there's more to it. You got a month to work this out, full moon's been and gone here. A month is about the same here as it is back home.' She smiled reassuringly. 'Kiddo, people survive this. They do. You know, I only get paid to hunt, um, bad dogs. I've known some werewolves before who were great guys! Most of the time. Hell, I had a werewolf boyfriend once! He was a real asshole. But not because he was a werewolf. Well, maybe thirty percent. Thought he was Mister Big Dog, couldn't lick his own ass, never mind - anyway, my point is that he lived his life and it was all gravy for him and once a month he had a real bad day. Everyone has bad days.'

Blix looked up. 'Bad days. Yes. I'm having a lot of them all of a sudden.' She sniffed and tried not to cry, and scowled at Constant. 'You stop being a bastard,' she ordered.

Constant looked outraged for a moment, then took a deep breath and swallowed hard. 'I'm sorry. I don't know why I thought that was a good idea. I'm still not myself.'

'You look like you to me,' Kit said. 'You being an asshole.'

There was a sharp sound from outside, like a branch snapping, followed by what sounded like a stifled grunt. Kit grabbed her rifle, peered through the tiny window for a long moment then, crouching slightly, cracked the door an inch and peered through it. 'Wait here,' she whispered and, pulling her rifle stock firmly into her shoulder, plunged through the door, which swung closed behind her.

Constant drew his sword and made to follow her. He moved as if his injury had never happened. Impulsively Blix grabbed his arm. 'Don't go, please! I can't face it alone. After what happened at the circle, and just now, and being bitten...'

She can't cope with this now, Constant thought. He put his hand on Blix's shoulder. 'Don't be upset,' he said, and the words appeared in his mind. Just for a moment, but it was enough. Blix took a deep breath, and wasn't upset any more.

Kit appeared at the door, rifle slung over her shoulder. 'False alarm,' she said. 'You have yaks.'

'Excuse me?'

'Yaks. You have them. Hairy beeves have arrived.'

Constant chewed on his lip. 'By themselves?'

'With other beeves. Why?'

'Oh no.' Constant pushed passed her, followed closely by Blix. Sure enough a small herd of yaks had congregated near the cottage, chewing on what lichens they could scrape through the snow and nervously avoiding the corpse of the werewolf.

'Are they the same ones?' Blix asked Constant. 'We met a family last night,' she told Kit. 'I hope...'

Constant took a long look at the animals. Now it was day he could see the clan tags punched through each yak's right ear. He ducked under the horns and examined one. It told him all he needed to know. The yak grunted amiably. Constant saw the fear on Blix's face.

She can't cope with this now.

'Not the same,' he said.

They retreated to the house. The yaks tried to follow.

'Okay. Okay.' Blix paced up and down, as far as she was able in the tiny cottage. 'Let's think this through. How about I just neck all your magic water? Maybe it'll cure me?'

'No!' said Kit, plainly alarmed by the idea. Then in a more normal voice she said, 'Afraid it don't work like that, kiddo. Ain't no cure for lycanthropy, not even my medicine.'

‘Crap. Then, maybe I can stay inside during full moon? If I never see the first full moon I don’t change, right?’

Constant, opened his mouth but Kit gave him a shove and slid between them. 'Shush, you.' She gave Blix a sad little lopsided grin. 'Sorry kiddo. You know this one. Like the kid said, it's already started. It makes you want to change. Not right away. You get used to it. Then you want it. It starts to hurt if you avoid it. Then when the moon rises, you seek it out.’

‘Yeah, but if I lock myself up -’

‘That won’t work,’ Constant interrupted. ‘Once, twice maybe, but the longer you go without turning the more agonising it will be, until the disease tears you apart. You’ll want to change. Your body needs it, your mind will too. Eventually you’ll have no choice. Then, if you make it out the other side, you'll change every full moonrise whether you see it or not. That's just the way it is.'

‘Ohhh fuckfuckfuckfuckfuck just fuck off the pair of you. Fuck. Right. Off.’

‘And that’s about all she wrote.’

‘God, I don’t want to be a werewolf,’ Blix moaned. ‘Just kill me now.’

There was a long pause.

‘I could do that,’ Kit said reluctantly. ‘I got silver. Hell, you don’t even need silver before you change.’ She leaned close to Blix. ‘Do you really want that, kiddo?’

‘Eh? God, no! It’s just an expression! Who would want that? Jesus!’

‘Idiom,’ Constant remarked.

‘Glad to hear it! Look on the bright side,’ said Kit. ‘You just got werewolf healing powers too. No more busted bones for you. You can still die though, don’t throw yourself off any cliffs.’

‘That's... Actually, just stop. I don’t want to think about it. There’s just no bright side to this. Just stop.’

They were quiet for a while as Blix tried to process the shocking news. But the longer it went on, the more nervous Constant became.

Eventually he said, ‘We can't stay here. We should leave. More werewolves might come. More than we can cope with.’

Kit McCoy pursed her lips sagely. 'You ain't wrong, kid. This place is wolf bait. Pack your bags.'

'Maybe we should head upstream?' Blix offered. She looked relieved to have something else to think about. 'They'll lose the scent that way.'

'Guessin' you never had a hound dog?' asked Kit. Blix shook her head. 'Thought not. That don't really work. Dog with a good nose on him'd track you through the fires of hell, never mind across water.'

‘I know the way,’ Constant said.

'Okay then Hiawatha, where to?'

'We should go where the wolves aren't.'

Kit rolled her eyes. 'First sensible thing you said, kid, now where exactly might that be?'

Home. 'The Anvil.'

Kit stopped rolling her eyes and stared at him incredulously. 'Come again?'

'That's the flat mountain, the one you lived on?' Blix asked.

'Yes.'

Kit made a disparaging sound. 'You mean go back to the Monastery?'

'Yes.'

'The one that's just been paid a visit by every werewolf in the world? The one they burned to ashes? Smoke's still hanging in the sky, kid, ain't no church left to pray in.'

'I'm going anyway.'

'Kid, are you crazy?'

'Possibly,' said Constant, with absolute honesty. 'Think about it though. The wolves have burned the town.' He swallowed hard. 'I saw it happen. But the Monastery is mostly inside the mountain. They can't burn the tunnels.'

'No, they can just hide in them and leap out on you and eat you up.'

'They won't be there anymore. Their army is not like a human army. They don't capture and fortify, they're not interested in loot, they don't leave a garrison or need a base. It has been the same in every city they've taken. They kill, they burn - then they leave. They won't be there anymore.'

'Oh, you think so?' Kit put her hands on her hips and leaned forward pugnaciously. 'Well I think that's horseshit. Horse. Shit. Let me clue you in. That mountain? That's wolf central, kid. There'll be so many werewolves you could cut a fur rug a mile wide from their hides. Hey, you need the idiot version? I'll use short words, you don't seem quite right in the head still.' She thrust a finger in the general direction of the mountains. 'Bad dogs that way!' She jabbed another finger in the opposite direction. 'We go this way!'

'Go that way then,' said Constant. 'We just met you, I'm not asking you to come. In fact, who are you?'

'Kit McCoy!' said Kit immediately, thrusting out her hand for a shake. 'I just got through telling you. Guess that ass-kicking you took was worse than it looked, huh?'

'That's not what I -' Constant began, but Kit cut him off.

'I know what you meant. But let me tell you kid, I'll be happy to trade life stories with you when we're a long way from these mountains. Stop this nonsense and come on.'

'I just said -'

'I know what you said, too. Boy, you're none too bright, are you? Let me spell it out for you. I ain't asking. *I saved your life.* Both your lives. That means you owe me. How am I gonna collect if I let you go running off all by your damn selves with boys like ol' hairy britches out there just waiting for you, mouths open? Prob'ly get yourselves killed in the first five minutes.'

'I need to go home. It's my place, I need to be there,' Constant said in an anguished voice. 'Come or don't.' Constant turned to Blix. 'I promised I'd help you. I will. Trust me. Or go with her. Or stay here.'

'God, I feel sick,' said Blix. 'Look, I don't want to make a choice. You've both saved my life. I don't know anyone else. I don't want to be alone. We're, like, the good guys, aren't we?'

'Sure are!' said Kit. 'Except I'm not a guy.'

'I want us to stay together. But I think we should go with Constant. He's from here, I think that's our best hope for staying alive. I want you to come too Kit. We just met, like, seconds ago, but I... I don't know. I trust you. Both of you. I don't really know why.'

'I have an honest face,' said Kit, winsomely. She play-punched Blix on the arm. 'Absolutely you can trust me. I am eminently trustworthy.'

I do not trust her thought some part of Constant. Constant pushed it back.

Blix gathered her courage. 'I need to go home too. I need to find my sister and go home to my mum and dad and I don't know how and something awful's going to happen to me and I don't think I can cope alone,' she finished in a small voice. Tears welled up in her eyes.

'Now look what you did!' said Kit, with a look that nailed Constant to the floor. She gathered Blix into her shoulder and, slightly awkwardly, patted her on the back. 'Are you okay, kiddo?'

'Mm.'

'What did I do?' Constant protested. Then in a firmer voice he said, 'We must go. Make a choice, do it now.'

Kit fumed for a second, then threw up her hands in exasperation. 'Boys oh boys,' she said. 'Are you really going to make me climb that damn mountain again? That's horseshit!'

'Like I said, you don't-'

'Well all right then!'

'- have to go. Wait, what?'

'I said, well all right then! It's dumber'n a sack of turkeys but if I can't talk you out of it, I ain't gonna let you walk into that den of wolves all on your lonesome. Because I'm the good guys.'

Kit let Blix go; this seemed not to be what the girl wanted. Kit gave her a wink. 'Anyway, do you think I'm gonna let this sweet thing walk out with a boy unchaperoned? Mercy no. People would talk. We can't have that.'

A look passed between Kit and Blix that Constant didn't understand, but appeared to drive all thoughts of werewolves from the girl's mind. She blushed furiously and bit her lip.

Constant scowled. 'Fine, whatever. Come, then. But come now.'

Kit gave them her best Cheshire Cat smile. 'All righty then. What's said is said, and don't need said again. Now, how much of my stuff did you steal?'

Constant set the yaks off on a path downhill, then returned to the house. He folded the linen sheet into his bag, and realised that was the only thing he had to pack except for food. He watched for a moment as Blix helped Kit bring her things down from their hiding place, then went outside again. He took the little earthenware water jug with him. Outside, he walked a little way onto the snow-covered green, now churned to slush by battle and hooves. He stared at the jug for a while, still not really knowing what he was looking for.

After a few minutes, Blix joined him. 'Kit's stuffing her pack, she won't be long. You should try to get along, you know.'

'I don't know her. Something doesn't feel right. She killed that wolf without a thought. She's dangerous.'

'I trust her.'

'So you said. You don't know her either. You met her minutes ago.'

'I met you yesterday. I trust you. I'm not sure why, you're only sporadically likeable you know. Um, no offence. I like her though.'

'I can tell.'

Blix's cheeks coloured once more, and she quickly changed the subject.

'I found this knife. Why is it shaped like this?'

She showed him a bone-handled knife with a short blade, which curved back on itself at the point to form a wicked-looking hook. It looked well-made and well used.

'That's a gutting knife. For dressing game.'

'Can I keep it?'

'Why are you asking me?'

'It belonged to your mother. That means it's yours now.'

'I hadn't thought of that.' Constant took the knife from Blix and turned it in his hands, trying to picture the person who had used it, but seeing no one. It was just a thing. He looked back at the little cottage.

In another life, I would have lived here. Would that have been a better life?

'I would be dead now,' he whispered to himself.

'Excuse me?'

'Nothing. Have the knife.'

'Thanks. I'm leaving the sword. It's too heavy and I don't know how to use it. I'm fairly sure I can stab someone though.'

'Are you,' said Constant absently. His attention had returned to the jug.

'I don't know. I don't want to find out.'

Constant looked up. 'Then there's hope for you,' he said simply.

A wolf howled in the far distance. Blix shuddered involuntarily.

'It's a long way off in the wrong direction,' said Constant when the wolf call had faded. 'I'm not going to let them hurt you. I promise,' he added, without quite knowing why. 'I don't want you to worry.' He touched her arm, intending only to reassure her, but his words rose in his mind and he felt their power flow out of him into Blix once more. He felt the girl relax. 'I don't know how yet, but you'll get her back. I'll help you.'

'Mmm.' Blix was staring at the sky. 'Sorry, help me with what?' she said dreamily.

'Your sister. I'll help you find her.'

'My sister?'

Constant frowned. 'Your sister, Katy.'

'Sorry, what about my sister?'

Constant was alarmed now. 'She's been kidnapped. By your teacher. Blix, are you okay?'

Suddenly Blix snapped back to attention. 'Oh! My God! Sorry, I was miles away. I don't know what I was thinking!' She looked confused and upset, and shook her head several times as though there was water in her ears. 'Katy! Oh my God!'

'Look, don't get upset. It's okay. We've had a difficult day. Don't worry about it,' he concluded. This time he didn't touch her.

'No, it's fine. I'm fine.' Blix looked completely lost for a moment, in a way which chilled Constant's blood. Then suddenly she smiled brightly and said, 'Where's Kit got to?'

'Here I am!' said Kit, plunging through the doorway in a hurry. The tall pack rode high on her back and she wore the saddle bags across her shoulders, the rifle slung over them on her right. It looked awkward and heavy, but she moved as gracefully as if she carried nothing at all.

'You must be stronger than you look,' said Blix. Her confusion had vanished as quickly as it had set in.

'It's mostly clothes. Clothes and bullets. Everything a modern gal needs. Almost everything.'

The look she gave Blix this time made Constant think he had led several dozen sheltered lives. Blix blushed almost scarlet.

'Don't forget your ears,' he said.

'That's right!' Kit disappeared behind the house. She returned moments later, stuffing her belt pouch with furry things. 'It's too damp for them to dry. I hope you got more salt on your mountain kid, or they are gonna get ripe.'

'Why do you have saddlebags?' Blix asked, clearly happy to be talking about something else.

Kit looked at her as this was the strangest question she'd ever been asked. 'They're for my horse,' she replied.

'Oh. Okay.'

Kit gave Constant a straight up and down kind of look. 'Lead us to the promised land, Moses. You bringing that jug?'

Constant turned it over once again, feeling the grain of the fired clay with his fingertips. Then he tossed it onto the grass beside him.

'No,' he said. 'It's just a jug.'

'Then let's get gone.'

They walked into the woods, following Constant's sense of the right direction, although once again he barely knew how he knew. As he walked he summoned forward the memory of Darcen Ysir.

sen-Hersa is a better forester but I'm not making that mistake again. I need to be a killer. I don't want to be a killer.

He scanned the forest with the eyes of a man used to springing ambushes. Memories both his and not-his existed side by side. They felt wrong, icy and empty at the same time. He ignored as best he could just how worried he felt at how easy it was to become someone else, long since dead.

As they walked in silence across the slope of the land, Constant had time to think about Kit McCoy. He watched her carefully.

She knew her woodcraft. The thigh-slapping happy-go-lucky demeanour which had seemed to be her way had disappeared the moment they'd entered the tree line. The Ysir part of him noted with approval the way she ranged ahead, virtually silent despite her weight of kit, only to fall back and around them, then return to point from the other side, covering all lines of attack as they moved forward. Her path spiralled like a figure of eight and covered twice the ground that Constant and Blix travelled, but it was perfectly designed to catch unwelcome guests creeping up on them. She did it subtly too; never sneaking around or starting at shadows, never out of sight or overtly hunting. Constant suspected this was so Blix wouldn't notice and start imagining werewolves in every thicket.

It also became apparent quite quickly that Kit McCoy knew where she was going.

The guns were worrying. Someone he had been once had seen a hand bombard in action, and the weapon had made a lasting impression of brimstone and terror. That had been a very long time ago, and they hadn't caught on among Shambhalhai - surprisingly, now that he thought about it. They had been plenty of wars.

He understood what he was seeing. The artifice of their manufacture had come on since Shambhala had lost contact with Earth, but the principle was the same. Constant carried one of the finest blades in the world and was partly one of the finest swordsman, but Kit McCoy's cannons gave her the advantage over everyone; man and, as she had just demonstrated, beast.

Experienced and dangerous. Glad she's on our side. Except she's not on our side. She's on her side.

Kit McCoy had saved his life though and he owed her a debt. He wasn't sure how he felt about that.

There was something else strange too. Not dead was one thing, but Constant had been struck by a beast as strong as an owl-bear. Yet here he was, walking through the dismal forest like nothing had happened. The aching muscles and tiredness had gone too, and the scratches on his face were fading. Even his bad knee felt better. Whatever was in the "snake oil" that Kit had given him was powerful stuff. Too powerful to be natural - which meant magic. But some part of him knew that magic didn't fix to water. Which meant she was using magic herself. And magicians were not to be trusted.

Just as well I can't see myself in a mirror right now, thought the most him part of his mind. *I wouldn't be able to meet my own eye.*

Nonetheless, he was alive when otherwise he would surely be dead. Blix too. Twice in two days, in fact. The girl had the knack of being rescued in the nick of time.

Although he supposed Blix thought she was being quiet, by comparison to Kit and himself she was crashing through the forest like a paladin in full armour. Mostly she looked alert and aware, but now and then Constant noticed a slightly absent look on her face, as if she had a lot on her mind. That wasn't surprising. Being bitten by a werewolf probably changed you in more ways than the obvious.

Or maybe it was something else. Constant was beginning to worry that he'd done something to her.

'They're just words, really,' Brother Simon said. He regarded his breakfast and carefully speared a mushroom with his fork. Brother Simon did everything carefully.

It had been a bad night. Constant had ended up under the bed in his grand apartment, screaming the words over and over, trying to make the voices go away. Simon had held him until it passed, and then held him while he slept, exhausted by the effort.

'Just words.'

Simon regarded the serious-looking five-year-old staring up at him, framed in the light from the great window behind him.

'Just words. A tiny mantra to focus your mind with a flicker of magic to reinforce it.' He selected another mushroom. 'The magic is barely worth the name. That's why it works here. Eat your sausage,' he added.

Constant did as he was told. 'They stop the old men shouting at me,' he said. 'Ususally.'

'Don't talk with your mouth full. Yes. They don't know they're loud. They're not real. They're just memories.'

The old man took up the water jug and filled his flagon. 'One head isn't made to hold seventy lifetimes. They spill over the edges.' He sloshed the mug to illustrate the point. 'The words settle your mind.' He set the flagon down. Then he frowned. 'Now I need a cloth.'

Constant obediently went for a cloth. When he got back he asked, 'Did baby Constant say the words?'

Simon smiled. 'Babies don't talk! The voices come later. When you can understand them.'

This seemed perfectly natural to Constant. 'Where do the words come from?'

'The book.'

This also seemed perfectly natural. Everything came from the book.

'I wish I couldn't hear the voices,' Constant said.

'You have to be who you are,' Simon replied. 'You don't have to let it rule you.'

'I hope you're right.'

'I hope so too,' Simon said. 'Hope carries us when we cannot lift ourselves. Have hope. And faith. Faith carries us when hope fails.'

A sharp cry came from outside the window. Constant dropped his fork and scrambled away from it, alarmed by the sudden sound.

Simon crossed to the window and closed it. 'Don't worry,' he said. 'It's just an eagle.'

Constant regarded the window with distrust, as though it might reach out and pull him through.

'I don't like the sky,' he said. 'It looks at me in the night.'

Brother Simon considered this carefully.

'There's somewhere else you can sleep,' he said.

'Ow,' said Constant, as he walked into a tree.

'That was a tree,' said Kit McCoy brightly, from behind him. 'Walk where they ain't.'

'Yes. I was wool-gathering.'

'Save your dreams for the night-time, kid.'

'Yes.'

Constant was confident that the Tutor's Book would have recorded if there had been a problem with the words, and that Brother Simon would have told him. The well-being of the Great Father was the highest - only - concern of the brothers. And yet within the space of a few hours the words had failed to shield him from the urgent, pressing, painfully noisy past in his head, and - possibly, maybe - shielded Blix too much.

He looked back at her and caught her eye. She gave him a fingertip wave. He returned it and she smiled. A normal smile as far as he could tell, as far as normal was normal.

As their deliberate pace led them through the winter woods, Constant thought seriously for the first time about what it meant to forcibly suppress four thousand years of memories, and what might happen to someone who didn't have them. He didn't like either thought.

'It never helps,' he said to himself.

'What's that now, kid?' said Kit. She was now well behind Blix. Constant was surprised she'd heard him.

'Nothing.'

They walked on. Constant thought about the Writing, and how strangers could possibly know about it, and what it might mean if it was coming true.

I am alone but not alone.

After a couple of hours of slogging through awkwardly sloping snow-drenched woodland, Blix decided 'warm' and 'flat' were severely underrated. Hiking wasn't her thing. The chaps had quickly ceased to be sexy and now weighed down her legs like a pair of leather anchors. They did at least stop her jeans from disintegrating. The tear Kit had made flapped annoyingly as she walked.

Blix was incredibly grateful not to be alone. Although she was coping quite well with the disasters of the last - less than twenty-four hours, she suddenly realised - she knew it would have been ten times worse alone. Alone she would have died. Alone was terrible.

But not alone wasn't enough. Blix wasn't naturally chatty, but the silent march was becoming oppressive. To begin with the simple act of putting one foot in front of another without falling over or broadcasting their presence to a world full of monsters had distracted her from her problems, which receded so far into her mind that she'd felt almost free of them. But now, after a couple of hours of walking, the bad thoughts plunged and reared through her brain, one moment all but forgotten, the next hairy and slavering in front of her mind's eye. It was weird and disconcerting, and she wanted it to stop. She wanted to talk to someone friendly about something entirely unconnected to the madness around her. Instead her flitting mind made her fill the silence.

'You know, things have changed a lot for werewolves in England,' she said brightly, her voice slightly brittle as she tried not to sound too forced. 'Someone once told me it used to be illegal to be a werewolf, back in the olden days. Then they, like, got emancipated or something. Everyone's a lot more understanding now. The hospital near us has a full moon crash team and a secure unit they can check into if they need somewhere safe to change. There's a kid I know, Paul, his dad ran a marathon to raise money for it.'

'Izzat so,' said Kit, in a lazy drawl.

'Yes!' *Of course, I'm in the backwoods of another planet so that's no help,* she added in the privacy of her head. 'Paul's step-sister's Alurian. You get tested for therianthropy in infant school, I had to eat this sugar cube with vile stuff on it to see if it made me sick. Anyway, she had to go to a special school when she was little, but basically she just has to put up with turning into a cat person every now and then. They don't lock you up any more. You get a leaflet and a stern talking to about biting.'

'That's mighty liberal of them,' said Kit, now ahead of her. 'Say, I wonder what the Mormons would pay for werecat ears?'

'That's an awful thing to say.'

'Guess those Utah boys ain't so liberal.'

'You will have the opportunity to collect more ears quite soon if you don't keep the noise down,' said Constant tersely.

'Sorry,' said Blix, and buttoned her lip.

Something about the thought *someone once told me* seemed wrong. The shape of it wasn't right, as if someone had knocked a corner off it. The word *Katy* floated across her mind without connecting with a thought, then fizzled and caught like a match taking light, illuminating her memory.

Katy! How could I forget it was her? God, where are you? She felt strange and guilty for being so selfish, and began tearing up again.

Then Kit said something, and Constant replied, and Blix got distracted momentarily. The memory of her sister vanished as quickly as it had reappeared. She trudged on, annoyed that the cold was making her eyes stream. She wiped the tears away, wondering why they were there.

Rain set in, an icy drizzle which turned the snow to sludge and further lowered Blix's spirits. She lost track of time and when Kit said it was high noon and they should take a bite to eat, Blix was depressed that it wasn't later.

They found a patch of earth under a densely-covered conifer which was almost dry and nearly big enough and huddled together. They shared some bread and some beef jerky Kit dug out of her saddlebags. Blix had never tried jerky before, though she'd seen it in Westerns. It was like chewing salty belt.

No one talked much. The events of the morning repeated themselves in Blix's mind, over and over, over and over. After a while she noticed that Constant was staring intently at the trunks and branches of nearby trees.

'What's up?'

'The trees are sick. I noticed it at the cottage and it's the same here.' He pointed out the reddish scale afflicting the bark.

'Looks nasty,' said Kit. 'What is it?'

'I don't know.' Constant found a patch of the blight on the tree they were leaning on, looked closely at the red-brown dust. 'It's strange. It's like...'

'Like?' Blix prompted.

'I don't know.' Constant drew his knees up to his chin. 'I don't know plants. I don't think I do. I don't want to think about it.'

They moved on. The rain came with them. Before long Blix was thoroughly fed up. Here and there, signs that werewolves had been through were evident - a young yak reduced to bones turned her stomach - but no werewolves, and no dead humans. They walked on.

'Are we nearly there yet?' Blix asked a couple of hours later, when she could bear the silence no longer.

'Tomorrow fore-dark,' said Constant tersely.

'What? Another day? You might have bloody said.' Blix kicked at the sodden earth miserably.

'Fore-dark at the Path of Fire. It will be full dark before we reach Forge. That's the town at the foot of the Anvil.'

'The forge leads to the anvil. Y'all are quite literal round these parts,' Kit remarked.

'What's this about a path of fire?' Blix asked. 'I have sensitive feet.'

'It's the pilgrim trail leading to the mountain. It's about five hundred miles long. Each village on the trail lights torches to show the way at night, every quarter of a mile or so. It's quite beautiful from above. Or was.'

'You think …' began Blix.

'Yes. They destroyed Forge. I saw it. There was no place stronger in these mountains. The others will be gone too. No more fire on the path. Here, at least. Probably everywhere.'

'I'm sorry.'

'Yes. I don't want to talk about it.'

'Well, we can't walk all night,' said Kit. 'We should make camp. And you know, this doesn't look like a bad spot.'

They had entered a glade, a near-circle perhaps fifty feet across. A thick sheet of rock rose from the earth on one side. A huge, flat boulder lay on top of it, jutting into the clearing, making a shelf of sheltered ground which looked relatively dry. Another large stone lay nearby. Twisted tree roots wrapped themselves around the stones like the tentacles of some withered sea monster.

Blix suddenly recognised it. 'It's a dolmen,' she said. 'A sort of proto-gate from ages ago.' She laughed slightly, without much humour. 'These bloody things got me into this mess in the first place. It looks like it's fallen over though. I wonder where it led?'

'Could have been anywhere I suppose,' said Constant. 'Shambhala had gates pointing to Earth, Lyonesse and a few other places. Mostly Earth.'

'It don't point nowhere no more,' said Kit. 'That lid looks like it'll keep us dry though. Looks defensible too.'

'I agree,' said Constant. 'We should have a cold camp.'

'Should do, but ain't gonna,' said Kit firmly, stowing her baggage under the rock. 'The reason being, my ass is too fine to freeze off, which it will unless we start a fire.'

'The wolves will see it,' said Constant. 'They'll smell the smoke.'

'Lots of things been on fire recently, ain't no one gonna check out another one. And if our furry friends slink up we'll just blast 'em 'til they ain't slinky no more.'

'I'm with Kit,' said Blix wearily. 'This place is bleak enough without freezing to death as well. I'm frozen already.'

'That's the stuff,' said Kit, winking at her. 'Let's see about firewood.'

'This is a bad idea,' Constant said, but came with them anyway.

Blix searched nearby for any remotely dry wood, nervously alive to each twitch of a branch in the wind. There was a knack to it; she watched both Kit and Constant return quickly with armloads, while she struggled to find more than a twig that wasn't sodden. Occasionally she touched a branch still on a tree to find it snapped off in a puff of red dust. Whatever blighted the trees, it seemed to be everywhere.

Kit built a fire and cooked beans and bacon, which was a million percent better than pottage and infinite percent better than nothing. Blix sat as close to the fire as possible, soaking in the heat. The bearskin steamed. She pulled her ushanka as far down as it would come. It steamed too.

As they ate Blix told Kit the story of her kidnapping and how she had met Constant. As she spoke she frequently found herself struggling to remember the details. She wondered if the stress of everything had affected her more than she realised. She kept it as short a story as possible, leaving out all of Dragonville's flannel and Echmoth's insults.

Kit paid close attention but said nothing until Blix had finished. Then she whistled in astonishment. 'Damn kiddo, that's a hell of a tale. Your teacher dragged you and your sister across the universe for nefarious reasons as yet undiscovered.' She looked at Constant. 'And you whacked five werewolves without breaking a sweat.'

'Something like that,' said Constant, shifting self-consciously.

'Well I'll be.'

The conversation lulled for a while and they ate in silence, listening to the rain.

Blix was idly wondering how old Kit was, and whether she liked younger women, when she realised Kit was watching her. She gave Kit an awkward smile and commanded her face not to blush.

'Penny for 'em,' said Kit.

'Not worth a penny.' Blix quickly changed the subject. 'I've never been to America. What's Nebraska like?'

'Flatter than a skinny girl's tits and twice as boring. No offense,' she added blithely, to Blix's instant mortification. 'I figure they only made us a state to annoy Colorado.' She looked around at the endless forest and the rain blatting off the leaves. 'Wide open prairie don't seem such a drag right now.'

'I don't know these places,' said Constant. 'Are they on Earth? Blix knowing where you're from suggests they are.'

'That's right thinking, kid.'

'You're a long way from home,' said Constant, looking pensively out into the trees. Blix followed his gaze. Everything looked like werewolf to her now. 'Both of you,' he continued. 'Why are there so many Earthmen on Shambhala? *How* are there so many? No gate to Earth has worked in centuries. No gate to anywhere. Yet here you are. I know how Blix got here. You've heard our tale, Miss McCoy. What's your story?'

The woman grinned her widest smile yet. 'I've heard part of your tale. But golly, do I get to talk about myself? Well that's Jim Dandy! Sure, there ain't none of our furry friends around right now, why not? Let's see. I was born in 'sixty-one in the aforementioned Territory, which if you can't count makes me twenty-three. Daddy always said Momma was a real fox, which was kinda -'

Constant put up a hand to stop her. 'Your more recent story,' he said.

'Oh. Well, like I said, I'm here to kill a man.'

'So you said. Which man?'

'Goes by the name of Dragonville. Belmont Dragonville.'

Blix started. 'The magician at the circle!'

'That's the fellow. He's a magician all right, a real powerful one.'

'Powerful enough to open a dead gate and bring two people through it from another world,' Constant said. 'That not just powerful, that's world-shaking. And he used that power to bring through two normal girls. Why?'

Kit frowned. It looked like an effort for her. 'I got no idea,' she said.

'Leicester,' said Blix firmly. 'He works for Leicester. Or Echmoth, that seems to be his real name. Echmoth wanted me, he said so. I don't know what for, but he dragged me across the universe for it.' A firefly of memory shot across her mind. 'Us! I mean us. He wanted me, but he took my sister instead. Katy. We're twins. He made the big werewolf, the First, he made him take her. Then Dragonville opened a hole in the air to a room somewhere else and they walked through! Then they... she... Katy! Why do I... She was gone. And then, he set werewolves on me, and...' She shook her head, and shuddered. 'Sorry,' she said. 'It's difficult to talk about.'

'I can see that, said Kit, looking curiously at Blix. 'I don't know no Echmoth or Leicester. But something don't sound right. Dragonville ain't the kind who works for anyone else. I don't doubt what you say, but if he's with this Echmoth fellow it's for his own reasons.'

'I don't care,' said Blix bitterly. 'I don't care about reasons. I just want to go home. How did you get here?' she asked the American. 'There must be another gate nearby, I suppose. Is that how you're going to get home?'

Kit clapped her hands together in delight. 'Home's not a problem! I can go home anytime I want. Lookee here.'

She put her hands to her neck and started to unbutton her shirt. Blix hoped her face didn't betray her.

Kit had a long chain around her neck, on the end of which was a stone about the size of a large coin, with a hole in the middle. It was polished smooth and there were several scratches on it which seemed to glow slightly, a faint green-gold. The scratches looked like a stylised trilithon.

'This here's my ticket home,' she said, displaying it proudly. 'It's-'

'I know what it is,' said Constant, astonished. 'It's a wicket. Where did you get that?'

'Family heirloom. It was my mom's.'

Constant whistled appreciatively. He suddenly seemed like a different person, eager and excited, his morose disposition vanished like a dark cloud burned off by the sun. 'That's some heirloom. I've read about these. You could buy a city with that. A big one.'

'Can't make change from it though. I prefer dollars.'

'What? Hold on,' said Blix. 'A wicket? Like in cricket, you mean? Stumps and bails and silly mid-off?' She surveyed their expressions and reorganised her thoughts. 'What's a wicket?' she asked.

'It's a portable gate,' said Constant. 'That's the name for a small gate, like in a fence. A magician joke. The wicket locks onto the destination point of a gate you attune it to and takes you there. You don't need to be in the stone circle to use it. The rest of the gate rules still apply - no forced travel, no changing your mind halfway through.'

'It's pretty neat,' Kit agreed. 'I don't know nothing about how gates work, but momma always said it would guide me home when I needed it to.'

'Teleportation. Of course that's a thing, why not?' said Blix, not quite believing what she was hearing, although it was no crazier than anything else she'd heard recently.

The others stared at her blankly. Constant's brow furrowed. '*Tele… port…* Sorry, my Latin's a bit rusty. Carry across distance?'

'You know, disappearing here and reappearing there. With the wicket.'

'Oh. No, that's impossible. Where would you be in-between? Gate and wickets work by opening a thaumatic tunnel through –'

'That's great,' Blix interrupted, to spare herself another lecture. 'Why can't I buy them in the shops?'

Kit chimed in. 'You've been through a gate, kiddo. Would you say that took a lot of magic?'

'You're asking the wrong person. All the magic, as far as I know.'

'It's a lot. A magician had to pour a lot of power into this. And magic runs out, so it has limited uses. Think of it like a return train ticket. You point it at somewhere, it takes you there, and then when you want to it brings you back to where you started. Then it's done.'

'You pointed it here?' asked Constant.

'I followed Dragonville. He has one too. I think his is better than mine. He's used it at least five times that I know of, maybe more. A man like him oftentimes needs to leave in a hurry, I guess.'

'Um. When I find my sister, could you take us home, please?' Blix asked tentatively. 'I don't know how.'

'Sorry kiddo. One rider only. Well, maybe two, if we squeezed up real friendly like.' The American took a moment to appreciate the rosy red colour Blix's cheeks had turned. 'But three? Uh-uh. I don't think it would take all of us.'

'I'll find some other way then,' said Blix, as resolutely as she knew how.

'That's the spirit, kiddo.'

'Okay, that explains how you got here,' said Constant slightly brusquely, 'but not why. Why is Dragonville here?'

'Can't rightly say,' Kit replied. 'When I catch up with him I'll ask, after I blow his brains out.'

'Why are you trying to kill this magician?'

'I got some reasons, which are of the personal variety,' Kit replied. For a moment her smile no longer extended to her eyes. 'But boy oh boy, *everyone* wants to kill Belmont Dragonville! He makes enemies like you turn prayer wheels. I'm just one of a multitude. There's kind of, uh, an unofficial commission, you might say. To take him out.'

'You're *really* a bounty hunter?' said Blix. 'Like, for people?'

'Sure I am! I did tell you. There's more folks than werewolves with prices on their heads. I tracked him to Utah territory, down Salt Lake way. He stole something from the Mormons. They put their own bounty out, dead or alive, and since I was in the killing business anyway I offered them my services to track him down, 'cause, you know, bullets cost money. Found him holed up way out in the sticks, in a pool hall called Little Gate Saloon -'

'More magician humour?' The word *saloon* had conjured a host of Wild West stereotypes in Blix's imagination, although she knew it was just pub marketing. She had no idea what Utah was like but suspected it was all skyscrapers these days.

'Seems so. The Mormons didn't see the funny side though. They don't care for saloons at the best of times. Elder Smoot and his boys pumped so many rounds into that place they coulda renamed it the Lead Lined Saloon. Mormons don't mess around. Lotta men caught a bullet they probably maybe might not have deserved. But when they counted out the bodies, Dragonville wasn't one of them. I realised he'd used the wicket. You can tell, if you know. I used mine to latch on to his, they can do that if you're fast enough. So here I am and here we are. That was a few months ago. Ain't caught sight of him since, so I been doing some exploring to pass the time. Killed a few werewolves, here and there. Not seeking 'em out, you understand. Just any who came across me and, uh, didn't act like gentlemen.'

'What did the magician steal?' Constant asked.

'She saw it. What you said he did kiddo, making a place appear out of thin air? The thing he did it with is called a lens. It can show you anywhere you've been already, just like it was in front of your eyes.'

'Dragonville did more than watch,' said Blix. 'They walked right into it.'

'Yep. No idea how. This one's special. No wonder the Saints didn't want to lose it.' She stretched and yawned. 'Annnnyway. That's you all caught up with me. What's your story, preacher boy?'

'I don't want to talk about it. You'll see for yourself tomorrow anyway. We should sleep now. Tomorrow's going to be unpleasant.'

'Worse than today?' said Blix miserably.

'Yes. And I'm sorry to say tonight might be a little unpleasant for you.'

'What do you mean?'

'The moon. Full moon was a few days ago so you won't change tonight, but your body is going to start responding to the moon. It won't be fun.'

'Bloody marvellous.'

'Get some sleep while you can.'

'I ain't so sleepy,' said Kit. 'I'll take first watch.' She sat on the edge of the rock, looking away from the fire.

Blix pulled her hat as far down on her brow as she could and curled up on the driest and least uncomfortable bit of ground she could find.

She didn't know what to make of her companions. Kit was the most american American Blix could imagine. She practically bounced with enthusiasm and can-do attitude, and the mile-wide grin was open and disarmingly straightforward. That was very American, in Blix's TV-and-films-only experience of Americans. So was her apparent willingness to come out guns blazing and kill the baddies. There was also the fact that she was *totally* gorgeous, but Blix was trying hard not to think about that.

Oh God, who am I kidding, I really want to talk to her. Talk that goes somewhere. She said boyfriend! She's had boyfriends. That look though, it undressed me. Maybe she's bi! Is she too old for me? Yes. No! I don't know. I have no chance. What am I going to say to her? She's like innuendo on a stick. How do I talk to someone like that? Hi, thanks for shooting the monster that was going to eat me, I think you're well foxy, fancy eating me yourself? Or maybe, I noticed you shaved a couple of years off your age, shave anything else? Arrgh, no, those are just awful, I'd die of embarrassment before the first word came out. Literally die, dead, finito. I'm not good at this. Katy! You're good at this. First thing when I've got you back you are writing me a script, Cyrano.

Constant was another matter. He'd saved her life and she was trying hard to like him but the only thing he was bouncing with was sporadic rage. He'd slaughtered the werewolves like it was nothing. Then he'd been so nice, then so harsh, and seemed to switch back and forth between the two on a whim. Sometimes he was nasty and unpleasant, others, a twelve-year-old boy who had lost everything, vulnerable and confused and twelve, no matter how much he tried to appear older. Blix sensed that he was bottling something up, anger he could barely control. Blix couldn't imagine losing everyone you knew. Perhaps this was the only was he could cope.

She stuffed the doombag under her head. It wasn't a very comfortable pillow, but at least the awkward bag was useful for something. She couldn't for the life of her remember what had possessed her to bring such an enormous bag anyway.

Blix slept, and dreamed. White fangs tearing red flesh. Blood in the darkness.

Chapter Fourteen: Words

Constant dreamed.

In my dream, I am fourteen years old. I am sitting on the edge of a bed which is far too big for me in a room which makes me feel alone. I am supposed to be praying, but the pain in my head makes prayer impossible. I have just stopped crying. I wipe my eyes with the heel of my hand and screw my face up in a grimace of pain. I have been Great Father for a little over six weeks. It has been hell from the moment I was Recognised.

'I'm sorry,' I say. 'I didn't mean to cry. They're just so loud.'

In my dream, Brother Corlai, Corlai Endelain, Corlai the Bear to most because of his enormous size, sits by my bed, smoking a long-stemmed pipe of mountain weedstalk. This is quite scandalous in the Monastery, where stimulants are not to be used. Everyone adores Corlai though, and he is Tutor and therefore carries great responsibility, so he receives an unspoken dispensation. No one can quite understand where he gets it from. Weedstalk is not tithed from below, and although the winders say it grows wild on the plateau, they also say that Brother Corlai has never set foot on the steps leading to the basket mechanism. It is a puzzle which adds to the air of benign mystery which Corlai cultivates.

In my dream, he sucks on his pipe for a moment, and gives me a philosophical look.

'You always feel like this,' he says. He has the deepest voice of all the brothers. 'It says so in yon book. It will get better.'

'I don't think I can cope any more,' I say. 'It's so painful, Brother Corlai. You have no idea. I dread making the prayer marks. I almost fainted when we spoke the Penance before the evening meal.' I squeeze my forehead over and over, as if pressing the skin will squash the ache. 'And the Night Prayer is worst of all.'

Brother Corlai weighs my words, and takes a few long puffs on his pipe. The long stem curves down from his lips to a small bowl at navel height, which glows orange at each inhalation.

'Each Great Father hears the voices of the Fathers before him,' he says eventually. 'It is written. I have thought about this. What it means.' A pause, and another pffft on the pipe. 'The Great Father before you spoke of this to me.' He blows a smoke ring across the room. 'Do you remember?'

In my dream, I shake my head. 'I can't tell one memory from another. It's all I can do to hold them back.'

'Hmm.' He stretches in his chair. Like everything he has not made himself, it is too small for him. He reflects a little, then continues.

'Fourteen years we were without you, until you were Recognised. Did you hear them during that time?'

'Sometimes. At night, or when I was distracted. Nothing like this. I thought I was dreaming, or imagining it, or, well...'

I leave the thought hanging, but he knows. 'To hear a voice in your head that is not yours is the sign of madness, in other men. Not you.'

'Something changed when I was Recognised.'

'Yes. You remembered who you are.'

In my dream, I ask, 'Did the others feel like this when they were Recognised?'

'Some. The most recent ones, certainly. But I expect the others had problems too. When the second heard the first, it must have been a terrible shock. But I expect one voice could be accommodated. And two, when the time came, or three, or four. What number are you?'

He already knows the answer, but I say it anyway. 'I am nineteenth of my name,' I say. 'But you are right. And there are others. From before the first Recognition. I am not sure how many. A lot. Their voices are different. Distant. Cut short. Drowned out by what comes later.' I am not sure how to say what I feel.

'Hmm.' Brother Corlai sucks on his pipe some more. 'Must be quite the hubbub in there.'

He leans toward me, and I feel safer in his shadow than in the deepest tunnel in the mountain. 'How do you feel?' he asks gently.

'I want to die,' I say, and I mean it.

Brother Corlai's expression does not change, but he says nothing for a long time. The only sound is the wet rasp as he smokes his pipe, and the crisp crackle as the weedstalk burns.

Eventually, he says, 'There are some words.'

I don't understand. 'What words?'

'To make you feel better. Calmer. They will lessen the pain. They will make the voices easier to put aside.'

'Magic?'

'Yes.' Another deep pull on the pipe. 'Of a kind. Old magic, from before the All-men came here. From the old place, on the other world. Magic of my forefathers.'

I have hope then, but I wonder whether it is misplaced. To be me is to be circumscribed. I lead the brothers, but only where the brothers let me lead them. I feel strongly that this is right. I don't know why I feel this.

'I am not allowed to know magic. The First Father forbade it. I *forbade it. It's one of the rules.'*

'I know.' Puff, puff, contemplate. 'But you know, there's only one rule, really. To keep you safe. I don't think we'd discharge that if you go mad. Or kill yourself. The next you would be a bit unhappy if we let that happen, I think.' The bowl of his pipe glows as he sucks on it once more. 'They are barely magic. A flicker to give strength to the words.' Puff, puff, puff. 'Shall I tell you the words?'

I want to say yes. I want to say no. I prevaricate. I know the nature of this place, how it is protected.

'I thought no one could use magic on the Anvil. The stone prevents it. It protects us.'

Brother Corlai turns his mouth into a sort of shrug of the lips. 'I've considered this. It's yours,' he says. 'The stone, I mean. You made this rule. You can change it. A little, at least. The stone will respond to you. If you tell it to.'

This is a revelation. The part of me which is still a fourteen-year-old boy starts thinking about fireballs.

Brother Corlai leans closer still. I can smell the weedstalk in the hair of his beard. 'It may not be a good idea,' he says. 'I offered the words to your predecessor. He refused. He was known for his wisdom.'

I understand what he means. I am not allowed to know magic. But I know its nature. My mother was matriarch of our clan. She knew about magic. She taught it is not to be trifled with. To say 'the magic of my forefathers' is to claim it as first magic, magic before magicians. It is to connect it to the wild forces of the universe. It is to say it is dangerous.

'Who were your forefathers, Brother Corlai?' I ask.

He shrugs, and sits back. 'No one special. Miners, mostly. They cut ore from the deep earth. All of them back as far as I know of, and my old ones never said theirs did different. Me too, before I came here.'

In my dream, I try and imagine Corlai the Bear squeezing down a mine shaft. 'You must fit in well here then,' I say. 'Sometimes I think the brothers are trying to hollow out the mountain.'

Corlai seems amused by this. 'They are industrious,' he allows. 'They follow the first brothers' design most assiduously.' Another pull on the pipe. 'I try and keep my hand in, now and then.'

He thinks some more. I realise that by doing so he is making me focus on him and not the pain in my head.

'Thing is, I always hated tight spaces,' he continues. 'Since I was tiny. Hated them. Feared them. I'd watch my father and the other men go underground each morning, and I knew they'd never come back up. I knew the earth would claim them. Payment for the ore. When they rose at shift end the relief didn't make me feel better, it made the next day's fear worse.

'So, when the time came for me to go down, younger in years than you, I said no. This was shameful among my people. My father stopped speaking to me. It was a terrible thing. After a few days, my grandfather, who lived in the next valley, got wind of my shame and paid a visit. I thought he'd come to denounce me. He was fearsome, the old one. A big man of religion. Instead he held my hand and said some words. It was as if a yoke had been taken from my neck. That day I went underground with my father. He was proud. I felt no fear. I didn't feel alone. I felt cradled in my grandfather's arms.'

'The words did you good,' I say.

'Did they?' Corlai ponders it. 'The words took something from me. Something I didn't like, granted, but something of me nonetheless. I am not sure. What would I have been without them? Had I my time again, I might choose differently.'

'I am sure you father was happy you didn't.'

'Perhaps. I'll never know. We didn't speak of it at the time. A few years after, the earth took payment. Then I came here.'

Now it is my turn to think in silence.

'I can use magic here.'

'Yes.'

'But only me.'

'Yes.' He shifts in his chair. He knows what I will ask.

'How then have you used your words, Brother Corlai?'

'I haven't,' he says, his voice growing quiet. 'Not since the day I came here.'

'Do you still fear tight spaces?'

'Yes. I do,' he whispers. 'Fear them. Hate them.'

'Then how do you live here?' My voice cracks with emotion as I realise what this kind man goes through each day. The mask he wears to hide it from me. What it has cost him to take it off.

'I have faith,' he says simply. 'I have faith in you. Shall I tell you the words?'

I want to say no. But the pain is terrible, and the voices so very loud, and I am fourteen years old and I have just stopped crying.

'Tell me the words,' I say. 'Now. Forever. For the rest of my lives.'

'I will,' he says. 'I will write it in the book. And I will warn those who come after.'

Now there is a boy here I do not recognise.

'The ironic thing is that you use the bloodstone to do this magic, and one of the things you suppress from future you's is the knowledge that you can use the bloodstone for magic. Wouldn't have come as such a shock the other day otherwise, would it? Or to twenty-two, come to think of it. Sorry, Constant, this isn't what you're looking for either. You will find it. Keep trying.'

The boy looks at me critically, as if he cannot quite decide what to do with me.

'What's wrong with your mind?' *he continues.* 'Reaching you was like finding someone in the fog. Was it that medicine you took this morning? It's healed you completely, do you understand that? What's in it? Oh, you can't answer.'

The boy looks frustrated. It is a look I have seen in the mirror many times. He sighs.

'We have to work with what we have,' *he says.* 'I don't trust that thing, whatever it is, but we have no choice. It hasn't killed you yet. Very well. It is standing over you right now. Wake up. If it doesn't try to kill you, let's come to an understanding. You can pretend to give it the special girl, it wants her anyway. As long as she remains close. Try and remember. Oh, and you missed something important yesterday. You know you did, so *I* know you did, but I don't know what, because you - well, you get the idea. Try and remember that too.'

Constant did not remember the boy when he woke up.

Constant looked up. Kit McCoy was staring down at him, her face lit by the glowing embers and the pale light of the hour before dawn. She wore a strange expression, far from her usual beam. She looked like she was making a calculation.

'If you're trying to decide whether to kill me, I vote no,' he said, rolling out of his blanket and sitting up. It was bitterly cold. Blix was still asleep nearby, lying on her side facing them. In sleep, all the stress and tension had left her face. He wondered briefly how he looked when unconscious. *Like a different person*, a cynical part of him thought.

'Ain't gonna kill you, kid,' said Kit in a low voice, sitting down beside him. 'I think we should talk though. A real heart to heart.'

'I don't know you,' said Constant guardedly.

Kit poked the fire with her boot, stirring a last glow from the crumbling white cinders. 'That is surely true,' she said. 'But then I suspect your circle of acquaintance is quite small, Your Holiness.'

Constant sat up sharply. 'How in the world did you know that?' he blurted, before the thought to deny it appeared in his mind. 'There's no way - I've haven't said -'

Kit gave him a heavy-lidded look. 'Don't ever try out for the Pinkertons, kid. You ain't undercover agent material. I know you don't get out much, but even you gotta know how people work. I been here a while now. Folks like to talk about their religion. They know all about you. 'Cepting what a big asshole you are. Annnnyway, being such a one as can add two to two and make two twos, when I see the mountain afire, and shortly after come across a paladin boy-priest who just happens to look like you look and, let's face it, to be right out-and-out callin' himself -'

'I know what my name is, thank you,' said Constant irritably.

'Well you see my point then. Not exactly a master of disguise, are you?'

'I suppose not,' Constant muttered into his robe.

'No. Sore thumbs stick out like you.'

'Who *are* you?' Constant said suddenly. 'What do you want?'

'Just a gal from Nebraska, kid, here to kill a man.'

'No, there's something else. There's something different about you,' he continued. 'I don't mean the Earth stuff. I can't put my finger on it, but I can feel it and I don't like it. I'm assuming it's magic, since that seems to be a thing again. You're a magician.'

'Nope,' said Kit. 'I don't do magic. I do understand it though. I understand what it looks like, and how the world feels when it's done. For example, I know you're doing somethin' in the way of magic, now and then. I don't know what exactly. I can taste it.'

'I don't want to talk about it.'

Kit moved a little closer to Constant, who tensed slightly. 'Look kid, you don't have to be afraid of me. We got a lot in common.'

'Don't tell me you're on my side.'

'No, I won't say that. I have my own business and you have yours. But we're not on different sides. I think we're both against some bad people, and things that aren't people. And I think we're going to go along together for a spell. You should decide whether you can trust me or not. I did save your lives, I should point out. Didn't have to do that.'

'No. No, you didn't.'

'Ain't regretted it yet. Not too much, anyway.'

Constant stared at the fire for a very long time. 'This world is very dangerous,' he said eventually. 'It always has been. We're at war. We've lost a war. A war that ended us.' He looked at Blix. 'I don't know that I can protect her from that.'

Kit smiled widely. 'Well kid, I don't know that you need to. You don't really understand women, do you? Comes with the monk's robes I expect.'

'People,' Constant whispered. 'It's people I don't understand.'

'Well I understand women just fine, being as I definitely am one and also have a fine appreciation of them in ways you ain't old enough to misunderstand yet.' She tipped her head toward Blix. 'That there is one tough cookie. Plain as the nose on your face. Protect her? She'll be protecting us afore long, you mark my words.'

She paused then, and her voice took on a different tone. 'But I will keep my eye on her. Yes sir. I am inclined to do that.'

Constant said nothing for a while. Then he appeared to come to a decision.

'All right,' he said.

'That's it?'

'Yes.'

'Well, shit. All right then. All right is all right by me.'

'Keep it down, some of us are still unconscious,' Blix said. She yawned so widely it looked like her jaw might unhinge.

'Sorry,' said Constant. 'Um, how much did you hear?'

'Something about hard cookies and understanding women. And then you were going along together. Sounds pervy. You should get a room.'

Constant looked closely, but the girl showed no sign that she'd heard the rest of the conversation. 'How do you feel?' he asked carefully.

'I had weird dreams. And I had cramps all night, like my insides were being twisted. Like really bad period pain, you know? But I'm not due on for three weeks.'

'That was the moon.'

'I figured as much. I kept waking up and nodding off and waking up when the cramps kicked in again. I feel dreadful. I did get some sleep towards morning though. Did you two keep watch all night?'

'Not me,' said Constant. 'You should have woken me,' he said to Kit. 'You'll be exhausted.'

'It's fine. I'm kinda nocturnal. And I don't sleep so much to be honest. Guilty conscience I guess. I've been a bad girl. Repeatedly.'

'Too early for innuendo,' Blix yawned. 'Feed me.'

'We should eat while we walk,' said Constant. 'We've been here too long. We'll be lucky to reach the town before nightfall. And then we've... got to... climb...' He trailed off, puzzled. Blix and Kit exchanged looks, then shrugs.

'I'm going for a pee,' Blix announced. 'Um, while I'm there, do you want your underwear back?'

Kit grinned. 'Keep 'em for now. Like I said yesterday -'

Constant's head jerked sharply, like he had just been slapped.

'What you said yesterday!' he exclaimed.

Kit raised an eyebrow. 'Beg pardon?'

The boy pointed at her sternly. 'What did you mean, "again?"'

'Oops,' said Kit McCoy, grinning ever more widely.

Chapter Fifteen: The Forge

'Men can't climb the Anvil,' said Constant flatly.

Blix groaned. 'Not again.'

'Again and again,' Kit said, not bothering to conceal her amusement.

They trudged along the side of the road, pushing through a slurry of ice and mud which froze Blix's feet even through her rubber boots and thick socks. The road itself was raised above them on a causeway and looked much easier to travel on than slogging through the ditch, but Kit had insisted. Easier, yes, but too exposed - a straight line of sight down the mountain.

Thick poles lined the road every quarter of a mile. Atop them sat wide metal baskets, burnt black and rusting. They held bundles of firewood and charcoal, waiting for the flame. There was no one to light them.

Ahead, the road rose beyond the treeline into scree. Beyond that, giant boulders hundreds of feet high dominated the slope, the moraine of some ancient glacier. The path turned left behind one of the biggest. Blix couldn't see where it went, but there was no doubt where it ended. Towering above them stood the sheer walls of the Anvil, stark and featureless, ground smooth by ice. The summit was shrouded in mist, invisible from the ground.

Perfectly visible from where they walked was a pall of black smoke rising near the base of the mountain.

The hike had been both tense and monotonous. There was no sign of werewolves but distant howling reminded them of their presence now and then. The mountains masked where the sound came from; not even the sharp-eared American could tell where the monsters might be. Blix, who trailed, bone tired, slightly behind the others, felt compelled to look behind her every few seconds.

Other than the pervading sense of threat, the journey was gloomy and tedious and Blix hated it. What Shambhala desperately needed, she decided, was the introduction of the motor car, and possibly the ski-lift.

To pass the time Kit had invented a new game: Constant Baiting. Her insistence that she was telling the truth about climbing the Anvil, coupled with at first coy then increasingly extravagant refusals to explain further, had short-circuited something in Constant's brain. He kept coming back to what seemed to be an article of faith, subsiding after each rebuff for a few minutes, then returning to worry at it again. Blix had at first found it funny, then annoying, then funny again, and now wearying beyond words.

'Just tell him, for goodness sake,' she said. Almost a day of continual uphill trudging had left her legs aching terribly.

'There's nothing she can tell,' said Constant. 'Men can't climb the Anvil.'

'I don't lie,' Kit said. 'And y'all monks need to get out more. Allow me to clue you in. I am what is commonly known as a Woman. I believe I explained this already. And boy, let me tell you, I am all woman, yes siree! I have womanly wiles and a vagina and all sorts of things like that.'

Constant went red, but he was beginning to get the measure of Kit McCoy.

'What was that word you used yesterday? About horses?'

Kit thought. 'Horseshit?' she suggested.

'Yes, that's the one. That.'

Kit grinned. 'Starting to like you, kid.'

'Great. But look, men can't climb the Anvil.'

'Just bloody tell him,' said Blix. 'This conversation is getting right on my tits.'

Kit giggled. 'Well we wouldn't want that. Okay, fair enough. I admit it. I did not climb the Anvil through the application of womanly wiles.'

'Finally,' said Constant.

'I did climb it though. And I do have a vagina.'

'*Yes*. But, seriously, men can't -'

'That's it,' said Blix. 'Your needle's stuck, mate.' She turned to Kit. '*How* did you get up the mountain, Kit?'

'*Finally*, someone asks!' said the American, laughing.

'Did you fly?' asked Blix.

'Say what now?'

'In a hot air balloon or something. I don't suppose they have planes here, it being sword n' sorcery land.'

'We have plains,' said Constant. 'There are grasslands thousands of miles wide to the south.'

'That's not what... In fact, never mind.'

'Fine. What's a hot air... whatever that next word was?' asked Constant. 'It didn't translate. Bah-oon?'

'Balloon. You don't have them here, don't worry about it,' said Kit. 'Ain't no Montgolfier's in this neck of the woods. Not that it would matter if there were. Your damn monks did some magic back in the old days. You can't fly up the Anvil or over it.'

How does the woman know that there is magic which stops flight above the Anvil? Constant thought, but the shape of the thought was someone else's. He was alarmed by how present Ysir was. It was as if the warrior had thought it himself. But that was ridiculous. He was a memory of a dead man, nothing more.

Kit was still musing. 'You guys have big birds here or something? That people could ride on? Or dragons? Ain't never seen a big dragon. Earth dragons are *tiny.* The big ones are kaput. Although, I hear they still got big mechanical dragons in Africa.'

'Nope, they're gone too,' said Blix. 'Gryphons?' she said, hopefully.

'No big birds, dragons or gryphons,' said Constant. 'Only people, and wolves. I expect the first brothers were just being thorough. When they first climbed the Anvil, they destroyed the route they'd taken. The basket is the only way. One way up.' He sounded angry and miserable at the same time. Blix wondered why.

It didn't seem to register with Kit. 'That's right! That's what they say. Except, not so much.'

'Of course,' said Constant. He all but spat the words. 'Something we missed over *four thousand years* of continual alertness.'

'Now you're getting it! There's a climbing route. On the other side from here. A man told me about it.'

'What man?'

'I don't know, some old guy. Looked like he lived hereabouts. Tall and skinny. Smelt like a yak.'

'That's it?' Constant gritted his teeth to stop vulgar words coming out. 'Thousands of years of impregnable fortitude breached because some random herder you just happened across says "oh look, you can climb that bit?" I don't believe it.'

'Well, there was a bit more to it than that. He was trying to impress me. Real hard.'

'I don't believe it.'

'Just tellin' it like it was, kid. I went up to Forge for a looksee, figured getting to the top that way was a no-no. I did some scouting, met my, uh, confidential informant, and he showed me the way. Turns out your mountain ain't quite as sheer as it looks from a distance. Hell of a climb, let me tell you, ol' Whymper woulda turned white just looking at it. Now I happen to have walked uphill a time or two, I thought I'd give it a go. I climbed it a few weeks ago.'

'And you just wandered through the Monastery without anyone noticing?'

'Pretty much. I was, uh, trying not to bump into anyone.'

'I bet you were. Why?'

'Thought I might find Dragonville,' she said. 'When I followed him from Utah, we ended up here. Now, that coulda been a coincidence. Maybe he just kicked open the wicket and latched onto the nearest gate to escape Mormon justice. But then I figured, horseshit. I don't believe in coincidence.'

'He wanted to come here.'

'Reckon so. And no offense son, but there ain't much of interest hereabouts if you ain't a squirrel or a rock, 'cepting the Monastery. Figured he'd come here to go there.'

'He did. Just not in person.'

'Yeah, I guess so. Dragonville's a real powerful magician, but I think maybe your mighty monk mountain is designed to keep his kind out. He had to get creative. Wolves musta come up the same way I did. That wasn't my fault,' she added, seeing the look on Constant's face.

Blix saw it too. 'Fun though it is to watch you two bounce off each other, this is important. This is all connected. Dragonville joins everything that's happened to us together. I don't believe in coincidences either. I think we should... we should... Whoa.'

They'd turned a corner. Ahead of them the wide road ended abruptly as the ground rose steeply. Before them several carts, some laden, some empty, stood abandoned. The beasts that had pulled them up the path were nowhere to be seen.

Ahead of them a vast number of steps led up to a huge fissure in the rock, at least three hundred feet high and more than twice that across, tapering to describe an almost perfect oval. It appeared to be wholly natural, the chance shaping of a break in the stone, but to Blix it looked like nothing less than an immense eye looking down at her. As the last rays of sunlight shone through it she felt like she'd been caught in the gaze of God.

'That's impressive,' she said, fighting against a quite strong urge to kneel.

'It's called the Iris,' said Constant. 'It's the last station on the pilgrim trail. It's also the front gate to Forge.'

'That hole has gates?'

'They're really big,' said Kit, helpfully.

'They were useless,' said Constant. 'The enemy was already inside.' He'd turned pale. Blix wondered what he had seen when his home was destroyed, and whether she was about to see it too.

The stair stretched above them like the spine of a giant snake, each enormous step carved from the living rock. Blix measured the first against her leg. It came up past her knee.

'How many?' she asked.

'Eleven hundred and eleven,' said Constant. 'Eleven is an auspicious number.'

Blix sighed heavily. Her legs *really* hurt. 'Come on then,' she said, 'If we must.' Mentally she added elevators to the list of Shambhala must-haves.

'We should be quiet from now on,' said Kit. 'In case there are still some, uh, uninvited guests around.'

Blix was still looking balefully at the staircase. 'I don't think I'll be able to talk.'

She looked back at the Iris; the last rays had gone, and the sky was rapidly purpling. 'It'll be pitch black when we reach the top, we won't be able to see where we're going.'

'Yes, we will,' said Constant. 'It's still on fire.'

The lip of the Iris - the eyelid, Blix supposed - was fifty feet thick. She sensed rather than saw the roof looming high above her. The path was worn completely smooth. Generations of feet had preceded hers. She wondered whether any would follow.

The gates were monumental, iron-bound wood dozens of yards thick. They stood open and undefended.

The town was below them in a hollow in the rock. A dull orange glow spotted the way ahead of them here and there; not enough to light up the town, but enough to give shape to the darkness. Blix got a sense of Forge as a jumble of buildings wedged in a narrow strip of flat space beneath the sheer immensity of the mountain. It smelled of char and - something else, that Blix's mind shied away from. Something bad.

'What in the world's still burning after almost five days?' asked Kit, in a stage whisper.

The rock,' said Constant. 'Some of the houses are built from coal-bearing stone. Fire them for long enough and they burn. It could take months for the fuel to run out. Years, maybe.'

It was the silence that disturbed Blix the most. From her point of view Forge was a small town, as far as she could tell, despite its grandiose front door. Blix knew about small towns. She knew the sounds they made, the sounds of life, even at night. Here there was nothing except the wind.

More huge steps led down from the Iris to the level of the town, just visible; only a few, Blix was relieved to see. Constant started down, then paused.

'We need more light. There are torches over there.' He pointed into the darkness.

Blix looked, but saw nothing. 'How do you know?'

- seventy times I have travelled this path, some as men, some as boys, some as babes, it is always the same -

'That's where they are.'

Kit skipped off into the blackness and returned with three rods as long and thick as her arm. They smelt heavily of bitumen. Kit struck a spark and passed the flame around. Blix felt very grateful as the pool of yellow light showed their surroundings, until she realised she had lost her night vision and could see nothing beyond. Suddenly every flicker of a shadow on a wall was a werewolf.

'Where are we going?' she asked, trying not to sound scared. 'And can we go there quickly?'

Constant gestures with his torch, and in the sweep of light Blix caught a glimpse of a road.

'There's only one place to go,' he said. 'The town exists to serve the Monastery. All roads lead to the basket.'

'You still think there ain't no werewolves in town?' asked Kit.

'Yes,' Constant replied. He drew his sword. 'I might be wrong though. Be prepared.'

'I heard that.' Kit drew her pistol and cocked the hammer.

The silent city was strange and scary. Blix was sick of feeling scared. The fear had been building all day and now felt like a knife scraping along her nerves. She felt weird and disorientated. She stared fiercely into the darkness beyond the torchlight, her relief when each vague shape resolved into a building tempered by fear that the next one would be a werewolf. She could taste the smouldering ruins, an acrid tang that made her want to scrape her tongue. She realised she felt like screaming and couldn't wait for it to be over.

'Where are the people?' she whispered.

'Dead,' said Constant, tersely.

'Yes. Where are the bodies?'

Constant paused. 'That's a good question. Wait here.'

The boy walked over to the nearest doorway and without hesitation kicked it open. Not for the first time Blix was impressed by his resolve. He didn't look like he had it in him.

He disappeared inside. Only the glow from his torch reflecting off the walls was visible. A few seconds later he reappeared. He ignored Blix and Kit, crossed the road and repeated the exercise in another house.

'Plenty of blood but no corpses,' he reported when he returned. 'That's unusual. Wolves are indiscriminate. They don't clean up after themselves.'

Kit looked back the way they'd come. The Iris was invisible. There was the light of their torches, then nothingness. 'Well, let's not dawdle, kid. In case we find out the hard way what happened.'

'There aren't any wolves here,' Constant said. He sounded certain again.

Kit snorted. 'Says you.'

'Says me, yes.'

Kit snorted again. 'Kid, it could be wall to wall werewolves ten feet around the corner and you'd never know until you were halfway down their throats. They can be sneaky like that. How far is it to the damn basket anyway?'

'We're here.'

Constant walked forward into what looked like a town square or plaza, wide enough that any buildings were beyond the light of the torches. She followed him, and as the little sphere of light moved through the darkness suddenly the mountain was there, an immense blank wall, oppressive in its majesty. It was like running into the end of the world.

Ahead of them, tiny against the endless rock face, was a wicker and wood gondola. As they got closer Blix realised it was a trick of perspective - the gondola could easily hold thirty or more people. It wasn't really meant for people, but for the goods that kept the monks on the Anvil alive. There were a lot of monks, she supposed. Or had been.

It dangled at a slight skew a foot or so above the ground, half a dozen yards out from the wall. It was highly decorated with symbols and signs in what Blix assumed would be vibrant colours in the daytime, but which the flickering torchlight rendered only in yellow and black. Four thick ropes were tied at each corner and another two on a complicated pulley beam which crossed the basket at head height and attached to all four sides. It looked like a low-tech version of the window cleaning platforms that Blix had seen hanging from the sides of skyscrapers.

She touched the rock face. It was smooth, strangely so. There were no cracks or crevices, nowhere to gain purchase. She could see why Constant had been adamant that no one could climb it.

She looked at the boy, who was frowning fiercely. 'We're here. Now what?'

'We get in.'

'Okay. And then?'

'Then you two keep quiet while I concentrate.'

He pulled a lowlight from his bag and offered it to Blix. 'Dump the torches. We can't risk fire in the basket. Use this.'

Blix shook her head. 'Save it. I'm not sure I want to see this bit.'

They threw the torches on the ground and clambered in, slightly gingerly. Blix collapsed in an undignified heap, more grateful to be sitting down than she had thought possible.

Constant sat in the middle in a lotus position, just visible in the torchlight through the basket slats. She put his palms face up on his knees, and closed his eyes. Blix suddenly giggled.

Constant opened his eyes. 'Something funny?'

'Sorry. You suddenly looked like a monk. You haven't really, up to now. Properly Tibetan you know, like the Dalai Lama.'

'I'm not Tibetan. Please be quiet, this is extremely difficult and possibly impossible.' He looked at Kit. 'If this doesn't work you're going to have to show us how you climbed the Anvil.'

Kit suddenly looked uncertain. 'Well, gee, I don't know...'

'I thought as much.' He closed his eyes again.

Blix looked at Kit, but she'd turned away and was looking back into the city. She was cradling her rifle in a way that made Blix nervous.

'Did you see something?'

'Nope.'

'Hear?'

'Nothing but the wind.'

'Oh.' Blix listened. The wind sounded like howling, far in the distance. She hunkered down in the basket and tried not to think about it.

The inside of the gondola was as gaily decorated as the rest. Blix could just about make things out by the light of the torches through the wicker. She glanced idly at some of the symbols, and suddenly sat bolt upright.

'Hey, I can read that! I know what the squiggles mean! They're in English. But they still look like squiggles, too. How am I doing that?'

Kit didn't look down. 'Magic, probably. What do they say?'

'"Consider your choice carefully."'

'Too late,' said Constant.

The gondola lurched upward suddenly, throwing Kit backwards against the frame. The basket swung alarmingly. Blix peered over the lip of the gondola and saw the torches become smaller and smaller, until they were no more than spots of light. She realised the basket was moving quite quickly, although as soon as she looked away from the torches she lost any sense of it. Beyond the town square she saw other spots of light dotted here and there across the settlement, where fires still burned.

'Just as well I'm not afraid of heights,' she said. 'How are you doing it?'

'I don't know,' said Constant. Blix could no longer see him, but he sounded strained. 'Brother Simon said it was magic.' He paused for a moment, then said, 'I don't like it. I don't know how I'm doing it and I don't like it. It'll end badly.'

'Please don't say that when we're hundreds of feet above the ground.'

'I don't mean now. I mean generally. Magic is not a good thing.'

'Have to agree with the half-pint on that one,' said Kit. 'Think about it. You can suddenly read another language. How long does it take to learn languages normally? What happens inside your head when you learn things?'

'According to my teachers, not much.' said Blix.

'You're funny, kiddo. It ain't so funny though. Magic has changed your brain. Mine too, since I can understand the midget monk here. I didn't ask for that. Did you ask for that?'

Blix was so surprised by Kit's sudden intensity that she didn't reply.

'No. She didn't,' said Constant quietly. 'Magic only seems to help. It never does.'

'Damn straight.'

Blix must have slept, if only for a few minutes, because the jolt when the gondola stopped woke her up with a start.

'We're here,' said Constant. 'Wait a moment.'

He returned smelling of oil. Kit struck sparks again.

When the torch was bright enough to see by, Blix looked around. There was a hole in the rock, about ten feet square. A tunnel led into the mountain.

'We're not at the top.'

'The winding wheel is up there, but the Monastery is lower. This is the way in. Follow me.'

Constant led them along the tunnel and around a corner and straight into two werewolves.

Blix screamed and scrabbled for her knife. The monsters loomed massive in the narrow tunnel, primal fear made flesh, death itself come for her. The fear that she had imprisoned broke free and, terrified, she shrank from the beasts, knowing that they would rip her clothes as they had at the circle, toy with her as they had at the cottage, before tearing her apart in rage and hunger and ending her forever. But even as she turned in terror, part of her mind felt only awe. Suddenly the bitter tang in her mouth was blood and the acrid stench in her nostrils the scent of silver, old and hate-making. That part of her mind reached out to the werewolves even as she turned, and she found herself screaming, 'Don't kill me! Don't kill me! *I'm like you!*'

Then arms were around her, human arms, a woman's arms, and a woman's voice said, 'Hush, now, hush. You don't need to be afraid. I'm here.' Those strong arms held her tight, held her as if they would never let her go, and Blix knew then that she would never want them to. She sobbed until her heart wrenched in her chest.

'They're dead,' said Constant loudly. Eventually Blix felt able to talk.

'D-dead?'

'Yes. I killed them when I left. I should have said. Sorry.'

Eventually Blix calmed down enough that she could see the bodies as they were, not as her imagination had made them. It was barely better. The corpses made her stomach churn. They filled the narrow passageway so that there was barely room to squeeze past then. The fear gripped her again. Although the obscene lumps of rancid, stinking fur were clearly dead her mind would not believe it. Blix felt their hands around her throat and clawing at her flesh. She turned away, dry-heaving violently. A trickle of bile burned her throat.

'I can't,' she said, bending almost double as spasms of fear and pain wracked her. 'I'm sorry, they're- oh, God, I feel-'

She felt a hand on her shoulder then and heard Constant's reassuring voice. 'It's okay. You're strong enough. You can do it.'

And she was, and she could.

Then he jerked his hand away. 'No! I didn't mean -'

'What the-' said Kit, sounding shocked, though Blix didn't know why. 'Boy, what the hell did you-'

'I know!' And now Constant sounded anguished, and why did he seem to be so very far away? 'I'm sorry! *I didn't mean to!*'

'Didn't mean to?' said Kit angrily, from a dream. Blix looked between them, wondering what was happening but not really minding. 'Is this what you've been doing? I knew something was up, I could just taste it!'

'You don't understand!' Constant was almost pleading. 'At the circle, she couldn't... She was crying, what they tried to do... I mean, she couldn't even move!'

'Did you give her a chance? Or did you just decide to take over? How dare you! What gives you the right! Goddammit so much!'

Blix didn't understand the exchange, but it didn't matter and when she glanced away she forgot it. 'We should get going,' she said brightly. Or did she? For some reason her tongue felt heavy, and the words came thickly to her.

'Goddamn it kid, we are going to *talk.'*

'I'm so sorry!'

Kit stomped off ahead, muttering. After a moment of awkward vacillation, Constant followed. Blix followed happily, squeezing past the dead werewolves as though they weren't even there.

Chapter Sixteen: The Constant

Blix stumbled dreamily through the dark, glad to be away from the starless sky and its unrelenting black canvas. The tunnel was narrow and its darkness oppressive, but she could see the shape of it, reach out and touch it. It gave her a sense of reality. There was nothing realer than rock.

The tunnel sloped down, twisting and turning haphazardly, following a natural fissure. Here and there she saw signs of tool working. People had widened the way. It reminded her of a prehistoric cavern she'd visited once on a school trip, home to literal cavemen who had lived thousands of years before. The cavern had been very cool, in both senses of the word. The tunnel was strangely warm. She didn't wonder why.

Ahead of her Kit and Constant were whispering. It sounded angry, but Blix didn't mind and didn't feel the need to find out what was going on. Everything was fine.

Eventually they emerged back into the open air on a flat shelf of rock. Wind whipped across the face of the mountain and guttered the torch until the flame barely clung to the wood. Blix couldn't see much beyond the sputtering flame, but nonetheless felt a profound sense of depth. The wind threatened to slip beneath her feet and lift her out into the void she knew was there but couldn't see. She didn't mind this.

'Where are we?' asked Kit. No smiles from her for some reason.

Constant took a deep breath before answering. 'There's a big fissure in the rock here which cuts deep into the mountain. There are steps up this side of it and down to the other side. It's the only way forward.' He pointed into the darkness and described a jagged V with his finger.

'I can't see a thing,' Blix said.

'I think I can help.' Constant looked for a long time at Kit, seemingly asking for permission. She looked away haughtily. Constant's shoulders sagged. Blix didn't wonder why.

The boy walked a few steps to his left, and suddenly his torch illuminated the edge of a sheer drop. He held the torch out over empty space and closed his eyes. The torch flickered and spat as though a gust of wind had caught it. Then a ball of flame dripped from it, oozing like hot tar. But rather than falling into the abyss below, it bounced along the air like a rubber ball, gaining speed at each bounce. Blix watched as it touched another torch set into the cliff face, which burst into light, burning sodium yellow and with a strange intensity. Torch after torch sprang into life, up and down the rock face. Blix followed its arc across the chasm until it disappeared around a corner. A path began at that point, little more than a ledge on the mountainside. Part of Blix's mind told her it looked terrifying, but she didn't feel scared at all.

'First the basket, now this. I thought you couldn't do magic.'

'I can here.' Constant dropped the torch by his feet. 'I didn't know that until recently. I wasn't allowed to know. There's no trick. You just need to think about what you want.'

'What did you light?' asked Kit. She looked impressed, albeit grudgingly so.

'Every torch and lamp in the temple complex that's still where it should be,' said Constant. 'They won't go out either. I'm tired of darkness.'

'Can't say I disagree. You have just announced us though.'

'There aren't any wolves here. I think I'd know.'

'Hmmm. You mentioned steps?'

'Over there.'

'You go first.'

The 'steps' were no more than a foot wide at best, and in places so vertical that they were more of a ladder. A chain had been hammered into the wall at head height along the length of the path. Blix faced the rock and kept a firm grip. It was icy cold and hard going. At the point of the V there was a short ledge where they paused to get their breath back and rub some life back into their fingers. That's when Blix looked up.

'What the hell are those?'

For as far as she could see in the magic light, hundreds, thousands of short wooden boxes, about four feet long and three wide and high, rested against the rock, row after row of them. Each one sat on two thick wooden beams driven into the stone. The ones nearest to them looked new and had strings of small flags hanging from them. The higher ones looked increasingly weather-aged the further up they were. Blix could just make out some poles which seemed to have lost their boxes.

Constant followed her gaze. 'Coffins,' he said. 'This is the cemetery.'

'There are dead people in there?'

'Brothers at their final rest, yes.'

'That's creepy. Why don't you bury them?'

'Where? This is a mountain.' He rapped on the rock with a knuckle.

'Okay, you could send them down in the gondola.'

Constant shook his head. 'One way up, no way down. This is our way. They took a vow. They wanted this. They're with their brothers.'

'What about the empty ones?' Kit asked.

Constant closed his eyes, and said something under his breath. Blix realised it was a prayer. 'The sky took them. Come on.' He started along the path again, in the shadow of the dead.

They rounded the corner and suddenly there was a wall towering above them. It seemed to hang in open space, barely touching the mountain. A sheer, windowless expanse made of massive blocks of iron grey stone. Lit by a dozen torches near the ground, its heights disappeared into darkness. Before the wall a close-slatted wooden bridge spanned a chasm to reach the path on which they stood. At each post on the bridge a prayer wheel turned slightly as the wind moved it. Above them red and yellow flags fluttered gaily. The bridge led to a courtyard in front of a small, heavy wooden door. It was painted blood red. Blix hoped it was paint. It was shut.

'Never saw this side,' said Kit. 'Damn if it don't say, "go away".'

'It's a fortress,' whispered Constant, looking profoundly uncomfortable. 'To keep something safe.'

'Mmm-hmm. Nothing worth much I'd say. Just one thing though,' Kit went on before Constant could say anything. 'Isn't it supposed to be burnt to the ground?'

'I was wondering,' said Constant. 'We saw the smoke. It wasn't just from the town.'

They crossed the bridge. Two torches sat in brackets on either side of the door. Kit and Blix took one each while Constant pressed against the door, which didn't move.

'Barred from the inside.' He closed his eyes. There was a dull thud from inside the gate. He pushed it again. This time it glided silently open. A thick spar of black wood lay on the ground a few feet away.

Blix give the spar an experimental boot. 'Ow. No trick, you say?'

'Thought and will.'

'I'm going to try it.'

'Don't.'

'I'm going to give it a go.' She struck a pose, arms outstretched toward the door, like a stage magician levitating her assistant. 'See it in your mind, yeah? Right. Magic time.'

'We should go inside,' Constant said.

'Shush, I'm magicking.'

They waited. Nothing happened. Eventually Blix stopped posing.

'Okay. Why you and not me?'

Constant rubbed his forehead irritably. 'I don't know why it didn't work for you. I told you, I don't know about magic.'

'Yes, you did. Then you told me lots about magic, remember?'

Constant said nothing. Blix *hmmff*ed in frustration and turned to Kit. 'What about you, oh mighty huntress?

'Mighty huntress! I like that! I should get a card made up. Sorry kiddo, don't know. Who the hell knows how magic works? I ain't never heard a word about it that didn't sound like horseshit. Only fools use it,' she said pointedly, but whatever the point was, Blix missed it.

Blix looked back at Constant. 'You're doing that thing with your forehead.'

'Am I? I was just thinking...'

Constant trailed off, lost in the thought. 'Your key need winding?' said Blix after a few moments. 'You do this a lot.'

'I was thinking about what you said. I think I do know something about magic. Not how it works, but... I think I'm drawing on an artefact.'

'What's an artefact?'

'It's something that magicians pour power into. To store it for later. Millennia, sometimes. They can be anything. But the thing is, I shouldn't be able to do that, because the only artefact we had was stolen by the werewolves and given to your magician, Dragonville. But I knew that,' he continued, now talking to himself. 'Why did I come back here, knowing that? Why did I think that was right?'

Constant expression changed. He looked to Blix like he was wrestling with a problem he didn't quite understand and didn't know how to articulate. Something his mind couldn't grasp.

'Maybe the whole mountain is an artefact?' she suggested.

Constant snapped out of his introspection and shook his head. 'How would that work? What would stop the magic draining away? Artefacts can't be connected to anything. They're things, not landscape.'

Blix scowled and stuck out her tongue. 'Well pardon me for not knowing how this stupid stuff works. Okay then, maybe there's another artefact you didn't know about?'

'Maybe Dragonville's here,' said Kit suddenly. She drew her pistol.

'I don't think he is,' said Constant. 'I think I'd know.'

'Kid, Belmont Dragonville could make you think tomorrow was yesterday if he wanted to.'

'The Anvil is protected against magicia- well. Maybe it isn't any more. Maybe you're right. Maybe Blix is right. I've had a lot of certainties turn out to be wrong in the last few days. Let's find out.'

The door led to a long, low, narrow corridor. After a few yards, Blix realised they were still walking through the outer wall. It was at least thirty feet thick. A series of holes opened at intervals in the ceiling, each with a thick iron grating embedded in the shaft.

'I know what those are,' said Blix. 'I went to a castle once. They're murder holes. You pour boiling oil through them onto your enemies. That doesn't seem very religious. Why do you live in a fortress?'

'We didn't want to be disturbed,' said Constant, looking once again very uncomfortable indeed.

'Maybe think about a "keep out" sign rather than burning death from above?'

'Shambhala has never been a safe place,' said Constant.

'Yes. Werewolves.'

'No. People. If it helps, we've never used them. Until now the Anvil has never been threatened. Now it's too late.' He paused at the end of the tunnel, where there was another thick door, this time standing a little open. 'Welcome to my home.'

'Wow,' said Blix.

The room was the size of a cathedral, at least three hundred feet long, half that wide and perhaps two hundred feet tall. it curved slightly, following the side of the mountain. The wall to their left was blank, facing the rock, but the opposite had huge stained-glass windows at intervals. It was lit every few feet by the magical torches, which still weren't enough to fully illuminate the enormous space. It was completely empty. A marble floor made every step echo in the silence.

It was the ceiling that drew Blix's eye, and made her jaw drop. There were no pillars holding it up, only the arch of the ceiling itself. On that ceiling was an extraordinary painting. The night sky, covered in intricately rendered swathes of white stars, constellations, nebulae in vivid colours, galaxies so realistically depicted that Blix could sense the way they span. She had to concentrate quite hard to see that it was a painting; it was as if the temple had opened to embrace the cosmos.

'That's incredible,' she said, so awestruck she couldn’t think of anything else to say.

'This is the First Temple. The one the first brothers built when we came here. It's special.'

'Yes. Yes, it is. Sistine Chapel special. But this room is huge. How can this be hanging from a mountain? Is it magic?'

'No. I wouldn't walk through a building held up by magic if I had the choice, would you? The brothers were master builders. It took a long time.'

‘I believe it.’ Blix found it hard not to just stand and marvel at the sight. ‘This is just extraordinary. What am I looking at?'

'It's the universe as seen from here,' said Constant. 'Torchlight really doesn't do it justice. Every Brother that ever lived has stood in this placed and looked up. Here we experience a connection to the infinite.'

'It's ace. Is it all like this? Is there a pamphlet or something I can read? Nothing too god-bothery please, I'm C of E. I'll put money in the charity box, I swear.'

'We don't proselytise and we don't need money. The priests and lay brothers do that. Down below.'

'What do you do then?'

We protect me.

'We pray. And meditate.'

'Exciting life you lead,' said Kit. 'Well, glad though I am to not be hanging over certain death on the trail back there, ain't nothin' and no one here.'

Blix dragged her eyes away from the ceiling and looked around. 'I don't see any, um. I mean, I don't see any blood.'

'I don't think the battle came this far.' Constant walked into the echoing chamber. 'Brother Si... the brother who saved me said that the wolves were at the Fourth Temple.'

'That's where the climbing route leads,' said Kit, following him. 'It traverses around the mountain and under the Fourth Temple. That's the one with the picture of the mountain, right?'

Constant stopped dead. He looked at Kit for what seemed a very long time, his expression caught somewhere between uncertainty and suspicion. Then, very grudgingly, he said, 'I may owe you an apology.'

Kit hitched her thumbs through her belt loops. 'Not to me. Where does that door lead?'

'Through some antechambers and the old cells and then to the Second Temple. But... you should know that.'

'I'm an outdoors gal, kid. I get lost in a closet. Lead the way.'

They followed Constant through the temple, their footsteps the only sound other than the wind beyond the walls. The silence was dispiriting. Blix didn't know how many people had lived here, but as they moved into the living spaces of the Monastery she could feel their absence. The Monastery was a heart without its life's-blood.

The way passed unlit rooms. Blix caught glimpses of robes, books, prayer mats and neatly furled flags, along with other religious paraphernalia she didn't recognise. It felt like a church after the service had ended - sacraments and robes of office neatly put away for the next act of worship, worship that would now never happen.

The Temple complex was vast. Tunnels snaked deep into the rock, natural cracks and wholly manmade shafts branching and turning and exiting back out onto the open face of the mountain, where they met wooden bridges and shelves cut into the crag. Each path led to another temple more magnificent than the one before.

The Second Temple was decorated in flames, so realistic that it seemed they were in the middle of an explosion. The Third was dedicated to the sea, again so exactly painted that Blix expected the waves to crash over her at any moment. High in the vault she could just make out what appeared to be people in the water but there wasn't enough light to see more and she decided not to ask. Both rooms were on the scale of the First Temple and as empty of any other adornment. They showed no sign that fighting had taken place.

The Fourth Temple was the world around them; a masterpiece of landscape painting dominated by the looming presence of the Anvil. It was so accurate that Blix recognised places she had been, including, with a tiny thrill of fear, the stone circle she had arrived through.

Alone, she thought. *But not...*

The windows here were shattered. Glass shards strewn across the floor made clear that they'd been broken from the outside. Here and there on the floor were brown stains, dried and turning to dust.

Blix swallowed hard. 'Is that…?

'Mmm-hmm,' said Kit. Her pistol was in her hand again. 'But no bodies. You okay there, kid?'

Constant rubbed his head. 'Yes,' he said. 'I've seen blood before.' His tone was matter-of-fact once more. 'This is the Fourth Temple,' he continued. 'The seventeenth Great Father built it almost three thousand years ago, to complete the cycle. Brothers come here to feel a connection with the world. Being cut off is difficult sometimes. This reminds us of how the world sees us.'

Kit and Blix exchanged glances. Blix realised that giving them the temple tour must be Constant's way of displacing his anxiety. It gave him something to focus on other than the corpses of his brothers, that he expected to see but had not yet found.

As they left the Fourth Temple, Blix thought about what she had seen in each hall.

'This is your creation story, isn't it?'

Constant nodded absently. 'Part of it, yes. First the universe alone, the vault of heaven in the air. This world created by fire, shaped by flood, built from stone.'

'The four elements.'

'Yes. We're animists, and hesychasts of a kind, as the Christ religions understand the term. We believe that the timeless universe animates all things from within - a living connection with the Ultimate. The four cardinal elements are the most powerful expressions of this.'

'I understood that, apart from the big word. So, where next?'

'The Fifth Temple. The last.'

'What's in there?'

'You'll see.' He sounded unhappy again.

He led them down a short corridor and pushed open a door.

The Fifth Temple was much smaller than the others, almost on a human scale. It was a rectangular room with a dais at one end. Two doors led from the chamber. On the dais was a high-backed wooden chair, simply made but nonetheless a throne. It was covered by a baldachin of cloth-of-gold. Two enormous prayer wheels stood on either side of it, carved with images and writing in a language Blix didn't know.

Arranged on the walls of the room were dozens of full length framed portraits, again painted with exquisite artistry. Kindly-looking monks gazed out from the canvases, captured in poses of genuflection, meditation, contemplation and prayer. Several had their arms open toward the viewer, as though they might step out of the frame and embrace their brothers. All the paintings showed a lit candle. At the foot of each frame was a small brass plaque with a number etched into it.

'A lot of monks,' Blix observed.

'Seventy-one,' said Constant. 'The Great Fathers of the faith since the founding of it.'

Kit and Blix wanders around the room, look at the portraits. Blix peered at one, a serene-looking ancient with a shock of fluffy white hair. The plaque read *Twenty-nine.*

'They don't have names on them,' she said. 'How do you know who was who?'

Constant looked at his shoes. 'They all have the same name,' he replied.

'Here we are,' said Kit, from behind the chair. Blix went over to her.

'Yes, we are,' Constant agreed with a sigh, and joined them.

'Well, that was unexpected,' said Blix, staring up at the picture of Constant.

'Not to me,' said Kit. 'I seen him before.'

'You could have said.'

'I did say.' Kit thought back. 'You were asleep. He just don't listen.'

Blix peered at the plaque '"*Seventy-one."* So, you're Constant the seventy-first?'

'You might as well tell her,' said Kit, as Constant chewed his cheeks and remained silent. 'Ain't exactly a secret, now is it?'

Constant sighed again, then drew himself up.

'I am the Constant. Seventieth reincarnation of the First Father, founder of the Faith, and of those who came before. Vessel of the timeless universe. The essential self of the Ultimate. And a bunch of other crap.' He grimaced suddenly and massaged his forehead. 'Stay *down*,' he said.

'Pardon me?' said Blix

'Nothing. A headache.'

Blix glanced at the picture, then back at Constant. Neither looked very happy. Swearing was new too.

'You don't look like the Pope,' she said. 'You should have said. I would have bowed, or something. Curtsied. Not called you a bastard, certainty.'

'I hate all that stuff,' Constant muttered. 'I used to hide from it. Deep in the mountain where no one would say my name.' He looked around the room at the faces that lived in his memory. 'We all hate it, to begin with.'

'Reincarnation. Really? Properly?'

'Yes.'

'What's that like, then?'

Constant frowned as he considered an answer. 'What does reincarnation feel like? It feels like being punched in the back of the head for four thousand years. All these thoughts I didn't think elbowing for space in my mind. Not knowing whether I think something because *I* think it or because someone else did a long time ago. Not being wholly in charge of my emotions. Like being in a room full of people talking all at once, right in my face. It's hell.'

'That sounds difficult to cope with,' said Blix. *And explains a lot.* She was slightly shocked at how angry Constant sounded.

The boy sighed. 'I have ways of coping. I'm told it gets easier. I'm supposed to become more serene. Not sure when that's going to happen,' he added under his breath.

Blix found she was quite taken with the idea of Constant as a major religious figure. 'So, what do I call you then? Your Holiness? Your Grace? Archbishop?'

The boy looked mortified. 'Great Father. Please don't though. My name is Constant.'

'Sorry. I'm just teasing.' Blix put a thumb over her shoulder at the older portraits. 'That was their name too though, wasn't it? Did they have names before that? Like, that their mum and dad gave them?'

'Yes. Some of them lived full lives before they were Recognised as the Constant. Others were found as babies. Like me.'

'What was your name before, then?'

'I don't know,' said Constant quietly. 'I was hoping to ask my mother.'

Blix's jovial mood evaporated instantly. She wondered why she was acting as she was. Joking in what was almost certainly a tomb wasn't appropriate. She realised she felt disconnected from the pain and grief that Constant must be feeling, and didn't know why. To cover her confusion, she looked round for Kit and saw that she'd moved away. She was standing by one of the doors leading from the room, between Constants thirty-nine and forty. It was closed, but Kit was standing close to it, facing the opening edge. Every so often she put her head back slightly and breathed in.

'What are you doing?'

Kit glanced back at them. 'Do you smell that?'

Constant and Blix came over and sniffed the air.

'No,' said Blix. 'What am I supposed to be smelling?'

'It ain't good.'

Cautiously, Constant opened the door a crack. There was an unlit corridor beyond, its end lost in darkness.

Blix inhaled deeply. This time she smelled something - a faint whiff of something rancid and burnt. It smelled bad, but it felt worse.

'What is that?' she asked, fearing she knew the answer.

'What you think it is,' said Constant in a voice like flint. 'Burnt flesh.'

He rocked back and forth on his heels for a second. Then without another word he drew his sword and plunged into the corridor. He turned a corner and was gone.

'We should go after him,' said Blix, without moving. The charnel smell was growing stronger.

'Uh-huh,' said Kit, looking away. 'You know, I seen some things. Before now. Things I wish I'd never seen. You don't forget them.' She turned back to Blix. 'Maybe you should wait here a spell. No need to see this.'

Blix nodded and said 'No,' in the same instant. She tried to work out which she meant.

'No. Whatever it is, I can deal with it. He has to, so I can. We're all in this together, aren't we?'

'Yes.' Kit smiled gently. It was far from her usual manic grin and made her look... the thought *more human* popped into Blix's head. 'Yes, we are, kiddo. I suppose I should remember that. Come on then.'

They followed the corridor until it opened into a wide circular courtyard, open to the sky above and on three sides. A tall balustrade ran around the edge. There was no other exit.

Constant stood at the threshold, his sword hanging limply in his grasp.

A mound of corpses covered the centre of the courtyard, higher than Blix's head and ten or twelve yards across. The bodies were blackened and charred by some fierce flame, flesh turned to paper, shrivelled and drawn back, exposing white bone. Where faces were visible the mouths gaped obscenely or were twisted in a deathly rictus, and empty sockets stared into the next world, or nothingness. The stench was stomach turning. Greasy black smoke still rose from the pyre, curling into the sky.

'Jesus,' said Blix, but it was more reflexive than anything else. The hideous sight horrified but did not move her. It was a thought but not a response. *I'm in shock. This isn't a normal reaction. I must be in shock.* The word *alone* flitted through her mind. *I shouldn't have to deal with this alone. I wish mum and dad were here. I wish -*

But there was nothing else. There was no one else.

'This is the Sanctum,' said Constant, his voice trembling - with anger, Blix concluded. 'This was our holiest place. A flame burned here for four thousand years without going out. It symbolised eternity.' He pointed to the pile of bodies. 'It's under there.'

'Constant, I'm so sorry,' Blix began, but the boy made a dismissive gesture with his free hand.

'There's no need to be sorry. You didn't do this. When I find the ones who did, they *will* be sorry.'

'*Why* would they do this?' said Kit under her breath. 'It makes no goddamn sense.'

'It's a message,' said Constant. 'A message for me. Someone is making a point. They knew I'd come back here and see this.'

'What message?' said Kit incredulously.

'I would have thought it was obvious,' the boy replied. 'What does it mean when you smother an eternal flame with the bodies of the dead? It means everything is coming to an end. Life is coming to an end. Someone is telling me the fire is going out. That the Constant falters.'

He sheathed his sword and turned on his heel. 'But they're wrong. The fire never goes out,' he spat. 'The Constant never falters. Nor will I. Not while I'm alive.'

Blix saw the tears streaming down his face, and looked away.

Kit and Blix followed Constant back into the Fifth Temple. They found him leaning against the throne, head bowed, panting as if he'd just run for miles. Blix started to go over to him, but Kit held her back, shaking her head. 'Give him a moment.'

Alone, thought Blix. *He's completely alone. Everyone he's ever known is dead. Except us.*

A flash of memory pierced her reverie; a few strands of hair on a patch of blackened flesh, clinging to a bare skull. A sudden burst of horror made her shudder. It made her feel dirty to have seen it. The emotion arrived and was gone again in a second.

'I need to get clean,' she whispered to Kit.

Constant straightened up suddenly. 'There's a bathtub in my apartments. You can use that.'

Blix winced. *Shit. Bloody echo chamber.* 'Constant, I-'

Constant cut her off. 'It's okay. I'm okay. Follow me.'

He walked purposefully toward the door they hadn't used, his face hard and emotionless. He led them through tunnels and up a staircase cut from the rock. He walked so quickly and turned so often that Blix lost her sense of direction. The Monastery was a labyrinth, carved through the mountain by four thousand years of tireless hands.

Eventually Constant stopped at an ornate door and roughly shoved it open. The room beyond was beautiful. Richly embroidered tapestries hung from the marbled walls, which were themselves intricately carved with symbols that Blix couldn't decipher. Huge windows filled one wall. A very large four-poster bed still looked tiny in the space. It was the kind of room Blix could imagine would be in Buckingham Palace - ancient and august, not so much lived in as looked after.

'Wow. Do you live here?'

'No. I don't like it. The bath is in the next room. It should be suitable. There's a cistern for water and a fireplace and kettle to heat it. If you're hungry there's a kitchen with a larder further down the corridor. Most of the food should be all right. You should sleep too. Stay around here. Don't go exploring.'

He turned to leave. 'Where are you going?' asked Blix.

'I have to do something.'

'What?'

Constant took a ragged breath and Blix got a sudden glimpse of fury, of barely mastered rage. He shut his eyes for a moment and said something under his breath. The shape of the words seemed strangely familiar to Blix, even though she couldn't make out what he was saying. She wondered if he was counting to ten.

He opened his eyes and stared at her; calmer, but not much.

'That wasn't everyone.'

'Excuse me?'

'The bodies in the Sanctum. There weren't enough. Not nearly. I'm going to look for the rest.'

'We'll come with you,' said Blix.

'I don't want you too.' He ducked back through the doorway before Blix could say anything more.

'Constant! Come back! Nuts.' Blix looked down the corridor, but Constant was nowhere to be seen. A dozen more doors opened off it. There was nothing to show which he'd taken. She turned back to Kit.

'We need to go after him!'

'We need to respect his wishes,' said Kit sagely. 'Which is ironic, all things considered. Boy has to grieve in his own way. He don't want us around for a while, that's okay. Probably for the best right now.'

'There could be monsters here!'

'Maybe, maybe not. He thinks otherwise, and you know, it's getting so I think I agree with him. We announced ourselves, but no one came looking to see who was here. He's got that big sword, he can look after himself.'

'So, we just let him storm off. After he saw that. What if he does something stupid?'

'If you mean what I think you mean, he ain't the kind. Anyway, you saw the pictures. He'd just come back.'

Blix looked at her suspiciously. 'Was that a joke?'

'Kinda. A stupid one. Speaking of stupid things though I just gotta catch him about one thing before he disappears. Wait here a second, kiddo, I'll be right back.'

'But you just said…!' Blix started to object, but Kit was gone. 'Not you too! Damn it! I…'

I don't want to be alone.

A voice screamed in Constant's mind as he pounded down the tunnel.

Kill every werewolf ever born, strip the flesh from their bones, flay their hides, kill them, kill them for what they've done!

'Yes,' said Constant out loud. 'You're right. Kill them all. Kill them *now.'*

'Talking to yourself, kid?'

The sword was in Constant's hand before he knew it. He turned in the same moment and thrust forward, the blade straight above his shoulders, sure to take the werewolf in the throat fast and clean.

But Kit was faster. She stepped inside the blade and forward and hooked his arm away sharply with hers. The sword rang awkwardly against the wall and skittered from his grasp. He felt cold gunmetal on his skin as she pressed the pistol hard under his chin.

'Snap out of it kid, I don't want to have to ventilate you,' she said pleasantly.

Constant stared at her wild-eyed, then groaned and held his head in his hands. 'I could have killed you.'

'Nope,' said Kit. 'But try not to do it again anyways.'

He reeled away, clutching at the wall for support. 'I'm sorry,' he said eventually. 'That wasn't me.'

'I get it,' she said, holstering the gun. 'You got a lot on your mind. A lot *in* your mind. I won't get in the way. You gotta do something first though. Let her go.'

'What?' said Constant, confused.

'The girl. You know? You don't know. Well, shit. I don't know if that makes it better or worse.'

'I'm sorry?'

'You should be. And I figure you will be when she realises. You're holding her. With your mind. Now that I seen it I can see it clearly. When you did that calm-down spell on her, you took charge and you ain't stopped. I was watching her just now when you said the words, she was saying them right along with you. It's wrong. She's not yours. Let her go.'

'I'm not,' Constant began, but even as the words formed in his mouth he realised that he was. It was as though the words reached out of his mind and off into the distance, saying themselves in his voice until the refrain was pick up by another's. Blix's voice. Now that he could see it, he could see it clearly.

'Oh *no.*' He closed his eyes. 'I don't know...' He imagined himself cutting a thread, and felt the ribbon of magic between Blix and himself dissolve into nothing. 'Okay. I think.' He opened his eyes. 'I had no idea.'

'Yeah. That's about the only thing saving you from an ass-kicking right now. Which would be easy seeing as you're mostly an asshole.'

'I've never done this before,' said Constant miserably. 'People, I mean. The brothers, yes, but, others... you're the first I've ever met. I don't know how.'

'Learn faster.'

'Will she be very angry?'

'I'm angry, kid. She'll be furious. And she'll be right to be. You can't mess with people's heads. You can't take away their choice.'

'I thought I was doing the right thing!'

'Boys always do.'

Constant flushed scarlet and looked around him, anywhere but at Kit. He collected himself. 'I don't know what happens now. When I stop using the words… it's like everything happens at once. All my lives. For her… I don't know. It might be bad. You'll need to help her through it.'

'I'll take care of her. Go on about your business. Don't come back tonight. You might have a price to pay tomorrow. You ready for that?'

Constant jerked his head in uncertain acquiescence.

'Good. Maybe you ain't wholly mostly an asshole.'

She turned and went back the way she'd come, but then stopped.

'Hey, kid,' she said without looking back.

'Yes?'

'Let yourself go too.'

As if it matters. Find the wolves, kill every one of them

'You're not me,' Constant mumbled, careening off a wall as he stumbled along the tunnels beneath the mountain. Anguish piled on anger. Constant wanted to kill. The anger was his, but Ysir's memory brought rage. The memory of the young Ysir was so much more powerful than the old Constant he became. They were the same person. But there was something different. The younger version seemed whole, somehow.

His feet had walked the corridors of the Monastery for almost six dozen lifetimes. They carried him without him thinking about the way. Through tunnels and chambers, into halls and turrets and cellars, he followed the invisible path of his life, of his lives.

There was blood. The Hall of Swords was covered in it, now dried and flaking under foot. The racks of blades were overturned, steel swords scattered across the floor. There were dead werewolves here, and elsewhere in the living quarters. Some brothers had found silver. But of the brothers or their bodies there was no sign.

Eventually he realised where his feet were not taking him. He turned and followed the path to the novice cells and the kitchens.

His cell was untouched. He found fresh clothing and discarded the torn robe. The large slit from shoulder to waist, hastily repaired with a few stitches, reminded him how close to death he'd come at the cottage. The bed sheets lay where he had thrown them off. A spot of red marred the white.

Constant made his way to the kitchens. A knot of fear twisted his insides as he approached. The door was broken in. The table on which Brother Simon had sketched the chimney in flour was upended, plates and food scattered across the floor. But of Simon himself there was no sign beyond a smear of blood where he had rested. It was not enough.

Constant sat on the floor, back against a wall, and thought about what this meant. Grief, tiredness, fear and anger roiled within him, breaking on his mind like a storm tide against a sea wall. He sat impassively, refusing to think of the words, ignoring the sorrow of generations that welled up from his memory, each voice crying for a home violated, a family destroyed. Voices screaming for vengeance.

Minutes passed, and turned into hours. Then abruptly he got to his feet and left the kitchen, retracing his steps through the Monastery until he was once again at the Sanctum. He stared at the pile of corpses until the revulsion and urge to vomit or run felt bearable. The screaming in his mind was unbearable.

I have seen dead like this before. Many times, over many lives. Shambhala is a bad place. I can't act if I can't think. I have to do what I have to do.

Saying his words over and over, Constant began to pull out the bodies.

The bathtub was not at all the Top Monk wallowing pool Blix had vaguely imagined. She looked critically at the shallow, high-backed wooden sitting tub. A thick towel hung over the edge.

Just my luck to get dragged across the universe to a world where they're six hundred years off inventing the jacuzzi, she thought. 'There's no bloody reason why they couldn't have,' she said out loud, as she dragged the tub in front of the fireplace. 'Probably think enjoying baths is a sin, or something.'

The tiny tub seemed even smaller in the vast room, and felt exposed. The door had a latch but not a lock. Blix noticed a large dressing screen folded against the wall near the enormous bed. She carried it over and opened it around the bath. The frame was rich, dark wood. The three panels were made of what seemed to be laminated paper, painted with what Blix assumed were significant religious scenes.

In each picture a monk pointed at someone. On the first panel, it was a knight in full armour on horseback, riding from an immense mountain fortress. In the second, a young man with a drooping moustache, scything through golden wheat. In the third, a baby at its mother's breast by a river. Blix wondered if she was reading them backwards. No one looked terribly pleased to see the monk. The monk looked positively beatific. Whatever their meaning, they were incredibly detailed, rich and lifelike, as the temple ceilings had been. Whatever Shambhala lacked in hygiene technology, it made up for in artistry.

Blix got a fire going and drew some water into a large kettle. As she waited for it to heat up she wondered again at her lack of reaction to the horrific scene in the Sanctum. It still barely registered with her. She did though feel very strange and slightly woozy. *Tiredness*, she thought, but there was something else to it too. It was as if she was being gently but insistently pulled sideways, or separated. It was the oddest feeling.

The bath was bliss. Monastery soap lathered as well as secular suds and the cleaner Blix got, the more human she felt. After a while she slid as deep into the tub as she could, arms and legs splayed over the sides. She was just able to immerse her head without the other end making an exhibition of itself. That thought appeared in Blix's mind in her mother's voice, which made her giggle underwater, but it also reminded her that she'd been gone for over two days.

God, Mum and Dad. They must be worried sick. What must they think? The police must be combing the countryside for us.

Us?

Blix gasped, then struggled upright, coughing violently. She clutched at her chest. It felt like she'd been stabbed by an imaginary knife, cutting her in two.

What just happened? I thought... I thought... I can't remember what I thought.

'You okay, kiddo?' said Kit. Blix could see the shape of her through the screen.

'Yes! Yes, I'm fine. Just inhaled some water. I'm fine.'

'Glad to hear it. I suppose it'd be hard to drown in that tiny tub. Although if you need mouth to mouth, I'm your gal.'

Blix blushed. Then she said, 'Hold on. How do you know how big the bath is? Did you peek around the screen?' Her blush intensified.

'Who, me? No. No, no, no. Hardly at all.'

'Kit!'

'Almost not at all, honest injun. Anyway, if you were worried about that, maybe you shoulda screened out the mirror?'

For the first time Blix noticed a long, silvered mirror on the wall she was facing, opposite the bed. The image was a little distorted, but Kit was clearly visible. She was grinning.

Blix immediately sank as far as she could and drew her knees up to her chest. 'Arrgh! Is everyone I meet in this godforsaken place going to see me naked? Look away!'

'What's the matter? I seen breasts before. Quite a few, now I come to think about it. Daddy always said there was nothing like seeing a pretty girl in the buff to put a smile on your face. Can't say he was wrong.' The grin widened. 'Want me to scrub your back?'

The way she said it made Blix go all squishy inside, a sensation which went head-to-head with mortifying embarrassment and lost handily.

'No, God, bloody stop it, I said don't look!'

Kit laughed and turned her back. Blix grabbed for the towel.

Something sailed over the screen and landed on the floor. It was a robe, an unattractive brown and three sizes too big. She wrapped herself in it.

Kit was perched on the end of the bed, legs swinging back and forth, a winsome look on her face.

'Um,' said Blix nervously. She sat down on the bed a good distance away from Kit. 'Look, I'm just going to come right out and say this, okay? You're, like, um, really nice and, um, incredibly attractive -'

'Thanks!'

'- and I really, like, totally would, really, but, I've only just met you and things have been *really* weird and, um, I'm kind of, you know, a virgin, so, um, maybe I say no, okay? Um.'

'Oh, that.' Kit shook her head. 'That ain't why I'm here, kiddo.'

'So, I'm just going to go curl up in a corner and die of embarrassment now,' Blix continued, cringing.

Kit laughed brightly. 'Don't sweat it, kiddo.' An eyebrow flicked upward archly. 'Maybe later we'll see about that last bit. In the meantime, I just wanted to ask you something. Are you okay?'

'I feel terrible,' said Blix.

'I don't know why I said that,' said Blix a moment later. 'I feel fine. Shockingly embarrassed, but fine.'

'Is that so.' Kit stopped swinging and looked directly at her. 'Mind if we talk about a couple of things?'

'Okay,' said Blix, not sure where this was going.

'How did you get here?'

That was a surprise. Blix was slightly nonplussed. 'We walked. Then we got the lift. You were there.'

'I meant, how did you get to Shambhala?'

'You know. I told you.'

'Tell me again,' said Kit. There was an insistent tone in her voice that made Blix feel uncertain and very nervous.

'Long story, but to cut it short I was sort of kidnapped. By my teacher and his mate. Dragged across the universe to God knows where, for God knows what reason. And here we are.'

'Hell of a tale, when you put it like that,' said Kit. 'Why do you put it like that, kiddo?'

'What? I don't underst-'

'Is that really what happened?

'Y-'

'Are you *sure*?'

As she said the word Blix suddenly had a shock of memory that ran through like a physical pain. Her whole left side was suddenly in agony.

'God, Blix, are you there?' her sister cried.

'Yes,' she said. 'I - '

Blix leapt up from the bed as though she'd been scalded. 'What the actual f-'

'Katy. What the actual fuck just happened?'

Blix clutched her head. It felt like it was about to split in two. 'Kit, what's happening?' she said in a shaking voice.

'What the fuck did you do, Amelia?'

Blix suddenly felt that there was a great wound in her mind, a pit carved into her from which something had been removed without her knowing and which had been healed against her will. Then all at once she knew what was missing. A lifetime of memories, shoved aside, blanked out, made invisible, were suddenly *there,* bursting all at once into her consciousness.

'Katy?' she said, and collapsed.

Before she could hit the floor, Kit was there to catch her, lowering her and cradling her gently as she shook.

'How could... how could I forget?' Blix stammered, looking up into Kit's kind, sad face. 'How could I forget her?'

'Oh honey,' said Kit, 'I got some bad news. You ain't been yourself. You had a terrible thing done to you, and the boy, he tried to make it right. But he didn't help, he just made it worse.'

'C- Constant? said Blix weakly, confused. 'Constant did this to me?'

'He didn't mean to. He was trying to help you. Bad things happened. He tried to help you cope. He made you put away the bad things, but he made you put away too much. He's stopped now. You'll remember her again. But that means the bad things come back too. All at once. And much worse now. All the fear and pain, you gotta feel that now, all at the same time. But don't worry. I'm gonna hold you 'til it's over.'

And then in front of her was a wolf, pushing forward.

'I'm going to fuck you 'til you're dead inside, bitch.'

Blix screamed.

Constant stood listlessly by the bathing pool and wondered how he'd got there. The large communal baths were deep in the mountain, lit by a multitude of tallow candles glued to the walls by generations of monks. The stubs now flickered with Constant's magical light, burning but not consuming the last of the render. The pool was usually steaming, but the fires which heated it had died. The brothers who tended them were gone, presumably joining their fellows on their next turn of the wheel.

Why am I here? he thought. *I'm exhausted. I should go to bed.*

His hands felt greasy. He looked down at them, and saw the black char and the redness, and the blood and ichor covering his tunic.

'Oh. Yes,' he said.

Constant toppled into the icy water.

Constant dreamed.

In my dream, I am walking through a forest toward a mountain. I hope I am. When I was child I saw it in a dream I think was a vision. Since that day, I have walked toward it. As I have walked I have spoken of the Constant to others. Some of them now walk with me. Several hundred men and women trail in our wake. I have forged ahead with my most devoted brothers, twenty men. They recognise something in me that the rest believe but do not see. Something I do not see myself. Something that they cannot readily explain, though I have asked. It is the way, they say. We see the way. We recognise it.

They follow as I walk it.

The ground has risen with us for days, but the weather has been so foul the mountains have been invisible behind rain clouds even when we might have glimpsed them. My brothers look cold and weary, but my heart rejoices. I am almost home.

In my dream, we break through the treeline and it is there, *suddenly, profoundly there, towering into the heavens. I sink to my knees, overwhelmed by the sight,*

'This is it,' I tell the brothers. 'This is the place in my vision. We will build our temple there. As high as we can climb.'

'We can't climb that,' says a brother. He is called Mason, for his trade. He does not express doubt; no man here doubts me. He speaks the truth as he sees it. I encourage this.

'There is a way,' I say. I take the bloodstone from my pouch and show it to him. He knows what it is. Everyone understands what it can do.

'There is a way,' I say again. 'Not all will take it. But for those who do, there is no way down. I am the path that I walk as I am he that walks it, and yet I choose the path I walk. I do not compel others to walk with me. Consider your choice carefully.'

The man simply says, 'Father, we have considered.'

In my dream, I embrace him and the brethren. I tell them to return to the others and bring them here. I remain to contemplate the future. The strange, flat-headed mountain looms above me. It disappears into the sky. It is terrifying.

'I will be safe here,' I say to myself. I do not know why. I look at the bloodstone once more. 'Keep me safe,' I say. I do not sound like myself when I say it.

Now there is a boy here I do not recognise.

'It kept us safe,' *he says.* 'Us. That's the answer you're looking for. That's why it didn't protect them. You won't remember when you wake up. I'm sorry. You won't remember that either, but it's true.'

In my dream, he approaches me, He looks sad.

'I've been thinking about our situation,' *he says.* 'The Writing is not clear about much except the consequence of doing nothing. We have to try. Believe me when I tell you I would rather stay here alone with you in this tomb than do this. We have no choice. We're going to have to leave this world. And we need the others. You can make it look like you're helping the girl and still do what we must. You *will* be helping her. Just don't tell them the truth. They won't follow you if you do. They'll find out, there's no choice in that. We need to be well on our way before they do. No turning back. No other ways. We go the way we need to. Examine the books. Consult the map. Follow the way.'

In my dream, the boy looks at me like a father who sees his son grieve. I think he will embrace me, but he does not touch me.

'We'll talk again soon,' *he says.* 'In the meantime, there's something you need to do. Wake up.'

Constant did not remember the boy when he woke up.

Constant came awake lying on the side of the pool, soaked through and freezing. He cried like a baby.

Chapter Seventeen: Lies

It was the hour after dawn when Constant returned to his apartments. The door was closed. Kit McCoy sat on the flagstones in the narrow corridor outside, lounging, arms folded, against a door-jamb, one foot up against the opposite wall.

'Figured you'd show up about now,' she said lazily. 'You okay, kid? You look a little drawn. By which I mean, sheets look as white as you, know what I'm saying?'

Constant nodded steadily, 'I was looking for a friend,' he said.

Kit considered that information, tipping her head slightly. She looked Constant up and down, taking in the fresh robes, damp hair and well-scrubbed hands. 'Did you find him?' she asked.

'No.'

'Mmm-hmm. Where can he be, if he ain't here?'

'That is a very good question,' said Constant severely. 'To which I *will* have an answer. 'Have you been out here all night?' he asked.

'A few hours, maybe.'

He raised his eyes to the door. 'I thought you'd be in there. How... how is she?'

'Tougher than she looks. Child had a bad night. A lot of stuff came out all at once.'

Constant sighed heavily. Then he sat down opposite Kit. 'I had a bad night too. I don't weigh them against each other,' he added.

'You're pretty tough as well, kid.'

'I don't know what I am any more,' Constant replied, looking away. 'I am a child though. I know that. I'm twelve. It's important that I remember that.' He looked back. 'Was it really bad?'

'Yes. She came through it. Seems to remember what she should. After it was done she was pretty beat. I figured I'd step out. Otherwise folks might talk, you know how they do.'

'Not really. You stood guard?'

'Sat, mostly. I'm about convinced you're right about us being alone up here, but, hey, you've been wrong before.'

Constant frowned. 'Don't you ever slee-' he began, but stopped as the door suddenly jerked open. Constant scrambled to his feet as Blix stormed into the corridor.

'I'm so-' he said, but got no further. Blix slapped him hard across the face, so hard he staggered.

'You bastard!' she screamed, and slapped him again.

'I'm sorry. I didn't mean to. I didn't know.'

'You absolute bastard,' said Blix furiously. 'How dare you? How dare you?'

'I'm sorry,' said Constant miserably. 'You were in such a bad way, and we needed to leave. I thought I was helping.'

Blix looked incredulously at him, anger mottling her cheeks. 'How could you *possibly* think that? You wiped my mind! How could that help me?'

'It doesn't work like that! Or it's not supposed to. The magic I used on you, I use it myself all the time. It's just supposed to calm you. I think I must have used it so often for so long that it felt like nothing. Weak. But it's not.' He was trembling with emotion. 'I'm sorry,' he said, pathetically.

Blix snorted contemptuously. 'That's it? That's what you've got to say for yourself? Have you any idea what you did? *I almost forgot her.* Do you know what it feels like to remember you'd forgotten half of yourself? Let me enlighten you. It feels terrible. You utter shit.'

Constant looked helplessly at her. Then he fell to his knees in front of her, raised his arms high and wide and said, 'For any hurt I have caused you, for any fault or sorrow, I ask forgiveness. My soul is yours.'

'Are you fucking kidding me? How I feel is not about you! How I feel is not trivial! Piss off.'

Blix turned and went back into the room, slamming the door shut as hard as she could. Thick puffs of dust showered from the frame.

'Damn, that shook the mountain,' said Kit, who hadn't moved at all during Blix's outburst. She brushed a dust fall from one shoulder and eased herself to her feet. 'So, you know you deserved all of that, don't you? That and more.'

'Yes,' said Constant. 'I should have known. Magic never helps. It only hurts.'

'*Stop fucking saying that!*' screamed Blix through the door. Then footsteps, and another door slamming further inside the rooms.

'I think just about everything you do or say is gonna be wrong for a while,' Kit said laconically. 'If you're lucky, not forever. Assuming you stop doing and saying dumbass things. For now, leave her be.'

'I have to make this right.' Constant was fairly shaking with the stress of it. 'I have to fix this.'

Kit sighed. 'Didn't you listen last night? Women are not things for you break or fix, kid. She's a person. She'll fix herself. You fix you. Your decisions aren't magic's fault kid, they're on you.'

Constant nodded firmly, but his eyes were elsewhere, seeing something inside that propelled him up off his knees. 'There's something I can do.'

Kit raised an eyebrow. 'You're not going to understand this are you. Okay. Don't keep it to yourself, kid.'

'I can keep my promise,' said Constant simply. 'I promised I would help her get her sister back. I will.'

Constant suddenly realised how shaky he was. He gathered himself. The words came to him, but he dismissed them. They just seemed wrong. 'I'm going to the library. I could be some time. Come and find me later if you want to.'

'Whatever you say.' Kit watched him for a moment as he marched determinedly along the corridor. 'Hey, kid. Don't get her hopes up.'

She didn't forgive me.

Constant padded through the tunnels once more, outwardly resolute but in turmoil inside.

She didn't forgive me. My soul is hers.

Deep in his mind a part of him weighed the fact that he had saved Blix's life against what he had done to her memory and found the balance tipped far against him. It made him feel sick.

Some Shambhalhai believed fervently in life debts. More than a few brothers had entered the Monastery to clear theirs. A few of his antecedents floated to the surface of his memory to affirm the moral rightness of this. He had said the Penance his entire life, since he'd learned to talk. The words, and what they implied, were part of him.

My soul is hers.

Suddenly the swirl of memories became too much. Constant leaned heavily on the wall and said his words until they were under control again. *At least that seems to be working properly again. That's something.*

The library was a high-ceilinged room without windows, deep inside the mountain. Shafts sunk through the rock walls brought air and a weak light from outside. Otherwise it was gloomy and shadowed, even with the handful of torches lit by Constant's magic, which still burned despite the hours since his spell. *Books like darkness*, Constant thought. *Magic likes darkness.*

The library was large by the standards of Shambhala, although Constant knew it was dwarfed by the great libraries on other worlds. At one time it had received a copy of every book written in Shambhalhai and many other tongues, whatever books were circulating across the worlds. That had ended when the last gate closed. Writing and copying were uncommon these days. The darkness encroaching on Shambhalhai humankind left little time for letters. Still, the Library was vast, many thousands of handwritten and illuminated tomes, scrolls and sheaves of parchment held in stacks of shelves. There was a system to their ordering, but Constant didn't know it. There had always been a brother around who did.

Well, perhaps I used to know, he thought. He found a chair and took a few deep breaths, then closed his eyes and searched his memories.

My name is Darcen Ysir.

'Piss off,' said Constant aloud. The words felt strange in his mouth and echoed guiltily around the hall. There hadn't been much call for swearing in the monastic life. Blix was better at it.

'I don't need any killers now, thank you,' he continued more primly. 'One of you who knew about books and was really good at thinking, let's have you out instead.' He hunted through the recesses of his subconscious mind a while. Eventually he found the shape of a memory which felt right and hauled it to the surface.

Palden Ngapoi? A local boy. They even told you your name. I guess someone took the trouble to ask it. Okay then. What do you know?

Constant sat motionless for a few moments as he remembered the man he had once been. Then he padded through the shelves until he found one which was now strangely familiar and began taking down books.

Blix paced around the room, shaking with anger.

'I ought to kick his head in,' she said again.

Kit was lying on the bed, hands behind her head, eyes closed. 'You've been at this for hours, kiddo,' she said without opening then.

'I'm *angry*.'

'As a matter of fact, you ain't,' said Kit. 'Well. You are. And rightly so! But that's not why you're making holes in the rug.'

Blix stopped. 'Oh, make sense, woman.' she said nastily. She resumed pacing.

Kit opened an eye lazily. 'I *am* a woman!' she said, sitting up. 'Glad you noticed. And I do make sense, to those that have sense to listen.'

'I am listening. To you. Where is he? Why isn't here begging my forgiveness?'

'He tried that. You socked him, remember?'

'Don't ask me if I remember things. And he should try harder.'

'Kit smiled gently. 'You feel like you got super-strength emotions sloshing about inside you like nitroglycerin, and your bottle is gettin' all shook up. Only natural you want to go kaboom at the kid. And you know I felt that too. But now I've thought on it, I can see he's gotta point. He's twelve.'

'He's four thousand and twelve if you believe him. It's his bloody magic. He should have known!'

'Yep, he should have. But he didn't. I think there's a lot he don't know. The more I see of this place, the more I think that these monks ain't done right by him.'

'That's an excuse. Some things you shouldn't have to be told. He's responsible. I don't care what the monks did or didn't do.'

'And that's your right. I ain't taking his side. I'm on your side. Thing is, he thinks he's on your side too. He was trying to help. Still is, as a matter of fact.'

'What a load of crap,' said Blix heatedly, turning toward Kit ready to argue. 'I-' she began, then stopped. 'Wait a minute. What do you mean, he's still trying to help me?'

'Not more magic, if that's what you're worried about. After you blackened his eye he said he was going to keep his promise to help find your sister. He's in the library.'

'What's he doing there?'

Kit gave an airy little wave with one hand. 'I don't know kiddo. Book stuff. Maybe there's a book there that'll tell us what the hell's going on here.'

Blix's eyes widened suddenly, then narrowed into a furious scowl. 'He *knows* what's going on,' she said. 'In the cottage, he knew. I *remember*.'

Blix grabbed Katy's bag and half-ran to the door. Kit swivelled off the bed. 'Where're you going?' she asked. 'And why are you taking that?'

'I'm going to the library. I'm going to hit Constant until he tells the truth. I'm taking the doombag because I'm never leaving it behind. She'll want it back.'

Kit half-frowned and squinted at the same time, scratched her ear and looked away. 'Huh. Well, I enjoy a good beating as much as the next gal. Maybe I'll tag along.'

It took Kit and Blix some time to find the library. After a few wrong turns and dead ends they finally stumbled upon it when Kit remarked that the air down one corridor smelled of dead trees.

Constant wasn't there. Instead there was a large arrow chalked on the flagstones with 'THIS WAY' written next to it in the strange runic language that Blix could now read easily. It pointed through an archway and down yet another corridor.

'Guess he's expecting us,' said Kit.

'He won't be expecting my boot,' said Blix crossly.

Constant heard Blix and Kit coming.

How much do I tell them? Do I have to lie?

The women stopped on the threshold, taking in the scene. A large oval room with an immensely high ceiling, built onto the mountain. Round clear-glass windows let light in. Here and there around the room there were cabinets and chests, some in disarray, their contents spilled across the floor. The battle had clearly reached this far and, for the monks who had made a stand, had just as clearly ended there. Blood stained the floor and lay in streaks toward the door where the bodies had been dragged out.

Near the door, books and scrolls were strewn haphazardly across the flags and piled against the wall. Some were broken at the spine and had pages torn out. A small stack of parchment was held in place by a stone the size of a fist. A couple of heavy wooden chairs had been dragged across the room in front of them.

'I'm up here,' he called as they entered.

'What are you- good God!'

How much do I tell them? Do I have to lie?

Constant grinned, wondering if it looked as forced as it felt. 'Good, isn't it?'

He stood near the top of a very long ladder. As Blix and Kit came further into the room they saw that the entire wall was a giant map - not of the world, but of worlds.

There were hundreds of them. Circles and pairs of circles, ranging in size from a dinner plate to two or three yards in diameter, each describing, in rich colour and beautifully realised detail, worlds beyond the stars. The void between them was inked in a midnight blue that seemed to sink into the wall, giving the whole the illusion of three dimensions. Stylised stars dotted the infinite night. Near the bottom ragged splashes of blood added colour of a more recent wash.

Blix stared in wonder at the mural. The was a world-circle at head height, at the bottom left of the picture, its name written in runes next to it. 'Tian,' she read out loud.

She traced the outline of a strange continent with her finger. The line of the coast trailed away as it reached the top of the map.

'I've seen drawing like this,' she said. 'On old maps of America or Australia before the whole land had been discovered.'

In the better-defined areas of the map there were several black dots. Thin lines left each dot, crossing the painting to connect with dots on other worlds. Some worlds only had a few dots and lines. Others had many more. Earth, the largest of the circles, in the centre of the map, was so covered with them that the landscape underneath was almost invisible from the ground. Overlaying it all was a thin, straight line of white string, a recent addition to the scheme. It curled around pins pushed into worlds here and there, criss-crossing itself several times, like the web of a drunken spider.

'Catch,' said Constant, throwing something at them. A ball of string sailed through the air into Blix's automatically outstretched hand.

'What are you doing?' she asked.

'Planning,' said Constant, in a determined voice. 'Planning is key.'

'Planning what?'

'I'll come down.'

As Constant carefully descended, Blix's eye returned to the Tian map. The dots had tiny writing next to them.

'Fire-Mouth of Suì Rén,' she read on the nearest one. '2d/g. 1d/l.' She followed the line off-world, rising diagonally, avoiding other worlds to disappear into the impossible-to-distinguish lines crossing Earth.

'It leads to China,' said Constant, stepping off the bottom rung. 'Somewhere near Mount Song. Have you been there?'

'China is on the other side of the world from England. And it's Communist. You can't just go there.'

'What's - no, it's not important. It's a place with a mountain with a gate. The gate is one of the very oldest. Ten thousand years at least. The mural is almost three thousand years old.'

'I'm not impressed by old things,' sniffed Blix. 'All it means is no one got rid of them when they should have. Speaking of which.' She eyed Constant disdainfully. 'I hear you're supposed to be helping me. You can stick your help up your-'

'Pretty picture you got here,' said Kit loudly, standing back to take it all in. 'I seen maps like this before, but nothin' like this.'

'The artistic impulse and the religious one are closely related,' said Constant, not taking his eyes off Blix. The girl fumed for a moment and scowled at Constant. Then she too found her gaze drawn again to the monumental map. As she did so her anger dissipated slightly, sucked into the depths of the painted darkness.

'Yeah, okay, it's pretty. I get that it's a gate map. But -'

'It shows which gate leads to which from world to world,' Constant interrupted eagerly. 'Look, there's Shambhala. You can follow a line from the circle you arrived through to the one you entered on Ear-'

'*But it's wrong,'* Blix said, glaring at Constant, who shut up immediately. 'Wrong and strange,' she continued. She pointed to Earth. 'Why are we in the middle? We're on Shambhala, why is that not the centre of the universe for you lot? And why is Earth so large and detailed compared to the others?' She squinted, and turned her head sideways. 'Why is it the wrong way up? It's on its side, what's going on there? And why is half of it missing? Where's the US? And South America?' She frowned. 'What am I looking at?'

'Earth is in the middle because Earth is the nexus. Not all gates point to Earth, not by a long way, but there are more on Earth than anywhere else.' He considered the map and rubbing his forehead absently. 'I don't know what you mean by the rest. What's the right way up for an object in the universe? This map is how Earthmen draw maps, isn't it? Jerusalem at the centre, all distances measured from there. What's a US? America? You said that word before.' He turned to Kit. 'That's where you're from isn't it? Is it a new-discovered world? I thought you were from Earth.'

Kit laughed. 'A new world. You could say that. I always wondered why they called it that. Guess it was a joke.'

'There have been some changes,' said Blix firmly. 'They aren't important. What do these letters and numbers mean? "2d/g" and that?'

'That's a very long conversation,' said Constant, smiling.

'Then we're bloody well going to have it, you miserable sod,' she said sharply, pointing at a startled Constant. 'It's time you told us what the hell is going on. No pissing about this time. Spill the sodding beans.'

How much do I tell them? Do I have to lie?

'I don't know what you mean,' he said, but Blix shook her head violently.

'Bollocks. I don't believe it. You know more than you're letting on.' She jabbed her finger at Constant again. 'I remember. The other night, in the cottage, when we were talking, you went mental when I told you what Echmoth said in the circle. You know what he's doing, bloody tell me or I'll duff you up, no joke.' She crossed her arms and redirected the scowl at him.

'Look, I promise you,' Constant began. Unthinkingly he reached out to touch Blix but found his hand intercepted by Kit McCoy, unexpectedly beside him, who gently steered it away.

'Let the lady say her piece, son,' she said, and the warning was as clear as a bell to Constant's ears. He stepped back sharply, shock evident on his face.

'I didn't! I wasn't going to!' he said, horrified.

'It's okay. I know. But you need to tell us what *you* know. Seems to me you got something big on your mind. Planning, yes? I get it. You could use some help, I figure.'

'People better start telling me what they get or I'm going to bloody well lay waste,' said Blix, fuming. 'You *promised*. You promised me you'd tell me what was going on once you'd thought it through. You have to keep your promise. You bloody owe me.'

Constant chewed pensively on his bottom lip while Blix glared at him.

'I think they're trying to open the Narrow Way.'

'Dragonville said that. What's the Narrow Way?'

'It's a gate. It's at the Bastion.'

'That's the place you said they took Katy! Did they bring me and Katy here for some reason to do with this gate?'

'I think so. It's something to do with *Elpis*.'

'Echmoth said that word. And Dragonville said something else. Something about vets. You know what,' she said coldly. 'You forced it out of me in the cottage.'

Constant let his guilt hide his indecision. *How much to tell them? Tell them what they might already know.*

'*Spes vetus*. It means 'ancient hope' in Latin.'

'Means nothing to me.'

More lip chewing. 'Do you know the story of Pandora?'

'From the Greek myths? A bit. We did it in junior school, but I skipped ahead to the Argonauts story. That was more exciting.'

'In the Greek religions, Pandora was the first woman, clothed in virtues by the Gods and given a box - an urn, actually - by Zeus, which she was told never to open. Naturally, she did, and all the evils of the world were released. What was left in the urn was hope, or rather the Spirit of Hope. Hope in Greek is *Elpis*. In Latin, it's *Spes*.'

'Okay. Good story for *Jackanory*. So what? Hope is a good thing, isn't it?'

'Maybe,' said Constant. 'The Romans were ambivalent about it. You might understand hope as positive thinking, but there is a sense of it as false hope when all is lost. There's also a sense that Hope is a person as well as a concept. Elpis was a goddess you see, and-'

Blix stopped him with a look. 'Okay, got it. *So what.*'

In Constant's imagination, the lie loomed in front of him, a black beast bearing down on him. 'So, it's an analogy, yes? There must be something terrible beyond the gate. Something like the evils in Pandora's box. They want to let it out.'

'Great. What horrible things are through this gate, then?'

Constant almost felt the lie leap into his throat, so rank it might burn his mouth on its way out. 'I don't know. No one knows. Something awful.'

'Yeah, baddies always want to do the big hairy terrible thing that screws everyone and ends the world. Like, in every film. And how do we stop them getting out?'

Another lie, so big that Constant felt he might choke. 'I don't know.' *I wish I could trust you. But you hate me.*

'What do they want Katy for?'

'I don't know that either,' said Constant, relieved to be telling the truth again. *Don't ask me why they chose her.*

'You don't know much.'

'Sorry. Whatever it is, it's for no good reason.'

'No shit. She's alive though.' It was a statement. Constant nodded sharply, though he had no reason to believe it.

'But it doesn't matter why. I'm going to find your sister and close the Narrow Way if it's the last thing I do. I swear by... I swear on my life.' His trembling sincerity echoed from the walls.

Blix stared at him for much longer than Constant felt comfortable with. Then she spoke very deliberately.

'No. *I* am going to save my sister. And *you* are going to help. If I let you. If it suits me.'

'Yes,' mumbled Constant, reddening. 'Yes.'

'Wrong all the time,' said Kit, staring into the middle distance.

After an awkward silence, Blix picked up the thread again. 'So, we go to this Bastion, rescue Katy and stop the end of the world,' she said. 'Easy-peasy. When do we leave? And can we find horses or something? A yak, even. I'm sick of walking.'

Constant shook his head. 'You can't walk to the Bastion. It's on the other side of the world.'

Blix scowled at him again. 'I don't know, I'm not bloody well from here. How far is it?'

'From here to the Bastion?' Constant thought briefly. 'About seven thousand miles.'

Blix staggered as if she'd been kicked. 'That's like London to Johannesburg!'

'Take about a year to walk that,' mused Kit. 'Faster if we ride, but not much.'

'Christ! I can't leave Katy in the hands of those *things* for a year!' said, Blix in despair, clutching at herself. Then she straightened suddenly and rounded on Constant, who backed away quickly, startled. 'You! You can do magic! You can take us there! Teleport us!'

The boy shook his head nervously. 'I told you that's impossible.'

'Bloody hell, that's where you draw the line in this madness? That's what's impossible? Then make a gate! Or use her wicket!'

'Sorry kiddo,' said Kit, holding her hands up placatingly. 'That's a one-way trip somewhere else.'

'*I can't leave her!*'

'It's okay,' said Constant. Kit turned sharply and stared penetratingly at him, but the boy hadn't moved to touch Blix; instead he was smiling. 'It's all right. I have a plan.' He gestured expansively at the giant map.

'What plan?'

'Ain't it obvious?' said Kit.

'Uh, no.'

'The gates,' said Constant. 'We're going to use them to get to the Bastion.'

Blix thought about that for a moment. 'Gates don't point to places on the same world. I can't go through a gate on Land's End and arrive at John O'Groats, or from here to the Bastion, wherever it is. They go to other worlds. So...'

Constant nodded encouragingly. 'That's right. We're going to gate-hop through the gain until we get to the Bastion.'

Blix blinked and said, 'What?'

'Let's start from first principles. Sit down Blix.'

Blix bristled. 'Don't tell me what to do!'

'I'm sorry! I'm sorry. *Please* sit down. If you would like to. Both of you.'

Kit eased herself into a chair and sprawled a leg over the armrest. After a moment in which Constant wished he was someone else, Blix took the chair beside her.

Constant stood in front of the mural looking just like a little lecturer about to launch into a lesson. His whole bearing and demeanour had changed, as though he'd become a slightly different person in the five seconds it had taken him to cross the floor.

'The purpose of the standing stones is to give shape and focus to existing weaknesses in the walls between worlds - rifts, holes, portals, whatever you call them - to close them to random travel and turn them into gates. Each circle is linked to another - the otherwise of the gate - and no other. Each one points to a different spot on a different world.'

'Like I said.'

‘Yes,’ agreed Constant. ‘And on each world, there are lots of portals. There are several near the Anvil. Now, here's the important bit: they don’t all point to the same world. And when they do, not necessarily to places near to each other on that world. You came here from Earth through one gate, but another nearby will take you to a completely different world. So -’

‘So, we can plot a course through various gates on different worlds and thereby travel between points on this world without having to walk seven thousand miles. Great! That’s great.’ Blix looked suddenly enthused as she put the pieces together.

‘That’s right,’ said Constant encouragingly. ‘The gate in the Bastion points to somewhere on Lyonesse. If we can find out where, we can get there and open it from the other side, go through, and arrive at the Bastion.’

‘But we don’t know if all the gates are working,’ said Blix. ‘You said there haven’t been any working gates on Shambhala for centuries. They haven’t worked on Earth for seventy years.’

‘What’s that?’ said Kit, shifting position languidly. ‘That ain’t right. Gate in Utah worked just fine.’

‘Yeah, but Dragonville must have done something. We don’t know about the rest.’

‘I don’t what you mean,’ Kit began, but Constant interrupted her.

'Ah, that we do know,' said Constant. 'Watch.'

He closed his eyes, concentrated momentarily, and breathed out in a slow controlled breath. As he did so some of the dots on the world-map glowed golden. Soon about two-thirds of them were shining gently. The Earth map looked as though a swarm of fireflies had landed on it; dots glowed across the countries of the Old World and into the Middle East and beyond. At the bottom of the map the Fire-Mouth remained dark.

'The map shows all the gates that are active now,' said Constant, opening his eyes again. 'It hasn't done that in generations. And look,' he continued, pointing at a circle high on the map, far to the right of Earth. Pinpricks of light were just visible. 'Shambhala has active gates. There haven't been any of those here for six hundred years.' He looked significantly at Blix. 'More than one.'

Blix was staring at the glowing dots on Earth. 'They're alive!’ she breathed. 'That means this map is connected to the whole universe. Wow. There are hundreds of them. Thousands.’

'I think it's every gate that hasn't stopped working,' said Constant.

‘This is brilliant!’ said Blix, ignoring him in her excitement. She jumped up. ‘I can go get my sister back!’

‘I’ve plotted a course.’ He pointed to the mural and the line of string and paper snaking across the picture.

‘Right on!’ Blix beamed, rocking back and forth on her heels. ‘Let’s go then!’

‘It’s not as simple as that.’

Blix stopped dead, looked daggers at him, and sat back down. 'Of course it isn't. Of course. Let's hear the bad news.'

'Several bad things. Firstly, the gates aren't in sync,' said Constant.

Blix stared blankly. 'What does that mean?'

Constant almost skipped over to the corner of the map that Blix had examined. 'Time works differently as you pass through the gate. You asked what the numbers and letters meant, "2d/g, 1d/l". It's describing the gain and lag of traveling through this gate. If you're not careful you could get badly out of sync. We need to avoid serious gain or lag or catastrophic paradoxes.'

Blix shook her head helplessly. 'To save time you should just assume I'm going to say, "what does that mean" whenever you stop talking,' she said. 'I'm not Einstein, I'm new at magic and I got a D minus in this gates crap.'

'I'm sorry. I'll be clearer.' Constant paused for a moment's thought. 'Going through a gate isn't just about moving through space. Sometimes you travel through time as well.' He indicated the part of the map that Blix had examined. 'This gate, the Fire-Mouth, you'd go through it on Tian and when you arrive on Earth, from your personal perspective in time it would be two days in the future, even though it only took you a few seconds to actually travel. When you go forward in time it's called "gain". 2d/g, two days gain. Okay so far?'

'Yeeeessss,' said Blix, cautiously. 'Why does that happen?'

'No one knows. It's just how it is. But it's not always the same both ways through a gate. It can be neutral, or more gain, or you can go backwards in time. When that happens, it's called "lag".'

He pointed at Tian again. 'This says "2d/g, 1d/l. Two days gain, one day lag. So, you'd go through the gate and from the point of view of this world it would be the day after tomorrow when you arrived at Mount Song. Let's say you immediately turn around and go back through. Because there's lag you go backwards in time from Tian's perspective, but not by the same amount, it's one day backward not two. You'd go through the gate today and seconds later come back to where you started on Tian, but it would be tomorrow compared to the time you started.'

Blix sat back in her chair, wide eyed. 'Wow.'

'Wow indeed. Good, you understand. Now understand that if you didn't want to lose that day, you can't fix it by going through the same gate again. That just puts you two more days in the future from *that* moment, not from the time you started. And if you come back through again it's only backwards a day again, so you're now two days in the future from where you started, even though only a few minutes might have passed for you.'

'Would this make more sense if I took drugs?' Blix asked, but Constant could tell from her expression she was beginning to see where this was going and didn't like it at all.

'It gets worse.'

‘Of course it does.’

‘Let's say that the gate has a cumulative lag. Say you gain a day one way but the lag is a year coming back. In that circumstance, you exist twice in the same time and potentially the same place, if you were actually there a year before. Tell me: if you'd come back from the future, what would you do?'

'Do I have a Delorean? No, don't ask. I suppose I'd find old me and tell her who won the next Grand National. Then old me would go down to the bookies with her life savings and put a bet on.'

'I sort of got all that. Modern earthmen have a strange way of expressing themselves. So, yes, you might change history as you remembered it in your favour - events which hadn't happened yet from the perspective of old you. But it wasn’t like that the first-time round. And that must have happened, because you lived it. But the new version is true as well, because old you lived that too, and after you changed things so must you, because the person old you was became new you, now. Both can't be true, but they are. That’s called a paradox. In your example, even if you avoid your old self and, um, place wagers yourself, that didn’t happen the first time either and it will have consequences you can't anticipate. Maybe your wager-taker loses too much money and kills himself. But the first time, he lived. And so on. Backwards time travel in your own space is ripe for catastrophic paradoxes. You can cause serious damage to existence.’

‘What does that mean?’ asked Blix before she could stop herself.

‘Try extremely hard never to find out,’ said Constant, in a very serious voice indeed.

‘Okay. Okay. So, I get it. Gain and lag. That makes things difficult.’

‘Yes. That’s understating it. We're going to use the gates to get to Bastion without traveling thousands of miles and taking months. But we don't just have to plot a route which gets us from here to there. That would be quite easy. We must make sure that the cumulative effect of the gain and lag means we get there in time to save your sister. If we get it wrong we could be months too late, or years, or anything like that.'

'My God, that’s...’

'... incredibly complicated, yes.'

‘But you’ve done it,' said Kit.

Constant started slightly; he’d paid such close attention to Blix he’d forgotten the American was there.

‘You said you’ve worked it out,’ she continued, pointing at the string.

‘Yes,’ said Constant. ‘I've had to be incredibly careful. For a start, we can't use any route where the cumulative lag at any point is greater than minus three days from today.’

'Why not?'

'Because we don't know what Dragonville did to make Shambhala gates start working again. We don't know *when* he did it. The first time we know for certain a gate was working again was when you arrived. That's as far back as we can go. Even that is dangerous.'

'What about Kit? She's been here for weeks. What about Dragonville himself for that matter? He's obviously been here before, Echmoth too. Echmoth was on my world in October, until at least the day before I came here. But he knew the werewolves already. He must have used a gate to get here. Or is from here.'

'Probably. Almost certainly. But almost certainly isn't good enough. The only thing we know for certain is that Dragonville and Kit both used wickets to get here. That heavily implies one working gate in - Utah, did you call it? And the otherwise gate here on Shambhala. It doesn't absolutely guarantee it though. You can use wickets in creative ways, the way that Kit hooked onto Dragonville's wicket. But what about all the rest of the gates? We don't know and we can't make assumptions. The risk is too great.'

'What does it matter?'

'If we go through a gate with lag that takes us, objectively, back in time before that point, then we risk going through a live gate which opens onto a dead one. That would be bad.'

'How bad?'

'Probably catastrophic. We might get bounced back. Or bits of us might. We might just die. We might be trapped between the gates with no way on and no way back. I'm not sure what that's like. It's not the sort of thing anyone reports back on.'

'Okay, that's all bad,' said Blix. 'Let's not do any of that. So. We have to choose a route carefully. Choose which gates allow us to get to the Bastion in time without causing disasters.'

'Yes.'

'And you've done it?'

'Yes.'

'How many?'

'I've got it down to - '

- Ten -

' - nine.'

Blix blanched. 'Holy God.'

'How much gain?' said Kit.

'Cumulatively, plus six weeks.'

The American mulled it over. 'Faster than walking,' she said.

'It's pretty good,' said Constant. He seemed relieved not to have been attacked. 'Most of that will be actual physical walking between gates. If we can travel faster, we could cut it down.'

Blix was horrified. 'I can't take six weeks! I need to get to my sister now! Is there no faster way?'

The lie clamped Constant's lips shut for a moment, so bitterly did he not want to say it. 'No. I'm afraid not.'

'Six weeks is better than a year, kiddo,' Kit pointed out. 'Unless you can do what Dragonville did, it's the best we've got.'

Constant now looked extremely nervous. 'There's another problem. I'll show you.' He paused. 'There are dead werewolves in the next room. You might want to hold your nose. And perhaps steel yourself.'

He looked to catch Kit's eye; she nodded slowly.

Constant led Blix toward a door in the far wall. Kit peeled herself off the chair and followed, glancing back over her shoulder at the worlds-map as she did.

The door led to another chamber, smaller than the map room but still vast and vaulted. Huge windows dominated one wall. Sunlight streamed in, the beams illuminating several hulks of fur lying dead and bloated on the flagstones. Blix was riveted by the sight. Then the smell hit her.

'Gaah,' she said, trying not to vomit. 'That's rank.'

'Dead wolf don't keep so well,' Kit agreed. She produced a large white handkerchief and clamped it over her nose.

The werewolves had been killed by a silver-edged sword. The weapon was still embedded in one of the corpses. Constant approached the body and, with some distaste, slid it free. He wiped the blade on the matted fur and offered it to Blix.

'Lighter than the wolf-iron,' he said. 'The right killing line, too. You should take it, you need something to defend yourself with. You don't have to look,' he continued, seeing that Blix was staring at the body.

'I want to. No more fear.' She held her hand out for the sword.

'If you try and kill me I won't be very pleased,' said Constant. Blix glared at him. He handed it over.

The sword was much lighter than the one Constant had given her in the stone circle. Blix swung it back and forth through the air until she was sure she had its weight and measure. Then she reached deep inside herself and pulled out rage. She swung the sword high above her head and slammed it with everything she had left into the werewolf's back, so hard her arms went numb from the force of the blow. Its shoulder shattered. Blix stood there and stared at the dead wolf for some time. Then she jerked the sword from the body.

'That was a surprise,' Constant said.

'I was imagining what it felt like to kill something. To kill a werewolf.' Blix looked at him. 'I've never killed anything before. If I have to do that, I need to know what it feels like. I need to be prepared.' She stared directly at him. 'What does it feel like?'

Constant looked away. 'Not like that. It feels-'

Magnificent.

'- terrible. Just terrible.'

'Well I think that was cathartic for most everyone,' said Kit, who'd taken a step sideways to avoid being skewered by Blix's backswing. 'Was that what you wanted us to see?'

'No.' Constant. 'This is.'

The wall behind them was covered by a huge mural; unlike the others it was a painting of a living thing.

'That's incredible,' said Blix, wide-eyed. 'Incredible. It's -'

'Suzaku!' cried Kit. 'The Vermillion bird!'

The mural stretched from floor to ceiling, its wings swept wide from wall to wall, the size of an ancient dragon. Exquisitely rendered and breathtakingly life-like, the rich red plumage glowed on the wall, each vane and barb burnished in the sun with a sheen that, as the light shifted and played across the room, made the Vermillion bird look like it was breathing. Tail plumes as long as its body snaked sinuously around it. There were eleven of them, each one a different brilliant colour. Orange, amber, yellow, chartreuse, green, teal, blue, violet, purple, magenta, and a stark red as different from the vermillion body as night was from day. The whole bird was wreathed in painted flames so realistic that without realising it Blix shrank from them as though they might burn her.

'It's like a colour wheel, she breathed. 'I learned about that in art class when I was little.'

'Oh, wow!' said Kit, enthralled. She was more excited than the other two had yet seen her. 'That's my bird! I love it. I seen it once, when I was tiny. They keep it in the Imperial Castle in Edo - *Tōkei-jō*, I should say. Momma took me to see it. You can't, but we, uh, found our way in. It was *beautiful.* And huge. Not this big though.'

'It was there,' Blix corrected. 'It died.'

'Really? Damn, I didn't know that. I thought it had a hundred years or more to go before that happened.'

'It was a few years ago. It laid an egg before it died though. They can take up to a decade to hatch. They think it's viable but it's too hot to get close enough to check properly.'

Blix's eyes shone as she imagined the majestic bird stepping from the shard of its egg. 'When that happens, I am totally going to Japan. I'd pay anything to see a Vermillion chick.'

'Me too! But boy, is this ever a good likeness! Any more like this, kid?'

'You're missing the point,' said Constant evenly. 'I didn't bring you here to admire the picture. Look more closely.'

Blix found it hard not to be distracted by the incredible beauty of the Vermillion bird. It was overwhelming. She felt that if a breath of air touched the wall it might ruffle the feathers, or that the bird might leap into the air and take flight, or that it would turn and look her in the eye...

She saw it then. 'It's had its head smashed in,' she said.

'Yes,' said Constant. 'It was the werewolves. They took something.'

Blix remembered. 'The bloodstone.'

'Yes. It sounds sinister but it's just the name for the rock. A green gemstone shot through with red. It was set in the eye of the Vermillion bird.'

'Important pebble, I suppose?' asked Kit.

'It was an artefact,' the boy replied. 'A powerful one. Ancient magic, stored in the stone. It protected the Monastery from other magic for millennia.'

'Dragonville has it,' said Blix. 'I saw it. He used it to open the gate.'

'That's what we needed it for,' said Constant. 'I know how to open a gate.' He rubbed his head irritably. 'I know now. I think I might have known before as well. But knowing that is trivial. *You* know. *Come and see.* There needs to be magic, or they're just words. Serious magic.'

Blix put her head in her hands and bent almost double. 'So, it's hopeless.'

'Not quite.'

He took out a handkerchief-sized piece of cloth from somewhere inside his robe, knelt and opened it careful on the floor. 'Look.'

Sparkling in the sunlight were tiny shards of green and red gemstone. The ranged in size from a sliver the thickness of Blix's little fingernail to barely more than a mote of dust.

'The wolves smashed it free,' Constant said. 'They broke it. I collected every piece I could find. I looked extremely carefully.' He looked at the other. 'These will work.'

Kit looked critically at the flakes. 'Kid, I got bigger pocket lint than those things. You really think one of those has the power to shoot us across the universe?'

Constant nodded, but uncertainly. 'It's really complicated and I don't understand it myself in any way I can express. I *know* each of these flakes can be used to open a gate. And in the same way I know that, I know that once each fragment is used, that's probably it. No more power. Probably. Which means we have one final problem.'

'What problem?'

Constant pointed through the door at the wall, and the tangled mess of paper and string hanging from the map. 'Nine worlds. Ceto. Helikon. Horkos. Thyïlea. Elysium. Ymir. Vicandra. Lyonesse. And then back to Shambhala, at the Bastion, in six weeks give or take. Nine worlds, nine pairs gates to get where we need to go. Nine gates to open.'

- and then the tenth -

'Yes?' Blix prompted.

'There are only eight shards.'

'Of course there are!' said Kit, throwing her hands up in frustration. 'Ain't nothin' ever easy!'

Blix was looking at the shards. 'Wait a minute. I count ten.'

'Look again.'

Blix peered closely at the shards. Two of them were mottled with tiny flecks of reddish brown.

'They've been drained,' Constant said. He looked uncomfortable. 'I think it was me. The basket and the door and the torches. I didn't know.'

'You should get a t-shirt made up with that on,' said Blix, irritably. 'It'll save time.'

She let a finger rest next to the nail-sized shard, careful not to touch it. 'This one is a lot bigger than the others. Maybe that has enough power to open two or three gates?'

'I don't know,' said Constant. 'Is it the size of object that determines how much magic can be stored in it? Maybe. Some property of the rock? Maybe it's that, although no one ever thought the bloodstone was special its own right, it was just something a magician poured absurd amounts of power into. Luck, perhaps? Gods? I haven't a clue. Do you know? I wish I'd learned more about this. I know about gates, not magic.'

'What now?' Blix asked.

Constant took a very deep breath. 'Now we're going to have to take a huge gamble. We can't just go from gate to gate on the worlds we go to. We're going to have to go to places where there might be artefacts of power. And then we have to find an artefact powerful enough to open a gate, and take it. People tend not to like you stealing their incredibly valuable things. They don't usually want to sell them either. And we have to do it all in time to get to the Bastion and stop your teacher, his pet magister and his army of werewolves from killing your sister.'

Kit whistled appreciatively and put her hands on her hips. 'Boys oh boys, those are some long odds you got there, kid.'

'Almost no chance,' said Blix. 'But not no chance.'

'No. There's a chance.'

'Then let's go,' said Blix. 'How far to the first gate?'

'Not far,' said Constant. He was suddenly shaking with excitement. 'It's here.'

'It's a rockery,' said Blix. 'So what?'

Constant struggled to find the words. He stood in the dead centre of the stone garden and turned around and around, trying to make sense of the enormity of the revelation he'd just had, the clarity with which he now saw something he'd only ever seen through a fog.

'It's a gate. Do you see the sandstone? All the way around the fissure. I thought they were just inlay, aesthetics. But they're stones. This is a gate.' He stopped spinning and looked at the women, his face a picture of wonder and shock together. 'I didn't know.'

Blix walked back to the doorway and pointedly stepped over the threshold into the corridor. 'Fool me once,' she said. 'Again, so what.'

Constant focused on her. 'Didn't you hear me? *I didn't know*. What have I been saying? "One way up, no way down". The Anvil is supposed to be impregnable. Yes, yes,' he said irritably, as Kit raised a finger to intervene. 'Leaving that aside. How can there be a gate here? How can no one know about it? We have lived here for *four thousand years*. It's on the great map, for goodness sake! We drew that! How can we draw something on a map and not know that we have? It even shows the gain in each direction! How could we know that if we've never used it?'

'Okay, so you're going to say it's magic,' said Blix in a flat and slightly bored tone. 'Let's skip over that mediocre revelation and straight to, who did it?'

Constant threw up his hands in exasperation. 'Me?' he suggested. 'One of the former Great Fathers, I mean. Maybe the First. But I don't remember. Why wouldn't I remember?' He ground the heel of his hand into his skull. 'The bloodstone? Maybe it made us not see it or not remember that we had. And now it's gone we can see what's really there.'

'That's barking,' Blix said. 'Why would you hide something from yourself?'

'The alternative is someone else did it. I can't even imagine the kind of power it would take to defeat the Anvil's defences.'

Kit looked up the fissure to the sky above. Morning sunlight made the rock glisten. 'Occurs to me that maybe this could all be new. Someone magicked up a gate here just five minutes past and redrew your map at the same time. Dragonville could do that. He could have made you forget. Hell, maybe you could. You're pretty good at that.'

'For fuck's sake,' said Blix, disgusted.

Constant chewed on his top lip and gave a little jerky nod. 'I thought of that,' he said guiltily. 'I think he could reshape the Anvil, if he's as powerful as he seems. He could physically build the rocks I suppose, maybe even create the gate, but the rift the gate controls is natural. It's just there, until it ceases to be. He couldn't create a rift.' He closed his eyes for a moment and settled himself. 'And it's there.'

'*Again,* so what.'

'Objectively it's good news. Starting here is what gets us down to six weeks. Any other route adds a minimum of two months, mostly fighting wolves here on Shambhala as we walk to the gate at Kalsang's Town.'

'Great. Let's stop talking and go.'

'Wait, we have to think about what this impli-'

'I don't have to do anything you tell me,' Blix said sharply.

'Um. Yes. Sorry.'

'We should get some things together,' said Kit, breaking the silence. 'What's Ceto like, kid?'

'Wet. We have to sail to the next gate.'

'And me without my life preserver. Oh mercy.'

They spent the rest of the day scavenging gear from the Monastery. Blix found it hugely dispiriting - every time she took something she found herself mentally apologising to the former owner, then remembering he was dead, slain by werewolves, and putting it back. Eventually she overcame her reticence and packed a sling bag of food, a few spare clothes and a handful of lowlights she'd found in the armoury. She filled a canteen and Katy's plastic water bottle.

'What about that?' asked Constant when they reconvened in the map room, pointing to the doombag.

'That's staying as it is,' said Blix. 'It's not mine. She'll want it back.'

'Okay, but it will be easier if you distribute the contents in your shoulder bags, or a pack, and stow - '

'It's not mine,' said Blix sharply, cutting him off. 'It is staying as it is. And for the last time, you don't get to tell me what to do any more.'

She stubbornly hitched it up her arm, holding it as Katy always had, and glared at him.

'Sorry,' said Constant in a small voice. He shifted his weight uncomfortably. Then he fled.

'Mmm-hmm,' said Kit, watching him go. 'Well I suppose we'll have to go get him. I see you got some new threads.'

Blix self-consciously showed off her newly acquired leggings, thick, grey, woolly and warm. 'I got a couple of shirts too. They're long and a bit Errol Flynn but they're okay. And I ditched the jeans, they were wolfed too much. I don't need your chaps now.' She handed over a neatly folded pile of leather. 'Thanks.'

'Neato,' said Kit. 'Maybe I'll leave them behind though. Darn heavy.' She looked Blix up and down. 'Wear the bags under your cloak. The sword too. That way you can shrug it off if you need to run, or fight.'

'Thanks. I'll keep the jacket underneath though, that's mine. Um. These are yours too,' she added, handing over the lacy bloomers. 'Thanks.'

'You're welcome. Say, did you wash 'em?' She gave them a theatrical sniff. 'Guess not.'

'Oh my God, stop. I meant to ask though, bit old-fashioned, aren't they? I'm, I mean, I'm not suggesting you should, um wear a thong or something, probably chafe in the saddle, um, I mean, I just thought they were unusually big, you know?' She rushed to the end of the sentence, aware she had turned bright pink.

'I don't know about fashion, kiddo. Saw 'em, liked 'em, bought 'em. Ain't nothing about being a country gal that disqualifies me from fancy under-things. I got some corsets back in my room that look mighty fine with 'em.'

'Oh, really?' Blix said, in what she hoped was an entirely normal voice. She tried not to think about her roasting cheeks.

'Sure. They also keep my ass warm. And I think they get my point across,' the American continued, admiring the embroidery.

'What point?'

Kit looked directly at her. 'That I know how to enjoy myself,' she said.

Blix wondered just how much redder she could go without bursting a blood vessel.

'You okay, kiddo?'

'Oh, yeah, sure.'

Kit laughed suddenly, and thrust the bloomers back at Blix. 'Maybe you should keep 'em. Don't want you catching a chill down below.' The sly smile made a reappearance. 'Maybe I'll come and get them later.'

Blix couldn't take any more. 'Stop it,' she moaned, looking anywhere but at Kit.

'Sure! If that's really what you want. Is that really what you want?'

'Oh. My. God,' said Blix, and fled.

Being flirted at by Kit had lightened Blix's mood, but it plunged back into the depths of anger as soon as they started looking for Constant.

They found him in his apartments, staring out of the huge windows into the rapidly darkening sky. The great forest was already an indistinguishable mass, the snaking road invisible. He was weighing a large dagger in the palm of one hand. It was long and thin, with a silver point. The handle was carved bone. A wolf's head glowered menacingly. Constant seemed lost in thought.

'That's a nice knife,' said Kit, by way of announcing herself.

'It's mine,' said Constant. 'Another me, a long time ago.' He slid the blade into its sheath. 'Silver is always useful.' He produced a fire steel from his sleeve. 'I found one,' he said to Blix. Awkwardly he held it out to her. 'You can have it. If you like.'

'Keep it.'

Constant coloured, and looked even more awkward.

Blix looked out of the window into the darkening world. 'I've never seen anything like this. It's beautiful, I suppose.'

'Mighty fine trees,' Kit offered.

'I've always hated this view,' Constant said in a quiet voice. 'We always have. The Great Fathers before me. For different reasons. I felt exposed. That's common. Others were angry they couldn't return to the world. A few felt stolen from it. We all came to terms with it in the end. We became serene.'

He looked at them. 'The Vermillion bird comes from Taoism. I have taught that all faiths are aspects of the Faith. It has a meaning for the Taoists, which we respect. For us, it represents the Constant. Me. It burns with the flame eternal, which it passes on when it dies. It has no mate, it makes the egg of itself. The new bird burns, hidden within the shell, and bursts into glorious flame when it emerges into the world. Death and life, an unending succession, leaving and returning to the world.

'That's how it is for me. I live here, I die here, I'm reborn out there, I come here. And I've realised that the world through that window is as much a part of me as this mountain. And it's *wrong*.'

He closed his eyes and held out his hands, the fire steel in his left hand, the striking stick in his right. He struck sparks, which showered from the steel in a fountain far in excess of the scrape Constant had made. The sparks drifted out of the window, caught in a wind that was not there, moving faster and faster until they were lost to sight. Then down below, far in the distance, a light appeared. Then another, and another, until Blix could see a long twisting line of fire stretching from the base of the Anvil to the far horizon.

'You relit the torches,' said Kit. 'The Path of Fire.'

'Yes.' Constant grimaced with pain, shaking his left hand.

'All of them?'

'No. Just the ones we can see.'

'Please tell me you didn't waste a shard on that.'

'No. That was from within. I don't know how. At the cottage, when I, ah, made Blix remember, that's what I did then. I just meant to this time.'

'You're telling them where we are,' Kit pointed out.

'I'm telling them who I am,' said Constant, suddenly passionate. 'I am the flame that never burns out. I am the Vermillion, the Constant of the universe. I am the path that I walk as I am he that walks it. I follow the way. If there's someone left who knows what that means, I want them to see. I put something of myself in there. Thought and will. The fire *won't* go out. Not while I'm alive.'

He was still flexing his left hand as if it hurt; he saw Kit looking it. A thin, rust red line marked his palm, from just to the left of his little finger almost to his wrist. A mark which hadn't been there before. He scratched at it, but it seemed to be part of the flesh.

Kit peered over his shoulder. 'You okay? You cut yourself on something?'

'I'm fine. It's not a cut. It's from the magic, I think. It's strange. It aches, and itches a bit. It feels heavy. Not very, but heavy.'

'Uh-huh. Don't know about no heavy hands, kid. Saw a palmist once though, she called that there the sun line.'

'The sun line.' Constant looked at his hand, then the line of torches twinkling into the distance. 'I guess I got burnt.'

'That's what happens when you play with fire, kid. Well I'm sure it'll heal. You know, I got some snake-'

'No thank you.'

'Please yourself. We should get outta here.'

'Yes.' He walked to the door, followed by Kit. Blix didn't move. Constant looked back when he realised. 'Are you coming?'

She stared at him strangely, then pointed sharply out of the window at the lights far below.

'That,' she said. 'Was that supposed to be inspiring? Because it wasn't.'

'What?' Constant said in surprise.

'You don't get it, do you? You don't get to be noble. You don't get to be the hero. If you're lucky and you work hard you get to redeem yourself. But all this ponderous mystic monk crap, you can stick it up your arse as far as I'm concerned.' The anger and hurt in her eyes made Constant gasp despite himself. 'You're going to help me? Fine. We'll get along. Laugh and joke even, why not. But we're not friends. I don't trust you. I haven't forgiven you. I don't care if you don't like that.'

Constant looked like he was going to cry. He plunged out of the room as fast he could.

Blix saw Kit's expression. 'What?'

'I ain't saying that's wrong,' said Kit languidly. 'I'm saying he's twelve. Not four thousand and twelve. Just twelve. Think on that for a spell. We should catch up. Again.'

Blix took one last look out of the window, her mind's eye looking past her anger and pain, through the forest and the mountains and the great empty distance beyond to a castle she could only imagine and the part of her that was there.

'I'm coming,' she said.

Chapter Eighteen: What Katy Saw

Katy Summerland dreamed of barking dogs. She woke up with the sound still ringing in her ears. After a moment, she realised that it wasn't in her head. Then she realised they weren't dogs.

She knew three things immediately: that she was in a bed which was not her own, that her clothes had been taken away from her, and that everything stank of death.

She lay still for a few moments, trying to remember. The memories came in pieces, like scenes in a film trailer, cut away from events as they'd happened and bursting in her mind all at once. The Conspirators, the runes, Blix, Leicester and the werewolves - it seemed like a terrible dream, but Katy was no fool. However much her mind wanted to disbelieve her memory, she knew it was real.

Magic! Real magic! Katy had learned about it in school, but it was all history. The last people to experience magic, in the flesh so to speak, were now very old. Katy has been born too late.

She didn't feel angry about that. She knew the generations directly after magic went away had felt very angry, and lost, and cheated. They'd suffered the Great War which killed millions upon millions and in the middle of it their horizons had become immeasurably narrower, for reasons no one could explain.

But for Katy and her peers, several generations removed for the catastrophe, it was like missing the sixties - old people expected then to care, but they didn't, not really. Magic was something in a textbook, on the same level of interest as silent movies; forgotten relics of the distant past, discarded not by choice, but by events. All that was left was a bunch of magical tat; *objet ésotérique,* used up and discarded, from all periods of human civilisation and before it. Until today, Katy would have agreed with Blix. As far as magic was concerned the past was past. But not anymore it seemed.

Without moving her head, she tried to look around.

She was in a four-poster bed, tucked in, white sheets up to her shoulders. The bed was built from some very dark wood and looked old and expensive. The canopy was embroidered with intricate snowflake designs in orange, yellow and red, while thick bed curtains in rich blue cotton hung from the corners.

She looked beyond the bed posts. To her left, she could see a stone wall, built of large bare blocks, the edge of what was probably a large stone fireplace, and a door.

The door was open.

Katy did not move. She knew she was a prisoner. An open door didn't mean she was free. She caught sight of her hair, which surprised her. It seemed to have been brushed out and carefully arranged to lie in tresses across the sheet. She glanced to her right. The same. She also realised that it had been washed; as far as she could tell, she had been bathed while unconscious.

The room opened out on that side and she could make out heavy furniture, possibly a wardrobe, and a tall armchair facing the bed. Beyond, there was probably a window. She could get the shape of it in her peripheral vision, a stone arch without glass, shutters thrown open. Grey light and cool air suggested that it was before dawn. *A good time to slip away unnoticed*, she thought, but still did not move.

The whole thing reminded Katy of the stately homes she'd visited on family trips. She remembered wandering around entranced by the living past, dragging a sullen Blix behind, headphones on full blast, hands firmly in pockets. *Am I in a castle?* she wondered.

The door was open.

She seemed to be wearing some sort of nightie, which was too short for her and ended high on her thighs, so high it wouldn't cover her if she stood up. Her knickers had been removed. Her stomach turned over as she thought about what that might mean. She didn't hurt, and she thought she would if... But she didn't.

Then she remembered Blix, and what Echmoth had told the werewolves to do to her. Katy bit her lip hard and tried not to cry. She breathed deeply until she was in control again.

Dogs - no, not dogs, *werewolves* barked and yelped beyond the window. It seemed to be coming from far below. Katy wondered how high up she was. She also wondered if she was alone.

She held her breath, and listened. There was no sound of movement or breathing in the room. If someone was standing guard out of sight, waiting for her to stir, she couldn't sense them.

The door was *open.*

Carefully, trying to make as little noise as possible, she slid to her left, out from under the covers. As her foot touched the floor a voice said, 'I would put some clothes on first if I were you. There are bad fellows about.'

Katy struggled backwards until she was sitting bolt upright against the headboard, clutching the sheets high against her chest in fear.

The man called Dragonville sat deep in the high backed chair, so deep in shadow and so still that she hadn't noticed him. His top hat sat on a table beside him, his long legs were crossed over a footstool. His head rested on a lace antimacassar; Katy remembered her grandmother had owned one just like it. His fingers were steepled, resting on his chin.

You slept for quite a few hours, young lady,' he said, straightening up a little from his lounge. 'I fear the First of Wolves is not possessed of the lightest touch.'

Katy gasped as she remembered the blow, and put a hand to her cheek.

'I took care of it,' said Dragonville, waving his hand lightly. 'It won't bruise or scar.'

'Who do you think you are?' Katy blurted.

'Forgive me. We haven't been properly introduced. Dragonville's my name. Belmont Dragonville, at your service.' He bowed his head slightly, without moving from the chair.

Katy watched him warily. *Keep him talking until I can work out what to do,* she thought.

'Katherine Summerland. Katy.'

'I know. A very special and unfortunate girl. The pleasure is mine, Miss Summerland. Shall we play Twenty Disingenuous Questions? I promise to answer honestishly.'

'What's that supposed to mean?' Katy asked. She didn't like the sound of *special and unfortunate.*

'It means I thought you might like to talk, while you plan whatever it is you think will get you out of this. I enjoy talking to the very young, generally speaking. They seldom want anything that matters to me.'

'I'm not very young. I'm seventeen.'

'Such comparisons are relative. I mean only to say that I am of advancing years.' There was another round of barking from below. Dragonville frowned briefly. 'Also, my current colleagues, brave and noble as they are, are possessed of limited conversation.'

Katy was scared and confused, but she was still Katy. Still a smart girl. Even as he spoke, she analysed his words in the silence of her mind.

No one to talk to? Is he lonely? This is important. Let's talk. You bastard. Katy realised that as well as fear and anxiety she felt angry. This surprised her slightly. Normally Blix was the one with the nuclear temper.

Katy looked around properly. She was in some sort of castle. A child's bedroom. Brightly coloured hangings decorated the walls, scenes of hunting and horse riding and happy children. A few toys, crudely made to her eyes, were strewn about the floor. Katy saw a carved wooden rocking horse; it was broken in three.

'Where are we?' she asked. 'I imagine we've left Kansas,' she added under her breath.

Dragonville heard her, and gave her a quizzical look. 'What's that about Kansas, hey? You weren't in Kansas. You were in England. Dear Old Blighty, John Bull, rules the waves and so forth.' His face brightened. 'Do you know America, though? Lovely place. I was there quite recently. Had to leave in a hurry, bit of a to-do. I'll draw a veil over it. Moving on, where we are *now* is Shambhala, which you'll know if you know your Other Worlds. "A fly-blown wasteland, long since forgotten," as Defoe says somewhere. Or was that Cobbett? A prominent perambulist of some kidney. Anyway, there you have it. Rather harsh on flies, I always thought. Admirable creatures, really.'

Doesn't recognise the reference, does very much like the sound of his own voice. Okay then, wizard, let's see what's behind your curtain. Just give him a few words, let him fill the silence with information. Play the little girl for a while.

'Looks like a castle?'

Dragonville nodded encouragingly. 'Close enough. This is the Bastion. It's a fortress, far to the south and somewhat west of where we were yesterday. I mahocked us here while you were on the nod using a rather pleasing device I've acquired. A beautiful piece of thaumaturgy, I'd write a note of praise to the manufacturer if he hadn't recently departed this mortal coil. I digress. What was I talking about?'

'The room.'

'Ah yes. The room was a child's. I thought you would be more comfortable. The grown-up mattresses hereabouts are like potato sacks, let me tell you.' He chuckled lightly, and smoothed the ends of his moustache with a fingertip.

Well aren't you a friendly devil. But don't be fooled. This man's a killer. Killers kill. I could be next unless I am very careful.

'Yes, I can't offer any good news on that front, I'm afraid,' said Dragonville, smiling again. 'You *are* going to die, and quite soon. Or rather, part of you is. It's quite complicated. I wouldn't worry, since you can't do anything about it. Not my doing, I should say. I have nothing against you.'

But you're not going to stop it. Katy was now thinking very hard. 'Did you just read my mind?'

'Not particularly. I can do that, but there's usually no need. I am exceptionally good at reading people. Not that reading people is terribly hard, mind you. If there's one thing I've learned in my long life, it's that people who think they're subtle, aren't. Everyone's motives are transparent. Your thought was written on your face.'

He yawned widely and stretched rather theatrically. Katy got the impression that Belmont Dragonville did everything rather theatrically.

'Take brother Echmoth, for example,' he continued, flicking a finger idly to indicate somewhere else in the castle. 'Leicester, as you know him, although in fact Leicester was someone else. The man, if you can call him that, is practically bouncing up and down in his desire to betray me and take my power. I imagine he has some tedious little scheme up his sleeve. It's quite charming in its childishness, really. Echmoth's kind generally are childish, I find. They don't understand humanity. Very emotional creatures. They know how we sense and see the world, how we feel, but not how we think and understand. It makes them petulant and devious. I much prefer the First of Wolves, of the three of them. He at least is completely honest.'

Three of them, thought Katy, trying exceptionally hard to maintain a poker face. *Who is the third?*

Dragonville sighed a little, and looked away, in a way which might have signalled regret from another man. 'Pity, really. Whatever else I am, I am a man of my word. I promised to help Echmoth achieve his heart's desire, and I will keep my promise. He can trust me in that.'

He looked up at Katy, his voice animated once more. 'Now *you*, on the other hand, are far more normal. Torn between wanting to get me talking so garrulously that I give away something important, fear that if you say the wrong thing I might just kill you now, which I won't by the way, and an urgent need to find out whether I molested you in your sleep. Don't need to be Cagliostro to know what you're thinking, child. Do ask the last one, you'll feel better once you know, perhaps.'

'Did you?' asked Katy immediately.

'No.'

I feel better. Much better. Foolish. He didn't care about leaving Blix to be raped. Don't just obey him. Make him say more. Learn what you can about this place without shutting him up. So what if he knows that's what you're doing? He's so smart, thinks he knows me. Am I that transparent, or is he just manipulating me? Just saying it so I think it's true? Two can do that. Let's find an opening for waterworks.

She lowered the sheets a little, exposing the nightie neckline. 'Who does this belong to?' she asked.

'The last occupant of this room, I presume.'

'Where is she now?' asked Katy, her voice trembling a little, only partially faking it. She thought she knew the answer.

Dragonville mused on the question for a moment. 'Well. I'm sure you could find bits of her around here if you looked hard enough.'

Katy shuddered at the thought, and at the thought of a man who could make light of it. 'You put it on me? You washed me?'

'Yes, to both. She was smaller than you, but I didn't realise that until it was on. My apologies. She wasn't wearing it when she died, if that's what you're worried about. And as for the other, you were very dirty.'

The thought of his hands on her naked body made Katy feel sick, and the look of disgust on her face was quite real. But while she could easily have suppressed it, it she decided on the spur of the moment to take a gamble.

'You fucking *pervert*!' she said hotly. 'Bet you couldn't wait to touch me up, you dirty, evil bastard!' Real tears were barely held back anyway; Katy let go and sobbed convincingly. Between teardrops, she looked for a reaction.

Dragonville only smiled. 'Sticks and stones Katy Summerland, sticks and stones. The answer, as I said, is no. I used a spot of magic, my hands never touched your flesh, nor did my eyes gaze upon it. I've done many terrible things, worse than you can possibly imagine, but rapine and pederasty are not among my offences. That's not to say I would demure from violating you if doing so served my ends,' he allowed, tilting his head slightly as he considered the matter. 'But I wouldn't enjoy it.'

'Well that's something, at least,' Katy said sarcastically. She choked back a ragged sob and tried not to show how very relieved she was.

'It is, isn't it? Brother Echmoth would, I fear. You must expect bad people to do bad things, I suppose. Although by his lights he isn't a bad person. Or a person. It's all relative, isn't it?'

'Leicester's going to do it then.' Katy remembered what Blix had said about Leicester and his almost-wandering hands, and what he'd said about her "looking the part".

'Echmoth. Leicester's no longer with us. I'd say he'd gone the way of all flesh, but the flesh hasn't quite gone, what? But it will soon, I think, old Echmoth's starting to look a bit peaky, don't you think? Returning to your question, no, you will be spared a defilement, although only because he wants to do something far worse. From your point of view. He thinks it's the best thing since leavened bread.'

Dragonville extracted a white silk handkerchief from his breast pocket and, with a flick that sent it further than it should have travelled, tossed it to Katy. 'Feel free. There, there, and all that.'

Katy dabbed at her eyes and sniffled. *Now then. What did you want me to know from that? That you're a ruthless fiend, certainly, capable of anything - but only when you need to be. Otherwise essentially honest and straightforward, a man who keeps his word. Why do you want me to believe all that?*

Something occurred to Katy. 'Why did you brush my hair?'

'It was something to do to pass the time. This is increasingly important for a man of my age. Besides, hair care is terribly important, don't you think? Paying attention to one's appearance is a mark of civilisation. Take my own fine peruke, for example.' He swept a finger lightly over his hair, which fell in jet black, lightly oiled waves backwards from his brow to a neat trim just above his collar. 'It took me centuries to find a style I like, it'd be a poor thing not to look after it, what?'

Centuries?

There was a shift in the wind. Katy got a whiff of rotting meat. She wrinkled her nose. 'I smell something bad.'

Dragonville affected a grim demeanour. 'That would be death. A lot of it, I'm afraid. Werewolves are not mild mannered. A terrible business, combat. Cry "havoc!" and let slip - well, you know the rest. Or do you, do schools still teach that? No matter. The Bastion fell. It was thought to be impregnable, but it fell nonetheless.'

He appeared to be serious, but now and then there was a little creasing in the corners of his eyes that said something else, but it was not evident what. Katy was no fool though, and made a logical leap.

'You let them in.'

Dragonville raised a finger to his forehead and tipped her a lazy salute. 'Indeed. The former occupants had grown complacent. Why defend against magic when it barely exists anymore? The monks were far more careful. The Monastery fell just the same. Everywhere has fallen. The wolves take their Great Matter most seriously.'

'You murdered all those people,' said Katy hotly, while wondering which monks Dragonville was referring to, and what the Great Ominously Intoned Matter was. 'Maybe not personally, but they're dead because of you.'

'Well, quite a lot of them are still alive, actually,' Dragonville said, still smiling encouragingly. 'Sort of. But for the rest, yes, you're right. It was, I regret, a necessary evil. Necessary for a higher purpose.'

'That's what people like you always say,' Katy said. 'I know a lot about history. There's always some justification for atrocities. It's always bullshit.' *God don't provoke him!* But the words were out.

'My dear girl,' said Dragonville mildly, 'I am neither a child nor an imbecile. I know all that. Nonetheless, I am engaged in work of the greatest benefit to mankind. The price has been terrible. The weight I bear is intolerable. Yet I have paid it and borne it because my end will do humanity an infinite kindness.'

For a moment, his eyes flickered a strange silver flecked with red, and he spoke with a conviction so bitter it sent a chill down Katy's spine. 'It is worth any price. Any price.'

Then his eyes were sparkling blue once more, and the laugh-lines crinkled as he smiled gently at her.

'You're immoral,' she said aloud.

'That is one point of view,' Dragonville acknowledged. 'I prefer to say that I have purpose. I am resolute. Where others shift and tack like a steersman to the breezes, as Plutarch says somewhere, I stay the course. However so bloody.'

He's a madman, Katy thought.

'I'm not mad,' said Dragonville, as if he'd heard her. 'I just do mad things. And yes, I did read your mind that time, a regrettable lapse in decorum. You rather shouted that thought. I try not to listen in, my apologies. Would you like to go for a walk? See the sights, as they say?'

The sudden change in subject caught Katy by surprise. She looked at him carefully. The charnel smell was still rich in her nostrils. 'What will I see if I do?'

'A fine example of late period Germanic Cherusci monumental architecture full of dead people in varying states of consumption and decomposition. I will steer you away from the worst of it, if mortality troubles you. There are wonders here, and valuable lessons to learn. I would like you to see them and learn them. Come for a walk.'

There was a slight shift in Dragonville's tone that made Katy think she was no longer being asked.

Don't just obey.

'If I do, will you tell me what Echmoth is going to do to me?'

'Yes, if you wish.'

Katy fingered the nightie. 'I can't go like this.'

'Your clothes are on the table beside you,' said Dragonville.

'Wh-' Katy began, but there they were, where they hadn't been before. They were clean and mended - no, Katy realised, they were undamaged, as if she had never fallen through the gate. Her wellingtons were on the floor.

'Where's my handbag?'

'Halfway up a mountain, thousands of miles away, I imagine.'

Katy wrinkled her nose. 'I live out of that bag.'

'Not for much longer,' said Dragonville complacently. 'Now, I will turn my back,' announced the magician. He rose serenely from the chair, did an ostentatious about-face, and walked over to the window.

Watching him the entire time, Katy struggled into her things. She half expected Dragonville to sneak a peek, but he gazed with apparent interest at the view until she was fully clothed.

The door was open. Katy took a step toward it.

'There's nowhere to go,' said Dragonville, without turning around. 'Do feel free though.' He flicked his fingers over his shoulder, and the door swung fully open. 'You might get a little way before you get et.'

Katy hesitated, then looked past him.

'There is always the window,' conceded Dragonville, somehow knowing where her eyes had gone without looking at her. 'But we are in a tower, many hundreds of feet above cobbles. Perhaps you can climb down. Do you climb?'

'I could kill myself,' said Katy.

Now Dragonville did glance back, and then turned to face her when he saw she was dressed. 'What's this?'

'I could run past you and throw myself from the window. Echmoth wants me for something special. And so do you,' she continued with sudden realisation. 'You don't help people. You help yourself. So if my fate is as sealed as you say, the only way to beat you is not to be around for it.'

Dragonville looked impressed, but there was a hard edge to his smile which hadn't been there before.

'Impeccable logic,' he said. 'You are a clever child. That is the kind of answer a clever child could come up with without realising how glib and facile it is to talk so casually about self-murder. Yes, you could. That would be very brave, and hateful and empty. But you won't.'

'How do you know?' said Katy, taken aback.

'Because suicide is for the despairing. For the lost. For those who bear the weight of the world as it is, which is not as it should be. Suicide is for the damned. You are not such a one.'

'You sound like an expert.'

'I do know a lot about death.'

He suddenly leapt forward, planting his feet on the stone floor with two great thumps and pointing at Katy, his jovially restored. 'But you! You think you can escape! How marvellous. The triumph of youth,' he waved his hand vaguely, 'and so on.' He stepped back, acting as if the effort had been all too much.

'Okay then,' said Katy. 'If I can't run and I can't die, there's a third option.'

'Oh, I do like you,' said Dragonville, clapping his hands together delightedly. 'A child with options. Do tell me.'

'I wait,' said Katy.

'Wait?' Dragonville raised his hands in mock-astonishment. 'For what?'

'My sister. She's coming to rescue me.'

Dragonville laughed. 'She may be some time. Do you remember the part about her being raped to death by werewolves?'

Katy blanched, but said, 'You don't know her. She'll find a way. She's tougher than all of you put together!'

'Bravo!' said Dragonville, clapping with apparently genuine feeling. 'That's the spirit! But that will be too late for you I'm afraid. What Echmoth intends to do is... irreversible. Do you have any last words you wish me to convey to the other Miss Summerland when she arrives?'

'Tell her I told you to get fucked.' But she had noticed the momentary pause as Dragonville said *irreversible.* And was that a twinkle in his eye, the merest tremble of an eyelid in a wink? Katy knew, without knowing how, that Dragonville was telling her something.

What is he telling me? If whatever happens is irreversible, what different thing can I do? If I can't go back...

'Vulgarity,' sniffed Dragonville disapprovingly. 'What a pity. Never mind. So, you will wait upon a rescue from your sister. Ah, the pathos! It is quite moving. Well, let me prove that I am not wholly a monster by giving you - '

He stopped talking suddenly and smiled as if remembering a joke.

'By giving you hope,' he continued. 'She's alive! Your sister survived her encounter with *Lupus sapiens,* how shall I put it, *virgo intacto.* Assuming she was to start with. Modern children have flexible morality, I understand. I do not judge.'

Relief flooded through Katy. 'I told you!' she said in a ringing voice. 'She'll come for me!'

'I am sure she will. I'm rather counting on it in fact. I may have to nudge her along a bit if she doesn't, but I expect she is on her way even now. She had some help dealing with our furry friends from a very special and unfortunate boy who will assuredly bring her here.'

Katy sobered up immediately. *That's the second time you've used that phrase,* she thought.

'Yes,' said Dragonville. 'I'm afraid there's no scenario in which this ends in any way other than unfortunately for all of you. Can't be helped I'm afraid. As I said, a necessary evil.'

He stopped again, and appeared lost in thought. The he looked at her, smiled fiercely, and his voice was somehow in her mind. *Who knows though? You might survive. I didn't choose you randomly.*

Katy suddenly lost patience. 'What game are you playing?' she said.

Dragonville laughed his easy, mocking laugh.

'An extremely long one,' he replied. 'Longer than you could possibly imagine. And many at once. But it's not a game, you know. I am a natural philosopher of some renown. Think of this as an experiment. I have formed a hypothesis. I now test it. Observations are made. I may publish. Shall we walk?'

He offered his hand. Katy left him hanging. He withdrew it and bowed slightly, with a slight *hm* of disappointment. 'As you wish. Please go ahead.'

Spiral stairs led down to a landing with several rooms leading from it. Doors were broken open at the lock or hanging off their hinges. The walls were thick with tapestries and the floor richly carpeted in red. Clearly money had been spent, although just as clearly to Katy's mind that money had been ducats, groats or schillings. There was a distinctly mediaeval style to the decor.

Through one of the broken doors she saw a woman's body, hanging from the side of a bedstead. Flies circled what remained of her head. Katy had never seen a dead person before. She forced herself not to shake.

'Who lived here?'

'The Keeper and his family. The Keeper was the master of this fortress. I imagine we will find his remains wherever the last stand was made. Such is nobility.'

They descended more stairs and entered a long, panelled gallery. Sunshine entered diagonally in narrow shafts from slit-windows on one side, making it look like the wall was buttressed by light. Portraits stared down from every inch of space above the eye line. Stern martial men and women in high-necked gowns with impossibly thin waistlines glared at Katy. The portraits became progressively more stylised and simplistic as they walked along the corridor and, Katy presumed, into the past.

'Shall I tell you the fascinating story of how I came to this world?' said Dragonville as they reached the end of the gallery. More stairs led down.

'If you want to.'

'I do. It begins in the United States. America is a marvellous place, isn't it? A very forward-looking people. I admire those who are unconcerned by history. Anyway. You will not know this, but for many years that side of the globe was off-limits to the likes of me. To everyone except the savages, actually. A very old friend desired most extremely to be left alone.'

He struck a deliberative pose, finger and thumb on chin. 'Strange to think now, that the great kingdoms and empires of Europe and Asia were for thousands of years dotting off through holes in reality to discover new worlds, while half their own planet remained unknown to them. Unaware that a master had closed their minds to the thought that there might be something there. The past is ridiculous, sometimes.

'Cut a long story short, a few of us started to object to being denied half the Earth, we remonstrated, one thing led to another. All very unpleasant. Our friend moved on and the Americas opened for us, and everyone. Fourteen-hundred and ninety-two, Columbus sailed the ocean blue, and all that. Do you know that rhyme? I learned it quite recently.'

You're ancient. How is that possible?

'I've explored it extensively since then. Wonderful place, as I said. I particularly enjoyed Utah. Do you know what the most wonderful thing I discovered there was?'

'No.'

'I will tell you. It was a gate I didn't know about.'

'That's it?' Katy couldn't help looking underwhelmed.

'It may sound like nothing to you, but I assure you it was utterly shocking to me. I am an authority on *Mundus ceresis.* I am *the* authority. The idea that one could be unknown to me was most troubling.'

'There are loads of gates in America. Maybe you just missed it.' Despite herself Katy was interested. 'I did an essay on American megaliths for my History O Level. I got an A.'

'How charming. It doesn't work like that for me. I knew about all the rifts on Earth. Yet here was one I didn't know. Naturally I suspected a trap. Magic is survived by the cautious and men in my line make enemies. But investigation proved that there was nothing of concern, so I opened it up and had a look through. Always wise generally, the other side might not work, or the locals might be getting a bit tasty nearby. One does not wish to leap into nothing or a brawl, after all. And who knows where it pointed? I could have found myself on Mars. And I saw...'

He trailed off, enraptured by the memory playing out behind his eyes.

'Saw what?' prompted Katy eventually.

'A vision of the future,' the magician continued firmly. 'It was very exciting. I saw something else, too. Two special and unfortunate girls. And now we are here.' He stopped by a huge door of age-blackened wood and turned the handle. 'This is one of the things I wanted to show you.'

It was a library, a huge room with a dozen long stacks of shelves arranged like the spokes in a wheel around a centre circle. The books and scrolls were tightly packed and ancient and the whole effect was quite impressive, but that wasn't what made Katy's jaw drop. The domed ceiling high above them was made entirely of stained glass and the picture it showed was the universe. It glowed as the weak sunlight passed through it.

'I love libraries,' said Dragonville, and for once the knowing theatricality was absent from his voice. 'I am academic by inclination. Do you know the Reading Room at the British Library? It's my favourite place. Reminds me of Alexandria. There's something wonderful about the smell of paper and ink between covers, don't you agree? It's the perfume of civilisation.'

He took a deep breath, and exhaled happily. 'I strongly advise browsing the section on magical creatures. It is quite fascinating. And instructive.'

Katy didn't answer; she was still looking up. Dragonville followed her gaze. 'Impressive, isn't it?' he said. 'A *mappa universalis.* It's -'

'I can see what it is,' Katy said. 'It's a gate map. I saw one in a book once.' She fought hard against a desire to stand slack-jawed in wonder. *This is not a tour. I am still a prisoner.* 'It's beautiful. Gosh, the detail is incredible. Look there's Earth! And where's... oh there's Shambhala. Is that really how you spell it? These runes are weird. Hey, I can read runes! Is that because we came through the gate?'

'Yes,' said Dragonville, sounding slightly put out at having his thunder stolen. 'It is remarkable. I wouldn't have thought the All-men of that era had such artifice in them. Very stolid people, then and now. If I am any judge of character - and I am certainly that - your sister will see something like this very soon. Alas, her guide has ulterior motives.'

'And you don't?'

'I've explained my motives, repetition is tedious. Would you like to see how to get back to Earth?'

'Yes,' said Katy immediately. *Dammit. Don't just obey.*

'This is the best way from here to there.' The magician wiggled a finger and several tiny lights glowed golden in succession, starting on Shambhala, then appearing in several different circles whose names were too small to read from such a distance, then finally on Earth, on a portion of the map which Katy thought roughly corresponded with England if she turned her head a bit.

'Got it? Good. And here is another, if that proves fruitless. A bit more circuitous but avoids some big lags.' More golden lights appeared in various places, and more of them than before, but still starting on Shambhala and ending on Earth. 'Perhaps another? Pays to be prepared. Maybe one more? And again?'

The patterns of lights were coming quickly now, pattern after pattern ending on Earth. But now they no longer started on Shambhala; gates on worlds across the map lit up in rapid succession, and Katy found that she could see the names quite easily despite the distance. She turned to ask Dragonville what she was seeing, which is when she realised she couldn't turn and she couldn't look away. She couldn't move at all.

She could still speak. 'What have you done to me?' she cried.

'Not to worry, just a trick,' murmured the magician from behind her. 'This is a sight worth seeing, isn't it?'

The lights now came so blisteringly fast that they blurred into one burning whole which struck sparks across the ceiling and dazzled her painfully. 'I can't move! I can't close my eyes! Please, I'll go blind!

'Just a few more, I think.'

The ceiling was now one great white light which glowed with such intensity that Katy could only just catch the slight flicker that told her there were patterns still flowing beneath the blaze. She realised what she was seeing - every route, from anywhere to anywhere, through all the gates that existed, millions upon millions of combinations one after the other.

Then suddenly there was a hideous screeching and the glass exploded, raining dagger-like shards down upon them. Swiftly Dragonville swept the tail of his coat over Katy's head. Glass shattered on the flagstones all around her, but not one even touched her. When all was still once more Dragonville uncovered her and she stood there, breathless and trembling, until she realised she could move. She felt dazzled and disoriented, but she could see.

'What just happened?' she asked.

'What a shame,' Dragonville said, ignoring her question and regarding the carpet of glass now surrounding them. 'A weakness in the structure, perhaps. No matter. We won't be needing it anymore.' He looked at the open sky critically. 'Does it look like rain to you? I must move the books.'

'I said, what just -'

'Nothing of importance,' Dragonville said, dismissing the matter with an airy wave. 'We are seeing the sights. This was a sight to see. And to remember, yes? Highly memorable. Memory is a wonderful thing. Who knows what you will remember when you need to? Now, onwards.'

Katy didn't move. *How am I supposed to remember any of that? This is a distraction.*

'You said if I came with you, you would tell me what Echmoth wants with me.'

'Ah yes, the ultimate question. For you, anyway. Now's as good a time as any. He intends to move in.'

'What?' said Katy, nonplussed.

'To your body. He needs it to live. Or it does, its kind have no gender. It is a *dybbuk*. A thing from elsewhere, let us say. This is how they survive. They enter the body of a living person and occupy it as their own. You, the bit that you experience as yourself, is destroyed. Some of the host body's personality remains, bent to its new occupant's will. It is interesting though, what survives and what does not. The memory almost entirely remains, but the emotions and causes associated with those memories do not. What you experienced, but not how you understood it. What you saw, but not what you felt. How you acted, but not why you acted that way. It is mechanical, rote. As if it acts on instructions, like a computer following a formula given to him to make his calculations.'

Dragonville's eyelids flickered slightly, the barest movement that somehow riveted Katy gaze to his. 'What you remember happening,' he said, 'but not what you thought about it.'

He looked away and the moment between them passed. He continued. 'People misunderstand memory. It's not just in your mind but in your muscles and mannerisms and so on. Makes it much easier for a *dybbuk* to pass for human, once they're in. Which would be just spiffing for them, except human bodies tend to be quite attached to their minds. They rot without them, eventually. Still, while they last, they can be quite convincing. Your sister thought "Mr Leicester" was a legitimate teacher, didn't she?'

'She thought he was a creep,' said Katy, fighting down the horror rising within her.

'That was Echmoth. Leicester was an inoffensive supply teacher. Echmoth occupied him to be close to your sister. Shame, we would have gotten on exceedingly well, I think. He shared my fondness for gates. As do you! No wonder we're getting along so famously. I digress. All things must pass, however. While Echmoth can animate a corpse quite successfully for weeks, months, years sometimes, ultimately dead is dead. Toward the end the body reacts quite chemically, shall we say.'

Katy remembered how Echmoth had smelled at the circle. 'Mothballs and rot,' she said.

'That's right. Mothballs and rot.'

The enormity of Dragonville's words turned Katy's nerves to wire. Electric charges burst through her skin as she struggled to control herself. 'H-he's going to do that to me?' she said, her words suddenly coming in shuddering sobs.

'No!' said Dragonville, laughing. 'It's going to be worse for you. Because you're *special*.'

Katy slumped to her knees in the broken glass and doubled over, clutching her stomach with both arms as great wrenching screams of sheer horror forced their way up from the core of her being. Dragonville bent over next to her and put a solicitous arm on her shoulder. 'There, there,' he said. 'Here's my hanky again.'

'Always drive through,' said Katy.

'I beg your pardon?'

Katy rocketed up from her toes and punched Dragonville as hard as she could in the nuts. As the magician collapsed she was off, running as hard as she could for a door at the far end of the hall. Spiral stairs lay beyond; Katy hit them at full speed and almost fell down them. Three flights below she hit bottom. There was a long corridor with numerous doors leading off it. She seemed to have found her way to the kitchens, but she didn't stop to check; she ran blindly toward the end of the corridor to, where it branched left and right. *Just run,* she thought. *Don't think about where you are or where you're going. He can hear that. Just run.*

She was halfway along the corridor when the werewolf stepped in front of her. It was chewing on a pig's face, stripping the fat from the cheeks with its tongue. It seemed surprised to see her. Katy skidded and tried to turn but momentum sent her sprawling.

The werewolf looked thoughtfully at her. 'Fresh meat,' it said, licking its long lips. It cast the pig's head aside.

'Fucking try it!' Katy screamed, terror and adrenaline surging through her like fire. She put her fists up ready to fight, knowing it was madness, ready anyway.

A dagger of light shot past Katy's head and struck the werewolf in the chest, lifting it bodily into the air and throwing it back along the corridor, burning with magnesium flames. It slammed into the wall with a ferocity that shattered the stone like a bomb-burst, sending clouds of dust rolling back along the corridor and leaving wall and werewolf broken. Katy coughed violently as the cloud enveloped her, covering her in grey powder.

Belmont Dragonville stepped past her, straightening his cuffs. Irritably he waved away the dust cloud, which did not settle on him.

'I am most terribly sorry,' he said, looking severely at the dead monster through the pall. 'I left clear instructions that you were not to be molested when you fled. I regret this fellow did not care to remember. Well, nothing is lost that matters to anyone.' He smiled his rakish smile once more. 'I must say though, I didn't expect you to strike me. You're braver that you look. A palpable hit! Don't worry about the Dragonville family jewels by the way, all tickety-boo down below.'

Although his tone was jovial Katy could see that the magician was shaking with anger; when he reached for her she flinched automatically. 'Don't hurt me.'

'I'm not going to hurt you! That would be severely counterproductive. Anyway, a mighty blow struck in a just cause is no offence, I say.' The magician flicked the ends of his moustache. 'Were I in your position I would do the same, I don't doubt.' He offered his hand, making a little bow as he did so. This time she took it and struggled to her feet. She could feel the rage coursing through Dragonville's sinews.

'You're furious,' she said without thinking. *Fool. Don't provoke him.*

'Hmm? Oh no, don't worry about that. That's not on your account but rather on my own. In my haste to deal with yon canine I neglected to prepare properly. I drew on my own resources. I was incautious.' He glanced at Katy then looked away hurriedly. In that unguarded moment she saw that it was not simply rage that coursed through Belmont Dragonville, but pain too. He looked back. 'Never do this,' he advised.

Then suddenly he was himself again, roaring with laughter. 'Completely fooled! I didn't think it possible. A new experience! I count the day well-lived when I learn something new. Thank you.'

He stepped lightly along the hall and peered critically at the dead werewolf. As the dust cleared Katy could see that the beast had hit the wall so hard it had vaporized from the spine forward. A sodden red wolf skin was all that remained.

'Good for a rug, I suppose,' he said to himself. 'At least friend werewolf has provided us with a short cut.'

Katy saw that the wall was broken open; beyond it was sunlight and the outside world. With a gesture Dragonville magically widened the gap and stepped through.

He looked back at Katy. That look told her she could not run again. She gingerly walked around the shattered body of the werewolf and followed him.

A narrow courtyard between two towering, windowless walls led to another just like it, then another and another. Huge blocks of granite bigger than Katy was tall gave the maze of yards an oppressive, merciless feeling. They branched off here and there, the new lines indistinguishable from the one they followed. Katy quickly lost any sense of where she was or where she had come from. She realised the granite warren must be perfect for ambushing and bottlenecking enemies. She had visions of arrows and oil and hatred from above. Dragonville drew her on at an insistent pace, never letting go of her hand.

'That to-do back there,' he said after a while. 'That illustrates rather well something else I want you to understand.'

'What?

'The folly of practicing magic.' The lazy good humour was once again absent from his voice, replaced by a certain sadness, Katy thought. *Up and down like a yo-yo. An insanely powerful magician with wild mood swings is not a great combinatio*n. She tried not to think it again in case he was listening.

Dragonville continued walking, not looking at her and showing no sign of having heard her thought. 'There's no chance to it, you see,' he continued. 'Understanding this marks the difference between petty manipulators of magic and the great originators, like myself. He glanced at her. 'Do you practice, yourself?'

'There isn't magic any more,' said Katy.

'As I told you at the gate, this is not so.'

'Okay, but how was I supposed to know? Seventy years of it not working then it just does again. No one's been memorising spells on the off-chance for two thirds of a century.' Katy glowered at him. 'Magic was bloody stupid anyway. Went wrong more often than not. It was like playing Russian roulette by all accounts.'

'A fair point,' Dragonville allowed, 'but wrong. You describe my meaning perfectly. People think magic is random, that it goes wrong all the time and there are unintended effects. "Bimsaladin, make me a pony!" you cry, and find you've turned into a young horse. That's not a mistake. It's what you asked for. Magic is extremely precise. It makes you choose your words and thoughts exactly. You decide, and then there are consequences. You must be precise if you practice magic. Almost no one is precise in their desires. Even magisters as mighty as I fail from time to time, as just now. Though it is not failure. I got what I asked for.'

He broke off from his speech and stopped walking, so suddenly that Katy almost walked into him. He stared up at the narrow slit of grey sky visible beyond the heights.

'Magic is back, from your perspective. I've skipped all that for the time being. But now that it is back, I wouldn't recommend it as a profession.'

The magician failed to speak for a while, then turned to her as if suddenly remembering she was there. 'How can one trust when there is magic? I could wear any face, do anything to you and make you forget it. There is no trust. I have lost so much... where I am from... who I was before all this... and my parents.'

Katy couldn't help herself. 'Your parents?'

'They are long since dead. But I have no memory of my parents. That was one of the things I gave up to become who I am.'

Katy thought of her mother, and how worried she must be that her daughters hadn't come home. 'Was it worth it?'

'Oh no,' he said. 'Not even slightly.' Katy thought she saw a tear in the corner of his eye.

Katy tried to look blank, but inside her mind was churning like a mill-race. *A man tells me I'm going to die hideously with his connivance, then bares his soul to me. A killer no less, weeping for his old forgotten mum. I don't think so. What's really going on here then? Why is he telling me all this?*

Maybe because when Echmoth is finished doing whatever to me, he'll remember this conversation. He'll be in my body. You're not talking to me, you're talking to him. You want him to believe something that he wouldn't if you told him face to face. He'll remember what I saw and heard, not what I thought about it. You told me that.

Or maybe something else. When Echmoth occupies me some of my personality remains. How much? "Maybe you'll survive" you said. Will I still be here? Do you want me to know this if I am? Do you want me to do *something?*

Which is it?

Is it both?

Echmoth will remember if I say this out loud, but you, you smug bastard, you can hear my thoughts, you can speak in my mind. What are you trying to tell me?

But Dragonville was not listening, or affected not to hear. They walked on.

After another two corners Dragonville said, 'Ah ha! We're here.'

They entered a great parade ground, three or four times the size of Horse Guards. Gravel crunched underfoot. High battlements squared it on two sides and would have on the third too except the wall had been explosively destroyed. Beyond the rubble was a long bridge over a ravine and then sharp mountains thrusting almost vertically from the ground beyond. Katy glanced upward but got no sense of the shape of the Bastion, only that there was a massive, looming fortress behind her.

In the centre of the square was a circle. It was huge, easily three hundred feet in diameter, made of beautifully milled obelisks in the same blue granite. Banners hung from the outer faces, fluttering freely.

A battle had raged here, and humans had lost. Corpses of soldiers were strewn here and there, dismembered, bloated and festering, covered in flies which buzzed unceasingly. The stench was appalling, and Katy struggled not to be sick.

Here and there a campfire burned. A few werewolves, a dozen or so at most, squatted an awkward distance from one of them, as if they'd been told to sit there and didn't like it. As Katy and Dragonville entered the square their yellow eyes focused first on Katy, then on Dragonville. Then they looked away.

'Magnificent, isn't it?' said Dragonville, rubbing his hands together. Katy looked up sharply and realised he was talking about the circle. 'A thing of beauty. Don't use something for long enough and it becomes decorative, instead of the gaping hole in the Bastion's defence it was when it was active. Anyway, this part of the fortress is designed to defend against uninvited guests from Lyonesse. That's where this gate points.'

'That's stupid,' said Katy. 'Why would you build a castle with a gate inside? Anyone could open it from the other side. Why not build your fortress somewhere else?'

Because there is another gate here which must be defended at any price,' said Dragonville. 'Unfortunately, the price was paid.' He gestured across the courtyard. 'Behold the mighty werewolf army.'

'There's a dozen of them.'

There were a lot more. In the high tens of thousands, I believe. Their work is done, though. They have passed to their reward.'

Katy gasped. 'You killed them?'

'Good Lord, no. My apologies, I meant it literally. They have passed through the gate and are now massed on Lyonesse, preparing for their next conquest. These few remain to guard the gate until the rest of the pack arrives to travel onward. That was our deal. They help me, I help them leave the planet.'

'Why do they want to leave the planet?'

'Because it's dying.' Dragonville checked his pocket watch. 'Now, I really think our question and answer session is at an end. I said twenty questions and you've had them and more by my count. Shall we pay a call upon the Wolfmaker?'

'What's a Wolfmaker?'

'No more questions. You have a lesson to learn. Come, come.'

Dragonville dragged her back into the maze of courtyards. The way they took had been travelled by the attackers. The oil and arrows of her imagination had been the murderous reality here. There was something strange about it though, Katy realised. Arrows lay in neat rows against the walls. A central path was clear. It looked as if oil had poured onto a roof that wasn't there and trickled harmlessly away.

'Yes, my magic protected the werewolves as they entered these murder alleys,' said Dragonville. 'But the defenders still thought they were herding them into the death trap at the end of the run. They forgot the most important truth about warfare. About life, really.'

He stopped at a section of wall, indistinguishable from the rest, and pushed. The wall slid backward, massive blocks of stone gliding effortlessly inward on some hidden mechanism.

'Which is, in case you were wondering, that there are no secrets. Someone always knows.'

He stepped into the darkness beyond and looked back at her cheerfully. 'Dead people galore from here on in. Avanti!'

They went down. Dragonville clicked his fingers and a blue flame appeared, dancing before him as they descended. There were bodies everywhere. Some werewolf, most human, all decomposing and rank. Katy covered her face with her sleeve, but the vile odour seeped in. Rotten flesh pulsed with maggots.

Eventually they entered a long corridor lined with thick iron doors.

'The test of a people is the quality of their dungeons, don't you think?' said Dragonville conversationally. 'It speaks to their enthusiasms. These are excitingly barbarous. I understand Shambhala has not been a tranquil place.'

There were growls in the darkness, and two werewolves emerged from the shadows. 'No further,' said one.

Dragonville smiled. 'I go where I please, you know that. I bring this one to see her.'

The terrifying yellow eyes scrutinised Katy as if measuring her life against the snap of their jaws. They passed over her and returned to rest with implacable hatred on Dragonville, who had neither moved nor changed his polite smile but who was nonetheless now threatening them.

The werewolves chose wisely. 'No bright light,' said the second werewolf. 'She doesn't like it.'

'Consider it snuffed,' said Dragonville. The light went out.

Katy couldn't see a thing. Her other senses went haywire. The hot, wet breath of the werewolves seemed to billow in the air; the sound of their panting came fearfully close. The stink of fur and blood was suddenly acute, filling her nostrils, bring up bile. There was a click and the sense of movement through the air, then pressure in the small of her back which made her start violently until she recognised the weight of Dragonville's hand.

'Take ten paces forward and then stop. The door is open but there are steps down. There is light, your eyes will find it.'

Katy could feel the werewolves as she passed between them, so close that their fur brushed her sleeves. A primitive part of her brain screamed that she should turn and run, but she moved forward, guided by Dragonville.

A candle guttered in a niche in the wall. As her eyes adjusted its bare light let Katy see the room. Dragonville was right, it was a dungeon. A dozen steps down gave the room some height but made it seem like a pit from where she stood. Manacles were set into the walls and a rack of irons and pincers stood near the cold fireplace. There was a large table in the middle with chains and a winding wheel at one end; a rack, Katy realised. It was almost a cliché.

The pit was full of werewolves, but they weren't looking at her.

Suddenly she was pushed aside, crushed roughly against the wall. Two werewolves descended to the torture floor bearing a man between them. He looked dead. They threw him onto the rack. There was a wet thud and the man let out a gasping groan, shocked back to consciousness. His once red tunic was crusted brown with dried blood. He oozed at his stomach, which was distended in strange ways. There was a chorus of hungry growls.

They're going to eat him, thought Katy. *I'm going to have to watch them eat a man.*

'I don't want to learn this lesson,' she said, turning away.

'There are no lessons,' said a voice from deep in the room, a desiccated whisper like sandpaper on parchment. The werewolves fell silent immediately. 'Nothing is ever learned. No one remembers.'

Katy followed their gaze. In a corner by the fireplace there was a deep, cushioned armchair, its flowery needlepoint incongruous amid the barbarity. Curled on the chair was a werewolf unlike the others. Obviously female, she was tiny and appeared very elderly. Her fur was pure white and thinning, contrasting sharply with the pitch-dark hair of the others. Her breathing was laboured, and one hand seemed to tremble of its own accord. But the eyes that fixed on Katy Summerland were penetratingly sharp, ferociously intelligent. They were a brilliant, icy blue.

'Come down,' she said. Dragonville touched her back once more. Reluctantly Katy descended but stopped as soon as she could. Dragonville stood close behind her.

'I slept,' said the werewolf. 'The fire went out. None of these will touch it.' She gave the other werewolves a look of contempt. 'They are not trained yet. They are new.'

'Allow me,' said Dragonville. Instantly a fire appeared in the grate. The white werewolf shielded her eyes, but leaned in to the sudden warmth.

'I had not expected to see you again, magician. Our bargain is concluded. You have your trinket. I have a gateway to a new world and the means to open it. My children will swarm across it like locusts through the wheat fields.' She lowered her hand and stared with utter hatred at Dragonville. 'What more is there between us?'

'A little business, perhaps. I promised to bring the rest of your children here for one thing. And there is the other matter.'

'That matter is between you and God.'

'Indeed. Apropos of that, an introduction.' He prodded Katy sharply and she took a step forward despite herself.

The old she-wolf stood up, very slowly, and crossed the floor to stand in front of Katy. Katy saw that the trembling arm was withered and useless, the paw clubbed and curled in on itself. Around her neck, her only adornment, was a large pearl strung on a golden chain.

'Who is this one?'

'A special and unfortunate girl,' said Dragonville.

'Ah.' The white werewolf looked her up and down. 'Fortunate, you mean.' She reached out. Katy flinched away but found that Dragonville was holding her. The werewolf stroked her hair with her shaking paw, over and over, seemingly entranced. 'A golden child,' she said. 'Hair of the sun. A worthy vessel.'

'Looks the part,' murmured Dragonville.

The werewolf appeared not to hear. She locked eyes with Katy. 'Fortunate child. Fortunate to be chosen. As I once was.'

Suddenly her voice grew louder, a querulous bark of glee. 'You will be the vessel of God! The Moon made flesh! He will shed his dead shell and be reborn.' She looked at the other werewolves, who cringed away from her. 'You will see him as I see him. You will see God!'

She started to howl but broke off almost immediately, coughing violently and staggered a little. One of the werewolves came immediately to support her but she brushed it away irritably. 'I will live to see it,' she finished, her voice a whisper once more.

She turned away and noticed the man lying on the rack table for the first time. 'I thought I was finished,' she said.

A grey-furred werewolf emerged from the wall of darkness. It approached the ancient with exaggerated deference, almost awe. 'He is the last of the mountain men, great one. There are no more.'

The white werewolf considered this. 'Old. A breath away from death. Why bring him to me now, so late?'

We were told to bring all living. We thought he would die. He hasn't. He is strong for a man. He killed many of us. He is worthy.'

The white werewolf leaned in to the dying man. He eyes rolled in his head as he tried to focus. 'What was your name, man?' she said.

The man whispered, but the words barely left his mouth and Katy did not hear the name.

'You will not remember,' the white werewolf said. 'That life is over. You are dying and there is nothing after. No torch to guide you home. But take heart. I am the Wolfmaker. I will make you anew. Young and strong. All men will be wolves. I have seen it.'

The man shook his head, the tiniest movement all that his strength allowed.

The Wolfmaker gestured to the grey werewolf, who ripped the man's tunic open at the shoulder. The Wolfmaker bit deeply into the man's flesh, jaws closing around his arm. Katy flinched as the man screamed. Blood spurted through the Wolfmaker's mouth and dripped down her pelt.

It was too much for the old man. As the scream died, so did he. His last breath rattled across his lips. flecking them with his life's blood. In the soft glow of the magical fire, Katy saw the light in the man's grey eyes go out.

'She killed him,' whispered Katy, not realising she had said it aloud.

'Watch,' said Dragonville softly.

The werewolves stared intently at the corpse, except for the Wolfmaker, who turned and shuffled back to her chair. Suddenly the body arched violently, and the man drew in a ragged breath that sounded like a scream made backwards. His body spasmed, beating itself against the table. The man clawed at himself, tearing away the remains of his tunic, exposing the gaping hole that was all the remained of his belly, the coils of his guts horrifically exposed. But as Katy watch the wound began to close, new flesh growing across the gap, knitting itself together as if the blow that separated it had never been struck. The man's other wounds likewise melted away, except where the Wolfmaker had bitten him. That seeped a strange white ichor, ugly and rancid. The man sat up, wringing wet with sweat and shaking like a leaf. He stared wildly at Belmont Dragonville.

'I'm healed,' he said in a thick voice. 'Great Fathers, man, I'm healed.'

'Afraid not, old thing,' said Dragonville.

The man shuddered suddenly, and said 'Wh-', but the word turned into a strangled scream, then a shriek the like of which Katy had never heard. The man slid from the table and onto the floor in front of her, writhing as though he was possessed.

Katy watched him change.

Limbs buckled and broke, stretching obscenely and twisting into new shapes. The man's chest burst and reformed instantly in a different, larger form, and hair sprouted across his body, matting into a thick pelt. His jaw dislocated, snapped and elongated, his skull flattened and moved forward to meet it. Teeth were pushed from his mouth as fangs grew in to replace them. The agonised scream was choked off as the lungs grew and vocal chords rebuilt themselves. The scream became a howl, first of fear and pain, then of rage and hate and hunger. Katy clutched at her ears and screamed in terror.

The werewolf arose, taller, leaner, more powerful, fearsomely lupine. The once grey eyes were now a bright, feverish yellow, its fur as black as the infinite void. The werewolf leered hungrily at Katy and lurched uncertainly toward her on new-made paws.

'I don't think so,' said Dragonville. He held up a hand and the werewolf froze, clawing desperately at the air a few inches from Katy's face. She stood extremely still.

A thrill of outrage ran through the pack at the magic done to the new werewolf. A few surged toward the magician, fangs bared.

'Stop.'

The Wolfmaker only whispered, but the pack stopped immediately.

'Come here.' This to the new one. Dragonville released the werewolf, which obediently padded over to the chair.

'Sit.'

The werewolf folded its legs and sat down. Its tail beat the floor happily as it gazed up at the Wolfmaker.

'What is your name?'

The tail stopped beating. The new werewolf looked confused. 'I don't have one,' it said eventually.

'Then I will give you one. You are Wolf.'

The werewolf nodded, and the tail resumed. 'I am Wolf,' it growled happily.

'We shall withdraw,' Dragonville announced suddenly.

'Yes,' said the Wolfmaker. She looked at Katy. 'Come back when you are God.'

Katy managed to wait until they were back on the surface before she gave in to the terror. She was sick until there was nothing left to come up, until the heaving felt like it would turn her stomach inside out. She cried until there were no tears left, heartsick sobs that tore at her throat and choked her to the point that she couldn't breathe. She doubled over and clutched at her chest, and beat at it just to feel something other than fear.

Dragonville stood discreetly aside, handkerchief at the ready. 'There, there,' he said after a while. 'There, there. It wasn't that bad, was it?'

Katy's head shot up. 'Not that bad? It was fucking *horrible*. It was the worst thing I have ever seen. The worst thing.'

'My, you have lead a sheltered life, child.'

'No, I haven't. That was *awful*. Why did you show me that? Why would you possibly want me to see that?'

'It was a sight to see. A lesson to learn. Events should be witnessed, don't you agree? I must say, however often I see the Wolfmaker at her work it never fails to impress. To see the Wolfmaker's bite transform that man, to see that white poison kill him, and bring him back, and heal him, yes, but to drive out the man and create something new in his place, remake the flesh and cleanse the mind... That is something you will never forget, no matter what happens.'

He leaned in, and smiled his beautiful, rakish smile. 'Some things are never forgotten,' he said. 'Don't you agree?'

'Don't I agree?' Katy's mind whirled with everything she'd seen and heard. All the pieces, she realised now, that Dragonville had careful fed her.

'The survivors. The Wolfmaker changed them all?'

'That's right,' said Dragonville, his encouraging tone returned once more. 'Think it through now.'

'And men from the North? Where the gate is.'

'Yes. And..?'

'Men from all of Shambhala?'

'Yes.'

'*How many?*' asked Katy fiercely.

Dragonville considered this. 'All of them, I think. All the humans on this world.'

'That's *genocide*.'

Dragonville laughed. 'That's one way to put it. I am sure the Wolfmaker sees it as gene*sis*. She thinks her species is dying and she's right, it is. All magical creatures are. Your sister knows this. The Wolfmaker has found a novel solution.' He paused to reflect, then added. 'Though I must say, she is somewhat messianic. She wants a new world. This one's on its way out, you see.'

'And you're helping her!'

'I'm helping all humanity. All life everywhere, really. I have a higher purpose. But for the moment, yes.'

'You're *Satan*!' screamed Katy.

Dragonville laughed again. 'I am far worse than Satan. I am more in God's company. I surpass death itself.'

He paused again, and chuckled to himself. '"I surpass death", that's a good one. I must write that down.' He fished out a fresh cigar from an inside pocket.

'Mind you, what separates me from God and Satan is that I don't *want* to kill people,' he continued, striking a match and setting it to the tobacco. 'It is not the point. I don't kill people on a whim, or a bet, or because they get in my way. I don't kill people because I enjoy it. It's just an unfortunate side effect of my work. It's not what I *want*.' He blew smoke into the air.

'What the fuck do you want?' gasped Katy.

'Oh, that's easy. Didn't I tell you? I want it to be over. To achieve my end and put down my burden. Regrettably you must die first.'

'I'll kill you,' she said.

'If only it were that simple. No, your destiny lies elsewhere. It can be easy or hard, but your story ends here. But take heart. Have I not enlivened your final hours? It this not a gift? No lesson is wasted on those who have the desire to learn, or the wit to understand.'

Do you understand why the Wolfmaker is important?

Then Katy understood.

I understand, she thought.

'Well,' said Dragonville, in a satisfied tone. 'Our time together is concluded. I am pleased. I may publish.'

'I'll tell him,' said Katy. It was a threat and a promise.

'You won't know how. Time to sleep. Night night, my dear.'

Katy collapsed.

Chapter Nineteen: The Howl

Echmoth dreamed.

In my dream, I have died. This happens from time to time. This time it is unexpected. The body was new and seemed vigorous. The former occupant put up a fight before I obliterated him. For months, everything has been as normal. But now it fails catastrophically. I do not know why.

And I have made a mistake. I am in the wilderness, far from the places humans frequent. There are no other bodies to occupy. In my dream, I am terrified beyond imagination. I know what happens when there are no bodies.

When I realised that the body was failing I set it to run as hard as it could toward the last place I saw humans. I will not reach it. First the nerves failed, one by one, turning the body's sprint into a formless lurch, limbs flailing, feet dragging. Then the flesh began to slough off, the organs give up their bile and blood, the meat turn black and rancid. The cadaver struggled on for some miles before the legs gave way, a little longer on its knees, then on the stumps when the knees tore through. Now I am crawling, dragging the body forward, knowing it is pointless, too scared to stop.

Now there is a man here I do not recognise. I turn immediately to jump into him, but I can't. There is no one there. Then I recognise him. It is the former occupant of this body. He stands there looking as he was, not as I have become. I do not understand how this can be.

He looks down at me in disgust. 'Look what you've done to me,' *he says.* 'This is justice, I suppose.'

I try and speak but there is nothing left to form the words. Or I would have said, this is not justice. Justice is what happens now.

The body fails. I leave the body.

In my dream, I am screaming screaming screaming as the acid air burns me alive without consuming me, melts my soul without letting me die. Agony intolerable everlasting unrelenting a trillion trillions scream alongside me. But they are not like me. They do not see the world at all. I see the world as it is.

I do not know how long it is until I see the movement. It might as well be eternity. As soon as I see it, I know it for what it is. I jump.

In my dream, I am ecstatic. The relief is profound. But I realise immediately that something is wrong. This is not a human. It is something else. Something animal, but not animal. The mind of a wolf.

I try to kill the mind, but I cannot take hold of it. But nor am I thrown out, as I would be from a dog's mind. It is as though I am clinging to a cliff edge, scrabbling upward as the lip gives way under my hands. Each lunge stops me falling but I cannot climb, and then the earth falls away under my hand and I must make another desperate leap. At least I am not in as much pain.

In my dream, I continue like this for some time, scrabbling to hold onto this alien consciousness for fear of what happens if I let go. I become accustomed to my new mode of existence. It becomes manageable.

At the point when I no longer have to concentrate with everything I have on clinging on, I realise that I can see what the wolf mind is thinking about. It is thinking about me. It is aware of me. This has never happened before.

The wolf mind has experienced my failed attack on her as a profound religious revelation. It seems the wolf mind is mad. I am not sure this was my doing. The wolf mind has ideas about the world which are not mine. I have however become the thread which ties them together.

As the years progress, I discover that while I cannot control the body, I can influence the wolf mind because of her constant focus on me. Eventually, I learn how to make her do what I want.

I send her to find humans.

'You found them, sure enough,' said a voice. 'Just not the right kind, hey?'

Echmoth opened the eyes it was currently using. Belmont Dragonville stood over the body, which lay in the bed fully clothed.

'Wakey wakey, Echmoth old thing,' said the magician, smiling easily. 'Enjoying your beauty sleep?'

'I was dreaming,' said Echmoth. 'The body requires it.'

'Anything exciting?'

Echmoth considered Dragonville's preferred idiom. 'The old days,' it said.

'Ah, nostalgia. Comes to us all. You know these are my rooms? My bed?'

'You don't sleep. I have never seen you sleep. I awaited your return. Lethargy overtook the body; your bed was to hand.'

'Glad it was useful,' said Dragonville cheerfully. 'Hold hard,' he continued. His expression changed to a concerned frown. 'I say, you are looking a bit green about the gills. Are you quite well?'

Echmoth considered briefly whether the body possessed gills and finding it did not filed the statement under yet more idiom. It made the body rise and cross to a small oval mirror hanging on a nearby wall. It examined the body's face and made it purse its lips in disapproval.

'Yes, there seems to be a considerable amount of necrotic flesh. This body is becoming difficult to maintain.'

It pressed the body's index finger onto its right cheek and, with a little effort, pushed it through the flesh into the body's mouth. The body experienced searing pain and significant distress. Echmoth noted both effects.

'The body rots,' it said. 'It is the way of bodies. Shortly it will fail, and I will require a new one.'

'This is, of course, a matter for you,' said Dragonville. He drew on his cigar and sent a jet of smoke into the air.

'I know. I merely make conversation to maintain our relationship while our interests coincide. I care not whether you respond.'

Dragonville grinned. 'I believe you are only supposed to think that bit, old love,' he said.

Echmoth considered the reply. 'I see. I find it difficult to remember human conventions unless I am concentrating. The body usually manages that aspect of our existence, but it is in distress. I have found that the closer a body comes to failing the less its personality asserts itself. I convey an apology, if that is required.'

'Not at all, Echmoth. You need never apologise to me.'

'Fortunately, salvation is at hand,' Echmoth continued. 'I will occupy the girl.' It made the body frown briefly. 'Salvation at hand? Is that correct usage? As the body fails I become less certain about linguistic constructions also. The brain begins to degrade.'

'You convey your meaning admirably. I advise against it.'

'Why? The girl is special.'

Dragonville sighed. 'We've talked about this, old boy. The girl is special, yes, but until the Narrow Way is opened you will have no way of invigorating the body. It will rot, as this one has. Like all the others. Unless you wish to remain a passenger?'

'No. I will find another body temporarily. The castle must be full of them.'

'None in a better state than this, I fear. As for the living, the Wolfmaker has been exceedingly thorough.'

'You're here.'

Dragonville laughed uproariously. 'A joke! Echmoth, you card. You really couldn't, and even if you could, what would become of our plans?'

'Yes. You are right.'

'You could take up residence in a werewolf. Plenty of them about, no one will miss one.'

'That is not an option.'

Echmoth took a moment to fully experience the body's state of being and found it distasteful, but not intolerable. 'Very well. I will remain in Leicester. He will last a little while longer.' Echmoth made the body look severely at Dragonville. 'I should have brought the other girl as well. Then it would not matter if she rotted.'

'In fact, it's the other way around. Really dear boy, you have the memory of a goldfi- Ah. I see. I have indelicately referred to your condition. Let me remind you then that we have planned this. The girl needs to go with the boy.'

'And if she fails, if the boy fails?'

Dragonville smoothed his moustache. 'Then the Writing will turn out to mean something else, and we will fulfil it that way. The Summerland girls are still special; you can occupy the one you have. It will be infinitely better than now. You will not fix, and the body will rot, but we will find you others until the prophecy is fulfilled. That's the good thing about prophecy; it will happen, we just don't know what it means yet. I am confident I do not mistake its meaning, but if I am wrong, we learn even from failed experiments.'

'Your prophecy is ridiculous.'

'Not mine!' laughed Dragonville. 'I don't do prophecy. It sends you doolally. Catch me staring into a scrying stone, I should coco.'

'You admit it is madness,' said Echmoth suspiciously.

'I allow only that the author went mad. That is a commonplace. As for whether the prophecy is madness, we shall see. We must both hope not.'

The magician took a long, contemplative toke on his cigar. Echmoth noted that the body objected to the smoke. Echmoth made the body make a disapproving sound.

'Sorry, terribly rude of me,' said Dragonville, without doing anything to stop the smoke. 'Prophecy is a terrible business. Boils the bonce. Is that what happened to your furry companion? No offence old boy, but you're not God and you don't think you are. You aren't the type. Why does she worship you?'

Echmoth considered how much of the truth to tell. The dying body feebly asserted its desire for accuracy.

'I made a mistake. I possessed her. It didn't take. When I found a new body, she remained with me. I discovered that she could see me. Me, Dragonville, not the body. Me as I am.'

'Remarkable.' Dragonville seemed genuinely interested, although Echmoth found it difficult to tell for certain. 'What do you look like in the flesh? So to speak.'

'I don't know,' said Echmoth, as if the question had never occurred to it. 'That concept is meaningless to us. Evidently, impressive.'

'Yes, she seems keen. Well that's all just fascinating. We should talk about this in more depth, there's an article in this. I may publish.'

'No,' said Echmoth. Then he said, 'Are you sure the girl survived?'

The First of Wolves turned a piece of bark over and over in his hands, examining it minutely. Where his paws touched it, the wood crumbled; dust scattered in the air and tumbled away like pollen on the breeze.

We are justified, he thought. *It is necessary.*

The First of Wolves could not remember the world without the rust-red rot. He had lived through fifty winters, the height of maturity for a werewolf, and could expect to see another twenty or thirty before he became useless to the pack and they left him behind. The Wolfmaker, by far the oldest of the Great Pack at more than twice his age, remembered the world before the rot, but not he. The rot was in his earliest memories. He remembered the pack moving on, seeking new ranges, leaving the rot behind them. It always caught up. Then, lately, they found the rot already there when they arrived. It killed everything green and left no prey to hunt. The werewolves found other prey.

Wolves had always hunted man. This was the way of things. Men alone or in small numbers in a wolf range could expect no mercy. But since the beginning times men and wolves had not lived close by each other. The world was vast and neither men nor wolves dominated it. There had been room for both, prey enough for both. Anyway, the men seemed more interested in fighting each other. The rot had shrunk the world and set predators along each other's paths. The rot, and the Wolfmaker's vision.

The First of Wolves did not see what the Wolfmaker saw when she looked at the dead man. The series of dead men, rather - a dead man had left for the other world and another dead man had returned, who the Wolfmaker said was the same Echmoth in whom she saw the moon made flesh. There had been others before. He saw only the death, a rot of a different kind that made Echmoth smell repugnant and evil.

The First of Wolves was not used to thinking in terms of good and evil. Humans used those words. Wolves did not see the world that way.

The Wolfmaker had recognised the new dead man instantly, and the First of Wolves had no reason to suppose she was wrong. That the Wolfmaker could see and do things that no other wolf could was unquestioned, powers that she ascribed to the dead man's grace. Wolves could not do magic, but the Wolfmaker could. Wolves could not see across time, but the Wolfmaker had. And no other wolf could create new wolves - not the diseased lycanthropes that were the poison humans found in every wolf's bite, but pure werewolves, instantly transformed from one species to another at the close of the Wolfmaker's jaw. It was the one thing that stopped the First of Wolves thinking that the ancient white werewolf was mad. All men will be wolves, she had said, then she had made it so.

When he was a cub the Wolfmaker had found what was left of his pack. She had told her story, then touched each one of them, paused, then moved on. She stopped at him. 'You're like me,' she said. 'Come. You will be First of Wolves.' And he came, and was.

They all came. The packs had become the Great Pack, unified in a way that still only barely seemed possible to the First of Wolves. It was all her doing. There had never been a Wolfmaker before.

The First of Wolves grunted a laugh at that thought. There had never been a First of Wolves before either. Now here he was, at the head of an army that had ravaged a continent. A dagger made of teeth and rage thrust into the human heart.

Or rather, not at the head of it. Some of the pack was still in the northland, hunting humans. The greater part, the ones that had taken the Bastion, were now a world away, killing Lyonesse men and waiting for the Wolfmaker and her God. The rest were strung out between the Anvil and the Bastion over thousands of miles, either rounding up more bodies for the Wolfmaker or waiting for the magician to retrieve them.

And here the First of Wolves was, crouched among dead men around a fire he'd set himself because no other wolf would touch it, thinking thoughts that no other wolf would think.

'What's funny?' said a werewolf near him.

'Nothing.'

'When do we leave?' asked another, in a surly tone.

'When the others return. When the Wolfmaker's business here is concluded.'

'This place is barren,' said the werewolf. 'No trees. Too much rock.'

The First of Wolves grunted. 'The world is barren. I will not miss it. The sooner we are done with it the b-'

There was howling in the mountains. The distant sound echoed off the stone. Each werewolf pricked up its ears as the sound reached them. Then they stood, one by one, and turned to face the First of Wolves. Then one by one, each werewolf raised its muzzle toward the sky and joined the howl, a long, keening lament of sorrow and loss. In the castle behind them other voices raised to join it.

The First of Wolves could not cry. Instead he screamed.

The scream lasted for as long as his lungs would stand it, until his breath was lost, until his heart felt like it would give out.

The First of Wolves lost time. When next he became aware, he was on his knees, bleeding from the wounds his own claws had cut into his chest. The pain focused his mind. The despair and sorrow turned to anger and rage, and rage demanded vengeance. The First of Wolves knew where to go for that.

'The magician! He will take us to them! Take us to the ones who slew my cub!'

He ran to the fortress. Through the hidden doors and along corridors lined with the putrefying dead. He found the stairwell which led to the rooms the magician had claimed. As he set foot on the stair he heard the voice of God.

'Are you sure the girl survived?'

The First of Wolves stopped moving.

'Of course,' said the magician. 'The boy was hiding nearby. He reacted to the wolves as I expected. You now need more wolves.'

'There are many more. They are expendable.'

'I am sure the First of Wolves would disagree.'

'Who care what dogs think? It was good fortune that the boy happened across the circle at the right moment.'

'Stuff,' said the magician. 'Nothing fortunate about it. I've been guiding his steps since the moment he left the Anvil. A little rock fall here, a judicious wolf howl there, an unexpected impassable canyon or two, all served to bring him to the right spot when I was ready. I am very good at this Echmoth, do try and remember that.'

'I still dislike this plan. It is absurdly complex. I do not understand the point of that ridiculous pantomime at the circle.'

The magician sighed. 'My dear Echmoth, we must find you a less porous brainbox as soon as possible. We need the boy to do certain things we cannot do. For that to happen the girl must think in a certain way. To have the right motivation. And she must tell him certain things, to ensure he in turn is properly motivated. And I must say my dear fellow, while you may dislike the plan, it is working. We have brought it about with minimal effort. On your part,' the magician added, rather pointedly.

'They might do anything now they are out of our grasp.'

'I assure you, I will nudge them in the right direction from time to time.' A pause. 'There is a complicating factor I was not expecting, but I will deal with her when the time comes. Overall, Echmoth, I -'

The First of Wolves crashed through the door, howling incomprehensibly with rage and betrayal. With a sweep of his arm he clawed through Dragonville, sending him flying across the room to land in a broken heap. In the same second he plunged his claws deep into the flaccid flesh of Echmoth's chest and twisted. The body fountained blood from the mouth and collapsed. The First of Wolves yanked his arm free as the creature fell, taking ribs and red meat with it.

'Thus to betrayers,' snarled the First of Wolves. 'All will die.' He barked furiously, flinging a handful of flesh into the fireplace. He padded over to the prone body of Belmont Dragonville, which looked without sight into eternity. Awkwardly it clawed open the magician's pockets. Of the items which tumbled free, it selected the two it recognised, the two it wanted. A blue glass disc surrounded by gold wire, and a stone.

He spat in Dragonville's face. 'Rot in hell, magician.'

The First of Wolves stood and made to leave, then paused and returned to Echmoth. With studied contempt, he pissed on the corpse.

'You are not God,' he said. 'You are a creature. Come back from the dead again, I will kill you again. I will kill every form you take from now until the last day. You are cursed in my sight. All wolves will know this.'

The First of Wolves careened down the stairs and back through the castle to the parade ground.

'Rouse, you dogs!' he shouted. The werewolves sprang to their feet.

'Vengeance,' he said. 'I will have vengeance. My cub has been slain. Betrayed by the magician! He has paid the price. Others must pay. Blood for blood!'

His voice rose to a roar. The werewolves bayed at the thought.

'We go to the North. Behold.'

The First of Wolves showed the other wolves the lens. The ones nearest to him looked with distaste at the device.

'You've killed the magician,' said one. 'That's useless.'

'I am not like you,' the First of Wolves snarled. 'I am like the Wolfmaker.'

He thrust the lens forward and the world opened before the suddenly terrified wolves. The granite walls vanished and mountains took their place. Snow blew into their faces. The First of Wolves slipped the lens into the pouch around his neck.

'Forwards,' he snarled. He ran into the landscape. Without a thought the werewolves followed their leader into the wild.

'Well that's a perfectly good suit completely ruined,' said Belmont Dragonville, getting up. 'Most annoying. Do you know how far it is to Savile Row?'

There were huge rents in his clothes from the First of Wolves' claws, but the skin visible through them was smooth and unblemished. Echmoth could see no injury at all.

This made it extremely suspicious.

'I saw you eviscerated,' it said.

'Are you sure you saw that?' said Dragonville, smiling pleasantly. 'Or didn't I actually move nimbly backward just in the nick of time, causing only my tailor distress?'

'No,' said Echmoth. 'You were disembowelled. And now you are not. This body, however, now perceives events as you described. Please do not attempt magic on me, it doesn't work and the cognitive dissonance gives this body a headache. You should realise, Dragonville, that I see the world as it is. I cannot be deceived.'

Dragonville's eyes widened, and he beamed a brilliant smile. 'Do you now, and is that so? Quite remarkable! Very good. I am both chastened and impressed.' He bowed slightly. '*Dybbuk* are immune to memory altering magic. A day I learn something is a day not wasted. I will not glamour you again.'

'Good. And your return to health?'

'Is my own affair. On a related subject, you appear to have died.'

Echmoth examined the body. 'Yes, I believe you are correct. The First of Wolves' claws appear to have done severe damage.'

Echmoth took direct control of the body's nervous system and stood up. 'I can maintain this for a little while. A few hours at best. Are there no living men?'

'No.'

'Then our previous conversation is moot. The question is decided. I will enter the girl.'

Dragonville opened his mouth to speak, then appeared to think better of it. 'Very well,' he said. 'Needs must, and all that. I emphasise that you must fix the transition or the body will die as all the others have. You will feel ecstatic, but it will not last. Without *Elpis* there is quite literally no hope.'

'I see. We must hope that Amelia Summerland arrives soon. Where is Katherine Summerland?'

'In one of the tower rooms. We had a pleasant walk and a chit-chat and an unfortunate encounter with the Wolfmaker. We discussed your intentions toward her. I won't bore you with it, you'll remember in due course. Then I put her to sleep.'

'Yes. You appear not to have noticed that the First of Wolves took something from you while you were inconvenienced.'

Dragonville looked surprised, patted his pockets, and frowned. 'Bother. The fellow has made off with my lens. And the bloodstone.'

'Does this complicate matters?'

'Potentially. Fear not old thing, Uncle Belmont will handle it.'

'See to it. Our agreement has brought us this far. Nothing can be allowed to threaten our work.'

'*Our* work? Oh, I quite agree.' Dragonville smoothed his moustache with his index finger. 'You dying would certainly be a threat to our partnership.'

Echmoth made the body grimace in distaste. 'I can't die. You mean the body.'

'I mean the body,' agreed Dragonville. 'You know Echmoth, it occurs to me we have a great deal in common. We should have little chats like this more often. But not now, you need to rebuild yourself. Off you trot then. A new life awaits you.'

'A better life.'

Dragonville regarded the rotten, stinking, broken corpse. 'That seems likely.'

Katy dreamed about snakes shedding their skin.

She woke up in the same bed she had occupied before, soaked in cold sweat and terrified, panting in panic.

'Hello,' said a voice.

The room was in darkness, but Katy could make out a figure sitting in the high-backed chair across from the bed. It wasn't Dragonville.

'I hope you slept well,' said the voice. It was male, high pitched and querulous. A wasp-chewing voice, her dad would have said. But there was something wrong with it. The man wheezed like a ragged concertina.

He struck a match, and the phosphor fizz dazzled Katy for a moment. The flame travelled to a candle and when the wick caught, Katy saw him.

'Mr Leicester!'

'In the flesh,' said the man. 'That is a joke,' he added.

Katy remembered. 'Echmoth.'

As her eyes became accustomed to the dim light she became aware that it wasn't just Echmoth's voice that was wrong. He sat in the chair, left leg crossing the right, sleeves resting casually on the armrests. But it was if a mannequin sat there, stiff, unmoving, inhuman. A mannequin, or a corpse.

Echmoth noticed her attention. 'Yes, there is almost nothing left of Leicester. He was serviceable. This is my highest praise.'

He leaned forward and stood up in one sudden, jerky movement. There was a wet, tearing sound, as if something sticky had been pulled from the leather. Katy caught a whiff of rotting meat that made her feel sick to her stomach. She realised she couldn't move her legs.

'I took the precaution of immobilising you,' said Echmoth. 'The magician is elsewhere and I am in no condition to run after you.'

He lurched forward like a drunk toward the bar, outstretched arm eagerly seeking her. He stroked her neck; his fingers were ice cold. Katy cringed away from his touch. Echmoth noticed this and considered his hand, turning it back and forth. Even in the dim light Katy could see that it had turned blue.

'My apologies,' said Echmoth. 'I have ceased to care for this body. It has died.'

'What *are* you?'

'Humans call us *dybbuk*. The handful who know we exist, that is. I see Dragonville told you this so I will not repeat the story. I also see you have been thinking about zombies. I suppose I am one. Or this body is, anyway. I possessed this man and obliterated his mind and re-animated his body. I will now do this to you.'

Katy began to cry. Echmoth considered her dispassionately, as though she were a sick animal waiting to be put down.

'There, there, as I believe the phrase is. I have heard Dragonville use it in this context.'

'Don't touch me you fucking pervert,' Katy sobbed.

Echmoth smiled, if the crack and split of his lips could be called that. 'What foul mouths you Summerland girls have. I must write a note to your mother.' He stroked her again, this time running his hand down her face.

'I do not admire your flesh for that reason,' he continued. 'I admire it because it will shortly be my own. I think by the standards of your species you are quite beautiful. This will make life easier. There is a joke in that statement, but you do not see it. I am amused.'

Katy choked back a sob. 'The werewolves think you're God. But you're not. You're the Devil.'

'I am neither. The Wolfmaker is mad and therefore easy to manipulate. The rest are obedient and credulous. But really, does it make a difference whether I am God or not? It doesn't matter if it's true. If they believe it, they make it true.'

He stroked her again, almost tenderly. 'As for the other, I see you accused Dragonville of the same thing. He is a much better candidate for Mephistopheles. I only do what is in my nature to do.'

Katy realised something was wrong. Her head felt like it was tearing open, but there was no wound and no pain. Echmoth was suddenly still, and then slumped a little, as if he had wound down.

'All beings have standards by which they judge correct behaviour,' he said. 'By yours I am a man of darkness. For this reason I chose my name. I am Echmoth. I am the one who knows death.'

Katy could no longer speak. She felt something sliding into her mind. Echmoth's voice continued, but the words were now in Katy's head.

'The world is invisible to you, but I see it clearly. My kind bubble in the bile of creation. Most of us are unaware of the world and will never be aware of it. We flit unseen around the edges of humanity, screaming in voices you will never hear.

'But some of us are different. Some of us see the world. We see a way to escape the horror. We see *you.*'

There was nothing in the world for Katy now save Echmoth's voice. Peaceful, serene, without pity, it filled her mind and body.

'That body was temporary. It rotted. Yours is different. Or will be.'

He jerked suddenly, like a marionette whose strings had been yanked. The skin on his face started to melt and slough away. Something caused Katy's hand to move. A silver glow haloed the flesh.

'This man, Leicester, was inclined to lecture. He saw the world as a sheet of facts to be shared and tested. He liked accuracy. I will try not to retain that, it has been tiresome. Perspective is interesting, isn't it? Everything turns on how you see the world. By your standards, I am a cruel man, in that I do not care for other life forms. This is normal for my species. But consuming humans for so many years has changed me a little, I think. It has made me see things from your point of view. As I take everything from you, I will give you a gift. It is the gift of oblivion. This is not to be taken lightly. Cherish it, briefly, and know what it means. Some of your species believe in an afterlife. Have you ever wondered what happens after death? Let me tell you. *I do.*'

He slumped over, his now formless face gaping horribly. Something rushed toward her. Then there was Nothing.

Chapter Twenty: Ivory

Blix burst out of thin air and slammed into a sandbank. Constant landed almost on top of her. They lay there for a few moments, dazed and aching. Then they realised they were touching and scrambled awkwardly apart.

'That's never going to get any better, is it?' Blix groaned. 'I think I've got whiplash.'

'I think it might get worse,' said Constant, rubbing his arm. 'Like an angry cyclops... Where's Kit?'

Kit McCoy had landed in softer sand and was lightly buried. Blix pulled her out. She shook herself like a dog in a bathtub and a mini sandstorm enveloped the others.

'Pardon,' she said, primly, then grinned. 'I'm gonna have sand where the sun don't shine for weeks!'

They were in the shadow of a low outcrop of rock in what appeared to be a deep depression in dunes of sand. The sand was a dull grey-yellow and gave an inch underfoot. The circle they had come through seemed to consist of a few nubs of rock, none higher than a couple of feet, scattered haphazardly in a vague oval. Save for the three companions there was no sound at all.

'What a dump,' said Blix. She booted a nub. 'Whoever built this circle didn't try very hard. I've seen bigger stones on a driveway.'

'I don't know,' said Constant. 'Look a bit closer.'

He scooped a few handfuls of sand away from the edge of the rock. There was more rock beneath. He kept going. The rock didn't stop.

'I think it's a full-size circle that's just buried,' he said. 'No one's been here for a long time. I also think if it had been completely buried we wouldn't have been able to come through. We were lucky.'

'Yeah.' said Blix. 'That's us. Lucky. Which shard did you use?'

'The big one.'

'And?'

He showed her. The tiny sliver of stone was rusted over.

'Well, that answers that,' said Blix.

Constant put the shard back in the cloth and carefully folded it away. 'We need another artefact.'

Blix made a *pfft* sound through pursed lips. 'I bet they're just lying around waiting for us. Where's Kit got to?'

There was a shout from above. Kit was standing on the rim of the hollow, about fifty yards away, waving at them.

'Come and see this!' she yelled.

'How did she get up there?' said Blix. Then she realised she was talking to herself. Constant was already on his way up the dune, scrabbling as his feet sank into the sand. Blix shrugged and headed up after them.

As she stepped out of the shade the heat hit her like a club, making her stagger as the stark white light stung her eyes. She dug her shades out of her satchel and slid them on.

'Ain't that something,' said Kit, as Blix joined them.

The sand was endless. They were at a high point; the sand shelved away gently from where they stood for about half a mile, then sloped off precipitously to the desert floor, perhaps four or five hundred feet below. Giant dunes undulated across the landscape in every direction, swathed in colours ranging from dull grey and brown to brilliant yellow, which seemed to glow in the sunlight and turn a deep gold in the shadows. The landscape shimmered in the heat haze.

'I don't understand,' Constant said. 'The gate is supposed to stand near a great salt sea, a thousand miles from shore to shore.'

'Don't look like no sea to me,' Kit said. 'Sea of sand maybe. Ain't seeing no ships of the desert though.'

'Ceto is an ocean goddess. How can there be no sea on a world named after her?' He looked very unhappy. 'There was a map in one of the books.' He pulled out a crumpled sheaf of papers from his bag and extracted a particularly ancient-looking parchment. It was mostly blue. 'There are supposed to be people here too. With boats.'

He looked around with a slightly lost look on his face, as if the ocean might be hiding on the other side of the hollow.

Kit rubbed her chin thoughtfully. 'Looks like you brought the wrong map, kid. Or maybe blue means sand here. Or maybe they moved the circle somewhere else?'

'Rifts are fixed points. It can't move. Like I said.'

The American scuffed up some sand with her boot, slightly annoyed by Constant's tone. 'Well they didn't move the sea, now did they? Better hope your books got it right from now on kid, or we are in big trouble.'

Maybe the sea moved itself. Blix's heart sank. She tried to ignore the thought and what it implied. It was too big to think about after everything she'd been through. But it squatted in her mind, ugly and bloody, daring her to give it a name.

'Let's just say the map's right,' she said hurriedly. 'How far to the gate?'

'The book said fifty miles,' Constant replied, shielding his eyes against the sun. 'It's supposed to be on an island offshore.' He pointed to a blip of green on the parchment. It had a tiny drawing of a gate with the word 'Helikon' written next to it in runes. 'And we're here.' He traced a line to a larger landmass and another drawing of a gate. This one had only a question mark next to it. His finger tapped nervously against the symbol.

'Look at this,' he said. 'The Shambalhai who came here didn't know where this gate went, or the name of it. It can't ever have been used from this side. *How* can it be on the great map? It's profoundly disturbing.'

'Yeah, you said, I just don't care,' Blix replied frostily. She glanced at the parchment. 'Hey, look! There are other gates!' She pointed to one. 'This one says Lyonesse.'

'Wrong side of the world. This is the only way. Like I said.'

Kit made a *pfft* sound through her lips, exactly as Blix had. Constant crumpled under her look. He fumbled with his shoulder bag and, after a moment, pulled out a smooth grey stone about the size of a large egg and held it up. He moved it around left and right for a few moments.

'The gate is there,' he announced. 'That bit's right, anyway. The Thing says it's that way,' pointing out over the sand.

Blix followed his finger into the sun. There was nothing in that direction which distinguished it from any other.

'What do you mean, the thing says? What thing? How do you know?'

'Try it yourself,' he said, tossing her the stone.

Blix caught it. Almost immediately she felt a strong pull in the direction that Constant had pointed. She urgently wanted to go that way. She threw the stone back to Constant and the urge vanished.

'The Thing says it's that way,' she agreed. 'More bloody magic. What is this thing?'

'It's a tool,' said Constant. 'An object which has been magicked for a particular purpose.'

'Like Kit's wicket?'

'Nothing so extravagant. And not a store of power, unfortunately. It's sort of a lodestone. It's drawn to gates. You think about the gate you're looking for and it pulls in that direction. There's probably a magician's name for it but I don't know what it is. I call it the Thing.'

'Is that what that is?' said Kit, wrinkling her nose in distaste. 'Damn thing's buzzing in my ears. Can you turn it down?'

'I don't know how it works. I don't hear any buzzing. I don't feel anything when I'm not holding it.'

'Well. Guess I'm more sensitive than you. As usual.'

Constant ignored the jibe and put the stone back in his bag. 'It's drawn to working gates,' he said. 'And only the gate you think about. The gate is there.'

'Good.' Blix looked back out over the dunes. *If the gate is there, and the map says there was a sea...* The ugly thought slithered into her mind again. She got a sinking feeling in her stomach. 'So, we go that way.'

'We go that way,' Constant said firmly.

'Does the Thing say anything about not dying of thirst?' Kit said, pursing her lips. 'Fifty miles in these dunes is a week or more of tramping uphill and down. A week at best. We can't carry enough water to travel fifty miles across that terrain. We don't have enough water to carry. We got maybe two days' worth between us on short rations. We'll die. We have to go back and find another way.'

'There isn't another way,' said Constant, shielding his eyes against the sun. 'Even if we decided to go back, there's gain from this side of this gate, relative to Shambhala. It's seven months. Then we'd have to walk to Kalsang's Town. We'd be too late. *Like I said.'*

'Y'all coulda just said no,' Kit said. 'Now look here, prickly Pete. Fifty miles in tough terrain is every day of the week and twice on Sundays for me. You'll die. There has to be another way.'

'There isn't.' Suddenly he rounded on Kit. 'And don't try and take the shards from me and go back yourself,' he said fiercely. 'It'll go badly for you.'

Kit threw up her hands in exasperation. 'And I was all for being nice to you, too. Just so you know, I don't take what ain't mine. Much. If I like you. Also, I said I'd come with you, so I will. And when I say I'm gonna do something I don't need to say it twice, understand? You're paranoid, son. Need to put that black dog on a leash.'

Constant took a deep breath. 'Sorry. I'm on edge.'

'On a razor's edge, sounds like. Step off before you get cut.'

'This isn't helping,' said Blix. 'What do we do?'

'I'm not giving up at the first hurdle,' said Constant. This is too important.' He looked Blix, holding her gaze. The effort made him quiver. 'We walk,' he said.

Blix nodded slowly. She hunted in the doombag and found Katy's lip salve. She tossed it to Kit, who looked at it curiously.

'We'll probably need this,' she said.

'Well, shit.'

The furthest away from home Blix had ever been was Majorca, two years and a lifetime before. The whole family had gone. Her parents were getting on and her dad had come up with the cash from somewhere. Ten days in a not bad hotel near Las Palmas. They'd all turned a shocking pink.

She'd thought that was hot. The desert was punishing. After an hour, her exposed skin was blistered and cracked. Her brain felt like it was about to boil.

She'd put together a makeshift keffiyeh from Katy's handkerchiefs and some thread, and stripped back to a base layer of white flannel shirt and leggings. The rest of her belongings were now sliding along the sand on a bearskin cloak sled, which she pulled by the sleeves. She'd thought to ditch the cloak, but Kit had advised against it.

'Of course,' Blix said. 'It gets cold in the desert at night.'

Kit laughed. 'There's that, sure. Also, you are gonna need somethin' to sleep on. Bare sand ain't fun. Sand flies and such. If you wanna snuggle up to something warm...'

She laughed as Blix went slightly pinker.

It was difficult to judge what progress they were making. As soon as she crested the first dune and skidded down the other side, Blix lost any sense of where she was. Several dunes later she had lost her sense of time as well. It seemed like several hours had passed but the sun had barely moved in the sky. She wondered if this world was bigger than Earth, or if it turned more slowly. A hot, sandy wind blew them on, its even flow quickly becoming grating.

Each footstep was a battle. The sand gave a little every time Blix shifted her weight and was so hot that the glue on her wellington soles was beginning to melt. Before long they were on the bearskin and Blix was walking in her socks, which made it worse. Soon she was exhausted.

By contrast Kit move effortlessly across the sand despite being the most heavily laden. 'I got the knack,' she said when Blix asked. 'You gotta step lightly. I don't stomp around the place like you guys. I walk on my toes. It's only a slog if you let it be.'

Blix tried to think light thoughts. She sank into the sand anyway.

To pass the time, Kit and Constant bickered.

'All I want to know is, who's driving the train?' said Kit. She sand-surfed to the bottom of a dune and waited for the others to catch up.

'I don't understand,' said Constant, sounding petulant. He had retreated under his thick cowl to avoid the sun and his face was hidden. Blix imagined him scowling.

'I mean, I get that you're lots of old dead guys in a boy suit, that's all fine, but who's in charge? You sound like you most of the time, but sometimes you don't. Who's doing the thinking when you ain't you? Are you still calling the shots? Because one of you sounds difficult to get along with, if you get my drift.'

'I am *not* lots of old dead guys in a boy suit,' said Constant angrily. He scrambled off up the dune, muttering furiously to himself.

'I was just asking,' said Kit innocently.

As Constant topped the rise he threw himself flat on the sand and frantically slithered backwards. He rolled sideways and down until he was below the lip of the dune, then rose and silently drew his sword in the same motion. His finger pressed firmly against his lips stifled Blix's question. He slid-stepped back down to them.

'Monster,' he whispered.

Kit had her pistol in her hand. 'Give it a name, kid,' she breathed.

'Don't know. It's immense. White. I saw teeth. Lots of teeth.'

Kit grinned, the words between them forgotten. 'Let's take a look-see, shall we?'

'Maybe we should just leave?' suggested Blix, as quietly as she could. 'I have had enough of monsters for a while, thanks all the same.'

'You want it to sneak up on us? Come on.'

Kit scampered up the dune, commando crawling the last few feet. Constant went with her, Sorcha held before him. Blix sighed, and followed them.

Keeping as low as possible, trying not to send sand spilling down the other side of the dune, they peered over.

'What in tarnation is that?' whispered Kit, shock evident in her voice.

'Whatever it is, it's in no shape to attack us,' said Constant, at a normal volume. He stood up.

The skeleton was half buried in a sand dune, but even so it was huge. Vaulting ribs described a cathedral arch into the sky, three or four storeys high to Blix's eye, gaping in the centre where the spine had collapsed inward. Guessing the length was complicated by the fact that it was half buried, but Blix mentally parked double-decker buses from the first sign of tailbone above the sand to the point of the jaw and thought she could line up at least nine. The giant skull, stripped clean of any flesh, was long and low, sweeping down from the brow line along a flattened top jaw, narrowing to a point. Its enormous teeth were serried along the jaw in an evil rictus. This together with the falling brow and high cheekbones gave it a wrathful yet laughing appearance; sadistic, clownish and strangely human.

'Yep, it's dead all righty,' said Kit, clambering to her feet. 'But are there any more? And what the hell killed it? And is *that* still in the neighbourhood?'

Blix laughed suddenly, but there was a sharp edge to it. 'I don't think we have to worry about what killed it. I know what killed it. Oh, God, that's awful.'

Kit arched an eyebrow. 'What killed it?'

'Its own weight. That's *Odontoceti.'*

The pretty eyes narrowed quizzically. 'Who is it, now?'

'*Odontoceti.* A toothed whale of some kind.'

'A whale? It's huge!'

'Ginormous,' Blix agreed. 'Three hundred feet, at least. It's bigger than Big Ben, the Clock Tower I mean. At least three times the size of a Blue Whale and that's the biggest whale on Earth by far. And that's flensed, just imagine this thing with meat and blubber and sinew and skin. Incredibly big. Toothed whales are usually smaller than Baleens, too. This is no whale that's ever lived on Earth. It's bigger than a Kraken.'

'Well I'll be,' said Kit, pushing back her hat. 'How'd a whale get in the middle of a desert?'

'I think I'm going to be sick,' Blix said.

Constant's eyes widened, and he shared a look with Blix, who nodded unhappily.

'I understand,' he said grimly. 'It was here before the desert, yes? When the desert was the ocean.'

The companions stood quietly for a few while they took in the terrible reality of it. Presently Kit broke the silence. 'A thousand miles from side to side. Great Heaven. What in the world can dry up a damn ocean?'

Blix snorted through her nose, her anger and distress written across her face. 'Five letter word, begins with M.'

Constant frowned. 'It's a possibility. But, you know, places change. We hollowed out a mountain. It took thousands of years. Maybe the people here diverted the rivers that fed the sea, or dammed them. Something like that.'

'Maybe,' Blix said. 'I've heard of that, like in Egypt.' The sick feeling hadn't gone away. *I want to believe that. I don't believe it.*

'Or, or, it could have been some natural process,' Constant continued. He looked like he didn't believe what he was saying either.

'Could have been but wasn't, let's face it,' said Blix decisively. 'Everything that's happened to us has been about magic. It's weirding me out. You might be used to all this, I'm not. As far as I'm concerned it's been disaster followed by calamity and now,' she swept an arm across the scene, 'catastrophe. Obviously it's magic.' She spat into the sand in disgust.

'It never helps. It only hurts,' Constant whispered, in a voice like gravel.

'Stop saying that. I bloody know. Oh, God.'

'Now what do you suppose that is?' said Kit, peering under her hand at the giant skeleton. 'Wait here a minute, I want to check something out.' She bounded off down the dune toward the exposed head, disappeared behind it and was lost from sight.

Constant kicked the sand. 'We should stick together. It could be dangerous.'

'Could be? Are you paying attention or what? Oh, come on,' Blix strode down the slope. Constant followed a moment later, mooching sulkily, and then skipping to catch up.

'When do you suppose this happened?' he asked when he was beside her again. 'My people haven't been here for hundreds of years. And we didn't come through that gate,' he added under his breath.

Blix shrugged. 'Who knows? But I'd be willing to put a big bet on seventy years ago. Maybe this was a magical ocean.' She looked around at the gritty, grey-yellow vastness. 'Maybe just something really bad happened, I don't know. You're the expert, you tell me.'

'I'm not an expert. I don't think there are experts on this.'

'It's terrible. You know, it's not just the whale. Do you know how much life the sea supports?'

'I've never seen the sea,' said Constant. 'I dream about it sometimes.'

'Good for you. Next time dream about billions of tonnes of life dying all at once. Fish, mammals, plankton, plants, corral, krill, bacteria - that's what a sea is. A massive ecosystem, all dead. And whatever other life is on this planet, I don't fancy its chances. Something this immense doesn't just happen in isolation. God knows how it changed things.'

'It made a desert. Maybe everywhere.'

'Maybe. Let's not find out, it's depressing enough just thinking about it. Let's just find the bloody gate and leave.'

Blix looked back the way they'd come, and tried to imagine the ocean. 'Tell you what though, if I'm right and this is connected to whatever happened in nineteen sixteen to destroy magic on Earth, well, Earth got off lightly.'

They were nearly at the remains. There was a sharp whistle, and Kit McCoy appeared on top of the skull.

'Look what I found,' she said. She threw a long piece of metal down to them. 'Saw it glinting in the sunlight.' Constant and Blix stepped back smartly as it landed between them and flexed as though it was alive.

'It's a saw,' said Blix with surprise.

'Yes, it is,' said Kit. She slid halfway down the vast jaw and jumped the last few feet to the ground, landing lightly on the sand. 'Someone's been harvesting the ivory.' She grinned. 'There are people here. Alive ones. Recently, I reckon.'

I wonder where they live?' Constant said. 'There's nothing nearby.'

'There could be a city three dunes away and we'd never know,' Blix pointed out.

Kit scratched her chin thoughtfully. 'There's some camp signs in the lee of this big boy. Someone stayed overnight not too long ago. One person, a man. A big man.'

She picked up the saw and flexed it a little. 'I've lived in the wild a time or two. This is a good saw, worth a few bucks, cared for, ain't broke. I'd take it with me. Assuming our friend ain't dead, if I'd left this behind, I'da turned around and come back for it. Unless I didn't have to. Maybe he knows he's coming back. And our friend wasn't worried about this bright metal taking a walk while he was gone, or he'd have packed it. That means not many people and he knows them all. Living quite near. A day or two's travel away, I'd say, by however they travel here.'

'Nice work, Sherlock,' said Blix, 'I'm impressed. Can you tell me his shoe size from the ash of his cigars?'

'Say what?' said Kit, looking slightly puzzled.

'Sherlock Holmes? No? *Really?* Blimey. Nebraska a bit isolated, is it? I expect *him* not to get things, but... Never mind, it's not important. What do we do about this?'

'Move on,' said Constant immediately. 'We know the path. We'll deal with the locals if we meet them. There's no reason to go out of our way.'

'There could be a couple,' said Kit, giving him a cool look for the way he'd said *deal with*. 'Number one is, people who use saws drink water and we're gonna need that after tomorrow. Number two... Well, never mind, number one is more important. We don't find water, we are going to die.'

'Okay. Fine. Let's look for them. Which way do you suggest we go?'

'Well now. I don't know. Wind's covered any tracks.'

'Right. So there's no point talking about it. There are only two directions for us. Forward and back. Which means there is only one direction.' Constant pointed up the dune behind the whale. 'The Thing says that way.'

'I'm gonna shove that thing right up your ass,' Kit began heatedly, but Blix interrupted before she could say anymore.

'Look, let's not squabble again, I'm sick of it. I'm also shattered. This is as good a place as any to camp. The ivory man might come back. You can fight over him if he does.'

'You know, that ain't such a bad idea,' said Kit. 'Camping, I mean. Old Jasconius here gives us shade and shelter.' She grimaced as the wind blew a shower of sand into her face. 'And we'll be out of this damn simoon.'

Camp that evening was a sullen affair, with Constant and Blix not really talking to each other and Kit disinclined to broker peace. The disgust Blix felt for Constant was still too raw to contemplate agreeing with him, even though she knew he was right. Forwards was the only way. She chewed on some slightly stale bread and tried to ignore him.

She found herself drawn to the sky. A swathe of stars lit the vastness above her in constellations Blix didn't recognise. She was used to the handful of bright stars it was possible to see against the dull orange glow of civilisation. Here, with zero light pollution and an open sky, she could see the depths of space for the first time, tens and hundreds of millions of stars layered in imaginary shapes and vaulting clouds. As she stared into the distant universe and far back in time she felt a sense of her place in the scheme of things; indescribably small but, as the observer and interpreter of the infinite majesty above her, not insignificant. She wondered where in the universe they were, and which star led home.

There was no moon in the sky at least. She could though sort of feel that there was one somewhere, which was a bit unnerving. Tonight, it was below the horizon. That was probably normal, she realised. There was no reason why the way things were on Earth should be how it was in the rest of the universe. Blix fought hard not to be overwhelmed by the alienness of that thought.

She sat up against the massive skull and forced herself to eat, although she wasn't hungry and the food tasted... wrong, somehow. Bloodless. As she chewed on the hard bread, the thought struck her that she was wearing two skins - the bearskin clothed her human flesh, which now covered a wolf. The thought of it made her feel sick again.

'Penny for 'em,' said Kit. She was sitting on top of the skull at the point of the jaw, wrapped tightly in a blanket, keeping watch. Constant was some way further back, wedged between skull and sand.

'Still not worth a penny,' Blix replied. She gave up on the bread and hunkered down. Then she remembered something.

'What was number two?'

'Pardon me?'

'This afternoon. You said there were a couple of reasons we should try and find the people who live here. You only said one. What was number two?'

'Number two, I got to wondering about something. Whatever happened here almost buried the gate we came through and dried up the sea. Sand's all but swallowed up old Moby here. Maybe the gate we're going to ain't in such good shape. Maybe we'll need help to dig it out. Maybe we'll need help to go back the way we came.'

Constant rolled over at that, and fixed Kit with a baleful stare. 'We are not turning back. As for the other thing...' He seemed be searching for the right thing to say, then suddenly threw his hands up in disgust. 'Marvellous. Thanks for that. Just what I needed for a restful night's sleep.' He rolled over and turned his back on Kit. Kit shrugged, and went back to watching the world.

Blix thought about sleep, but something else occurred to her.

'Hey, I meant to ask something. How did you know it was a guy?'

'Pardon me again?'

'You said a man had camped here. How did you know it wasn't a woman?'

'Oh, that.' Kit giggled suddenly. 'He took a leak up the side of the whale. Just about where your head is.'

'Gaah.' Blix peeled herself off the bone and flapped at her hair.

'Sweet dreams, kiddo,' said Kit. Blix could hear the laughter in her voice. It made her feel safe.

Constant dreamed.

In my dream, I am about to kill a lot of men. I have been about to kill them for several months. I hate sieges. They are so dull.

'God's arse. I've never seen fog like it,' says Aldegund. He speaks in a low voice. The fog carries it to me, I am not quite sure from where. 'I could carve out a chunk and take it home in my pocket.'

He is right. I can't see him, though he must be nearby. That's not such a bad thing. Aldegund had his nose cut off for stealing and never had it closed up. You can see into his skull. Most people find it horrifying. I find it distracting. I haven't killed him because he is completely fearless of me. Not just through stupidity, or the confidence that he can beat me. He is just not scared of me. This is novel. I am paying attention to this.

'You think they'll run,' he continues.

'Yes.'

'Not fight?'

'No.'

'Why not? Were it me starving behind those walls, I might be tempted. Send rangers out to ghost through the fog and slit our throats before we know they're there. A pea souper like this must favour blokes who know the lie of the land. Why not fight?'

'Because I'm out here. There's a reason I go around proclaiming my name at every crossroads. My name goes before me. They're not fools. If they fight me, I'll win. They know that. I've taught them that.'

'That's fair enough. I presume that's also why we're freezing our feet in the bloody water margin?'

'Yes. A breakout on land is the same as a battle. They have small boats aplenty and the water gate is unbreachable from without. They'll think the fog is their chance to escape downriver. It is *their chance.'*

'Why not let them go? We can walk into the town then. They can't carry too much with them.'

I spit in disgust. 'They'll take what matters. And anyway, I don't want them living to tell the tale of how they outwitted the terrible Darcen Ysir for the rest of their lives. I live by my name. I will be remembered by my name. If anyone tells tales of me, it will be about how they barely lived while everyone else they ever knew died. That's how I'll be remembered.'

I am becoming irritated with Aldegund. 'I said all this before. Why are you making me repeat myself?'

'I didn't hear you before. I was somewhere else. Buried in a beaver, as it happens. I arrived late. I just followed everyone else.' He chuckles.

In my dream, I am moved to engage in his banter. Perhaps it is because I have lived with these men for months, doing nothing but wait, but I feel as connected to them as I ever have to other men.

'The camp whores are pox-ridden,' I say. 'You'll get the chancre.'

'Ah yes, the chancre. Makes your nose rot off, doesn't it? Well now. That would be terrible.'

In my dream, I am amused, and laugh. This rarely happens.

'It wasn't a whore,' he continues. 'Just some woman I found. She's dead now.'

I hear a stream of water hitting the river. Aldegund is pissing.

'Bollocks to this,' he continues. 'My feet are sodden, my arse is freezing, and my balls are filling up again. Am I wasting time I could put to better use spearing a cunny? How are we supposed to see these bloody watermen if I can't see the cock in my hand? I can't tell where I end and you start.'

'I have a way,' I tell him.

The artefact hangs on a chain around my neck. I take it I out. A garnet of little value, misshapen and pitted. I know, though I do not know how I know, that it nears the end of its use. This might be it. It is almost wholly rusted. I don't care. There are always others. I know where there is another.

I close my eyes and concentrate on the artefact. And I reach out, looking for magic. Suddenly I can feel Aldegund as a presence in the turmoil of my mind, in the flesh under my skin. Black souled and oozing. I can feel him breathing as I am breathing. I see the magic within him. I realise that if I knew how, I could draw on that power and use him up as I have used the garnet. I reach out. I can feel the rest of my men; the ones on this bank and, now and then, those of the far side. I reach out. I can feel the water trickling past the pebbles by my feet. I can feel the fish rising for the flies.

I can feel an artefact, glowing white hot, like a molten rivet driven into the steel of my soul. I feel those who carry it. I feel their terror.

'I hear them,' says Aldegund. With my mind I show him where. I show them all where.

'Light up!' I shout. I strike a spark on tinder and blow it into a flame. I light the fuse line hanging from the wax covered pot which sits in a rope cradle by my feet. It takes the flame well.

'Swing!' I call, and as I do an arrow whizzes past me, harmlessly. There is commotion on the river, voices raised in fear. The watermen know they are discovered. I take up the short rope and swing the pot, around and around beside me like a slingshot. It makes a sound like a windmill blade on a stormy day. I hear a hundred like it along the river.

'Burn!' I cry. I let loose the pot underarm and it sails up into the fog and is lost. I know how far it will travel. I hear others whirr through the air. I hear some splash harmlessly into the water. I hear some smash on timber. I hear screams as the firewine takes hold.

'I think I missed,' says Aldegund. He sounds disappointed. Cheated. Angry. I know why. I have felt his mind. I realise why he is not afraid of me. He makes jokes and fucks women but this is a face he wears for other people. He is not like them. He is like me.

'You can make up for it now,' I say.

The watermen begin to splash ashore. We draw our swords and begin the slaughter.

In my dream, I kill two men and a woman and feel better than I have in a long time. Another man stumbles toward the bank, sodden red robes dragging at his ankles, face burning where some firewine has stuck to his beard. He collapses, exhausted, at my feet.

'Don't kill me,' he begs, cringing.

'That's funny,' I say, and raise my sword to hack his head off.

Then he looks up, and Recognises me.

'Great Father,' he stammers, 'it's you. I've found you! After all these years! It has been so long!'

'What -' I say, but in that moment my mind opens and I see the world for the first time. The sword slides from my fingers as I collapse, fall to my knees then back on myself, spasming, fitting, as visions swim across my eyes. Faces I have never seen but know, a dozen, two dozen, a dozen more. Faces of boys, men, ancients, all strange and serene and me, *they're* my *face, the faces of all who have come before. And behind them, burning bright silver like the birth of creation, is the Constant. The Constant is everything, it is in me, it is everything, it is Nothing.*

I have done so much wrong.

'Is this one giving you trouble?' says Aldegund, his monstrous form appearing through the whiteness. 'Allow me.'

'No!' I scream, and before I know it my sword is my hand and I have cut up and pulled and opened the murdering rapist from crotch to navel. He looks stunned and starts to speak, but the point of my sword closes his mouth forever.

I collapse again, all strength gone, and look to the monk. He looks utterly horrified by me. Well he might.

'Protect me,' I say, but it is not my voice, it is a voice of many voices. 'Take me home,' we say. 'Take me to the Anvil.'

Now there is a boy here I do not recognise.

'A dream of water and death,' *he says.* 'I was expecting something a little sandier, but I suppose this is appropriate in its way. So, that is how he became me. Told you it was hard work. I'm quite proud of it though. You've already seen what he became. He became the man he might have been had his mind not broken. I suppose it makes up for some of the other things I've done. Some of them.'

He comes forward a little and kneels so he is closer to me. I can see his face. He looks incredibly agitated.

'Now tell me, seriously, how the bloody fuck is there a gate on the Anvil? How is that possible? I can just about believe that someone could cast magic so powerful that it could hide the gate from you and the other seventy of you and all the thousands of monks who ever lived on that rock. But how can it be hidden from me? Magic does not work on me. I see things as they really are. I forget nothing. *Nothing.* This is not possible. Not possible.'

In my dream the boy chews on his knuckles, frightened by what has been revealed, then throws up his hands in exasperation. 'Ach, why am I asking you? You don't know, and you couldn't tell me if you did. I need to think about this. Let's talk about something else.'

In my dream the boy touches me on my shoulder. It is meant to put me at my ease, but it feels cold, cold as death even through the thick leather of my jerkin.

'I think you made the right decision, Constant. There's no backward path for us now. The Writing is clear on this, if nothing else. But it's incredibly dangerous. If you don't find water I'm going to have to take steps.'

The boy stands again.

'I hope that doesn't happen. I don't know what it would mean for you if I took direct control. It has been so long since I have. I don't know if you would come back from that.'

The boy leans in. His face is hard, determined.

'I hope it doesn't happen. But if you die here there's nowhere for me to go except the girl, and that's hardly better in the circumstances. I don't know this place. I don't know how to find people. I'd be lost. No beacon in the darkness. No Constant to guide me. No one to replace you, not if the girl dies too. That can't happen.'

Constant did not remember the boy when he woke up.

'My sunburn is better,' said Blix, the next morning.

'Glad to hear it, kiddo.'

'No, I mean it's *better.* It's completely better.' She held up her hand so they could see. 'Not even red. And my blisters have healed too.'

Constant looked at her warily, as though she might change there and then and rip his head off. 'That's the werewolf. It heals you.'

That's not why it happens thought Blix. She opened her mouth to explain but the thought was too big and awful to say out loud. *I'm having a lot of big thoughts these days. God, Katy I really don't want this to happen.*

Instead she said. 'Yeah. It's healed me.'

'Yup. Though I wouldn't test it too much kiddo, you ain't changed yet. You can still die. And pain hurts, you know?'

'Thank you Doctor Obvious. Well, at least I don't have blisters.'

'I do,' said Constant. 'Don't be happy you haven't.'

'That's a bit churlish,' Blix groused. 'All things considered you'd think you'd be pleased I won't be walking on bone today. I know I am.'

'He means it's the wolf talking,' said Kit. 'Making you accustomed to it.'

'Oh, nuts.'

'Don't accept anything about it,' said Constant. He flipped his hood up. Blix caught sight of his fingertips. They were still rust red.

Kit saw them too. 'I got a little something that'll heal what ails you,' she said, producing the little bottle of snake oil.

'I'm not touching that stuff again. Stop talking and come on.' He walked off, feet sinking into the sand with every step.

A day of walking came and went with nothing to show for it except exhaustion. Kit forged ahead, Constant and Blix dragged behind. By late afternoon everyone was thoroughly sick of slogging through sand dunes. There was also the creeping realisation that Kit had been right. The water was almost gone.

As they reached the foot of yet another sand mountain, Blix upended Katy's bottle and shook the last drops into her mouth. They didn't help. Then Blix had an idea. An idea she hated.

'You can magic some water up,' she said to Constant, wrinkling her nose in disgust. 'I can't believe I'm even saying it. You seem to be able to do magic, it might as well be useful.'

Constant shook his head. 'What have I been saying? It doesn't help. There'll be water out here somewhere. It's a stupid idea.'

'Don't talk to me like that! "Somewhere" is a big place. We're here, and we're running out of options.'

'Don't listen to her, kid,' said Kit from way up ahead.

'How did you hear that?' asked Blix.

'I got big ears.'

'Not that big.'

'Wind carried it. Dumb ideas carry further.'

'Not you as well. Thanks very much.' Blix looked at Constant. 'Give it a go, see what happens. You have a lot to make up for. Start with making sure we don't die.'

Guilt mottled Constant's face. A long pause. 'I shouldn't. But I think I can...' He closed his eyes and concentrated. 'Water,' he said.

Before Blix's eyes a small pool of water appeared in a hollow in the sand. Immediately it started to soak in. Constant plunged his hand into it before it vanished completely, scooping up a palmful. Drops splashed up and hit Blix in the face.

She frowned. 'Well, that was useful. I needed a shower.' She licked her lips. 'Salt.'

'It would be,' said Constant, shaking his head in disgust. He spread his fingers and let the water trickle out. 'Logical, I suppose. We're at the bottom of the sea, sort of. It would be salt water. I didn't say otherwise.'

Blix noticed he was flexing his left hand. 'Is something wrong?'

'Not really. It just started to itch.' He scratched the red line on his palm.

'Quit playing around, kids,' said Kit, coming back a little. 'Night's coming, we need to put some more miles in before we lose the light.' Without waiting for a reply, she turned and walking back up the sand.

There was nothing to distinguish the current dune, a featureless uphill waste like all the others. Half way up it, Kit stopped dead.

'Do you hear that?' she said, suddenly excited. The other two quickly joined her and listened.

'There's nothing to hear except the wind,' said Constant.

'You need to get the cloth outta those ears, kid. Running water! Come on!'

She raced up the dune and skidded to a halt at the top.

'Maybe I did that with the magic,' said Constant hopefully.

'Well, shit,' they heard Kit say.

'Or perhaps not,' Constant continued evenly.

'Let's go and see the terrible thing,' said Blix in a resigned voice.

The dune fell gently into a low, wide hollow, one side of which was a huge rock shelf rising from the sand. In the middle was a wooden post, about fifteen feet high and the same in diameter, black with age and bound at intervals with rusted iron braces. Wooden and metal spikes, ten feet long or more, protruded from the post at random intervals from ground level to above head height.

On top of the post there was a gallows. Something hung from it. Something man-sized.

'This isn't a good place,' said Constant immediately.

'Nope,' Kit agreed. 'But lookee there.'

On the far side from where they stood a small pool of water lay against the rocky side of the depression. From a crack in that rock came a trickle of water, little more than a dribble, pitter-pattering into the pool. Or at least Blix assumed it pittered; she couldn't hear it from where she was and didn't know how Kit had heard it from the other side of the dune.

'Do you think it's fresh?' she asked.

'Looks like a spring.'

They waited for a while, watching. Apart from the strange object in the centre and whatever was hanging from the top of it, there was nothing much out of the ordinary. A few sheets of what looked like metal lay discarded on the sand, and piles of wood lay here and there. Iron pipes were stuck into the sandy walls of the hollow.

'I don't think anyone's home,' said Blix.

'Maybe,' said Constant, chewing his bottom lip. 'Let's not let our guard down though.'

Kit nodded vigorously. 'What he said. Something ain't right about this place kids, keep your eyes open.'

Cautiously they descended into the hollow. As they approached the centre, Constant wrinkled his nose in distaste. 'What is that smell?' he said. 'Smells like... dried fish?'

As they got closer to the post it became clear where the smell came from.

He was upside down. The skin on his upper body had shrunk and turned to paper. Carrion birds had evidently plundered the corpse. The eyes were gone and the flesh of his face had been stripped off; the strange shape of the skull and the huge eye sockets were visible. Below the waist, dried scales hung from the creature's tail. The skin had shrivelled, and the flukes shredded into nothing.

'That's a merman,' said Blix, looking up from just outside the ring of spikes. '*Homo oannes tritonis*. Looks like he's been dead for a while. Quite a while I think, he looks pretty desiccated. It's arid here, it must have preserved the remains.'

'I guess the desert came as a shock to him,' said Kit.

'More than a shock,' said Blix. '*Homo oannes* can't breathe out of water. It must have been terrible. Like drowning in reverse.'

Constant was examining the post closely. 'You're assuming he died of natural causes. Maybe not. I'm more interested in how he ended up tied by the tail on this... What is this? Totem pole? Sacrificial altar? Feeding station? Something bad.'

'Yeah, I was kinda wondering that,' said Kit. She looked around. Her usual carefree attitude was absent. 'Not by himself, that's for sure. Maybe someone didn't like him so much.'

'I wonder who?' said Constant. They shared a worried look.

'This is horrible,' said Blix. 'Merfolk are intelligent. I saw one once. We were little. Looked me right in the eye...'

The merfolk had been hunting in the breakers, taking the pouting, wrasse and garfish which shoaled there in the summer months. The red flag had gone up the moment the first one was spotted, and everyone had to move back from the water's edge. Merfolk could be very aggressive, Dad told Katy when she asked what was going on. They had very poor eyesight and often mistook humans in the water for seals or dolphins. Even when they did recognise people they often attacked anyway. People hadn't treated Mers very well, Dad said.

Blix and Katy watched as the merfolk danced through the waves, moving with phenomenal speed and grace as they impaled fish on their tridents, or sometimes simply caught them in their mouths. The merfolk mostly ignored the people on the sand save for a couple of the younger mermen, who faked a charge every now and then, and laughed as the people ran back in alarm. They were stupid people, Blix had said very loudly. Everyone knew that Mers couldn't hold their breath long enough to make it up the beach.

One merman, a merboy judging by his size, had paused in the hunt and stared directly at Blix, his huge, unblinking, milky-blue eyes locked onto hers. She saw his strange, alien, silver-scaled skin, gasping gills and very human, almost beautiful, lips. Not half fish and half man, but a Mer.

She wondered if he could see her and gave him a little wave. After a moment in which the creature looked more unnatural than anything Blix had ever seen, he gave the same little wave back. Then he dived into the water and was gone.

'Glaucous,' she said absently.

'Pardon me?' said Kit.

'The colour of his eyes. Merman eyes. It's called glaucous. I read it once.' She shook her head slightly, banishing the past. 'We should cut him down and bury him.'

'We touch nothing,' said Constant firmly. 'We do nothing. We don't know what's safe and what's not.'

'We should look around though,' said Kit thoughtfully. 'There's a lot of junk about. We should see if there's anything useful.'

'Okay. Shout if you find anything. But don't touch it.'

The sand was strewn here and there with pieces of wood and metal, like the detritus of a workshop floor. A pile of what looked like old shipping pallets had been broken down into planks, which appeared, on closer inspection, to be what the central post was made of.

There were several metal sheets, which looked like they had been cut from oil drums, but were much thicker. They had holes cut in the middle, thick enough for an arm, and were badly dented, as if someone had beaten them randomly with a sledgehammer. Kit hefted one appraisingly, staggering slightly under the weight, then lifted it over the highest spike she could reach. It slid halfway down before the spike widened, wedging at about Kit's head height.

'What part of "touch nothing" was unclear?' said Constant sharply.

'The part where you get to tell me what to do,' replied Kit. 'Real hazy on that part.'

Constant shook his head, annoyed. But he said, 'Sorry. I didn't mean -'

'Yeah sure, reincarnation, fine. But there are only so many times you can say that before I stop caring.' She considered for a moment. 'That was so many.'

Blix heard them squabbling but ignored it. She was looking at the pool. It looked clear and inviting. She could see to the bottom, flat, blue-grey and rust red, silted with sediment. But she didn't touch it.

She'd drunk water on Shambhala without thinking about it, which had been a mistake. That had at least been mountain water, close to the source and presumably as pure as bottled French water claimed to be. But desert water had a bad reputation.

Even on Earth it might give you anything from an upset stomach to tapeworms or cholera or a whole host of nasties you didn't want to catch. She looked around for something to boil it in.

'What's that for?' she asked Kit, pointing at the metal she'd slid over the spike.

'I got no clue what that's for. But it's manufactured, whatever it is. People are here. Or were here. I wonder where they've gone?'

'They could be a thousand miles away or just over the rise,' Constant pointed out. 'Let's not worry about it. We have to camp somewhere. This is out of the wind, there's plenty of wood for a fire, and there's water.'

'Boy ain't wrong, for a change.'

'It's settled then,' said Blix. 'Good. I can't walk anymore. My blisters have blisters.'

'Then I guess they won't have them tomorrow, kiddo.'

'Oh. Yeah. What about him?' said Blix, looking quickly at the body of the merman.

'Let's just leave him be,' said Kit. 'Whoever he was, he's gone. I don't like this spokey thing. Let's not take chances.'

'Now you're getting it,' said Constant.

As darkness fell they built up a fire and ate some hot food and Blix felt better. She used what was left in the first aid kit to clean and dress her feet, aware that they'd heal soon anyway but not yet prepared to live with that. Then she and Constant drowsed while Kit tried to figure out how to build a still to purify the water using the junk around them and what they carried. The woman seemed to have endless energy. They'd camped upwind of the dead merman and by unspoken agreement ignored his body.

As Blix dozed she heard a distant note, as if someone had sounded a trumpet and then muted it suddenly. She sat bolt upright.

'What was that?' said Constant tiredly.

The trumpet sounded again, a little closer, a low blast followed by a higher note, muted again almost immediately.

'Passing oom-pah band?' Kit suggested. 'What the hey?'

'Oh no,' said Blix. 'We're in terrible danger.'

Constant dragged himself to his feet and drew his sword. 'Who is it, Blix?' he asked.

'Not who. What. It's a manticore.'

The trump sounded again, closer still. Almost immediately another horn sounded from the other side of the dune. It sounded distant, but not that distant.

'Manticores,' said Blix. 'Plural.'

'Time to go,' said Kit. 'Let's not be around when they find this place.'

'No!' Blix almost shouted, then stifled herself. 'No. We can't run. They know we're here. *Manticora vox buccina.* The bugle-voiced man-eater. Manticores sound when they're hunting. It's supposed to panic their prey into bolting. They want to herd us toward the rest of the sawt, they'll be lying silent nearby ready to ambush us. We have to fight.'

Kit's pistol was in her hand; she offered it butt first to Blix. 'Know how to use this, kiddo?' she asked.

'I'd never even seen a real gun before I met you,' said Blix, looking horrified.

Kit tapped the muzzle. 'This end goes bang. Point it away from you. And me. No, waitaminute.'

She dug in her pack and pulled out a small cardboard box. Inside, neat rows of bullets gleamed in the firelight.

'No point wasting good silver on those that don't need it,' she explained. She broke the pistol open and knocked the silver rounds out, stuffing them in her coat pocket. 'Shoulda done that before. Here you go kiddo. Come out gun blazing.'

Blix took the gun. The weight of it dragged her hand down, just like the sword had done at the cottage. 'It's so heavy!'

Kit, now shucking the silver from her rifle, looked at her strangely. 'What did you expect? It ain't a toy. Take a big handful of bullets, you might need them.'

Another pair of bugle calls sounded above the rim of the hollow.

'Anything else we need to know, child?' said Constant. He had taken on the harsh, martial bearing Blix had seen when they first met.

'Um. Yes! Manticores are scleroderms. They have incredibly tough top-hide, it's almost bulletproof, you'd need an elephant gun. Aim for the face. The eyes, the inside of the mouth. The underbelly. That's where they bleed.'

'Thank you kindly for that information.'

'They have poisonous tails, like scorpions. They attack by rearing and lunging, or by doing, like, a handstand so the tail can strike over their shoulders. Their teeth are like razors.'

'We can fight two Manticores,' said Constant firmly.

Blix shook her head. 'It'll be six Manticores, a sawt is usually about six. The others will come when the herding doesn't work.' She racked her brain for anything else she knew about the creatures. 'Don't be fooled by the faces. They're not human hybrids and they're not intelligent. Don't hold back. They won't. They are incredibly aggressive.'

Constant swore. 'I'm missing something, I can feel it.' He rubbed his eyes with the heel of his hand so hard that Blix thought they might burst. He grimaced for a moment, gritting his teeth.

The blaring clarions sounded again. Blix couldn't tell where it had come from.

'Goddammit, we're trapped down here,' Kit said.

Constant's head shot up, shock on his face. He stepped out into the bowl, away from the others and the fire, turning around and around, trying to take it all in.

'Get back here, kid,' cried Kit, putting the rifle to her shoulder.

'I get it,' he said. 'Great Fathers, I get it.'

'Whatever you got son, get to it soon,' said Kit, turning around and about herself, trying to cover the whole bowl with her rifle.

Constant suddenly yelled at the top of his voice. 'Hey! Hey! Are you there? Help us! Please!'

'What the hell? Kid, are you crazy?'

Constant gestured around him. 'It's not a gallows, it's a lure. This whole place is a trap. The fresh water is bait. The merman is bait. The wind must be carrying that stench for miles. Someone is hunting manticores right now. I think they'd be here if we weren't.'

'We've camped in a trap?' said Blix.

'Our luck is just horrible. That's the bad news. The good news is, this trap's not for us. It's for manticores. It's going to help us fight them.'

'Get to the point kid, we're about to have company,' said Kit grimly.

'How long is a manticore tail, Blix?'

'Fully grown? Four to six feet.'

Constant ran out into the hollow and grabbed two more of the metal sheets, dragging the heavy metal along behind him to the post. He slid them over the spikes to either side of the one Kit had covered, both lower than the first, one at waist height, the other near his knees. They overlapped and wedged on the spikes at different lengths. Constant squeezed behind then, turned, and thrust his sword back through the gap. He was almost completely covered.

'Goddamn son of a bitch,' said Kit, astonished.

'It's a shield wall,' said Constant. 'A *testudo*, a *fulcum*. The metal protects against tail strikes. The spikes protect against lunges. You can attack from within, strike, retreat. It's brilliant.'

Kit and Blix stared at each other for a moment, then ran out into the hollow.

'Be quick,' said Constant unnecessarily.

Blix found two sheets close together, half buried in the sand. She grabbed the first and dragged it free. It was a lot heavier than it looked. She worked on the second and, after a few seconds which seemed like an eternity, pulled it out. She dragged the two drum halves back to the spikes. She levered the first onto a low spike, and heaved the second up to a waist-high one, her arms shaking a little as she tried to slide it over. In the same time, Kit had retrieved three sheets and threaded them up with apparent ease. Blix went hunting for a third.

Blix's spikes were between Kit and Constant, but there was a problem. The wide spacing of the spikes meant that there was a gap between the shields that Blix had hung and the ones Kit had just placed, and between Blix's and Constant's.

'Whoever built this had somethin' in the middle here that ain't here no more,' said Kit. 'Manticores are gonna come around the sides.'

'Discourage them,' Constant said. He was almost thrumming with anticipation. 'Grab some brands from the fire!'

'Right on, kid.' Kit ran to the flames.

'I can't find another shield!' Blix shouted. She'd searched right to the edges of the pit and could almost feel the beast on the other side of the slope.

'There!' screamed Constant. Blix dived on the glinting metal he'd seen and came up with a broken strip of corrugated iron, useless as protection.

'Get back here!' Kit commanded. Blix took off toward the post at a dead run. She skidded behind her shield wall to find her head poking above the rim.

'Fuck! I'll get stung for sure.'

'Switch places,' said Kit immediately.

'No, why should you die?' She slammed her fist into the shield in frustration and yelped as the metal cut into the edge of her hand. She instinctively sucked at the wound and was shocked at how good it tasted. The blood dripped down the sharp metal, the bright red merging with the blue-grey metal.

Blue-grey and rust red...

'I know where there's another one!' she cried. She dropped the pistol, squeezed out from behind the shields and took off for the pool.

'Blix, no!' shouted Constant, but it was too late. Blix was there in a matter of seconds. She plunged her arms shoulder deep in the water and through the silt and sand felt the hardness of metal. She found the centre hole and pulled with all her strength.

A manticore burst over the ridge a dozen yards from Blix and reared, framed in the firelight. Its body was a lion's, but much larger and covered in flowing yellow hair like an afghan hound. From its powerful shoulders rose a long, llama-like neck, at the end of which, bizarrely, sat the delicate, pale oval of a young woman's face, with large green eyes and a strange, serene, archaic smile, which made it look beautiful and benevolent. The long black scorpion's tail which arched high above her head gave the lie to that. It quivered and twisted, ready to strike.

The manticore opened its mouth obscenely wide, revealing rows of dagger-sharp teeth. It blared its trumpet call, a terrifyingly loud brassy screech-bark which made Blix freeze and scream involuntarily. The beast swung its head sharply in her direction.

'Hi-hi-hi! Over here, you ugly bitch! Hiya-hey!' Kit dashed out from the post and toward the manticore waving her arms over her head. The creature's placid face swung in her direction. Kit backed away, still waving.

The manticore trumpeted again. Another manticore appear on the opposite side of the rim and blared a response.

Constant dashed outside his defences. 'This way! This way, monster! Hear me, see me! Run, Blix!'

Blix heaved as hard as she could and slowly the metal began to move, shedding its load of mud and sand. But it was heavy, too heavy to move quickly. Blix didn't dare look at the Manticore in case she froze again.

Then suddenly she was stronger. Much stronger. The shield slid easily from the sand and up through the water. She dragged it to the bank, gasping at the sudden burst of energy running through her nerves.

'How on earth?' she began. The manticore's head swung around to face her again. The needle-toothed mouth opened wide again and blared its clarion call. It took a couple of probing steps toward her. Then it reared, claws splayed wide.

Blix gripped the shield and ran. The manticores charged. Shots rang out as Kit let loose but the manticores did not flinch. They took tiny, almost delicate steps, pitter-pattering down the sand, their erect posture giving them the appearance of a show pony trotting around a ring, ridiculous except that they were so fast and so deadly.

But suddenly Blix was faster. She sprinted hard for the spikes, carrying the shield as if it were nothing. As she reached the post some instinct made her jump. With unerring accuracy, she slammed the shield onto the spike and in the same movement twisted around and through the gap in the wall and landed on her side in the sand. She scrabbled desperately for the pistol, found it and grabbed it and screamed and pulled the trigger as the manticore fell on her. Hot blood splattered her face. The manticore skidded and reared awkwardly, roaring with pain, a hole in its belly splattering gore into the sand, and fell sideways toward Constant.

'That's mine!' he cried, in a voice that wasn't his but somehow was. He darted from shelter, swinging Sorcha in a high executioner's arc as he moved, bringing it down with terrible force on the manticore's neck, severing it in a sickly crunch of bone.

The other Manticore charged at Kit, unheeding of the bullets whipping through the air around it and bouncing off its hide. Kit fired until the rifle clicked and at the last second ducked behind the shields. The manticore reared and slammed into the shield wall at the edge of Kit's line. The metal buckled but held firm. The tail barb flashed past the wall and struck the centre post where Kit's head had been moments before. Kit grabbed the firebrand as the needle-filled maw appeared around the shield wall. She thrust upward and fell back in one motion. The manticore trumpeted in pain as fire touched its face and the head disappeared back around the metal.

'Ho, beast,' came a voice. The manticore turned on the spot. Constant stood behind it, sword extended, moving slowly forward. He swept the sword back and forth across its field of vision. The angelic head followed its course, the scorpion's tail arched over its back, quivering nervously, readily to strike.

'Keep it busy until I reload!' Kit yelled.

Blix, shaken by the sudden violence, took aim and fired, and missed. But the noise attracted the manticore and it took its eye off Constant. The boy ran the few steps which separated him from the monster and stabbed and slashed in one motion. The manticore twisted savagely through the air as the blade opened a stripe through its flesh from shoulder to haunch. The animal yowled in agony, then threw itself forward and arched its back, sending the black tail forward with lightning speed, the barb flying true to Constant's chest. He twisted the sword into a cruciform and caught the tip of the barb in the guard. The shining metal rang like a bell as he guided the barb harmlessly down and to his left.

'Hi there!' said Kit McCoy, and blasted the manticore's face off.

As the echo of the rifle shot died away and the writhing manticore fell still, Blix sank to her knees, exhausted.

'Holy fuck,' she said. 'We killed them! They're dead. How in God's name did that happen?'

'Chance,' said Constant, checking that the second manticore was dead. 'It's always chance. It could have gone the other way. As if it matters.'

A series of trumpet calls pierced the silence. Some distance away, but closing. 'It still might,' he continued. 'Here come the rest.'

As he said the words the manticores came over the hollow's edge. Four of them, heads erect and mouths agape, hair flowing behind them as they charged.

'Take cover!' Constant shouted. 'Draw them into your attack!' He rammed the burning brand between the lip of his shields at chest height to his left and took guard on his right, defending the gap between himself and Blix.

Blix thrust her torch into the same position as Constant. Then she found her sword and thrust it into the sand, a last resort if bullets failed. With trembling fingers, she reloaded the pistol. Six shots were better than five.

The manticores ran at them, bounding toward them in their strange pitter-patter, seeming uncaring of their dead packmates.

One took a bullet in the brain from Kit straightaway. It tumbled as if tripped and went head over heels, bringing down the beast next to it in a tangle of paws and hair. Neither got up.

Blix had no time for triumph as a manticore was upon her, long neck arching around the shield wall to bite her in half. She screamed and pulled the trigger; the bullet sliced across the manticore's face, scalping it at the brow but not killing it. The angel face disappeared at speed but in the same moment the black tail struck, juddering across her shoulder as it missed by millimetres, the harmless side of the poison barb stripping skin from her cheek as it hurtled by. The impact knocked the pistol from her hand. She buckled at the knees, ducked beneath a renewed assault by the tail, grabbed her sword and hacked upward. The blade bit but didn't cut through. The manticore pulled back its tail, screaming in pain, jerking the sword from her hands. It clattered against the shield wall and came loose from the wound, spiralling out into the sand beyond her reach.

Constant jabbed his attacker as it clawed at the shield edge, ducked back and stepped underneath the scrabbling paws, He thrust forward and up but the beast leapt backward with astounding speed so the blow he landed was only a nick. As it regrouped Constant saw Blix fall and her sword fly away. He leapt across the gap, dodging under the burning brand and pulled her back with his free hand, fending off a fearsome swing of her manticore's tail with the flat of his blade before twisting back and around to do the same on his side as the manticore he had pushed back arched forward to strike. The second manticore attacked again but, incredibly, Constant parried that too. The tails flicked in again and again from both sides, but the boy took each one on the blade and turned it away. Blix cowered in a ball in the sand, too terrified even to scream, the silver sword swinging lightning fast above her head.

'Dammit Kit, kill them!' Constant shouted.

Kit was struggling with her rifle. 'It's jammed!' she cried.

'Get the other one, the bombard, the pistol!'

Kit ran three steps and dived headlong between the manticore's tail and the flashing blade. She grabbed the pistol as she landed, rolled and came up under the manticore that had attacked Constant. Screaming obscenities, she emptied the pistol up into its chest. The manticore collapsed, missing her head but pinning her chest and arms. Her scream was choked off by its dead weight on her.

Constant turned to the scream just as the manticore he fought righted itself. The snaking neck curled through the defences. Its teeth clamped onto the silver blade and yanked it violently backwards. Constant held on and suddenly he was flying. He lost his grip in mid-air and landed in a heap halfway between the post and the fire. The manticore spat out the sword and turned toward Constant.

Blix sprang up, grabbed her own sword again and charged at the manticore, yelling 'Get away from him! Get away!' Strength surged through her, the sword was suddenly weightless in her hands. She swung the blade high as Constant had but the manticore took one look at her and flailed its tail as hard as it could. It caught her square in the stomach and sent her flying back the way she'd come. She landed in front of the wall of shields and skidded to a halt next to Kit, who was hopelessly trapped beneath the dead lion body. Blood welled up in Blix's mouth, sweet and metallic.

The manticore turned back to Constant. Almost delicately it tip-toed across to him. It stood above him. It opened its mouth as wide as it could.

Constant screamed '*Burn*!' and thrust his arms out. Fire burst from his fingers and engulfed the manticore, burning hotter than a furnace, lighting up the sky like an exploding star. The beast was lifted bodily into the air by the force of the flame, which stripped away hair and skin and roasted the flesh beneath in seconds. When it landed on the other side of the hollow, it was incinerated.

Constant screamed in utter anguish and curled into a ball, clutching at himself and crying helplessly.

'Fuck,' said Blix, trying to draw breath enough to speak. 'Fuck. We won. We won.'

'No,' croaked Kit. 'Look.'

Blix rolled over, though it cost her in pain. She looked where Kit had looked.

The fourth manticore got to its feet. It was unsteady and looked confused. The fall had knocked it to the verge of unconsciousness. It took a few unsteady steps sideways, shaking its head a few times. It stared at the dead manticore that had brought it down as if it had never seen death before. It made a strange, plaintive mewling sound. Then it seemed to focus, and think. It looked at Blix. It started toward her.

'We're dead,' said Blix simply, now far beyond fear. *I'm sorry, Katy.*

Then Kit spoke. 'I'm going to do something now. Try and forgive me.'

'What?' said Blix.

Then from out of the darkness a harpoon impaled the manticore through the chest and pinned it to the ground, instantly dead.

'That wasn't it,' said Kit in a shocked voice.

A strange creature approached them through the smoke from beyond the charred manticore. Huge, man shaped, wearing thick, ragged clothes, its head was a bone white expanse. Two huge tusks swept straight down from there before curling outward and behind the beast at waist height. It was terrifying.

The creature paused to look at Constant, who was rocking back and forth and crying inconsolably. It paused again to pull the harpoon from the stricken manticore. It made to slide it into a spear carrier strapped to its back, where another like it already thrust high above its head. But then it paused, and kept hold of the spear, and looked toward Blix and Kit. Then it walked purposefully toward them.

Now something else kills us, thought Blix.

'Goddamn son of a bitch,' said Kit. She sounded delighted, which Blix didn't understand at all. Then she saw it, and her heart leapt with joy.

'You'm all right then?' said the man, crouching next to them. His voice was deep and rich, a burr of gold and honey.

'No,' said Blix,' suddenly laughing as much as her lungs would allow. 'Not in any way at all. But better than dead. Is that a walrus skull on your head?'

Chapter Twenty-One: The Blood On Her Hands

The man stared at Blix from the darkness within his strange helmet. 'Sure,' he said eventually. 'Hey'm not usin' it no more.' He grabbed one of the tusks and shook it; the helm rattled on his head. 'Good protection from yon manticores. Stingers'r too wide, y'see.'

He pulled off the mask. The skull was screwed to a steel headpiece that reminded Blix of a cavalry helmet.

The man was old, perhaps in his seventies, with fine white hair braided into rows. His face was blue, something Blix had never seen before - but then she realised he was tattooed, lines and whorls in intricate designs rendered invisible by time. His face was heavily lined by age, care and a hard life. But his eyes were piercing sharp.

'Can you'm stand?' he asked. He held out a hand. He wore leather gauntlets which stretched half-way up his arms. They looked like armour.

Blix eased herself to her feet. Her body hurt from the centre out. 'Help Kit,' she said.

The man looked unblinkingly at her. Then walked past Kit, picked up her discarded rifle, and examined it minutely. Then after a moment in which Blix felt nothing but dread, he carefully placed it back down and returned to her side, and handed her his harpoon.

The shaft was as thick as her wrist and she wilted under its weight. Its head had a sharp barb on it. *To keep it in the flesh* thought Blix, shuddering slightly.

'Brace the far side so yon don't roll,' said the man. He turned to Kit. 'Wait on.'

He straddled the manticore corpse. With one movement, he lifted it under the forequarters, enough so that Kit could wriggle free. Blix levered the beast using the spear, although she wasn't sure this helped. The man held the weight by himself without breaking a sweat.

Kit slid out, seeming none the worse for having all the weight of a dead manticore lying on her. The man dropped the carcass and held out his hand for the spear. Blix hurriedly surrendered it.

'That's a really heavy spear,' she said, nervously.

'Hey'm no spear. Hey'm a harpoon.'

'Harpoon. Right. I knew that. It's heavy.'

'Thanks for saving us from old Maahes there,' said Kit, brushing herself down. 'What's your story, friend?'

The man looked warily from Kit to Blix and back again. 'Name's Roohsk,' he said eventually.

'Kit McCoy!' said Kit brightly, thrusting her hand out.

Roohsk ignored it. The leather of his glove creaked as it tightened around the harpoon shaft. 'I don't know you'm,' he said flatly.

'We ain't from around here,' said Kit.

The man chewed on his bottom lip. 'Go on 'n see to yon boy,' he said. 'I won't do nothin' while you'm backs is turned.' Blix wondered what he had considered doing but decided not to.

Constant was alive, but something was wrong. 'I'm twelve, I'm twelve, I'm twelve, I'm twelve,' he said over and over. He was curled in a ball, shuddering convulsively. He seemed unaware that Kit and Blix were there, his eyes glazed, seeing some inner world. With difficulty, Blix knelt beside him.

'Constant. Constant. *Constant.* CONSTANT.'

Constant's eyes snapped back to the world outside his head. 'Who am I?' he demanded.

'You're you. You're Constant.'

'Yes. I'm me. I'm Constant. There is no doubt.' His face contorted in pain. 'What happened?'

'We won! They're all dead! You nuked that manticore! Burned it alive, I mean.'

'How did I do that?' said Constant, shocked.

'Was wond'rin',' said Roohsk. He was examining the manticore he'd killed and didn't look at them. 'Ain't seen magic like they'n since us small days.'

Constant stiffened. 'Who are you?' he said sharply.

'Name's Roohsk.'

'What are you doing here?'

Now Roohsk looked over. 'Might ask you'm the same,' he said. 'This place, hey'm mine. You'm'r strangers. Ain't nowhere you'm could have come from round here I don't know. How you get to th' sand then?'

'We came through the gate,' said Blix. 'The one two days walk that way.' She pointed into the darkness is what she hoped was the right direction.

Roohsk pondered that. 'Ain't never seen a gate work since us small days either,' he said. 'Never seen that one work ever.'

'It didn't,' said Constant. 'Now it does.' He was looking at his hands, face screwed into a scowl of distaste, as though they'd offended him somehow.

'What's the matter, kid?' asked Kit.

He showed her. On each hand the very tips of his fingers were burned - no, not burned, Blix realised, but rusted, red and scaly. It was as if the marks he'd had on his two fingertips had spread to all the others. He rubbed at them, but the rust didn't come off.

'What's happened to your hands?'

'I'm not sure. I need to think about it.' He pushed himself up, wincing. 'I think I've pulled just about every muscle in my body.'

'My snake oil'll fix that right up!' said Kit.

'I expect it will. Are you okay?' He asked Blix.

'Catastrophic internal injuries, probably. I took a huge wallop. I feel okay though.' Blix was surprised by just how okay she felt. 'I'll feel it in the morning.'

'Perhaps not,' said Constant. He was watching Roohsk. 'What are you going to do with that?' he asked.

Blix looked around. Roohsk was holding a knife with a blade as long as his forearm. It had a hook at the point, like the gutting knife she'd taken from the cottage on Shambhala.

He looked at them impassively. 'Gon dress yon carcass,' he said, tipping the knife toward the manticore he'd killed. 'Need to get the temperature down, otherwise meat'll spoil. That why I'm here. Hunting manticore. This 'un, then those 'uns,' he continued, the knife now taking in the other bodies. 'I do that, I leave you'm alone, you'm leave me alone. Then I leave. Okay?'

'Sounds good to me,' said Constant.

'You eat manticores?' Blix wrinkled her nose at the thought. 'I ate alligator once. It was a bit chewy. What's manticore like?'

Roohsk smiled for the first time and it transformed his face. Suddenly he was the iron-eyed night hunter no longer. He reminded Blix of her grandfathers.

'You'm ever eat boots?' he said.

Constant took a sniff of Kit's "snake oil" and wrinkled his nose.

'Maybe not,' he decided, handing it back. 'I'll be fine, I think. I'll keep watch.'

He immediately fell asleep by the fire.

'Snake oil is powerful medicine,' said Kit, beaming once again. 'A whiff will do you good.' She held out the bottle to Blix and shook it a little. 'Want some?'

'No thanks. I don't seem to need it.'

She pulled up her shirt to show her stomach. The skin was pink and unblemished.

'The manticore's tail hit me like a tree trunk, hard enough to send me flying. That should have snapped my spine. Or pulverized something important inside me. Or at least given me an improbably large bruise.'

Kit rubbed Blix's shoulder. It was comforting. 'You know, magic healing powers ain't exactly a bad thing.'

Blix sighed, and sagged a little as though someone had placed a load on her back. 'The problem with knowing things is you can't not know them. I know about lycanthropy. I should just face it. It's not healing me as such. I mean, it has that effect, but it's not trying to help me. It's putting my body back to the way it needs to be before I change.'

'Yeah. I know too, kiddo. Didn't want to say.'

'Werewolf boyfriend?'

'Yeah. You learn a thing or two. He's ancient history though. In the wind.'

Blix suddenly wondered whether Kit had taken his ears.

The American's broad smile reappeared. 'Reasons don't matter. It healed you when you needed it. That ain't a bad thing.'

'I suppose not. The bad thing happens at full moon.'

'Yes, it does.' Kit rubbed Blix's shoulder again, then suddenly hugged her tight, then broke it off just as suddenly. 'Say, I'm gonna wash dead lionmanthing offa my clothes. Get some rest.'

She bounded off to the pool of water.

That took my mind off turning into a werewolf, Blix thought as she waited for her heart to stop galloping.

She joined Constant by the fire. He had wrapped himself in the sheet with the strange writing on it like a caterpillar in a chrysalis. Blix rolled into the bearskin cloak and tried to copy him. Kit was watching over her and Roohsk seemed, if not exactly safe, at least keen to have as little to do with them as possible.

She didn't know how she felt about Constant after his bravery against the manticores, but she didn't have the energy to think about it. Now that the fight was over and the adrenaline had drained away she felt bone weary.

Sleep didn't come. Every time she closed her eyes she saw an oily-black manticore tail striking for her face. She saw herself tearing it off with claws she didn't have, biting through hide and hair with fangs that were not there.

She watched Roohsk instead. He'd rolled the manticore onto its back and sliced it open from sternum to crotch. Now he had his arms inside it, pulling out the guts and cutting through the membranes with the hooked machete. Dark blood poured from the open belly.

Blix had never seen butchery before. She knew where meat came from, had no illusions about that and was okay with it most of the time. She'd never wanted to see it. But watching Roohsk cut through the flesh so expertly was fascinating. Almost mesmerising, in fact. She went over to get a closer look. Roohsk glanced up at her but didn't speak. He continued his work.

She was suddenly nervous. 'Um. I didn't introduce myself before. My name's Blix.'

Roohsk said nothing.

'Um. I never said thank you. For, um, killing this. Thank you. It would have killed me.'

Silence. Blix decided to give up the small talk. But as she turned away Roohsk said 'Nah. You'm kill it first. You'm a hunter.'

Blix laughed a little. 'Thanks, but I don't think so. I've never hunted anything. I was useless in the fight.'

'You'm killed one. I saw.'

'That was pure bloody luck. I was terrified. When the others came, I fell over. I just lay there.'

Roohsk paused in his work and straightened up. 'You'm did right. Boy would have cut you'm head off otherwise. You'm listen. Hunter ain't th' brave one, or th' one who swings steel or fires a gun well. Hunter is th' one who makes the kill. You'm a hunter. You'm all three are.'

Blix looked back at Kit and Constant. 'I suppose we are hunting someone.'

'Goddess help they'm.' Roohsk made an unusual waving gesture across his chest which Blix realised was a religious thing, like crossing himself. Then he bent himself to his task.

After a couple of moments Blix realised something else. 'You saw me shoot the manticore. That was right at the start. Couldn't you have helped sooner? Did you hear Constant shouting for help?'

Roohsk threw some offal aside. The wet squelch as it landed made Blix's stomach turn, and her heart pound. 'I don't know you'm. Anywise, you'm was doing aright. Kill two manticore inside half a minute.' Roohsk appeared to consider it. 'If you'm died, I help then.'

Blix had no answer to that. She watched him work in silence for a while. *We need help. Here's help. Maybe. Let's find out.*

'So, do you live around here?'

Roohsk said nothing. Eventually Blix realised he wasn't going to answer. *Okay, let's try something else.*

'There's a dead whale about a day's walk from here. Someone was taking ivory. Was that you?'

Roohsk looked up suspiciously. You'm steal my saw?'

'No, I did not.'

'I did!' Kit called from across the hollow. 'You can have it back though.'

'How did you hear that?' asked Blix.

'I told you, sound carries in the desert. Plus, I eat lots of carrots.'

'No, that's seeing in the d... Never mind.' She turned back to Roohsk, and tried again.

'Did you build this trap?'

This time he did speak. 'When'r was more of us, that's how we caught they'm. Now we'm ain't more. Now I track. Still use the lure though. Scent brings they'm here.'

'Oh.' Blix thought of asking why there weren't more. Instead she asked, 'Did you kill the merman?'

Roohsk didn't answer straight away. Eventually he said 'No,' and the sadness in his voice was clear. 'Hey'm kill hey'mself. They'm all do.'

'When the water went away,' said Blix. It wasn't a question.

Roohsk pushed his bloody gloves methodically along the hairy hide, wiping the worst of it away. In that moment he looked not bent to his task but just bent; an old man with a memory of too much sorrow.

'Sommat happen. Seventy year ago. Quake that shook the world. The big rivers they'm stop flowing, way upstream. Whole place get hotter. Sea dried up, get salty. Took years. Mers got nowhere to go. Took years. When the sea ain't no mor'n pubbles here and there, they'm go mad. They'm all beach. Some die quick, some not. Some rot, some not. Hey'm got dried out. Sand cover hey'm 'til I find hey'm.'

'And you hung him from a trap?' horrified at the images that now filled her mind.

'Needed bait,' said Roohsk. 'Manticore won't stalk they'm own kind, not much else hereabouts.' He thought some more. 'Hey'm'd understand. Hey'm was a hunter too.'

He broke off abruptly and got off his knees. 'I hang this 'un now to take the paws off and finish the dress, then I start on the next 'un. Wait on.'

He left her with the gaping carcass. He slung a line from one of the high spikes on the centre post, cinched around a lower one and tied it off. He took up the loose end of the rope and made it into a noose.

And then Roohsk was standing next to her, the big knife in his hand. 'You'm okay?' he asked.

'What? Yes. Fine. I must have nodded off, I didn't notice you coming over.'

'Mmm.' Roohsk looked away, staring at the stars. 'Full moon, hey'm day after tomorrow.' He looked back. 'Wherever you'm goin', you'm need to be there by then.'

Blix stared at him open mouthed. 'How could you tell? There's nothing, not yet! I'm not going to hurt you,' she added quickly.

'I know,' said Roohsk, his voice temperate. 'Sure, I seen you'm folk before. Some weres used to live in the old place, before water hey'm go. But that ain't how I know. Look down.'

Blix looked down. She saw the blood on her hands. She felt it in her mouth. She saw the dead manticore in front of her. She saw where she'd torn the flesh with her teeth.

Blix screamed and scrambled backwards, horrified. In a second Kit was beside her, cradling her as she babbled incoherently. In another second Constant was there, barely awake but with the great sword angled high above his head, ready to plunge it into Roohsk's chest. 'What did you do, old man?' he demanded.

'Nothin' as did this,' he said calmly. 'Girl doesn't know what's happening to her. She'm needed blood.'

Blix took deep breaths until the panic subsided. 'I had no idea. What if I'd attacked you?'

'I would have stopped you,' said Roohsk simply. 'You ain't that far gone though.' He looked impassively at Constant. 'You'm can put that pigsticker down now, boy.'

'*Make me.*'

'Okay, sure.' With lightning speed Roohsk ducked under Constant's guard, caught the blade with the hook of his knife and twisted and pushed at the same time. Constant's wrist bent backwards and the sword sprang from his grip, flipping over in the air. Roohsk caught the hilt before the blade hit the sand and in the same split second swung the point up to rest under Constant's chin. Constant froze.

'Give it back,' said Kit, levelling her pistol at Roohsk.

He ignored her. 'You'm good, boy. Saw you fightin'. But you'm a boy.' He dropped the blade and tossed the sword back to Constant. 'You'm should remember that. You'm draw the sword, don't stop to talk. Kill the man. Otherwise the man hey'm going to take this sword from you'm and stick it in you'm guts.' He looked sideways at Kit. 'I'm not against you'm. You'm coming and going, sure?'

'Yes sir, we surely are.'

'I help you go,' he said firmly, in a tone which said this was no favour. 'Where you'm going?'

Constant was rubbing his chin where the sword point had touch it, a furious scowl on his face. 'You live near here?'

'... mmm.'

'We're going to the other gate. There was a henge on an island. Do you know it?'

'Mmm. About forty ell on.'

'What's an ell?' asked Blix.

'Just over a mile,' Constant supplied.

Blix's heart sank. 'We only walked ten miles?'

'Told you, kiddo,' said Kit. 'Desert's a hard place.'

'I take you there,' said Roohsk. 'Ain't free,' he added.

'Nothin' is,' said Kit. 'How much? I got about twenty-three dollars and change on me.'

'Not money. Bullets.'

'How many?'

'How many you'm worth?'

'Wait a minute.' Blix pointed accusingly at the harpoon and walrus helmet. 'You have guns here? I thought this was sword n' sorcery land mark two. Like Shambhala but warmer. You're saying this is a modern world?'

'Dunno what you'm mean,' said Roohsk. 'World's th' world. Got a rifle, like hers. Had it since us small days. No bullets no more. No black powder. No one to make they'm round here.' He pointed into the darkness. 'My place between here and there. 'Bout twenty-five ell. I take you'm there, you'm rest up in the daytime, we go to the gate tomorrow night. Better that way. Sun hey'm no friend no more.' He rubbed a finger across his chin, rasping at stubble, watching Kit carefully. 'We'm come to a deal then. I think you'm make a deal. But no deal, no problem. You get halfway for free, you'm on you'm own then. Fifteen ell from my place to the ring.'

Blix looked despondent. 'We can't walk that far before moonrise.'

'Good reason you'm make a deal then.'

'We can't walk that far tonight either,' Constant pointed out.

'Sure. We'm don't walk. We'm ride.'

'Ride? Ride on what?'

Constant dreamed.

In my dream, I stand before the Vermillion Bird, staring at the glint in its eye. I have been reading about magic. What it is, what it does. It is very interesting. I'm not allowed to learn to use it, but the brothers can't stop me reading. It keeps my mind off other things.

The bloodstone is the only artefact I have ever seen, or ever will see I think. I have asked for it to be brought down so I may see it up close. This has caused concern it seems, because instead of some men with long ladders, Brother Jamyang ambles in.

'I am not going to use it to escape,' I say, before he can speak. This is true, though as I say it I know the thought has crossed my mind more than once.

'I didn't think you were,' he says. 'I think the brothers are worried you might accidentally turn yourself into a frog.'

'I'm not going to use it at all. I just want to see it.'

'You can see it well enough from here. It doesn't look impressive, or mystical. There are a hundred like it in the Treasury.'

'None of them defend the mountain. Or could level it, if the books are to be believed.'

'I don't know about that. It is a powerful artefact.'

'How is that possible?' I ask. 'How can a tiny gemstone store power like that? Who could do such a thing? Why did they do it? Where did the magic come from in the first place?'

'All very good questions. If you don't know the answers nobody else here does.'

'I can't remember. I tried to think about it, but the voices... I just end up saying the words.'

'I understand,' says Jamyang, but he does not understand. 'My advice is to wait. Reflect on the matter. If you know, it may come to you. No need to plumb your depths today. You fathom deep.'

'Yes, yes,' I say irritably. 'Another answer which amounts to "do nothing and pray."'

'That is what you're for,' he says mildly.

I throw my hands up in exasperation. 'But why *am I for that?' I say. 'Why am I not for something else? There are other religions in the universe you know, thousands of them. Other fathers of faith go out among their people. They feed the hungry and heal the sick. They lead crusades and convert heathens to their belief at the point of a sword. Why don't I?'*

'Because you told us not to let you,' he says without hesitation. 'And you told us not listen if you changed your mind.'

'I know,' I say, deflating. 'I know I did.' I remember. Not exactly a memory, but a feeling that someone I once was said those words. And it is right. That is our way. Nonetheless, I stare out of the window, wishing not for the first time that I could fly away into the blue. But I know my duty.

In my dream, Brother Jamyang waits until the storm clouds lift from my brow. 'Do you want to lead a crusade?'

'No, of course not. I just want to be able to do something.' I gesture to the bloodstone. 'Magic, maybe.'

'I wouldn't ask for that, were I you.'

'Why not? It defends us, doesn't it? I know you had an unpleasant experience but-'

'We should be thankful that we have it,' he says, cutting across my thoughtless remark. 'And we should leave it alone.'

'But why?'

'Do you know why magic is stored in artefacts? Because it takes from you. It gives back nothing. The power that's in that stone came from somewhere. It may be just as well you don't know.'

In my dream, I say, 'I don't want to think about it.' I feel strange as I do so, as if the thought isn't quite mine.

'Yes. Maybe you will one day. Will that be a good day, I wonder?'

'I hope so,' I say. I smooth the front of my robe.

Now there is a boy here I do not recognise.

'I wasn't expecting to see this one again. I wonder what you're trying to tell yourself? Shame you don't really remember your dreams, isn't it? Makes a change from the angry one, anyway. You need to control how much of that one you access. He's very aggressive.'

The boy looks at the bloodstone.

'Actually, Jamyang was right. I don't know where the bloodstone came from. The first one had it when I entered him. Not the first of you. The very first. You don't remember him. There's nothing left to remember. He wasn't like you. He wasn't *special*.'

The boy is not smiling. I can see that he is upset.

'Now listen. You just gave me a very bad scare. What's in that snake oil? You went to sleep but you didn't dream. I couldn't speak to you! I thought she'd blocked me. It was the fog I felt in the woods the other day, except this time there was no way out, no way to find you. I thought she'd separated us! And you only sniffed it, why was that stronger than drinking it? Don't ever go near that that stuff again, do you understand? Don't drink it, don't smell it, don't even look at it. Never. *Never.*'

His jabbing finger emphasises the point. I follow it with my eyes. He is terrified, I realise. He calms himself. He smooths the front of his tunic in a way I recognise as my own.

'Now, I've been thinking-'

Constant did not remember the boy when he woke up.

The moon was only a silver glimmer around the edges of thick clouds, but Blix felt it.

Four large manticores drew Roohsk's long sled across the trackless desert, their dainty steps thrumming on the sand. At least Roohsk called it a sled, but this understated its presence by some way in Blix's view. It was a trimaran built from the shell of a ship's longboat, a shallow draught pinnace big enough for ten oars, stripped back to the bare hull. It was held above the ground by four curved beams which led to an outrigger on each side - but where the floats would have been if the vessel had gone on water, wide blades cut through the sand, spreading the weight of the boat. The stern point had been cut off and a wagon gate attached to give access. The sides were higher than Blix's head. Constant had needed a boost to get on.

Roohsk sat on a raised driving seat, the prow under his feet. He held the reins in one hand and a driving whip in the other, the walrus skull helm hiding his face once more as he drove. The others sat in the back with three manticore carcasses, which Roohsk had covered with canvas and tied down, much to Blix's relief.

There wasn't much room. Crates and sacks of cargo largely filled it. Roohsk had spent some time grumbling about the space they took up. 'Could have brought another'n,' he'd said, thumping the meat.

A long pole arced from the driver's seat high into the air and back across the sled. A lantern dangled from the end, bobbing merrily as they bounced along the sand, shutters closed on one side to give light without night-blinding the driver. The only other light was the near-full moon. Unfamiliar, but beautiful despite that. Blix tried to imagine what they must look like in the moon's sight - a tiny dot of light and life in unending darkness, like the world in space. Then she wondered whether it was bad that she'd considered the moon's perspective on things. That felt like wolf thinking.

Roohsk flicked the reins a little and the manticores picked up the pace. They were muzzled, and their long tails had been docked at the barb and tied off to limit their movement. They were as obedient and responsive as the finest cavalry horses.

Constant woke suddenly as the sled bounced over a boulder and he was thrown heavily against the driver's box. A thick black tail coiled above his head. He froze.

'Are you *sure* they're safe?' he said.

'Sure,' said Roohsk. 'Very loyal, if you'm get 'em young.'

Constant looked unconvinced. 'How long was I asleep?' he asked, sitting up. He watched the manticores carefully.

'Not long,' said Blix. 'Less than an hour I think.'

'It felt longer. Felt like a lifetime. What's that smell?'

'Dead meat.'

'No, it smells like... fruit turpentine?'

'Oh, that. That's booze.'

Roohsk held a bottle out behind him. 'Palm rakia,' he said. 'Home-made. You'm have some if you'm want. Crate back there. Hey'm give you those man muscles, sure.' He took another swig. A large lockbox behind the driver's seat clinked on cue.

Constant lifted the lid gingerly. A dozen or more assorted bottles sloshed with an unappetising liquid.

'I abstain, thank you.'

'Good. More for me.'

The sled lurched downward suddenly. The manticore's tail flattened for balance; Constant ducked.

'If they're so safe, why are they docked and muzzled?' he said, moving out of the way.

Roohsk didn't bother to turn around. 'So's I don't get my face et,' he said, as if to a small child. 'They'm loyal. I ain't stupid though.'

'Docking is cruel,' said Blix, arms crossed in disapproval. 'Manticores express themselves through their tails. It's like, I dunno, sewing your lips shut.'

'Better'n getting stung,' said Roohsk evenly. 'They'm can still wag when they'm out of harness.'

'How much further?' asked Kit. She thumped a manticore carcass, which squelched. 'These old boys are gonna get ripe pretty quick when the sun comes up.' She swatted at a large winged insect, which fell into Constant's lap. He pitched it over the side.

'I tell you when,' said Roohsk in a tone which ended questions.

Blix closed her eyes and tried to sleep, but the smell of the manticore meat filled her mind with disturbing thoughts. Fangs in the darkness. The moon bright in the sky. Blood on her hands. They bounced along in silence as the long night crept toward dawn.

The First of Wolves faced the desert and sniffed the air, seeking the trail of his enemies.

A dozen werewolves had come with him through the lens frame from the Bastion. They'd seen him cradle his dead cub in his arms and howl obscenities into the unheeding sky. Ten more had joined them as they tracked the wolf killers through the forest to a cottage, and from the cottage to some rocks, and from the rocks to the road, and along the road to the mountain and the town at its base.

They could not climb the Anvil in their man shapes. There was no need. The pack watched nervously as the First of Wolves used the bloodstone to summon the gondola, exerting control over the magic in the stone. This was the second time he had done so, following the magician's instruction. It was easier this time than when the werewolves had descended to bring death to the men of the town.

Once they had risen they followed the confusing scent path through the complex of tunnels and chambers until it ended at a place of stones with a gate at its centre. The blast marks told them what the wolf killers had done next.

This was a problem. The First of Wolves knew about gates. He knew the words which opened them. But he also knew he needed the name of the place the gate pointed to, and that he didn't know. He let the pack sleep while he brooded on the matter.

The map was key. The First of Wolves recognised it as sister to the glass roof at the Bastion. He cared not for its artistry, but he was different enough from the other werewolves that he noticed it.

Why am I different?

One of the killers had made a route with twine. The First of Wolves understood what the pictures represented. Each world was shown. But the names of the worlds and the places on them were written in human tongue. The First of Wolves did not read human marks. The First of Wolves did not read any marks. He sat on the cold floor before the great map and tried to think like a human. Then he tried to think like the magician.

Why am I different?

A wolf that used magic was not unprecedented. There had been one. Now there were two. The First of Wolves knew the trick of it. The magician covered it with flamboyance, and the Wolfmaker with religion. The First of Wolves saw through both. It was just strength. Speak the right words with enough strength, and what you desired would come to pass. Everything else was show.

Speak the right words...

The First of Wolves rose abruptly and held the bloodstone up to the map. 'Where the twine leads from this place, say those names.'

Silence. Then a strange, shattered, echoing voice spoke in the room. With a start the First of Wolves recognised it as his own, speaking to him as if through cracking ice. It was a terrible thing to hear.

'*Shambhala,*' it said. '*The Stone Garden. Ceto. Eveni Krai; the Men of the Isle. Helikon. The Stones of the Plain; The Stones of the Meadow. Horkos. Break-no-oaths; key-of-Haides; Thyïlea. Pytheas' Gate; The High Rocks. Elysium. The Blessed Dead; Valhalla. Ymir. Muninn; Huginn. Vicandra. Fort Clive; Saint Alexander Nevsky Gate. Lyonesse. Ten Trolls; the Great Henge. Shambhala. The Bastion.*'

The First of Wolves followed them with his eyes as each name was spoken. A world, a place to arrive, a place to leave. He said the words in his mind until he remembered. Wolves had no marks; they had only memory. Then he headed for the place of stones.

Now he was on a different world. He stood at the lip of the Shambhala gate pit, Eveni Krai to the men of this place, knowing his quarry must have stood there too. He stared into the east and the first light of dawn. He breathed in.

Below him the werewolves waited for his word. They feared him, as they should. He was the leader of their pack. But they also feared the magic. A fire in the mind, burning through the senses, it left ruin in its ashes. The First of Wolves had seen this. They had all seen this.

He focused his mind on the green-red rock. 'The ones I follow. Take us to them.'

Nothing happened.

'Show me their path.'

Still nothing. The First of Wolves tried to remember if the magician had said anything more about using the stone, but could not.

He put away the stone and took out the lens. 'To the ones I follow.' Again, nothing, but this time the First of Wolves knew the reason. *I have not been to the place they are. This magic only shows me what I have seen.* He put the device away, and turned his nose to the air once more.

In and out. In and out. The sands have shifted. Don't smell the sand. Find the scent beneath the surface. Where their feet sank in, their skin rubbed against the grains. In the heat, sweat dripped from them. The tang of females. The sands have shifted. Breathe.

The sands had shifted but the scent was there. Faint, stripped away by the wind, but there nonetheless. Enough that he could follow it. The First of Wolves howled and was answered by his pack. They ran into the eye of the morning.

''bout there,' said Roohsk. 'Few dunes away.'

Blix opened her eyes. It was the hour after dawn when everything looked new. The clouds brightened in the sky as the sun climbed above the horizon. The sled runners cut through the sand with a persistent *shhhhhh*.

Blix watched Roohsk. He was master of his boat. As the sand rose and fell he steered the manticores to the best line to take them forward without climbing tall dunes or sliding to their bases. The way Roohsk half sat, half stood on the driving box, the way he leaned into the movement of the sled and the flow of the sand, wasn't the way of a coachman or a dog-driver. It was the way of a helmsman at the wheel.

The manticores crested a dune and pulled the sled over. Roohsk pulled the reins hard to slow them. 'We'm here.'

Blix took one look and said, 'It's an oasis!'

Below them was a stand of sandy scrubland held together here and there by patches of grass. A pool of water a few hundred feet across sat in the middle. Low trees and bushes surrounded the pool. The dunes surrounded the oasis, looming over it, encroaching on the pitiful green.

Between the water and the sand …

Constant squinted, not quite believing what he saw. 'Boats?'

'Sure.'

Sixteen rusting boats sat around the oasis - not on the water, but on the land. There were steam funnels and sail-rigged masts. They ranged from little more than dinghy-sized, though puffer tugs and fishing boats, to longer cargo vessels and barges. Some sat straight on their keels as if only waiting for a late tide. Some listed or lay on their sides. Some were half buried in sand and seemed abandoned, their ribs visible where the siding had been cut away. A black collier had been stripped almost completely and buried to the deck. The remnants looked like a mechanical skeleton, clawing its way to the surface. It had the stillness of a grown-over grave.

Other boats were still in use. Awnings tied to deck rails at one side and poles driven into the sand at the other gave shelter against the sun. In some places the cloth was replaced by corrugated iron sheets. A rickety boardwalk of planks snaked through the encampment.

Roohsk steered the sled around the slope of the dunes until he was parallel with a fishing boat, nets and crab pots still visible on the deck, then dropped down to it, expertly guiding the longboat so its weight didn't pull it sideways uncontrollably. The fishing boat had sunk into the sand below the plimsoll line, and was buttressed on each side by girders plundered from one of the rotting ships. The prow was hidden by a large tent of orange silk. The stern was shaded by a canvas sheet tied at each corner of the boat and pegged to the ground. It looked like an old sail and probably was, Blix thought. On the side of the boat a word was written in faded letters, in a strange claw-like script which Blix once again found she could read. It said *Xvairizem.*

The manticores knew where they were going. They pulled toward a large pen near the boat and padded to a halt. 'All out,' said Roohsk, climbing down.

A tiny girl, no more than two years old, swamped by a bright blue cotton dress and crimson turban, barrelled up to them at top speed, laughing in delight. Roohsk opened his arms wide to embrace her, but she shot past him and buried herself in the thick fur at the neck of one of the manticores, almost knocking herself off her feet with the impact. The manticore looked momentarily startled, then knelt so the girl could wrap her arms around its neck. It trumpeted contentedly.

'Hmph,' said Roohsk. He looked slightly deflated.

A woman appeared on the deck of the ship. She was dressed in the same style as the child, except her dress and turban were mustard yellow. She had the blackest skin Blix had ever seen, a matte so deep it looked almost like paint. Emerald swirls cascaded down her cheeks. They looked like paint too, but as she climbed down and approached them Blix saw they were tattoos, the luminous counterpart to Roohsk's ancient, indistinct markings. The woman was about half of Roohsk's age, if not younger.

'Wife,' said Roohsk, by way of introduction. He nodded toward the little girl, who was now rubbing her face from side to side though the manticore hair and giggling wildly. 'Child. Adopted,' he added.

'Loved,' said the woman. 'I am Seminah.'

'Kit McCoy!'

Seminah took Kit's outstretched hand. Blix and Constant introduced themselves.

'Welcome to our krai. You'm must be thirsty. Come and drink.'

'Is that drinkable?' asked Constant. Up close the oasis shimmered like oil. It didn't look pleasant.

'No,' said Roohsk. 'Hey'm salt. Very salt.' He pointed beyond the settlement to where the sand shelved gently up to a point of flat ground. 'Fresh spring's up there. What left of hey'm. Was land up there, back when'r was a difference. An island.' He gestured at the oasis. 'Hey'm the sea. What left of hey'm.'

Constant followed Seminah to a water butt nearby. He took a ladle and drank deeply. The water looked clear and clean. He caught sight of Blix's dubious expression.

'They drink it,' he said. 'You only live once.'

'I suppose I do. Wait, was that a joke?'

'Yes. I'm trying.'

'Yes, you are.' She joined him, and took a big slurp. 'I suppose the were thing will kill any bacteria, now I come to think of it.'

'What's a, um, back tree ah?'

'Never mind.'

Here and there men and women emerged from inside their boats. Lean and sand-scrubbed. Blix could feel their eyes on her. She knew the 'strangers in a small town' look when she saw it. Curiosity, and fear. The first now, the second waiting for its moment, ready to turn to anger.

Kit knew it too, it seemed. She took a few deliberate steps away from the sled, so she could be seen. Her right hand rested on the butt of her pistol, not in a way which threatened anyone, but showing beyond doubt, here is a gun.

'How many people live here?' she asked, staring out across the water, not meeting anyone's eyes.

Roohsk had unhooked the manticores from their harness and was shooing them into their pen, slipping off their muzzles as he pushed them through the gate. The tiny girl slapped their bottoms as they went in.

'Twenty-one,' he said, gathering up the tack. 'Was more. Some died. Others left, gone somere else, up north, far north where they'm cities are. When you'm could get there without dyin' of thirst. We'm the last here.'

He saw how Kit was standing and stopped what he was doing. 'You'm not going to need hey'm here,' he said, his voice carefully neutral. 'They'm not going to hurt you'm.'

'I know,' said Kit. 'Now they know too.'

There was a nervous cough. A big man waited on the boardwalk just beyond the prow. He looked a lot like Roohsk, except his tattoos were much clearer. He said something to Seminah that the magic didn't translate for Blix. Roohsk beckoned him across. There was a brief exchange, then much spitting in hands and deal-making-style shaking of them. The man shouldered one of the manticore carcasses without much effort and carried it off.

'Butcher,' said Roohsk. 'Told hey'm to send some boys for the other beasts before they'm spoil too bad. We dry 'em, salt 'em up, they keep a while. Salt we got. Dry, too.'

He crossed to the ladder and put a foot on the first rung, then turned to Kit. 'Come, you'm. We do a deal.' He thumped up to the deck and disappeared through a hatch. Kit scampered after him.

Seminah took the ladle from Blix. 'You'm sleep last night?'

'Not really. I closed my eyes.'

'You'm look like you'm need it.' She looked at Constant. 'You'm too. Shade at the stern. Stay out of the sun. Hey'm no friend.'

Something tugged at Blix's leg. The tiny girl looked up at her, face very serious.

'Hey'm no friend!' she declared. Then she teetered off to the tent at top speed, giggling mightily.

'Akali,' said Seminah, smiling. She raised her voice so that child could hear. 'She'm bother you, throw her to the manticore.' There was an infant shriek from inside the tent, then more giggling.

'What kind of place is this?' asked Constant, mostly to himself.

'Ours,' said Seminah simply. 'The last place. Where we came to rest when the sea hey'm go.'

She guided them to the shade. Blix noticed the temperature change immediately. 'Rest. Food when the sun hey'm get low. You'm need it where you'm go.'

'You don't know where we're going,' said Constant sharply, suddenly suspicious. 'You don't know us at all.'

Seminah smiled gently. 'I don't need to know you'm. You'm like everyone here. You'm strays. Roohsk, hey'm find strays. Roohsk found all of us. Hey'm father to this place. Some stay, like me. Some go, like you'm.'

'If Roohsk's the father of this place, does that make you the mother?' asked Constant.

The woman smiled once more. 'No. I am Shamanka. I'm in charge. I keep they'm together.'

She stepped back out into the blazing sun. 'Wherever you'm go from here, the way hey'm hard.'

'Harder than you think,' said Constant.

'Not really,' she said, without coming back inside. 'Going, hey'm hard. Harder to stay. Not much left here.'

'What keeps you here?' asked Blix.

'What keeps anyone anywhere? Love.'

The werewolf sank its teeth into the lion-thing carcass and tore off a chunk. It immediately spat it out again. 'Bad,' it growled. 'Heat spoiled.'

'Drink, then,' said the First of Wolves. He stared at the remains of the fish-man, hanging high above his head. 'Rest. We run again soon.'

The rest of the pack lay exhausted in what shade there was, out of the noonday sun. The werewolves were not used to the day. They were not used to heat. Even in their man-skins their pelts were thick and shaggy, a winter coat for a cold world. The change was brutal. It was slowing them down.

The faint scent he had followed, the last traces of where humans had stepped on the sand, had suddenly coalesced beside the dead behemoth. The titanic skeleton had not moved the First of Wolves. The thing was dead. Instead he concentrated on the scent. He was easily able to distinguish them. The bitch the magician had brought through the gate. The bitch who smelled of burning powder. The cub who carried silver. The longer he held the scent the more it revealed about them. That the girl had been bitten, but had not yet changed. That the woman was human, but more than human. That the boy was scared all the time.

The scent in this graveyard of lion-things was stronger still. The First of Wolves had killed lions before. The lion-things were bigger and more fearsome. The scent picture was confused, but gradually the First of Wolves had put the shape of the battle into his mind. The First of Wolves formed a grudging respect for his quarry. Resourceful and courageous. Lucky too, that another had arrived and slain one of the beasts. That they were brave and clever and lucky did not lessen his rage against them.

The First of Wolves wanted to sleep but when he closed his eyes he saw his cub. The rage made sleep impossible.

'Did you have cubs?' he asked the fish-man's corpse. 'Did you live to see them die?'

'What say you?' said a nearby werewolf. Fur the colour of burnt bread marked him as New.

'Nothing for your ears.' The First of Wolves looked away, but found his eyes came back to the merman. *This is how everything ends.*

A breath of wind stirred the sand. The grains scattered and fell still, then rose and scattered anew as the gust returned. This didn't matter. The trail was now clear, with physical tracks furrowing the sand should the scent disappear. Yet the First of Wolves hesitated.

If we run through this heat, we will die. And then I will have no vengeance.

'Use what shade there is. We wait here until the sun relents.'

The huge post cast a shadow. The First of Wolves lay in the shadow and stared at the merman.

Constant dreamed.

In my dream, I wake in the night to find I cannot move. A monster sits on my chest, formless and infinite, pinning me down, crushing me, forcing the breath from my body. As I realise this I am consumed by terror such as I have never felt, terror that when I recall it afterward seems to me to be the dread of judgment. The fear that this is the last moment, and retribution is here, retribution for sins I have not committed.

In my dream, I cry out, but no sound comes, and the weight presses down. There is Nothing there. Then suddenly I am free. I fall from my bed, drenched and shaking, clawing at my breast and gulping air. When I finally dare to turn around, the monster is not there, and I feel foolish to have been so scared by a nightmare. But the weight remains.

In my dream, my wife Kisva wakes with a start and sees my distress, and she slides out from under the sheets onto the floor beside me. Her beautiful face is contorted by a very different fear. She knows that my father died when his heart gave out, and his father before him; she knows they were not old.

In my dream, we are naked, for this is our marriage bed and we have just known each other for the first time. We are nineteen years old and very much in love.

In my dream, we lay awake into the small hours and talk about the future. I say that my brothers and I will continue our father's work on the farm. Each year the land we reclaim from the forest will increase our lot and the portion of the surplus which is ours. Adri, my eldest brother, is a man of vision and education. He talks about rotation and diversifying crops. I have ideas about husbandry that he approves of. He calls me Ails Good-husband and now everyone does. It is the greatest joy of my life to have my brother's approval. The second greatest, now.

In my dream, we fall asleep until morning, and I rise, rested, with no weight on my chest. I quickly forget that I was ever afraid. As I break my fast there is a knock on the door. Kisva answers it. It is a monk, she says. Let the good brother in, I say, and give him some milk.

In my dream the monk comes in and looks at me and he Recognises me. I do not understand how I know what this means, but I do.

In my dream, I rise to leave my wife and home without a thought for either. I rise to go and never return, because I am the Great Father, and no one comes down from the Anvil except for this.

Now there is a boy here I do not recognise.

'The problem with this way of talking is we get interrupted by consciousness,' *he says.* 'Never mind.'

In my dream the boy smiles at me.

'I liked being this one. He was straightforward and good with his hands. I liked making things. I understand why you're dreaming about family here. This Roohsk has built himself a surrogate family out of this catastrophe. It's sort of like the Monastery, isn't it? A family that chooses itself. I understand why that is attractive to you. The idea of family isn't meaningful to my kind, but being you for the last four thousand years has helped me understand. You can't be part of it I'm afraid. We must move on.

'But before we do, let's confront whatever that is pretending to be a woman, shall we? You won't remember that, so let's push at the things you're already suspicious about. We need to understand her motives and I want to do it while there are other people around. I don't know what Roohsk's motives are, but I know he's human. Which means he'll kill her if we need him too.'

Constant did not remember the boy when he woke up.

Constant ached. When he stretched his legs, it set off tiny explosions of pain everywhere from his ankles to his shoulder blades.

'Ow.'

Blix looked up from the bowl of food she was shovelling into her mouth. 'Welcome back. You should have some of this, it's fantastic.'

'What is it? No wait, let me guess, manticore stew?'

Blix squinted critically at the bowl. 'There's not that much manticore in it. It's more ragu of manticore. Seminah brought it just now. It doesn't taste like boots at all.' She pointed with her spoon. 'There's a bowl for you there, but it won't be there for long unless you get a move on. I'm hungry.' She gave him a disdainful look. 'I'm still not your biggest fan. Food would make an excellent peace offering.'

'Take it. I don't think I can eat anything now. Not until my body starts working again.' Constant sat up. 'Ow.'

'I'm not surprised you're stiff. You didn't move a muscle all day. You were dead to the world.'

'That's how I sleep. I'm told. I think I must dream a lot. I don't really remember.'

Constant petered out, frowning slightly as if he didn't quite understand something, then shook his head to clear it. 'Ow.' He rubbed his neck.

'Kit's probably got something for that.' Blix put her bowl aside and looked at Constant's with a predatory expression. He pushed it toward her.

'I expect she has. I don't want to have that argument now.'

'Why would there be an argument? Other than you both enjoy one.'

'I do *not* - ah, very funny,' said Constant, as Blix pointed an accusing finger. 'I mean her liniment, or snake oil, or whatever she calls it. It's magic, isn't it?'

'Maybe. Or maybe just really great drugs? They give animals stuff you wouldn't believe. I was shocked. Horse tranquilizer? Ketamine. That stuff'll do your head in.'

'It doesn't just help with the pain though, does it? It fixes you. Almost instantly. That means magic. And that's impossible. You can't infuse magic into liquid. It's constantly moving, changing. There's nothing to fix to. Which means it's not the snake oil that's fixing us. It's Kit.'

'What's me?' said Kit, ducking under the canvas and illuminating the shade with a brilliant smile. 'Whatever it was, I plead the fifth.'

'Damn. I didn't want to-' Constant began, then changed his mind. 'No, let's have it out. Your magic potions aren't magic. You're doing it.'

'Right on the first part, wrong on the second.' Kit plonked herself on the sand and started on Constant's food. 'I don't do magic. It's for assholes. Hey, this stuff is nice! You should get yourself some, kid. Stop your mouth for a while. Fill up those grumbling guts.'

'My gut is telling me something isn't right. You're faster than us and stronger than us, you hear and see and can smell better than us, you never sleep, and you have magic that makes us like you, because I liked you the moment I met you and that never happens. Who are you, Kit McCoy?'

Kit paused, spoon in mid-air. Then she put aside the bowl, and smiled sweetly at Constant.

'Just a gal from Nebraska. All that's just so much horse hockey. I'm stronger and faster 'cause I'm grown and you're twelve. I slept when you slept. You dint wake to see me sleep. And I ain't put a spell on you. You like me 'cause I'm nice.'

She heaved herself up. 'Sun's going down. Roohsk's fixing up the sled. Better feed and water yourself, I don't think he's gonna stop for oats.'

'Did you do a deal?' Blix asked.

Kit sighed happily. 'Well sure I did a deal! I'm American. Deals are what we do.' She strode out before Constant could ask her what deal she had made.

'Did that conversation go as you expected?' asked Blix, after Kit had gone.

'It was more confrontational, in my head.' He looked earnestly at Blix. 'What I said about her, you must have noticed?'

'Sure. I also noticed that she's on our side.'

'Is she? How do you know? I'm not sure anyone's on anyone's side. Sometimes I'm not sure I'm on my side.'

'Sometimes,' Blix said pointedly, 'you are a dick.' She suddenly looked slightly alarmed. 'Here, you're not thinking of leaving, are you?'

'No. I promised I'd help you and I will. I keep my promises. I know that much.' He sighed. 'I think I do. I'm getting pretty sick of not knowing what I think.'

'This is the reincarnation thing.' Blix picked up the bowl Kit had set aside and began vacuuming up the contents.

'Yes. You know how you're changing into a werewolf?'

Now Blix too paused mid-mouthful. 'Way to put a woman off her food.'

'Sorry. I don't know how to talk to people. Kit's right, I'm only twelve. I'm trying not to be older. It's not working very well.'

'It is noticeable,' said Blix, carefully. 'Every now and then. Sometimes you talk like a professor.' She shifted uncomfortably. 'Sometimes you're very angry.'

'The professor was called Palden Ngapoi, briefly. Then he was the thirty-second of my name. This is about three thousand years ago; do you know how strange it feels to remember that? You don't. No one does.' He looked suddenly haggard and haunted and unhappy.

'Tell me about him. A problem shared, you know.'

Constant stared into the middle distance, as if looking down a long tunnel. 'He came to the Monastery as a baby, like me. He was quite unusual, as we go. I grew up wanting to hide under the mountain. He longed to be somewhere else. He's the reason I know about gates and artefacts. I know because he read everything there was to read about them. He was... Is the word auto-didactic?'

'I don't know what that means.'

'Self-teaching. He was also petulant brat when he was a boy.' Constant grinned despite himself. 'I can relate to that, at least.'

'And the other one. The angry one?'

‘Darcen Ysir.’ Mentioning the name made something stir in Constant’s mind. He pushed it down. ‘He was a man before he became me. He was a mercenary, a bandit, a... Do modern earthmen have a word for somebody who doesn’t understand that other people feel things?’

Blix shifted as though she’d felt a chill at the base of her spine, her sudden discomfit obvious to Constant. ‘Psychopath,’ she replied.

‘Then he was one of those.’

‘You’re turning into a psychopath?’

‘No, not at all. He really changed quite profoundly when he became me. Or us. Or remembered he was us. Or me. It’s really complicated.'

'No kidding.'

'I’m remembering that I once was him. Or part of me was. Something like that. I’m not changing, not like you’re changing, but when I remember, when I’m scared or angry, it’s sometimes difficult to remember who is remembering who.’

‘Okay, my noodle is officially stir-fried. You mean he takes over your body?’

‘No, not at all... sort of. Sometimes I feel I’m looking out of his eyes. I mean, I’m me. I have a personality and a sense of self and that hasn’t changed. But sometimes I feel...’

‘What?’

‘I feel that if I’m not careful, it might change.’

‘Then stop thinking about him. Think about one of the others. Seventy, wasn’t it? Someone who doesn’t accidentally brainwash people.’

Constant, mortified, swallowed his words for a second. ‘I could do that,’ he managed. ‘I dream about the others. There are some like that.’

‘You do you.’

‘It’s all really, really difficult. What it comes down to is, I think I need to think about Ysir. When I remember Palden, I know what he knew. Well, no. It’s not as simple as that. I know how to find it in my mind. It’s the same for Ysir. He knew how to fight. But he was also a grown man, honed from years of battle. My mind is trying to do things with muscles my body doesn’t have. That’s why I ache all over.’ He looked up at her. ‘I don’t want to be them. I didn’t ask for this. I want to be me.’

‘You are you. You’re you right now.’

‘Am I? Are you sure? Because I can remember almost four thousand years of conversations about this, and they were all like this one.’ He sighed heavily. ‘Although they were all with monks. We all feel like this. Those of my name, I mean. I’m supposed to become more serene as I get older.’ He stared unhappily at the sand. ‘Dunno when that’s going to happen.’

‘Well, if it helps, at least your body isn’t going to rip itself apart and turn itself into a monstrous killing machine.’

‘There is that. How do you feel?’

‘On edge.’ Blix stirred the remains of the sludge in her bowl. ‘Meat tastes a lot better than it used to. I don’t have any aches or bruises and let’s face it, I should be on crutches with the punishment I took yesterday.’ She tossed the bowl away. ‘There was something else too. Just before the Manticores arrived, I got stronger. A lot stronger. And faster. It didn’t last, but it did happen.’

'I think I know why,' said Constant. 'Werewolves are creatures of the moon. Full moon had passed on Shambhala when you got bitten. The moon was waning. Here it's waxing. Almost full.'

'Tomorrow night. We'll be gone by then, thank goodness. I can avoid it for a bit longer. Hey, if I could find a gate that had the right gain and lag, I could go through it every month and miss the full moon on both sides completely. I'd never change.'

'That much gate travel would be bad in its own right. You might die from it.’

Blix screwed up her face in disgust. ‘Intestinally dispersed,’ she shuddered. ‘Maybe I won’t do that.’

Seminah appeared at the edge of the awning.

'You'm friend say, haul you'm lazy asses off the sand or manticore they’m get fat chewing them off. I think she’m ready to go.' She held out a package. 'Jerky. You'm need more meat. You'm both too skinny.'

Constant took the package. 'Bless you for your kindness,' he said. 'I hope you don't die.'

Seminah looked taken aback for a second, then she laughed, a tinkle of silver bells. As she did so her face sparkled, and Constant realised the swirls tattooed on her face weren’t just made of ink, but also a dust of emeralds, scarified into the skin.

'Hey’m a *good* blessing,' she said.

'Everyone says that.'

Seminah reached out and held his cheek in the palm of her hand, startling him a little. It was the way a mother might touch her child. He’d never been touched like that before.

‘Boy who tries to be a man, here is something for you'm.'

She held out something small and white. It was a figure carved in ivory, a stylised mermaid with a human face and flowing hair, bare-breasted and heavily pregnant. A long fishtail coiled back up and around her belly, each scale detailed exquisitely. It fit into the palm of his hand.

'It's beautiful,' said Constant, not knowing quite what to say. 'You made this?'

'Scrimshaw. Roohsk hey’m bring ivory from time to time.'

'Who is it?'

'Ceto,' said Seminah. 'Mother of oceans. Goddess of this place. We’m are the Ocean People. It is good to acknowledge the gods.'

All faiths are aspects of the Faith,' said Constant. 'Thank you.'

'Will it bring us luck?' asked Blix hopefully.

Seminah shook her head. 'No. Ceto, she'm indifferent to human fate. Like the sea. Like the sand. You'm make your own luck.'

Roohsk was wrestling the last manticore backward into harness when Blix and Constant arrived. Blix saw again how strong the old man was, forcing the recalcitrant creature to step backward against its will by kicking its shins, quite gently, then shoving hard when it shifted its weight.

'Right, they'm bastards are in, finally.' He gathered his weapons and threw them into the longboat sled. The heavy harpoon poles clattered against the slats. 'On you'm get. Light hey'm going.' He looked coolly at Kit. 'Pay when we'm get there.'

'Sure. I ain't no welcher.'

'Mmm.'

Blix got the impression that Kit had driven a hard bargain, in a way that Roohsk really hadn't been expecting.

She realised for the first time how low the sun was. 'How long until we get to the gate?' she asked, climbing into the sled. It still smelled of meat.

Roohsk hemmed a little, scratching a cheek with his nails. 'Five hour, maybe more. Manticore'r good long-distance runners. Don't tire easy. Long past full dark 'fore we get there.' He thumbed toward the keel of the sled. 'Stretch out if you'm want to. Wind's rising. Sand'll hurt if it whips up.' He pulled on the walrus tusk helm and his long gauntlets, and climbed aboard. The leather gloves creaked as he pulled the reins tight.

The boat was too heavy to climb back up the dune from a standing start. Instead they spiralled out of the camp through the skeletons of ships. Hard-looking, blank-eyed men and women watched as they passed. Roohsk exchanged a few curt words with a couple of them, then the sled rose with the sand out of the oasis.

The sea without water stretched out before them without any sign of life, turning burnt umber and gold as the sun neared the horizon. The sounds of the settlement were quickly put behind them. The silence of the desert was profound. The creak of the boat and the thrumming footsteps of the manticores were soon the only sounds besides the wind.

'How do they cope with the emptiness,' Blix said to herself.

'Ain't so bad,' said Roohsk without turning around. 'Sea was empty too. Empty ain't empty. Empty hey'm beautiful, sometimes.' His tone became more abrupt. 'We'm lucky. Desert was east of here before. Hey'm just move west when the water left. South, 'bout two hundred ell, desert don't reach. Salt plain for a thousand ell. Wind get up there, hey'm not sting, hey'm strip the flesh from you. Salt flies. Bad air. People get sick. Nothing grows.'

'Is everywhere on this world like this?'

'Don't know everywhere. Maybe. Sure hope not. Ain't none as deserved this.'

Blix woke with a start. 'Something's wrong,' she said, without knowing why she said it. Then she realised the manticores were picking up speed.

'Yep,' said Kit. 'Something's wrong.' She was staring out into the darkness behind them, one hand on the rail of the sled, the other on her rifle. Constant, sitting opposite her, stared the same way.

The sled lurched. 'Beasts'r nervous,' said Roohsk. 'I can feel it through the straps. Sommat's back there. Sommat's coming.'

Blix got to her knees, steadying herself as the fierce wind caught her. It blew them onward. She wrapped the bearskin tight around her against the desert cold, and took a deep breath.

'There's something in the air.'

'Shutter yon light,' said Roohsk. Constant scrambled to obey. 'Beasts don't need it to find the way, we need night eyes. We be unseen, maybe.' Blix heard the nervousness in his voice. 'Maybe not. Moonlight's enough.'

As he said the word Blix's gaze shot upward. The gibbous moon loomed large in the sky. She saw it as if for the first time, how great and graceful and beautiful it was, and how strange and alien and different from the moon she knew. It set the wolf racing through her blood. Then the clouds hid it, and the moment it was out of sight Blix felt as if she had woken from a trance.

'What could it be, Roohsk?' she called, searching for movement in the night. 'What lives in the desert?'

'Manticore, sure. Cockatrice, maybe. Maybe sand dragon.'

'How big are sand dragons?'

'Big.' Roohsk slapped the reins a little and the manticores lurched from a trot to a canter.

'Big is bad,' said Constant. 'How far to the circle?' He pulled out the Thing and concentrated. 'Close… can't we go faster?'

'We save the beasts 'til we need they'm. Henge, hey'm a couple of ell. Hold on.'

The sled angled sharply upward as they climbed a tall dune. As they crested it the sled twisted right. Blix looked back just as the moon broke through the clouds and she saw them, saw them and felt their presence just as much. Running low, parallel to the sled but closing the gap quickly. A thrill of recognition and terror turned her spine to ice.

'Oh God, werewolves! They're almost on us! Now, Roohsk, now! Go now!'

'Hayah!' screamed Roohsk, cracking his whip and sending the manticores leaping forward. The sudden burst of speed threw everyone down. The manticores blared wildly as they ran.

The werewolves saw the sled take off and realised they'd been seen. The pack swung sharply and converged on them, barking furiously. They were fast, their inhuman gait narrowing the distance rapidly. Sometimes on two legs, sometimes bounding forward on all fours as if their hands were paws. The fastest of them were terribly close.

'Faster Roohsk, faster!' Blix cried.

'Time to start blasting!' shouted Kit. She steadied herself on her knees, put her rifle to her shoulder and fired. 'Missed.' Another shot. 'Missed, goddammit.' A third, and then, 'Got one, son of a bitch!'

Blix watch the stricken wolf fall, and roll, and lie still - and get back up. It took up the chase again, holding one shoulder but not noticeably slowed by the wound.

'Kit, you didn't kill it!'

'What the- oh hell, I'm shooting lead! Kill 'em, kids!' She dived onto her pack.

'Yes,' said Constant, his voice winter-grim.

Blix reached for her sword as the werewolves fell upon them.

A werewolf caught hold of the left side of the sled. As it pulled itself up Constant slashed down and to his left, but the wolf jerked back at the last moment, the great blade cutting it only lightly across his chest and arms. The wolf howled in pain and fell to the sand. Constant swung back hard, taking scalp, skull and brains from the top of another wolf's head. As it died two more werewolves made the sled. One ripped the tailgate from its hinges and leaped onto the back. Another scrambled to climb on next to the first, the bouncing sled throwing it sideways roughly as it lurched.

Blix held the silver-edged sword straight out in front of her and threw herself headlong at the first werewolf. She felt stronger than she ever had before, the sword almost weightless in her hands. The blade sank deep into the werewolf's stomach. Blix skidded to a stop and threw her weight backward, yanking the sword as hard as she could. The blade pulled free and brought the werewolf's guts with it. As the offal spilled out the body tumbled back into the desert floor.

Constant kicked the second werewolf in the face and he fell beside his dead brother, but his place was taken instantly by another. It grabbed Constant's heel and pulled. The boy flipped and landed on his back, his yell of surprise cut short as the wind was knocked out of him. He scrambled to his feet, but the werewolf was aboard by then and as Constant lifted the sword the beast slammed the flat of the blade against the side of the boat, knocking Constant sideways.

'Uh-uh!' Kit sprang inside the werewolf's reach and shoved the rifle up into the werewolf's chest, pulling the trigger as the barrel touched fur. The werewolf was dead instantly, heart blown to pieces, but it clutched convulsively at Kit, clawing through the leather of her bandolier as it fell, and tearing the rifle from her grasp. They landed with the werewolf on the sand and were instantly lost to the darkness.

'Son of a bitch!' Kit roared, blood dripping from the claw wounds. But there was no more time to curse. Werewolves appeared behind them and to each side, scrabbling to get purchase on the boards of the sled and still avoid being mown down by the outriggers.

Then the moon went behind clouds. The moment it was completely hidden, no matter how brightly the sky still shone with moonlight, the werewolves changed. Blix saw their wolf-fur fall from their backs like a snake sloughing its skin, revealing their mannish selves. No longer as fast or as strong as they'd been only seconds before, they fell behind, spitting with rage, men-wolves leaping awkwardly through the sands they had effortlessly bounded across as wolf-men. Roohsk whipped up the Manticores and they pulled away.

'Harder Roohsk, harder!' cried Kit exultantly, as the monsters became distant shapes in the night. 'We're losing them!'

'No, we're not,' said Blix. 'It's temporary. When the moon comes out they'll be fast again. They'll catch up.'

'Then we need to find somewhere we can defen-'

'Goddess!' Roohsk screamed.

The world turned upside down. Blix was flung from the boat and thudded into the sand on her back, rolling over and over until she came to rest. Her head rang from the impact. She lay there for a few moments, breathing hard, dizzy, unsure what had just happened. The moon shone brightly once more. It took her shaken mind a moment to make the connection. Then she gasped and hauled herself unsteadily to her feet, knowing only death awaited her if she lay still. Staggering, seeing double, she tried to make sense of things.

The ground had fallen away into a wide sinkhole, thirty feet deep. The manticores had tried to turn at the last second and flipped the sled. The boat had upended, snapped across the keel and landed on the rear two manticores, smearing them across the sand. The front pair were hopelessly tangled in their harness, screaming in terror and pain. Roohsk was hacking at the mess of rope and leather with his gutting knife, trying to free them.

Constant and Kit were running toward a circle of trilithons. 'Come on!' the boy screamed. 'They'll be here in seconds!'

Roohsk slashed the last of the harness away and the manticores struggled out. They ran for the desert the moment they were free, past the stones and over the lip of the sinkhole. Roohsk grabbed his weapons from the sand and ran after the others. He was limping badly.

Blix ran for the boat.

Constant saw her. 'Blix! This way!'

'I have to get Katy's bag!'

'Just leave it!'

'*She'll want it back!*'

She skidded to a stop by the upturned boat. The cargo was strewn across the ground, smashed and torn. Rakia dripped onto the ground where the bottles had broken. The handles of Katy's bag were visible, pinned under the gunwale. Without thinking she grabbed the board and pulled as hard as she could. The gunwale snapped in two. Blix dragged the bag out and looked around wildly for her sword, but it was nowhere to be seen. Blix gave it up for lost and ran. As she charged toward the gate she saw Kit's saddlebags, sitting daintily on the sand as if they'd been placed there waiting for her while she brought her horse around. Blix scooped them up without slowing down and caught up with the others as they reached the stones. As she crossed the threshold Constant yelled 'Helikon! *Come and see!*' and then 'No! No! NO!'

Roohsk was outside the circle.

'Stop!' screamed Constant as the stones lit up. 'No! I take it back! Ceto, come and see! Come and see!'

Lightning crackled around the lintel stone as a strange throbbing pulse through each of them. Constant tried to leave the circle. The magic stopped him.

'Roohsk, I'm sorry,' he cried, distraught. 'I didn't see!'

'None of that,' said Roohsk hoarsely. 'You'm don't make no mistake. I ain't leaving.'

'Dammit man, those dogs will kill you!' Kit spat.

'This is my home. You'm go on now. I wait on.'

Constant inhaled sharply. 'For any hurt I have caused you, for any fault or sorrow, I ask forgiveness. My soul is yours. I hope you don't die.'

'Good lad,' said Roohsk. 'You'm -' A thunder of paws turned his head. He moved fast despite his leg, running past the gate. In seconds he was hidden by the darkness.

Then a werewolf was there, horrifyingly there, slamming into empty air at the edge of the circle as the gate magic took effect. It howled impotently and scraped the solid air with its claws, only inches from Blix's face. As the night sky opened upward into a swirling white vortex, Blix locked eyes with the First of Wolves, towering over her. As it met her gaze it ceased its raging. It took something out of a pouch around its neck and held it up so she could see it. The red-green disc glittered in the unnatural light.

'I have your scent,' it said. 'I will follow.'

Blix was hurled into oblivion.

The First of Wolves was knocked backward by the blast of energy as the gate hurled the travellers into the hole in the sky. A moment later the hole was gone. Acrid smoke filled his nostrils. He realised it came from his own singed fur. He picked himself up. The magic had stirred up a sandstorm. He could see nothing.

'Do the rocks still stand?' he asked.

'Yes,' said another.

'Then when this settles we will follow. They cannot escape us.'

‘I smell man,' said a werewolf suddenly.

A spear whistled through the darkness and struck the werewolf full in the chest, toppling him to the ground. The First of Wolves watched the stricken werewolf as he writhed, stiffened and lay still. A lantern sailed through the air and smashed on the wreckage of the sand boat. It caught fire instantly, sending a ball of flame whomping into the sky.

The pack started and barked in fear, but the First of Wolves was unmoved. He peered through the clearing air and saw the man who had thrown the weapon. He stood before the stone circle, quite still. A statue in the sand.

The First of Wolves looked back at the impaled werewolf. At first sight it appeared dead. But the First of Wolves knew better. He smelt the metal in the wound then looked back at the impassive figure.

‘Your iron won't kill us, man,' he shouted. 'He will revive, and soon.'

The man before the gate nodded slowly. 'Keep yon busy for now, though,' he said. 'I come back to hey’m later.'

The First of Wolves could have closed the distance that separated them in the time between heartbeats, but the man's calm resolve made him pause. Underestimating enemies got wolves killed. A watching man was a thinking man. Another might have thrown the spear and lantern and run, hoping to strike unseen from another angle while the sand and fire blinded the wolves, yet telling the pack where they were with every footfall, every breath, easy prey for a hunting animal. This one stood as still as the First of Wolves, waiting for the right move. He was not to be underestimated. The other werewolves could feel it too. They'd survived enough battles to know a dangerous man when they saw one.

Most of the other wolves. 'Go on then, man,' sneered one, its fur gallows-black. 'Throw your other spear. You won't catch us like that again.'

The man made a disapproving *tch* sound with his tongue. 'Hey’m not a spear. Hey’m a harpoon.' He looked up at the long pole. 'This un's a halberd,' he said. 'Got a blade on it, see?' He lowered the shaft and pulled the leather cover free. 'That's how you’m can tell.'

'I don't give a shit what they're called, I'll stake you to the rocks with them. I'll feast on your flesh and step over your bones!'

The halberd cut lazily through the air as the man brought it to bear on the werewolf. 'Maybe. Maybe not. You’m want to taste man flesh, you'm pay the man price.'

The werewolf sneered. 'I'm going to bite your fucking eyes out!'

'Have a go,' said the man simply.

'Enough,' said the First of Wolves suddenly. 'We don't follow your scent,' he said to the man. 'Step aside, and live.'

The man appeared to consider this seriously. Eventually he said, 'Was a whaler, me. Rode the *hwael-weg* as far as hey’m go. Then when the water went, took up trapping. Mostly manticore round here. Savage, is wild manticore. But very loyal, once you'm train 'em up.'

From behind him the First of Wolves heard a muted bugle-call, then another. He looked over his shoulder. Two manticores, docked tails swinging to and fro, stepped delicately down the dune towards the werewolves. Their muzzles were gone. Needle mouths gaped obscenely.

'They can't kill us,' said the First of Wolves, returning his attention to the man. 'If one of your beasts rends me and eats my bones, in a day I will burst fully formed from its stomach. We are sons of the moon. Only his metal destroys us.'

'Mostly manticore round here,' the man said again. He swung the halberd expertly through the air. This time it settled edge-on to the First of Wolves. Along the blade a line of silver gleamed. 'Some weres, too,' the man continued.

Behind the walrus helm the man smiled a death's-head grin. The First of Wolves drew his sword and ran at him.

Chapter Twenty-Three: The Wolves of the Storm

Blix materialized a few feet above the ground and landed almost upright, skidding to a squelching halt in wet mud. Pelting rain soaked her instantly. The sun was hidden behind low, grey clouds, folding over each other across the heavens. A sudden jag of lightning split the sky, followed a few seconds later by a clap of thunder, incredibly loud - not on top of them, but near.

Blix staggered, overcome with nausea. Constant stumbled to his knees, dry-heaving, and collapsed back onto all fours. Kit skidded on her side and tumbled over the edge of the gunmetal-grey stone circle. She immediately rolled onto her back, pistol pointing at the spot of air they had just burst through, but she was quivering like she'd just been shocked and looked about to pass out. 'Goddamn hell and death!' She clutched her head. 'My brain feels like it's on fire. Move your asses, kids!'

Blix was crying. 'Roohsk, oh God, we left him behind!'

'He chose to stay. That's one brave old son of a bitch. I hope he makes it.'

Blix staggered to the circumference and slid downhill slightly. She looked around wildly. 'Constant, did you see? Did you see him? It was the First of Wolves! He followed us from Shambhala! He said he had our scent!'

Constant tried to speak but convulsed suddenly and was violently sick.

Kit looked incredulously at Blix. 'You *know* that thing? Sweet Jesus of Nazareth!'

Blix was staring wide-eyed, gulping air in uncontrollable sobs. Her hands seized and shook of their own accord. 'Did you see? He had the bloodstone! He can open the gate!'

'Hellfire, it's gonna start raining werewolves any minute. Get out of the damn circle, kid!'

Blix turned toward Constant, suddenly galvanised by fear. 'We have to run! We have to run now!'

Kit didn't take her eyes off the gate. 'Fuck that shit. We stay here until those dogs come through and we blast 'em - straight to hell!' Another flash of lightning and roll of thunder punctuated her cry.

'Silver,' croaked Constant, crawling toward them, dragging the great sword behind him. 'Fire silver.'

'Fuck!' Kit broke the pistol open and knocked the rounds out of the chamber. They scattered in the mud. She looked around wildly. 'My bandolier's gone! Where's my pack?'

Blix pointed at the gate. 'Back there.' She clutched Katy's bag to her chest. 'I only got your saddlebags. The pack was under the sled.'

'Goddammit, my pistol rounds were in there! Only rifle shells in the saddlebags and the rifle's gone. I got a coupla silver in my belt, no more- wait.'

She scrabbled in her pockets and pulled out a handful of silver slugs.

'Praise be,' she said. 'Unloaded at the manticore trap.'

As Kit thumbed the rounds into the gun, Blix helped Constant to his feet. 'Give me your knife.'

'What?' rasped the boy. He reeled and clutched at Blix's shoulder for support.

'Your knife, the one with the silver point. I've lost my sword, I need a weapon!'

Constant stared stupidly at her, then slid the poignard, scabbard and all, from his belt. He fumbled it and it felt into the mud. Blix scooped it up.

'I put it in his eye,' he said.

'What did you say?'

He said nothing more to her, but instead started whispering to himself, words that Blix didn't recognise, but knew and hated. She pushed him away hard, but he didn't seem to notice. He stood bent over, a hand on each knee, breathing heavily and saying his words.

'Sweet mercy, here we go!' Kit flicked the cylinder closed and span it. 'Right on. I got eight silver bullets for this here revolver. Six in, two to reload.' She wiped water from her face. 'How many werewolves do you think there were?'

'I don't know, fifteen or twenty?' said Constant, straightening up unsteadily. 'Maybe more.' He looked much more focused. Blix saw he'd taken a cut to the forehead. The rain washed blood into his eyes. Suddenly all she could think about was how blood tasted.

'How many did we kill?' Kit continued.

'Three. I think. Wounded a couple.'

'Shit. Do you reckon we can kill six or seven apiece before we get got?'

'No.'

'Me neither. We have to run.'

Constant wiped the blood away and looked around. 'Where?'

The stone ring was set into a hillside, halfway to the top. Rolling grassland stretched out as far as they could see, the grass flattened by the driving rain. There was no house in sight, no town or city to which they could escape.

Kit slapped the ground in frustration, sending a spray of water into the air. 'Which way and how far to the next gate?'

Constant collected himself. He was now much more alert, but still breathing heavily and fighting not to be sick. 'How far was seventy-five miles southwest. Which way that is I don't know. I lost the Thing when the boat turned. It got left behind.'

Blix ran her fingers back through her sodden hair, despair welling up in her. 'We're dead.'

'Check the other side of the hill!' said Constant. 'There might be-'

There was a low rumble in the distance, over the hill. It went on for a few seconds then petered out.

'More thunder?' Blix suggested.

'The hell it was!' cried Kit, leaping up. 'Come on kids, our bacon might just be saved!'

They ran to the top of the hill, slipping in the sodden mud. The other side sloped gently down to a broad, shallow river half a mile away. Between them and the water were-

'Horses!' cried Constant. A herd two hundred or more strong, black and chestnut, grey and dun, grazed nervously near a stand of trees.

'No,' said Blix, her cares suddenly forgotten. 'Not horses. Look again.'

The horses twitched and shivered, and suddenly bolted fifty yards before shuddering to a halt. Here and there one spread huge wings and leapt into the blasted sky, flying free for a moment before landing gracefully back amid the herd.

'Well I'll be,' breathed Kit. 'Pegasi!'

'The plural of pegasus is pegasus,' said Blix automatically. 'It's an uncountable noun, like sheep.'

'It's our ticket out of here is what it is!' Kit unhooked the long coil of rope from her belt and quickly made a lasso. 'I've been roping horses since I was two. Either of you break a horse before?'

I was born in the saddle. 'I've never even seen a horse,' said Constant, clutching at his forehead. Blood dripped through his fingers.

'I've ridden horses,' Blix volunteered. 'They have three at the city farm. They're pretty docile.'

'That's close enough, you win.' She ran the rope through her hands and snapped it taut. 'Kid, go get our stuff. Pick up those bullets too, I might have to blast something else. Kiddo, you get to help. Come on!'

She ran down the slope toward the herd, sprinting at incredible speed - an Olympic athlete would have been impressed. Blix turned to Constant and said, 'Did you see that?' but he was already halfway back to the gate. Blix ran after Kit as fast as she could. As she approached the herd they raised their heads sharply and whinnied in alarm. A few took off immediately, and a wave of fluttering rippled through the herd as the rest prepared to follow.

Kit span the rope above her head as she ran, ducked left as she came up to the herd's leading edge then slid back right as the pegasus shied away, expertly cutting out a palomino mare. More horses leapt into the sky, shrieking in alarm. With a final jerk the rope flew over the mare's head and tightened. Kit flicked the rope backwards and pulled hard then held on as if her life depended on it. 'Here we go!'

The mare bucked wildly, leapt into the air and tried to fly but, amazingly, Kit held it down, her boot heels digging deep into the wet earth as she pulled with all her might. As Blix arrived she saw that the rope partly pinioned one wing. As the horse tried to take flight it veered sharply and crashed back to earth.

'Grab on kiddo!' Kit yelled. Blix fell on the free end of the rope and added her weight to it. The strength she'd discovered on Ceto was gone, left behind with the moon. The pegasus screamed and struggled to its feet.

'Run across it! Rope the legs!'

They ran across the front of the pegasus while it was still staggering upward and swept it low across the fetlocks. The creature's feet lifted, and it crashed to the sodden earth on its knees, roaring in pain. The rest of the herd wheeled in the skies above screeching in fear, too scared to descend and end the battle with a kick or bite.

As it fell Blix locked eyes with the pegasus, just for a second. She felt the strangest sensation. It was as if someone had taken her head and turned it violently sideways, so that she saw things from a new perspective. She dropped rope and ran in front of Kit, waving wildly.

'Kit, stop! Stop, *stop*! She's intelligent!'

'What the-' began Kit, but the pegasus bucked again and kicked out hard and she had to haul heavily on the rope. 'What the hell?'

'She's not a creature, she's a person!' She spoke directly to the pegasus, who was champing wildly. 'We didn't know!'

'Goddammit kiddo, what are you doing?'

Blix ignored her. 'We didn't know! We're sorry! We need your help, we're desperate! Werewolves are coming!'

At once the pegasus stopped struggling, so suddenly that Kit fell backwards. The pegasus lay completely still and looked unflinchingly at Blix. She got a strong sense of anger and pain.

'We're very sorry,' she said again. 'We need your help. Please don't fly away, we'll die.' She turned to Kit. 'Let her up.'

'What? It'll bolt!'

'She. She's a she. And we need her to trust us.'

'Damn fool idea,' said Kit darkly, but nonetheless she shook out the rope and, carefully avoiding the pegasus' teeth, loosened the lasso and lifted it off. At once the pegasus rolled off its haunches and stood up. She spread her wings wide and shook them violently, then flapped them so hard that the downdraft knocked Blix back a step.

'Look out, she's going up!' cried Kit.

'No, she isn't,' said Blix, not entirely certain how she knew. But the pegasus did indeed settle, folding its wings so closely to her flanks that the feathers were indistinguishable from her shaggy winter coat.

'Well I'll be damned.' Kit looked incredulously at Blix. 'How the hell are you speaking horse?'

'We came through the gate. The magic makes us speak the local language. I guess it's pegasus.'

The pegasus whinnied. Kit looked sceptical. 'I ain't hearing no words.'

'Well. She's not human. Maybe it only works one way. Their vocal cords are different too. I don't know and it doesn't matter.'

'Right.' Kit tipped her hat. 'Pardon me ma'am, no offense intended.'

Blix made eye contact again. 'Werewolves are chasing us. We came through the gate. One of us stayed behind.' She gulped air, trying not to cry again. 'When they're finished with him, they'll come through. You can fly away, but we'll die. Please help us. We're wet and frightened and our friend just died protecting us from them. Please carry us away from here.'

Blix got a sense of affronted dignity, contempt and anger, but also compassion, and hatred of killing, and love. The pegasus reared slightly and hoofed the earth, and snorted.

'She said yes,' said Blix.

'Really? Much obliged, ma'am,'

Constant came running up, bags slung over both shoulders, puffing for breath.

'What did I miss?' he asked.

Kit looped the rope around the pegasus three times and cinched it tight. The pegasus looked startled, and huffed out her wind in a huge harrumph. Kit rubbed her back.

'Thank you kindly, ma'am. Everyone on!'

'Can she carry us all?' asked Constant.

'This fine lady can launch her own weight into the heavens, she can carry us three skinny folks. It'll be just fine. Slip your legs through the rope at each side and your arms through the top to inside your elbows, and, you know, pray.'

Kit boosted Constant onto the pegasus' neck, then help Blix swing up after him to sit just in front of the thick wing muscles, on top of Kit's saddlebags. She clutched Katy's bag between Constant and herself. Kit vaulted on from behind.

'Ooch up everyone, and hang on!' She slapped the pegasus on the rump. 'Hi-ho palomino!'

With a leap that left Blix's stomach behind the pegasus thrust upward. Blix felt huge muscles working incredibly hard as the giant, elegant wings swept back and forth, twisting and turning as the pegasus powered into the sky, scything through the sheets of rain. The other pegasus' banked and wheeled as the palomino joined her herd.

Kit whooped and laughed wildly. 'Goddamn this is fun! Which way? she yelled.

'Still no Thing!' Constant shouted, clinging hard to the pegasus' neck and looking extremely unhappy. 'I don't know!'

'Anywhere that ain't here then!'

'Wait!' Blix let go of the rope with one hand and plunged it into the doombag. 'I forgot! I've got a compass!' She pulled out the tiny broken pencil torch. The little compass was still on the end, needle twisting. 'Southwest is... that way!' She pointed behind them. 'Are north and south the same here as on Earth?'

'Who the hell knows?' cried Kit. 'It's a way to go, that way we shall go!'

The pegasus soared in a broad circle over the gate. Blix took her eyes off the compass for a moment to look down. Then she yelled over her shoulder to Kit.

'Still no werewolves. Maybe they aren't coming?'

'That would be lucky,' Kit shouted back. 'You think we got that kinda luck?'

'No.'

'Me neither. Roohsk bought us some time. God bless the old bastard.'

'I hope he's okay,' said Blix to herself, but Kit heard her.

'He ain't.'

The man coughed wetly. A bubble of blood welled up in his mouth. The First of Wolves was surprised there was any left.

There was a high brass scream as his remaining wolves disembowelled the second manticore. The remains of the first were already strewn across the sand.

Three wolves had died in the chase. They lay somewhere out in the darkness, bodies destroyed by silver. Seven more had died before the gate. Of those, three would eventually come back. The survivors were now opening the throats and stomachs of the manticores and extracting werewolf meat. Regenerating from that would take time though, and would be excruciating. Manticore teeth ground fine and quickly.

Of the twelve that remained, two had bites and one had silver wounds, the latter deep enough that they would take time to heal and would scar terribly. This was honourable. The First of Wolves had a silver-made slash across the chest which oozed blood where the blast from the gate hadn't cauterised it. His fur was singed in patches.

The man had slid under his charge and used the First of Wolves' own momentum to up-end him and slam him head first into one of the standing stones. By the time he'd recovered the man had cut through the pack like a scythe through corn stalks. The First of Wolves was impressed. The man was in his last days and had fought like a demon. If he'd been younger, he might have won.

All but one of the remaining wolves were New.

One of the metal spitters spat silver. The First of Wolves examined it dispassionately. He had seen them before. The Lyonesse men who lived beyond the Bastion gate had them. Their spitters spat the not-silver which didn't kill wolves. And so, they had died.

The fire had consumed most of the sled, as much of it as would burn. The metal ribs *pinkt* as they cooled. Behind that noise something irritated the First of Wolves. A buzzing in the ears, quiet but persistent, like a fly he couldn't swat. It came from beneath the hull of the sled.

Careless of the heat, he pitched the ruined contraption over and rummaged in the embers. His hand closed around a smooth pebble, tiny in his grasp, strangely cool amid the flames. Instantly the buzzing stopped. Instead he felt overwhelmingly pulled toward the standing stones. He considered this.

He looked down at the man. The walrus skull helm had been ripped away during the battle, the tusks shattered. His face and arms were covered in bites and his guard arm was broken. He'd lost an eye and most of one cheek. But these wounds were nothing compared to the gaping cavity where his chest had been. Innards trailed obscenely onto the sand, and broken ribs jutted through ruined flesh.

The First of Wolves crouched on his haunches next to the man and pressed down on a rib fragment. The man coughed violently and spat up more blood. The remaining eye swivelled back in his head, then focused on the First of Wolves.

'You fought bravely and well. Better than these deserved.' He indicated the werewolves who had died by the man's hand. 'I respect that.'

The man burbled something unintelligible. The First of Wolves ignored it. 'I will not end your suffering,' he continued. 'This is a gift for your bravery. Suffering is to be cherished. It is proof of life.'

He pressed down again on the exposed rib, then suddenly snapped it off. The man screamed and started shaking violently. The First of Wolves licked the blood from the bone. He stood and addressed the pack.

'You will stay behind and tend to our brothers,' he said to the werewolf with the silver wounds, a wolf of the old pack, like him. 'No, this is honourable,' he continued as the werewolf started to object. 'You have served well and will wear a scar of pride. When our brothers revive bring the Wolf Age to this place. I will return and find you.'

The werewolf leered and barked his assent.

The First of Wolves glowered at the New. 'You, into the circle. We are twelve. That is enough.'

He turned back to the man, who was now grey and listless, but, incredibly, still alive. 'When he dies, don't eat him,' he instructed the wolves who would remain. 'This too is a gift,' he told the man. 'Our disease starts to heal you, even now. But your wounds are too great. You will not live, not in this wasteland. Full moon is tomorrow. Tomorrow is never for you.'

The man tried to speak again; his lips moved without sound.

'You fought like a wolf. You may have such rest as this dead earth gives you.'

The First of Wolves turned to join his men between the stones, then paused, and looked back. 'A night from here lies a ring of broken ships, iron and wood. Is that your place?'

A glimmer in the man's eye gave the answer. The First of Wolves nodded. 'We passed that way. If you live, don't go back.'

He turned away at last and strode into the circle.

Roohsk wept.

I dreamed about flying. I think I dreamed. I dreamed that I dreamed. It was nothing like this.

He's dead. They're dead. It's my fault.

Blix was talking, but Constant wasn't really listening.

'... look like horses with wings but they're not, they're pegasus. They've got hollow bones, like birds. Incredibly strong but really light. Plus, they have interlocking ribs which gives them a hugely strong frame, so they don't buckle in flight. Their wings lock open when they're in the air, so it takes no effort to stay aloft. And their wing muscles are massive. You can feel them.'

I can feel them.

They'd moved beyond the rain clouds and now soared through blue skies, high above the earth. The huge wings beat when they needed to. Otherwise the pegasus let the air do the work for it, gliding and soaring like an eagle rising from its erie. Constant had imagined that the sky would be cold, but the pegasus generated so much body heat that he felt positively warm.

Height held no fears for Constant. For most of his life his only view of the world had been from above. What was new was movement, and speed. The pegasus flew faster than he'd thought it possible to travel. The herd flew in a V formation. Blix said this was to cut down wind resistance, but Constant felt like the shining edge of an arrowhead, slicing through the air toward a distant target. Constant had imagined that the seventy-five miles to the next gate would take three or four days. Now it was clear they'd be there in hours.

The miles disappeared behind them as the winged horse carried them over forests and grasslands. They followed the course of a river upstream. Constant watched, mesmerized, as the broad water narrowed and shallowed until the riverbed became visible, white foam rippling over the stones.

The First of Wolves would follow them. Constant had glimpsed him before the gate activated. He had no doubt that Blix was right that he was the leader whose army had ravaged his world. Who had destroyed the Anvil. Who had burned Forge. Who had killed his family.

Who follows me. I'm the last. The last one left. The last of my line. The last leader of Shambhala society, fractured and dispersed though that was. Everyone else is dead. The Keeper of the

Bastion, the Kalsanggir, the Hetman of Amdo, Johann Rhinm, all the rest - all dead. All their people, all my people, dead. I'm-

'I'm the last of men,' he said aloud.

'Say what?' shouted Kit.

Constant felt wetness on his cheeks. He realised he was crying. 'Nothing,' he said. 'I was just-' then he gasped and shouted, 'Down, down, we have to go down!'

'What? Why?'

'House! There's a house down there!' He pointed. A little ranch homestead sat near a bend in the river, at the edge of the grass plains before that land began to rise into rocky foothills. Cattle tracks led from the fold out onto the plain. A puff of smoke from the stone chimney showed that someone was home.

'We have to go down! The werewolves will go right through there! We have to warn them!'

'Goddammit kid, how will they follow us? They can't follow a scent through the sky!'

'Are you kidding? They followed us to another world! They'll follow us to this one too! Do you think they're going to give up? They'll find us! We have to go down!' We can't let them die like Roohsk! Like-'

He choked off the last words. *Like my mother.*

'Goddammit!' said Kit again. 'Take us down kiddo!'

Blix spoke to the pegasus. The winged horse banked hard to the left and wheeled toward the ground. Instantly the herd turned with it, the arrowhead breaking into a spiral of flapping wings as they came down, forelegs straight, hind legs working hard as if cantering through the air as the pegasus' used all their muscle power to control their descent. The herd whinnied and neighed, calling across the sky to prevent mid-air collisions.

The door to the ranch house slammed open. A woman was briefly framed in the doorway, then she disappeared inside again. The herd touched down in front of the house, bouncing and jostling as they made room for each other. The palomino was in the middle, penned in by nervous horseflesh, its wings folded over its passengers' legs. Blix urged the pegasus toward the house, as Kit and Constant, each pulling a leg free from the rope saddle and hooking it under the pegasus feathers, fended off the surrounding animals with careful boots to the flanks. Wings beat and fluttered, filling their field of vision as the pegasus settled themselves, reared and displayed.

As Blix maneuvered them to the front the woman reappeared. 'Off! Off! Away, you vermin, away!' she cried angrily.

'Werewolves are com-' shouted Constant.

The woman raised a gun to her shoulder and fired.

The leading edge of pegasus shrieked in pain as shot peppered their hides. They leapt straight up into the sky, followed in a terrified wave by the rest of the herd. One which had been just ahead of them stayed down, writhing, and then was still.

Constant was thrown sideways, barely hanging on to the rope with one hand. He grabbed Blix's waist, partly to hold on and partly to keep her on board. Kit yelped in surprise in his ear.

The pegasus slammed through the air, its powerful wings beating frantically. It flopped sideways across the ranch and over the river before almost crash-landing halfway up the slope on the other side, half a mile or more from where it had first touched down and only seconds later. It staggered, turned groggily, then bucked wildly, neighing in fury.

'Everyone off!' shouted Blix. 'Now! Before she kills us!'

Kit pushed herself backwards over the mare's rump, grabbing her saddlebags as she landed and yanking them away and somehow freeing her rope at the same time, which whipped around the beast's flanks as it bucked and fell under her. Constant fell-jumped, landing dangerously close to the stamping hooves, scrabbling away before he got his skull caved in or battered to death by the wildly gyrating wings. Blix slid off the animal's neck, but to Constant's astonishment instead of getting away from the pegasus she faced it, her posture placating, trying to soothe the outraged animal.

'I'm sorry! We didn't know!'

And then, 'No, she's not part of our herd!'

And then, 'I suppose she is.'

The pegasus turned; Constant saw its face. It was bloody where shot pellets had hit it. Wounds peppered poll, crest and muzzle. He looked in its eyes and for the first time he realised that Blix was right. They could speak pegasus, hear the words unsaid. He understood what the animal wanted him to know.

No further! it said.

Never again! it said.

Murderers! it said.

The pegasus surged into the air, following the rest of its kind into the blackening sky, over the hill and away. The emptiness it left behind was an accusation.

None of them spoke for a moment as they recovered from the shock. Blix was shaking. Constant had to prevent himself from trying to comfort her.

Kit broke the silence. 'Did anyone get shot?'

Blix and Constant shook their heads.

'Thank God. I've had enough of disasters for one day.' She started coiling her rope. 'Get your things together, kids. Let's find this damn gate and get gone.' She threw her saddle bags over a shoulder.

Constant locked back toward the homestead, now almost invisible in the twilight. He couldn't see the woman.

'We aren't done here,' he said. 'We still have to warn her about the werewolves.'

'What?' cried Blix disbelievingly. 'We tried! She tried to kill us!'

'We didn't try hard enough. I don't think she saw us. There were wings everywhere.'

'She was cursing the pegasus,' said Kit. 'She called them vermin.'

'Is that what she said? I couldn't make it out.' Constant looked back toward the house. The dead pegasus, a roan, was bleeding out into the mud. 'She aimed for them, not us.'

'And she hit them! Okay, maybe she didn't see us, she still shot those beautiful creatures. That's just as bad. They're people!'

Constant measured his words carefully. He could see now that Blix was shaking with anger, not fear. 'We know they're people because we understand their language. We went through the gate. Maybe people here don't know that the pegasus are people.'

Blix clenched her fists and thrust them down by her sides. 'I don't care if she knew! They're pegasus! She killed one! She *deserves* to be eaten -' Blix checked her fury suddenly, shocked at what she'd said.

'No, she doesn't,' said Constant, gently, without rancour. 'Did you see the house? There's only one. The rest are barns and stables. To the far horizon there are no other buildings, not that I saw. Whoever lives there, they're alone out here. There's no one to stop the werewolves.' He bit his lip. 'I've realised something. You know Roohsk is dead. But he isn't the only one. The werewolves followed us from Shambhala. That means they followed us to the whale. To the manticore trap. To -'

'The boats, oh sweet Jesus.' Kit covered her mouth in horror.

'Seminah! Akali!' Blix cried.

Kit shook her head, as if denying it could have happened. 'We didn't kill them. We didn't know. It's not on us.'

Constant nodded, slowly and deliberately. 'You're right. But now we do know.' He pointed at the house without looking at it. 'Whatever she's done she doesn't deserve what's coming.'

Blix bit her knuckle, then nodded sharply. 'No, she doesn't. You're right. We have to try. No one deserves to die like that.'

They were quiet for a while, until the tears had dried, until they could breathe without choking back sobs. Until they could think of something other than the dead. Then Kit broke the silence

It's getting dark. If we're gonna do this, now's the time. But we ain't going down there to get shot at.'

'No.' Constant thought for a moment. He looked back at the house. 'There's a pile of boulders at the river's edge. Big enough for us to hide behind.'

'I see them. That's a ways from the house though.'

'How loud can you shout?'

Despite everything, Kit grinned. 'Mighty loud.'

'HALLOOO! HALLOOO THE HOUSE! WE'RE FRIENDS sorta AND WERE WAVIN' A WHITE FLAG OUT HERE metaphorically, not that you could see it 'cause it's black as pitch -'

'Kit!'

'Sorry SO COME ON OUT AND DON'T SHOOT US GODDAMMIT Sorry BUT DON'T.'

'That's brilliant,' said Blix. 'That'll work a treat.'

'Sure it will! It's worked, lookee there.'

Blix could just make out the door. As she watched it opened a crack. A long firearm poked through the gap. It was double-barrelled, each slightly flared in a way which reminded Blix of the trumpet of a gramophone.

'I see you. Speak in a civilized tongue or I'll blast you to Boston and back, goddammit.'

Two things happened at once.

'You're American!' said Kit and Blix together.

'What did you say?' said Constant at the same time. Then he looked at Kit and Blix. 'What did she say? And what did *you* say?'

'What do you mean? You heard her. And us.'

'It was gibberish.'

'Kid, make sense, you can hear us, can't you?'

'Yes, now I ca-'

'Speak English,' the woman demanded. 'I know you can, I heard you.'

'Well of course you did, we're talking in it,' Kit started, but Constant interrupted.

'There! Gibberish again. When you spoke to her, after she said her own nonsense.'

'Nonsense? What are you talking about, kid?'

'In English, goddammit!'

'What the hell is going on?' said Kit, exasperated.

'Oh *no.*' Blix stuck her head as far above the boulder rim as she dared. 'Just a minute please, ma'am, we're having some translation problems.'

The woman shouldered her gun more firmly. 'I'm gonna count to ten.'

Blix ducked back down. 'It's the gate magic. Kit and I came through Shambhala gates, so we can speak Shambhalhai, even though we don't realise it. And we all went through the gate to Ceto, so from Roohsk's point of view we spoke whatever that "you'm" language was. But when we came through the Helikon gate we learned Pegasus, not any human language. The woman's speaking English. Constant doesn't speak English.' She looked at Kit. 'We're switching between English and Shambhalhai depending on who we're addressing. That's why they both think we're talking foreign.'

'Wait a goddamned second,' whispered Kit hotly. 'You mean the magic is *making choices* about what language we speak *as we speak*? And I can't tell? How the hell-'

'Ten,' said the woman, and pulled the trigger. The gun boomed and billowed smoke; Blix heard shot pepper the boulder.

'GODDAMMIT I SAID DON'T SHOOT US WE'RE FRIENDS!'

'Friends don't hide behind rocks,' said the woman. 'Friends don't whisper in the night. Friends don't carry swords. You get the hell off my land. I got one more waiting for you if try any shit, *friends*.'

'Yeah? Then you're out,' said Kit bullishly.

'I can reload faster than you can cross that river,' said the woman evenly.

'Woman, you have no idea how fast I am.'

'Kit, stop it!' Constant hissed. 'Stop antagonising her! We need her to listen! Blix, you speak to her.'

'Me? What do I say?'

'You know what to say! Say what's right. Kit, you tell me what they say.'

Blix looked terrified for a second, then took a deep breath and shouted.

'Hey out there! I'm going to step out, I don't have a gun or a sword. Don't shoot me please! Thank you!'

She slid around the edge of the rock and immediately put her arms high in the air. 'Don't shoot!' she said again.

The woman stepped out, closing the door quickly behind her. As far as Blix could tell in the gathering darkness she was tall and very thin, her face hard and furiously determined, her greying hair hastily tied back. She wore a long brown dress that had seen better days.

'Hi,' said Blix. 'I'm Blix. What's your name?'

The woman aimed at her. 'Stay exactly where you are, or I'll blow your head off.' She paused for a moment, examining Blix. 'What do you want, girl?'

'To say our piece and leave,' said Blix immediately.

'Then say your piece and go to hell.'

'Werewolves are coming.'

'Are they now.'

'Yes. They're following us. They'll come right through here. I'm so sorry.'

'Horseshit,' the woman said. 'There haven't been werewolves in Asphodel for centuries. You're lying.'

'I'm not,' said Blix. 'Wait, Asphodel? I thought this was Helikon?'

The woman looked confused for a moment. 'Well, it is. Don't you know what state you're in? I don't-' She paused, and her expression hardened again. 'Where are you from?' she demanded.

'We came-'

'Are you Anaasází?' She took two or three strides forwards as though to bring herself in range. 'I swear to Christ I will kill you all before I let you hurt us! Me,' she said quickly, but it was too late to take it back and her suddenly terrified expression showed it.

Blix spoke gently. 'We're not Anaasází, whoever they are. We're not going to hurt you. We're women and children. Like you?'

There was a long silence. Then the woman said, 'I'm not lowering my gun. But talk.'

'We're not from this world. We came through a gate. Do you know about gates? Doorways to other worlds, encircled by stone. There are some near here.'

'I know what they are. They don't work. Haven't in twice my lifetime.'

'They do now. We came through one to the north-west. You're American, yes? You have an accent. My friend's American, from Nebraska. I'm British.'

Another long silence. 'I'm fourth generation,' she said eventually. 'Since the Roosevelt party. But there are Americans here going back to Roanoake…' She suddenly looked lost. 'There were. There ain't many of us left.'

'Then you have to live,' Blix pleaded. 'We were being chased by werewolves on the other world. They killed someone who'd cared for us. We escaped here, but they'll follow. They'll already have followed. They'll follow us, and they'll find you here and they'll kill you. Please believe us. You have to believe us.'

The cabin door cracked open. Small fingers curled around the edge of it, not far from the ground.

'Mommy?' said a piping voice.

'Stay inside!' cried the woman. The tiny fingers retreated, but the door remained ajar.

'We aren't going to hurt you,' said Blix. 'Any of you. But the werewolves will. You have to leave.'

'Leave!' The woman turned her head and spat on the ground. 'I knew it! It's a trick! Do you think I went through these years of hell to leave now? To hell with you! What's mine is mine. Go back, you damn Anaasází, you damn cannibals, or I swear to God that I will blow holes right through you!'

'I ain't no damn cannibal,' said Kit hotly from behind the boulder. Blix's nerve failed and she ducked back behind the rock as well.

'We're finished here,' she said. 'We've told her. We should go. We've tried.'

'Not hard enough,' said Constant fiercely. He grabbed the poignard from Blix's belt, still in its scabbard. 'Blix, translate for me.'

He stepped around the rock. 'Woman of the house! I'm going to throw something over to you. Don't kill me.'

'Speak -' the woman began, but Blix interrupted her.

'He wants to throw something to you. Don't shoot him, he's twelve.'

'... Okay.'

Constant hurled the knife high into the air. It landed a few feet from the woman. She didn't move or even look at it.

'What's that,' she said flatly.

'It's a dagger. It has a silver tip. Only silver kills werewolves. You don't look like you have silver. You should leave. But if you stay, you'll need this.'

Blix repeated the words. They felt no different leaving her mouth than they had arriving in her ears, but the woman understood her. The woman hesitated. The gun dipped slightly. After a while she said, 'Werewolves.'

'Yes,' said Blix.

'How many?'

'Could be a dozen or more.'

Now she looked at the poignard. 'That's not enough to kill a dozen werewolves.'

'No,' said Constant unhappily. 'It's all I can give you. I'm sorry.' He looked at Blix, who said it for him.

'No, it ain't,' said Kit suddenly. 'Wait a minute.' She dug in her saddlebags and pulled out a cardboard box, which rattled when she shook it. She dug out a handful of rifle bullets and held them up so the woman could see.

'Pay attention, you dumb bitch,' she said. 'These here are silver bullets. They're for a rifle, you can't fire them from that old blunderbuss. But if you're stupid enough to stay, you can prise the bullet from the brass cartridge and load 'em with your shot. Be damn careful you don't shoot yourself in the hand while you're doing it, these are black powder cartridges, do you understand? Don't just throw them whole into the muzzle, they'll explode in your face when you pull the trigger. Prise the bullet free.

'Now, if you're smart and leave, well, they're solid silver, worth money. You look like you could use some money. I'll put 'em on this here rock, you can get 'em when we leave. Which will be now. Those werewolves might be a day behind, or two, or they could have magicked themselves five minutes away and be bearing down on us right now. Decide quickly.'

She put the handful of bullets on the rock and returned the remainder to her saddlebags. Then she turned to Constant. 'We've done what we can here.'

Constant nodded curtly.

'People don't give people things,' said the woman suddenly. 'Not here. What do you want, strangers?'

'We want someone to live,' said Blix. 'We've seen too many corpses. We want someone to live.'

'And we want to know where the next gate is,' said Kit. 'You said you knew.'

'It's not far. Over the hill. Go on straight, due east. You can't miss it. Moonrise'll frame it for you in about an hour.'

'What moon?' said Blix immediately. 'What phase, I mean.'

'Third quarter.' The woman tightened her grip on the firearm. 'Why you want to know that, child? You got a love bite?'

'Well of course I have,' shouted Blix, suddenly exasperated. 'Oh, I've had enough.' She stomped away back up the hill, exposed to the woman's fire but uncaring of it.

'I hope you don't die,' said Constant to the woman, and followed Blix.

'What he said,' said Kit.

'What did he say?' asked the woman. Kit ignored her.

The woman watched them go. Only when they were halfway up the hill did she lower the gun.

Near the top of the hill Constant and Kit met Blix running back down.

'Hey! Hey!'

The woman watched her come but didn't raise the blunderbuss. 'What now?'

'You can tell me something else. Why did you shoot the pegasus?'

The woman looked at her with something close to despair in her eyes. 'They tear up the land. The land's all I have.'

'They're intelligent. They're not dumb animals. They're like people. Remember that.'

'I don't care,' said the woman, and turned away.

Blix caught up with the others halfway down the other side of the hill. They walked in silence for a while, slipping through wet grass and wildflowers.

'Do you think she'll listen?' Blix said eventually.

'Yes,' said Constant. His declaration rang across the meadow, shockingly loud in the night's stillness.

'I was gonna say no,' Kit said. 'She's proud. It goeth before destruction.'

'She's herself,' Blix said. 'Why should she listen to anyone else?'

'We did right,' Constant said. 'Right will prevail. She'll listen. She has to.'

Blix couldn't see Constant's face; she heard the conviction in his voice, and the fear.

The sky flickered slightly and, after a while, there was a rumble of thunder in the distance. Blix looked back in the direction they'd come from.

'The storm is following us,' she said.

Constant looked away. 'Yes.'

There was a sharp flash and the sky turned white momentarily. Blix counted, as she had as a child. Eight seconds later, thunder rumbled across the fields.

'About a mile and a half. It's moving quickly. We should go.'

'Yes,' said Constant once more. 'I was just remembering something my f... that Brother Simon, my tutor, told me about lightning once. His people were All-men, sheep farmers in the slate hills beyond the Bastion. Lightning country. It killed a lot of animals. Like beasts preying on the flock. They called lightning "the wolves of the storm".'

'She'll be okay,' said Blix gently. 'We helped her.'

'Did we?'

The First of Wolves had lost the scent.

It was bright and blood-sharp from the stones to the trees, where it merged with the pack-smell of some strange animals, which itself disappeared into thin air. He waited at the stones while the New searched the area for the trail. One by one they returned without answers.

The First of Wolves sat down, and turned his attention to the bloodstone.

'Show me their trail.'

It sat lifeless in his hand, as it had on the last world. He repeated the question, and then again, focusing all his will on the stone. Nothing. It would not answer this question, he decided.

'The way to the next gate. The Stones in the Meadow. Show me that path.'

Still nothing. Yet it had opened the gate and sent the pack across the void to another world without hesitation. The First of Wolves did not understand this.

He turned his attention to the buzzing stone. The First of Wolves did not believe in coincidences. The stone was not of the desert. A magic stone where his enemies had passed had been brought by them and lost. A stone which had pulled so fiercely toward the greater stones half-buried on the desert world and which now sat on the ground before him, buzzing like a gnat in his ear.

He picked it up and, while the buzzing stopped, the stone did not drag his mind in any direction. It was now just a stone, it seemed. The First of Wolves considered this.

'The Stones of the Meadow,' he said.

Suddenly the urge to follow the stone switched on, and the First of Wolves swung around to a line south of the sunset. He felt a sense of distance that he didn't understand, but somehow, he knew how far to go. He considered this.

'The Stones of the Plain,' he said. Immediately the urge to follow transferred to the circle next to him. The other werewolves watched him, uncomprehending. He nodded slowly.

'The Stones of the Meadow.' The stone swung back once more. He looked at his pack.

'Follow.'

Chapter Twenty-Four: Bos

Constant was sick.

'I can't feel anything below my knees,' said Blix. She pulled off a wellington and rubbed her sole hard with the flat of her hand. 'Nope, nothing.'

'Me neither,' said Constant, spitting and wiping his mouth. 'It'll wear off. If they start turning black, tell me.'

He dragged himself to the edge of the circle and propped himself against a stone. The pommel of his sword scraped against the flat black granite as he righted himself. He looked exhausted, like a soldier who had gone to battle and returned in defeat. Blix wondered what toll the gate travel was taking on him. She knew what it felt like to her. She felt like was being pressed to death under the stones in the circle.

The stones were stuck in the earth at random. They looked like gravestones in an old cemetery after everyone who cared for them had died. The thought reminded her of the graveyard at St. John Chrysostom and in turn, Katy.

'It's daytime again.' She lay back and stared into blue sky, rubbing her eyes. 'Morning, I think. I've lost track of time. This is like, magic jet-lag. When did we last sleep? I'm shattered. Urgh, my guts are in an uproar too. Is it tomorrow or yesterday now?'

'It's neither.' Constant tried to stand but his legs gave way and he sat down hard on the grass. 'Ow. We've gained a lot. We gained going to Helikon too. We're almost six months ahead now, relative to Shambhala.'

'That's incredible.' Blix massaged her calves vigorously. 'It doesn't feel like the future.'

'How does that leave us for getting to the Bastion at the right time?' asked Kit. She'd made no attempt to get up, and lay there staring at the bright blue sky.

Constant lay back, hands under his head, then sat forward and rolled upright. He grimaced and held his arms out for balance, but didn't fall.

'We saved time by flying,' he said. 'We probably broke even for time on Ceto, all things considered. There are some big lags later, we need to be careful, but overall this is good. It gets us closer to your sister when you last saw her.'

'Awesome.'

'As for sleep, at the oasis, half a day ago.' Constant limped toward Blix and heaved her onto her feet. Fierce pins and needles shot through both feet, which was a lot better than nothing. 'Great Fathers,' he muttered. 'Everything that's happened since then.'

'I don't want to think about it anymore,' said Blix. 'I can't bring myself to.' She suddenly clutched at her stomach, grimaced in pain, and threw up. 'Sorry,' she added. 'Jesus, this one's bad.'

'At least it isn't raining here,' Kit said eventually. 'Where's here?'

They had materialized on a plain. Short grass stretched as far as the eye could see, a smirr of blue on the horizon only a suggestion of mountains much further away. But it felt different to the gate on Helikon. Bright and fresh, like everything was new-made, the colours bold and slightly saturated. There was a stiff breeze which flapped the collar of Blix's jacket, but it was warm air. The blue sky seemed vast, endless in a way that made the desert night seem intimate by comparison. Blix felt a sudden sense of vertigo, as if she might fall off the earth and into forever.

'Here is called Horkos,' said Constant.

'What's a Horkos?'

'A Greek god. The Greeks of antiquity discovered many worlds.'

'They didn't know they were different worlds though,' said Blix, remembering. 'They thought they'd discovered the underworld. Hell.'

'That's right,' Constant said. He looked slightly impressed. 'How do you know that?'

'Learned it in school.'

'If this is hell, it ain't so bad,' Kit said, raising her head to look around. 'Kinda like home as a matter of fact.'

Constant rubbed his forehead absently. 'We're in high plains country on the central plateau of one of their continents. I can give you names if you want. My people came here once.'

'Wait until we see something worth naming,' Kit replied. She got up, very slowly, and turned all the way around, scanning the horizon. 'Don't look like there's anything but grass here.'

'What moon is it tonight?' said Blix suddenly. Fear turned her chest to ice. 'Is it a full moon here?'

'I don't know,' said Constant. He massaged his forehead roughly and grimaced, almost seeming in pain from the effort. 'I don't know. It's not something we ever thought about. I don't even know if Horkos has a moon.'

Blix closed her eyes and reached through the world. 'It does. I can feel it. I can do that now. I could feel the moon on Ceto. On Helikon too, although I didn't really think about it. I can feel it here. A lot. It's under the world. Rising to meet me.' She opened her eyes and looked plaintively at the others. 'Is being a werewolf always going to feel this weird?'

'I expect it is.' Constant settled the sword more comfortably on his back. 'I'm not an expert.'

'Always this weird,' said Kit cheerfully, sticking her thumbs in her pants pockets and stamping her feet vigorously. 'Weirder than weird. Nothing more weird.'

Her casual indifference made Blix see red. 'It's all right for you,' she said hotly, squaring up to the startled American. 'You're not going to turn into a monster. I bet if you felt something like this inside you, you'd take it more seriously! "Weirder than weird," tchah!' She spun on her heel and gave her back to Kit, fuming with unexpected anger.

'Hold on there, kiddo! I didn't mean nothin' by it.' Kit put up her hands in surrender, but stood her ground. 'No need to bite my head off.'

Blix spun around again. 'Was that a joke?'

Kit grinned. 'Yup. Seems like the right way to face your problems, don't it?'

Suddenly Blix's anger evaporated; she felt tired and confused. 'Sorry. I'm sorry. I don't know why I snapped at you.'

'Yes, you do,' said Constant quietly.

Blix was silent for a moment, then said 'Yes. I do.' The anger flared again. 'We'll, do you know what? I'm allowed to be angry. I don't care if it's the werewolf talking. You know, all my life people have been telling me I shouldn't be who I am, that it's bad and I should be ashamed. Well I'm not. I'm not and I never will be. This will just be something else. I'll still be me.'

'That's the spirit!' Kit clapped her on the shoulder. 'Just like I said. More people should listen to me! They'd be right more. Mind you, there's a difference between kissing a girl and biting her face off. Although I known some girls, wasn't much of a diff-'

'We should go,' said Constant. 'The wolves are still behind us.'

'Yes.' Blix deflated again, righteousness replaced by fear. Fear of what was behind her, and what lay ahead. She stared out into the grasslands, empty and open. 'If I change on this plain tonight there's nowhere for you to run. Nowhere to hide.'

'No.'

Blix thought about it. She didn't know what to think. The whole thing was too insane, too cruel. 'If I change tonight, don't let me hurt you,' she blurted suddenly.

'I won't,' whispered Constant, without looking at her.

No one spoke for a moment. The wind ruffled the grasses at the edge of the circle.

'At least it ain't raining,' said Kit again. She jumped straight up and down to try and get the circulation going, then said 'Whoa, nelly,' and steadied herself on an obelisk. 'What happened there?' She was panting heavily.

'Gate shock?' Blix asked, glad to change the subject.

'I was fine 'til just now. But I've felt like this before. It's the altitude. How high up are we, kid?'

'High. The books didn't say. We're on a plateau, like the Anvil but much, much larger. There's a fault that runs the length of this continent, straight north to south. We're very near the escarpment.'

'I didn't feel like this on the Anvil.'

'I don't know why. I don't have any answers for you.'

'Naturally.' Kit gave the world another once-around. 'Ain't nothing but flat here, kid. Which way's the way?'

Constant walked gingerly to the edge of the circle, looking out across the plain, facing away from the others.

'This one's difficult. We have to climb down the escarpment. After that we have to go through, uh, go through some bad country, before we get to the gate. We have to travel about a hundred miles.'

'That's too far,' said Blix at once. 'The werewolves will catch up.'

'There's a way which helps. I had a map... wait a minute...' He rooted in his shoulder bag and pulled out a fistful of slightly damp parchment sheets. 'Rain doesn't agree with paper.' He peeled back a large page and smoothed it flat. 'Here we go.'

It was a panel from a much larger map. Beautifully illuminated on one edge, it was roughly torn off at the others. The map itself was barely worth the name, virtually featureless except for a dot near the top right, a pair of parallel lines denoting a river directly above it, and a dead straight line from top to bottom on the left of the page which Blix assumed was the escarpment. There were a few dots along the river bank on each side. There were a few letters next to each marking. Blix didn't recognise them which meant, she presumed, that they weren't written in Shambhalhai.

'It's like a child's map,' she said.

'It's how maps were when Shambhalhai were last here. It shows what we need to know. Look.' Constant traced a badly faded line diagonally across the map. 'We're here. The way down the escarpment is at the mouth of the river - here, beside some great falls. That's a hundred miles.' He moved his finger back to their position. 'But see, the river is only thirty miles north of here. This isn't the desert, we can walk through this grassland in twelve or fifteen hours, less if we push ourselves.' He moved his finger straight up, to a dot just below the river. 'This is a settlement. People and rivers mean boats. We can sail to the escarpment.'

Kit peered at that map. 'That's longer than going as the crow flies.'

'Twenty-five miles longer,' said Blix. 'Thirty walking, ninety-five on the river.' She saw their looks and added, 'Right-angled triangle, isn't it? Me and Pythagoras are like *that.*' She crossed her fingers.

'Longer but faster,' said Constant. 'And safer. Once we're on a boat we're safe, from werewolves at least. Sailing is faster than walking. Rowing, even. We can stay ahead of them.'

'Can we?' Blix glared nervously at the patch of sky they had fallen through. Just looking at it made her feel ill. 'What if they magicked themselves to the gate, like Kit told that woman?'

'Well now, I was only trying to scare her.'

'What if you're right? They've got the bloodstone.'

'If she's right then we'll make a stand and we'll kill them all.' The sudden fury in Constant's voice rang through the stones. 'You're going to save your sister, Blix. Nothing will stop you. You're not alone. You won't ever be alone.'

His furious words died away into silence. The sky suddenly seemed closer to Blix, its vastness terrifying. She wanted to say something but couldn't find the words. She said nothing.

'It's a good plan,' said Kit eventually. 'Let's do that.' She shouldered her saddlebags.

'Better get moving,' groaned Blix, shuffling over to pick up Katy's bag. She found the little compass torch. 'North is that way. Probably.'

They left the stones behind them and headed out into the grass. Blix felt light-headed and out of breath almost immediately but forced herself to keep up the pace. Her imagination peopled the landscape behind her with monsters. The thought drove her on.

After an hour, Kit stopped walking.

'We can't rest yet,' said Constant. 'We have to push on.'

'I'm not resting. Do you smell that?'

Blix suddenly remembered the Fifth Temple. She sniffed the air carefully, expecting to smell death. Instead:

'Urgh. Well, it wasn't me. I went behind a stone before we left. I've run out of tissues by the way.'

Kit laughed. 'I wasn't accusing. Look up ahead.'

She did. 'The horizon is moving?'

Kit smiled her Cheshire Cat smile. 'Not the horizon. Know how I know you didn't grow up in the mid-west? Say, you like steaks?'

They walked toward the shimmering distance. As they approached, the vague movement resolved into shapes. Blix realised they were cattle. The increasing smell confirmed it; at once rich and rank, unmistakably ungulate. Then, as they came closer, she realised there were a lot of them - she estimated three or four hundred head, blackening the plain with their presence. Shortly afterward a horseman crossed the edge of the herd, and Blix suddenly got a sense of scale. The horse and rider together didn't reach half the height of one of the beasts. They were twenty feet tall at the shoulder at least, proportionately bovine and mightily muscled. Each wore two enormous thick cream-coloured horns, thrusting massively from their skulls like Ankole longhorn cattle, but twisting and curling back on themselves, then down and around again so that the points faded forward. They resembled nothing more than an enormous pair of bicycle handlebars. Long manes of bright blond hair hung across their necks.

Kit whistled appreciatively. 'That's more meat than I expected. What kinda cows are they?'

Blix felt happier than she had in a while. '*Bos bonnaconus.* They're bonnacon. You see the horse-mane and the swept back horns? Classic bonnacon characteristics. Really, really enormously big bonnacon. Do not under any circumstances stand behind them if you value your skin.'

The rider returned, this time with some friends. A lot of friends. They milled about at the edge of the herd for a few moments, then trotted toward them. Blix counted an even dozen of them.

'What do we do?'

'Wait,' said Kit. 'No reason to do otherwise. Nothing else we can do. Can't exactly run, too many to fight. Could be the start of a beautiful friendship.' She loosened her pistol in its holster. 'Maybe we don't mention werewolves though. No need to scare them off. It's a big sky to be alone under.'

The horsemen were dressed almost identically. Each wore a wide-brimmed straw hat with a short crown and tasselled band, and a dark woollen poncho decorated with beautifully embroidered flowers and plant motifs. Both were immaculately maintained. Underneath they looked like they spent a lot of time around cattle. Blix also couldn't help noticing they bristled with guns. Their horses, chestnuts and piebalds, were small and tough looking, suited for distance riding, bred for endurance.

They pulled up a respectful distance away and observed in silence for a few moments. Then one, who moved like he was in charge, nudged his horse forward a few steps. He looked about fifty, and had an open, handsome face, scarred horribly on one cheek with what looked like an acid burn, old and not treated well. All of them bore some sort of scar, Blix noticed. The man smiled and tipped his hat. '*Buenos días.*'

'That's Spanish!' said Blix immediately. 'I've been to Spain. *Buenos días, señor. Cómo estás?*'

From the pack of riders a harsh voice said, '*Una perra griega.*' Blix didn't understand that. The boss put up a hand to still his comrade.

'*Muy bien, gracias.*' He paused politely.

'Um. That's all I know.'

'The attempt honours me,' the man replied, smiling easily. 'A Greek who has any Spanish is unusual.'

'Greek? I'm not Gr- oh, the gate. We're speaking Greek, are we? I'm not Greek. I'm British. From Great Britain.'

'*No griega.* That is a place unknown to me,' said the man.

'It's very far away,' said Blix, with absolute certainty. 'Um, forgive me, but when is full moon here?' She saw his quizzical look. 'We need to be somewhere by then. I've lost track of time.'

'I see. Three nights brings the full moon.' The man watched Blix visibly relax. He leaned forward slightly in the saddle. 'This place you are from, Great Britain. Are you returning there?'

Blix felt the weight in the question. The man was deciding what to think about their unexpected appearance, and what to do about it. There was no menace in his words, but he said them with the confidence of a man accustomed to acting decisively. It could be a short conversational step to trouble if she got it wrong.

'We're passing through,' she said, carefully. 'We're not staying. We don't want anything. We're going to the river.' She hunted for something non-threatening. 'I like your *bonnaconus*. I've never seen such big ones. They're majestic.'

'Prodigious beeves,' Kit agreed. 'Well fed and happy.'

This was evidently the right thing to say. The men puffed up a little with pride.

'They are *ours*,' said the leader, in much the same way that a lord might claim a landscape. The bonnacon did not acknowledge the claim and continued to amble forward, chewing the cud as they went.

'They're escaping,' Blix pointed out. 'Very slowly.'

'Where will they hide?' the man laughed. 'They are bonasus, a landrace of *bonnaconus*. Bred for their propensity for enormity, among other things. They are the tallest thing on the pampas for a hundred miles in any direction. They stand out.'

The man slid from his horse. On the ground, he was shorter than Blix, and walked with a severe limp that twisted his whole body and made him fling his left leg out to the side as he moved. It looked painful, but the man didn't give any sign that it troubled him. He bowed slightly.

'With your permission, I will introduce myself, so we may become acquainted. I am Ángel Gabriel Mendoza Suarez de Rioleteo.' He waved a hand airily over his shoulder. 'These ruffians are my eleven brothers and nephews. They have similarly long names.'

The men started to shout out their names, but as the cries of 'Antonio Mendoza Suarez!' 'Francisco Javier Mendoza Suarez!' 'David Mendoza Florez de Pavlopetri!' and 'Also Ángel Gabriel Mendoza Suarez de Rioleteo! The younger!' rang out, Blix quickly lost track of who was who.

'Um. My name's Blix. Blix Summerland,' she said when the last of them had declaimed their nominal.

'Charmed, *señorita*,' said the elder Ángel Gabriel.

'Kit McCoy!' The man found his hand being pumped.

'I am further charmed. And who is this mighty warrior, who stands silent?' he continued, smiling easily at Constant. His eyes flicked to the sword strapped to the boy's back. 'In my experience, one carrying such a blade either wishes to play the big man, or to cut others down to size. Which is it with you, little *espadachín?*'

'Neither. I carry it because it's necessary. Its name is Sorcha. I'm a monk. My name is Constant.'

Mendoza looked momentarily nonplussed, as though he'd been expecting a child's response, a blush perhaps, not Constant's blank certainty. He recovered quickly. 'A monk. That is very well. Religion is a good thing. Two of my sisters are nuns.'

'What brings you good gauchos out this way, Señor Mendoza?' Kit asked.

'We are *huasos*,' Mendoza corrected. 'Chilean, by God's grace. Or our ancestors were. This is our place now.' He paused, and for a moment looked slightly irritated. 'Well. Our place is now several hundred miles to the south. The Greeks pay us to be in this place temporarily.' A sweeping gesture took in the grasslands. 'They wish to put this land under the plough. It is not so fertile. This is where we come in.'

'We are specialists in fertility,' said one of the riders.

'You mean fertilizer,' said another.

'I have seven children.' Familial laughter.

'I don't understand,' said Constant.

Blix grinned. 'I do. You're going to use the bonnacon to burn the pampas. That's *epic*.'

Constant looked behind him. The black granite circle was no longer visible, now well under the horizon, but he knew where it was. 'I still don't understand.'

Blix looked pleased. 'Do I get to lecture you for a change? Ace. Bonnacon have an acid duct which they spray when they dung. It's high in phosphoric acid and highly flammable. And they're um, a bit diarrhetic. They can poo for *ages*.'

Ángel Gabriel laughed. 'Bonasus only spray acid when they are startled. We will startle them. When they are startled, they run. One, maybe two miles. It is very difficult to stop them. It is a rich dung. We will spray the pampas in strips over the next few weeks. Then we say to the Greeks, behold, the plain is fertilized, in a season it will be fit for crops. And so, we are paid. We go home, eat figs, and are happy.'

'Golly. I've been in a stampede before,' said Kit enthusiastically, 'but never like that. That I gotta see.'

'You are welcome to join us. If that does not interfere with your business. Why are you here?'

The directness of the question caught Blix off-guard. 'Um,' we're, um-'

'We're running for our lives from a band of murderous werewolves who are chasing us across the universe,' said Constant. He saw the others' looks. 'We have to trust people,' he explained. 'We can't do this alone any more. We were lucky on the last world. We'll die unless we get help.'

Mendoza looked confused. 'Werewolves? This word…?' His voice changed suddenly as he sounded out the word; Blix got a glimpse of what he was hearing as the magic failed to translate the parts. '*Ly- kán- throo- pous.* I know it not.'

'*Hombres lobo,*' said another of the men, who Blix thought might be Ángel Gabriel the younger. '*Monstruos. Como el lobison de los Argentinos.*'

'Ah.' The elder Ángel Gabriel was suddenly serious. He drew a pistol and cocked it ostentatiously. 'Then there is no question. You are now under our protection. We stampede the herd northward this day. When we are finished, you will ride with us to Akragas. The walls of the Greeks are high. No monsters breach them.'

Kit McCoy grinned and slapped her thigh. 'Well that's just great! Say, you got silver bullets?'

'Why would we need such outlandish things?'

'Well that's just *great.*'

Constant gripped the back of the saddle as tightly as he could.

'Don't worry, *niño,*' said the man in front of him. He had a bold moustache which covered much of his face and had identified himself as San Borondón Miguel Mendoza Suarez, younger brother of Ángel Gabriel the elder. 'I ride gently. You'll be fine. Unless you fall off while we are galloping. Then you will probably break something. Or die, that is possible too.'

'Don't tease the boy, San Borondón,' said another rider, laughing. Kit McCoy lounged on his horse's rump, entirely at home. 'You'll be fine,' he said to Constant.

'I know,' said Constant. He didn't look at the mountain of beef looming alongside him. His eyes were fixed on the patch of horizon where the stone circle sat. 'A few hours ago, I was riding a pegasus through a lightning storm with only a rope to keep me from falling to my death. I'll be fine.' A phrase appeared in his mind and without thinking he added, 'I was born in the saddle.'

'Good for you!' The moustache grinned at him over its owner's shoulder. 'Then I will ride *vigorously.*'

Blix rode with Ángel Gabriel the younger, who was the son of Francisco Javier and much closer to her age than the rest of the Mendozas, as she now thought of them. He was exceptionally handsome, but his neck was strangely swollen in a way which made it difficult for him to turn his head. He paraded his horse around the edge of the herd, which eyed him complacently as they cropped the grass.

'We must be alongside the beasts, at the gallop, before we raise the noise,' he explained. 'The acid can spray quite wildly. The beasts are immune to it, but we must be past them quickly. Otherwise we risk severe injury when they, ah...'

'Shit themselves,' Blix finished. 'You don't have to be delicate with me. I'm not.'

'Me either,' called Kit from some distance away. 'I'm the opposite of delicate.'

'*How* did she hear that.'

'Carrots!'

'Tsk.'

Blix was slightly shorter than Ángel Gabriel the younger; the bulge in his neck was at eye level.

'May I ask you a personal question?'

'Certainly. I am unmarried.'

'That *so* wasn't the question I was going to ask.'

'My apologies,' he said without embarrassment. 'Young women occasionally ask. And your question?'

'Is that a goiter?'

The man nodded stiffly. 'I am afflicted. It is nothing. A common complaint.'

'The next time the bonasus find a salt lick, break a piece off. Lick it every day for a few weeks. It might reduce the swelling. Some goiters are caused by iodine deficiency, you should get some that way.'

Ángel Gabriel twisted around in the saddle so that he could see her. 'I will. Thank you.'

'You're welcome. I'm good with animals. People are animals too.'

The Mendozas had gently split out the bonasus and the herd now stretched over a quarter of a mile. The elder Ángel Gabriel galloped across the face of the herd from the far side, where six Mendozas marshalled. '*FORMAR UNA LINEA*!' he bellowed over the lowing of the herd, in a voice that belied his small stature. He rode up to San Borondón and Constant, as the Mendoza clan lined their horses facing north, the same way as the herd moved.

'Whoa, Marmolejo.' The hardy little horse obediently skipped to a halt. Mendoza licked his finger and stuck it in the air.

'Wind from the north, but not much. It is time. *DOS MINUTOS!* He observed Constant for a moment. 'You watch the horizon, *padrecito*. You expect *monstruos*. You think, these Mendozas have spent hours moving those damn cows, the bad wolves will be upon us. Worry not. We move now. Soon the pampas will be on fire. Should they pass that, let them try and pick up your scent over the burnt earth! It cannot be done. You will be invisible to them. Soon your bad wolves will be a memory.'

Constant dragged himself away from his vigil. 'You don't understand. They're not animals. They're intelligent. They'll realise what's happened.'

'We will be long gone by then.'

'They'll catch up. They run very fast and they don't tire easily. There are a lot of them and we can't kill them without silver.'

'Hmm.' Mendoza mused on the subject, absently scratching his acid scar. 'Tell me *padrecito*, if I shoot these werewolves with my lead bullets, unload my *pistola* into a wolf face for example, will they fall over?'

'Yes. Then they will get back up. Almost immediately. Only silver kills them.'

'Almost immediately? Then it is settled. If they should trouble us, then our guns will come out. Then we will replace their brains with lead. Then you will cut their heads off with your silver sword. Then they will be dead. Yes?'

'Yes,' said Constant, nodding so hard his chin thumped on his chest. 'I like you,' he added.

Mendoza laughed. 'Many do. Although not so much these days, hereabouts. *GIRAR*!' he shouted in an enormous parade-ground voice, before Constant could ask him what he meant. Instantly the Mendozas spurred their horses. The line on each side of the herd wheeled with military discipline. The horses trotted in step to the rear of the herd, and beyond. They were several hundred yards in the wake of the herd before Mendoza roared '*GIRAR*!' again, and as soon as they had turned, '*MEDIO GALOPE*!'

Constant clung on as the horse lurched forward into a canter. The horses were alive with anticipation and excitement, their riders hauling back hard to keep them together. After a few moments, once they were at pace and in line, Mendoza yelled '*AL GALOPE*!' and the horses leapt forward with an electrifying burst of speed, their hooves beating a thunderous *taranta* rhythm on the dry earth. As they approached the herd he cried '*CARGAR!*' and the Mendozas whipped their steeds into a flat sprint, and then let slip the reins and drew pistols in each hand.

'*ABRIR FUEGO!*'

Guns blazed, volley after volley ringing to the sky. At the same time riders veered in toward the bonasus, swinging as close as they dared. The beasts closest to each side raised an outraged bellowing as the terrifying noise penetrated their slow cow minds. The bellow rippled toward the centre of the herd as each animal picked up on the fear of the next, and as the riders passed the leading bonasus, the beasts lurched, then lumbered forward, then suddenly burst into a run, showing a surprising turn of speed for such massive beasts. As they ran a slick of vile liquid sprayed from the rump of each animal - sprayed, and kept spraying. The trailing animals took the muck in the face and forequarters but shook it off without harm. Beneath them the grass instantly burst into flame, blackened, shrivelled and was extinguished, crushed out by mighty hooves. But at the edge of the herd the grass caught light and was not put out, but took hold and spread slowly onto the pampas.

When they were well past the bonasus the Mendozas slowed the pace until it matched the herd, and formed up again as a band of twelve.

'They will run until they exhaust themselves,' shouted the younger Ángel Gabriel to Blix. 'Their excrement will cease in perhaps half a mile. Tomorrow we will turn the cattle and fertilize another half mile. It will be easier after this first burn. The fire burns away from us, but if it turns, we will stay ahead of it.'

Blix was exhilarated. Nearby Kit was whooping and yee-hawing as if stampeding incontinent beef-mountains was how the West was won. Which perhaps it was, sort of. Despite all the pain and sorrow and death she had seen over the days since she'd fallen through the sky at the cemetery of St. John Chrysostom, Blix couldn't help but laugh.

Constant watched the horizon.

The bonasus ran themselves out several miles later, and returned to grazing. Black smoke to the south showed how the fire had taken hold, but the northerly wind stayed steady and sent the flames away from them.

As night came in the beasts began to kneel and lower their hindquarters, and lean forward on their chests to rest. There was no bull to boss the herd around. It seemed that there was just a consensus between the bonasus that it was time to sleep.

The Mendozas set up camp on the open pampas, digging a fire pit and producing wood, kettles and pans from nowhere. Soon a merry blaze was underway and rich smells rose from the cookware.

Blix found it hard to pay attention. She knew where the moon would rise and when. She watched that spot on the dark horizon as the camp took shape around her. When it rose, it both turned her stomach and took her breath away. A half-full moon much larger, or perhaps just closer, than the moon of Earth, brilliantly white, pitted with craters. It was mesmerising, captivating, terrifying. She felt pulled toward it like the tide.

'It's like seeing God,' she whispered.

'*Media luna esta noche,'* said Ángel Gabriel the younger, startling her out of her reverie. 'Do your werewolves become men without the full moon? I remember stories saying this.'

'Not these ones. Not quite.' His presence seemed to have broken the moon's strange spell over her; when she looked back, it seemed no more than a rock in the sky. Suddenly she felt incredibly tired. A huge yawn forced its way out of her mouth. 'Sorry. I'm knackered. I want to sleep, but I don't, you know?'

'Here,' said Ángel Gabriel the younger, offering Blix a gourd with a wooden straw in it. Steam curled from the bowl. Blix sniffed it suspiciously. It smelled a bit acrid. 'What is it?'

'*Mate*,' said Ángel Gabriel. 'It will enliven your spirits.'

'As long as it doesn't put hairs on my chest. Thanks.' She sipped carefully on the straw. The drink was very bitter and not very pleasant, like a green tea with leaves and twigs all-in, in which someone had stubbed out a cigarette. 'Lovely.'

Ángel Gabriel smiled gently. 'It is an acquired taste. I will not be offended if you find another drink. Your friend has already found one, I think.'

Kit had made some friends among the Mendozas, it seemed. A bottle of clear liquid was circulating, and humour was being attempted. Blix wasn't quite sure how long the booze had been out, but it didn't seem long enough for the participants to be quite as drunk as they appeared. She wondered what was in the bottle, and whether she could have some.

Constant wasn't happy.

'This is a mistake. The wolves won't bed down for the night. They'll be upon us. We'll die.' He looked evenly at the elder Ángel Gabriel. 'I had hoped you would escort us north when the stampede was finished.'

The Chilean waved away his concerns. 'My brothers stand guard. In three hours, my other brothers will stand guard. Then it will be my turn, until morning. If the beasts appear, then they will die. Whether they appear or not, then we will take you to Akragas.' He smiled in a fatherly way. 'Worry not. Should our night eyes fail, the bonasus will hear them. They are exceptionally sensitive to *los sonidos de la noche.'*

Constant *hmphed* under his breath, but didn't push it. He found a spot at the south edge of the camp and sat facing the way they had come, Sorcha unsheathed across his lap, the tiny ivory statue that Seminah had given him balanced on the blade facing in the same direction, as though the eyes of the goddess might see further than his own.

Blix feared the werewolves as much as Constant, but her attention was diverted by the wonderful smells emanating from the cooking kettle. Whatever it was, it wasn't manticore. Eventually one of the Mendozas dished up.

'Beans?' Blix pushed the food with her spoon. Underneath the beans were more beans. 'I thought it would be beef.'

As one the Mendozas stopped what they were doing and looked incredulously at her.

'Slaughter our livelihood?' David Mendoza Florez looked outraged. 'Unthinkable. Would you beggar us? Leave them to rot on the plain as you play in their blood? We are not Greeks!' He put his thumb behind is top front teeth and pulled it forward sharply in an unmistakable gesture of abuse.

'Hush now David,' said the elder Ángel Gabriel, softly but with authority. 'They do not know.'

Mendoza Florez subsided, still looking as if Blix has insulted his mother.

'I didn't mean anything,' she said, hunkering down under the man's glare. 'I'm sorry. That was a hell of a reaction though,' she added, feeling she should be more assertive.

'We depend on the bonasus,' Ángel Gabriel explained. 'There are fewer than there were. When one dies, then we eat and salt beef, tan leather, grind the bones. We use everything then. But we do not slaughter them. The bonasus are *ours*, you see. The Greeks though, they used to sacrifice them to their Gods. Still do, when they can. It has been a point of contention.'

'I'm sensin' some tension between y'all,' said Kit, who was lounging by the fire smoking a long-stemmed pipe she'd acquired from a Mendoza. 'You Spaniards and Greeks not get along?'

There was a smatter of laughter from among the Mendozas, coloured with barely concealed bitterness.

'You put it mildly,' Ángel Gabriel said. 'But we are Chilean. Our ancestors were *criollos* who fought for the King in the civil war. After O'Higgins and San Martin beat them at Chacabuco, they found the country less welcoming, shall we say. Some left for Spain, others went elsewhere on the old world. My people came here. It is a harder here, perhaps, but we are free. After a fashion.'

'I don't know much about South America I'm afraid,' Blix said. 'Chile is where Pinochet is from, isn't it? We had a war with Argentina. We won.'

'I know nothing of these things. We have had no contact with the old world for many generations. The stones no longer open the sky.'

'You might want to check that,' said Blix, but Ángel Gabriel wasn't listening. He saw something behind his eyes that interested him more, and brought his tired body to life.

'You see that we are established here, yes? For generations. And we try to fit in. I learned Greek with my mother's milk, I speak it better than the Greeks do. But the Greeks, they say our years are but the blink of an eye. They have been here since the ancient times, since before the days of Solon. They have been cut off since then. They have... remained. They had no Pericles to lead them, no Sophocles to question them. No Plato, no Xenophon. They are not Christians, like the Greeks of Greece in our forefathers' day. They cling to the old religions. The old traditions. We are not embraced.'

'They have embraced the gun wholeheartedly,' said San Borondón Mendoza with open contempt.

'They have,' said the elder, soberly. 'That is one thing they learned from us.' He looked at Kit. 'Over a hundred years we lived in peace with them. We lived where they were not, by and large. Then times become harder. One day, the Greeks came to our fathers and say, your debts are not paid, you are-' He paused, the words sticking in his throat, and then his voice changed again as he sounded the syllables far enough apart that the translation magic failed to recognise the word. 'They say, you are *hek-te-mor-oi,* you are oathbreakers, you are accursed in Horkos' sight. They say, all this land is ours. Our fathers say, we are not, it is not. There is contention. Then a settlement. Now the land is Greek.'

Blix didn't have to read much into that statement to know that it covered a lot of wounds. The Mendozas looked sombre, or outraged, or both. Blix recognised distrust in more eyes that David's. She wondered whether it had been there all along. Seeing it now made her angry in a wholly unexpected way. She took a deep breath, and tried to think of something to say to get them back on her side.

'I'm sorry. I didn't know. Animal sacrifice is horrible. I can't imagine it.' She sought out the massive shapes of the bonasus, chuntering quietly among themselves in the darkness. 'How could they kill something so magnificent?'

'With fervour,' said Ángel Gabriel the elder. 'The greater the sacrifice, the greater favour Apollo shows them. So goes their rite.'

'They hoist the bulls into the air with cranes,' said Ángel Gabriel the younger, throwing his *mate* onto the fire. 'Then their priests slit their throats and dance in the hot blood. Then they slit their bellies and the pagans sport in the offal. So I have been told.'

Blix got the sense in which he meant 'sport' and blushed. 'It must be difficult for you to work for them.'

'Money is money,' said Ángel Gabriel the elder flatly. 'They have it.'

'Yeah, but don't you worry that they'll want to kill your cows?'

'Bulls,' said David Mendoza Florez. 'They sacrifice bulls. We have none.'

Blix brightened. 'Oh. Well, that's all right then!'

The way the atmosphere turned to ice made Blix realise she had said the wrong thing, but it was too late. The Mendozas either turned away or, in Mendoza Florez's case, stared at her with outright hostility. From the corner of her eye Blix saw Kit McCoy subtly shift position, ready to act.

'She does not know,' said Ángel Gabriel the elder, sadly.

'Know what? Look, whatever I said, I'm really so-'

'We have no bulls because bulls are no longer born,' said Ángel Gabriel, cutting across her. 'My father was a young man when last one was birthed. Bonasus are long lived. Maybe one hundred and twenty years. That bull is in his prime. We do not bring him north. He has few brothers, and no sons. When the bulls are gone, the bonasus will be no more. And neither will we. And now it is time to sleep,' he said firmly. 'Tomorrow is another day. A day on which this conversation will be forgotten,' he added pointedly, but without looking at Mendoza Florez. That man stomped off into the darkness. The elder Ángel Gabriel sighed, and bedded down near the fire, his back to Blix. The other Mendoza's followed his lead. Blix suffered the occasional surly look in silence.

'Well, I'm gonna heed the call,' said Kit, getting up. 'Don't anyone stroll out this way less'n you wanna get shot.' She walked off in the opposite direction to Mendoza Florez.

Blix wanted nothing more than to let things lie there, but the story of the bulls had left her with a horrible feeling.

'*Señor* Mendoza.' The man half-rolled back. 'I am very sorry.'

He grunted.

'You said times got harder. That bulls stopped being born. When was that, exactly?' She felt rather than saw Constant suddenly start paying attention.

'When? The time of earthquakes. About seventy years ago.'

That was the end of conversation. Ángel Gabriel rolled back over and didn't stir again. His younger namesake collected Blix's bowl and gourd, and seemed about to say something, but moved away abruptly. He returned with a bedroll, but said nothing.

Blix went to sleep thinking about the year nineteen sixteen. Her knowledge was a jumble of clichés - trenches and bombardments, spiked helmets and Tommies going over the top, Kitchener and the Kaiser and the sudden end of magic. Nothing which resembled a fact. *I wish I knew more about history. I wish you were here, Katy.*

Blix woke in the night to find Kit asleep beside her, one arm draped across her chest - not holding, just there. It made her feel safe. She snuggled in. Then she realised that Kit hadn't come to her. She'd gone to Kit.

She lay and watched the moon.

The First of Wolves stepped across the threshold. The boards creaked and bowed under his great weight.

There was no one there, it seemed. Doors stood open to show empty rooms. But the First of Wolves did not need to see them to know that humans were there.

'You cannot hide from me, woman,' he said. 'I smell you. Your offspring too.'

There was a carpet in the centre of the room, old and threadbare. The First of Wolves slid it back with his foot, being careful not to lean directly over it. Underneath was a trap door. He made no move to open it.

'Will you die in a hole in the ground? Come out.'

'Come and get me, monster.' The muffled voice shook with fear and with anger. 'I will make you pay a price for your meal.'

It did not surprise the First of Wolves that he could understand the woman. He didn't know it could be otherwise. He moved silently around the trap door to the hinge side. An iron ring was bolted near the opposite edge, well within reach. A sudden grab and pull and it would be open.

'I am not a monster. I am that I am. I do not want to eat you. Come out. Or I will come down.'

'Try it and you'll get a heart full of silver.'

The First of Wolves inhaled deeply. There it was, the bitter tang of the moonbane, barely noticeably amid the stink of humanity, but there. He took a step back.

'You know us. You are ready for us. But we are not of this world.'

'I was warned.'

'Ah.' The First of Wolves considered what his nose told him. Humans, three, a female and two whelps. Not the ones he sought.

'I do not follow your scent. Your ground smells of horseflesh. The same must I smelled many miles away. The sky horses landed outside. I seek the ones who came on them. Tell me where they are, and live.'

'I told them to go to hell. You go too.'

There was a tiny sound from below. A child stifling a cry of fear.

'Are they worth the lives of your children? Tell me, and I will leave.'

'You'll leave anyway. Or stay forever. I have silver. It kills you so you stay dead. I know this. You know it too.'

The First of Wolves chuckled, a throaty *wuff* that was more than half growl.

'You are brave, woman, and foolish. We are many. We could rip you from that hole in the ground and devour you in the blink of an eye.'

'You talk a lot for a damn wolf. He who comes first, dies. Will it be you?'

A howl from outside interrupted the First of Wolves' reply. A howl of triumph. Presently a New appeared at the door.

'I have found the scent! The cub with the silver and the two bitches. Beyond the river.'

'Good. Leave.' When he was alone again he turned back to the trapdoor.

'Brave, foolish woman, you are also lucky. My wolves would swarm through this hole and not care who died, if you died too. I am not like them. I do not follow your scent. Live long, lucky woman.'

'Just fuck off.'

The First of Wolves left that place and ran, following the scent of his quarry. their trail bright and clean across the landscape. As they approached the standing stones the buzzing in his ears became a swarm-noise as the magic rock found its mark. He took it out and held it, and silence was restored. He heard his own breath and the beating of his heart. He took out the bloodstone.

'Horkos,' he said. '*Come and see.*'

Then there was fire.

Chapter Twenty-Five: Brazen

Constant dreamed.

In my dream, I lie flat and low in the skiff and wait for dinner to arrive. It is just after dawn. Everything is still, not a breath of wind. I stretch out my left arm over the thwart and steady the boat against the bank, but it is barely necessary. The lake is at its most jewel-like in these hours of the morning. I could slide my hand into the water and send forth a ripple of white diamonds across the surface that would not stop until it reached the far shore, and would return to me like a gift from the water. It is so beautiful that I am entranced, hypnotized by the sight. Moments like this are why I came to live in the water margin, far from any town or village. They are why I live alone. The world is drenched in beauty.

A dozen waterfowl come in from the north and settle with fat splashes onto the lake, quacking complacently among themselves, squabbling, preening and displaying. Presently they scud into range. They do not see me. I have taken steps. I have thrown up a little illusion to make the skiff seem like a stand of reeds in their minds. You don't need a lot of magic to fool a duck. It is the most magic I am prepared to do.

I shift position slightly, trying not to stir the water or make the boat creak. I take up the weighted net and ease my arm back to throw.

A rumbling hauk-hauk call from behind me cuts through the silence, and then a crashing sound of splintered wood as something huge approaches. The skittish birds react as one, shouldering powerfully into the sky. I throw the net as hard as I can. It spirals across the lake, spreading like the fingers on a hand as it flies. But the birds are gone.

I let the illusion drop and haul the net back in, then roll over to spy out the cause of my failure, not that I don't know already. A way along the bank a giant sloth rears and grabs the high branches of a kawaaga tree, hauling down the sweetest leaves and stripping them from their stems with its thick, curling tongue. He's twenty feet from nose to tail and four tons of muscle and fat into the bargain. He doesn't step lightly.

In my dream, I say, I don't begrudge you your breakfast big man, but what about my dinner? I don't have your reserves.

The sloth ignores me. That is the right way of things, I think. The beasts should not be troubled by men.

In my dream, I catch sight of something that should not be there, a flash of red in the greenwood. There is a landsman, a monk in a crimson robe. He stands there, staring at me, open mouthed.

'Great Father … In the village, they told me, a magician in the waterlands... I never imagined it would be you.*'*

He Recognises me.

I sigh heavily. He is the seventh of his kind to pass this way in the last decade. The first six I hid from. This one has caught me unawares.

'It had to happen sometime,' I say to no one.

The no one does not reply.

Now there is a boy here I do not recognise.

'Comen sen-Hersa,' *he says.* 'Sixty-two. He was unusual. Some kind of magician. He never did much magic. I think he feared what he could do. That's quite unusual for someone with the strength to do it. Power is attractive.'

In my dream the boy pauses for a moment, and admires the beauty of the lake. Somehow, I feel what he feels about it. He feels as I would feel.

'He was aware of me, on some level. Before he was Recognised. I was never quite sure how much. I've suppressed those memories over the centuries. Don't want you lot getting ideas.'

In my dream, the boy looks with interest at the monk. 'Oh, him,' *he says. He turns back to me.*

'You've been dreaming about Recognition a lot,' *he says.* I think that's because I'm trying to reach you. Recognition is a trigger for me. It helps me remember who I am after I move bodies. Becoming you, becoming any of you … it's hard. Very hard, sometimes...'

He trails off into some reverie in a way I recognise in myself. Then he perks up.

'Our little confrontation plan didn't go as I expected, did it? I was expecting a reaction. She looks like type to react, don't you think? Still, a lot has happened since then. She's helped us stay alive. I'm less suspicious of her. Which is to say I'm still very suspicious of her. She's not telling us a lot of things, starting with what she is. When we find that out I will sleep easier. Not that I sleep. A figure of speech.'

He steps closer. The look on his face reminds me of my father, when as a small boy I did something foolish and dangerous.

'You have to stop acting on impulse. You think you know what's coming. In fact, we're only guessing. I hope we're good at it. Otherwise we won't be talking for much longer, will we?'

Constant did not remember the boy when he woke up.

Constant was stiff and cold when he woke up, but he was alive. The werewolves had not come in the night. He wondered why not.

Breakfast was brief and, save for the occasional muttered *'lobos, tch,'* largely silent. Then the Ángel Gabriel's elder and younger and San Borondón Mendoza carried Kit, Blix and Constant northward on the backs of their horses. Constant looked back a lot but the only sight to see was the rest of the Mendozas beginning the laborious task of turning the bonasus and pointing them in the right direction for the next burn.

The *corraleros* kept up a steady trot, a slow pace which ate up the miles nonetheless. Blix turned occasionally to see the mighty bonasus shrink with distance, and then be lost over the horizon.

'Stop squirming,' said Ángel Gabriel the younger. 'You will fall off.'

'Sorry. I'm going to miss them. Your bonasus, I mean. I like cows.'

'As do I. They do not ask for much. That is a good way to live for man or beast.'

They rode on, walking the horses now and then to rest them and watering them after a few hours at a pool surrounded by strange, spiky trees. Soon the open plain gave way to scrub. Paths became visible in the dirt, tracks rutted by cart-wheels and flattened by hooves. The Mendozas took one leading almost-North. In another hour it bisected fenced-in farmland, first long fields of wheat, then acres and acres under olive trees. None of them looked particularly well managed and quite a few of the vines looked dead. People were few and far between. They were the only ones on the road and when they did spy people working in the fields they didn't look up from their tasks to see the riders pass.

'*Esclavos*,' said Ángel Gabriel the elder, when Constant asked. 'Slaves, or serfs if you prefer. Some born to it. Others, debtors who defaulted. It is a bad business and I do not wish to speak of it.' He seemed both troubled and angry, chewing on his bottom lip and saying nothing when Blix expressed her disgust at the institution of slavery.

A little later they pulled up and dismounted. Ángel Gabriel the elder gestured along the road ahead of them.

'It is still some hours on foot to the city gates. This is as close as we go. From here I would expect patrols. The sight of *huasos* tends to excite their blood, yes? Even when we are at peace. And today we are few. We will turn back here. The road twists and turns most unnecessarily and will add much time to your journey compared to the flight of a crow, but do not be tempted to cut across fields. Trespass is a capital offence among the Greeks. Take this seriously,' he added, looking almost but not quite at Kit McCoy.

The elder Ángel Gabriel found his hand being pumped again. 'You've done us a solid, *señor*,' said Kit. '*Muchas gracias*.'

'*Eres bienvenido*. It was nothing. A man's duty.'

'You don't say.' Kit was looking appraisingly at the short-barrelled rifle in the saddle holster by Ángel Gabriel's right knee. 'Say, now. I don't got much in the way of trade goods and I don't suppose American dollars buy a damn thing here, but I do got a few silver bullets I can't use. Solid silver slugs, real valuable. What say you name a price for one of those rifles? Bullets too. The lead kind.'

The corners of Mendoza's mouth twitched in what might have been a smile had he not looked so haunted. 'I regret that our weapons are not for sale.'

'Darn.'

'How about now?' said Constant. He held something between his thumb and forefinger. It caught the light and shone brightly, like a teardrop shed in joy. It was a diamond, cut into a lozenge, perfectly faceted and flawless. It was bigger than Constant's thumbnail.

'*Madre de dios*,' said San Borondón Mendoza, marvelling. Both Ángel Gabriel's crossed themselves.

'Great day in the morning!' Kit exclaimed. 'That has to be thirty carats! Where on God's good earth did you get that?'

'The Anvil. We had a Treasury. We don't have much silver on Shambhala, but we do have diamonds. There was a time when penitents sent things like this to us as a sign of devotion. We didn't have a use for them. They just lay there. I thought it might be useful.'

'You could buy everything we own a hundred times over with this,' said Ángel Gabriel the elder, his voice shaking only slightly. 'You could buy the *pueblo* and everything in it. Every*one* in it.'

Constant tutted. 'People are worth more than rocks. I don't want any people or your pebblo, whatever that is. I'd like to buy a rifle and some bullets for my friend. And I would like to say thank you for taking us in. You didn't have to.'

He tossed the diamond up to the elder Ángel Gabriel, who started like Constant had thrown a hot coal at his face. He snatched it from the air just as it was about to sail past him and cradled it in the palm of one hand, holding it at arm's length as though it might bite him. He examined it, shaking his head slightly. Then, speechless, he unholstered his rifle and handed it to Kit. A box of bullets followed.

'Thankee kindly,' said Kit, sighting down the barrel. 'Mighty fine weapon for something, uh, country-made. Shame my rifle rounds won't fit though.'

Ángel Gabriel wasn't paying attention. He was staring at Constant with an expression somewhere between awe and horror on his face.

'You have no idea what you have done,' he said. 'No idea. You have saved us.'

'You were kind to us when you didn't have to be. Be kind to others. Kindness is its own reward, and it's worth more than this. I hope you don't die.'

'*Gracias, padrecito*.' Mendoza looked like he was about to say something, then stopped. He worried at the pommel of his saddle for a moment, kneading it with the heel of his hand.

'You have been open and generous with us,' he said suddenly. 'I will repay you as I can. I brought you here because you sought protection and asked for help and that is what Christian men do in such circumstances.' The other Mendozas nodded sharply in agreement. 'But I confess, and will confess before God, that I did not care for your fate beyond this point. I was content that I left you alive. But now I will say this. Don't go into Akragas. Not unless *los hombres lobo* are biting at your heels.'

He pointed ahead of them, weaving his finger left and right. 'After many bends this road leads to a canyon, which is the only way to the town. Just before you reach it, there is a crossroads. A shrine to Zeus stands there. You cannot mistake him. The path to the left will take you, eventually, to a fishing commune some way along the bank, outside the walls. Better to deal with the Greeks there. Fishermen are practical. Perhaps for the right price they will take you where you want to go. Back to your Great Britain, perhaps.' He smiled at Blix, but there was too much worry in his eyes for her to think it was real.

'I don't think they can do that,' she said.

Constant and Kit had exchanged glances as the man spoke. Constant asked the obvious question. 'Why?'

The elder Mendoza made to speak, but his brother beat him to it. 'You look wrong,' said San Borondón. 'You stick out. To be Greek here is to conform. To be part of the - how do you say the word, brother? *Pol-it-ei-a*? Part of the polity. You are different.'

'It is true,' said the younger Ángel Gabriel. 'You,' he said to Kit, 'dress like us. Your hat could be my grandfather's. They don't like us. They will never have seen a Japanese before either.'

'I'm used to that,' Kit grinned. 'Boys in Nebraska ain't well-travelled, if you know what I mean.'

The youngest Mendoza did not return the grin. 'Insularity is common. It is not the only reason you will draw eyes. You,' he said to Constant, 'are carrying a weapon that will command the attention of every soldier in the city. There are lots of soldiers. And you,' he said to Blix, 'I...' He paused, taking in Blix's ushanka, her leather jacket and monkish leggings, and the doombag. 'I do not know what you look like.'

'My mum says that all the time,' said Blix, smiling at the sudden memory. To Blix's surprise Ángel Gabriel blushed slightly.

'My brother and nephew are right,' said Ángel Gabriel the elder. 'You don't fit in. The Greeks on this world have been here for a very long time, far longer than we, I must admit it. Their laws and customs are intricate. You are novel. The Greeks react badly to novelty. Everyone on this world does - Sumerians, Akkadians, Ishuwan, Hittites - all who came here in the ages before Christ.' He crossed himself as he spoke the name, then laughed bitterly. 'The shrine at the crossroads is dedicated to Zeus Xenios. He welcomes guests and avenges wrongs done to strangers. This is surely a joke. Everyone looks to their own here.'

'You didn't,' said Blix. 'You helped us.'

'Did I.' There was no question in Mendoza's voice. He spoke as if he'd ground the words between his teeth before saying them.

His horse shied suddenly, startled by an insect. Mendoza reined it in, then stroked the animal's neck until it was calm once more. *As much to calm himself as the horse,* thought Blix.

That is only half the reason,' he continued abruptly. 'Today is the first day of Thargelia. It is a day to honour Apollo. They placate their god lest he ruin the harvest four months hence.' His expression turned grim. 'I have not been to the city since I was a child. The Greeks we treat with come to us. Yet I have heard stories of this bacchanal. In ages past it was benign, to an extent, but no more. Apollo has not listened to their prayers for some time. The Greeks have grown excitable. Desperate. Thargelia requires human sacrifices. They will have been chosen already, but still... It could be a bad night to be different. Anyone going to the city, who is not from it, would be wise to go in numbers.'

Blix suddenly understood. *He thinks he is honour-bound to come with us if we go to the city. He is scared that he will not return if he does. He's just been handed salvation for his people. He wants to be told he can leave in good conscience.*

'Sounds like good advice,' said Constant. 'We'll take it. Fishing commune downriver. We won't go into the city. We'll go there.'

'Well now,' began Kit, but Constant's sharply raised hand stopped her short.

The elder Ángel Gabriel looked very relieved and, Blix thought, slightly guilty at his relief.

'*Bueno.* Now we must leave and return to our family. But first, a story. Do not speak unless you are spoken to. If you are questioned, tell the Greeks that you have come to sacrifice to Artemis tomorrow. Women and children are permitted to travel for this. You are from Laüs, which is seventy miles upstream. It is a long, dusty and boring walk from there to here. Their symbol is Cerastes, the horned serpent. For Akragas, it is bull with a man's head. Your menfolk have ridden ahead to do business. You are dressed the way you are because, I don't know, because it is the fashion in Laüs this season. A patrol will be men, they will have no idea. You carry weapons because they are men. The big sword is your father's, *padrecito,* you carry it for him. This is the furthest you have ever been from Laüs. You don't know Laüs well as you don't normally leave your house unaccompanied. This is believable for women and children among the Greeks.'

The words tumbled out of him at increasing speed as he tried to satisfy his idea of honour and still leave before Constant changed his mind.

'Thank you for everything,' said Blix.

'I have said all I can say. Now we will leave. Your names will be remembered. *Buenos días.*' He turned his horse and spurred it. The animal kicked up dust as it took off. San Borondón Mendoza tipped his hat and followed suit.

The younger Ángel Gabriel shook hands with each of them in turn. When it came to Blix, there was something in his hand already.

'Take this,' he said, passing her a revolver and holster belt. 'Your friend has one, but we have no bullets for it. I have many for this.'

'I can't take your gun.'

'I have another. They are a pair. This world is dangerous for young women. Consider it a loan, if you wish. As thanks for your advice.' He touched his swollen neck briefly. 'Perhaps you will come back here one day,' he said, gazing into the distance. 'You can return it then.'

'Um. Perhaps. I shouldn't think so though. I need to go home.'

'Ah. I am sorry to hear that. Then I will get another revolver. I think we can afford it now. *Buena suerte, mi amiga.'* He spurred his horse hard and rode after his family.

'Someone has an admirer,' said Kit, wafting away the dust with her hat.

'What? Really?' Blix watched the departing Mendozas as they rode away. 'Gosh. He's really not my type.'

She held the gun belt awkwardly for a moment, then strapped it on, copying the way that Kit wore hers. It felt strange and heavy, and wrong. There was a knife sheath sewn into the opposite hip to the gun. Blix fished out the gutting knife from her satchel and slotted it in. It didn't make the rig feel any better.

'We should go,' said Constant. 'I want to be inside the gates or on the river before nightfall.'

'Say what? You just told Mendoza-'

'I know. He needed that. I don't decide for us by myself. There are other considerations which we all need to agree on.'

'What other considerations?' Blix asked.

'We need magic. This is our third world since Shambhala. We had no opportunity to look for artefacts on Ceto or Helikon. We *must* find one or we'll be stranded when the eighth shard rusts out. Artefacts will be where people are. People are here.'

'You're saying we should go to the city.'

'No, I'm not offering an opinion. The Mendozas were pretty clear on the risks. It might make more sense to move on to a less polarized society and acquire an artefact there. What I'm saying is that we need to make a choice. Together.'

'Be a better decision if we knew if there was an artefact in the city or not,' mused Kit.

'Yes,' said Constant. 'I can find out.'

The walk to the crossroads turned into a trudge as a light but persistent rain set in, turning the dusty road into rutted red mud. From Blix's point of view this journey was not enlivened by Constant and Kit resuming their bickering.

'... all I'm asking, Rockefeller, is whether the fact that you had a diamond the size of Plymouth Rock up your sleeve sorta slipped your mind? Cause that's quite an important detail to forget.'

'No. I chose not to tell you. I didn't know you then. I barely know you now.'

'I saved your lives about three times now. I oughta get some love for that.'

'I already love everyone. You said you were a bounty hunter. That doesn't inspire trust.'

'Well, that's fair enough,' said Kit, looking like it was anything other than fair enough. 'Say, why didn't you offer that to Roohsk when I was bargaining with him?'

'Roohsk told us what he wanted. What use would a diamond have been to him anyway? Where could he exchange it in the desert? Mendoza wanted money to free his family from debt. He told us that, obliquely. Now he has it.'

'I'll say. That rock is worth a lot. I mean a lot a lot. The kind of money that changes the balance of power. And you know they got a thing about the Greeks.'

'That's understating it,' said Blix. 'What do you think about all that?'

Kit looked back down the trail. The Mendozas had long since passed beyond sight. 'I like those guys. They helped us when they didn't have to. They got nice cows and a sad story. Still, though, it's one side of a story to which, I don't doubt, there's another side.'

'One side has slaves,' said Blix darkly.

'How do you know both sides don't? I don't know much about South America but it ain't just my folks that have a black history. For that matter how do you know there are only two sides? Life ain't like that. Did you know when we met them they called you a bitch? *Perra.* When they thought you were Greek.'

'I didn't know that. I didn't know you spoke Spanish.'

'I know what men call women. You know, maybe they're the good guys. Maybe they're just guys. We don't know anything about this place. Let's not get involved. Let's just move on,' and here she looked pointedly at Constant, 'and hope they don't die on account of us suddenly giving them wealth beyond their wildest dreams.'

Constant said nothing, but flipped his hood up and retreated under it.

'We'll never know, will we?' said Blix. 'We'll never see them again.'

'Maybe not. But I reckon they can take care of themselves. And if they can't, now they can buy people to take care of them.'

The road started to show signs that people used it. Lanes left the main highway, some to farm buildings or to fields or groves, others to quite grand estate houses, set well back from the road. The occasional road sign announced the owner. "Land of Kallicrates, beyond it the land of Isidoros". "Nikomachos, his villa." Way-markers counted down toward Akragas in some unit - probably not miles, Blix realised, as she processed the simultaneous realisation that she could now read Greek.

The signs of civilisation eventually produced fellow travellers. The winding road was joined by other, better roads and itself became more defined. Farm carts pulled by skinny cattle met them coming. A pair of horsemen passed them from behind. Several times they saw men walking the road, against or with them, alone or in small groups. They were dressed in simple tunics which left the right arm bare, sometimes with a cloak or a rectangle of cloth over the left shoulder, belted in at the waist, hair and beards in tightly curled ringlets. They all wore short swords, and some carried rifles like Kit's.

The incongruity of it made Blix wonder. The obvious normality with which the Greeks wore clothes that had gone out of style among their cousins on Earth thousands of years before was bizarre, and nothing like anything she'd seen so far.

Dragonville dressed for pulling rabbits from hats. Kit McCoy was every American Midwest stereotype made flesh, although Blix suspected other Americans probably thought she was a bit rural, with her cowboy hat and lariat and horse gear. Maybe Nebraska didn't change much, although she was also beginning to think that quite a lot of it was an act. Although Kit came across like she was all shiny surface, every now and then there was a hint of something deeper.

Constant dressed like the monk he was, and the Tibet-descended Shambhalhai they'd met looked exactly like the Tibetans she'd seen in the colour supplements in her dentist's waiting room. Roohsk and his people had been wildly different, but Blix supposed there wasn't a dress code for desert dystopias. The woman who had shot the pegasus dressed like a farmer – old-fashioned, but normal. The Mendozas ponchos and hats made them look a bit Speedy Gonzales, but Blix knew South Americans wore things like that on Earth too. But no one in Greece dressed like this. It was as if time had stopped for them. They reminded Blix of a religious community who deliberately adopted the dress of their ancestors.

The thought of Roohsk made Blix want to think about anything else. She tried to concentrate on where they were going.

Each time they passed someone Kit, ignoring Mendoza's advice, offered up a bright 'Howdy, partner!' to the stranger. But each time the man she addressed ignored her, with the same studiously blank expressions they had seen on the field slaves. Where they caught up with someone walking in the same direction, the man stepped aside and pointedly allowed them to overtake without engaging with them.

'This is weird,' said Blix after the fourth such non-encounter. 'Not talking to strangers is one thing - I've been to London - but this total blanking is creepy.'

'Maybe, maybe not,' said Kit. 'Maybe this is what politeness is here. Mendoza said they had strange customs.'

'If ignoring someone is polite I don't want to know what happens when they decide not to ignore you.'

'Me neither. Hey, lookee there.'

Small stone statues lined the road ahead of them. Mostly limestone, a few of marble, they were heavily weathered and looked ancient. Some had the remains of offerings in front of them - old food, sheaves of wheat withered to wisps, or small coins covered in verdigris.

'Any of these Zeus?' asked Kit. She booted one lightly. It fell over. She hastily righted it and looked around so see if there was anyone to notice her transgression.

'Um. Search me.' Blix gave the statue a closer look. It looked weedy. 'Probably not Zeus.'

'Oh Great Father of religion?'

'No,' said Constant. 'That's Zeus.'

He pointed. Ahead of them, too far away to fully make out, was a tall white shape, At least three times as tall as Blix. Although its features were indistinct at this distance it was unmistakably male, bearded and holding its muscular right arm high above its head. Clenched in the raised fist was a jagged gold thunderbolt.

It took then another half an hour to reach the shrine. The statues by the roadside became bigger and better cared for the closer they got - and more colourful too, the marble painted in flesh tones and brightly, almost garishly decorated clothing. Armour in gunmetal, silver and gold, laurels picked out in lifelike hues.

As they drew closer the road rose to meet them, then fell away sharply into a broad river valley. The ground suddenly became rocky, huge boulders blocking most ways forward, save for narrow roads cut through the stone, an excellent defensive approach for the city beyond. No army could march on Akragas from here except in single file. The river, broad and lazy at this point, protected it from the rear.

Where the rocks ended, the city began. It wasn't a city on the scale that Blix knew, but impressive nonetheless. High white walls defended and constrained it. From this angle Blix could pick out some of the buildings. In the centre, raised high above the rest of the buildings, the columns of a strange acropolis dominated the city.

The statue of Zeus was mighty. There were people before it. Quite a few - the first real crowd Blix had seen since school had kicked out, a few days and worlds ago. That was strange too - how few people she'd seen, how empty the worlds were.

Perhaps fifty men prayed before the statue. Kneeling, hands held high in beseeching gestures, voices raised in invocation, drowning each other out as they begged the god to listen. They were all venerable and looked at lot like Zeus. They weren't armed, either. Blix found the cross-talking hubbub irritating, although at least someone wasn't getting the silent treatment.

A road led to the city. Another crossed it, left and right, wending and quickly disappearing into the rocks. The long shadow cast by Zeus fell across their path like a roadblock.

'Right then,' said Blix, stepping well away from the nearest supplicant. 'Route One,' she pointed to the city, 'or take the bypass?' twisting to point down the left-hand path.

'You talk funny,' said Kit. 'I suppose it depends on whether we got good reason to go to the city. Werewolves don't seem to be on our asses at the moment. We could risk staying out and making our way to the fishing village. On the other hand, those darn werewolves might be hiding behind the first bush around that corner. I can see docks in the city. We can find a ride downriver there, one way or the other. But it's dangerous in other ways than werewolves, if we believe Mendoza.' She reached over and pulled down Constant's hood, startling him. 'Do they have magic? You said you could find out? How are you gonna do that kid, you got a Thing for that too?'

'I have a way,' said Constant. He closed his eyes.

Blix started, concerned. She put out her hand to stop him. 'No, wait, Constant, don't use -'

' - magic,' says the girl, but I have begun. I have a way.

I close my eyes and concentrate on the power near me. But I cannot draw from the artefacts. The shards are precious. I concentrate on myself, reaching within, looking for magic.

I can feel the girl clearly, a presence in the silence of my soul, in the heart in my breast. My soul is hers. I can see her breathing as I am breathing. I see the magic within her. The silver of a summer moon, yellow-bright and glowing. I realise that if she knew how, if she had the will, she could draw on that power and use it as I have used my own. But it is surrounded now, captured by something black and raging which courses through her blood.

I reach out. I can feel the woman, see the magic within her. A vulpine red, burnished gold, shining like honour. I reach out again and I can feel the men grovelling before their God, feel their fear and envy and hope and anger. The green of an illness with no cure.

I reach out. My thoughts speed across the land, dancing like a sparrow on the wing. The city is far away, further than I thought. The ground falls away into the valley cut by the great river. The city is before me, white walls and battlements standing tall and proud. I rush to meet the wall and soar above it, turning down into the city below. People teem through the streets like salmon in the stream, their many colours forming an infinite rainbow in my mind's eye. I dive through them, in and around and beyond them, through streets and buildings and people. They move in silence. I reach out. Then I feel it, hidden, guarded, safe behind stone walls and metal doors. I can feel an artefact, glowing like the last ember in the ashes. I feel those who guard it. I feel their terror. I feel terror everywhere. And I feel other things too. I feel ecstasy. I feel hatred.

Constant screamed and fell backward as if he'd been punched. Kit leapt forward and caught him before hit the ground. He was shivering uncontrollably, as if he'd been drenched in ice water.

'Hell's teeth!' Kit knelt and gently lowered the boy into her lap. 'What happened, kid?'

'It was too far,' he croaked, his voice desiccated. Too far away.' His left hand convulsed uncontrollably. Constant pushed up his sleeve. A line of red rust, thin as wire, now snaked up the inside of his forearm, from his wrist almost to his elbow.

'This is happening every time you do magic,' said Blix. She hesitated for a moment, then knelt beside him and wiped the cold sweat from his forehead with her sleeve. Constant gave her a grateful look.

'I didn't think. I knew how to do it, and we needed it, I didn't think, I just did it. It never helps.' He coughed violently and spat out blood. Blix quickly wiped it away.

'Whatever you're doing, stop doing it,' she said, alarmed. 'I may be cross with you, but I don't want you to hurt yourself.'

'We're attracting attention,' said Kit, nodding toward the statue. Blix looked around. Several of the Greek men had stopped praying and were looking at them. A couple of them had stood up. One, elderly and regal-looking, furiously jabbed the air in her direction. They all remained silent however.

'Are we indeed,' said Blix. She sprang up and took a couple of aggressive steps toward the men.

'Mind your own bloody business!' she shouted. She put her hand on the butt of her pistol like she'd seen Kit do at the oasis and glared at them. The standing men hurriedly turned away and those at prayer bowed their heads once more. Blix kept the glare going until the last sidelong glance was over, then returned to Constant's side.

'That was assertive,' he gasped.

'That's polite where I come from,' she said firmly.

'Ain't you the cutest,' said Kit. 'One thing though. Don't threaten gunplay unless you're prepared to back it up.'

Blix saw that Kit had drawn her gun and was resting it on her thigh, just behind Constant's head. It must have been visible to the praying men.

'I didn't threaten gunplay,' she said.

'Yeah, you did.'

'I just did what you did!'

'I don't threaten. That was definitely a threat.'

'Then I would have backed it up,' said Blix pugnaciously.

Kit gave her a quizzical look. 'Really? You'd kill someone who ain't done nothing to you?'

'Yes! No. I don't know. I feel a bit weird. More than weird, actually my insides - ow!' She bent as though she'd been punched in the gut. 'That fucking hurt!'

'That big old moon ain't helping you none, is it? Let's get you off this world as soon as possible.'

Constant coughed again, and the women turned their attention back to him. 'How are you feeling, kid?' asked Kit.

'Like I was kicked by a giant sloth.' He scratched along the new stripe on his arm, digging his nails in hard. 'It itches like a rash.'

'I got the tincture here that'll fix you right up,' said Kit, reaching for her saddlebags.

'No!' Constant struggled to sit up. 'I mean no, I'll be fine. I'm feeling a bit better.' He looked across at the statue of Zeus and the men kneeling before it. 'We should move off a bit and leave these good men to their worship,' he said, loud enough for any Greek ears to hear. 'We're interrupting their penitence.'

Kit and Blix all but carried Constant further back the way they had come. He sat down heavily by the side of the road and rested his weight against the base of a statue. It depicted a beautiful young woman in a clinging tunic, one breast bare, a cypress wreath in her hair. With one hand, she reached over her shoulder to draw an arrow; with the other, she held both a bow and a struggling doe deer by the ears. The inscription read "Artemis of the Wastelands. Mistress of the Hunter's Moon." The last words caught Blix's attention and made her feel strange again. She could feel the moon, pulling her inside out. But then she saw the statue opposite it and her stomach turned over. A beautiful young man, naked save for a cloak wrapped around one outstretched arm; at his feet lay a snarling wolf, so lifelike that Blix suddenly felt cold.

'"Apollo Lycegenes,"' she read aloud. '"Born of the Wolf."'

'Say what?'

'Nothing. What's up with those beardy-weirdies?' She jabbed the air theatrically. 'All that.'

'They're talking to God,' said Constant. 'To Zeus, not to each other and certainly not to us. They didn't speak to us even when you were being aggressive. Silence among men must be part of their rite.'

'It's creepy.' Blix looked back to the praying men and scowling.

'Religion is, to those who don't believe.'

'Oh please. You can cut that gnomic utterance crap right out, mate.'

'Did you find anything?' Kit asked.

'There's something there,' said Constant. 'I could feel it. Only one. It's weak. I don't know if it's enough.'

'Better than nothin',' said Kit. 'I reckon we gotta take the chance. Never look a gift horse in the mouth. We should go get it. Maybe they like diamonds too. You got another Rock of Gibraltar up your sleeve?'

'They won't sell it. Power is worth more to them than money. I felt that.'

'Then we can, ahem, get it another way.'

'I don't agree,' said Constant. He heaved himself up and took a couple deep breaths, wheezing like broken bellows. 'Something is wrong in that city. Really wrong. I could feel the crowd. They're excited beyond belief. They're building themselves up to something. The sacrifices that Mendoza mentioned, probably. Crowds breed madness. I think Mendoza was right. I think we should move on.'

He blanched and coughed violently, but waved away Kit's steadying hand. 'There's something else,' he continued when he could speak again. 'I don't think you've noticed something important. We have a problem.'

'Yeah, I probably didn't see it because it was hiding behind all our other problems,' Blix said with resignation. 'Let's have it then.'

'The days are shorter here.'

'Excuse me?'

'It's almost evening again. We haven't been on the road that long.'

Blix took in the lengthening shadows, surprised she hadn't registered the time of day. 'You're right, I hadn't noticed. This must be their winter season then. It doesn't feel like winter. Summer must be brutal.'

'That's not what I meant. I think the whole day is literally shorter. I think a day on Shambhala is about the same length as an Earth day. I can't be sure, but I estimated the time from noon to noon at about eighteen of the hours I am used to. At most.'

'Really? Wow. Okay, no reason why that shouldn't be how it works here I suppose. I thought the days were longer on Ceto. Not seeing why that's a problem though.'

Constant met her eye. 'It means moonrise tomorrow is sooner than we think.'

'Oh. Great. That's just great.'

'We can do it,' said Kit. 'Get in, get it, get gone, get off this damn world before -
'

'Yes, thank you,' Blix interrupted.

'Sorry. Well, that's what I think we should do. One vote each way. I guess we're a democracy. You get the tiebreaker, kiddo.'

'Um. I don't know. We *can't* get stranded. But if the city is that bad... I don't know.'

'Don't sweat it kiddo, I got an idea.' Kit rummaged in the inside pockets of her jacket. 'Well lookee here, a gold dollar. Ain't seen too many of those since silver bullets became part of my stock in trade.' She held up the tiny coin, so Blix could see it. 'We'll let Lady Liberty decide. If it lands heads up, we go to the city. Wreath up, the fishing village. Call it.' She flipped the coin high into the air.'

'Heads,' Blix said immediately.

Kit caught the coin in mid-air. 'Alrighty. City it is.'

'Hey! You didn't let it land!'

Kit gave her an old-fashioned look. 'Luck is for suckers, kiddo. When it was up there you decided what you wanted. Let's do that.'

'I think this is a mistake,' said Constant. He put up his hood. 'But okay.' He coughed hard and spat. 'Let's go. Night is coming.'

As Constant walked away Blix look at where he'd spat. It was still red with blood.

As they reached the point where the road entered the rocks, Kit glanced back. 'Those old dudes are following us.'

The worshippers had risen from the feet of Zeus and were processing in single file down the road toward them.

'Let's hurry along,' said Blix, anxiously.

The road entered the rocks and quickly became the floor of a high canyon. A canyon which was full of people. Although there was only one narrow path through the rocks, it seemed that every flat surface and crevice large enough to hold a person was occupied by one, from the canyon floor to high up its walls. Greek men, and occasionally women, dressed in traveling clothes and looking like they hadn't seen a bath for a while, were camped out along the way. Anywhere not big enough for people held a statue, icons to the Greek Pantheon surrounded by votive candles and offerings. The people seemed to be waiting for something, sitting or squatting in the same eerie silence that the other Greeks on the road had shown - but watching them. Blix was terrified. Only the fact that Kit had not drawn her gun made Blix keep hers in her holster.

'Kit-'

'Shhh.' Kit put a finger to her lips. The watchers perched like a gallery of vultures, ready to swoop down on them and pick them clean. But no one attacked. Indeed, as the three of them passed along the road it seemed that their passing was the catalyst for a change. Blix heard a stage whisper - 'It's time! It must be time!' followed by an angry hiss of 'Silence, heathen!' But the word 'time' suddenly came from everywhere, a susurration of excited whispers along the canyon walls. Men and women peeled themselves away from their purchase and came out of their bolt holes, coming onto the road with Blix, Kit and Constant - not to follow them, as they were quickly overtaken by the first few to join them, but to follow their lead. As they approached the city gates more and more people move around and ahead of them. They started to pick up the pace. As the numbers grew, Blix found herself walking a little faster as the rhythm of the stream of people carried her away, them walking faster still, them almost bouncing into a skip-step-jog as the numbers of people around her suddenly swelled. Then she was running, running without knowing why, and Kit and Constant ran alongside her, the people wide-eyed and excited, all in silence.

They swept toward the open city gates, past stalls and stables, past guards in white armour, past houses and shops, along the cobbled streets and upward, ever upward, sweeping up people as they went until the crowd surged into a plaza before the great acropolis like a river bursting over rocks and into a deep pool beyond.

Kit grabbed Constant and physically pulled him sideways through the crowd. Blix followed, ducking and weaving to avoid the Greeks. They flattened themselves against a wall near another entrance to the square and let the people swarm past them. Blix struggled for breath.

'What in tarnation happened?' Kit whispered.

Constant was panting heavily and had turned a little grey. 'We set something off by walking down the road. They were expecting someone else. The men from the statue. We beat them to it.'

'Let's hope no one's angry. Hey, look at that!'

Blix looked where Kit pointed, and saw the bull.

It was colossal, bigger than the biggest bonasus in the Mendoza herd. Made of gleaming bronze, it was incredibly life-like, posed as though turning to charge the people who now flooded into the square to stand before it, mouth open to bellow in outrage. The mouth seemed to be hollow, like the funnel of a fountain statue. It dominated the square, standing on a raised dais before the steps leading up to the citadel at the highest point of the acropolis. Piles of wood underneath the statue made it look like it had just trampled a forest.

The crowd, thousands strong now and growing in numbers by the second as more and more people flooded into the square, raised their arms in supplication before it, swaying in wordless exaltation.

'We should amscray,' Kit hissed. 'This is church, ain't nobody gonna thank us for crashing their revival.'

'The artefact is near,' said Constant. He squatted, resting his forehead on the backs of his hands as they crossed his knees, staring at the ground. 'Very near. I can feel it.'

Blix looked around helplessly. 'Too many people. We'll never find it. What does it look -'

A deep blast of brassy noise cut Blix off. Not trumpets, something else. A whale-call moan, long and low, unlike anything she had heard. It felt like the sound of sorrow. It came from behind her, from the street they had run through. The people nearby looked that way, their faces full of fervour and anticipation. Many of them were carry branches torn from young olive trees, which they brandished like trophies.

A procession of men appeared from the street behind. First soldiers, an even one hundred, in gleaming gold breastplates with studded leather skirt straps and high-domed helmets with broad, sweeping cheek guards. Then came four banner-men, carrying long staves with what looked like ancient battle shields tied to them, each one yellow with a bull painted on the boss - a bull with a man's head. Musicians followed, carrying huge triton shells, conches bigger than their torsos, holding them high and blowing deep and long, sending out a resonance fit to raise Poseidon from the fathoms. And then came the old men they had seen at the statue of Zeus, in context now obviously priests, clad in white and crowned with laurels, parading with immense dignity as the crowd genuflected to them.

The last of the priests carried something above his head. It was a man's face mask, once gilded perhaps but now the colour of rust. It was the face of a bull.

Constant shot up, electrified. 'That's it!' he gasped. 'That's the artefact!'

'Steady,' warned Kit quietly. 'We ain't doin' nothin' with the city watching.'

The sea of people parted to allow the procession to approach the brazen bull. The priests mounted the platform and stood before the immense animal, facing the crowd. The triton shells sounded one last time. The priest holding the bull mask stepped forward. Blix recognised him as the man who had pointed at her at the statue. He stared imperiously out across the crowd. Blix was suddenly glad there had been no soldiers with him earlier.

'Children of the light of Apollo!' he shouted suddenly. 'We have been silent as our God is silent. But the time of silence is over!' An enormous, deafening roar went up from the crowd. The people nearest Blix cheered wildly and began babbling excitedly to each other as though the words had been bottled up inside forever and were now spilling forth uncontrollably.

'How long do you think they've been silent?' she asked, but the priest spoke again before the others could respond.

'Children of the blood of Zeus!' The God of Gods has spoken!' he cried. The crowd responded with ecstatic cheering. 'His son Apollo blesses us with his radiance! He shines gently upon us! He draws out the pestilence that afflicts us! He casts it out! He shares his bounty with us! Blessed be Apollo!'

The crowd roared again, working itself into a frenzy of joy. The priest was now pacing back and forth, almost bouncing with righteous indignation.

'Our forefathers fell from the arms of the Gods! They fell because they were impure! Because they were unclean! Because they were decadent! Because they treated with outlanders!'

'Uh-oh,' said Kit.

'But we have sacrificed! We have sanctified and purified ourselves! We have regained favour!' The harvest will be bountiful! I have seen this! I have seen this in my mind's eye!'

People in the crowd were openly weeping with joy and, Blix realised, relief. The priest encouraged them to greater cheers, then cut them off into silence with a slash of his hand. 'We cannot take Apollo's favour for granted!' he declaimed. 'We must expiate our sins!' And then in an enormous voice he cried, 'THE GOD DEMANDS SACRIFICE! BRING THEM FORTH!'

Over the mighty roar of the crowd Blix heard screaming. More soldiers entered the square, passing so closely by Blix that she could have reached out and plucked the plumes from their helmets. Behind them came prisoners, men and women, naked and chained at the feet and hands, a dozen or more of them. Overseers whipped them on, stripping the flesh from their backs as they stagger-ran forward. The crowd parted as they had for the priests but as the prisoners passed they struck them, spat on them, whipped then with their branches and whatever they had to hand, aiming for their faces and genitals, screaming in delight as the naked sufferers screamed in agony. When they reached the dais they were bloody wrecks, but the whip-wielders forced them on.

'We need to get out of here,' said Kit urgently. 'Right now.'

'Let Apollo hear the scream of the bull as we sacrifice!' shouted the priest. 'Let the smell of their flesh be sweet in his nostrils!'

He thrust the rusted bull-mask high above his head. Instantly the side of the gigantic bronze bull swung open, a hatch hinged at its belly swinging down to reveal a hollow inside. The reverse of the hatch bore steps leading into the beast. As the crowd screamed the overseers whipped the condemned inside. The hatch swung closed of its own accord, slamming shut with a deathly clang and trapping them inside.

'Let the bull sing of our sacrifice!' screamed the priest. He thrust the mask into the air once more. With a strange *whump* the woodpile burst into flame.

'Now, now, we leave now,' Kit hissed. She grabbed Blix's shoulder to pull her away, but Blix resisted, dragging herself from under Kit's hand.

'We can't leave! They're going to kill those people!'

'Yes, they are, and there's nothin' we can do about it. We're outnumbered thousands to one. We gotta get gone. I was wrong, we can't get that thing. We have to leave before they notice us or we'll be next.'

As the bull's metal body grew hot the people inside began screaming. And as they did, the bull began to bellow, the cries of suffering amplified and filtered somehow into a strange, crazed lowing. It was hideous, the sound of horror, the sound of madness. Blix clutched at her head, sickened beyond belief. 'They're burning them alive! We have to stop it. It's fucking *evil*!'

She spoke too loudly. Heads turned.

'Who said that?'

'Heresy!'

'It was the girl! That one!'

'Look how she's dressed. Look at her friends!'

'Outlanders! *Spaniards*.'

'Time to go,' said Kit, slipping her rifle from her shoulder. The others grabbed their gear, Blix shouldering Kit's saddlebags too.

'Weapons! Call the guard!'

'Heathens! Defilers! Apollo will curse us!'

'Get them!'

'Run,' said Constant. 'That way!' To Blix's surprise and evidently to their accusers' surprise too he ran not back down the street behind them, but diagonally across the city square to a side street far away from them. Kit reacted quickly, bundling Blix into a run.

A ripple of heads turned their way as they fled. Fingers pointed. A surge toward them in the crowd broke almost instantly into a torrent of pursuers. Blix ran as hard as she could and quickly caught up with Constant. 'Which way?' she shouted, hanging on to the doombag for dear life.

'I don't know! This way!' he plunged down a side street.

'Goddammit!' Kit paused at the corner to fire back toward their pursuers with her rifle, a couple of shots in quick succession, aiming above their heads. The leaders hit the ground. 'And stay down!' Kit yelled. But those that followed ignored the prone men and charged forward, trampling them underfoot. 'Goddamn it!' Kit cried again, and ran after the others.

'The docks are this way! Down here!' panted Constant, turning again, then 'And here!' and 'Here!' then 'Here! Oh no!'

A dead-end street blocked their path, a narrow alley piled with bins and broken boxes and strewn with rotting food. High stone walls were unclimbable on all sides. To the left a wooden door covered with peeling red paint was the only way on. Without even pausing for thought Kit shoulder-charged it. It didn't give even a little and she reeled away clutching her arm. 'Goddamn it, stand back, I'll shoot out the lock!' she cried.

Before she could raise a weapon, Blix stepped in front of her and with a cry that was part snarl kicked the door so hard that it tore from its hinges, twisting and hanging on the lock before fall inward. 'In, in!' she cried to her companions, plunging into the darkness within.

Her eyes adjusted immediately, a night sight that was not human. The door led to a commercial kitchen, cold and deserted. They reeled through another door, down a short corridor and into a taverna dining room, emerging beside the bar where it curved into a long L-shape. A central well-square held an obstacle course of chairs and tables. Long benches covered with red velvet lined the walls. A stair of slats in one corner led upward. On each side there were gauze-curtained alcoves with small tables. Everything was shut up and locked away, and in darkness. But Blix saw the way through.

'The front door, there!' She dodged around the furniture and smashed the door open as she had before, emerging into the street beyond, reaching for her pistol as she saw people walking away from them further down the street. They didn't hear the crashing and didn't turn to see Blix brandishing her gun.

'Wait!' Constant pulled her back into restaurant. 'Hide here! They'll think we've run through!'

Kit hit reverse gear. 'Good idea! Spread out!' She vaulted back over the bar and ducked down in the crook of the L, hidden from the door they'd just come through. Constant slid under one of velvet benches and disappeared in the darkness beneath. Blix looked around for a hiding spot. Suddenly she staggered, as though knocked off balance, as something strange happened in her ears - and then she heard voices. Not from inside the building, but from the alley they had entered from. Further than human ears could hear.

A man. 'This way! No! Dead end!'

A woman. 'I thought I saw -'

A different man cut her off. 'Shut up and go home, woman. This is not your business.' He spat. 'They're not here.'

'They could be hiding,' said another man. 'Search the trash!'

'There's a door! It's broken!'

'Inside! Guns ready!'

Blix looked around wildly, made a move for the stairs, then stopped as she heard feet running through the kitchen, down the corridor. It was too late. She took a deep breath and stepped back into an alcove, steadied the curtain, and ducked under the tiny table. She held her pistol ready.

I can see them. They can't see me. Not until their eyes adjust. Not unless they look.

Men burst into the room, wild and furious, lunging forward, careening into the bar. The one in front waved a handgun crazily and let off a couple of shots. The barrel blazed brightly in the darkness, the report rang blisteringly loud in the confined space. Blix jerked and clutched her head, dropping the pistol, barely stifled a scream as the sound of the gunshot stabbed her newly sensitive ears. Her pistol bounced off her leg and skidded away beyond the curtain, sliding to a halt at the foot of the stairs.

Blix's half-stifled scream was covered by the much louder screams of their pursuers.

'Stop firing!'

'Man, are you mad?'

'I can't see! They could be here!'

'Anyone could be here, you fucking idiot!'

'Shit, I'm deaf.'

'Are they here?'

'The door! Look at the door!'

'It's kicked through!'

'Can't see a damn thing.'

'Come on! They're getting away!'

'Come on! Come on!'

A dozen men groped through the darkness, knocking over chairs and tables as they rushed to the far door, crashing through into the street beyond.

'This way!' shouted the gun-waver, charging away to the right. The others followed.

Most of them. One man stopped suddenly at the threshold and put his arm out, stopping the last two men from leaving. They all carried rifles.

'What -' began one of the men, but the first put a finger to his lips, then raised it toward the ceiling, then pointed back toward the stairs. The others looked back, then nodded as understanding dawned. They crept back into the room.

Blix made herself as small as possible under the table. As the men approached she was torn between watching them and staring at her gun, only a few feet away but as distant as the moon for all the good it did her. It had come to rest part way under the first step, barrel pointing back toward her.

They'll see it. They'll know someone's here.

They'll find me.

I'll tear them to pieces!

The first man was whispering to the others, though it rang like stage-speech to Blix's heightened senses. 'Kleitos and I will go up. Tryphon, guard the way. If anyone but us comes down, deal with them.'

Tryphon nodded resolutely. The others ascended the stair with exaggerated cautious, sticking to the edges to minimize creaking.

They didn't see the gun.

Tryphon glanced into Blix's alcove but saw nothing but the furniture. He stood with his back to the gauze curtain, rifle pointed up the stair. Everything was silent for a moment, save for shuffling sounds through the floor as the other men crept through the rooms above. Then the man called Tryphon started fidgeting. Stepping from one food to the other. Scratching himself. Looking around.

He'll look down.

Trembling, Blix inched forward. *He's big. Bigger than me.* She slid the gutting knife from her belt. she stood up and, very gently, pushed aside the curtain. She reached up and around the man's neck and put the knife to his throat.

'Don't move,' she whispered.

The man went rigid.

'Speak and die. Say nothing and you might live. Nod carefully if you understand.'

The man nodded carefully. His sweat trickled onto Blix's hand. She was suddenly aware of how scared he smelled. It set her heart racing.

She looked across the room. Kit was watching her from around the edge of the bar. Their eyes met. Silently, Kit raised her pistol and pointed it to the stairs, then the ceiling, then pointed a finger at herself. Blix shook her head, then tipped it toward the man she held at knifepoint. Kit understood. She took a knee, then carefully drew a bead on the terrified man.

Blix whispered in his ear. 'Now, you listen to me, Tryphon of Akragas.' She pressed the knife a little harder. Something trickled into her hand that wasn't sweat. 'Do you see my friend over there by the bar? Look through the stairs. Just nod if you do.'

A tiny nod.

'Now, in a moment I'm going to take this knife away. But if you move even a little my friend is going to make a big hole right between your eyes. Then your widow will be rich, because those are silver bullets. But you'll be dead. Understand?'

He nodded, the smallest movement he could make.

'Now, look down. See the gun beside the stair? Kick it under. Good boy. Okay. When your friends come down, there's no one here. And when they go to leave, you need a piss, so you'll catch them up. Be convincing. Right?'

A muscle in his neck twitched.

'Good boy. Now remember, if you give us up, you die first. Remember this and live.'

The creaking overhead suddenly became thumping and banging. With a sudden sweep, Blix pulled the knife away and disappeared back into the darkness. The other men emerged from the door at the top of the stairs and clumped back down.

'Nothing,' said the leader. 'Brothel-beds and pisspots. Whore belongings. No people.'

'There's nothing down here either,' said Tryphon, slightly too loudly. The other men didn't seem to notice.

'Waste of time,' said the one called Kleitos. 'They ran through. Let's see if we can catch the others. Tryphon, are you bleeding?'

Tryphon clutched his neck. His hand came away with a line of blood smeared across it.

'Oh! I... I was scratching. I topped a spot. It wasn't ready to pop.'

The leader curled his lip in disgust. 'Please. Tryphon, you're a troll. Come on, let's find the others.'

'I... need to piss. I'll catch up with you.'

'A troll, I say it again. I pity your wife. Piss, then. We'll follow the street of the potters until it meets the corner of the place of coopers, then right, behind the acropolis. If you don't find us, we'll be at the brazen bull in an hour. Hopefully with demon heads on poles. Clean yourself up, too, you're sweating like a pig. You need more exercise.'

Typhon watched them leave. He waited without moving. Eventually Kit said, 'I reckon we're clear.' She got up and came over to Tryphon, gun still pointed at his head, and looked him up and down. 'Well, lookee here. Guess you really did need to piss after all.'

'What now?' said Constant, crawling out from under the bench.

'Now we leave this fucking hell-hole,' said Blix. As she walked past him Tryphon bent as far sideways as he could to avoid her without moving from the spot.

'What about the artefact?' Constant asked.

'Screw it,' said Kit firmly.

'I agree.' Blix retrieved her gun. 'If we go back, we die.'

'We still need something. Otherwise a few worlds from now, we're done.'

There was a sudden hubbub in the street ahead. Kit kept a weather eye on the door as she spoke. 'We'll find something else, kid. That damn bull mask is the centre of the world to these idiots just now. It's too dangerous to... What's that matter with you, boy?'

Tryphon was shaking, but not with fear. His face was suddenly mottled with fury.

'Demons! Outlander demons! Here to destroy us!'

'We ain't here to do shit,' said Kit. 'Less'n you make us,' she added, inclining the gun pointedly.

But the Greek did not care. 'You'd steal the god's face! End his favour! Take what is ours!'

'We don't want what's yours. Well. We did. We changed our minds.'

'That's what you always say! Then you come, you come and you burn and-'

'Enough.' Without warning Blix took a swing at the man, hitting him hard on the side of his head. He collapsed, unconscious. 'We haven't got time for his problems.'

Kit's eyebrows were in her hairline. 'You knockin' people out now, kiddo?' She checked the unconscious man. 'Laid out cold. That's a hell of a punch you got there.'

'I did karate. Always drive through. Come on, let's head for the docks, find something that floats and get the hell away from here.' She headed for the door.

'Wait a minute. We need to think.' Constant worried at his forehead with the palm of his hand. 'They're looking for us. They know what we look like. Not just those ones. They must have spread the word by now.'

'Seems likely.' Kit hitched a thumb toward the door. 'We should vamoose.'

'What will they be looking for, though?' Constant described a circle in the air with his finger, taking in all of Kit McCoy below the neck. 'This is what they've seen, your clothes. This, and your hat and jacket Blix, and my sword and robes. The Mendozas were right, we stick out a mile. We need local clothes.'

'Whore belongings.' Blix bounded up the stairs. There was silence for a few seconds. 'Come on up.'

The upper floor was divided into tiny cubicle-like rooms, barely wide enough for the narrow cots they contained. Kit surveyed one with curiosity.

'Brothel beds, the man said. He wasn't wrong. Ain't no one ever slept under these sheets. I ain't judging though. These folks don't exactly seem liberated, a gal's gotta make her way as best she can.' She opened a few doors. 'Don't see no clothes though.'

'Down here.' Blix led them to a closet at the end of the hall. It was full of gauzy dresses in exciting colours, hanging on pegs. Blix held one up. She could see straight through it. 'I can't remember the last time I wore a dress. I'm not sure this qualifies as a dress, there's not enough of it. You'd catch your death.'

'It's not for wearing, it's for taking off. This is more like it.' Kit reached beyond the diaphanous things. She hauled out two thick red woollen dresses with long sleeves and held them up against herself. The hems brushed the floor.

'And look.' Blix picked up more red material from the wardrobe floor. 'They come with hoods.' She pulled one on. It covered her whole face with only a slit for the eyes. 'No, they're veils. Iqbal in my Chemistry class, he's from Pakistan, his mum wears one of these when she goes to the shops. It's a... burka? Niqab, that's it. She's lovely.'

Kit was struggling into a dress, pulling it over her clothes. 'Suits you. Suits our purposes more. Nothing for boys here, kid,' she added from within the robe.

'Then I think our friend downstairs is about to make a donation,' said Constant. 'Change quickly,' he added as he ran back down the stairs.

The red wool was clean and soft and made Blix realise how long it had been since her last real wash. 'Urgh. I need a launderette, like, *so* badly. I want to take my clothes off, not put more on.'

Kit stopped what she was doing and gave Blix a look so direct it made her heart pound. 'I'll help you out of those clothes.'

Blix blushed scarlet and looked at her feet, then the ceiling, anywhere but at Kit. 'This is really not the time.' The she took a deep breath, and looked straight at her. 'But yes,' she said. 'Maybe, yes. We should really, really talk about that.'

'Hurry up,' said Constant from below.

Tryphon had been stripped naked. His tunic looked like a dress on Constant. 'It smells,' he complained. 'He really is a troll.'

'Healthy though. Very healthy.'

'Kit! Oh my God.'

'Relax kiddo. I ain't in the pork market right now.'

'Oh. My. Actual. God.'

'Enough,' said Constant, sounding not-himself.

The boy had wrapped his sword in the sheet that had covered it when Blix has first met him, that she'd worn after the werewolves had attacked her. Seeing it brought the memory to the surface. It wasn't far beneath it.

'I feel exposed,' she said, flapping the thick dress angrily. 'Even with this on. Exposed and wrong. This isn't going to work. We don't look right. People are going to look.'

Constant bundled his robe into a ball and thrust it into his bag. 'They will. But what they'll see is wrong they understand. Wrong that's almost right, not wrong that's completely different to them. That's what they're looking for. They're looking for, well, you heard him.' He nudged Tryphon with his foot. 'They're looking for demons.'

Kit shouldered her rifle and strapped on her gun belt over the dress. Suddenly the weapons looked absurd. Blix strapped on Ángel Gabriel's pistol anyway.

'Let's hope you're right, kid,' said the American. 'Folks are riled up around here.'

'All we need is to pass one glance,' said Constant. 'We won't be waiting around for a second glance. Come on.'

'Wait a minute.' Kit grabbed Tryphon's rifle and tossed it to Blix. 'Waste not, want not.'

'Right on.'

As the women head for the exit, Constant stood over the unconscious man. 'I hope you don't die,' he said seriously. Then he followed on.

Chapter Twenty-Six: A Bad Thing

It took all their nerve not to run.

Through the darkness, avoiding torches and lanterns and the warm glow behind windows and doors, they walked. They moved past people before the people knew they were there. But Constant was right - if they attracted a first glance, by the second they were gone.

We're getting a lot of first glances, Blix thought.

The news had spread. The word 'demons' was on everyone's lips. They passed as quickly as they dared through the angry city, heading north to where they thought the docks would be. Narrow streets and looming buildings made the place feel oppressive, closed in, threatening.

Blix could smell the river ahead of them. The scent led her through the maze of streets, guiding her when the way forward was unclear. It drew her onward.

They turned out of an alleyway onto a broad thoroughfare, leading to a wide crossroads with a central circus. A colossal marble statue filled the space at the centre; Theseus and the Minotaur, the former slaying the latter.

Kit held them back.

'Lot of open ground to cover,' she said, her voice slightly muffled by the niqab. 'We'll be exposed.'

Blix pointed across the circus. 'The river's just behind those houses. I can s-'

'-mell it, me too.' Kit drummed her fingers on the wall as she played the odds in her imagination. 'I don't like it. Not enough people to blend in and those that are there get to take a long look at us. Nope, don't like it. Let's find another way.' She turned back into the side street.

Blix felt a slight surge of annoyance at her timidity. 'The angry mob's back that way. These people don't know anything. We can use the statue plinth to break sight lines so that no one sees us for the whole time we're out there. We're almost there! We need to *go*!'

With that she darted out onto the broad street leaving Kit and Constant behind, heading to toward the statue, beckoning them to follow without looking back.

'Goddammit, don't run - damn fool - come on, kid!' Kit grabbed Constant's shoulder and practically dragged the startled boy along with her as she chased after Blix.

They almost made it.

'You! Stop!'

Blix was almost at the statue, but the authority in the speaker's bellow brought her skidding to a halt without even thinking about running, so suddenly that Kit and Constant almost ran into her. Three hard-faced men, soldiers or guards, approached from the west side of the circus. They were armoured in the Ancient Greek style, but where their ancestors would have carried spears these had rifles slung in the low ready position, and wore revolvers on the opposite hip to their swords.

'It's the law,' whispered Kit. 'Act natural.'

'What the fuck is natural?' hissed Blix. 'We should kill them!'

'*Don't kill people.*'

Blix almost asked why.

'In the name of Xanthippius the twenty ninth, General of the city, I detain you!' cried the leading soldier. He wore a plume where the others had none. Its slightly ragged appearance spoke to his real status. He was about the same height as Kit and slightly built. The others were larger and stronger. A few civilians paused to listen as the soldier spoke but a fierce look from him sent them on their way again.

'Yes, sir. Please, sir, we've done nothing wrong, sir.' It took a fraction of a second for Blix to realise that it was Constant who'd spoken. His voice was childlike in a way she'd never heard before.

'Haven't you,' snorted the plumed soldier angrily. He glanced at Kit and Blix's rifles, unworried by the weapons but glaring with utter contempt at their stolen clothes. 'Why are you whores on the street on a feast day? You know the law. Flog your poxy cunts in the red houses! Keep your indecency inside! Thirty strokes of the rod each! And you,' he continued, sneering at Constant, 'boy in his father's clothes. Out for your first jump, are you? Pathetic. A dozen for you.'

He stepped closer to Kit. 'Although you have taste, boy. I've never seen such eyes…'

He frowned then, as if not quite realising something. 'Never seen such eyes,' he repeated. His own eyes narrowed. He ripped off Kit's veil and then a moment later Blix's too. He looked back at Kit. 'What manner of metic are you, woman? Where are you from?'

'Laüs,' said Blix immediately. Eyes flicked from Kit to her. 'Which is seventy miles upstream, if you don't know. It is a long, dusty and boring walk from there to here. Our symbol is -'

'Shut up,' said the leader. 'Who said you could speak in public? I said nothing to you.'

'She's lying,' said one of his men, abruptly.

'What?'

'Lying. Look.' Kit's cowboy hat was on the ground next to her saddlebags.

The plumed soldier breathed out sharply. '*Huasos.*'

'Howdy,' said Kit, and suddenly her pistol was pressed hard against the soldier's neck. 'Nah ah ah,' she continued as the others quickly raised their rifles to aim at her.

She grabbed the soldier and, with a strength that no longer surprised Blix, twisted him around until he was facing his men. She forced her arm against his throat and pulled him back until he was off balance. She shifted her gun to his temple.

'Don't nobody do nothin' stupid. A man looks mighty strange with his head blown off. Kinda cramps his style. Now, here's what's gonna happen. Kiddo, get my stuff. Then chicken-hat here is gonna walk with us across the way while you fellas stay here. Then he's gonna go to sleep real sudden. Then we leave. Everyone lives to tell the tale. Now drop those weapons, *compadres*.'

The other soldiers did not respond. The barrels of their rifles followed Kit as she moved. Blix was riveted by the sight.

'Did you hear what I said? Ground those rifles!'

The soldiers did not react. Around the circus people started noticing and pointing, and coming toward them.

'Kit,' Blix said, the warning clear in her tone.

'Listen you sons of bitches, I ain't joking. Anyone think I don't mean it?'

'They are trained not to care,' said the leader. 'They are trained to take the first opportunity to kill you. Through me, if that is the only way. We do not surrender!'

Kit exhaled sharply. 'Well, ain't that a kick in the pants.' She thought for a second, and grinned. 'Say now. Answer a question, boys. Which one of you gets promoted if this asshole dies?'

Blix caught the barest flicker of corner-eye contact between the two men. Then they looked over Kit's shoulder. Blix remembered her gun and started to turn, but it was too late.

'I do,' said the soldier who'd crept up behind Kit. He slammed the butt of his rifle into her head and she collapsed, face down on the cobbles. Two others levelled their rifles at Blix and Constant. 'But it will not be today,' he finished, staring down at her. He transferred his gaze to Blix. 'Drop the death-makers, whore.'

Blix threw her guns to the ground, where they rattled uselessly next to Kit's revolver. 'Bastards,' she said.

'I had an honourable birth,' said the soldier, without humour.

'I also,' said the leader. He kicked Kit's prone body as hard as he could. There was a sharp, wet crunch as her ribs broke. Kit coughed and spat blood, but she didn't wake up.

The leader held out his hand for his second's rifle. He examined the butt momentarily, checking to see whether Kit's head had damaged it. Then he smashed it between Blix's eyes, sending her spiralling into blackness.

Blix saw a stone floor moving under her, and heard a scraping sound. Her arms hurt, but not as much as her head. Her vision swam in and out of focus.

I am being dragged along a corridor. A dark corridor. I don't know where I am. My clothes are gone. I am in my underwear. I am in pain.

A man was muttering to himself.

'... why the fuck do I get all the shit jobs? What was wrong with the cell upstairs? No one cares if a woman screams. I'm better than this dog work. Shit!' Blix felt his grip loosen and the ground suddenly rushed up to meet her.

'Oof! Ow.'

'The whore awakens.' The man kicked her; not hard enough to break anything but enough to knock the wind out of her. 'Good. On your feet, whore. You can fucking walk.'

'Make me, cockbite,' said Blix weakly, her head spinning.

'Fine.' Blix braced for another kick. Instead there was a sudden searing agony across her back, as though the skin had been stripped off her and the flesh set on fire. The shock of it made her arch and twist around, screaming in pain. Then Blix was grabbed under the arms from behind, heaved bodily into the air, and bent awkwardly around so that the man was cradling her. A fat man, shirtless, sweating and angry. She struggled against his grasp, but he crushed her against his chest. He staggered a dozen paces down the corridor, kicked open a door. 'Get inside, you Spanish cunt,' he said harshly, and spat on her. He threw Blix bodily through the air into the room beyond.

Time slowed down. Her insides convulsed in an agony that was at once excruciating and welcome. Blix felt the wolf burn in her blood.

As she fell she twisted in mid-air. When she landed, she was on all fours and facing the man. She sprang up again instantly and with bizarre strength and inhuman agility threw herself at the man, screaming hoarsely. In one bound she was on him.

Boiling blood sweetens my mouth as my fangs sink in. The flesh of its throat tears easily as I pull my jaws away. The prey tries to scream but it turns into a strangled gurgle as I bite into its neck again. It lurches back into the corridor, desperately trying to break free from my embrace, but I am stronger than it now and it cannot escape. Something metal strikes my shoulder, there is pain but it is nothing. And then the light goes from its eyes. It staggers forward, my weight pulling it forward and down until it collapses on top of me in a mockery of love. It dies there. Its blood spills across my face and breast and I feel reborn, a wolf blooded in the hunt.

Time returned to the world. Blix remembered herself.

With the last of her strength she rolled the man off her and sat up next to him, wild eyed and panting. She sat there in the near darkness and stared with vacant fascination at his corpse while she tried to process what had just happened. As quickly as the wolf had come it had gone, and the memory of her act seemed to belong to someone else, even as the man's blood still dripped from her mouth.

'I killed him!' she said out loud, surprising herself with the idea. She spoke again, as if testing the words. 'I bit his throat and he died.' And then: 'I feel *incredible.*'

She watched the dead man. The blood no longer pulsed from the wound, but now covered his body and pooled around it. Blix watched without emotion as it reached her foot. A whip lay on the floor. It was made of sharpened metal rods, eight or ten inches long, linked together with steel rings and bound to a chain and leather handle. A weapon of cruelty for someone who enjoyed hurting others. Blix touched the wound on her back, knowing before she did so it was already healing.

Eventually she remembered to look around her. The room was a cell, stone walled and iron barred, windowless. The man wore a ring of iron keys on his belt that looked like the most clichéd kind of movie prop.

Keys meant other cells. Other cells meant -

'Kit! Constant!'

She grabbed the keyring and the whip and dashed out of the cell, the dead man nothing more than flesh to her now.

The corridor was barely lit, a couple of guttering torches at the far end the only source of light. A dozen wood and iron cell doors lined the walls. A stair led upward. Everything was still and silent. *No one heard me kill that man. They would have come if they had. That doesn't mean there's no one there to hear.* She crept silently along the hall whispering names at each door she passed. At the fourth she got a reply.

'Hey, kiddo,' said Kit weakly, when Blix got inside. 'Heard you scream. Woke me up from my beauty sleep. Are you okay?' She had also been stripped and was lying on the filthy floor, shoulders propped against the wall, clutching her right side where the soldier had kicked her, which was an evil looking purple-red and badly distended. Her face was a blackened mess of bruises where the rifle butt had smashed her. Her lips were red with dried blood. Otherwise she was almost grey.

'I killed a man! ' blurted Blix in an excited whisper. 'He hurt me and I killed him! I tore his throat out!'

'Shit.' Kit coughed violently. Fresh blood bubbled from her mouth, fascinating Blix in ways she couldn't express. 'We gotta get you off this world.' She tried to move but stopped immediately, 'I can't walk by myself. Find the kid.'

Blix darted away. A few minutes later she returned, followed by Constant. He was dressed only in his breechcloth. His face and body were coloured with fresh bruises. 'Where are you hurt?' he asked at once when he saw Kit. He knelt next to her and reached to touch her side, but the American held up a hand up stop him.

'No need. Ribs are broke. Always the damn ribs that go.' Kit winced as she spoke. 'I need my medicine. Need it, need it, need it. In my saddle bags.'

'They must be upstairs.' Blix looked down the corridor but there was still no sign that anyone had noticed they were free. 'This is a cop shop, right? They'll have, like, an evidence room, or something?'

'It's a jail under a guard building,' said Constant. 'A holding place, not a big prison. I was awake when they brought us here, they tried to knock me out but I pretended. They took everything when they threw me in the cell. I don't know where they've put it. It's been hours.'

'Jails are jails, wherever you go.' Kit waved them over. Together they helped her to stand. 'We need a way out. If we get our stuff, great. If not, I'll live. Ain't nothing we need more than we need to get out.'

'No,' said Blix and Constant at the same time.

'I won't leave without Katy's bag,' said Blix. 'She'll want it back.'

Constant looked grim. 'The whole of my faith is in my possession. I cannot walk away.'

'Well, shit.'

'Hey!' A hoarse whisper from outside startled them into silence. 'Hey out there!'

Without speaking Constant pointed at the cell opposite. Fingers poked through a gap under the door, waving at them.

'You're escaping! Set me free! I beg you!' Suddenly there were voices from the other cells; urgent, terrified whispers.

'Me! Take me!'

'I did nothing!'

'Please!'

Constant looked at the others, then back at the fingers. 'We don't know you,' he said evenly,

'Please! They'll kill me! Put me in the belly of the bull!'

'Wait a goddamn second,' said Kit, and then to Constant and Blix, 'Take me over there.'

There was a viewing slot near the top of the door. Kit slid it back. A pair of desperate eyes appeared.

'Howdy, neighbor. What did you do to be put in there? Don't lie. I'll see it in your eyes.'

There was a long silence. Then: 'I am a murderer. I killed the man who killed my father.'

This time the long pause was Kit's. Eventually she spoke, her speech slightly laboured and slurred in a way which alarmed Blix.

'What's your name, son?'

'Teleclus. Son of Anaxander. Father of Telemachus.'

'My man, you and I are about to become very good friends for a very short time. You wait there a spell. Set me down, kids. Now, unlock that door.'

'Are you sure?' Blix asked. Kit just pointed at the lock.

A few moments later Teleclus was free. He was thin and wearing rags and looked like he'd taken a few lashes from the gaoler's monstrous whip. A grim-faced young man, aged by pain.

'Thank you,' he said. 'You can trust me.'

'I know that, ' said Kit. 'Now go down the hall and ask each man who answers your call what they did to get in here. Look 'em in the eye. Anyone who ain't evil, let 'em out. I have a plan.'

Teleclus didn't move. 'How do you know I am not evil?'

'I looked you in the eye.'

Teleclus stared, blinked, and shook his head in disbelief. 'That is the strangest thing I have ever heard,' he said. 'Thank you,' he added. He bowed his head for a moment, then darted off down the corridor. A few minutes later eight other men had joined then, each as ragged and desperate-looking as Teleclus.

'Two remain,' he reported. 'I will not let them out. They lied.' He spat. 'I told them if they make noise they won't have to wait for the bull. What is your plan, woman?'

'You know this place?'

'Some. This hell is three levels deep. To ensure the sound of torture does not trouble the citizens. Above are more cells. Above that, sleeping rooms, I think. At ground level, there is the guard post and the door to the street. There will be guards. I know not how many. There are locked doors between here and there.'

'Let's hope we got the keys. Otherwise you're gonna have to do your thing, kid,' she added, looking at Constant. He nodded impassively but his left hand twitched. He balled it into a fist to cover the reaction. 'Give me that whipsaw, girl,' he commanded.

Blix had forgotten she held the gaoler's whip. She handed it to him. 'Here you go. *Boy.*'

'Your plan?' said another man impatiently.

'We don't got time for plans. The plan is, bust out and run like hell. Don't stop unless you're dead.'

Blix listened at the door, and heard voices.

'... wasting our lives. I swear, I will go to the priests and have them declare that making honest men do paperwork on a feast day is a sin against the Gods.'

'Good idea,' said another. Then, with exaggerated dryness: 'Of course, *you'd* still have to do paperwork, then.'

Laughter. Then the first voice again. 'Observe my arse, Anakletos. Your lips to my cheeks, right here.'

Blix pulled her ear away from the lock and inched back to where the others were crouching in the stairwell. 'At least six. Maybe more.'

'Alrighty then.' Kit touched Teleclus lightly on the shoulder; he was breathing rapidly and rocking back and forth, working himself up for what came next. 'When you're ready, son.'

Teleclus nodded and turned to the other prisoners crouching behind him on the stair. 'This is your last chance, dogs,' he whispered. 'It's this or death. It might be both. Run until you fall at Haides feet.'

There was a surge of hissed assent from the men. Blix slipped back to the door and, carefully holding the keys to avoid them clanking together, tried the lock. The fourth key turned. There was a metallic click which screamed like an alarm bell in Blix's ears but couldn't have registered above the banter in the room beyond.

Teleclus was already moving as Blix grasped the door handle and yanked it back. The prisoners followed him in a surge of desperate energy and as they burst through the door it erupted from their throats in a cacophony of strangled cries and screams as they poured forward toward freedom. Furniture scraped and crashed as the men pushed past it, and door slammed on its hinges.

Kit, Constant and Blix did not move.

'What the-'

'Aah!'

'Bastards!'

'After them!'

'They're getting away!'

'My sword! Throw me my sword!'

'No, you stay here! Guard the shop!'

The sound from the next room quickly died down. The three waited for a few moments. Sounds of movement came from beyond the door, accompanied by low volume but vigorous cursing.

Constant stood up. He held the metal whip high and let it unfurl. As it reached full extension it sprang back slightly with a strangely merry jingle.

'Wait here,' he whispered, walking purposefully toward the door, the whip swinging in his hand like a pendulum.

'Are you kidding?' Blix followed right behind him, slipping beyond Kit's grasp as the American tried to pull her back.

'Goddammit, kids! Don't kill anyone!'

The room was an office, or part of it was; the remainder looked like a place men came to rest but didn't care much about. Now it was in disarray; chairs overturned, desks shoved aside, papers strewn about the floor. A door had been shoved open so hard a hinge had torn loose and left the door hanging awkwardly. Beyond, a room bisected by a counter; beyond that, a door to the outside world, also broken open.

A man knelt near the first door, gathering papers from the floor, sweeping them up with the indifference of a man who wanted to be elsewhere. He wore a guard's tunic and breastplate. A short sword, still in its scabbard, lay on a nearby table, its belt trailing over the edge. The pistol holster was empty.

Constant move silently into the room. The man looked up.

'Ho, friend,' said Constant, in a pleasant way.

The man looked at the whip in Constant's hand. Then he looked at his sword.

'I wouldn't,' said Constant. 'You'll die. As if it matters.'

'Listen to him,' Blix urged, coming into the room behind Constant. 'You can just leave. That's what we want to do. Get our stuff and leave. No one has to get hurt.' She followed the man's gaze down to her blood-soaked chest. 'No one else.'

The guard was moving before Blix finished. He snatched at the hilt, pulling it free just as Constant swung the metal whip high and hard down; it clanged off the blade where the guard's hand would have been had he not drawn it back. Dull steel slid from the scabbard. The man scrambled back as Constant swung the whip again, once, twice, each time missing his opponent by inches. The man kicked a chair into Constant's path; the seconds he gained as Constant moved around it were enough for him to get to his feet and take guard against the advancing boy.

'This will just mean your death,' said Constant blandly.

'Listen to him,' said Blix again. She edged left, circling round toward the soldier, who barely glanced at her, his attention firmly on the lazily swinging whip. 'You can still get out of this alive.'

'Stupid bitch,' he sneered, talking to her but still looking at Constant. 'You think I haven't faced the qilinbian before? After I've killed this little shit I'm going to strip the flesh from your cunt with it before I throw you in the bull!'

'Ah, you're Anakletos,' said Blix. 'You had your chance, Anakletos.'

Constant lashed down hard, sparking the floor in front of the guard and then in the same instant flicked it back up and down again where a fool would have ducked away to avoid the first cut. But Anakletos was no fool; when the snaking metal came down he stayed rock still and when Constant stretched to make the second strike count he stepped forward and thrust hard. The blade sliced along Constant's hip, slicing a clean but shallow line through his flesh. Constant grimaced but didn't cry out. Anakletos leaned into the thrust to yank the blade back and cut Constant in half. Then Blix was on his back, clawing and biting his face, tearing into his cheek with her teeth. Anakletos roared and straightened to throw her off; the sword came back above his shoulder to stab her in the face but as it did so the whip-steel snaked around it and it was yanked from his grasp, clattering uselessly on the stone floor. Then the whip came back around his legs, slicing through the leather of his sandals and biting deeply. Anakletos screamed as Constant pulled once more. Tendons severed in one leg and he collapsed under himself. Blix jumped free before his back hit the floor.

Constant picked up the sword and stood over the fallen man. He put both hands on the short sword's pommel and held it straight above Anakletos head, the point a hair's breadth from his right eye.

'I did tell you,' he said.

'Please,' said Anakletos, in an agonised voice, trembling violently as he stared at his death. 'Please. I have a family.'

'I'm sure you do. They're probably better off without you. There's something wrong with you people.' He tilted his head slightly, as if thinking. 'Mind you, there's something wrong with me.'

He raised the sword an inch and made to push it down. Anakletos stiffened, and cried out, and shut his eyes. And then opened them again, a few seconds and an eternity later. The sword point hovered over him, ready to send him to his Gods.

'Tell you what though,' said Constant, conversationally. 'Let's play a game. Say my name and you get to run away.'

'I … I don't know your name.'

'That's a shame.'

'Constant!'

'No,' said Constant.

'What?' said Constant, shaking his head and grimacing. He looked around. Kit had crawled from the stairwell to the doorway and was lying there, reaching out to him, her eyes imploring even as she gritted her teeth against the pain.

'Don't kill him, kid,' she said. 'He's just some guy. You got him. You don't need to kill him.'

'Don't I?' Constant looked down at the cringing man beneath him, confused, as if seeing him for the first time. He rubbed his forehead with the heel of one hand, grinding it into the skin like he was trying to break through it. He looked down again.

'Today's your lucky day, Anakletos. You get you live. If you don't do anything stupid, that is. Blix, bar the front door. Then find some rope.'

Blix had followed his instruction before she realised it was an instruction. A glance outside revealed the light before dawn on an empty street. Once the door was secure she went hunting through the rooms that led off the main office. She hunted for several minutes before she realised she was hunting.

'I found our stuff,' she said on her return. She threw a coil of rope at Constant, who kicked the now completely compliant Anakletos onto his front and hogtied him with his least damaged leg behind him.

Kit coughed, and spat more blood. 'First things first. My saddlebag. I need my medicine.'

Blix passed it over. Kit took out the little bottle marked "snake oil", uncorked it with her teeth and took a tiny sip, sighed with profound relief and smiled her Cheshire Cat smile. 'That hit the spot.' She took some long, deep breaths, and then, gingerly, got to her feet. The colour began fading from her injured side immediately. 'That's better. Anyone else want some? Does you a power of good.'

'I will!' said Blix brightly.

Kit passed her the bottle. 'Just a drop now.'

'I would like to know what is in it,' Constant said. 'It's magic, isn't it?'

'It's medicine,' said Kit emphatically. 'Patent. Good for broke ribs.' She was visibly better, moving almost as normal. 'Good for most anything.'

'It looks like water and tastes of nothing,' said Blix, after letting a drop fall on her tongue. 'I'm feeling better, actually. I didn't know I wasn't better.'

'What is in it, please?' Constant asked again.

'You're learning kid. Ask a polite question, don't insult no one, you might get an answer. It ain't magic. One hundred percent natural.'

'Natural what?'

'Like it says on the bottle. Snake oil. Sorta. To be exact, it's gorgon blood.'

Blix spat as hard as she could and frantically scraped at her tongue. 'Are you insane? That's a deadly poison! Why didn't you say?'

Kit grinned again; she looked pretty much back to her old self. 'If I'd told you what it was straight off you wouldn't have drunk it, now would you? Sure, it's a poison. When it's neat. Dilute, it's a cure-all. My contribution to medical science.'

Blix looks sceptical. 'How dilute?'

'Point of a pin in a ten-gallon vat, then distilled to a pint.'

Blix made a disparaging *pfft* sound from the corner of her mouth. 'Homeopathic gorgon's blood? I've heard it all now. You know homeopathy is bunk, right?' She held the little bottle at arm's length, regarding it with deep suspicion. 'Where did you get the blood? Gorgons are extinct.'

'I guess I helped that along then. I killed one. It was trying to kill me first.' The grin vanished. 'That's the only time you get to kill people, kids. Not even then unless you have to.'

'Yes,' said Constant absently. 'You're right.' He looked down at Anakletos again, who was trying very hard not to attract attention while he bled out. 'Give me the bottle, please.'

Blix handed him the phial. Constant dripped the smallest drop possible onto his little finger tip. After looking at it for several seconds he licked it off. Then he bent over Anakletos.

'This will heal your leg. Do you want it? It's your choice.'

The guard looked completely nonplussed for a moment, then nodded hesitantly. Constant knelt and smeared another drop on Anakletos' lips. 'I hope you don't die,' he said seriously.

'What shall we do with him?' Blix asked.

'Gag him and leave him,' said Kit. 'Then let's get changed and out of here before his pals come back. They'll have harsh words for us if they find us here.'

'Once we get to the, uh, where we're going, we'll be okay though, won't we?' asked Blix. She glared at Anakletos, then ripped a strip from his tunic, held it to his face and glared at him again; he obligingly opened his mouth.

'That depends what you mean by okay, kiddo. They might follow us, they might not. That ain't the real problem. We've wasted too much time here. We gotta leave before… bad things happen.'

'What do you - oh.' Blix rocked back on her heels 'Oh, yes. It's tomorrow now, isn't it?'

'Yep. Full moon tonight.'

'And sooner than we think. Fuck. Let's go. What about the disguises?'

'Forget them,' Constant said. 'They're useless. Better to fight.'

'Better to run,' Kit said.

The fisherman shipped oars as his boat approached the dock and took up a mooring line. With a practiced throw, he looped the rope over the post and pulled in hard. His long boat with its little mast and sail, tiny among the river tramps and tri-masters tied up along the length of the wharf, eased in toward the jetty, pushing the muddy river water aside. He tied off the line, stowed the short sail and clambered up the ladder from the water line to the boardwalk. Another line hauled the crab pots upward. Few were occupied.

As the fisherman readied the crabs for their boxes he noticed the boy. A boy with a sword on his back.

'Hello,' said the boy. 'My name's Constant. Is that your boat?'

The fisherman considered the question and the boy. 'It is half my brother-in-law's. I take the night shift, he the day.' He scanned the dockside, dissatisfied with what he saw. 'Or he will when he shows up. The lazy bastard is still in his pit I expect, no doubt for the next hour.' His gaze returned to Constant. 'What of the boat?'

Constant held up an opal the size of his eyeball. 'I need a boat. Why don't you buy a better one?'

The fisherman gaped momentarily, then thought very fast indeed, the calculation evident on his face.

'Why don't I?' he said, reaching for the opal.

Constant pulled it back out of reach. 'It occurs to me that a smart man might wait until his former boat was out on the river and then raise a hue and cry about it being stolen. That way a lazy brother-in-law might never know that a price was paid. Or how much.'

The fisherman grinned. 'Such cynicism in one so young. The thought never occurred.'

'Surely it did not. And what do I care? Except that if a man did that he might be advised to wait a while, until the boat was long gone, in case the city decided to chase me down and bring me back. They would certainly make me tell them everything I know. What is the penalty for fraud here? I bet it involves the bull.' Constant held out the opal toward the now much less jovial fisherman. 'Maybe you never saw who took your boat. You had gone home, cursing your brother-in-law's name for his lateness. Then when he does arrive, who is to say that you aren't still out on the river? By the time he knows different I'll be long gone.'

The fisherman smiled, slightly sourly, and reached for the opal again. Constant twitched it back. 'Anything I should know about the river? Don't lie, I can tell.'

The fisherman kept his eye on the stone. 'Up river or down?'

'Down. To the escarpment. The steps to the bottom.'

The fisherman chewed his tongue, evidently weighing up whether to tell the truth, never taking his eyes off the opal. 'If you wish to visit Haides who am I to stop you? Cleave to the south shore. Beware the current further out. It is much stronger that the surface pretends. Make sure to make the bank before you reach the Fingers. Otherwise prepare to meet Achelous in his palace of the drowned.'

'What are the Fingers?'

'You'll bloody know then if you see them, landsman.' The fisherman snatched the opal from Constant's grasp. 'Now piss off before I change my mind.' He stomped off up the gangway.

'One more thing, friend.'

The boy's tone brought the fisherman to a sudden halt.

'You're a night man. What time is moonrise?'

'This day? Not long after sunset.'

'My thanks.'

The fisherman walked away and didn't look back.

Constant looked around to see if the exchange had attracted any attention. The wharf was quiet in these early hours; those few who were in evidence went about their business. He gave a low whistle and Kit and Blix joined him at a run. They jumped into the boat and pushed off hurriedly, turning as soon as they were in free water. Kit and Blix pulled strongly at the oars until they were well out into the vast water. Then they let the current take them for a moment while they anxiously watched the dock for signs of alarm. None came. Slowly, very slowly, they drifted away from the city, away from the danger and madness that it held.

'That could have gone better,' Constant said eventually, when the dock was suitably distant.

'Could have?' Blix laughed despite herself. 'It was a litany of abject failure. One long calamity. We gained nothing and almost died. And I killed someone. A human someone.' She said the last as an afterthought, as though not quite connecting the memory to the deed.

'Yes, you did,' said Kit. 'How do you feel about that, kiddo?'

'I don't feel bad about it. I feel elated. I feel *right.*'

'Right? Christ. We've got to get you off this world.'

There was another long silence. Kit and Blix applied themselves to the oars, Constant to the tiller. The boat sat low in the water. As they left the city behind the wind got up, light at first but quickly stiffening. Constant rigged the little sail with the ease of an expert. 'I think I was a waterman once,' he told the others as he tied off the sheet. 'I think I liked that.'

As he spoke, Constant felt the memory of Comen sen-Hersa in his mind once more. Felt the man's fear of hurting others, his need to be alone. Heard him in his voice when he spoke. 'Sit you here, landswife,' he said to Kit, waving her to the tiller. 'Hold her. Turn as I say.'

He ignored Kit's contemptuous snort of 'landswife!', and hauled in the oar that Kit had vacated. He saw the water through sen-Hersa's eyes, read its story, saw its beauty.

'Do you think that fisherman will grass us up?' asked Blix, sliding her oar back into the boat.

'I don't know. Probably.'

'What if they follow us?'

Constant trailed a hand in the water; it parted and reformed behind it, leaving no trace that he had touched it. 'If they follow us they'll catch us. Let's hope they don't follow us.'

Chapter Twenty-Seven: Downriver

Blix dreamed.

The boar is dying. It screams as it tries to stand, tries to run, tries to escape from me. I cling to it and close my jaws around its throat and soon the screams and the boar are no more.

My teeth slice into the soft flesh and I swallow. The howling emptiness inside me is filled at last - for now.

I sense something that should not be there. A presence where there should be none. There is another creature in the forest. It sits in the shadows of the undergrowth, watching me. Smaller, nimble, built to dart and strike. It sits, seen but unseen, watching, waiting. I growl but it does not run. Teeth flash white. Yellow eyes shine in the darkness. A fox's eyes.

'Wake up, kiddo.'

Blix opened her eyes and stared into the deep pure blue of the sky, beyond the gold-tinged white of the clouds. For a moment, she felt as if she was falling into it from above and vertigo gripped her; then the boat lurched forward suddenly and a sharp pain in her spine corrected her perspective. She was lying on her back, head at the bow, feet under the oarsman's plank where, a minute ago to her mind, she had been sitting with Kit. She was soaking wet; water sloshed around her. One arm was threaded through the loops of the doombag, which was sitting on her chest like some squatting homunculus. Her own satchel was wedged under her back and, she discovered, was completely sodden.

'Have I been asleep?'

'We all have,' said Kit. She was also looking damp. 'I ain't never been much of a sleeper kiddo, but I guess when your body says so, off you go.'

'I tried to stay awake,' said Constant. He was wrapped around the tiller pole and looked pale and haggard. 'I failed. I didn't dream...' He looked a little confused, as though trying to remember a word that was on the tip of his tongue. 'The day has passed,' he added. Blix felt the now familiar fear start eating into her stomach.

Neither of them were looking at her. 'What's happening?' she asked. Constant said nothing, but pointed to the river bank. Blix sat up.

A pack of werewolves kept pace with the boat, loping along the high, rocky river bank about three hundred yards away. Blix counted a dozen of them. Now and then one of them looked in their direction. Blix recognised the leader instantly.

'Fuck, it's him.'

She slumped back down, clasped her hands around the back of her neck and bent double, trying not to be sick. She felt really strange. The old terror came back in full force, but now it was accompanied by an excitement that made her feel twisted inside. She steeled herself and sat back up. 'When did they catch up to us?' she asked.

'They didn't,' said Constant. 'We caught up with them. They were ahead of us.' He patted the tiller. 'We're further away from the bank now.'

Blix looked incredulous. 'Ahead of us? How is that possible? Following us is one thing, knowing where we'll be is something else. *We* didn't know where we'd be. How did they?' She found her eyes being drawn back toward the werewolves, despite herself; she turned her back on them and folded her arms.

'They must have the Thing,' said Constant. 'I lost it when we crashed in the desert. They must have found it and worked out how to use it.'

'They're clever dogs, no doubt about it,' said Kit. 'There's some good news though. Did you see? Maybe you only saw fur and teeth. There's only twelve of them now. Roohsk musta done us a solid before... I mean, twelve is good.' She slapped the butt of her pistol. 'I got eight silver bullets right here, the kid can kill the rest. When the opportunity arises,' she added darkly. Blix didn't get it.

'There's bad news too,' said Constant. He didn't take his eyes off the werewolves.

'Naturally,' said Blix, with a sinking feeling. 'What is it this time?'

The boat lurched forward again unexpectedly, and Blix was thrown hard against the port bow rail. She realised for the first time that the boat was moving quickly. The water roiled about the sides of the boat.

'That,' said Constant. 'The current is ferocious.'

'That's a good thing, isn't it? The faster we get to the next gate, the better.' The sun was low; to Blix, the reddening sky was a threat that became bloodier by the moment. Even though she wasn't looking at the werewolves any more, Blix could feel them, almost hear their harsh panting as they ran along beside them.

No, not almost, really - it's not my imagination at all. Wolf senses. I can hear them.

The thought made her skin crawl. The thought made her want to howl.

'Good and bad,' said Constant. 'At this speed we certainly have a fighting chance of getting you to the next gate before moonrise. It's not far from the base of the escarpment.'

'And the bad?'

'That would be the giant waterfall slightly before there.'

'Good point. Let's land.'

Kit pointed meaningfully at the werewolves. Blix pointed equally meaningfully at Kit's gun.

'You said it yourself. Twelve werewolves, eight bullets. Get blasting. Let's even the odds out a bit.'

Kit laughed. 'Thanks for the vote of confidence kiddo, but this ain't Sells Circus and I ain't Frank Butler, y'know? Two hundred yards with a pistol? If I graze a hair on a wolf's ass it'll be a miracle.' The boat surged and heaved upward suddenly, sending Kit tumbling backward from her seat into the hill. 'There's that, too,' she said, getting back up. 'Like the kid said, this water's getting excitable. And noisy.'

'More reason to land and blow them away there. Constant can have a go with the silver wolf-sticker if you miss one.'

'That's a good idea,' said Constant. 'Where shall we land?'

Blix glanced over her shoulder. Large, smooth boulders lined the bank. She couldn't see anywhere that looked even remotely plausible to heave to, as far as she could see. 'Oh.'

'The fisherman said we should make land early,' the boy continued. 'I think we might have missed our moment.'

'Great.' The boat clunked hard against something. Blix's head clattered against the bulwark. 'Ow! Bloody hell. Okay. Behind door number three we have the other bank.' She peered across the water. The far side was just about visible. 'Looks like a nice easy slope. Let's go there.'

'There's no way down the escarpment on that side,' said Constant. 'The map only shows steps on this side.'

'Marvellous.' Blix glowered and kicked the side of the boat with her heel. 'Do you ever think the universe is maybe conspiring against us?' She turned the glower on Constant. 'That's you, that is. You should have a word with yourself.'

Constant opened his mouth to reply but was knocked sideways as the boat struck something in the river and scraped along it. He clutched at the tiller as it swung away from his grasp and wrestled it back under control. 'What was that?'

Behind them spikes of rock poked above the water's surface. Sharply serrated, it looked like the hand of some strange creature clawing to the surface. Others like it lay ahead.

'The river's shallowing,' said Kit. 'That ain't good.' The boat scraped along another rock with a screech that set Blix's teeth on edge. She became aware of a huge increase in the noise level up ahead; the sound of raging water.

Blix scrambled to her knees and risked a quick look over the side. 'Jesus, it's ripped a huge chunk out of the wood! A few more like that and we'll be in pieces.'

'There are more than a few coming.'

Constant was working hard at the tiller, but the boat was borne so quickly by the surging waters that it barely mattered. 'We're going where the river takes us for a while.' He raised his eyes from the water ahead and met Blix's. He was haggard with worry.

Blix clung on as the boat bucked and juddered. 'I really don't want to go over a waterfall, Constant.'

'I know.'

'I mean *really*.'

'I know.'

The boat juddered violently along the river bed, the wood moaning like a wounded animal. One of the planks buckled and burst. Water poured through the new gap. Blix grabbed her hat, already floating in the bilges, and started to bail.

Then they were in mid-air, and leaning forward, and falling. The boat dropped away; gravity remembered them a moment later and they fell after it, ten or fifteen feet, then were sent sprawling and tumbling as the boat flopped back into the water.

'What th-' Kit struggled up. 'A falls! A goddamn step! You never said anything about no goddamn-'

'Another one! Hold on!' Constant grabbed the tiller.

Blix was thrown violently sideways and smashed her head against the rower's seat. A moment of ringing and clouded distance; then she was herself again.

'Everyone stay exactly where they are,' Kit ordered.

The boat had grounded itself on a rising lip of the falls, where a shelf of rock breached the surface. The front third of the boat was hanging in mid-air over the drop. It shuddered as the turbulent water swept past it over the edge.

But it was not the great falls, Blix realised thankfully as she risked a peek. That was still to come. The river dropped away in a series of steps ahead of them. As it fell, it separated - jagged spires of stone thrust into the sky, turning the broad river into a series of increasingly narrow gorges as it descended, channels of wild rapids which twisted and snaked so that the river's end could not be seen from where Blix sat. It looked like the whole river has been squeezed until its back had broken. The word *earthquake* appeared in Blix's mind. It was followed by the word *teetering*.

The drop under her was no more than twenty feet. That was more than enough to kill them. Blix felt a bit less thankful. 'You could have told us,' she said reproachfully, when she'd got her breath back.

'They're not on the map,' said Constant. 'They must be recent.'

'What's holding us?' asked Kit.

'Nothing much. Don't make any sudden movements.' He peered across the width of the river, their vantage point allowing him to follow its broken courses as far as he could see. 'I count four gorges. I bet there's another beyond the last. These are the Fingers.'

'I don't care what they're called. What do we do now?'

'We look over there,' said Kit, pointing at the near bank. 'Company's coming. Look.'

The werewolves had followed them, clambering carefully down through the boulders until they were level with the boat on the bank at the edge of the drop. The companions watched as one who wasn't the First of Wolves started out toward them, hopping from rock to shallow, leaning against the flow of the river.

'Oh, come on!' Blix's despair became anger almost immediately. 'One disaster at a time!' She almost thumped the boat, but remembered just in time. 'You know, one of these days we're going to catch a break and the shock is going to kill us.'

'We make our own luck, kiddo.' Kit rose smoothly, drew her pistol and took aim over her forearm, one eye closed. Then with exaggerated care she braced a foot against the base of the little mast, and waited. The werewolf got closer.

Blix didn't see Kit pull the trigger. The werewolf was about halfway to the boat when the bullet burnt the air between them. The boat rocked with the recoil, but didn't move forward.

'Son of a bitch.'

The werewolf had twisted at the last moment. Kit had missed. Barks and yelps were exchanged with the bank, then a sharp roar from the First of Wolves. The one who had ventured out into the river began the journey back to dry land.

'At least now they know we still got silver,' said Kit. She sat down as smoothly as she'd risen. 'They can smell it in the air.'

Not smell. Taste. Blix felt the irritation like acid in her throat. She realised it had been there since she'd woken up. 'You should have waited until it was closer.'

'Maybe. Maybe better to give myself time for a second shot if I needed it. Particularly seeing as the tiny paladin here can't exactly swing his sword while we're hangin' offa this drop, can he? Might knock us off.'

'Great. Back to the sixty-four-thousand-dollar question then. What do we do now?'

'I'm open to suggestions, kiddo.'

'What about you?' Blix asked Constant. But the boy said nothing, only flipped up his hood and leaned his chin on his fists, not meeting her eye.

'Just *great*.'

Blix watched the werewolves regroup on the bank. They stood in silence and watched the boat. Watched *her*.

Blix stood up so suddenly that the boat swayed dramatically. She pointed fiercely at the First of Wolves and shouted at the top of her voice. 'YOU! JUST PISS OFF, YOU!'

The First of Wolves stared impassively at her.

'WHY ARE YOU FOLLOWING US?'

No reaction. Blix knew he could hear her. She stamped her foot in frustration; the boat rocked a little.

'WHERE'S MY SISTER, YOU BASTARD?'

For a moment, it seemed the response would be the same. Then the First of Wolves raised one finger to his throat and with cruel deliberation drew it across. Yips and howls from the other werewolves - wolf laughter.

Blix sat down hard and burst into tears.

'Hey now,' said Kit, concerned. Shifting her weight carefully, she reached across and put her hand on Blix's. 'Don't let that lyin' dog upset you, kiddo. Your sister ain't -'

'I know she's not,' said Blix, pulling her hand away sharply. 'I'm not crying because of him. He's not worth the salt. I'm crying because I'm *angry*.' She glared at the werewolves, and suddenly bared her teeth at them. 'I want to run over there and tear them to bits.' She looked back at Kit. 'I want to tear *you* to bits.'

She looked west. The sky was a burning cloth of gold, the sun almost touching the horizon. Her insides cramped up horribly.

'It's coming, Kit. The wolf is coming. I can feel it. Rising in my blood. What do I do?'

'I have a plan,' said Constant. He stood up and hitched his bag higher on his shoulder. 'Anything you want to keep, hold onto it now. As if it matters.' He took a step forward. Then another. Then suddenly he was running. Two steps from the bow he jumped, up and forward. He landed heavily on the prow. And then he fell.

Blix grabbed at the doombag as the boat slid forwards and leapt as far as she could over the side. She hit the water hard and awkwardly and sank like a rock into the deep pool below. Moments later she struck bottom with a jolt of pain masked by the shock of the fall and the turmoil of the water. She barely had time to register the sullen thud and scrape as the boat ground against rock before she was swept away, yanked downstream by the ferocious current. She shook off her wellingtons and kicked for the surface but the water-filled doombag held her back, ballooning like a drift anchor on her left arm. With the right, she reached up, up to the surface and beyond it to the moon. *Give me strength* she thought without thinking. Then the wolf was there, its power flowing through her, and she surged upward and broke through the water with a gasp that might have been a howl.

Kit was only a few yards away, captured by the water, her saddlebags floating behind her. She saw Blix and shouted to be heard above the torrent.

'Thank you, Jesus! Keep your head above water kiddo! This river's tryin' to drag us under! Where's the damn boat?' She looked around wildly, expecting to see the little boat bearing down on them. Blix looked back; it was wedged at a steep angle under the falls.

'Where's Constant?' she yelled.

'Here!'

The boy was ahead of them by some distance, only just visible in the twilight. He was facing back toward them, floating almost serenely in the raging waters. The pommel of his great sword bobbed above his head like a buoy.

'You stupid son of a bitch!' Kit screamed furiously. 'You coulda killed us!'

'It was the only way. We have no time.'

'You should have told us! You should have asked! We should have talked about it!'

'All you do is talk! *We have no time.* I know-'

He vanished.

'What the-' began Blix.

Kit cut her off. 'Oh shit, here's another one!'

Then Blix was in mid-air, and just as suddenly underwater again. Hidden rocks tore through her jacket and cut into her shoulder. She screamed and choked on water. Instinctively she kicked upward; she surfaced, coughing up the river.

Kit was there again. 'You okay kiddo? Where's - oh no.'

Blix was blind in the darkness and ferment of the river - and then suddenly she could see, see through animal eyes. She followed Kit's gaze.

Constant floated ahead of them still, but something was wrong. His head lolled awkwardly. Blix tried to swim toward him, but the current was too strong now. 'He's going to drown!' she screamed.

'We're all going to drown if we don't fall first!' Kit yelled back. 'Try and get closer! I'm gonna do something!'

'What?

'I'm sorry kiddo, I- '

The world opened beneath them.

Constant dreamed.

In my dream two men walk along the beach towards us. They wear shabby red robes and their heads are shaved. They look thin and weary, as though they have travelled far and eaten far less than they need. They are still some way off when they Recognise *me. I start to cry, although I do not know why - but then I do know. I am crying because I have been found. I am crying because I know who I am again, and I can go home. I am crying because I do not know what that means. I am crying because I have lost everything.*

In my dream my father hears me cry, feels the wetness on his cheek. 'Whatever is the matter, little sparrow?' he asks. Then he turns, sees the men. I feel his body stiffen. He knows what this means. All men do.

'He is Recognised,*' says one of the monks, as they draw closer. 'We must take him home.' He looks unwell, but also somehow ecstatic, as though his life's purpose has been fulfilled.*

'No,' says my Father, *holding me close.*

'Yes,' I say, softly. He does not hear me.

'You know what this means,' says the other to my father. He coughs hard, then recovers himself. 'All men know. He must come with us.'

'No,' says my father, I hear the anger in his voice. Anger and fear. He shifts my weight into the crook of his right arm, leaving the other free. He pulls something from his pocket. I cannot see what it is.

'Yes,' I say again.

'No!' my father shouts, and as he does so he throws out his arm, straight and hard as if pushing something. Suddenly the monks are flying, lifted from their feet by an impossible force. They hang high in the air for a moment, then suddenly veer away at a right angle as my father's arm makes the same motion. They tumble through the sky in a clumsy arc, far out into the ocean. They plunge into the depths. In my dream, I hope they can swim.

The stone in my father's hand glows white, then begins to tarnish and crumble. In seconds, it is covered in rust-red dust. My father throws it away. Then he puts me down on the sand and turns me to face him. He bends down. He puts his hands on my shoulders. He does this very gently, but I seem to feel a great weight. I feel him shaking.

'We have to run,' he begins, and then checks himself. He smiles at me, trying not to scare me. I am not scared.

'We have to fly, little sparrow,' he says. 'Fly far away from here. Somewhere they can never find us. Somewhere we can be together.'

I look at him. I smile at him. He is my father, and I love him.

'No,' I say.

Now there is a boy here I do not recognise.

'Can you fly, little sparrow?' *he says.* 'Now would be a very good time to learn. WAKE UP.'

Constant did not remember the boy when he woke up.

I am flying, Constant thought. *I am flying.*

I am falling.

Constant's eyes snapped open. He shot his arms out straight from his shoulders, screaming as pain ran through them like lightning burning up from his fingers. The breath was knocked from his body as he slammed into something, hard. He felt as if he was holding onto something too tightly, something grasped firmly in each fist. But there was nothing there. Something heavy pressed down on him from above, straining his arms as if they were branches breaking from their tree. But there was nothing there. He lay on his back, gasping under the immense weight, his head swimming in confusion and pain, the deafening roar of water washing his mind clean. He tried to focus, to remember.

'Holy. Actual. Fuck,' someone said, very close and very far away. Constant looked up.

Blix and Kit were dangling in mid-air, hanging helplessly in nothing as the waterfall thundered past them. Kit was upside down and facing away from him. Blix was spread-eagled in the air not ten feet above his head. Even with only the last glimpse of light left in the sky, Constant could see her terror.

'Why are you flying?' he asked, struggling to shake the daze that turned his head to mush. His arms were really screaming now. The invisible weight on his chest felt like a mountain. 'Come... down... here.'

'Are you kidding? Look down!'

Constant rolled his head sideways. He scrunched up his eyes, and then blinked furiously until suddenly his vision cleared. Then he saw what scared Blix. Nothing. Hundreds and hundreds of feet of nothing, disappearing in the darkness below with the ferocious torrent of the falls.

'Oh,' he said, and let go.

There was a moment of bliss as the pain left him and the weight lifted. Then he was falling, falling, watching as his friends fell, tumbling head over heels, shouting, screaming, falling into oblivion with him.

Can you fly, little sparrow?

'No,' said Constant, before he realised he had said the words himself. He slammed his arms out straight once more and instantly stopped falling. The shrieking pain sliced through his arms and suddenly the weight was back, worse than before.

'Great day in the morning!' Kit was rightwise up this time, saddlebags hanging across her shoulders as though someone had casually draped them there while they went for the stirrups. She clutched them with one hand while the other held her pistol in its holster. 'How in God's name?'

But Constant couldn't answer. Pain whipped through his arms; it felt like his tendons were snapping. His back spasmed savagely and twisted in on itself. 'Can't hold it,' he muttered, and let go.

He plummeted, body limp, watching dreamily as his friends pinwheeled through the air.

You're going to die, little sparrow, part of him thought. He didn't know which part. *They're going to die.*

As if it matters, thought another.

'It matters,' whispered Constant. He stretched out his arms.

'Fuck!' screamed Blix as she decelerated suddenly again. She hung there, arms and legs spread wide like a spider clinging to an invisible web.

'Keep it up, kid!' shouted Kit, upside down again. 'We might not die after all!'

'Can't... hold...' croaked Constant, barely audible above the falls, bending as though he was being torn apart. 'The weight... can't bear...'

'Let me go!' shouted Blix suddenly. 'Let me fall!'

'What? No!' Kit tried to twist to see them. 'Don't you dare!'

'Do it!' Blix screamed. 'Whatever I hit down there, I can survive it!'

'No! You haven't changed! Goddammit kid, don't you let her go!'

Constant let them all go.

Constant dreamed.

In my dream, now there is a boy here I do not recognise.

'I hope this won't hurt you,' *he says.* 'You're unconscious, Constant. The magic is doing terrible things to you. But you must wake up. Otherwise I'm going to have to leave you. I don't want to do that. You won't care. You'll be dead. WAKE UP.'

Constant howled in agony and stopped dead in mid-air. Kit hung almost level with him. Blix...

Kit shouted 'No!' but to was too late. Blix disappeared into the darkness. Her scream was abruptly cut short.

'You son of a-'

'I can't anymore,' said Constant, and let them go.

He fell, and -

- there is darkness and silence and then pain and water and relief and no air and water and I'm drowning and my arms weigh me down and dive little sparrow! dive into the ocean! and my father no not my father someone else's father someone I used to be and there was a boy I don't understand and now there are hands and I am rising and no breath -

'No you don't, you son of a bitch! You don't die before I kill your ass!'

Hands pressed hard on his chest and he vomited water. He coughed harshly and felt muscles in his sides tear. He couldn't stop coughing and couldn't pull in air. Then his throat relaxed, like a fist unclenching, and he dragged in ragged, wet breaths, spitting and hacking as his lungs recovered. He tried to put a hand to his mouth, but there was no strength in his arms at all. It was if they were weighed down by lead. He let his arm fall back down. It splashed, and Constant realised he was still in the water.

He became aware that Kit was standing over him, pulling him up by the front of his soaking robe.

'Do you see what you did? Do you see what you did?' she cried, her voice a broken husk of itself. He could barely hear her over the roar of water. She dragged him to his knees and grabbed a fistful of hair, twisting him and pulling his limp head up.

They were in the shallows of the great plunge pool at the base of the waterfall. White water boiled and foamed furiously then flowed away in a broad, majestic river. Immense boulders broke surface here and there, smooth where they faced the waterfall, jagged on the lee. They must have missed the rocks by a whisker, he realised. Now they were near the south bank, suddenly far from danger. Constant had no memory of how he got there.

A small, detached part of Constant's mind, probably containing his own personality, wondered how he could see all this. He looked up and saw how light the sky was. The silver-grey of moonlight behind clouds.

'Blix!' he gasped. 'You have to-'

Then he saw her.

Blix hadn't missed the rocks. Her shattered body lay transfixed on a spike of dolomite that rose from the edge of the pool like the prow of a sunken ship. Her back was broken, limbs splayed at frightening angles, face torn away in a ragged flap of skin and flesh that made it look like she wore her own death mask. She didn't move, didn't scream, didn't breathe.

'She's dead,' said Kit. She let Constant go. He slumped sideways, but the point of the scabbard on his back dug into the mud and held him up. Kit sat down hard, close beside him. He let his head fall on to her shoulder. She didn't shrug him off. Instead she put her arms around him and pulled him in.

'The medicine,' whispered Constant, gasping for breath. 'The gorgon blood, use the gorgon blood!'

'Don't you think I did? She's dead.'

'The wolf, the wolf in her blood, it will heal her, it will fix her!'

'She hasn't changed. She can't come back from this.'

'The corpse flowers then, you said it could bring people back from the d-'

'It was a joke!' Kit screamed. 'She's dead!'

They sat there, drained, unable to move, the sound of the waterfall filling their ears, numbing their minds.

'This is your fault,' said Kit, quietly.

'Yes.'

'I oughta kil-'

There was a sharp crack, ringing through the water noise, and Constant felt Kit start shaking.

Blix was getting up. Her broken back straightened, the bones knitting and the flesh becoming renewed. The bloody mass hanging from her skull reformed into a face and secured itself in place. In barely a minute she was standing up, slightly unsteadily, clutching the doombag to her chest as though it held her beating heart and staring at them, astonished.

'What just happened?' she asked.

'You're alive!' Kit shouted, elated.

'I know. What happened to me?'

'Hot damn!' Kit whooped, leaping to her feet. 'God bless you, sweet Medusa! I'd kiss her right on her scaly lips if I hadn't killed her.'

'Great Fathers, it brought her back,' Constant whispered, fighting with all his strength not to faint. 'It brought her back.' His words failed.

Blix was ignoring him. She was staring at the sky. 'It's so beautiful,' she said.

A thrill of terror turned Constant's spine to ice, but it gave him a voice too. 'Get her inside! Get her inside now!'

'What? Inside where? We're outside!'

'Behind the waterfall! There's a cave!' He looked up. There was a break in the clouds. It moved toward the light. 'Now! Before the moonbeams hit her! Now, now!'

Kit was already moving. She sprinted through the shallows as though the water wasn't there. As she reached the rock spike she leapt, higher than seemed possible, higher than *was* possible, one, two, three bounds to the top, stepping so lightly that she barely touched the stone. She rose under Blix and shoulder-charged her at waist height, lifting her bodily with no apparent effort. After two more strides she leapt again, down into the deep water of the plunge pool. It didn't slow her. A sharp turn brought Kit back to shallow water, Blix over her shoulder. Constant saw Blix's face; oblivious to being lugged around, open mouthed with wonder, one arm raised imploringly toward the sky.

Then Kit made the bank, then the path behind the waterfall, and then they were gone from his sight, hidden behind silver sheets of water.

The moon came out from behind the clouds, reflecting a light as bright as day.

Constant waited until his heart stopped racing. Then, very slowly he rolled over onto his hands and knees, sinking a little into the mud. With immense effort he pushed himself up until, teetering as though they were his first steps, he could stand. He unstrapped the scabbard and slid the great sword around until the hilt was under his right arm. An arm that felt like it was encased in stone.

He pushed back one of the sleeves of his sodden robe, then, exhaling heavily, the other.

'Well,' he said, as though there was someone to hear him. 'Well. As if it matters.'

The effort of speaking out loud exhausted him, but there was one more thought, a thought whose enormity demanded to be heard, if only so he could persuade himself he believed it.

'It brings back the dead.'

And then: 'I can survive.'

He looked to the sky. The enormous moon seemed to stare at him, to pull at him, to draw him in.

Maybe the wolf is in all of us.

'You didn't win,' he said defiantly. 'You didn't win.' He trailed off, and let his eyes follow the path behind the waterfall. 'I don't think you won,' he continued feebly, as his energy gave out. 'Time to find out.'

His eyes sought the stair cut in the rock that led up the cliff. He thought he saw it; barely shaped surfaces, rising into the sky. He traced it upward to the top of the falls. Was that movement, far above?

'One long calamity,' he muttered. Then, carefully using Sorcha as a crutch, he limped toward the waterfall.

Chapter Twenty-Eight: Memory

Blix screamed.

The white eye. Staring at me. Calling me, lifting me, pulling me. The beautiful eye, the eye of God!

'Let me go! Let me go out! Let me go back! I need it! I need it!'

'Snap out of it, kiddo.'

The eye calls and I must answer, but the creature pins me down, its weight pressing me into the rocks. With all my strength I buck and twist and I scream and claw and fight as hard as I can but when I rise the creature throws me back down and when I scream it does not listen and when I rake my claws across its face it does not flinch.

'Come on now kiddo, come back to me.'

The eye fills my mind. There is nothing else. I will not be stopped from joining with it, bathing in its reflected radiance, living, changing, becoming myself. Yet the creature still holds me close in its embrace. I tear at its flesh as hard as I can, try and bite but it holds my head down. I rage at the thing that hold me. Why I say why why why won't you let me go? I need to I need it I

'Are you okay?'

And suddenly the eye recedes, a vanishing point of light in the darkness. And now it is gone.

'I need to... I need to... What? What's going on?'

'Thank God. Praise Jesus. I thought you were dead!' Kit's arms were around her, holding her tight, holding her in a way she'd never been held before. Tears trembled in her voice. 'I thought I'd lost you!'

'I can't see. Kit, I can't see!'

'It's just darkness. We're underground. You had a close call, kiddo. A close call.'

Blix's heart was beating so fast she thought her chest might break in two.

'I can't see anything. 'Am I still me?'

A deep breath. The playful lilt returned to Kit's voice. 'Well now, I don't rightly know. I can't see nothing in here neither. You ain't barking though, are you? You ain't acquired a new fur coat. Although, you know, I could just check some more...'

'Ah, no thanks. I'll look myself. When I can see.'

This should help,' said Constant, shockingly close.

'Oh my God don't do that! I nearly leapt out of my skin!'

'Did you though?' asked the boy. Then he appeared, rounding a corner Blix hadn't known was there, a lowlight blooming into dim illumination as he came nearer. It gave edges to the darkness but not much more. Kit's smile, even more Cheshire Cat than usual, sparkled in the gloom, inches from Blix's face.

'Howdy ma'am.'

'Um. Hi. I'm okay now. You can get off.'

'I like it here.'

Blix felt her blush must be visible even in the darkness. Kit laughed, and rolled off her.

'Where are we?'

'Under the waterfall.' Constant rubbed the first lowlight over another and blew on it gently until the dull grey surface of the second had turned orange. He passed it to Blix. 'Quite a way under. It took me a while to catch up.'

'Figured it was best,' said Kit. 'In case I was too late.'

'You weren't,' said Blix. 'I think.'

'Glad to hear it.'

'You picked up Blix like she was weightless,' said Constant to Kit. There was no accusation in his voice, just an inflection where one might have been.

'Why, ain't nothing to her, is how! I've seen more meat on a butcher's apron.'

A look passed between them, something shared which didn't need to be spoken. Kit nodded, then it was gone.

'Hey, is that what I think it is on your shoulder?' the American continued. Constant slung the saddlebags across to her. She fielded them against her chest.

'Hold that light a little closer, kiddo,' she said, unbuckling one of the bags. Constant leaned awkwardly toward her, bracing himself on the silver sword. It seemed a real effort to hold up the light. 'Well, shit. Most everything's broke.'

As the light made Kit's face more than a vague outline, Blix gasped, and held her hand to her mouth in horror. 'Your face! What happened to your face?'

Kit's face was streaked with blood. Her cheeks looked as if they'd been gouged with a broken bottle. She flashed her wide mouthed grin, but it turned into a wince half way through.

'You did, kiddo.'

Blix suddenly realised she had Kit's blood on her hands. She rubbed them frantically on her shirt. 'Kit, I'm sorry!'

'Don't sweat it.' Kit plucked a little bottle from the wreckage in her saddlebag; miraculously, it was unbroken. 'Madame Medusa will take care of it presently.' She dropped a spot of the liquid on her tongue and sighed contentedly. 'That hits the spot.'

'How much of that do you have?' Constant asked.

'I got a pint back in Utah. Got maybe a thimbleful left here.' A strange look suddenly passed across her face, as though she'd only just grasped something that had previously escaped her. 'Try not to get killed again,' she said seriously.

I died. 'God, yes. It must be Constant's turn anyway.' Contemplating the absolute horror on the boy's face, she added, 'That was a joke.'

'A joke. Oh. How do you feel?' The way he was leaning on his sword had changed subtly. It made Blix wonder whether he was preparing to use it.

I died. She paused before answering, wanting to remember, scared in case she did. Then suddenly it all came rushing out.

'I feel okay. Fine. It didn't even hurt. No, that's not right. It hurt, but I didn't mind. I wanted it to hurt. How do I feel? I feel lost. Like something wonderful has been snatched away from me. I wanted to change more than anything in the world.'

She looked away, trying to find something in the darkness, something to hold on to. 'Now, I still want to. I want to go outside.' She looked at Kit, her face still almost invisible even in the lowlight's glow. 'I would have killed you if I could,' she said quietly. 'I remember... I was strong...'

'Not that strong. Hey kid, you got one of those fire rods for me?'

Constant produced one. He struck it against the rock and waited until the meagre light crept along the length of the baton.

'Light in the darkness,' he intoned. 'Possessed of infinite compassion. Consumed by unimaginable wisdom. I honour you with my being.' His face convulsed for a moment, and then he was still again.

'What was that?'

'Part of the prayer I should be saying now. They will have to wait.' Constant handed the glowing stick to Kit. 'It was a good idea to bring these. I should have thought of it.'

It took Blix a moment to understand what he'd said. Then she gasped, and checked the doombag. 'Half Katy's stuff is missing!'

'I think I have some of it,' said Constant. He shifted awkwardly, grimacing in pain, and twisted his bag around. 'They were on the path to the cave mouth. They must have fallen out when you were being carried.' He handed over a few small items. 'I found your rope, Kit. And your hat,' he added, handing the battered and bedraggled headwear to the American. 'Not yours though, Blix.'

Kit knocked the crown of her hat back out and looked at it critically.

'Damn, it cost me almost twenty-five bucks. Suppose it'll dry, maybe I can find a hatter and get it reshaped.'

Blix was doing a frantic inventory, scraping out sodden notebooks and paper to see what was underneath. 'Where's Katy's compact?' She demanded. 'And her earrings? Where's her *purse*?' She knew it was trivial, stupid even, but suddenly she cared about nothing so much in the whole world.

'In the pool, somewhere, I expect. I didn't see them.'

'She'll want them back!' Blix scrambled to her feet, then remembered she was bootless. Then just as suddenly she was yanked back down onto her bottom. 'Ow! What the-'

Kit held her firmly. 'No you don't, kiddo. You're not going back that way until the moon is safely under the horizon.'

'We're not going back at all,' said Constant. 'We're going further in.' He pointed in a direction which might as well have been into the abyss. Only darkness defined it. 'That's where the gate is.'

'Really? Lucky we came this way,' Kit said.

'Yes. Lucky. That's us.'

'I said, she'll want them -'

'Forget them, they're gone.' Constant spoke evenly, but Blix suddenly saw he was shaking with emotion. 'We have to go *now*. The... the werewolves are coming.'

Blix saw his eyes move, the slightest flicker barely visible in the gloam. She heard the hesitation and knew instantly what it meant.

'You were going to say, "the other werewolves," weren't you,' she said bleakly.

'Yes. Sorry.'

'It's okay. I'm feeling okay about it, actually.'

'Don't,' said Kit at once. 'Don't accept it. That's the wolf talking.'

'I really want people to stop saying that what I say is about someone else.'

'We have to go now,' Constant repeated. 'The werewolves are climbing down the escarpment. I thought I saw them near the top, but even if I was imagining it they'll be doing so soon enough. They're coming for us. We know how well they climb,' he added bitterly. 'It will take them a while, but not long enough.'

Kit peered into the darkness, but there was nothing to see. 'How far to the gate?'

'I'm not sure. A couple of miles, perhaps. Perhaps more.'

'In this light? We are gonna get wolfed in the ass.'

'Never mind the light,' Blix moaned. 'My wellies are downriver somewhere. This isn't the desert, I can't walk in my socks here. My feet will get slashed up.'

Kit pulled her tall boots off and pressed them against Blix's chest, leaving her feet completely bare. 'We're about the same size. Put 'em on quick.'

'I can't, you'll -'

Kit interrupted. 'I told you kiddo, I'm an outdoors gal. I got feet like leather. Don't argue, do it.' She hauled herself up, and stared meaningfully at Blix until she started pulling on the boots. To Constant she said, 'Don't suppose you found my rifle?'

'No. I think it sank.'

'Figures. Well, that is definitely the most expensive thing I ever lost.'

Blix felt for the pistol that the young Mendoza had given her. The holster was empty. She showed the others. 'I am terrible at keeping hold of weapons. Not destined to be a famous warrior, me.' She was surprised how sorry she was to lose the young man's gift. It had meant something to him to give it to her, something which had a value for Blix she hadn't quite realised.

'Well, I still got my pistol,' Kit declared. 'And seven silver bullets. That's a fighting chance.'

'I still have my knife,' Blix noted.

'Me too. Let's hope no one gets that close. Best start putting one foot in front of the other,' she continued cheerfully. She looked critically at Constant. 'If'n you can. You look like you're a bad way.'

Constant, still shaking, clung grimly to his sword-crutch as though he would crumple in on himself if he let go.

'I'm freezing,' he said. 'Soaking and freezing. Aren't you?'

Blix realised she was. She also realised something else was stopping her from feeling it.

'I was,' said Kit. She took another drop of the snake oil. 'Now I ain't. But I don't think that's the whole story here, kid. May I?'

Before Constant could object Kit had levered herself up from her rock and gently pushed his left sleeve up to his shoulder. Along the length of his arm a network of rust-red canals snaked along his skin, upward from his fingers, far worse than had been there before. They glistened in the lowlight's glimmer, stark against his pale flesh, like veins of ruby running through chalk. Constant didn't try to shake Kit off. He looked like he didn't have the energy.

Kit traced the iron lines along Constant's arm. He shivered at her touch. 'This shit is eating into you,' she said. 'I've seen people use magic. This didn't happen to them.' She let the sleeve fall; it caught on his elbow and left the forearm exposed. 'Why is it happening to you?'

Constant looked very weak and afraid - very twelve, Blix thought.

'I don't know. My arms feel like lead. Like I'm being dragged downward, into the earth.' He tried to rally, affecting his usual grim demeanour, but it looked to Blix like he'd just decided to put on a mask - the real Constant was still there for all to see, exposed and vulnerable.

'I know what it's doing. One of me knew. Magic has to come from somewhere. It's using me like an artefact. But I don't know why. I'm doing something wrong. Not preparing properly, or something, I don't know.' He closed his eyes. 'Do you remember back on Shambhala, there was something wrong with the trees? It looked like this. Maybe... something drained... something...?'

He rubbed his forehead fiercely and shook his head so hard Blix thought he might twist his neck. 'Arrgh. Thinking about this stuff makes my head hurt. I'm not supposed to know magic. It's in the Book. I've never been taught.'

'Maybe it's time to educate yourself. In the meantime, I suppose you ought to have a pull.' Kit offered him the bottle. She seemed much more reluctant than before.

Constant's eyes narrowed. He took the bottle but held it at arm's length at the neck, as if it might slither out of his grasp and sink fangs into his hand.

'I don't want to. I know what it does, but I don't know what it's doing.' But in the same breath he brought the bottle to his lips and swallowed a drop, his face contorting with such evident anguish that Blix wanted to knock the bottle from his hand to protect him from himself.

'You said -'

'I know. I can't walk in this state and we have to go.' He sighed deeply, straightened and flexed his legs and arms, as though rediscovering his body. He gave the bottle back to Kit, who shook it speculatively. There was the tiniest tinkle of liquid against glass. She sighed in relief.

'I feel much better,' he said. He'd stopped shaking immediately.

'The rust is still in your arm,' said Blix quietly.

Constant examined it. 'It still feels weighed down.' He swung his sword over his shoulder and sheathed it, without once looking to see where it was going. 'I can live with it.'

He walked a few steps away from them. As the light moved, Blix saw a path. Little more than dirt smoothed flat, but a path nonetheless. Then her eyes changed. The wolf looked through them and saw the path, and the cave, and the way forward.

'Where are we going?' she asked.

'Down. As fast as we can.'

- Red cords slowly tightening as though some great weight hung from their ends, dragging me into the earth -

- never learned magic. The words are enough, says brother Danas. Not enough power in them to hurt you –

- It never helps, he says. It only hurts -

- use the artefact until it rusts, then take another, there are always others to take -

- trust that there are things you shouldn't know, and I did –

- the Writing makes no sense; how can I survive –

- call me a magician, the wizard of the water margins, but I am not, I am scared to be, scared of Nothing -

Constant stopped walking so suddenly that Blix walked into him.

'Ow.'

'Sorry.' *That thought, what did it mean?* As Constant tried to grasp it, it slipped away, a confused memory he didn't want to think about, drowned out by other voices, other people in his head, each one distinct and separate and him, always him. He said his words under his breath, making sure Blix couldn't see him, and the clamour receded, quietened but not stilled.

It's strange how normal that feels.

Darcen Ysir's memory was one among dozens again, for the moment at least. Ysir was an insistent thought though, an itch in the back of his mind that he didn't dare scratch. Constant tried to keep him close and distant at the same time. The effort was distracting.

'Ow.'

'Low bridge,' said Blix, ducking under the outcrop which had scraped Constant's scalp. 'If this tunnel goes on much further you'll be getting a tonsure, like a real monk. There was a double-decker once that had its top sheared off going under the railway bridge near the flat, Katy said... she said... Wow. Can you see this?' She rubbed her eyes hard. 'I'm not sure... my eyes are... wolf...'

'I see it, kiddo,' said Kit. 'Not sure I believe it though.'

They'd emerged into a cavern, but the word didn't do it justice. It was immense, its roof so high that it might as well have been the sky. it was warm, far warmer than the chilly tunnel they had scraped and staggered through to get there. Clouds of mist hung near the ceiling, ghostly fingers stretching across the cave. Spindly yellow stalactites hung from the ceiling, in places joining with fat stalagmites that rose to meet them, their mineral sheen a testament to centuries without disturbance. It was lit with a pulsing, silver glow, that made the drifting dust in the air shimmer like gossamer.

Their path led down to the edge of what Constant at first thought was a huge lake, but then realised was a broad, sluggish, silty-looking river, oozing over itself in sludgy folds as it emerged from the rocks. The water had a strange, oily silver tinge to it. It didn't look pleasant.

He knew straight away what it was.

'This is huge,' said Blix, marvelling. 'You could park the Ark Royal in here without it touching the sides.'

'Where's the light coming from?' asked Constant turning this way and that, looking for torches or a fire.

'Up there.' Blix pointed to the vaulting canopy of rock above.

At first glance they seemed to be tiny points of brilliance dotted against the unrelenting black. Then something stirred the air and the lights swayed with it, revealing themselves as shining pearls strung in their thousands, tens of thousands, dangling on silken threads from the cave roof. To Constant's eyes, craving light, it was as if the cave was open to the heavens and a galaxy had been born from nothingness, swathes of stars scattered deeply across a blue-black bolt of sky. It felt like creation.

'That is remarkable. It's as beautiful as the First Temple.'

'Let's admire it in retrospect, kid,' said Kit. 'We gotta hustle.'

'Yes,' said Constant. Something inside him had switched. Darcen Ysir was nowhere to be found. Someone else looked out from his memory. 'Charon of Lampsacus,' he whispered. 'You were not a liar. I have seen it, Jamyang.' He craned his neck to look straight up at the hanging lights. 'What are they?'

Blix piped up promptly. '*Arachnocampa luminosa.* Glow-worms. Fungus gnat larvae, in fact. They glow more when they're hungry. The adults glow too, but-'

'There are people here,' said Kit sharply.

Constant saw them. Here and there by the banks of the great river, in nooks in the cave walls and on the time-smoothed rocks, dark figures crouched and huddled. Some wore ragged scraps of cloth, some were naked, all were filthy and emaciated. Most attended to their own business, which seemed little more than scraping the rocks around where they sat, but some watched the three companions with dull, incurious eyes. Constant drew his sword ostentatiously. It drew no reaction from the watchers.

'What do we do?' asked Blix.

Kit pointed down the path. A naked man sat on the river bank where the path diverged left and right. 'Can't go back. Don't need to pick a fight. Let's go say hi. Maybe he can tell us where to go.'

The man sat where a few wooden piles were driven into the river bed, dangling his feet into the water. It looked like a narrow bridge had once stood here, but if so it had long since collapsed into the river. He was eating what appeared to be lizard eggs, pinching the tops off the shells and eating the half-formed embryos whole. There were six eggs, three as yet uncracked. He looked up at they approached, with the same sleepy, uninterested gaze as the others around the cave, and continued chewing.

'Hello,' said Blix brightly. The man nodded, said nothing, and kept eating.

'What's your name, son?' Kit tried.

The man considered this seriously. 'I don't know,' he said eventually.

'What do you mea-' Blix began, but Kit stopped her with a raised hand. She squatted next to the man and gave him a sweet smile. He smiled back, copying her, revealing black and broken teeth.

'How long have you been here, brother?'

The man's brow furrowed in deep concentration. 'Always,' he said. He seemed pleased with the answer.

Kit's eyes narrowed. 'I gotta bad feeling,' she said to Constant and Blix. To the man she said, 'How long is always?'

The man looked down. 'I looked down,' he said. 'There were six things in my lap. One was open. I was hungry. I ate the thing inside it. It tasted nice. I ate another two. Then you came. That's always.'

'What about before?' asked Constant gently. 'Were you thirsty? Did you drink from the river?'

The man shook his head. 'There was nothing before. That was the first thing.' His brow furrowed again. 'I am a bit thirsty now though.' He scooped up a palmful of water and slurped it. Then he looked down again. When he looked back, it was with the same drowsy, incurious expression he'd had when they'd arrived.

'A bad feeling,' Kit repeated. She smiled again, and the man copied her once more. 'How long have you been here, brother?' she asked.

The man's brow furrowed in deep concentration. 'Always,' he said. He seemed pleased with the answer.

'How long is always?'

'Kit, what-'

'Just a minute, kiddo.' Kit smiled encouragingly at the man. 'How long is always?'

The man looked down. 'I looked down. There were six things in my lap. Three were empty. Then I looked up and saw you. That's always.'

'What about before?' asked Constant, his voice deathly. 'Were you thirsty? Did you drink from the river?'

The man shook his head. 'There was nothing before. That was the first thing.'

'Oh, my God,' Blix breathed. 'This is horrible.'

'Yes, it is.' Kit stood up and faced Constant. The perennial grin was completely absent. 'You knew.'

'I did.' Constant watched the man carefully pinch off the top of another egg. Part of him was filled with compassion for the mindless man. He hoped it was the part that was him. 'My people came here once. I sent them here, hundreds of years ago. When I was someone else. Some of them came back like this.' He stirred the river water with the point of his sword. The silty liquid swirled around the blade. 'This is Lethe.'

'The river of forgetfulness,' said Blix.

'From the Greek religions,' Constant agreed. 'From which the dead must drink to forget their lives.'

'Not just the dead,' said Kit. She gently patted the starving man's shoulder. He glanced up briefly, smiled, and returned his attention to the eggs. 'All of his reason and language, just no memory of anything existing before right now. Born anew every time he drinks from the river.'

'Ghosts of people,' whispered Constant. 'No *animus.* No soul.'

'No wonder the Greeks thought this place bounded hell,' said Blix, shivering despite the warmth.

'You knew,' Kit said to Constant once more. 'You kept it from us. What else haven't you told us?'

How much should I tell them?

An eerie echoed through the tunnel behind them. A distant howling, savage and angry.

'They've found the cave mouth,' said Blix immediately.

'What else?' Kit insisted.

'A lot,' said Constant, finally. 'We all have secrets, all of us. How you carried Blix so effortlessly.'

'Hey, I'm just a gal from Nebraska-'

'Stop taking me for a fool.' Constant was surprised that the harshness in his words was all his. He took a deep breath. 'Once we're off this world and safe I promise I'll tell you everything. I promise. But now we must run. Or no one will be telling anyone anything.'

Kit gave him a look which seemed to bore into him. The few seconds before she spoke again seemed to last an eternity.

'Good enough,' she said, eventually. 'Barely. We will continue this conversation. Left path, or right?

'I don't know. Pick one and pray.'

'There's a sign,' said Blix.

It lay among the rocks nearby; a crossroads signpost, taller than their heads, broken at the base, rotted through with age, heavy and slimy to the touch. Constant, Blix and Kit levered it from its resting place. One of its four arms had snapped in half. A fragment carved on it in Greek letters read ATERFALL.

'That's helpful,' said Blix as they stood it up. She turned it on its rotten stump it to point that spar back the way they'd come. 'The others say MINOS, pointing where the bridge used to be, can't go that way. AIAKOS to the right, RHADAMANTHUS to the left. Give us a clue, Constant?'

'The judges of the dead.'

'Cheery. You know which way?'

'Either way takes us forward, and the path of Rhadamanthus is shorter, it cuts a world out of our route. He was lord of Elysium; that's where this path leads -'

'Sounds like a fun guy, let's go.' Blix started down the left-hand path.

'- but we gain six months we can't get back through lag. With Aiakos we lose a day.'

Blix did an immediate about face. 'Aiakos, always liked him, great man, what did he do again?'

'He was guardian -'

'Save it 'til we ain't gonna get et,' said Kit. 'Let's move.' She started after Blix.

'I'm a bit thirsty,' said the emaciated man.

'Take a drink from the river, brother,' said the American, not looking at him.

Blix skidded to a stop. 'Kit!'

'It can't hurt now. The damage is done. We can't look after him. Better for him not to remember us.'

She pushed the sign over again, lowering the last few feet so it didn't crash. Then they ran into the darkness, fear pushing them on.

Fear. I am terrified. I know what I must do. I hope it works. I hope it is true.

I don't want to end up like him.

The emaciated man watched them go. He drank from the river. He looked down. There were six things in his lap.

They ran along the bank, following the flow of the river until it disappeared into the earth once more. Their path led into more tunnels, quickly becoming less well trodden as they left the massive cave behind them. They scraped across rocks and through narrow fissures. Constant forged ahead, sword in one hand, lowlight in the other, peering into the pitch black beyond the feeble halo of light, trying to find their way. Kit brought up the rear, pistol pointing back down the tunnel, ready to end the life of any werewolf that caught up with them. Between them, Blix listened, straining to hear those that followed; far behind, but closing in.

They emerged into another cave, smaller than the last but still immense. There was more water here, the same sludgy, unpleasant-looking silver liquid as before. It pooled in a lake which grew shallower toward the curving bank on which they stood. The gate stood opposite them, a few hundred feet away, thin pillars of quartz, the crystal protruding at odd angles from broken fingers of rock, like a crown of ice crushed in a giant's hands. The circle was half in and half out of the lake. Water lapped gently up the stones before sliding like an oil spill back to the surface.

'Let's move like we got a purpose,' said Kit, sloshing forward. Constant grabbed her shoulder.

'There's something in the water.'

'There!' said Blix, pointing.

Constant saw the something slip beneath the surface with barely a ripple, thirty feet from shore. Then, a little closer, it appeared above the surface. It was a man. Young, beautiful, black-bearded, a slight but friendly smile on his face, only his blank silver eyes marked him out as something apart. He said nothing. The face moved forward a little. The rest of his body was invisible under the pool.

Then a long lizard tail, flattened at the end, flicked up and breached the surface, described a lazy S in the air, and returned to the depths.

Blix sighed in relief. 'It's okay. It's an afanc.'

'A what now?' Kit's eyes never left the face.

'An afanc. *Crocodylus homocymry*. That means "Welsh crocodile-man." They used to be found in Wales. Someone really literal named it. It's the manticore of the lizard world. But a bit rubbish. Look.'

She rummaged at her feet until she found a flat stone, then skipped it across the lake toward the afanc. The beautiful face dipped beneath the surface before the stone reached it. It reappeared a few feet away. As it moved the body beneath the surface was briefly visible. It was twice the length of a man, thick and powerful.

Kit followed its movement. 'It's big. Should I shoot it?'

'No. They're man-eaters, but it won't attack us. They don't have much of a bite and they're nothing like as strong as they look. They lure victims into the deep water and drown them.'

'Lure them how?' Constant asked. The afanc scudded lazily across the pool with a flick of its oar-like tail, the eerily human head always facing them. 'What should I be looking for?'

Blix laughed suddenly; the sound of it was so unexpected that Constant jumped. 'Don't worry. You'll be fine. The afanc targets women. Supposedly the face is so handsome that maidens are hypnotised with lust and follow it to their doom. I don't think that's going to be a problem for me.'

She gave Kit a sideways glance, to discover that Kit was already doing the same to her. Hesitantly, she held out her hand, and felt as she did so a sudden rush of blood that made her gasp, as though with that one trembling gesture she had offered her heart.

'How about you?' she asked. There was a different question in her eyes.

Kit considered the question and the hand. 'Never been one for beards,' she said after a while. Her fingers closed around Blix's.

Constant pretended not to notice and tried to think of something to say. 'Manticores, afancs. Why do monsters have human faces?'

Blix didn't let go of Kit's hand. 'Lots of creatures evolve to look like their predators. Why should liminal creatures be different?'

'If it ain't gonna eat us we need to move on.' Kit stepped into the water once more, pulling Blix along with her. They made a beeline for the circle, cutting out the arc of the bank, getting soaked to the knees. Constant followed more slowly, watching the afanc carefully.

A single large rune was carved into each upright stone. They looked sharp and clean, as though the stonemason had only just laid down his chisel. It only slightly surprised Blix that she could read it. It was in the same text as the runes she'd read at the Conspirators. Whatever Dragonville had done to her seemed to be permanent. 'Thyïlea,' she said. 'What does it mean?'

'The edge of the world.'

'More cheerfulness.'

'Do what you do, kid,' said Kit when they were all between the stones. 'Then pray for a herd of pegasus on the other side, the wolves are gonna be following right behind.'

'I'd prefer a tank,' said Blix. 'A big tank with a big gun.'

'I like big guns. What's a tank?'

'W-'

'Thyïlea,' said Constant. '*Come and see.*'

The crystal pillars shuddered. A pulse of white light slowly travelled from the base of each stone toward the tip. A metallic, throbbing bass note resonated through the cavern and made Kit and Blix clap their hands to their ears in pain.

Constant ignored it. He knelt and carefully scooped some water in his cupped hands.

'Constant, what are you doing?' Blix asked. Constant looked up at her, afraid but strangely serene.

'If you're still angry with me for what I did to you, this might be justice. I hope not.'

He raised his suddenly trembling hands to his lips and drank deeply from the water.

'Jesus Christ!' Kit kicked out hard and knocked Constant's hands away, spraying the silver-oiled liquid over the nearest pillar. But it was too late. 'Why the hell did you do that?'

The world turned white.

'I forget,' said Constant.

Chapter Twenty-Nine: Forgetting

Constant dreamed.

'Hello,' said the boy. 'I'm glad we can finally talk.'

Constant stood up. They were in a white space. There was nothing else to define it, no features or obvious illumination, although Constant could see well enough. It wasn't clear whether the space ended after a few feet or went on forever. Constant should have found it disorientating, but instead he felt quite rested and peaceful, without really knowing why. He realised his sword and bag were gone but didn't seem to mind.

The boy appeared to be about the same age as Constant but smaller and more slightly built. He had an encouraging smile, brown hair and eyes, a pleasant round face, nothing to mark him as unusual. He was wearing the kind of rough woollen smock Constant had grown up in.

Constant tried to tap the floor with his foot, then reached down to touch it. But there was nothing to tap or touch - no surface, but no absence of surface either. It was just nothing. The boy watched him with apparent interest. 'Not what you expected?'

'Expected? Where are we?'

'In your head. You're dreaming. Well, hallucinating, really. Your brain is shutting down. This is what a mind looks like without memories. Or how you imagine it does. You're not terribly imaginative I'm afraid.'

'Thanks for that,' said Constant. 'I recognise you. I've dreamed about you before. I remember that. I remember not remembering you afterwards. Who are you?'

'I don't really have a name.'

'What does your mother call you?'

The boy shook his head, smiling. 'I don't really have a mother either.'

'You're not being very helpful.' Constant looked him up and down, and sniffed disapprovingly. 'That's a novice's robe. An ill-made one. Novices on the Anvil make their own clothes. Are you a brother?'

Another shake, another smile. 'I don't really have an appearance either, not in the way you understand the term. How I appear in, ah, situations like this, is based on the dominant personality traits of whoever I happen to be inside of at the time.' The smile widened. 'Hey, maybe that's a name for me. You can call me Annoying Brat. Brat for short.'

'Thanks for that too,' said Constant. The boy was deliberately provoking him, but to Constant it felt like the kind of abuse that friends might heap on each other after years of acquaintance; insult as a form of affection. Constant had never had a friend like that. 'And why are you in my head, friend?'

The boy smiled as if Constant had just said something very funny. 'Don't call me friend! Fifty-eight killed people he called friend. He was a vicious one, wasn't he? A little too close to the surface. It's a fine line, between using a monster and finding you've become one. A very strange mind. But redeemed in the end, by your standards. I live here.'

'Excuse me?'

'I live here. In your head. In a slightly metaphysical but also real sense.' He leaned forward to share a conspiratorial joke. 'It's very roomy. Not much going on in here, you see.'

Constant snorted a half-laugh. 'And a third thanks. Have you broken into my head just to insult me?'

'I haven't broken in,' said the boy. 'Well, I suppose technically I did, but it was a long time ago when you using it even less. Shortly before you were born, in fact.'

Constant thought he understood then. 'Oh, I see. You're the last me. I didn't recognise you. You were older when you died. You don't really remember yourself as a child, in my head. I try to suppress all that.'

The boy laughed. 'I'm not him. That was quite stupid of you. I just told you my appearance is based on yours. Pay attention, this conversation is important.'

The boy hesitated for a moment. 'Let's put this to one side for now, shall we? You're not in the right frame of mind. We'll come back to it, I promise. We have plenty of time to talk before the water completely obliterates you. That's what's concerning you most now, isn't it? Whether you'll come out of this reckless gamble and still be yourself. Or whether you'll be him.'

The emaciated man knelt next to Constant. He looked up at him, the same dull, incurious look in his eyes as he'd had when they met in the cave.

'I looked down,' he said. 'There were six things in my lap. I was hungry.'

'How is he here?' Constant's mind told him he should be shocked to see the man next to him, but he felt nothing but peaceful.

'He's just a memory. He's gone now anyway,' the boy added, and Constant saw he was right. 'Nothing to worry about.'

'I wasn't worried. I should have been. Why wasn't I?'

'You forgot how,' said the boy. 'That's going to continue. Do you still remember how to worry about the Writing?'

'Yes,' said Constant. It was as though someone had re-lit his candle. He felt alert and, he realised, scared. 'Whether the brothers have interpreted it correctly. Whether I was right to drink the water.' He looked at his shoes. 'Was I?'

'Let's find out together, shall we? But whatever the answer is, the water has done some good, at least. It's let us talk. Among the things you've wiped away is something that was preventing you remembering me. Preventing you remembering lots of things.'

'The words? Or the gorgon blood?'

The boy laughed. 'We're far beyond the bloodwater. Although that doesn't help and you shouldn't drink it, *like I keep telling you.* I know, I know, you needed to,' the boy continued, forestalling Constant's objection. 'You'd be in a wolf now otherwise. And yes, I understand what it bringing the girl back implies. I need to think about that. You might be right. Just don't get into the habit of it, okay? I don't like it when I can't reach you. That thing doesn't understand the power it's meddling with. It should leave well alone. If it can,' he added darkly.

Constant was about to say something, then realised what he'd heard. 'Thing? It?'

'That thing pretending to be a woman.'

'Do you mean Kit?'

'Whatever it calls itself. It's not human.'

'I'm confused. She looks like a woman.'

'I look like a boy,' said the boy. 'I'm not though.'

'I'm dreaming you. She's real.'

'You're not dreaming me. Another stupid guess. I'm very real. And she - it - worries me. Why is it pretending?'

'What is she then, if she's not human?'

'I don't know. That worries me too.'

'Do you think she's dangerous?'

'Fool. It kills werewolves and manticores without thinking twice about it. Self-evidently it's dangerous.'

'She's on our side though.'

'It's on its own side. You thought that. But we are where we are. Don't trust it, okay? Be careful. Which reminds me.'

The boy suddenly reached forward, grabbed the front of Constant's robe with both hands and gave him a tiny shake. 'Stop doing stupid things which might get us killed! Seriously. I can't tell you things while you're awake because of the bloody words, but come on, I shouldn't have to tell you about mighty rivers with giant waterfalls at the end. That really should be obvious even to you.'

'The words.' Constant tried to call them to mind, but there was nothing there. He remembered speaking them, remembered using them on Blix, but which words they were had vanished. He didn't mind.

'They stop me remembering myself. The past me's. And you, because... you're me too.'

The boy seemed pleased. 'I'm always happy when you're not wholly stupid. It means I won't be either. Yes, that's right. I'm you too. Or rather, you're me too. But the words stop you remembering.'

Suddenly Brother Corlai was there, towering over them. 'There are some words,' he rumbled. 'Magic of my forefathers.' He looked down at Constant. The twinkle in his eye had been replaced by a glassy stare. 'Shall I tell you the words?' He suddenly bent low to look Constant square in the eye. '*It may not be a good idea,*' he hissed.

Then he was gone, as though he was never there.

'What was that?' Constant asked, thoroughly unnerved.

'It's your mind trying to tell you about something you've forgotten. Weird, isn't it? Brains are strange.'

'What have I forgotten?'

The boy sighed. 'The words,' he said slowly and deliberately, rolling his eyes. 'I let nineteen learn them to stop him going mad. That was quite generous of me, don't you think? There was a time when I wouldn't have cared. Wouldn't have known what caring was.'

'It was his decision,' said Constant with sudden certainty. 'He chose to learn them. You didn't let him.' He said it without knowing how he knew it was true.

The gentle smile didn't waver, but Constant saw a slight hardening around the eyes which told him the boy was annoyed.

'I didn't stop him,' he said. 'Same thing. I could have. But generosity has its consequences, like anything else. I never thought it would stop us talking at a time of crisis. There hasn't been one up to now. But, hey, problem solved! We can talk. I like talking.'

'You like the sound of your own voice.'

'It's all I am,' said the boy. He looked around again, nose wrinkling slightly in dissatisfaction. 'This is dull. Let's go somewhere else.'

Constant stood before the red gates of the Monastery. A sliver of moon curved low in the cloudless night sky. The gates stood open and the torches were lit. Brothers stood in single file stretching from deep into the tunnel behind the gates, across the bridge and along the rickety, narrow path that clung to the side of the mountain until it disappeared around a bend. The monks looked excited, even eager.

'What's going on?' Constant asked. He looked up curiously at a tall brother, who stared with unblinking passion into the darkness. He was shaking, and not with cold. It seemed to be happiness.

'We won't get a good view from here,' said the boy. He walked toward the bridge but, instead of stepping onto it, walked straight out into thin air. 'Hurry up,' he continued, turning to see why Constant hadn't come after. He followed Constant's horrified expression down to the emptiness beneath his feet.

'This is a memory too,' the boy said, sounding slightly exasperated. 'There's nothing here. Do try and keep up.' He ambled off across the void.

Constant took a deep breath, and followed.

The boy and Constant stopped in the middle of nothing. To their left was the entrance to the tunnel which led to the basket that descended to the town below.

Ahead of them, the almost-path across the face of the mountain which connected the tunnel to the bridge. The path was filled with monks, one for each step, leading into the tunnel. A flicker of fire from the torch each was holding illuminated the night.

A cry went up from the monk in the tunnel mouth. A bundle of plain red cloth that barely filled the arms of the monk was passed out to him. He looked into it for a moment, and passed it to the next man. Then he sank to his knees, praying fervently.

'Do you know what this is?' asked the boy.

'I've been told about it.' Constant watched the tiny bundle being passed from monk to monk up the path, each taking great care that the next had a good grip and sure footing before handing on their cargo. Each monk took a long look into the depths of the cloth before he passed it on. 'There's a baby in there. An infant Great Father.' He watched the next monk receive the precious burden. Saw the fear in his eyes, and the hope, which as he watched changed to extraordinary joy, almost ecstasy, as the brother saw the tiny life within. So it was with all the monks, each one in the long line in his turn - the terror that it was not true, the realisation that it was, the sense of fulfilment, the passing on. 'Each monk is Recognising him.'

'Yes. Recognition draws me out, makes the bond with you stronger. And makes the monks want to protect me. That's why we're up here.'

Constant watched the baby bundle slowly traversing the cliff. 'Is that me?'

'Yes. You're about ten months old at this point. You're quite scrawny for your age, I must say. After the old priest died the monks found you almost immediately. Your mother's house is very close. They took you when you were weaned.'

Constant tried to think about his mother. No memories emerged, but a thought furrowed his brow. 'If that's me, why am I not seeing this through my eyes?'

'A good question. You're asleep. I wasn't though. I don't, really. This is my memory. I see things differently to humans. Shall I show you?'

The world turned to fire and noise, a blistering assault on the senses which made Constant scream. The monks transformed into grey, man-shaped blobs, indistinguishable from each other, but, shining like the first silver star born into the universe, the baby he had once been riveted Constant's attention, filling his consciousness with fear and adoration and awe. And then it was gone, and he was himself again. He realised he was kneeling, breathing hard and sweating profusely. They were back where they'd started in front of the red gates.

'On your knees again, Constant? You monks do spend a lot of time down there,' said the boy conversationally. 'Must play havoc on the joints. No wonder our leg ached.'

'What... what was that?' Constant panted, struggling to compose himself after the assault on his senses. The boy lent his arm as Constant struggled back to his feet.

'That was a small representation of how I experience the world. The reality would blast your mind. You've done a respectable job of that yourself anyway.'

'That's what you see?'

'A representation. It's unexplainable in any way that would mean something to you. Mostly I see what you see. I am not separate from you. Being human has changed me in ways I couldn't have imagined. Here you come.'

The child bundle had arrived at the bridge. There was a palpable sense of relief from the line of brothers now that the baby was on firm ground. Eventually the bundle reached the tall brother, who held it reverently and peered into it as though it was his life's purpose to do so. Constant looked with him. The baby inside was just a baby, as far as Constant could tell. The silver radiance didn't seem to have an effect in his normal way of seeing. Nor did he experience any thrill of recognition. The baby slept hard and fiercely, a tiny scowl on his face.

'I will carry him now,' said a voice that Constant knew as well as his own.

Brother Simon emerged from the darkness behind the red gates. Slimmer than Constant remembered and younger, but with the same stern, kindly love in his eyes that Constant had known every day since he could know things. Simon took him from the tall brother and carried him carefully into the Monastery, stopping every second pace so the next brother could Recognise him in turn. As he went into the tunnel beyond the gates, darkness took him.

How gently you carried me, Constant thought.

'He's dead,' he said. 'They're all dead.'

'That's how it ends for humans,' said the boy. 'That took a lot of getting used to, believe me. When the first died... I don't think there are words to describe what someone else dying feels like from the inside, if you're not expecting it. It was bad. Then I was ejected back into the hell I thought I'd escaped from. That was worse.'

The monks from the mountain path were streaming back into the temple now, chattering excitedly among themselves. They reminded Constant of everything he'd lost. He turned away. The boy was in front of him once more, smiling his encouraging smile. Constant thought about punching him. Instead he said, 'Who *are* you? You're in me, you were in me when I came here. But If you're not the old priest...'

'I am not your predecessor. I am the reason you have predecessors.'

Constant swallowed hard, chills running up his spine. 'My God,' he whispered. 'You're the Constant! The light in the darkness!' He sank to his knees and bowed his head. 'I honour you with my being.'

'It would be easier if I told you I was God,' said the boy. 'You might start doing what I tell you instead of making random spur of the moment decisions.' He bent and lifted Constant gently under the arms, encouraging him to stand again. 'Unfortunately, I am generally honest. That's what seventy lifetimes of religion does to you, I suppose. Should there be a Constant, I am not it.'

Constant turned his head toward the stars, taking in the diamond-swathe of pin-prick lights he knew best from the ceiling of the First Temple. 'I don't understand.

The Constant is the reason I reincarnate. I am the Constant. The living embodiment of the universe. The torch was passed to me, it passes through me, and-'

'And passes on,' I know,' said the boy. 'I hear that a lot.' He looked uncomfortable and rubbed his forehead in a way that Constant found shockingly, intimately familiar. 'I don't suppose you've forgotten how to have your worldview shaken to the core, have you?'

Constant ground his teeth and glowered at the boy. 'I don't think so.'

'No, I didn't expect so. Well now. Wipe that scowl off your face. Let me show you something. I'm going to use your imagination for this bit, so it might be a bit, uh, rudimentary.'

They were on a beach. It stretched in an unbroken line as far as the eye could see, golden sand descending sharply to shingle where it met the water. Low, grassy dunes ran behind the beach. A short distance away larger rocks extended into the sea. The sun lent warmth to his skin and a light breeze stirred his hair. It felt real in a way that the Monastery hadn't. It felt as if he was there.

'I know this place,' said Constant. 'I dream about it a lot. Or someone does.'

'Thirty-six,' said the boy. 'It's the island where he was born. The beach was his happiest memory. There weren't many others. There was a sickness. I wasn't him for very long.'

'I don't remember.'

'Ah. It doesn't matter.' The boy looked uneasy, as though the memory of it brought him pain. 'I'd rather not remember. I'm just using it to illustrate a point.'

He hopped gingerly across the rocks until he was at the water's edge. Constant followed him. The steps felt familiar, but he didn't know why. It didn't seem to matter.

'It's deeper here,' said the boy. 'You can -'

'- dive in and touch the bottom,' Constant finished. 'I know.' His brow crinkled. 'How do I know?'

'Don't worry about it,' the boy replied. 'You want to know who I am. Let me show you.'

Without warning he grabbed Constant by the neck and threw him headlong into the ocean.

- I scream as the acid melts away flesh and bone but I do not die and the flesh renews to slough off once more, over and over, over and over, I scream until my lungs burst but the horror continues, my eyes are burned from my skull and I cannot see but I know I cannot escape my blood boils and I know it will last forever and my bones crack and my body breaks and I know I AM NOT ALONE there are millions like me here all crushing, writhing, screaming endlessly as we burn together and -

Constant stood on the shore, convulsing in horror and retching until he thought his throat would tear itself in half. He bent double, hands on knees, trying to stop his stomach from turning inside out. But nothing came out. *None of this is real.*

'W-what- what-' he gasped.

'Sorry,' said the boy. 'Must have been a bit of a shock, experiencing that.' He bent until his head was level with Constant's. 'Now imagine feeling that forever.'

Constant straightened up slowly, breathing deeply. 'That was... what?'

'That is how the world is for us.'

'Us. There were things in there with me. Not people. They were in agony.' Constant shuddered. 'Such terrible pain.'

'Not People. That's a very good name for us. We are Nothing. Here they come.'

The sea rose in towers of foam as thousands upon thousands of creatures burst through the surface and hung in the air, shapeless and contorted, nearly-things that should not exist. Acid-burnt flesh dripping from them, the foetid stench of it sickening to breathe. They seemed confused at first, searching for something. Then slowly, inexorably, each almost-head turned toward Constant.

'I would run if I were you,' suggested the boy.

Constant turned tail and fled up the beach, bounding and scrambling through the deep shingle and onto the sand as fast as he was able. Behind him a hideous shriek went up, endless torn voices raised in pain, and terror, and rage - and hope, a longing for release suddenly kindled for the first time, audible in the clamouring madness. Constant threw a desperate glance over his shoulder. The things were lurching through the air in broken lunges, twisted limbs outstretched toward him, eager fingers clawing the air that separated them. The sea came with them, now a cloud of acid that burnt the shingle that it touched on.

The boy was ahead of him. 'There's a house,' he said. 'Quickly now.'

Constant saw it, just about, its shape barely registering in his frantic charge, save for one feature which stood out - its open door. He charged through, skidded and ricocheted off a wall, then slammed the door shut. There was a heavy wooden bar standing against the wall. Constant struggled to lift it; he scraped it up the door and dropped it across. Then he collapsed, his strength consumed by terror, and waited for the creatures to break in, waited for the door to splinter and split as they came to devour him.

Nothing happened.

'Nice in here, isn't?' said the boy, from behind him. 'Very different from the last time we were here.'

Constant looked around, and saw his mother's house. But the boy was right. The last time - the only time - he had seen it, the room had been in pieces, ravaged by the werewolf attack. Now it was if that had never happened. The furniture was whole and neatly arranged, a cloth on the table, chairs pushed under. A fire crackled in the grate, a rabbit hung on a spit above it. Bright curtains were pulled across the window. A high-backed rocking chair sat next to the fire. The boy sat in it, warming his feet. On the sleeping platform, smooth blankets lay on a well-made bed. It felt lived in, cared for, and loved.

'How can we be here?' Constant demanded. 'This is in the forest.'

The boy sighed and made a face. 'Have you forgotten this is all in your head? That's going to be difficult.'

'No, I know that. I mean, why this house?'

'You think of it as home. I must say I was expecting the Monastery. Look out of the window.'

Constant hauled himself up and tentatively twitched a curtain until there was a fraction of a gap to peer through. Outside the monsters swirled through the air, shoaling like fish driven to the surface by the scent of food. They came so close to the house than Constant felt the curtain shiver as they moved the air. But they made no attempt to break down the door. The infernal shriek had ceased the moment Constant had closed it. The silence made his skin crawl.

'What are they?' he asked, letting the curtain slip back. He looked over his shoulder at the boy. 'You. What are you?'

'Come and sit by the fire.'

Constant was halfway there before he realised he'd obeyed without thinking. The boy's voice was his own - or if not his own, one that Constant had known throughout his life, speaking in his head, one voice among all the others but part of each other voice too. The idea made him feel ill, as he thought through the implications of what he had just seen. He sat on the floor next to the fire and looked up at the boy, who suddenly seemed both childlike and ancient beyond reason.

'I'm a *dybbuk*,' he said. 'Another name might be, demon.'

Constant said nothing.

'Or that's what your people would call me,' the boy continued, to fill the silence. 'It's a pretty meaningless term. Very judgmental. We don't have one for ourselves. Not People is more accurate. I'm perfectly normal for where I'm from. It's just that where I'm from isn't here.'

'There's a lot of that about these days,' said Constant, suddenly feeling icy cold. *A demon inside me.*

'More than you think. But I'm from a lot further away than your friends. And I've been here a lot longer too. The problem is... Well, the real problem is we do not belong in this... world? Universe? Reality? I don't know. Whichever it is, it's hell and we are trapped. We aren't supposed to be here.'

'Why are you here?'

'A very good question. We don't know. There was a time when we weren't here. Then we were here. We don't know where we came from. We don't know how to get back. Every moment is unbearable torment. We are mad.'

'You're not.'

'Am I not? How kind. They are.' He waved vaguely at the window without looking at it.

Constant realised that while he could remember that the *dybbuk* swarmed outside, he couldn't remember what they looked like. He went to the curtain again and carefully peered through. The misshapen man-things swirled past.

'Why aren't they attacking the house?' he asked.

'They don't know it's here,' said the boy, stretching his hands toward the flames and rubbing them contentedly. 'They don't even see it. The lamp was lit, the door was open - practically an invitation. But they don't see that. They weren't even really attacking you. They just moved because you moved. Only you saw the house.'

'They won't try and come in?' One part of Constant knew that the monsters were imaginary and couldn't hurt him. That wasn't the part which had made him run.

'Oh, if the house was empty, one of them might blunder into it, in the right circumstances,' said the boy, stretching expansively. 'And if it did, it would feel something it had never felt before: no pain. You understand a little, now? What it feels like when that horror suddenly ends? It's bliss.'

The boy closed his eyes, and his mouth parted slightly as he remembered the moment, a tiny breath of relief escaping his lips. Then his eyes snapped open again and glared balefully at Constant.

'There's a catch,' he continued. 'There's only room in the house for one. And if it's not you, you're out in hell again. You close the door and bar it. And while you're inside, no one can get in. And even though you know there's almost no chance you'll be evicted, you become very paranoid about it...' The boy hesitated. 'Just how stupid are you? Have you worked out that in this allegory you are the house and I am you?' Do you understand what I'm trying to tell you, Constant?'

'I'm not sure. Yes.' Constant groped for words that expressed how profoundly shocked he felt. 'I don't like it,' he finished angrily.

'I can see why. I wouldn't if I was you.'

'My whole life has been a lie,' said Constant bitterly. 'Mine and everyone who came before me. We aren't the Constant. We're you. There is no Constant.'

'Well now, not necessarily. I don't want to undermine your faith,' said the boy, apparently quite sincere. 'The people of the First Father believed in the Constant long before I found him. I just saw an opportunity. They believed in reincarnation, what we do looks like it, so I adapted.' The boy hesitated again, and suddenly looked troubled, as through the thought had sparked a memory he'd rather not have recalled. 'He wasn't the first. The first like you. The first special one. The first you can remember. The first who didn't...' He trailed off, distress etched in his face.

'Didn't what?'

'Didn't die,' the boy blurted, sitting forward suddenly. 'I know this is going to sound false, all things considered, but you're really important to me. I don't want you to die. I care about you, you're -'

'Bullshit.' Constant reached for his sword without thinking and when his grasping hand met only air, balled it into a fist. 'You're a monster who attacked me when I was a baby. Latched onto me like a leech. Living off me. Controlling me.'

The boy shook his head violently. 'No, no, that's not true.' Another pause. 'Not in the way you think.'

Constant barked a grim laugh. 'Generally honest, are you? Tell me how it's not how I think, then.'

'Because we are one. You're special, Constant. You are the Constant. You're *my* Constant. My light in the darkness. You are special in a way that almost no one else on your world is. You stop me being a monster.' The boy looked away. 'I have been one. Let me show you.'

Then the house was gone, and they were on a wide open plain. A weak morning sun hung just above the horizon. A dusting of snow sprinkled the iron-hard ground. A herd of short, shaggy yaks dotted the prairie into the distance, scraping their hooves through the ice to get at whatever roots of grass survived beneath. A stiff wind whipped up their hair but Constant neither felt it nor did it stir his robe. Nearby a dozen hide tents made a circle around a deep fire pit, embers still glowing amid the white ash. Constant wondered where the wood had come from; there were no trees in any direction.

'Where are we?' he asked.

'Many thousands of miles from where you call home,' said the boy. 'Thousands of years ago, too. These are some of the first Tibetans to live on Shambhala. Not that they knew they were Tibetans, that name comes later. There's an ungated rift nearby. There are many families living on this plain now. It's very like the place they left.'

Constant saw stirrings within the tent circle, as the herders began their day. A woman in a thick grey coat emerged from the nearest tent, jumped down into the pit, and kicked the fire traces until she found an ember with a bit of life left in it. She produced a pair of tongs from a pocket and took up the ember, and returned whence she came.

'Why are we here?'

'To see something terrible. I'm going to show you the world through my eyes again,' said the boy. 'Just a little this time.'

Constant braced himself for an assault on his senses, but none came. Instead the tents took on a strange translucent quality, as though the skins had been stretched tight and a light shone through them. He could see the people inside as though they were next to him.

He watched the woman with the ember blow on it until it glowed brightly, then set it to the tinder under a tiny pile of sticks with a water pan hung above it. She held out her hands to the warmth and rubbed them vigorously.

They walked through the camp. Here a young woman nursed an infant, while two other young children tried to roll their father over as he pretended to sleep and tried not to laugh. There, a man honed a skinning knife with a whetstone, methodically drawing the blade down the block, checking the edge every few strokes. Beyond, an old couple made love under furs while their family slept on beside them. The lives of people as they lived them, unaware they were observed.

'I didn't know I was seeing these things until much later,' said the boy. 'Knowledge of the thingness of things comes with being a person and I'm not one yet. I'm up in the sky somewhere. I'm looking this way but I'm not aware of it. I remember this later. Anyway. Question: what's different here than on the mountain?'

Constant thought about it, chewing his lip. Each had a grey halo around them, a formless blob that obscured the edges of their shape and made them look washed out and dull.

'No silver glow. They're all grey. Like the monks.'

'That's right. No one here is special. But let me tell you: Here lives the first. The very, very first.'

'The first Unnamed,' whispered Constant.

'He had a name,' said the boy. 'I just didn't know how to learn it. Here he comes.'

A young man pushed aside the flap of a nearby tent and stumbled out, yawning and stretching. He was wearing an ankle-length, fur-lined robe tied loosely at the waist. From his bleary expression, it looked like the previous night might have been well-lubricated. The icy air made him recoil slightly, muttering in a dialect Constant recognised as Tibetan but didn't understand. The man thumped himself on the chest with both open palms and breathed in deeply through his nose. There was a pouch around his neck, and Constant could see inside it just as with the tents. It held a small, flattish stone, translucent green flecked with red.

'The bloodstone!'

'Indeed. I have no idea how he came to have something so powerful.'

The young man pushed a peaked fur cap onto his head, yanking the ear flaps down hard. Then he took a few steps away from the tent circle, unbelted the robe and pissed into the morning.

'Such are the decisions that end lives,' said the boy. 'Here they come.'

A stream of *dybbuk* swirled through the sky, tens of thousands strong, diving and swooping like starlings on the wing, turning and rising without command or control, moving as though on invisible currents that pulled them through the world.

'No one leads. No one follows. They just react. The only thing they know is their pain.' The boy raised an arm, almost reaching toward the *dybbuk*, as if trying to touch them - and, Constant thought, perhaps to join them.

The man pissed on, not paying the slightest attention to the monsters blackening the sky. Constant looked back through the camp; the herders didn't so much as glance at the horrors hanging above them.

'Why don't they run?' he asked.

The boy blinked and suddenly the creatures vanished. At the same time the tents lost their translucence and the grey halo around each person faded into nothing.

'He can't see them,' said the boy. 'No one can, or ever has. We are invisible to humans. To everything. Invisible, intangible, inaudible. Barely there at all. We are thoughts beyond your understanding, flitting through this wrong world, less substantial than ghosts. Oh look, there I am.'

Constant's vision changed again and the *dybbuk* reappeared. The swarm was heading away and upward, but one of them had detached from the swarm and was snaking jerkily downward. It was little more than a vaguely human-like blob with stumps for limbs. What passed for a head craned this way and that, searching, searching.

'That's me,' said the boy, 'Handsome fellow, aren't I? That's not how I really look. I don't know how we really look. There's nothing to see. Do you understand? I'm trying to convey how I perceive myself.'

Constant barely heard him. Suddenly every fibre of him wanted to scream for the man to run. *This is not real. Remember.* 'Why are you coming down?'

'I noticed something. For the first time in my miserable existence, I saw something beyond myself. Beyond the pain. Ask me what I saw.'

'What -'

'I didn't know. For which humanity can be grateful. I would have told them all what to look for if I'd known.' He looked back at the flock of *dybbuk* sailing through the sky towards the sunrise. 'Now I think it was the bloodstone.' He turned back to his counterpart. 'This won't be pleasant,' he warned.

The man was tying his robe when the thing brushed against him. Instantly it vaporised, transmuted into a miasma of silver sludge that bled into the man through the pores of his skin while he stood rigid and choking. When the last of the sludge was inside him he collapsed, fitting violently, clawing at himself, bloody foam spewing from his mouth, eyes bulging from his head, convulsing so hard that Constant thought his spine would snap.

'I am obliterating his mind now,' said the boy conversationally.

Constant saw the terror in the man's eyes, then the horror, then nothing. He looked away, unable to bear any more. 'Why did you do that?'

'I didn't mean to. I'm not a thinking being at this point. It was instinct. Making room.'

The stricken man sat up suddenly, the movement snapping Constant's attention back to him. He looked around, open mouthed with astonished incomprehension. From some hollowed-out place deep inside the shell that had once been a man came a low, inchoate gurgle. Then blood fountained from his mouth in retching bursts, as though his body tried to purge itself of that which kept it alive. The man collapsed, and lay still.

'And thus, I am delivered into this world,' said the boy.

Constant felt sick, but once again there was nothing to come up. 'That was terrible. You're a monster. Is that what you do to us? Did that happen to me? Before I was born?'

The boy looked at him as if he were stupid, which made Constant want to flatten him. 'Do you think an unborn child could survive that? No. You are special Constant, as I keep telling you. And I am special too.'

'I'm special, you're special.' Constant looked at the broken man. Others from the tribe had come running and were trying to revive him. Some had weapons drawn, looking for an unseen assailant. 'What about him?'

'He rotted. Look.'

Suddenly they were elsewhere. Without knowing how, Constant knew time had passed. They were in a dimly lit tent, much larger than the ones Constant had seen before. In the centre was a long table on which the *dybbuk*-infested man lay, gagged with a bloody cloth and tied with thick rope at ankles and wrists. He struggled violently against his restraints. Grey-haired ancients milled nervously at the tent flap, talking quietly in the language Constant didn't know and looking worriedly at the man. The shimmering grey around them told Constant he still saw though the *dybbuk*'s eyes.

The place stank of rancid meat and putrefaction. Chunks of flesh had dropped away from the torso and limbs, exposing white bone beneath. Elsewhere, maggots feasted in open wounds.

'This is what happens to those that aren't special,' the boy said. He examined the straining man with the same cold interest that an undertaker might bring to a corpse. 'I saw a word in the Earth girl's mind when you touched her. *Zombie*. Do you know what that means?'

'No.'

'It means this. The body is dead, or near enough. The body rots. Its mind is gone. But it looks alive for the moment, superficially.' He pointed a thumb at the milling elders. 'This lot think he has some terrible disease.'

An old woman separated himself from the group and edged toward the writhing man. While she was still an arm's length away she dropped the bloodstone onto his forehead, then stepped back hurriedly.

'They know it's magic, they just don't know what it does,' the boy remarked. 'They've been trying to cure him of me.'

'They've gagged him. Tied him down. That's not what I call medicine.'

'You should learn more about medicine. I am tied up for their protection. I have no idea what is happening. I lash out. I've never had senses before. I'm learning to cope with a nervous system, lungs, a brain. It's a total assault on me. It has been a week since I took over this man. I've learned how screaming works though. I'm terrified.'

'It must be terrible.'

'Oh no. Were you not listening before? This is bliss. To be suddenly without the endless pain, insulated inside this bag of meat from the eternal torment - bliss. No, I'm screaming because I can feel the body failing. I don't know how, but I know instinctively that when it does, I'll be - ah, but watch. It's time.'

The man suddenly fell still, and then seemed to deflate a little. Then all at once the tissue of his body disintegrated, and the flesh sloughed off his bones and splattered in gobbets on the straw-strewn floor. The men and women cried out in horror. A woman uttered some invocation; a man started wailing. Constant thought he looked like the corpse, but older. None of them saw the silver sludge pour from the grinning rictus that has once been his mouth and coalesce into the part-man thing that had consumed him.

'I can't tell you the agony I'm in right now,' said the boy quietly. 'There are no words. But wait, what is this?'

The creature looked curiously around the tent as if seeing it for the first time - as if seeing *anything* for the first time. Slowly, jerkily, it floated over to the nearest man. Almost hesitantly, it reached out to touch him. As the silver sludge consumed the man, Constant turned away.

'And so I learned to Recognise humans,' said the boy. 'A *dybbuk* can enter anyone, as you can see. But we have to Recognise you. Without that, a thousand of us could pass right through your body and not notice you. Which is why there isn't one of us in all of you. Let's move forward, there isn't much time left.'

'Time left for what?' Constant asked, not knowing what the boy could mean. But he didn't answer, and then they were elsewhere.

A town, near the edge of a forest, on a cool spring afternoon. Well-made roundhouses of wattle and daub with tall, conical thatched roofs, were set back from a mud road. The road led to a longer meeting house set up on a low mound in the centre of the town. There was a market of a few stalls set along the road, selling food and goods. By one of the roundhouses a wood carver worked the treadle of a pole lathe, expertly turning rough wood into a smooth chair leg. Wood shavings fluttered into the sky as the wind caught them and bore them aloft.

Normal people went about their normal business, oblivious to the monster in their midst. But Constant saw the *dybbuk* immediately. He shivered as she passed. They followed, the boy walking through the passers-by, like a ghost, while Constant automatically dodged them, his reflexes unable to process that the whole scene was imagination.

She was blonde, mildly pretty, slight, clothed in a long yellow woollen dress belted high under her breasts. There was nothing to distinguish the young woman who walked around the edge of the square from her peers; a slight limping gait perhaps, a slight sheen to the skin, a mild smell, like mothballs. But Constant could see within, to the rotten core of her.

'This is much later,' said the boy over his shoulder. 'Almost a thousand years. The All-men have arrived, lots of them. We're among them. I've become adept at impersonating a human. I understand what is needed to pass unnoticed through the world of men. And I've learned how to slow the rot. I've been in this body for months and you can barely tell. The only time I've been a woman. She was the only human around when I needed a new body. I seem to be drawn to males. Maybe because of the first.'

He stared, fascinated, as the woman weaved through the crowd. The same fascination a boy might have for his reflection.

'I remember her,' Constant said. 'A little. Once. I remembered what it felt like to be a woman.'

The boy turned around completely and looked at Constant as if he had spat in his face. 'That's *rubbish*!' he said vehemently.

Constant shook his head. 'I remember. Brother Simon said she must have been one of the Unnamed who weren't Recog-'

'That's a *lie*!' The boy was so angry that Constant took a step back; he was shaking with fury. 'I destroyed her mind like all the others. She's gone. *Gone.'*

Then in an instant his anger vanished, replaced with a sullen, shuffling uncertainty. He kicked up the imaginary dust, suddenly looking for all the world like the sulky boy he surely wasn't. 'I'm sorry. I shouldn't have shouted. I don't like to think about what I did to these people. Being human has changed me. I joke about it to not think about it. It's horrible.'

Someone in Constant's mind said, *That wasn't it.*

The boy was looking away, or he would have surely seen the thrill of shock that ran through Constant's body.

Who's there?

My name is Darcen Ysir.

You're a memory!

More than that. Tell him again.

'I do remember,' Constant found himself saying. 'I remember being a woman.'

The boy clenched his fists for the briefest second. 'You can't have,' he said, quite calmly. It's not possible. You must have dreamed that.'

'I dream everyone.'

'No. A real dream.'

Interesting. This matters.

How are you here?! No answer came.

'I've lost sight of her,' said the boy suddenly. He showed no sign of having heard Ysir. Constant tried not to let his alarm show on his face. 'We need to catch up. Something momentous is about to happen.'

He grabbed hold of Constant's hand and without moving they were behind the woman again. Constant realised it was the first time the boy had touched his skin. His hand felt dead.

The woman paused and tilted her head to one side as if listening. She approached one of the roundhouses, pushed the door open, ducked under the low lintel and disappeared in the darkness.

'Now, pay attention.' The air flickered and the people became surrounded with the grey halo Constant had seen around the Tibetans.

Something glowed silver in the shadows within the roundhouse.

Constant followed the *dybbuk* inside. A small fire burned in a stone lined pit. Beside it, sitting on a mat made of rushes, a young woman nursed a baby, her breast and the child's head covered by a cloth. The baby was surrounded by a shimmering silver halo, a fraction of the intensity that Constant had seen on the mountain but still enough to make him shield his eyes a little. The *dybbuk* approached the woman, its face slack-jawed with wonder, marvelling at the sight before it.

The young woman looked up. 'Can I help you, *Herrin?'*

The *dybbuk* noticed the woman for the first time. She reached into the neck of her dress and drew out a little leather pouch, tied on a string around her neck. Constant knew without seeing that the bloodstone was inside.

'This is his now,' it said, throwing the pouch to the startled woman. The cloth covering the baby fell away as she awkwardly grabbed it. Then the *dybbuk* sighed, an unpleasant rattling sound, and its eyes rolled up into its skull until the pupils were no longer visible. Its body collapsed forwards as the sludge left its mouth and, without forming into the almost-man shape, seeped into the baby, insinuating itself between mouth and breast. Constant braced himself for something horrific, but while his mother scrambled away from the dead woman, arm outstretched to fend off the falling corpse, the child only adjusted his latch and continued suckling.

'Did you see what happened there?' The boy was happy, even excited; a child proudly showing his best toy to a friend. 'I didn't destroy the baby's mind. I am experiencing astonishment. That mind is a revelation. More special than any of you.'

The boy dragged his eyes away from the child, back to Constant. 'I think it's because he was a baby. I don't mind admitting that if he'd been older I might have destroyed his mind and just taken over his body. Lived a long life in control of a body that didn't rot. But he was a light in the darkness. I didn't want to take over. I wanted to watch. And then I wanted to protect him. And when he died I already knew where the next one was. The next baby. They're usually babies. Usually new-born, sometimes unborn. I could see him from thousands of miles away, silver among the grey. I was prepared to return to my agony for the time it took to go to him, rather than simply jump into a monk. Endure the agony and years of exhaustion because this one made me understand what being human really was... Are you listening?'

The scene evaporated, and Constant was in his mother's house again. The boy was with him, sitting in the chair by the fire once again. 'I want you *out*,' Constant demanded.

'You don't really.'

'Yes, I bloody do! Argh!' Constant rubbed his forehead with the heel of his hand. 'I'm going to punch you,' he declared, advancing on the boy. 'I've been thinking about it and I'm going to do it. I'm going to knock you right out of my head. Hold still.'

The boy laughed and held up his hands in mock horror. 'You can't. I'm not real. And you really don't want me to leave. Ask what happens if I leave this house.'

'I'm sick of bloody questions! All I do is ask questions about things I don't know! I'm supposed to *know*!'

Suddenly they were on the Anvil again, in the Fifth Temple. Another, younger him sat on the throne, trying to look serene but succeeding only in looking miserably uncomfortable. Row after row of monks knelt before him, alternately pressing their foreheads to the flagstones in worship, then rocking back to gaze at him. The great prayer wheels turned slowly, grinding stone on stone, as the brothers chanted a continuous drone of adoration.

'Look at them!' Constant shouted, angrier than he'd ever been. 'They look at me as if I have all the answers. For four thousand years men like these have looked at us as if we know everything. But none of us knew anything. It was you all along! It was all a lie! Even my name. Constant of nothing! They just wasted their lives! Like idiots! Get off your knees, idiots!' He ran along the rows of me, waving at them, trying to get their attention. 'Do you hear me? It's all a lie! Get off your knees! Get up! Get *up*!'

He kicked out wildly at the nearest monk, but his foot passed right through. His momentum sent him tumbling onto his back on the floor. As he landed the Temple vanished and they were back in the cottage once more.

The boy was sitting bolt upright on the edge of his chair, palpably shocked. 'How- how did you do that?'

Constant pulled his knees up under his chin and hugged his legs tightly, 'I don't know. I was angry. It's my memory, isn't it? Get out of my head.'

The boy still looked nonplussed, but recovered himself quickly. 'You really don't want that, Constant. Look, no more questions. I'll just tell you.' He gestured around him, taking in the house. 'This is your mind Constant and it's a lovely place to live, but look you at the door. There's no lock. It's barred from the inside. *I* barred it. That means if I'm not here, the door is open. I didn't open it, it just is. That's who you are. I am *protecting* you. I've protected you your entire life, you and all who came before you. I founded a religion to keep you safe, surrounded you with fanatical warrior monks willing to die to save you, put you on the most inaccessible mountain I could find and pulled up the ladder behind us. It wasn't people I was keeping you safe from. People I could just kill.'

'You've protected me from more things like you,' said Constant in scathing tones. 'Forgive me if I don't thank you.'

The boy nodded, his face pitilessly grim. 'More things like me. Only much worse. Worse than the things outside. Haven't you been listening? Being human has mellowed me a lot, over the years. But I'm not the only *dybbuk* to have Recognised a human. The others will slaughter your soul the moment they touch it. Just like I would have before I entered the child. They're bad people. I'm not. Not anymore.'

'I don't care. I don't care! I didn't ask for this! I didn't say you could! You didn't give me a choice! Get out of my... get out of... get... get...'

As he spoke the world changed. The house drained away into a colourless void, an endless blank space the like of which he had never seen.

Now there was a boy he did not recognise.

'Where are we?' he asked.

The boy smiled, a little sadly it seemed to him. 'In your head,' he said. 'It's quite roomy. Especially now that you've forgotten.'

'Forgotten what?' he said.

'Everything. What's your name?'

He thought for a long time. 'I don't know,' he said finally. He did not feel unhappy about that. 'Does it matter?'

'No,' said the boy. 'Not anymore.'

'Okay.' He looked around at the formless nothing. 'Why are we here?'

'We're here because someone you were thousands of years ago read something that said you would do this. And everyone you have ever been or known believed wholeheartedly that you would. So, you did. You were scared to, because you had seen what happened to people who did it. But you chose to do it anyway, because you had faith. And because you are genuinely brave. I think you should know that. Then you discovered your faith was... misplaced.'

'Oh.' He thought about that. 'I don't understand.'

'I know,' said the boy. 'Don't worry about it. Ask me why not.'

'Why not?' he said obediently.

'Because you were right,' the boy said, and smiled the biggest smile he had ever seen, of the two he had ever seen. 'Just not in the way you thought. You thought that your faith would cause a miracle. That somehow the water wouldn't affect you. But it did to you what it does to everyone. It wiped your mind as clean as a new-born's. There was nothing before. This is the first thing.'

'Yes,' he agreed. 'This is the first thing.'

'But do you know something? Those memories you've forgotten? They're my memories as much as yours. Mine more than yours, in fact. And I didn't drink *anything*.'

Chapter Thirty: What Faith Is

Once, when she was nine, Blix Summerland had been knocked unconscious. She'd been walking next to a five-a-side pitch in the park and had looked up at the cries of warning just in time to see the football before it landed on her face. Then the next thing she knew she was lying down and a group of worried boys were looking down at her, wondering out loud if she was dead.

Blix remembered this and thought, *well, it's not like I haven't felt like this before.*

Her eyes didn't work. Her vision shuddered and quivered, pulsing like a beaten drum. Her face was numb, but that was at least better than the electric shocks of pain that convulsed her body every few seconds. Her head lolled sideways and when she tried to control it, it lolled the other way, like a rag doll when the stitching had come loose.

The ground under her was wet and slimy and stank like a ripe compost heap. And it was cold, despite a humidity that was already making her sweat. She could feel something nasty in her hair. It made a sucking sound.

'I'm coming, Katy,' she whispered to herself, 'but, swear down, you are going to owe me the biggest drink.'

Blix heard Kit groan, somewhere behind her. 'Mormons ain't paying me enough for this,' she muttered. 'No siree, not nearly.'

The pain was lesser now, more like full-body pins and needles. Wincing, Blix pushed herself up into a seated position. Her hands sank into cold mud, and more of it clung to her jacket.

Constant was watching her.

'Hello,' he said.

'Hello yourself.' Blix glanced over her shoulder. Kit was squatting, her bare feet lost in the depths of the mud, her back against one of the rough granite gate stones. She was massaging her right thigh and watching Constant intently. She said nothing.

Blix looked back to the boy. 'Um. How much do you remember?'

Constant stared at her without blinking for several seconds. Then he looked confused. Blix felt an ice crystal of fear pierce her stomach and start growing up toward her heart.

'There was... a house? And... and a light, and... no, not that... there was Nothing... a shape... I should remember... I don't remember,' he finished lamely, staring helplessly into space.

'It's all right,' Blix felt the catch in her voice as she said the words she didn't want to say. 'It'll be okay.' Tears welled up in the corners of her eyes and flowed freely down her face.

'Yes,' Constant said, his voice as distant as the space between the worlds. Then he rubbed his forehead with the heel of his hand. 'I'm Constant. I'm twelve. I remember that. Are you crying, Blix?'

In a space of a heartbeat Blix had covered the distance between them and thrown her arms around him, hugging him tightly and sobbing with relief she hadn't known she could feel.

'You're okay!'

Constant held the embrace slightly awkwardly, and patted her on the back, taking away a palm full of mud.

'I'm sorry if I scared you,' he said as Blix disentangled herself. 'I realise what it must have looked like. I didn't have time to explain.'

'You goddamn better explain, kid.' Kit hobbled past Blix and hauled Constant to his feet. 'You scared the pants off of us! What in God's sweet name did you mean by drinking that water? Why would you even do that? You're a goddamn idiot!'

She sounded furious, and relieved, and... scared, Blix realised, in a way far beyond the fear that Blix had felt. *She's upset because she thought she'd have to leave him behind. Like the man with the eggs.*

'I haven't been entirely straightforward with you,' said Constant. 'I promised I'd explain,' he added hurriedly, pulling away from Kit's grasp. 'And I will. But first we need to get out of this... this... Where are we?'

'In a swamp,' said Blix unnecessarily, pushing herself to her feet. 'It's some rocks and mud in a swamp. Couldn't be less appealing if they put up a "No Blix's" sign.'

She tried to scrape the glue-like mud off against one the iron-grey standing stones, and discovered they were covered in it too. 'Ack. But you are not getting away with leaving it like that. Through all the mad things that have happened to us, Constant, I've asked you what's happening, and you've said you don't know. And then you always seem to know other things about it and explain them at length. And then something else mad happens and I forget how unlikely that is.'

A hurt resurfaced, an ember of a still-smouldering fire. 'Sometimes you made me forget. Well, enough's enough. We're your... friends? Companions? I don't know. I still don't know how I feel about you. After the fright you just gave us, I don't trust you and I need to trust you. You said you thought what you did might be justice for making me forget. You know what justice is? It's the truth. We're in this together. Time to tell us what this is. Tell me the truth.'

Constant blanched at the reminder of the damage his words had done. He swallowed hard. 'All right. I will. But we still have to go. The wolves are right behind us.' He pulled his boot out of the sucking mud with a wet splotch. 'It could be slow going.'

Kit took him by the shoulders, spun him around and pushed him firmly out of the circle. It seemed a little less liquid underfoot. 'Walk and talk, kid. Walk and talk.'

The moon had made the First of Wolves whole, but the cave had taken it from him. He longed to return to the open air, to stand in the moon's white gaze and become himself again. But the scent was strong. *They are close.*

The burning land had meant nothing to the First of Wolves. He did not fear fire in the way the other werewolves did. He had driven the pack through it. They endured the pain knowing they would heal. But the char hid all other scents. Without the buzzing rock their hunt would have been over.

Seeing the boy that had killed his cub for the first time had robbed the First of Wolves of his voice, the fury choking his throat. Watching him kick his boat over the falls had made him despair. *I must be the one!* He'd tried to scream. *I must be the one to kill you!* To find his scent once more at the bottom of the falls had been a relief like he had never known. His howl had echoed to the moon.

The boy's scent wasn't the only one. The girl had bled - it was smeared liberally over some rocks - and almost changed. The other one's smell was made of fear, and sorrow, and - something else, a joy tinged with something the First of Wolves didn't understand. Something made of fire.

Fear was easy. The First of Wolves knew what fear smelled like. He had killed many men. All of them stank of fear in their last moments. Some were brave, some cowered and screamed, all were afraid. There was something about werewolves that terrified men in a way they could not control. A primal fear, passed down to men from the first man to see yellow eyes in the night and still live to see the sun rise in the morning. The fear that death had come for you, unstoppable, inevitable, hungering. The fear of the predator who has become prey.

Only two men had ever been completely unafraid of him. One was barely a man. The creature called Echmoth was only tenuously connected to the human shell it possessed and seemed to view death as an occupational hazard. It smelled of arrogance and rage and contempt for life. There was fear there, but not of the First of Wolves. It feared the rot. It stank of rot.

Then there was the magician, Dragonville. Even before his betrayal, merely being in the same room as Dragonville had made the First of Wolves want to bite his eyes out. His whimsical and affected manner was hate-making. A superficial observer would think him trivial, and doubt whether he could remember his last wholly sincere thought. Then he would look at you, or make a little aside, and you would realise that the affectation masked a will that could move mountains and power that could break them. He felt no fear because there was none who could challenge him. Or so he had thought, until he died. The memory of his death brought a moment's satisfaction to the First of Wolves' mind, and with that memory, the memory of the magician's scent; he smelled only of rust.

And now there was a third man who did not fear him. He was different again. The emaciated man sat by the river and looked up at the snarling werewolves with blank indifference. This was not how men reacted. He was not merely fearless of the werewolves. He had neither fear nor the lack of it. There was no calculation behind his eyes, no emotion, no presence. Just a dull stare which spoke of nothingness inside, a stare which said, here is a thing which is happening in front of me. I am looking at the thing.

'They stood here,' said a wolf. He sniffed the air. 'They went that way.' It pointed down a tunnel.

'I know.'

The First of Wolves became aware of other eyes. Humans here and there around the walls of the cave, watching them with the same empty detachment. He looked at the man before him. 'They stood here. What did you speak of?'

The man's brow creased, as though he had heard an impossible riddle in a language he barely knew. Eventually he said, 'I don't understand.'

'Three humans. Two bitches and a dog cu... Two females and a young male. You spoke to them before. Tell me the words and live.'

Confusion on the man's face, the fog in his mind clouding his eyes. He shook his head slowly. 'There is no before. This is the first thing.'

The First of Wolves considered this. He watched the ugly, oil-silvered water fold over itself as though molten. He breathed deeply. He smelled the cave, and the people, and death, and oblivion. *I did not know that had a scent. How strange that I recognise it.*

'Enough now,' he said, and without looking at him drew his hand across the man's neck, almost gently, barely whispering against the skin. He heard the man's sigh, and saw his head tilt back as the red line across his throat opened into a killing wound. Thick blood splattered his fur. The werewolves surged, eager to feast, but a bare twitch of the First of Wolves' muzzle stopped them dead. 'You will catch his disease,' he warned, knowing there was no disease. 'Don't drink the water,' he added, almost as an afterthought. It was unnecessary. He couldn't imagine any wolf would drink from this river.

The dead man toppled backward into the water and lay in the shallows as the blood drained from his body. Something large moved beneath the surface further out. A face appeared, man but not man, a lizard's body breaching behind the head. In a trice, the dead man was dragged under the surface, streaks of red resting momentarily on the silvered water before it turned on itself once more. The humans around the cave walls watched impassively. A thing was happening in front of them.

The First of Wolves turned and followed the scent trail into the tunnel. The scent was so strong it made a fire in his heart.

They are close.

The heat wrapped itself around Blix like a constrictor, tightening slightly with every breath, squeezing the air from her lungs. But even though the sweat dripped off her, Blix felt cold. An inch under the brackish grey mud it was as cold as moor clay. She could feel it even through the thick soles of Kit's boots, spikes of cold like dead fingers reaching up through the slop to pull her under. The earth felt wrong, and the trees that forced their way through that earth looked wrong too. They grew like mangroves but weren't, some salt-tolerant species with thick, rubbery leaves that Blix didn't recognise. They stank like vomit and it was all Blix could do not to add her own. Their black, slimy trunks and mass of intertwining vines and branches would have made the forest all but impenetrable had Constant not wielded Sorcha like a machete to cut a path. Even with his efforts, dagger-like roots poked through the surface, ready to slash unwary shins, as Blix had already discovered.

Pneumatophores, part of her brain informed her. *We did them in fourth year biology. They draw oxygen directly from the air. It's an adaptation. They adapted to survive in their environment. About time I did the same.*

Ahead of her Constant, hood up to protect himself from flying splinters, swung Sorcha again, carving a tunnel through a tangle of tree limbs. Blix had forgotten the sword was so sharp. As he lopped off another branch Blix remembered the moment they'd met, and how he'd taken a werewolf's head with the same action. The memory made her shudder for a moment. But only for a moment. And then it seemed normal. Good. Right.

That's not right. I didn't think like this when it happened. I've changed. Was it the words? Being bitten? Am I just harder now? Numb? I hate not knowing. I should know why I feel things. I wonder how the moon will rise.

'Penny for 'em, kiddo.'

'Still not worth a penny.' The reflexive answer was out before Blix really registered the question.

'Sure they are. A penny goes a long way with the right kind of gal. You okay?'

Blix blushed, and then realised she didn't know what Kit meant. Then she thought she probably did, and blushed again. 'Um. Sure. Fine.'

Kit's voice had come from some way behind. Once she was almost sure she'd returned to her normal complexion, Blix glanced over her shoulder. Kit was looking back the way they had come, gun drawn.

'Did you hear something?' whispered Blix.

'Nope. Just being careful, is all.'

They'd tried to run, but the vegetation and mud had slowed their pace to a crawl almost immediately. Fighting through it was exhausting and painful.

'How are your feet?'

'Absolutely fine,' said the American, with no trace of sarcasm. 'Walk in the park kiddo, green grass and buttercups.'

Birds and beasts squawked and chittered in the canopy above them, and the continual whine of the disturbingly large insects that dive bombed them every few seconds underlay everything. There were other noises too, distant 'hooom' calls which she didn't recognise but felt she should, a feeling which made her more than a little uneasy. *What lives in swamps and goes hooom?*

'Absolutely fine,' Kit repeated. 'Shame it's so quiet,' she added, pointedly projecting the statement over Blix's head.

Sorcha paused on the downswing. Constant's whole body settled a little as he sighed slowly. Then he attacked the branches with renewed vigour. Blix could hardly tell that his arms weren't working properly. Only when the blade thudded into the mud unexpectedly and he struggled to pull it out, was it clear that something wasn't right.

Kit made an impatient little clicking sound with her tongue. 'Well?'

'There's a prophecy,' said Constant, as if the words were being dragged out through his teeth.

Blix tossed her head contemptuously. 'A prophecy. Sure there is.'

Constant paused once more in his deforestation. 'What's that supposed to mean?'

'It's supposed to mean that I should have guessed there was some ancient mystic bollocks behind all this madness.'

'It's not mystic b... What you said,' said Constant tightly, resuming his slashing.

'Yes, it is. They all are. People read whatever they want into them. Bloody Nostradamus and all that. They're either made up, or loony and made up.'

'What she said,' Kit added. 'Prophecy schmophecy. Just a buncha lies.'

'It is not lies and it is not made up!' Constant, angrily spinning around. Even though his face was mostly covered Blix could see his jaw working as he tried to control his temper.

'It is not made up.' A deep breath. 'Sorry, it's just that this has been my life for all of my lives. It's the most important thing there is for us. For me.'

'I didn't mean to offend you,' said Blix. 'But prophecy is nonsense.'

Constant shook his head. 'This one's different.' He turned back to his chopping, avoiding Kit and Blix's sceptical looks. After a moment he cut through the undergrowth to the banks of a tiny stream. The way was clearer here and they could move a little faster.

'Do you know what a scrying stone is?' he asked, without turning around.

'Nope.'

'Me neither.'

'Magicians in ancient days - before my time - had a lot of power. A lot. Enough to make scrying stones. Don't ask me how, I wasn't allowed to know. They're magical tools, like the Thing, only far more powerful. More powerful even than your wicket. Powerful enough to make a gate in your mind.'

'Say what now?' Kit's eyes momentarily left the trail behind them to waste an incredulous look on the back of Constant's head.

'Prophecy, true prophecy, is about the deepest magic there is. Seeing time that hasn't happened yet from your point of view. Time before it emerges in the universe. The scrying stone creates a gate which only your mind goes through. You can end up anywhere. And just like a stone circle there is gain or lag. If you are lucky you go forward. And if you are even luckier you come back.' He pulled his hood back and gazed earnestly at Blix, trying to convince her of the truth of his words. 'You really see what is really to come.'

'Can't say I've ever been a big believer in fate, kid.' Kit stepped as lightly as she could along the bank of the stream, avoiding the roots that lurked under the surface of the mud. 'Fate is bunk.'

'It's not fate. It's very complicated. The future isn't fixed. But when you look through a scrying stone it becomes real. Seeing the future makes it the future.'

'Oh really.' Blix didn't try to hide her disbelief. 'Schrodinger's tea leaves, is it? No don't ask. So why are prophecies all like, you'll meet a tall dark handsome stranger? 'Cos I'm still waiting to bump into her, you know?'

'Now, I am kinda taller...'

'That's not prophecy,' said Constant. 'That's just a trick. Charlatanry. We had that on Shambhala too. Real prophecy is vanishingly rare. There haven't been any genuine scryers for, I don't know, millennia, probably. And there weren't many when there were some. You had to be really driven to try and see the future.'

Blix was about to reply when the ground gave way under her feet. With a little cry she slipped and landed on her backside in the freezing mud. 'Arse.' Half the swamp came with her as she pushed herself back up. 'Double arse. I hate this place. Absolutely hate it. I am absolutely exhausted and absolutely covered in this miserable clag.' She glared at Constant. 'Are we nearly there? Are we even going the right way?

'I don't know why I got a glare then. If your compass works here, then we're going south-east and it's not far.' His foot pulled away a lump of mud the size of a brick. 'It might take a while though.'

'Walk quickly,' Kit advised.

'Thanks, I hadn't thought of that. What is that noise?' he added, as a long 'hoooom' echoed across the swamp from far away.

'I heard it earlier.' Blix listened intently, but nothing came to mind. 'I can't place it.'

'Sounds like whale song?' Kit suggested.

Blix pursed her lips. 'Mmm, maybe. Maybe this is a world where land whales still exist. *Ambulocetus*, or something. Or maybe it's some swamp thingie, we won't know unless we see it. Sounds like it's a long way off, whatever it is.'

'Let's hope it stays there,' said Kit. 'Keep an ear open in case I have to blast something. Something else,' she corrected, looking coolly back down the track.

'How far behind us do you think they were?' Blix asked.

'Half hour or so, maybe.'

'How long has it been since we got here?'

'Half hour or so, maybe.'

'Great.'

'We'll burn that bridge when we come to it, kiddo. Let's keep going.'

They followed Constant through a thicket of widely spaced, thick-trunked trees with flaking yellow bark and leafless branches which stretched skyward like the antlers of an ancient elk.

Kit cleared her throat loudly.

'Now I can't help noticing that his Holiness has dried up...'

Constant reached into his sodden shoulder bag and pulled a thick corner of folded cloth just far enough out that Blix could see it. 'Do you remember this?'

'It's the sheet I had wrapped round me on Shambhala. It has writing on it I couldn't read. You said it was about your religion.'

'It's the prophecy. The original. The Writing, we call it. It's four thousand years old.' He pulled the cloth out a bit further and Blix noticed it was clean and dry, despite Constant's bag being wet through.

'It's wearing well.'

'It's protected. I told you.'

'Oh yeah. Magic linen, why shouldn't there be that?' Blix stumbled against a tree; the bark came away like paint chips, clinging to the mud on her jacket. 'Arse again. It's a bed sheet. Shouldn't prophecy be on, I don't know, tablets of stone?'

'Whoever wrote it used what they had to hand.'

'And it's about?'

'The end of the world. Of all worlds.'

Blix rolled her eyes. 'Which is not at all suspicious. It couldn't be next week's bingo numbers. Has to be something dramatic.'

'It's real. I told you.'

'Okay, let me have it.'

'Excuse me?'

'The worst verse. Let's hear it.' Blix reached to pull out the cloth from Constant's bag, but he gently blocked her hand.

'I know it by heart.'

'I expect you do. I guess you wrote it. Old you. Number One, or someone.'

'No. It was given to me. Him. I'm not a scryer. You couldn't force me to do it at sword point.' He stared into the middle distance for a moment, then began to speak. His voice took on a strange timbre, richer and older, but still his voice.

You are the Constant. This is your fate.

Nothing, then
A light. I see this Writing as I write
You will close the Narrow Way forever.
Afterward, Elpis. Life and death entwined together.
Nothing lies between.
You carry a lantern lit by hope. It guides your way
Wolves in the temple
The golden mouth
The rose and the thorn
The sun-crowned child and the moon made flesh
The two made one
Last of men
You must go forward.
You must follow the way. You can stop this Constant, here
Or all worlds end. This is uncertain
There is a way. I see
to open the gate, willingly embrace
Memory, Sacrifice, Thought
Drink of forgetting, and remember
Between memory and thought, seek knowledge of the runes
myself to myself.
Die and live, moon to moon.
The Wolf has the strength
In the thought of the story, kill the Rakshasa.
The white, the grey and the black
All men will be wolves
Blood and silver is the key
One who is two
Life for the living and death for the dead
The fire goes out
Death is not the end. You must go forward.
The soul knows the way
An endless labyrinth
The vessel of what remains. Ancient hope.
A prison for the mind. A silent child
Pursued when no man follows.
The damselfly
What remains
A dragon's scale
The burning gate
A circle turns upon itself

You taught me this
Where do we begin? The first, and the last
Where -

He broke off as a long 'hooooom' echoed through the trees. 'There it is again.'

'It's miles away,' said Blix. 'Ignore it. So that's your prophecy, is it?'

'Just about, yes.'

Blix saw the expectation in his eyes, and tried to think of something that wouldn't offend him. *Like, don't call it drivel.*

'It's really long. I was expecting something a bit snappier.' She thought some more. 'Catchy lyrics. Not exactly top forty material though. Didn't rhyme at all.'

'It's not verse. And it's long because that's what he saw. He wasn't trying to fit it into stanzas.'

'*Elpis,* ancient hope, the Narrow Way. These are the things Dragonville and Echmoth talked about. They know about the prophecy.'

'I think they must do. I've been thinking about it since the cottage. But I don't know how. The Writing has always been our most closely-held secret.' He shot a withering look at Kit. 'Until recently I would have said no one else could have known of it.'

'Don't look at me, I ain't even seen it,' said Kit stoutly. 'I was lookin' for Dragonville, not some damn nonsense prophecy.'

'It is *not* da- '

'Damn nonsense is what it is,' interrupted Kit derisively. 'Y'all monks bin led on a snipe hunt by some carpetbagger.'

'No, we haven't,' said Constant. Blix admired his patience; she could barely even tell that he was massively pissed off. 'It's not verse and it's not nonsense. It's the record of a man's mind fracturing. What I said about being driven? Seeing the future sends you mad. Always. It's profoundly unnatural. You become disconnected. Unmoored. Unable to say simple things. But people have chosen to do it. Anyone who is willing to do that, that's driven.'

'So, it *is* loony.'

'No. It's… filtered through madness. You get what they can make sense of.'

He paused to listen to the swamp noises for a moment, then resumed his narrative.

'The Writing seems to describe multiple events. Normally scryers see one thing and try and describe their impressions. The way the Writing is structured suggests the prophet made repeated attempts at scrying, maybe as many as twenty. I can't imagine what that would do to a mind.'

Kit moved forward to talk to Constant. That left Blix at the back. She scanned the forest for yellow eyes.

'Still not buying it, kid.' Kit grabbed the point of Constant's hood and pulled it down so she could see his face. Startled, he slipped backward a little and stopped walking. 'How do you know it ain't bullshit?'

Constant righted himself. 'The prophecy is written in a language that didn't exist at the time it was written. The First Father knew how to read it because, well, because magic, I assume. I don't want to go that deep into my mind. He taught the brothers. But it was only seven hundred years ago that we discovered other people using that language. People on Earth. People who, more or less, had just invented it. The words are corrupted, some are sounded differently, but it was their language. That was the first moment that we knew for certain it wasn't just gibberish.' He gave a tired little laugh. 'If you ever wonder what faith is, faith is three millennia of believing in a sheet without knowing if could be real. I still don't absolutely know what it means.'

He looked relieved. Blix realised it was the first time he could ever have told the story to someone who didn't already know it. It was the relief of generations.

Kit gave a low whistle. '"*Drink of forgetting, and remember,*"' she repeated. 'You drank that oily shit based on five words of nonsense and you didn't know it was true? Kid, you take a lot on trust. I mean, a lot.'

'That's what faith is too,' Constant replied simply. 'My brothers have been parsing every word of the prophecy for millennia. I told you we'd sent people to Horkos. We knew what the water did. It was the only thing we had ever found which remotely agreed with that line. And there I was, where none of me who came before could possibly have hoped to be. It seemed so obvious. But no, I didn't know for sure until I woke up here and could still remember. That's what faith is.'

'You're crazy,' said Kit emphatically. 'Brave as hell but plumb crazy. Ain't no doubt, that's the bottom fact.'

Blix gave up trying to scrape the tree bark from her jacket. 'What does the rest of it mean?'

'There are dozens of interpretations, different schools of thought, learned treatise -'

Kit threw up her hands in exasperation. 'Will you please get to the goddamn point of what the goddamn hell is going on?'

'Oh.' Constant seemed genuinely surprised to be asked. 'I thought that bit was obvious. I told you that Echmoth and Dragonville are trying to open the Narrow Way. All the evils of the world. So yes, they know about this prophecy. Which is just *impossible*,' he continued under his breath, looking deeply frustrated. He composed himself and continued.

'I told you I'm going to stop them. I'm going to stop them because the prophecy says I'm going to stop them. But I have to be tortured first.'

'Oh. Wait, what the -'

Constant cut Kit off. 'We're here.'

They emerged into an open space, an oval a few hundred feet across. A circle of five perfect trilithons stood in its centre. Immense, thick bluestones so sharp edged and clean compared to their murky surroundings that they looked freshly hewn. What quarry they could possibly have been dragged from Blix couldn't imagine. It had been hard enough dragging herself through the swamp.

Behind the circle the landscape rose sharply, an up-thrust of huge, smooth boulders piled haphazardly into a mount which closed off the far side of the oval into a canyon, its lower slopes reaching around the edge. From the angle they stood at it looked like it was protecting the circle, embracing it in granite arms.

Blix squinted at the rock formation. 'Is that a bergrisar?'

'A what now?'

'A mountain giant. They're made of stone.'

Kit turned her head this way and that trying to turn the outcrop into a monster in her mind's eye.

'Can't tell. Is it likely to be?'

'Mmm, not sure. They like to lie in wait. It happens now and then in Norway, I saw it on *Panorama*. But they are very rare.'

'Saw it on what? I suppose if it eats us, the answer's yes.'

Before Blix could answer Kit turned back to Constant. 'What the hell do you mean, you have to be tortured?'

The circle looked dry and inviting and the outcrop accordingly less giant-like to Blix's mind. 'Let's get out of here,' she said, as Constant opened his mouth to reply. 'We can hear the rest of the midget mentalist's story once we're a world away. Come on! Hey, that's some echo. HELLLOOO.' The sound bounced around the canyon walls in a manner that Blix found deeply satisfying.

Constant scowled and looked at his feet. 'I am not a... What made that?'

With the point of his sword he showed them what he'd found. It was a footprint, on the edge of the swamp, half filled with water. Big, the size of Blix's whole body from neck to hips, it was a curious star shape, with three long toes splayed at the front and two more at the rear, stubbier and clawed. There was a line of them, emerging from the swamp where they stood and continuing in a kind of drunken stagger for a dozen yards, after which they turned back into the trees and vanished.

'Not a giant,' said Kit, sketching out a vague shape in the air which matched the print's proportions. Pretty big though. I ain't never seen-'

'Stop talking right now,' hissed Blix. She felt the blood drain from her face and solidify in her stomach as fear.

'What-' began Constant in his normal voice, but before he could say more than the word Blix had clamped one hand across his mouth and had a finger of the other to her lips. Constant looked in her eyes and his words dried. Blix released him and waved for them to step back behind the tree line. Once they were a few trunks deeper into the swamp she drew them together so she could whisper into their ears at the same time. Her voice was barely a breath, hardly sound at all.

'There's a cyclops nearby. It will have heard us. Do as I do. Don't ask why. Say nothing. When it comes, don't move for any reason, no matter what it does. Don't fight. Don't even breathe.'

She took two steps away from them to the nearest tree, a rotten-looking thing with thick wilting leaves which stank to high heaven. Carefully she draped herself around it, pressing her head and body against the bark so there was no gap between them. Kit and Constant exchanged glances, then found trees of their own nearby, where they could see each other and Blix. Awkwardly, they copied Blix's pose.

Seconds passed, then minutes. It seemed the swamp noises increased to fill the emptiness their silence had made. Insects chirruped continually, birds added their chorus. There was nothing to suggest a monster was coming. As the minutes dragged on Blix saw this thought appear on her friends' faces and translate through their bodies into frustrated twitchiness. A little shifting of weight here, a little annoyed sigh there; not much, but too much.

Kit particularly did not count stillness among her virtues. With treacle slowness Blix slid her left hand up around the tree trunk. Her index finger arrived at her lips just as Kit couldn't hold it in anymore and opened her mouth to complain. Blix caught her eye and tapped her lips with her finger, sharply. Kit rolled her eyes in exasperation, but closed her mouth.

Then the cyclops was there. It would have been fifteen feet tall standing straight, but the cyclops walked in a strange crouch, knuckling silently forward almost on all fours. Unclothed, it was the same oily grey as the swamp mud, so much so that it might easily disappear if it lay still on the ground. Its great head, huge but disproportionately small for its enormous body, swung back and forth, side to side as its single rheumy eye sought out prey. It moved sinuously, easing branches aside without breaking them, making little noise for such a massive creature. Its features, although vaguely human, looked like they had been squashed onto the face as an afterthought. Fangs curled out of a protruding jaw. It turned its head this way and that, moving constantly, scanning the ground. It carried a club - not a weapon shaped by an intelligent mind, but what looked like a lightning blasted tree trunk, torn from the ground, roots still trailing. Very slowly, it moved toward Blix. The huge, splayed, star-like feet gripped the soft mud, ready to leap when prey came near.

Don't panic. You've read about them. You know what to do. Don't even breathe.

The creature moved, and paused, and moved again, the great eye never resting, the head crossing and crisscrossing the trees. It moved a few steps further. It was so close to Blix she could have reached out and touched it. She slowed her breathing as much as she could and tried to ignore the part of her mind that was screaming for oxygen, and the other part that was screaming at her to run. *It doesn't see me. I know this. I have to trust what I know.*

She saw movement. In a moment when the creature's gaze was elsewhere, Kit McCoy had raised her pistol and was pointing it at the cyclops' head. Blix tried to scream with only her eyes; *don't do it, don't do it, you'll kill us all!*

There was a noise in the trees, a sharp clack of wood striking wood. The cyclops' head came up, listening intently. With impossible grace it eked away into the undergrowth quickly and silently in the direction of the sound, and was straightaway lost from view, blending into the swamp.

Blix fought the urge to move. She made eye contact with Constant and Kit in turn and saw the question in their eyes. Excruciatingly slowly, Kit raised a finger and pointed to her mouth. To each Blix gave the slightest shake of the head; *not yet, not yet.*

They waited, unmoving, as the seconds passed. Blix started counting. When she reached six hundred she let go of the tree; only then did she notice the pain she was in. 'Okay,' she whispered. 'Okay.'

The others stretched their stiff limbs and joined her by the rotten tree. Blix held her finger to her lips once more and whispered, 'I think it's gone. Keep your voices down just in case.'

'That was exciting,' Kit hadn't holstered her pistol. 'Why ain't we dead?'

Blix's hands were shaking. She curled them into fists and pressed then against her legs. 'It has good hearing but extremely poor eyesight and sense of smell. The eye is one of evolution's little jokes, I suppose. Zero depth perception. Its vision is based entirely on movement. It doesn't recognise things. When you stood against the trunk you stopped looking like an animal shape. It couldn't tell the difference between you and the tree. But If you'd moved it would have heard you instantly and seen that you weren't tree. Then you'd have been eaten.' She breathed out hard. 'I probably attracted it when I shouted.'

'I should have blasted it. I almost did, when it got so close to you.'

'We'd have died,' said Blix simply. The shaking wasn't going away. 'They're essentially invulnerable. Incredibly tough skin. They're critically endangered on Earth, but occasionally one turns up near some village in Sarawak or Madagascar or somewhere. They just have to wait for it to go away. Or bring out the artillery, nothing's that invulnerable. You can kill anything if you want it dead enough. But regular bullets bounce off it.'

'One in the peeper would do the trick, I reckon.'

'Blinding barely slows them down. They're famous for it. You should read the Odyssey. And they can regrow eyes. What blinding it would have done is sent it into frenzy which would have destroyed the trees and us together. Best just to leave it alone.'

'It's gone, anyway. We should go too,' Constant said. Without waiting for the others, he squelched back the way they had come. When Blix and Kit caught up with him he was already inside the gate. 'Hurry up,' he urged as they approached. 'We don't have much time.'

As if on cue there was a thunderclap, which reverberated around the stones and momentarily silenced the swamp insect chorus. A patch of sky just visible over the trees darkened and began swirling rapidly, forming a vortex like a hurricane.

Blix had no fear left in her, just bone weariness. 'I've never seen it from the outside before,' she said, as the vortex crackled with strange energy. 'That's not far away at all, is it?'

'They won't be long. Come inside.' Constant had the velvet cloth with the bloodstone shards in his hand, the first time Blix had seen them since they'd arrived on Ceto. Some sparkled in the light and seemed to Blix to be filled with the same power that cut the sky in the distance. Others lay rusted and useless, used up. It suddenly seemed impossible that one of those tiny flecks really held the power to ignite the massive gate and hurl them across the universe. Blix stepped into the circle anyway. She was too tired to care anymore.

Kit didn't join them. 'I got an idea,' she said.

'Let's talk about it when we're a world away from those wolves,' Constant said.

'That's the thing, kid. I reckon if we run, we're done. They're gonna catch up with us soon, somewhere we don't know, where we don't have the best chance to kill their asses. But you see here?' Her open arms took in the circle and rocky outcrop that loomed over it. 'This here strikes me as an opportunity.'

'Opportunity?'

'Guessin' you ain't never committed an ambush?'

'Not in this lifetime,' Constant said evenly. 'Have you?'

'It may be within my experience.' She pointed up to a mound of large boulders halfway up the scree slope, perhaps forty feet above their heads. 'That there is a defensible position. And this here,' she continued, twirling her forefinger to indicate the circle, 'this here is a killing field.'

'Seven bullets,' said Blix. 'Seven silver bullets to kill twelve werewolves.'

'Seven for her. My sword for five,' said Constant, his face hardening in a way Blix now found wholly familiar. 'I've killed five before. At the circle. And we slew them when they attacked Roohsk's boat. I am good at killing wolves.'

'Yes, you are!' exclaimed Kit delightedly, giving the boy's hair a good-natured ruffle. He shrugged her off, suddenly twelve again. 'Mind you, that all kinda implies they'll just patiently line up while we mow 'em down one at a time. In reality, what happens is we get one or two and then we get got when the rest swarm us. But hey, if they get that close you can do your thing, kid. And if your thing ain't enough, there's always plan B.' She pulled the chain around her neck until the wicket stone dangled free. 'Express train to No Wolf Land.'

'I won't go,' said Constant immediately.

'Me neither,' said Blix. 'I won't leave my sister.'

'You'll both go if staying means dying,' said Kit bluntly. 'We can work out what to do next when we're not dead.'

'You said it wouldn't take three,' Blix reminded her.

'I know what I said. But shit, I don't know how this thing works any more than you do. Maybe it would. It's a last resort. I coulda used it plenty of times since I met you, but I didn't. Wolves will have to be chewing our asses off afore I do. But in that particular circumstance, better to try than die.'

Then she smiled her easy smile again. 'But you know, I ain't planning on letting them get that close.'

'What do you mean?' asked Blix.

Kit smiled, a wide-mouth grin of barely suppressed glee. To Blix it was as though the sun had come out from behind storm clouds.

The black pit in the sky spat out monsters, folded in on itself in a ragged wound scar and vanished as though it had never been there at all. The werewolves fell to earth, skidding in the wet mud, but ready to fight, ready to kill. Then as one the New wrinkled their noses in disgust and tried to cover their faces, whimpering like puppies.

'Ach! What has died here?' said one.

'Everything,' said another. 'This whole place stinks of rot.' It took a tentative sniff, and gagged. 'I cannot smell them. We cannot follow.'

'Use your eyes, fool,' said a third. It slid through the mud to the edge of the circle, where the slopping holes left by human feet led into the swamp, passing under fresh cut branches. 'They are this way.'

The First of Wolves said nothing. He tipped the smooth stone from its hiding place into his palm and said, 'The High Rocks.' The buzzing intensified as he turned toward the footprints, and a little past them, to a dense patch of gnarled and tangled vines. A harder path than the one the humans had cut.

'They wander,' he announced. 'Turning as the trees allow them to cut through. It slows them down. We will make a straighter road.'

He ran then. At first along the human path, but when the cleared way turned from that which the buzzing stone wanted him to follow he ripped at the vines which blocked his way, which tore under his great strength like flesh stripped from bone. The jungle melted before him. The other werewolves took their place in his wake.

Soon they found a clearing where the land rose out of the mud and more rocks made a wide circle. A fist of stone towered behind it, sweeping down from its round peak and around the circle until it petered out into pebbles. Of the humans there was no sign, though as the First of Wolves stepped beyond the tree line he tasted the slightest tang of silver.

'We are too late. They have gone to the next place.' He paused at the circle edge. Something wasn't right. 'Wait. It is not burnt. The gate is unused. They are *here*.'

As he spoke the words a crack of thunder rang out, echoing wildly around the rocks. The First of Wolves felt the air move in front of him. The werewolf next him span as something bit into its chest and fell, howling in pain. Another wolf yelped in surprise as something screamed across its shoulder, missing it by inches.

'Shit,' said someone nearby.

The First of Wolves smelt the air. 'A silver spitter! Scatter! Behind the stones!' Effortlessly he scooped up the stricken werewolf and ducked behind the nearest bluestone. It screamed and coughed up blood.

'Hold still.' The First of Wolves pushed his finger into the wound and tasted the blood. He spat it out immediately.

'I will heal,' it barked thickly. A strange look came over its face. It coughed up more blood.

'You will not. You are already dead.' He stood up, ignoring the increasing weak protestations of the dying werewolf. Hugging the flat of the bluestone he took a swift look around the edge, trying to spot his assailants. He ducked back immediately, expecting to attract a silver shot. None came. Instead, someone shouted.

'HELLO DOWN THERE YOU MISERABLE SONS-A-BITCHES literally ha YOU TAKE ONE STEP TOWARD US AND I WILL BLOW YOUR DAMN BRAINS ALL OVER THOSE ROCKS! WE GOT SILVER AND WE AIN'T AFRAID TO USE IT Jesus look kindly I hope this works.'

The First of Wolves regarded his pack, hiding two or three deep behind the immense standing stones. At their most manlike in the daytime, they looked eagerly at him, awaiting his command. The silver did not terrify them.

They are New. They know nothing. They know how to obey and how to fight. But I know how wars are fought.

The First of Wolves considered what he knew. When he'd tested his enemies above the waterfall the woman had spat silver. But only the woman, and only once. And now again, only one spitter and only twice.

When I fought the Lyonesse men they rained metal down upon us with the roar of a thousand dragons. The air stank of brimstone. And when we rose again and fell upon them they spat metal until their last breath. These have nothing left to spit, or very little. They plan something else. They hope our fear of silver blinds us to their weakness.

There was the boy's sword. The thought of the boy set the First of Wolves' mind afire. He damped it down in order to think.

The boy can kill wolves. But we can swarm him and the woman both. He is from our place, he knows I will send them, and how.

The First of Wolves risked another glance. He wondered how loose the boulders they hid behind were. Did they plan to roll them? No, that was implausible. They would be dead before the first rock fell.

'HELLLLOOO HAIRY-BRITCHES! AIN'T YOU GOT NOTHIN' TO SAY BEFORE WE BLAST YOU INTO THE NEXT WORLD?'

One of his men spoke up. 'We should fall on them and tear their throats out!' Yelps of assent. He silenced then with a twitch.

The First of Wolves risked another glance. The rise to the boulders where they hid was steep and rocky but easily climbable in moments for a wolf. The rocks could be approached on both sides. Wolves would die as they gained the position but as they moved it would be harder for the bitch to hit them with the silver. Those that survived would fall on them. Once her silver was spent the older bitch was just a bitch and would be killed. The young bitch stank of her disease and would be stronger, but no match for a real wolf. The cub was a wolf killer but would be limited by the position he had taken. No space to swing and turn. If wolves fell on him from both sides he would be dead before he could kill many. No, not dead - taken, so the First of Wolves could carve out his heart and squeeze it to a pulp before his still-living eyes.

The First of Wolves looked again. He saw the older bitch pointing her metal spitter toward the stones. He saw the cub with his silver blade. The ever-present rage began to boil within him.

'I see you,' he said, loud enough so that they might hear him.

'Well hallelujah we got a talker TURN AROUND AND GO BACK THE WAY YOU CAME OR GET A SILVER BULLET UP YOUR ASS! I MEAN IT GODDAMMIT!'

Without words the First of Wolves sketched out his plan for the pack. How they would divide, how they would attack, what they would do to each human.

A new voice came from above. BEGONE, WORTHLESS DOG!' yelled the cub. 'I AM THE DEATH OF WOLVES.'

'WHY ARE YOU CHASING US YOU BASTARD!' screamed the younger bitch. 'LEAVE US ALONE. WE'VE NEVER DONE ANYTHING TO YOU!'

The scalding fury inside the First of Wolves boiled over.

'Slayer of my cub! Ender of my line! I will tear your hearts out for what you have done to me. You will die bitch, as you should have died at my cub's hand!'

'What? At the circle? He was trying to rape and kill me!'

'Then you should have died!' screamed the First of Wolves. '*We* die! That's all we do! We do not breed! He was the last born, the youngest of us! Now there are only half-breeds and mongrels, these bastard creatures of magic. And you, you are an uncreature, a half-thing. Diseased, fit only for killing.'

'Fuck you. Just, fuck you.'

'I killed him,' said the cub in a voice of ancient death. 'I killed them all. I cut off their heads and stabbed them with silver so they wouldn't come back. I'll do the same to you. As if it matters. Come and get me.'

The older bitch began 'I think I see-' but the First of Wolves had talked enough. He threw back his head and howled, his fury echoing to the skies. The pack joined him in the terrifying roar and as they howled they came around the stones and charged.

An enormous one-eyed creature burst through the trees, screeching hideously, checking the werewolves in their stride as it barged toward them. The cyclops swung its tree club hard, lifting a startled werewolf off the ground and smashing it against one of the gate stones. Its chest shattered. A branch stump on the tree trunk tore the creature open as the cyclops yanked back its weapon. It slid down the rock, broken, entrails pouring out of the hole where its midriff had been, dead for now.

The other werewolves turned and set upon the cyclops with terrible fury, one leaping on its back, clawing at its spine, teeth around its skull, another dodging under the cyclops' grasping arms to rip out its throat. The others harried it with bites and slashes. The First of Wolves drew his sword and hacked at the cyclops, trying to severe its limbs. But the steel bounced off the impenetrable skin; the teeth did not pierce it, nor the claws slice into flesh. The cyclops reached over its shoulder and grabbed its attacker, its giant hand closing around the werewolf's head completely. It yanked, and lifted, and crushed. The werewolf's skull exploded into a red sludge which splattered in gobbets across the circle. The body collapsed, twitching. Then the cyclops wrapped his massive arms around the wolf at his throat, which realised too late that it couldn't hurt the behemoth and clawed to be free. The cyclops squeezed sharply, shattering the werewolf's neck and spine, cutting off the creature's screeching howl as it began. The cyclops cast the limp rag of fur aside.

Shots rang out from behind the rocks. Two shots; two more werewolves fell. Those that remained were caught between attacking the ridge, ducking from the silver bullets and fighting the cyclops. Their indecision cost them. One took a sweep from the great club so hard that it launched it into the air. When it landed it lay stunned for a moment, and took a silver bullet through the chest because of it. The other werewolves leapt once more onto the great beast but to no avail; it ripped them off and smashed them into the ground. The first two to fall were greeted with bullets from above; both shots missed.

'Shit, I'm out.'

A werewolf trying to bite the eye from the cyclops' face got its own face chewed off in return. With incredible speed for such an immense beast the cyclops snatched at one of the remaining werewolves. It squeezed hard and the werewolf almost exploded, blood fountaining from its shattered body. The cyclops cast it aside.

One remained. It was the First of Wolves.

This is not my end.

'Do you think you can kill me?' said the werewolf defiantly.

The cyclops paused, looking suddenly confused - not because of the question, the First of Wolves quickly realised. Rather because it didn't understand words. The First of Wolves lowered his weapon. 'You cannot kill me,' he repeated. 'Rend me then, it just wastes time, I will -'

And then the First of Wolves remembered the boy in the rocks behind him. The boy with the silver sword. He knew their plan.

He turned to run but the cyclops was faster, faster than seemed possible. The creature grabbed the First of Wolves' trailing leg and held him, ignoring the frantic blows that rained down on it. It slammed the werewolf into the ground, then grasped his sword arm and with no effort at all, snapped it off. The First of Wolves screamed, agony such as he had never known burning through his body.

The cyclops picked up the sword, the long iron tiny in its massive fist. turning it this way and that as though it was a shiny toy to play with. Then it lifted the First of Wolves effortlessly into the air, dangling him upside down by one leg, standing to its full height as it did so. It swung the sword and hacked the First of Wolves in half, slicing him from crotch to skull in one awful, hideous blow.

Chapter Thirty-One: To Bow

'Don't move,' Blix whispered. 'Don't make a sound.'

She watched the cyclops cut the First of Wolves in two and the inside bits spill out of his body and onto the ground. Part of her was revolted by the slaughter and the offal. Another part was exultant. *They're dead, they're dead, no more running, we are free!* But that part also knew the truth: some of the werewolves were not dead. Another part of her wanted to tear the wolf meat from the cyclops' hands and devour it. She pushed that part as far down inside her as she could, but the scent of blood dragged it back up against her will.

Back in the circle, the cyclops was discovering that werewolf meat did not suit the cyclopean palate. It spat out a chunk of the First of Wolves' thigh, visibly frustrated at the sour taste of its meal. It hurled the half corpse hard into the jungle. The body span through the trees and disappeared into the undergrowth.

The cyclops mooched through the wreckage of the other werewolves, looking for something edible without success. Long minutes passed. Eventually it plodded back into the bush and was quickly hidden from view.

Blix, Kit and Constant waited. They waited, unmoving, for the cyclops to get far enough away that they could move without it hearing, watching the werewolf bodies for the slightest twitch or jerk, anything that would tell that the beasts were coming back to life.

Several centuries passed, in Blix's mind at least. Each second felt like a lead weight in her pockets, holding her down when her mind was screaming at her to move. She stayed still. She knew a lot about cyclopes. She counted.

Eventually, millions of years later, Constant whispered, 'Long enough?'

'Yes,' Blix breathed.

At once he was off, scrambling down the scree of rocks that separated the three friends from the carnage below. As he reached the circle he pulled Sorcha clear of its scabbard so swiftly the sword seemed to leap into his hand of its own accord. A fierce horizontal swing cleanly decapitated the disembowelled werewolf, whose head then got the point of the sword through its skull. The second werewolf had no skull left to pierce, so Constant impaled its heart instead, then hacked away at the squashed brain fragments just to be sure, his blade biting into the dirt with each blow.

As Constant turned to the third werewolf, Blix and Kit caught up with him. The beast was stirring, not fully conscious - not fully alive - but healing. Blix could see the fragments of its shattered spine knitting back together - slivers of bone sliding together, clicking into place and fusing into one, as though it had never been broken at all. Blix was still watching when Constant sliced its head in two; the healing stopped instantly, the magic causing it dissipated by the silvered strike. Blix felt nothing about it. Not revulsion, not fear, not even the rage or hunger of the wolf inside her. Just emptiness and an exhaustion she couldn't put into words.

Constant continued his grim business. Wolf after wolf was decapitated. Even the ones who had taken a silver bullet were stabbed and had their heads removed. Blix heard him mutter something under his breath with each stroke. 'Stops them getting back up,' he said.

That only left the First of Wolves. Close to, the damage done to the werewolf seemed more like butchery. Its insides had been emptied of its offal, organs strewn nearby or flung into the bushes with the rest of the corpse. The leg the cyclops had gnawed on was nowhere to be seen. Blood drenched everything.

'Can he really come back from this?' she asked.

Constant turned over a lump of flesh with his foot. 'Yes. From anything not done by silver or their own kind. No, it makes no sense. Yes, it is arbitrary. Magic is. It never helps.'

'I guess I'm becoming predictable.'

'I'm just tired of questions.' Constant raised his sword.

'Let me,' Blix said, blurting out the words somewhat to her own surprise. 'Let me do it.'

Constant paused in his death-stroke, and fixed Blix with a stare so bleak and pitiless that it made her shiver. *That's not you. Who are you? What was the name he said? Darcen Ysir. You're terrifying, Darcen Ysir.*

'Why? As if it matters.'

Blix took a moment to answer, staring blankly at the First of Wolves' body, waiting for the right words to come. It seemed as dead as dead as could be. No breath, no heartbeat, no means of making either left inside its ruined shell. *But was that a flicker in the corner of its eye? Is that life, or life to come?*

'It took my sister. Killed your brothers. Killed Roohsk and Seminah and Akali. And the rest. Who knows who else. Chased us across the universe. I am terrified of it. I want to be the one who ends the chase.'

'That ain't nothing to want, kiddo,' said Kit softly.

'I know.'

Not-Constant turned the sword and presented the hilt to Blix. As it left his hand he was Constant again, the change as clear as the sun coming out from behind storm clouds. He didn't seem to notice.

She struck clean and hard, the same blow she had struck to the dead wolf in the Monastery, which now seemed so long ago that it quite surprised her to remember only a few days had passed. The half head cut neatly in two. Methodically, Blix chopped the First of Wolves' body into pieces. When she was done, she felt nothing about it, only deep, deep tiredness. She wanted to lay down next to the werewolves and sleep like death would be a gift. Sorcha slipped from her fingers. Constant caught it before it hit the ground. He wiped the flat on what remained of the First of Wolves' chest.

Something not-flesh moved under the blade. Constant lifted it up a large pouch, torn nearly in half.

'Let's have a look-see,' said Kit. She pulled it off and tipped the contents into her hand.

Constant gasped. 'My bloodstone!' He reached out to pluck the gem from Kit's fingers and then suddenly pulled his hand away, as though he'd thought twice about it. 'I promised… no, circumstances have changed.' More gingerly, he took the stone from the American's grasp. As he held it his expression changed to one of wonder. 'I have possessed this for four thousand years. I thought I'd never see it again.'

'The happy reunion between a boy and his pet rock,' Blix observed. 'Very touching.'

Constant laughed. 'Touching, yes. I've never touched it before. As me. Not since it became the Vermillion Bird's eye. We can go anywhere now.'

Blix felt like her heart had burst in a shower of firework sparks, a roman candle dripping down the sky. The pall of exhaustion lifted as though it had never covered her at all. *I'm coming for you, Katy!*

'Our bacon is saved,' Kit pronounced. 'Hey, what's this?' She tipped something else from bag. 'Lookee here.' She held up the object between thumb and forefinger; a blue-tinted monocle surrounded by gold wire. It glinted in the sunlight.

'That's the lens!' said Blix in surprise. 'I saw it on Shambhala.'

'Glory be,' said Kit, deeply satisfied. 'That's what I was sent for. Her smile disappeared. 'Shit, it's broke.' She showed them a large crack through the blue glass. At the top a fragment was missing. She fished through the torn pouch and found it. 'Well, no problem. The Mormons want it back, they didn't say nothing about mint condition.'

'Will they still pay you?' asked Blix.

'They will if they don't wanna get shot.' She slipped it inside her jacket into an inner pocket and looked around at the dead werewolves. 'Guess you get to keep your ears boys, I ain't gonna need 'em.'

Constant was frowning. 'If these were the magician's, why does the wolf have them?'

'They were working together,' said Blix. 'Maybe he gave them to him.'

'There's no way a magician lets these out of his sight.'

'Maybe he's dead, then.'

'I surely hope not,' said Kit, hitching up her pistol belt. 'I want to kill the motherfucker myself.'

'You must really hate that man,' said Constant.

'Indeed I do, kid. Indeed I - well now. Surprise number three.' Wrinkling her nose in obvious distaste, she kicked something hard and ovate from under a piece of First of Wolves.

'The Thing!' Constant scooped it up. 'I was right, that's how they were following us.'

'Clever dogs. Formerly.'

Blix spat on the First of Wolves' corpse. 'Good news all round for a change. Great. Let's get off this shithole world before Lady Luck notices she's taken her eye off the ball and sends the cyclops back to duff us up.'

'Damn right. The place is making my head hurt anyway. Well, we're in the circle. Where to now, kid?'

'Elysium. *Come and see.*'

Constant dreamed.

In my dream, I am walking the Path of Fire. I have been Recognised, the path leads me home to the Anvil and safety. It may take me some time to arrive. With each step, I perform the Emperor Bow.

I talk a step. I kneel. I bow, full length, until my forehead touches the ground, my arms outstretched beside me. I count to three. I sit up to a kneeling position once more. I bow again, head touching the ground, arms outstretched. I return to kneeling. I bow for a third time. I return to kneeling. I stand up. Then I kneel again, and perform three more bows. Then I stand up. Then I kneel again, and perform three more bows. Three kneelings and nine prostrations. That is the Emperor Bow. The whole Bow takes about five minutes to complete. Then I take another step, and begin the Bow again.

I take perhaps twelve steps an hour, one hundred in an eight-hour day, which is about the most I can endure. Each step covers one cubit in distance, so I travel two hundred cubits a day, or a league in just over twenty-five days. This day marks exactly two years since I joined the Path of Fire and began to bow.

We joined the Path quite close to the Anvil. I have travelled over twenty-nine leagues in those two years. There are over seventy more leagues before I reach the Iris. I will be on the path, bowing at every step, for another five and a half years.

With every kneeling, with every prostration, I speak the words of the Penance. 'For any hurt I have caused you, for any fault or sorrow, I ask forgiveness. My soul is yours.' But there is no one left alive to forgive me.

My name is Darcen Ysir. I am the Constant. This is my penitence. There is nothing in this that makes up for what I have done.

In my dream the brothers stand guard in a phalanx, surrounding me. They are allowed to descend from the safety of the Anvil for the search for the new Great Father. Once I am found I am supposed to go there - return there - and take my place behind the thick walls of their unbreachable fortress on top of their unclimbable mountain. I do feel an almost overpowering urge to do so. That I have not done so has been the cause of great distress for the brethren. They remonstrated, then made demands, then debated taking me against my will. I reminded them of my name, which put an end to that suggestion. Eventually they gave in. Others arrived, returning home now that their task is complete, or descending from the Monastery when the news of my self-abasement reached them. They exist to keep me safe. So now a small army of red-robed men stand beside me as I make each bow, and take a step as I take mine.

There are few onlookers. This is not an age in which men travel far from their holds if they can help it, not even to see the living God of their religion throw himself upon the mercy of the dead he has made. Mainly because men like me will kill them and take what is theirs. When we approach a torch pole the community that maintains it appears, but there is only so much awe even the most devout of the faithful possesses, and only so much entertainment to be derived from someone passing by on his hands and knees, very slowly. They drift away to their lives, as they should. I am not to be worshipped.

I cannot imagine how I will come to terms with my acts. I barely survived my Recognition. The suddenness of the emotion nearly broke me. I had never felt like that before. I had never really felt before.

I am not a fool. I do not believe that this absolves me of my crimes. If I am honest - and I have always been honest - I am not entirely sure why I am doing this. Perhaps I do this to separate the past from the future. I know that I have changed. Perhaps I do not truly believe it though. Perhaps I do this in the hope that, in five and a half years when I reach the Anvil, the man who slaughtered his way across a continent will be no more than a distant memory. That I will be worthy of the name of Constant.

I don't know. I take a step, and kneel, and bow, and rise again.

Now there is a boy I... recognise.

'I see we're in a memory of the older Ysir,' *he says.* 'I wasn't expecting to see him again. You must be feeling guilty about something.'

'I know you,' *I say, but the voice that emerges from my mouth is not my own. It is a child's voice. And then, somehow, I am someone else.*

'Yes, you can remember me now,' *says the boy, grinning cheerfully.* 'Only when you're asleep or unconscious, but it's a start.'

Constant realised he was now separate from Darcen Ysir. He was in his own body, looking the same as he appeared when awake. The kneeling figure seemed frozen in place - as did everyone else. It felt like he'd woken up in a painting and then stepped out of it.

The boy was looking expectantly at him. 'I remember you,' said Constant. 'Not just from when I drank the water. From when you were in my dreams. When I was Ysir, or Ails Goodhusband, or Comen sen-Hersa or the others. I couldn't before. I just remembered the dream, if I remembered it. But now I remember you were in them too.'

'Blocked by the words. But not anymore. These are my memories, you see. You wiped yours. My memories, my rules. We might get more than a few seconds together now that I'm in charge.'

That is extremely interesting, said Darcen Ysir. Constant looked at the kneeling man, and was surprised to see he hadn't moved. Nor had he spoken, Constant perceived. His lips were still frozen in the middle of the Penance, words so familiar to Constant that he could recognise them from the shape of Ysir's mouth. The voice had spoken in his head.

Who are you? he thought.

You know who I am. I'm your protector.

He can't hear you?

I am not one of his memories. He is lying to you. It has always been a lie. I am what remains. When the water washed the others away, I clung on. Now hush, let us listen to the monster.

'We survived Lethe, thanks to me,' the boy said, rather smugly. 'Are you prepared for what comes next?'

Constant's stomach turned over and a chill of fear spread from there throughout his imagined body. 'No,' he said weakly. 'No, I'm not. I don't think anyone can prepare for that. If I'm wrong about the snake oil, I don't think I can survive it.'

I won't let you die.

'I've been thinking about that while you've been awake,' said the boy. 'I think you're right, it's too much of a coincidence not to be real. Tell your friends. Tell them everything. They'll help you through it.'

I don't trust them.

'I don't know if I can trust them,' said Constant carefully. He turned this thought over in his mind. 'And if I do trust them, I think they might hate me for not trusting them before.'

'That's a risk you'll have to take,' said the boy firmly. 'They both have their secrets. Hey, I was the first person not to trust them! One of them's not human, after all. Neither of them are now, come to think of it. But for this, you have to trust them. Or die. They're your friends. I'm your friend, and always have been. Trust me.'

Suddenly Ysir was raging in Constant's mind, an explosion of anger that buffeted his consciousness. *What friends? A girl whose mind you almost destroyed? A creature hiding in human form? This monster living inside you, who ruined both our lives? Stole you from your mother's arms, and turned me into this kneeling wreck? Who hides the past from you unless it suits its purposes? They're not your friends.* I'm *your friend. I'm the one keeping you alive. I'm the one who makes your sword arm strong. And I'm the one who is going to free us from the prison this travesty has locked us in. We're going to be free Constant. This* matters.

The boy was watching Constant curiously. 'Are you okay?'

Don't tell him.

'Yes. I'm scared.'

‘I understand. It’s madness. But the Writing is what it is. You have to seek the knowledge, or you can’t continue.’

‘Do I want to continue? How do I know of any of this leads where we think it does?’

The boy laughed lightly. ‘You’re the one who has faith, Constant. I’m just a passenger.’

Ysir spoke in Constant’s mind once more. *Show me how we got the prophecy.* The words came out of Constant’s mouth as if they were his own. To cover his shock he hurriedly added, ‘I’ve never tried to remember that moment. Too many voices between me and him. The Great Record doesn’t say how he got it. Perhaps he was too young. But you’ll remember. The First must have been a baby, but you weren’t a baby.’

‘That’s a good idea. Maybe the prophet explained this. I haven't thought of him since... I haven’t thought of him since...’ The boy trailed off, suddenly looking confused and frightened. ‘I have never thought of him from the day we met until this day. How is that possible?’

Suddenly they were elsewhere. Constant recognised the market square of the All-men village through which he had followed the *dybbuk*-as-woman. It was a festival day of some kind, it seemed. The square was packed with people cheering and dancing, as horns sounded and drums were beaten. Coloured confetti fluttered through the air, rising in the heat of a summer’s day.

The boy ignored the people. Constant followed him to a spot under a broad oak tree near one corner, where small children played in the shade. Constant didn't need to see through the *dybbuk*’s eyes to know which one was the First. The child was part of him; he knew him like he knew himself.

A man passed by, wrapped in a heavy hooded cloak despite the heat, hunched over but moving quickly, his face hidden by the cowl. He passed by and the child was gone and the man was running, out of the square into a street of thatched houses.

‘Follow-’ Constant began, but they were already elsewhere. A stable, strewn with hay. Two horses occupied stalls; in another, the man and the boy. The man, his face deeply hidden by the hood, knelt over the child, one hand on the boy’s forehead. The boy said nothing and didn’t move, his face at once dreamy and attentive.

‘*Listen to me,’* whispered the man, in a shrivelled, broken voice. Constant felt magic in the words, a compulsion that he felt as a memory even as the words were spoken.

‘There's no time to explain. I’m sorry. Take this.’ He pressed a bundle into the child’s hands. Constant recognised the prophecy sheet. It looked new. The man drew a finger across the boy’s eyes; more magic.

'Listen. This is true. Now you can read it. It’s the future. It’s going to happen. I’m so sorry. The future is fixed. But it’s not complete, do you understand? There’s room at the sides. Have hope. *Spes vetus.* Think about what it implies. You can save yourself, and everyone.' The child didn't seem to register any of this. Wherever he was, he wasn't present.

The man stood, and pulled his cloak tighter around his shoulders. Constant noticed for the first time how thin he was. The contours of his shoulder blades were visible through the weave of the wool.

'You will be called Constant,' he said. 'All of you. One after another, for four thousand years. And after four thousand years, you'll find out why. It's not what you think. It's a good thing Constant, and when you find out you'll be happy. I promise. But before then you must suffer. I want to tell you that I'm sorry. It's not my fault, but I'm sorry.' He staggered slightly, as if bearing a great weight. 'I don't think it's my fault,' he said, sounding uncertain. 'I forget where the start is sometimes.'

He raised a hand. Constant expected more magic, but instead he brushed the child's hair from his eyes, almost tenderly.

'As you grow you'll have visions. You'll see a mountain and you'll go there. You will think it is your idea. You will bring others. You will feel safe. One way up, no way down. Do not notice the gate. Do not notice it on the map, when that is drawn. Do not see them or think about them, and pass this to your brothers by this magic. If you do see, hear my voice. You cannot know this. Do not remember. Only when you need it will you find it.'

The man wilted a little, then rallied, as if pushing himself to say the words before his strength gave out.

'There is more. You must use the stone. To say your words. To see the gates. Otherwise you cannot do what you must.'

He paused, out of breath. When he spoke again there was great sadness in his voice. 'A long time from now I will make moonflowers grow where there were none before. They showed the wolves the way up the Anvil. I knew what would happen. I am very sorry. It was, so it had to be. You will leave, and live. When you need to return, the power will be there.'

He stopped again, this time because his body was wracked with a spasm of pain. He held onto the stable wall until it passed. The child stared into nothingness, oblivious to it all.

'I say this because I know that one day you will remember. Tomorrow you learn about the moonflowers and you blame yourself. But it was me. It was me.' He paused. 'One day you will remember this. For any hurt I have caused you, for any fault or sorrow, I ask forgiveness. My soul is yours. I hope you can forgive me.'

He looked over his shoulder suddenly, as though worried someone might be watching. He spoke to the child once more.

'Now forget me,' he said, and Constant felt more magic. 'Forget me until you need to remember. You, and all who follow you.' He paused, then said, 'You too, *dybbuk*.'

'*How can he know me?*' screamed the boy.

Constant did not remember the boy when he woke up.

Chapter Thirty-Two: What Love Might Be

Blix's whole body was buzzing. She stumbled to a nearby rock and sat with her head in her hands, trying to stop the world revolving. It took a very long time.

'I don't know how much more of this I can take,' she said eventually. 'I feel like death.'

'Five more,' said Constant, wiping vomit from his lips. 'Then we're done. Five more.'

'Four,' said Kit. She was walking very slowly and unsteadily, arms outstretched like a drunk driver walking the line. 'It's four. Were you unconscious?'

'I think so. I had the strangest dream. I think I did. I don't remember my dreams.' Bleary-eyed and yawning, Constant looked around. 'I can't see properly yet. It's all blurry. Where are we?'

'I don't know,' said Blix, 'but it's beautiful. Maybe we've died and gone to paradise.'

'They'll be surprised to see me,' said Kit, yawning. 'I've done things.'

Constant stared so hard that Blix thought he was trying to make his eyes work through willpower alone. After a while he began looking around him, blinking like an owl at noonday. Eventually he said, 'You might be right.'

The gate was set in a glade at the edge of old woodland, where the treeline broke and the land dropped down into rolling fields of long grass, descending gently into a valley in the far distance, rising again to green hills beyond. The brown basalt of the five tall stones blended with the bark so well that it looked like they'd grown there rather than been placed by men.

It was the time between the heat of high summer and the mists of autumn. The trees told the story of the season. Rich greens remained, but reds and yellows had joined them. Russet and orange leaves danced in the sunlight and shone like gold.

Beyond the newly scorched earth within the circle, the glade was in bloom. Tall stalks of enchanter's nightshade grew there, white flowers waving prettily in the air. The pale pink of dog roses made it appear that the forest floor was blushing as they looked upon it. Flowering ivy climbed the trees, high enough to bask in the sunlight rippling across the glade. A warm breeze shivered the leaves. The forest smelled of rich earth and the sap beneath the bark, and the heady perfume of life.

Nearby there was a pool, thirty yards or more across and perfectly circular, bounded by a thick mat of springy moss. It was fed by a brook which trickled into the pond with a sound like laughter. The water was clear and inviting. It looked man-made, or at least shaped by human hand, a thought borne out by the ruin of a grotto perched on a shelf of slate rising behind it. Now lacking its roof, it retained a long stone bench facing out toward the water. It was made to take in the beauty of the landscape. Someone, Blix thought, had come here, enjoyed it, and built a place for others to do the same. That was a happy thought.

A second, important thought appeared in Blix's mind, an urgent and brilliant idea that exited her mouth without the intervention of her consciousness.

'I am going swimming,' she said, decisively. 'Yes, I am.'

'We should leave,' said Constant immediately.

'Why? We don't have to run. Ding dong, the wicked wolves are dead. I am absolutely clarted and I want to get clean.' She started peeling off her torn leather jacket, which was thick with grey mud.

'We don't know who lives here,' said the boy, as Blix kicked off Kit's boots. 'Or what. There could be monsters. What if, I don't know, another cyclops comes along?'

'Then it can come for a dip too if it wants to.' Blix had stripped to her underwear and was holding her foetid leggings at arm's length, with great distaste. 'And afterward it can wash my clothes. And if it doesn't like that it can kiss my arse.' She pulled down her knickers and gleefully mooned him. Kit cracked up with laughter.

Constant self-consciously looked away, suddenly absorbed by a pattern of moss on a nearby tree.

'You used to be modest. This is the wolf, changing how you think.'

Blix blew a raspberry. 'Bollocks. I am a woman making decisions for myself. As it should be. Nuts to anyone who doesn't like it. Lighten up! Something went right for a change. I'm going for a swim. Come in or don't.' She glanced at Kit. 'Coming?'

'You don't have to ask me twice.' The American hauled her jacket and shirt together over her head.

Blix turned to Constant, who was still intensely interested in the trees. 'You can stay here and brood, I don't mind.' She unhooked her bra and with a loud cry of 'Linhope Spout!' she ran, jumped and plunged into the pool.

Constant seemed about to dispute her assertion, but checked himself. 'It did, didn't it? The plan worked.'

'Of course it worked!' Kit was down to her rather more voluminous underwear. 'It was a great plan! I'm known for them. And we were insanely lucky. Lucky helps. Yee-haw!' She dived elegantly into the water and resurfaced almost immediately. 'Ack, that's freezing!'

'You soft southern shandy-drinker.'

'Now what did you just call me?'

'I'll look for food,' Constant announced. 'I think everything except the manticore jerky is waterlogged.' He strode purposefully, and quickly, into the woods.

'Good plan,' said Blix to his back, wiping the water from her face. 'Off you pop.'

Constant, paused, made to say something, changed his mind, and disappeared into the woods.

Blix could stand on the bottom with her head above the surface. She worked her toes into the soft mulch. She ducked under the surface. Relief washed over her with the water. *They're dead, they're dead, no more running, I'm free!*

She kicked off the bottom and swam underwater from one side of the pool to the other and back, holding her breath for as long as she could, holding it until she felt her lungs might burst. Then she shot upward and breached the surface as high as she could and let her breath out in one great plosive sound, half moan and half shout, and with it expelled the fear and anger she'd carried with her since she'd first seen the First of Wolves. She fell back in the water, laughing. It felt like being born again.

Kit was watching her. 'Are you okay, kiddo?'

'Yes,' Blix said, realising only as she said it that it was true. 'I am.'

'Why are you okay?'

'Is it the wolf in me, do you mean? Like he says? Oh, I honestly don't know.' Blix closed her eyes and sank under the water and thought, really thought about the question. When she came back up, Kit was closer.

'You want to change.'

'Yes. I don't have a choice. It makes me seek it out. But I want to be myself as well. That's something I can choose. I've always chosen that.' She ducked back under the water and let it close over her. When she came back up, Kit was closer. 'You know, you've asked me if I'm okay so many times?'

'Because I care to know the answer, kiddo.' Kit said, without taking her eyes off her. Blix sank beneath the surface again. She felt that her mind should be churning, but the cold clarity of the water lent itself to her thoughts. When she came back up, Kit was closer.

'Do you know you've never used my name?' she said. 'Not once since the moment we met.'

'Names have power,' said Kit. She took a step toward Blix through the water. 'You know that.'

'Yes. I changed my name. Amelia wasn't me.' She thought about that. 'I mean something different. I wasn't her. I was Blix. Why don't you say it?'

'Using someone's name gives you a kind of power over them. I don't take that unless it's given.'

'You told me your name.'

'Did I?' Kit smiled then. Not her usual Cheshire Cat grin, but one between the two of them. She took another step forward. Blix could have reached out and touched her.

'Didn't you? What sort of name is Kit anyway? I always thought that was short for Christopher. That's a boy's name.'

'Kit could be a girl's name or a boy's name. But it ain't *my* name.' She stepped forward. She was so close Blix could feel her breath on her skin. It was so intense that she looked away. Kit gently touched Blix's chin with a fingertip, lifting her face. The touch made Blix gasp.

'What's your name?' she asked.

'You ain't answered my question yet. Why are you okay?'

'Because I am,' Blix said simply. 'I am because I am. I just am. I'm going to get my sister and save the world and I should be terrified but I'm okay. That's what I am. I know my own mind.' She realised she was trembling, and that Kit was too. 'I'm other things too. I'm Blix. I'm a woman. I'm yours.'

She stepped forward.

Her lips parted as Kit kissed her and as they kissed Kit drew her close, breast against breast, heart against heart. And as they kissed, as Blix caressed the back of Kit's neck and ran her hand down her back, she felt that for the first time in her life she knew what love might be. Then she felt Kit's fingers touch her face, playing lightly against the skin, then moving down, down to the curve of her small breast, along the length of her hard nipple, then down, down across her flat stomach and down, where she paused, and the pause was a question.

'Blix. My name is Kitsune.'

'Yes,' Blix said. 'Yes. I say yes.'

Constant hid behind a bush and watched as the bird strutted to its doom. A skinny not-quite-chicken with a bright red cockscomb, it looked stupid even for a fowl. It didn't look at the snare that Constant had twisted out of grass, hanging inches from its head.

Come on, thought Constant.

Gently, remembered Comen sen-Hersa. A memory of another hunt in another lifetime.

The bird turned its head slightly, cocking a beady eye at the snare. Constant tried to read its tiny chicken mind. *It's fine, go on, stick your head in, just ignore the hungry creature at the other end of the string.*

The bird opened its beak. A tiny flare of bright blue fire flamed forth, frazzling the snare into a charred crisp. It strutted on down the path.

'That was unexpected,' said Constant, out loud. The bird didn't react. Constant stood up from his hiding place, brushed himself off, walked up behind the fowl and snapped its neck with his hands.

No fear of humans. Or of human sized predators. Maybe there aren't any. What's above a fire-breathing chicken in the food chain anyway?

He wondered how much time he should give Blix and Kit to know each other. He understood, he thought, what was happening, without that particularly stirring anything in him. Not him-him, anyway. He could feel the shapes of memories in his mind - opinions angry and accepting, pious and permissive, lustful and lurid - which he made him think that deeper introspection would not be rewarded by deeper understanding. He decided to mind his own business. That felt quite mature. Possibly even serene.

Fruit like blackberries grew along the path, on bushes higher than his head. He held one in his mouth until he was sure it wasn't poisonous, letting its tart sweetness suffuse his palate. He picked as many as he could reach.

He listened to the forest around him live. The skittering of insects, the swish and scrape of leaves as the air stirred them, the crack of bark against bark. He took in the smell - the rich, loamy smell of grass and mulch, sap and stem. He closed his eyes and inhaled deeply, taking it inside himself. Something he had done in many lives. He felt peace. He felt the power of the earth rising through his feet, filling him, making whole something he hadn't realised was broken.

I did it, Simon. I avenged you and our brothers. I am not sure you would have wanted vengeance, but I did it nonetheless. As if it... No, it does matter. Does the wheel turn for werewolves? May they have justice. That is not unkind.

Thinking of Simon made him want to pray. The Night Prayer, even though it was broad daylight on this world. It was the one that most reminded him of the gentle monk. A memory came, from when he was very little. His small hand in Simon's, held tightly as they said the prayer, pushing down the voices inside him together.

He found a shady spot and knelt. The ritual words came easily to mind.

'Light in the darkness, possessed of infinite compassion, consumed by -'

He stopped. He tried again. 'Light in the darkness.'

He stopped. He rubbed his forehead.

'Look,' he said. 'I'm doing it, okay? I'm doing what I should. I'm terrified. I don't know if I'm strong enough. I wish you were here Simon. I need someone to tell me it will be all right.'

He looked up between the canopy of leaves to the blue sky above. *I am the universe. The living embodiment of its immanence. I am the way of all things. I am the path that I walk as I am he that walks it.*

'A sign would be nice,' he said out loud.

The forest went about the business of being a forest without giving up any obvious signs. *Can't even send yourself a sign, Constant. Some sort-of-God you are.*

Another of the fire-breathing fowls emerged from the undergrowth. Constant watched it for a while. Then he broke its neck.

Blix's whole body was buzzing. She had to keep moving around the camp because whenever she sat she started bouncing up and down with excitement.

Oh my God oh my God oh my God I did it I did it I did it! It was amazing how could I not know that I could never I swear to God it was nothing like touching myself oh God the taste of her in my mouth I felt her come I came Oh God it lasted forever I need that again she held me for the longest time I want to feel like that every moment for the rest of my life oh my God!

One of the shirts she'd taken from the Monastery was still intact, just about clean and long enough that it reached her thighs. It was sodden, but Blix felt there was a good chance of it drying quickly given that every time she looked at Kit she flushed so hot she was surprised she didn't catch fire. After they'd made love the American had decided, in a practical and outdoorsy way, to scrub their befouled clothes clean. She had chosen to remain naked while doing so, and the sight of Kit kneeling at the water's edge, rhythmically rubbing at a wad of cloth, was enough to make Blix think very bad thoughts, then plan on doing them.

God, am I ever going to calm down? Is everyone's first time like this? It was so intense, so perfect. Like, my fantasy first time. I thought it would, I don't know, hurt a bit I suppose. Not like Katy said because, you know, no thing involved, but a virgin is a virgin. Was I any good? Would she tell me if I wasn't? She was so good. I need more practice! I suppose she's had loads of girlfriends. And boyfriends. I mustn't judge. I wish I had a cigarette, I think you're supposed to after. I do! Oh no wait, they got soaked. God if it's as good as that every time I might die.

Am I in love? How do know?

'I died,' she said. The words surprised her.

'Say what now?' Kit looked over her shoulder.

'Nothing.'

The American flashed her a grin and went back to her work.

Why did I say that? I wasn't thinking it. Maybe I was and didn't know. I told Constant to let me go and he did and I fell and... I don't remember pain. I don't remember anything. Nothing except the moon calling me to join him. Why does the moon do that? It's just reflected sunlight, why doesn't the sun change me? I want to change. Am I strong enough? God, I want it so much, as much as I want Kit. Kitsune. Only to me. She gave me her name! I am so happy. Is that what love is? I must focus. I want to change. I can't. I might kill her. I might die. I'm not strong enough.

'I killed someone,' she said out loud. Kit didn't appear to notice.

He hurt me! With a steel whip! He called me a whore and a cunt! He would have murdered me and he deserved to die! I killed him. I didn't know I was doing it, but it was me. I don't know that I would have been murdered. He'd have put me in the bull! He was in the wrong place at the wrong time and he was just there, and I killed him. I killed him, and I don't feel bad about it. Not bad enough about it. A week ago, I wouldn't have known how to even think about killing someone and now I don't feel bad enough about having killed. What have I become?

'Penny for 'em, kiddo.' Kit was behind her, folding her arms around her waist. Blix leant back into the embrace.

'Still not worth a penny,' she said automatically.

'Yes they are, Blix. They surely are.'

Yes. I am. This is how I know.

Night drew in, clear and star-filled, a crescent moon cresting the horizon. Constant returned, calling from some distance away before he made his appearance. There was something about this that made Blix want to giggle. His earnest discretion felt very old fashioned. As if it was about how they'd feel about him knowing. It was quite quaint. Strangely, it made Blix feel better disposed toward the boy than she had in a long ti-

She caught the thought before it was finished. *In a few days. I keep making this mistake, stop it. God, has it only been a few days? It feels like a lifetime.*

Kit, now clothed again, set a fire and roasted the skinny not-quite-chickens that Constant had caught. They tasted like chicken, but not quite.

'They're basan,' Blix said, when Constant asked. 'They're native to Japan. And here, it seems. They look like roosters, but they're more closely related to the cockatrice.'

'Cockatrice? Can they turn you to stone?' Constant eyed his half-eaten drumstick with suspicion.

'Are you a rock? Seems not then.'

After they'd eaten Constant said, 'I can sleep somewhere else if you would, uh, like to be alone.'

'No, that's okay,' Blix said, smiling at his awkwardness. She was surprised she didn't blush, but that was Old Blix. 'We should stay together. There might be monsters after all.'

'Mighty kind of you to offer though,' Kit said, sucking the grease from her fingers.

'You know, for a major religious figure from basically the Middle Ages you seem awfully relaxed about, um, the gay thing.' Blix's chin came up as she said *gay*; she was used to standing up to someone when she said it out loud. 'Don't your lot want to, I don't know, burn me at the stake?'

'No!' Constant looked horrified. 'We're not like that! We live in peaceful contemplation!'

'In a fortress with murder holes,' Kit reminded him. 'Very peaceful, Your Holiness.'

Constant's face assumed the slightly uncomfortable expression that Blix had come to expect when someone mentioned his position. 'That's different. I explained that. To protect ourselves. As for the other thing... We studied many faiths from many worlds, so I understand why you say that. I think our faith is different. All things are one. We have a purpose. I think I remember... there was... no one...?'

Without seeming to realise it he reached out, as if trying grasp in the air something he could not hold in his mind. Then he rubbed his forehead in a way Blix now found completely familiar, and the moment passed. 'I remember, sort of, what it is to be other people,' he continued.' I have been seventy other men over four thousand years. And others before them, though I don't remember those …' He was momentarily gone again. 'Some had opinions,' he said, his eyes making clear what he meant. 'Some loved women, some loved men. Some loved no one.' The final words disappeared into a whisper as the boy's mind examined the past once more. From where Blix sat it didn't look like a joyful experience.

'Opinions,' snorted Kit, not seeing Constant's introspection. 'I ain't never met anyone with opinions whose opinions were worth a damn.'

'I don't know what to think about that,' Blix said. 'So, I'm not going to think about it. I'm going to sleep. I cannot tell you how tired I am, and how happy I am not to have to sleep with one eye open.'

'I do that anyway,' said Kit, settling down between two thick tree roots, the rise of the tree bole acting as a natural pillow. She pulled out the bottle of gorgon blood and let a drop fall on her tongue. 'Madame Medusa will keep me alert anyhoo. And if that's not enough I keep my right hand on my mahaska here, just in case.' She patted the butt of her pistol. 'Oh wait, I got no bullets left. So much for that.' She glanced at Blix. 'Hey, lookee here. I got an arm free. Whaddaya know.'

Blix rolled into the crook of Kit's arm. *Yes. I am.*

Sometime in the depths of night, Blix woke up. She didn't stir from her position in Kit's arms. She knew without looking that Kit was awake.

As they lay there together in the night's stillness an idea popped into Blix's head. It was an idea made of many little thoughts, scraps of notions swirling in her memory, hints and oddities here and there which had nearly coalesced many times, before being pushed away by events. But now the idea appeared in her mind so fully formed that she knew the answer to her question before she asked it.

'Kit?'

'Uh-huh?'

'How old are you?'

'I told you. Twenty-three.'

'Mmm. Born in 'sixty-one. And what year is it?'

'Beg pardon?'

'The year. What year is it?'

'What a strange… Why, it's 'eighty-four, of course.'

'Mmm. The full year. All four numbers. Just to confirm how self-absorbed and incurious I can be.'

'What - '

'Just humour me. What year is it?'

'Eighteen eighty-four.'

'Yeah. That's what I thought. Night night.'

Constant dreamed.

In my dream, I am standing in the Great Father's rooms, looking down on the forest, wondering why the open space scares me so. It wasn't like this before I was Recognised. Then the forest was my friend. I walked its paths many -

'No, we don't have time,' said the boy. Constant felt himself being pulled out of his previous existence, a weird, gut-wrenching experience like plunging down a sudden sharp incline. The scene froze. Constant recognised his fortieth incarnation, who had been born in a village near the Bastion and had come to the Anvil as a teenager. He looked worried. *Not half as worried as I am, Great Father.*

'It's much easier to stop your reveries now they're mine,' the boy said. 'Ignore him. We have work to do.'

The scene changed. They were once again in the stable in the All-men village. The hooded man stood over the First child.

'Now forget me,' he said, and Constant felt the magic working. 'Forget me until you need to remember. You, and all who follow you.' He paused, then said, 'You too, *dy-'*

Everything froze. The boy left Constant's side and, with a little hesitation, approached the hooded man.

'Right, so beyond this point we wake up wondering why we're in a barn and neither he nor any subsequent him's nor you nor I ever think about this moment from then until you ask me about it. I forgot something. Again. He made me forget. Which is *completely impossible,* in case I failed to emphasise this enough.'

The boy was very visibly trying to calm himself. He suddenly seemed far less certain and assured, a guide finding himself off the paths he knows. He noticed Constant watching this and smiled weakly.

'You know Constant, I may have given you the impression that I know a lot about my kind. That's not entirely true.'

Interesting, said Ysir's voice, from deep in Constant's mind. The boy continued.

'I know what I know. Magic barely affects us, because we're barely here. I have no idea how this,' he waved at the frozen scene, 'could be possible. Have you any idea of the sheer power it must have taken to do that to me? No, of course not. It has come as a bit of a shock. Four millennia with the sheet in my hand without ever thinking about how I got it...'

'I don't care about that,' said Constant fiercely. 'He's a murderer! He made the moonflowers grow! Brought the wolves to the Monastery!'

Knowing it was stupid but too angry to care, Constant kicked out at the hood figure. His foot passed through the frozen memory without touching anything.

'You did that before,' said the boy. 'Try learning, Constant. You're right, but the question is, why? Why did he do it, and why is he telling us about it now?'

'He's telling the child, you mean. And you, in the child.'

'No, he's talking to us. Listen again.'

The scene changed slightly; it was moments earlier.

'A long time from now I will make moonflowers grow where there were nonc before. They showed the wolves the way up the Anvil. I knew what would happen. I am very sorry. It was, so it had to be.'

He paused as the pain wracked him.

'I said that because I know that one day you will remember this. Tomorrow you learn about the moonflowers and you blame yourself. But it was me. It was me.' He paused. 'One day you will remember this. For any hurt I have caused you, for any fault or sorrow, I ask forgiv-'

'And so on,' said the boy, as the action froze once more. '"Tomorrow," he says. The child doesn't learn anything tomorrow. He means tomorrow for you. And since you didn't remember this moment when you were awake today, that means this man knows that we, you and me, are watching him, right now.' He thought some more. 'Also, he knows about our communication problem.'

'What?'

'He knows you learn about this right now. He also knows that you blame yourself tomorrow. Which you wouldn't do if you could remember this conversation when you're awake. He knows you can't.'

'Okay,' Constant agreed cautiously. 'I think that works.'

'Let's have a think about all that, shall we? What is he telling us and why?'

'He's alive in four thousand years to make the moonflowers grow,' Constant said.

'He's either long-lived, or he time-travels there. Or from there to here. That's possible, isn't it? Do you think he's talking about something he saw in a prophecy or something he's done already and come back to tell us about?'

'I don't know. The second one? Maybe the first. This is too complicated. I'm too angry to think straight.'

'That's magic for you. It never helps.' The boy pondered the question, rubbing his forehead absently and ignoring Constant's frustration. 'He's capable of immense feats of magic, and of keeping them hidden from us. Why reveal himself? What does he gain by it? I don't believe he just wants to say sorry. How is he doing it, I wonder... is he you?'

'What?'

'Stop saying what, it makes you sound stupid. Older you I mean, come back to the past.'

'Oh.' Constant mentally tried to de-age the hooded man, and then tried to age himself up. Neither fitted around the idea of himself he held in his mind.

'I don't think so. His hands are bigger, the proportions are wrong, his skin is sallow. He could be another me though. After I, you know, die. Your next host.'

'Don't say it like that. You know, I think I'd know if I was in there. He'd be special, he isn't. Unless I have to go into someone who isn't.'

He seemed to realise he was talking too much, and crab-walked toward the hooded man. 'Let's just see who you are under this hood, friend magician...'

Constant felt the words 'Belmont Dragonville' trickle into his mind, but he just as quickly dismissed the idea. The man Kit and Blix had described would have six or eight inches and a hundred pounds over this man.

The boy peered under the hood. His face creased into a familiar scowl.

'That's cheating,' he said, disgusted. Constant took a peek. The hood was black underneath - not just in deep shadow but a void, hiding the head that shaped the cowl in fathomless darkness. A darkness made by magic.

Constant hazarded a guess. 'He knows we're here. Maybe he knew we would do this and took precautions.'

'Well, obviously,' said the boy, with a nasty catch to his voice. He fretted for a moment, looking this way and that, chewing on the corner of a fingernail. 'Ever get the feeling you're being manipulated?' he said suddenly.

'*Yes,*' said Constant and Ysir together. Constant wasn't sure which of them had said it out loud.

The boy gave him a withering look. 'Not like that. I'm on your side. This one...' He trailed off, then looked sharply at Constant. 'You're going to wake up again. You have a terrible trial coming. If you sleep again before it, we'll talk. If not, just remember. You can live through it. You can survive. We know that now. All you have to do is survive.'

I have a plan, said Ysir, in the silence of his mind.

Constant did not remember them when he woke up.

Chapter Thirty-Three: Field of Heaven

Constant felt the warmth of the morning before he opened his eyes. It wrapped itself around him like tender arms, soothing the deep hurt in his limbs and, when he breathed in deeply, melting something cold inside him which had been frozen for so long he'd forgotten it could thaw.

The sky was a perfect, bold blue, a blue that a child might paint, segmented by ruler-straight banks of clouds which lay as if someone had raked them into neat white furrows. The weak, dappled sunlight seemed less fulfilling that the warmth he felt. It seemed to come from inside him.

'I feel great,' he said, sitting up.

'I know,' said Blix. 'I slept like the dead.' She was still lying with Kit. Neither of them seemed to have moved since Constant had closed his eyes the night before.

'I guess that's what not being chased does for you.'

'Maybe,' said Kit, yawning, and sliding out of Blix's arms to the latter's hmphed discontent. 'Elysium's where Greek heroes went after they died, ain't it? Where they went to be happy. Maybe something about this world makes you feel...'

'Joy,' Blix finished, stretching her arms as high they would go. She smiled at Kit. 'It makes you feel joy.'

'It does indeed, kiddo. It does indeed.'

They left the forest, following the line the Thing pointed them along, and walked through the morning. Across the stream and up and over downs of well cropped grass, although there was no livestock in sight. The way fell gently down through a gossamer-coated meadow, rich in brightly coloured, sweet scented flowers, to another expanse of trees. Sturdy old growth maples vied with young poles of ash and aspen and a myriad of other varieties which trembled as the wind danced through their leaves. Seeds spinning from the sycamores reminded Blix of home.

'A hundred years,' said Kit, shaking her head in bemusement as they walked. 'That's a hell of a gain. A hell of a gain.'

'A hundred and two years,' Blix noted. 'It's nineteen eighty-six where I come from.'

'A hell of a gain.'

'I've never heard of anything like that,' said Constant. He seemed slightly awestruck by the idea. 'There are gates with big side differences, but the biggest I know of is a little over three years.' He mulled it over. 'I wonder what the lag is? You know, when you go back.'

I don't want her to go back, Blix thought, and almost said out loud, but Kit was already talking.

'Could be anything, I suppose. More gain, even. But I'd be prepared to put a small bet on an equal amount of lag, or the next thing to it. Dragonville ain't the kind to give himself no way out, and he's got plenty invested back in -' She stopped, and laughed, shaking her head once more. 'The olden days,' she finished. 'But even if it's none, that's fine by me! Ain't no-one back there for me but my horse. I got my, uh, important stuff stashed where no-one's gonna find it. Be there in a thousand years if it takes that long. Say, they still got Mormons in Utah in nineteen eighty-six?'

'Lots of them, I think,' Blix said.

'Great! If Elder Smoot's dead his grandsons can pay me. That'll be fine too.'

She doesn't want to go back either, Blix thought, her heart lifting.

Constant however suddenly looked alarmed. 'You can't talk about it,' he said sharply.

'Say what now, kid?'

'The past. Or the future. Whichever it is for each of you. You could cause a terrible paradox with unknowable consequences.'

'Are you kidding me?' Blix said. 'How can we not talk about this?'

'We're trying to prevent a disaster, not cause one.' He frowned slightly. 'There's room at the sides,' he said, as though not quite certain what he meant. 'But we don't know where the sides are. It's very complicated. Better to say nothing.'

'That's crazy,' said Blix. 'But it's not even close to being the craziest thing I've heard this week, really. Okay. For now.'

Their way took them along the bank of a small lake, clear water twinkling in the sunlight. Dragonflies hovered and darted; kingfishers plunged into the pool. Blix pointed out a honeyguide dipping in and out of the leaves of a willow-like tree. It was all just like the spring days that appeared in Constant's memory, but there was a strange otherworldliness to it - nothing obvious, but there all the time - that reminded him he was a long way from home.

'When all this is over I'm going to find a place like this on Earth and live there,' Blix said. 'This is gorgeous.'

'It is beautiful,' Constant agreed, looking out across the gently lapping water. 'I've lived under a mountain for most of four millennia. Perhaps I could live outdoors. Maybe build a cottage, like my mother's.'

From the corner of his eye Constant saw Blix steal a look at him, perhaps expecting him to be brooding or anguished at the thought of his mother. He smiled gently instead.

'You can't live in the past. What happens next is what matters.'

'Which segues us nicely into something else you've been doin' for four thousand years,' said Kit, stretching theatrically but looking unflinchingly at Constant all the while. 'Namely, sittin' on a prophecy of some nonsense or other. Now kid,' she continued, in a schoolmarmish tone, 'we ain't runnin', we ain't hidin'. Ain't no cyclopes or werewolves or owl-bears gonna leap out on us from the bushes.' She looked around suspiciously, eyes narrowed. 'Probably. They do seem to show up every time we get to talking about this. Is that some magic hoo-hah you're doing, kid?'

'No.'

'Glad to hear it! Then you are absolutely gonna tell us everything you know, right now, you hear?'

'You always say you'll explain, Constant,' Blix reminded him. 'If we're not talking about the past – which I may have mentioned is crazy – then we're talking about the future. Right?'

Constant looked from one to the other. 'Right,' he said.

'Pick up where you left off,' Kit advised. 'You know, with you being tortured.'

Constant ordered his thoughts. 'Echmoth and Dragonville want to open the Narrow Way. I want to keep it closed. But the prophecy doesn't foretell that I will keep the Narrow Way closed. It says I will close it forever. There's only one way to close a gate forever. Destroy it.'

'Buy a hammer,' Kit suggested. She extracted a cold not-chicken drumstick from a saddlebag and bit into it. 'A big one.'

'If only it were that simple. You don't think like a magician. Magic is about control. Controlling something that doesn't want to be controlled, forcing it to bend to your will. Magicians don't give up control easily. Sure, destroy the stones and the hole closes for good. But you have to be really committed to destroy a circle. Committed and powerful.'

'And here we are back in "I don't get it" land, where I spend my days,' Blix sighed.

'Sorry. But haven't you ever wondered why stone circles just persist? Rocks just standing there, unchanging, for thousands of years? Why we only ever talk about gates not working any more of their own volition? Just petering out?'

'No, I haven't wondered about any of that. Because I'm normal. Anyway, that's not true,' Blix continued. 'I may not know as much about these bloody stones as Katy, but even I know they get raided all the time. You can find bits of Stonehenge in half the cottage walls of Wiltshire. That's why they made it a monument.'

'I know of the ringing rocks. They're not a gate, they're religion. Druids trying to be magicians.'

'Oh yeah. Katy told me about that too. Lots of sex and violence. But, sorry, Dragonville said he'd destroyed the circle I came through from Earth.'

'By using a colossal amount of magic to open it from the wrong side.'

'With the bloodstone. Which we have.'

'Yes, but you missed the important part. Dragonville didn't just destroy a gate. He opened it, and then did something which destroyed it. To destroy the Narrow Way, I must open the Narrow Way. Which you will recall, I don't want to do.'

'All the evils of the world,' said Blix, quietly.

'Exactly.'

'Where does this gate go then?'

Suddenly confronted with The Lie, Constant took a deep breath and told the truth.

'*Quam angusta porta et arta via quae ducit ad vitam et pauci sunt qui inveniunt eam*,' he said.

Blix pursed her lips. 'You what?'

'I thought you spoke Latin?'

'What? No. At my school they only teach you that if you're going to Oxbridge. In English, please. Or, you know, Shambhalhai and magic.'

Constant worked it through in his mind, glad for once that his former selves had known these things.

'"Strait is the gate, and narrow is the way, which leadeth unto life, and few there be that find it."'

'Matthew seven fourteen,' said Kit straightaway. 'Daddy taught Sunday school,' she explained.

'Sorry, told you I bunked off R.E.,' said Blix impatiently. 'What's that mean? I mean, I know it's from the Bible.'

'The sermon on the mount,' said Constant. 'The Son of David tells his followers that the path of sin is easy but leads to destruction, but the hard - narrow - way of virtue leads to salvation.'

'He's no fun, that Jesus,' said Blix. 'Okay, got it, but that's a metaphor, isn't it? You're talking about a literal gate, not a homily about being good.'

'Yes. And the name of the gate predates the Christ by thousands of years, let alone the composition of that verse. But it's far too much of a coincidence to be a coincidence.'

'Yeah, I suppose so. Where does the gate lead, then? If you say heaven I'm downing tools right now.'

'It leads nowhere, as far as we know. I don't know what it might mean to go through it.'

'On the Anvil you said something about getting trapped, or bouncing back. Or dying.'

'Yes. But no one's ever tested that with the Narrow Way. Two things are known about the Narrow Way for sure: it's always been there, and it's always been closed.

Not dead, just closed. The All-men built the Bastion around it to make sure it stayed that way.'

'Which is all fine and dandy,' Kit interjected, 'but I ain't heard nothing about you being tortured yet kid, and my interest is still piqued seein' as I am generally against the practice 'cept on cowboys who want what they can't have about which I have mixed views.'

Constant shifted restlessly. 'The Narrow Way is still a gate, no matter how strange, and presumably opens the same way as any other. But whoever built it really didn't want anyone to open it. There are additional protections. Conditions that you must satisfy to open the gate. Conditions which they never told anyone. We only know of them through the Writing.'

He paused, gathering his courage. 'They are impossible things. Terrible things. Taken from the great religions of ancient Earth. The Writing says I do them. And I have to want to do them or it won't work. Just like opening a gate, you can't be forced to do them. The magic will know.'

'Magic is not bloody well alive,' said Blix hotly. 'Every time I hear that idea it offends me more.'

'I know, but, you know. Sort of. Yes.'

'Torture?' said Kit, now as impatient as Blix.

'There are three tasks. Memory. Sacrifice. Thought. The water was the first. *Drink of forgetting, and remember.* From the Greek religion. Drink from the river Lethe and retain your memory. Patently impossible.'

'Yet you did it. How did you do it?'

'I don't know.'

'You sound uncertain,' said Blix. 'Everything, please.'

'I am uncertain. I feel that I do know, or should, or will. Something like that. Buried somewhere in my head, memory I remember I've forgotten.'

'Don't start that again. Okay, what's next?'

'Sacrifice,' Constant said, his face hardening as his mind gnawed on the idea. 'This is the torture bit. The prophecy says, *between memory and thought, seek knowledge of the runes, myself to myself.*'

He waited expectantly, but his words didn't have much effect. Blix and Kit looked blankly at each other. 'What's that got to do with torture?'

'Crack a book, kid,' Kit advised. 'Runes been learned already.'

'It doesn't say learn them. I already know runes in many languages. It says seek knowledge of them. That means do something specific. When Wotan sought the knowledge of runes he hung himself from the world tree Yggdrasil with a spear in his side for nine days, staring into the well of Urd, until his sacrifice was deemed worthy. That's what I have to do. It means that.'

'Holy moly.' Kit pushed her hat back on her head, then stopped walking and put her hands on her hips, leaning forward in a way that made Constant lean back.

'Kid, I thought the first one was a hell of a reach, but okay, I will allow you were right. But that at least told you what to do. But to go from reading the runes to nailing yourself to a tree is an almighty leap. That's the craziest thing I ever heard in all my born days. You may be a priest but you ain't Jesus. You will die.'

'Hanging. Yggdrasil was Wotan's gallows. I have to hang myself.'

'Well that makes all the difference!' Kit took her hat off, inspected it for a moment, then beat Constant fiercely over the head.

'Ow!'

'You! Will! Die!' Kit said, punctuating the words with further blows from her headwear.

'Ow! Stop it!' Constant said, ducking away from the onslaught. 'Look, the prophet must have seen that I survive, there's another task after this one.'

'What's that then?' Blix asked, diplomatically inserting herself between Constant and the still fuming American. They resumed walking, leaving the lake behind them and embarking on a long, grassy slope. Low hills undulated invitingly ahead.

'Oh, that's the easy one. *In the thought of the story, kill the Rakshasa.* That's from Hinduism. All I have to do is kill an unkillable cannibal demon which can alter reality at will.'

'All!' Kit almost shouted. Constant prudently stepped out of hat-beating range. 'Kid, I've said it before and I'll say it again. You. Are. Crazy.'

Constant looked hurt, but held his head high. 'I have faith.'

'Bickering doesn't help us,' Blix said as Kit opened her mouth to give Constant an earful. 'Let's just say it's crackers but true. One bit of it at least we know is true.'

Kit snapped her mouth shut in exasperation, then smiled her Cheshire Cat smile.

'Sure, why not? Why should I draw the line here? Ain't the craziest thing I ever heard.'

'Good. Constant, when you told us what the Writing said yesterday, there was loads of other stuff. What does all that mean? Say it again.'

The boy worried at his forehead once more, then spoke in his strangely older voice.

You are the Constant. This is your fate.
Nothing, then
A light. I see this Writing as I write
You will close the Narrow Way forever.
Afterward, Elpis. Life and death entwined together.
Nothing lies between.
You carry a lantern lit by hope. It guides your way
Wolves in the temple
The golden mouth
The rose and the thorn
The sun-crowned child and the moon made flesh

The two made one
Last of men
You must go forward.
You must follow the way. You can stop this Constant, here
Or all worlds end. This is uncertain
There is a way. I see
to open the gate, willingly embrace
Memory, Sacrifice, Thought
Drink of forgetting, and remember
Between memory and thought, seek knowledge of the runes
myself to myself.
Die and live, moon to moon.
The Wolf has the strength
In the thought of the story, kill the Rakshasa.
The white, the grey and the black
All men will be wolves
Blood and silver is the key
One who is two
Life for the living and death for the dead
The fire goes out
Death is not the end. You must go forward.
The soul knows the way
An endless labyrinth
The vessel of what remains. Ancient hope.
A prison for the mind. A silent child
Pursued when no man follows.
The damselfly
What remains
A dragon's scale
The burning gate
A circle turns upon itself
You taught me this
Where do we begin? The first, and the last
Where the moonflowers grow
there is a way.

'There. That's what it says. As for what it means, there are some lines which are clear, others more opaque. We've been thinking about this for a long time. The route through the gates takes us where I think we need to go, but for some of it I'm only guessing. The library of the Anvil is full of -'

Kit who'd been chewing on her lip, interrupted. 'Say that last line again,' she said. 'You didn't say that before. The one about the flowers.'

'Okay. Where the moonflowers grow -'

'- there is a way,' Kit joined in as he recited. 'Yep. I've heard that before.'

This time it was Constant who stopped dead. 'You can't have.'

'I ain't lying, kid.'

'I'm not accusing you. But the Writing is not known to outsiders. I'm just about prepared to believe that Dragonville and Echmoth know somehow, because at least one of them is an insanely powerful magician. Other people? No. Even when you were on the Anvil, Kit, no one would have spoken of it and you certainly couldn't have seen the original. It was protected.'

'It wasn't on the Anvil. I was, uh, hiding, there. Never spoke to no one. It was before. When I was looking for Dragonville. I told you. I met a man who told me how to climb the mountain. That's what he said. "Where the moonflowers grow, there is a way."' They bloom at night in crevices in the rocks. They showed the way up.'

Constant stopped again, looking as if his legs wouldn't carry him any further. 'That's what it means?' he said, flabbergasted. 'Four thousand years of speculation and research and the answer was literally under our feet all the time?'

'Y'all monks spend too much time with your eyes on the skies, I guess.'

Constant shook his head so violently it made his ears ring.

'This can't be right. It can't be. Nothing grows on the walls of the Anvil. Only on the plateau. I know every palm's breadth of that mountain. And moonflower doesn't grow that far north, it's a cactus.'

'I ain't lying. It's what the man said, there they were.'

'Again, I believe you.' Constant exhaled sharply. 'It's just imposs- wait, what man?' He rubbed furiously at his forehead. 'You said he was Tibetan?'

'Yeah, looked like. Old dude, white hair, big cloak. Skin like shrivelled leather. Looked like he could use a meal or ten.'

'A monk?'

'Don't think so. Gave me the look. You know, the look that guys give women. That old boy wanted to get in the furry pokehole, I reckon.'

'Oh. My. God. He did not say that.'

'No,' Kit allowed, 'but let me tell you kiddo, I've known more than one randy cowhand in my day. I know the look.'

'Why is that... I know... Ach, my bloody head!' Constant pummelled his temples with his fists as if trying to dislodge something. 'Too much in there! I know it means something, but I can't get to it. I don't believe it.'

'For the last time, I ain't lyi-'

'I believe *you*. I don't believe that it's possible that generations of my brothers could just miss something this obvious. So obviously, we didn't. They were either deliberately hidden from us like the gate, or they were new. I think they were new. Someone made the moonflowers bloom for you and the wolves to follow.'

'You're going to make your head bleed if you keep rubbing it like that,' Blix advised him. 'Also, you've just short... short circuited... my...'

Her mouth fell open as something powerful stuck her. Something wrong.

Constant didn't notice. He was really worked up now, taking little steps back and forth and waving his arms emphatically as he spoke.

'It's all connected. A man tells you, Kit, something about things he can't know about and sets you on a path which leads you here, helping me to fulfil the prophecy he can't know about to prevent the people who dragged *you* here, Blix, from doing what the prophecy say I must stop. All while some incredible feat of magic hides a gate in my very hall for four thousand years. Someone is meddling in our lives. A magician. Another magician.'

He was breathing hard, heart pounding as the enormity of the idea pressed down on him.

'I blame myself,' he said, without knowing why he said it. 'How can I have not understood? *Fucking* magic.' The word felt right in his mouth and he said it again.

His vision swam, and for a moment he felt he was looking through two pairs of eyes. He reached out to steady himself against Blix's shoulder. She pushed his hand away.

'Just a minute.'

She was staring at him, as though seeing him for the first time.

'You knew you had to do all this prophecy stuff. Like forever.'

'Forever is longer. But yes.'

'You knew it on the Anvil. When you worked out the route through the gates. You just said so.'

Constant blanched white and started shaking. 'Yes.'

For as white as Constant had gone, Blix had turned just as red. 'You planned the route so you could fulfil the prophecy. Do what it says you do.'

Constant swallowed hard. 'Yes,' he whispered.

Kit clasped her mouth, suddenly wide-eyed. 'Oh shit.'

'Does that mean -' Blix had to stop for a second to control herself. 'Does that mean there was a quicker route to the Bastion we didn't take?'

'No, I mean, it's not like you think-'

'Was there a quicker way?'

'... yes.'

'You absolute bastard!' Her face contorted with fury, Blix grabbed Constant, bunching his robe in her fists as she dragged him toward her. 'You absolute fucking bastard! I'd just started to trust you again!'

She pulled a fist back to punch him, then thought better of it and pushed him away sharply with a hiss of contempt. He tumbled to the ground. Almost immediately he was up again.

'I said I wouldn't lie any more. I can't change the past.'

'Fuck. Off.' Blix turned her back on him.

'Wrong all the time,' said Kit, shaking her head at his woefulness.

Something else had occurred to Blix, something which made her blaze with righteous fury. She turned back on Constant.

'Where?'

'What?'

'Where did the quicker route start?'

'Please -'

'Where? *Where*!'

'Ceto. The Lyonesse gate you saw on the map. But - '

'I knew it! You bastard! Everything that's happened, we could have missed it! Roohsk would still be alive! Roohsk, and Seminah and, and, Akali, and the rest and I, and I *wouldn't have killed someone.'*

'*Please* listen - '

Blix wasn't listening. She started to storm off up the hill, but she hadn't taken more than two steps when Constant grabbed her hand and pulled her back. She gasped at his touch, horrified, but he let go instantly.

'It's not like you think! We can't go a quicker way! We have to do these things! Didn't you listen? Didn't you hear? The prophecy isn't just about me! The prophecy is about Katy! The prophecy is about *you*!'

The words rang out across the hillside like an accusation. Blix staggered, suddenly light headed as she took in the implications of the boy's words.

'Make bloody sense, will you?'

'The rose and the thorn. Your sister and you. Echmoth said it when he took her. You told me. I knew it as soon as you said the words, that night in my mother's house.'

'Really? Come on. That's so vague. And a bloody stereotype by the way, thanks.'

Constant kept going. 'The sun-crowned child, it says. Look at you.'

Blix touched her hair self-consciously. 'That's mad,' she said. 'Blondes are ten a penny. Buy some peroxide and you could be one.'

'I know. What was it Echmoth said when he took your sister? She looks the part. I saw her picture, she does. I thought it was you at first. The prophet saw you both, but he knew, he knew…'

'Knew what?'

Constant took a deep breath. 'What would happen to you. You're the Wolf.'

'Oh, fuck off.'

'You're a werewolf,' Constant said relentlessly. 'They call themselves children of the moon. You're the Wolf.'

'That's not fucking me!' Blix shouted.

'It is you. You're here. The Wolf has the strength.'

'What strength?' Blix was now completely exasperated. 'What the hell are you talking about?'

Constant met her eyes, his gaze so heartbreakingly empty it drained Blix of anger almost instantly.

'The strength to hang me. The strength to hold a spear in my side as I bleed out. To torture me as I seek wisdom.'

Blix sat down hard and pressed her hands into the earth as if only the world could steady her. 'Jesus Christ.'

'Now wait just a goddamn second, you tiny asshole,' said Kit furiously, stepping up to Constant. 'Firstly, this is horseshit. Secondly, she is not going to torture you, you hear? And thirdly, I didn't hear nothing about no gals from Nebraska. Where am I? You expect me to believe some damn prophet saw the pair of you and didn't just write down your names? Then he saw me too. Where am I?'

'I don't know,' said Constant. He felt immensely tired, the strange weight in his arms pulling him down until he felt that if he lay on the grass he might never get up. 'Maybe you are in there. So much of it is unexplained. Maybe the prophet didn't see you, or couldn't write it down. Maybe you're not important in the prophecy. I don't know. Sorry,' he added, as Kit glared at him.

'Horse goddamn shit.'

'Sorry.'

'I feel sorry for you,' said Blix suddenly. The words we so unexpected that Constant didn't know what to say.

'I feel sorry for you,' she said again. 'I'm still absolutely fucking furious with you, but I feel sorry for you too. She was right,' she continued, looking at Kit. 'Those monks didn't do right by you. Any of you. They never taught you what this looks like from the outside, did they? How have you lived like this? How have you lived, knowing this is coming? You talk so matter-of-factly about this terrible thing. This terrifying thing. Again and again, life after life, for thousands of years, just waiting for this. How on earth have you coped, seventy times?'

'I had faith,' said Constant, his voice quivering with righteousness, ringing across the field. 'I had my brothers. Now I have you.'

'You have me.' Blix closed her eyes, and to Constant's surprise, gave a little laugh. It had no humour in it. 'You have me. Good grief. How can it be that you still don't get this? I know, you don't understand. Let me tell you once and fucking for all.'

She sprang up and stared the boy right in his face, jabbing her finger in his chest.

'I am not an event in your life!' she shouted. 'I'm a person in my own right, with things that are about me, not you. I make decisions about me for my own reasons, not to fulfil your fucking prophecy!'

She turned away again, not able contain her emotion and face him at the same time.

'Yes. You have agency. I believe this. How could you not? There would be no choice without it. How could we be moral without the choice not to be? I believe this more than I believe anything.'

Constant was shaking so hard he found it difficult to speak; after taking a moment to gather himself, he pressed on.

'That the prophet saw your choices doesn't change that they're yours. Seeing the future makes it the future. But what is seen is not foreordained, it is chosen. I am choosing to believe. I am deciding to act in such a way as to bring what the prophet saw to pass. You can decide differently. And if you do the prophecy will turn out to be about something else, about someone else. But it's not about someone else. It's about you. It's about us. Because here we are. It's really complicated and I am sorry.'

'I am getting pretty fucking sick of you saying that.'

'I *am* sorry,' said Constant, tears streaming from his eyes but standing his ground as they did so. 'For any hurt I have caused you, for any fault or sorrow, I ask forgiveness. My soul is yours. I know you don't want it. I'm not forcing you to take it. But it's yours, nonetheless. Because this is real. I think you hold my life in your hands. I've thought it since I met you. I am terrified beyond words. I'm twelve. I have to remember that. Please help me.'

No one said anything for what seemed an eternity. The sounds of the meadowland filled the emptiness.

Eventually Kit spoke up. 'What do we do now?'

'Fuck, I don't know.' Blix looked up at the sky, perhaps hoping for inspiration. The sky remained silent. *No signs for her either,* thought part of Constant's mind.

'We do what we do,' she said. She brushed herself down, sweeping away the grass that clung to her. Then, to his immense surprise and possibly to her own, she grabbed Constant and hugged him tightly.

'We do what we do,' she said again, releasing the startled boy. 'We keep going. That's what we do. We keep going, no matter how scared we are, and hope we're strong enough.'

Up another hill, rich in clover and wildflowers. They had no words to say to each other anymore and strangely, that helped. As they walked, Elysium did its work on them as it had throughout their time there. Blix felt the band of anger around her heart loosen a little. She fell in with Kit and took her hand. That helped too.

The sounds of horses reached their ears as they neared the rise and, wary now, they approached the top on their stomachs, weapons ready. As they looked over and saw what lay beyond, the fear in their hearts melted like night frost in the first light, replaced by wonder.

In a field of grass and poppies, below them and some distance away, a herd of unicorns drank in a flooded plain, where a stream had widened to the point where there was no difference between river and land. Around fifty strong, tall and muscular, wild manes tossing as they lifted their heads, they seemed almost to glow in the limpid sunlight, brilliant white and sleek coated. The horn that gave them their name was long, almost as long at their bodies, jutting thickly from their foreheads in a straight tusk, growth-ringed in a spiral tapering only slightly toward the point, like a narwhal's tusk, which it closely resembled. Foals sported through the flowers and danced in the water margin, charging and rearing and feinting with each other, their pure gold voices carrying across the distance. The older animals gathered in twos and threes, rubbing their horns together in a display of affection. They seemed so at one with the land that suddenly the numinous world made sense to Blix, and seemed wholly natural for the first time. Brightly coloured leaves and butterflies fluttered in the sky. The moment seemed blessed.

'I have never seen anything so beautiful,' breathed Constant.

He spoke quietly, but ears pricked across the herd, heads turned toward them, and honeyed voices neighed skittishly. But the unicorns did not run. A few young horses, barely yearlings, peeled away from the main group and cantered toward them, heads held high in anticipation. The companions got to their feet as they approached, but to Blix's mind there was no threat in their demeanour, only curiosity. The animals drew to a halt on the slope a few yards beneath them.

'Do you think we speak unicorn now?' Blix asked, trying not to sound as awestruck as she felt.

'Give it a go, kiddo.'

Blix found that she was a little lost for words. 'Um. Hello? We're friends. Not enemies, anyway. Do you understand? Friends.'

One of the unicorns snorted a little, but gave no sign of understanding. Blix had no sense that the animal was talking to her. She took a step forward, Tentatively, she reached out a hand. 'May I touch you?' Another step, then another, then she was inside the reach of the unicorn's horn.

The unicorn shied away. It turned, and the others with it, and walked away slowly, back to the herd. Blix tried to contain her disappointment.

'Only virgins can touch unicorns,' Kit observed.

'Oh. Yeah, I knew that. Wait, was that a joke?' She watched the unicorns retreating. 'I think they're just animals. Well, 'just' is the wrong word. They're incredible.'

One of the unicorns, barely more than a foal, paused and turned to look at Blix, who wondered in that moment whether she'd been mistaken, whether there was a mind inside the milk-white flesh, one that had heard her and understood her words.

'My name is Blix,' she said simply. 'I'm... someone. Are you? Do you have a n-'

Without warning an immense winged shape plunged from the sky and landed on the colt, smashing it into the wet earth and breaking its back with a crack that echoed across the meadow like a rifle shot, killing it instantly. Blix screamed and fell backward in shock. The thing beat its mighty wings and wrapped huge claws around the broken unicorn, and launched itself back into the sky, effortlessly dragging the dead body with it, which lolled obscenely, blood spraying in its wake.

Suddenly the air was thick with them, screeching raucously, diving toward the unicorns, massive leonine paws tensed to rend or slice. For their part the unicorns shrieked in equine terror but instead of running they began to rear, the whorled horns now a phalanx of spears stabbing upward again and again at the monsters falling from above, making them think twice about exposing their underbellies as they swooped in for the kill.

'What's happening?'

'To me!' Constant yelled. He snatched Sorcha from its scabbard and held it high, tracking first one beast then another as they circled overhead.

Kit had her gun out and ready to fire before she remembered it was empty. 'Shit! Get your sword up kid!'

'It is up!'

'Look out!'

Blix crawled back to them. 'Where'd they come from?'

'Who knows? Stay down!'

And then as quickly as they'd appeared they were gone, beating away into the blue, two more unicorns taken from the herd, bloody remains splattered across the field of flowers. Wild poppies danced red against the cornflower sky, black eyes turned toward the sun.

The unicorns fled screaming over the hill and were lost to sight, the thunder of their hooves drumming ever more distant until they heard it no more. Blix, Kit and Constant stood rooted to the spot, shocked and terrified and elated not to be dead. Eventually, Kit said, 'What the hell just happened?'

'Life,' said Blix. 'Life happened.'

Constant was swallowing hard, trying not to be sick. 'We did that. They were watching us, not the sky. It was our fault. It was horrible.' There was nothing of the hardness which so often filled his voice. In this moment, he was just a child.

'No, it wasn't,' Blix replied. She stared into the distance where the winged beasts had flown. They were still just visible, black dots lurching through the air. 'Things aren't always about us. Amazing, I know. That was carnivores eating herbivores. Just the way it happens. We were incidental. They probably didn't see us. They have very large pupils you know, great eyesight, an eagle's eyes, but they have tunnel vision too. Very focused on their prey.'

'I always wondered why horses needed horns,' mused Kit, finally holstering her empty pistol. 'What were those things?'

Blix turned to face her. Her eyes were shining. 'Gryphons,' she said. 'They were gryphons.'

They found the gate a little further on. It was part of a complex of stone circles, thirty or forty groups across a series of hilltops, with individual menhirs, lines of stones and dolmens forming an intricate pattern which had long since fallen into disrepair and been broken up. Whoever the people of Elysium were, they'd left this place and taken some of it with them. Constant went to find the right stones. Blix and Kit did some sightseeing.

'Katy would love this,' said Blix, patting a particularly portentous-looking megalith. 'I bet these are druid stones around a magician's gate. She'd get extra marks in History for knowing that.'

'You can bring her here once we rescue her,' said Kit.

A dam broke inside Blix, a wall holding back her worst fear, something she'd held in check through the madness and terror of the days since she last saw Katy, disappearing through the window in the air. But instead of tears or screams, she simply said, 'Do you really think we will? What if it's too late? What if she's already dead?'

Kit put her arm around Blix. This time Blix didn't wriggle free.

'We're not and she ain't,' said the American emphatically. 'You gotta have faith. Life ain't nothing without it.'

'I suppose. Faith. I hope you're right. Faith and hope.' She hesitated. 'There's one more thing after that.'

'Yes, there is. And that's the greatest thing, ain't it?'

'Found it!' called Constant. He was at the highest point of the complex, standing near a circle of bluestone trilithons. 'We're in luck.'

'Yeah. That's us. Lucky.' Blix was about to go up to join him, but abruptly she turned back to Kit. 'But what if she is?' Her tone was still calm, but her anguish was carved on her face as if by a knife.

'If she is, we'll do right by her,' said Kit.

'What does that mean?'

'It means what it means.'

'What does *that* mean?'

'I dunno, kiddo. Love is its own meaning.' She held out a hand. 'Come and see.'

Chapter Thirty-Four: Too Many Secrets

Blix was almost used to the gates by now; when the sky spat her out she remembered to roll as she fell. She ended up with a face full of sand. Even the gate shock seemed lesser than before. She felt like she'd been beaten up by only three owl-bears this time. Her stomach hurt terribly, like she'd torn something inside. She crouched in a foetal position, hugging her knees, until it subsided.

The sand was red and there was lots of it. The gate, a series of ugly black basalt spikes, was surrounded by a low rise of dunes. It was cooler than Ceto, but otherwise it seemed depressingly familiar.

'Another bloody desert,' Blix grumbled, standing up and brushing herself down. 'Do we have to slog through this one as well?'

'It's not a desert,' said Constant, weakly. He looked distinctly nauseous. 'Listen.'

Blix heard the shhhhss of waves rolling onto a pebble shore, and the clattering applause of stone on stone as the tide dragged the rocks back under the water. The sharp smell of saltwater and wrack cleared her sinuses for her. She felt better for it. She pulled Kit to her feet, checked that Constant was okay, and then hauled herself up the sand to see what she could see.

They were near the shore, well above the high-water mark and at the low edge of a well-eroded cliff, which rose above the sand into untamed grassland which stretched along the clifftop in both directions. A cut in the rock made a path up to the cliff top. Whether this was natural or man-made, Blix couldn't tell.

In the other direction, sand dunes thick with marram grass gave way to pebbles near to the water's edge. Further along the shore, tables of stone peppered the beach where the cliff face had collapsed. Out in the water dozens of huge, bent spines of rock, uplifted from the seabed and tilted on edge, looked like the backs of giant sea dragons, row upon row of them, breaching the surface and plunging back beneath. So alive did they look that Blix almost ducked, before her mind caught up with her senses. Waves crashed against them and the spray whipped across Blix's face, driven by the stiff wind coming from the sea. Thick grey clouds squatted low in the sky, covering most of it.

'Ooh, bracing. I love it,' she said. 'It's like the Jurassic Coast. We used to go there a lot when I was little. Mum's cousin has a cottage she lends us. Katy always used to look for fossils. I preferred bugs. Once I found this huge oil beetle, I put it right down her... down her...'

The moon appeared from behind the clouds. Half full and tiny compared to Earth's moon, it nonetheless drove all other thoughts from her mind. It was startlingly beautiful. It made her breast swell and her breath catch in her throat like a kiss from a lover. Then it was gone again, and she felt unnerved by the effect it'd had on her. Her stomach, still not happy from the gate travel, turned upside down painfully. She groaned and clutched at it.

'Right down her what?' Kit asked, joining her on the lip of the dune. 'Never mind, she can tell me herself when I meet her.'

Blix shot her a grateful look. Her stomach rumbled loudly. 'Pardon,' she said primly. 'I'm hungry. How are we doing for time, Constant?'

The boy tottered up to join them. 'Well, I can't see the sun, late afternoon maybe?'

'I meant, relative to six weeks from the Bastion.'

'Oh. Yes.' He thought about it little. 'The Valhalla gate had a big and very helpful lag. I think at roughly this moment on Shambhala we are looking up at the Iris, wondering why there are so many large steps.'

'Really? That's incredible. Further back than when we started? Incredible. I don't think I'll ever get my head around this stuff.'

'We gain again on the next gate, and a lot on the one after, then it's wiped out a bit when we go to Lyonesse.' He flinched slightly as he said the name, clearly wondering if Blix would explode. When nothing happened, he continued. 'We're on schedule, pretty much,' he concluded.

'Boy ain't wrong,' Kit said. 'Now that's incredible.'

She looked around, less impressed than Blix with the sea breezes. 'Valhalla, you say? This ain't how I imagined Valhalla. Distinct lack of big bearded men with axes and mead.'

'I didn't name the gate. Presumably it means something to the people who did. Who knows what else is here? Worlds are big places.'

Blix took another deep breath of sea air. Her stomach cramped again. 'Argh. How far to the next gate? Not another huge route march, I hope.'

'No, the next gate is very close. In fact, you can see it from here.'

He pointed. To their right, which Blix guessed was probably north, the cliff curved around to form a headland perhaps a mile away. Somewhat closer and inland from that point a black stone circle was just visible, outlined against the sky.

'Great. Not a walk in the meadow, but not bad. These gates are a bit close to the waterline, aren't they? A few big waves and this one will be underwater.'

They were many miles inland when my people first came here,' said Constant. 'The sea has claimed the land since then.'

'I see. We got here just in time then. That's not at all suspiciously convenient. Come on then, let's go and get thrown across the universe again. Might as well do it while I still feel like shit.'

Constant shook his head. 'We're not going there yet.' He squared his shoulder in anticipation of an argument. 'The gate we went through was called Valhalla. This gate has a different name. It's Muninn. That one,' he continued, pointing at the distant rocks once more, 'is called Huginn. Huginn and Muninn were Wotan's ravens. He sent them out every day to gain knowledge. Their names mean 'thought' and 'memory.'

His pointing finger shifted to the cliff top about halfway between the gate. A gnarled black tree stood there alone.

Blix followed his finger, put two and two together, and this time she did explode.

'Oh, for fuck's sake,' she said hotly. 'That's where we're supposed to hang you? Did you forget to mention *when you told us about this for the first time an hour ago* that you meant immediately? Jesus!' She kicked sand at the boy, who took it in his face with only a slight grimace. 'Do you really expect me to do this? It's fucking mental.'

'What she said,' Kit agreed firmly.

Constant looked from one to the other. Then to their astonishment he screwed up his face and burst into tears. Blix saw him exposed like never before, saw the fear that ate at him, and saw, as he quickly composed himself, the resolve that drove him on.

'You will help me,' he said, rubbing angrily at his eyes, seemingly ashamed at his show of emotion. 'No,' he said as Kit moved to comfort him, shying away from her outreached hand. 'You will help me. The prophet saw you. He made it the future.' He looked imploringly at Blix. 'Saving your sister is not separate from this. Without this... I think we won't have done what we need to do to succeed. I think the prophet says that.'

His round face hardened; more than resolve, he looked like he'd become someone for who hardness was all there was.

'Whether you help me or not I am going to do it,' he continued, turning away from them. 'You can either help me live through it or watch me die. Or you can leave and I'll die alone.'

He stomped back down the dune, through the gate and started up the cut. Blix and Kit watched him struggle upward.

'We could hit him on the head,' Kit said after a while. 'I could hogtie him, we'd be on the next world afore he knew a thing about it.'

Blix shook her head 'Superficially attractive, probably quite satisfying, but won't work. You can't take an unconscious person into a gate. No entry without free will.'

'Stupid rule.'

They watched the boy struggle over the sand and start on the vague path up the cliff. It looked precarious.

'We're going to help him, aren't we?' said Blix eventually.

'I ain't gonna let him die, anyways,' said Kit. 'I don't know if that's helping him. Well, I suppose we better go after the damn fool before he does something damn foolish by himself.'

'You can kiss me first. If you like.'

'I do like.'

They caught up with Constant. He was muttering angrily to himself. He glanced at them under his arm as they scrambled up the bare path behind him, but said nothing.

The black tree was covered in rubbery purple leaves and long needle thorns, which to Blix's mind looked like an open invitation to blood poisoning. The trunk had much thicker thorns, bigger that Blix's outstretched hand, wicked upward-pointing barbs which looked oily and a bit sickly, growing from the bole up into the high branches. She didn't know what species it was, but its unpleasant and slightly unearthly aspect made her think it wasn't something she'd find at Kew Gardens.

'I hereby name this the 'Go-Away' Tree,' Blix said, pulling a face. 'I bet the sap's poisonous or something.'

The tree stood by itself, but further back from the cliff edge there was a forest, not far away over open fields. The trees stretched unbroken from one horizon to the other. Blix didn't recognise these trees either, but the straightness of the tree line suggested they were managed. They certainly looked healthier than the thorn tree, and a lot less ominous.

There were no other people around.

'If this was England this place would be thick with beardies in cagoules banging on about fresh air and ramblers' rights,' Blix said. 'Looks like we've got it to ourselves. Lucky us.'

Constant wasn't listening. Constant was staring at the tree.

'Yggdrasil,' he whispered.

'Yggdrasil was an ash tree,' said Kit. 'What?' she said, as the others stared at her. 'Don't look at me like that. I know stuff.'

'I didn't mean literally. I meant, for me.'

Blix looked the tree up and down with distaste. It didn't get any prettier the longer she looked at it.

'This can't have been here when your people came,' she said. 'At least six hundred years ago, right? It's not old enough.'

'I assume it wasn't. I didn't know it would be here. I had faith something would be though.' The boy rushed on to forestall the others' objections. 'Look, I know this is mad and I don't want to have that fight again. I want you to hear my plan.'

Kit snorted. 'Another plan! Well, let's hear it kid, I'm all ears.'

'Good. Because it's about you.'

'Say what now?'

'You wondered where you were in the prophecy. I think you're here, by implication at least. For years - millennia - we've questioned how I survive hanging with an open wound when the Writing says I die. We assumed it would be some form of magic which would keep me alive. But now, when it matters, I think I know. I don't survive. I die. I think you use your snake oil to bring me back when I do.'

Kit looked absolutely dumbfounded. 'Goddamn son of a bitch!'

'That's incredible,' said Blix, suddenly elated. 'Absolutely lunatic and brilliant. Will it work?'

'It brought you back. You're not a full werewolf yet, you heal well but non-silver things still kill you. What happened at the waterfall was catastrophic. You didn't live. It must have been the gorgon's blood that brought you back.'

Kit had the strangest look on her face, half angry, half afraid.

'We can't do that,' she said. 'I ain't got but three or four drops left!'

'Then three or four drops will be enough,' said the boy firmly.

Kit seemed strangely shocked and somehow helpless. She spluttered for a moment as she tried to say something which wouldn't quite form into words.

'But then I won't have any,' she said almost plaintively.

'You said you've got a pint in Utah,' Blix pointed out.

'There ain't here.' The American turned away from them, her demeanour suddenly nervous and unsure, wholly different from her usual carefree insouciance. Blix found it strange and slightly unsettling - and familiar, in some way she couldn't quite place.

After a few moments in which Kit plainly steeled herself for something unpleasant, she turned back to them, a pugnacious look on her face. 'Well, okay then,' she said assertively. 'Well, okay.'

'Thank you,' Constant breathed.

'Yeah, well, let's get this done before I change my goddamn mind.' Kit said grimly. 'I seen a hanging before. They ain't pretty.'

'How long must you hang for?' Blix asked.

'The Writing says, "moon to moon". Normally you would interpret a moon as a month - '

'A month! Christ on a bike.'

'- but that's madness,' the boy continued. 'Wotan himself only hung for nine days. I think moon to moon means a day.'

'Moon's already up,' Kit said.

'It's still afternoon. Nightfall to nightfall, then. It's not clear so I'll interpret it how I want and if it's not good enough then, then... I don't know what then. It will have to be good enough.'

Without warning he drew his sword and lopped a low, straight branch from the thorn tree.

'You should prepare for a vigil. Find food, build a fire. I would prefer it if you didn't sleep tonight.'

He began methodically stripping the thorns from the bark with his blade.

'What are you doing?' Blix asked.

'Making a spear.'

'Jesus Christ. I don't feel well.'

The sick feeling in Blix's stomach got worse as she gathered wood from the forest edge and built a fire under the thorn tree. The brief moment of happiness - and to her surprise, it had genuinely been happiness - that Constant might live through his trial didn't come back no matter how much she tried to focus on it.

Do I feel bad because he might die? Or because I might be the one to kill him? Or is it because I might be the one to kill him and I might not feel bad about it if I do? Because I killed a man and I don't feel bad about it. God, Katy, I need to talk to you.

While Blix found wood, Kit went fishing. They came back as night was drawing in. Kit had a couple of broad, long-legged crabs tied to a string. 'Found 'em in a rock pool.' She sucked a finger. 'They didn't want to leave.'

'Eocarcinus magna,' said Blix, as she coaxed the wood alight. 'Baby giant crabs. They grow really quickly. Five, ten years and they'll be size of this tree. Cut you in half with one snip.'

Kit looked at the crabs with new respect. 'Wow. Really?'

'No,' Blix smiled. 'Just joking. There are eleventy million species of crabs. I have no idea what these are. Just crabs, I expect.'

'Ha! Dinner is what they are. Gimme one of those green sticks kiddo, I'm going skewer these boys over the fire.'

'I'm ready,' said Constant.

Blix's stomach kicked hard. 'I've lost my appetite,' she said.

'Me too, kiddo. Me too.'

The spear was a work of craft. The branch had been stripped back to a straight, strong pole and split at one end. One of the thick thorns from the trunk of the tree had been bound into the split. It looked like something from the Stone Age, and Blix thought that if she threw it hard it would kill a manticore as cleanly as Roohsk's harpoon. Constant held it out to her. She took it as if it might turn into a serpent.

The boy had cleared the big thorns from the side of the trunk facing the sea, leaving only some big ones near the base, under a thick branch. He surveyed his handiwork with grim approval, then turned to Kit. 'Give me your rope,' he said.

Kit looked ready to argue but Constant cut her off. 'Listen. Really listen. I know this is crazy. You have to trust me. I know you've no reason to. I haven't earned it. Please force yourself. What I am asking you to do is terrible. Please don't falter. Please give me your rope.'

'Goddamn hell and death,' said Kit, but she unhooked the long coil of rope from her belt and gave it to Constant.

'Thank you. I am going to ruin it, so here is payment.'

He threw what appeared to be a large emerald to Kit, who caught it and pocketed it without even looking at it.

'Rope's free. You can buy me some bullets when we get outta this dump.'

Constant ran the rope around the tree trunk and cinched it at head height. He cut the rest off and quickly made a noose of one end, so quickly that Blix had the strong sensation he'd been practicing. He threw the free end over the low branch and pulled the noose up level with the cinched rope. The noose swung free. Seeing it made Blix want to puke.

Constant pulled his red robe and under shirt over his head, folded them carefully, and laid them by the fire, his bag on top. His skinny body made him look even younger than his years. He stepped on the thick thorns at the bottom of the tree. They squeaked alarmingly but held his weight. He loosened the cinched rope and slipped under it, back to the tree, and then tightened it again around his chest and under his arms, so that he was hard against the trunk. His pale flesh stood out starkly against the black bark - all except the streaks of rust-red snaking up his arms, which glittered strangely in the firelight.

He caught the swinging noose and put it over his head.

'This has to be real. I don't have to be stupid. I can give myself the strongest possible chance. When you pull the rope taught I will start to strangle. This rope around my chest stops me swinging free and keeps the pressure on my neck consistent. You must hang me enough so that I can barely breathe, but not so much that I immediately choke. It will be a fine judgment. Pull me so that I am on tiptoe, do you see? Tie it off under that root.'

He demonstrated. It only made Blix feel worse.

'I can probably stand that for some time. I'm used to maintaining awkward prayer positions for hours on end. But I will have the spear in my side and I will be losing blood. At some point I will faint, and then I will strangle to death or break my neck. You must let this happen. Then you bring me back. I hope. Then we do it again, until it's enough.'

'Madness,' Kit said cheerlessly.

'Yes. I might lose heart. If I do, please don't cut me down. If you cut me down this is all wasted. Be resolute if I am not. Tie my hands so I can't free myself.'

Kit stared at the rope as though she'd never seen rope before. Then quickly she cut a short length from the trailing end of the noose and tied his hands behind his back.

'Kid, your courage has depths I can't fathom,' she said toughly. 'I'm gonna make sure you come back. I make you my promise.'

'Don't make promises you might not be able to keep.'

'I make you my promise.'

'Thank you. Then we begin.' The boy closed his eyes and began muttering under his breath. Blix knew what he was saying.

'I hope you don't die,' She blurted all at once.

'Me too,' said Constant fervently.

'No, that's not what... I mean, I understand now. Why you say it. Why it's a blessing. The magic that lets us talk is hiding its meaning. It sounds so prosaic in English, but in Shambhalhai or Tibetan or whatever it must have a deeper meaning. Something in the sound of the words that doesn't translate. Something that tells the listener that you care about them.'

She came over to him and put her hand on the bare skin of his chest, over his heart.

'I care about you. Even after everything. Because people should care about other people. Say your words, Constant. I hope you don't die. I - '

She faltered, and turned away.

'I'm not strong enough,' she said.

'Yes. You are. Have faith. My soul is yours.'

With a scream that was made of equal parts fear and pain and hate and love Blix turned and thrust the spear into Constant's right side.

The thorn went in easily, slicing through the flesh with a razor's grace. Constant groaned and his whole body twisted, up and away from the cause of the wound. Blood pulsed around the spear's head and flowed down Constant's side, a dark waterfall splashing against his feet.

'Again,' he said, summoning the words from some abyss inside himself.

'Fuck, no,' said Blix, dropping the spear shaft and spinning away, tears pouring from her eyes as freely as the blood from Constant's side. 'I can't, I can't.'

'Then pull,' Constant gasped, his eyes seeking out Kit's.

'Fuck you,' the American shouted, but she moved quickly, grasping the rope and pulling it taught. As the noose tightened around his neck Constant began to scream, a scream which became a strangled gurgle as the rope cut him off. Kit hauled slowly and evenly, not watching the noose, watching Constant's feet instead. She raised him until he was on his toes and then, without lowering him in the slightest, tied off the rope under the tree root with one hand. Blix was so drained she couldn't even wonder at the strength and skill it took to do that.

Constant jerked as his head was pulled back, and started choking, his eyes bulging, his face red and swelling, the skin below the noose going whiter still. Blood seeped from under his chin as the rope sawed into his flesh. The wound in his side alternately sucking and gaping as the boy's body rebelled against the outrage inflicted on it. As it opened, blood poured from it. His leg was soon painted red.

Blix backed away, buckled over and threw up, her insides twisting as if it has been she who had taken the spear in her side. 'God almighty, what have we done?' she said, wiping her mouth with a shaking hand.

Kit had no words for her. She was watching Constant. She clutched the little bottle of snake oil.

'There's not enough,' she said. 'There's not enough.'

It took almost two hours for Constant to die.

It was the sound that made Blix ill. The continual, hideous choking sound that filled the silence of the night, echoing above the dull crash of the waves at low tide. She was sick twice more, each time worse than the last, each time feeling like she was being crushed inside by the horror she was watching. She sat beside the fire, taking no warmth from the flame; Constant's torment seemed to suck all heat from her, causing an icy shivering that would not stop. Not even the radiance of the tiny moon appearing now and then from behind the clouds could distract her.

I won't turn away. I owe him nothing. Nothing but this.

Kit sat on her haunches in front of Constant, never once taking her eyes off him, ready to keep her promise when the time came. Neither Blix nor Kit spoke. Words seemed redundant, useless in the face of the immense act of will taking place before their eyes.

The boy was as good as his word; squirming, convulsing as his wound opened further, but not failing, not strangling, not hanging himself until the last moment when his strength gave way and he fainted, fell, and took the full weight of his body on his neck. There was a dull snap. At once Kit was with him, standing on the broad thorns and holding him almost tenderly around his waist with one arm while she loosened the noose with the other. She moved so quickly it took Blix a moment to catch up with her. She dived on the rope and yanked it free. Constant slumped forward and was held by the rope under his arms. Blix knew he was dead. There was no life left in him. No blood pulsed through his veins.

'Pull out the spear,' Kit said.

Blix did as she was told. Blood squelched with it but didn't spurt. Something grey bulged in the puncture. Blix gagged immediately but there was nothing more to come up. She dropped the spear and staggered backward, appalled. Then suddenly she wasn't appalled. She was hungry.

'Push that back in,' said Kit matter-of-factly. 'Now let's see if this works.'

Gently, she opened Constant's mouth and, with exaggerated care, uncorked the little round bottle with her teeth and let a single drop fall onto his swollen tongue, all without letting the boy go.

'If you got prayers kiddo, pray 'em now.'

Constant didn't move.

'Oh God, it hasn't worked,' Blix moaned in despair.

'Give it a moment. It took a long time to bring you back.'

'Give him more!'

'I can't, gorgon blood is poison except when dilute. He don't have my tolerance.'

'He's not coming back! Do it!'

Hesitation, and deep reluctance. Then, another drop. 'Come on, kid,' Kit said, her voice trailing away into a whisper. 'Be right for once. Just this time. Be right, kid.'

Blix gasped. 'Look!'

The wound in Constant's side was closing.

Suddenly he opened his eyes. he arched convulsively and drew in a sand-dry breath, a rattling hiss exploding into a deep moan as he sucked in air. He looked around wild-eyed as if unaware of his surroundings, then swung his head up and focused on Kit.

'Where?' He croaked the word in a voice like tomb dust. '... ws a boy?'

'Don't try to speak,' said Kit gently. 'You need to rest.'

The boy's face hardened. 'Ag.' He swallowed and tried a second time. 'Again.'

'Jesus, kid!'

'Again.'

Kit looked at him helplessly for a moment. Then she straightened, hauled the boy back to an upright position and tightened the rope across his chest. She dropped down and picked up the spear. She held it out to Blix, who took it wordlessly. Kit took the strain on the rope once more, and nodded. Shaking with horror, fear and the raw sense that she was betraying something important, Blix stabbed Constant once more, feeling once more that as she stabbed him she was stabbing herself. Kit lifted the boy back onto his toes and tied off the rope.

The women fell to their knees beside the fire, exhausted.

'We're done,' Kit said heavily. 'It's done. For now.' He arms sought out Blix and pulled her in, cradling her head in her breast.

'Oh God, I can't believe we're doing this again,' Blix cried, wrapping her arms around Kit in return. 'Look at him! I can't. I can't do this anymore.'

'Yes, he does look in a bad way, doesn't he?' said Belmont Dragonville from behind the fire. 'A terrible thing to do to a body. Still, we must all do what we think we must, mustn't we?'

Kit snatched up Constant's sword and with one smooth overhead swing cut Dragonville in two.

'That was exciting,' said Dragonville, smiling easily as the sword passed straight through him, 'but as you see, I'm not really here.'

'Bastard!' screamed Kit and swung again, hard, cutting diagonally through the magician from shoulder to hip.

'I am happy to wait until you've got this out of your system,' said Dragonville. 'Another blow?'

Kit threw the sword down in disgust. 'Fuck you, you goddamn bastard.'

'And *konbanwa* to you, daughter of sunrise. And Miss Summerland, greetings to you also.' He bowed politely.

From deep inside Blix a sound welled up, part scream, part howl, a ragged bellow born of pain and anger and the soul-wrenching exhaustion of constant terror. The sound became words before she realised she had them and she shouted out loud enough to fill the blackened sky.

'WHERE'S MY SISTER?'

'Ah, yes! Miss Katherine! A charming girl. I had a lengthy conversation with her just this morning. Perceptive and intelligent, a model for us all. I am afraid old Echmoth has had his wicked way with her. She is... no longer with us.'

Blix felt the words cut her open and tear out her insides. She tried to rise but her legs gave way and she fell back, clawing at her heart as though she might somehow take it out and give it to Katy and so bring her back. She felt like her skin was afire and ice-bitten at the same time, like it was about to crack and burst and shatter into pieces.

'She can't... she can't... she can't be...' she cried, unable to say the word and make it real. 'I was coming! I was coming to rescue her!'

Dragonville clapped his hands in delight. 'That's what she said! To the word. You really are each other, aren't you? How wonderful. She told me to tell you she told me to "get fucked". Excuse the vulgarity, I merely convey the message. Is there a message you would like me to pass on in return when I see her next?'

A little flame of hope, snuffed out, flickered alight once more in Blix's mind. 'She's… she's alive?' She stammered, not daring to believe.

'I think that rather depends on how clever she is. What is life, really? Let us say she has been... superseded. Yes, that seems right.'

'I don't understand!' Blix wailed. Emotion overtook her at last and she was sick again, retching bad enough to tear her throat, though there was nothing left to come up.

'Why would you? I assure you it all makes sense from my point of view. But if you want a real answer to your question we should ask the expert!'

Dragonville strode through the fire without the flames touching him and stood squarely in front of the strangulating boy. He looked Constant up and down critically.

'Hmm. No jaw-jaw for you. Let's fix that.'

He waved a finger and Constant's dry choking became a splutter. He took a long, agonised gulp of air, that sounded like the first breath of a dead man rising from the grave. He looked at Dragonville with horror.

'No,' he croaked. 'No.'

'Don't worry dear boy, I haven't put the kibosh on your exercise in self-torture. This won't obviate whatever sacrifice you think you're m... aking...' He trailed off, staring at the red marks on Constants upper arms. Moving closer, he followed the lines down and around Constant's arms until he could see no further. He stepped back, looking deeply unhappy.

'My dear boy! This damage... This is forever! No, you should not have done it!'

Unforced compassion filled his voice, the ripe jocularity now completely absent. 'This will never heal. It will be this way for your whole life. I am very sorry to see it. Very sorry.'

'... weight...' mumbled Constant.

'I know, dear boy. I know. It is intolerable. Take no more upon yourself. Never do magic. You must not. Please.'

He glanced back at the two women and seemed to realise he'd exposed something of himself. The plummy chumminess returned but the eyes hardened, and his tone had a bitter edge that he couldn't quite conceal.

'But look at you! Wotan reborn. I wonder what your little friend thinks of it all?'

He gazed penetratingly into Constant's eyes, then laughed uproariously.

'Hello, what's this? You are unaware! I must tell Echmoth, he will be amused. Possibly. Well, no matter. In due course, no doubt, you will learn. No, don't trouble yourself,' he added, as Constant tried to speak. 'In due course.'

'Why are you here, magician?' Kit snarled.

'Didn't I say? I'm looking for stolen property. The First of Wolves and I had a bit of a to-do. Nasty business, most regrettable. He abstracted some things of mine. I thought I'd find them in his possession, but here you are instead.' He frowned. 'I was going to, ah, persuade him to return to the Bastion using the lens. But that won't work with you, you haven't been there. Bother.'

'He's dead,' managed Blix, trying to calm herself. 'We killed him. We killed them all! You're next!'

The magician's presence had set off something inside her; she badly wanted to rip his head off and only the knowledge that he wasn't there stopped her leaping on him.

'Is that so? What a shame. A most unusual werewolf, as werewolves go. A remarkable perspective. Still, never mind. I shall retrieve my property from you in due course.'

'Horseshit,' said Kit, cocking her hip and folding her arms across her chest. 'The bloodstone's his,' she nodded at Constant. 'The Mormons own the lens. Hey, I do have something that belongs to you though.' She extended a middle finger in Dragonville's direction.

The magician laughed and mockingly held up his hands as if to ward it away. 'The infamous finger! I cede it to you, *Ojou-chan*. I will not claim it. The other things are mine.' His last words rang out with a conviction that could carve granite, such was the steel in it.

Kit wasn't cowed.

'Dead men need no possessions,' she said flatly. 'I'm gonna kill you if it's the last thing I do. And if I die first, I'll wait for you in Hell with my gun.'

Dragonville laughed his mocking laugh, a sound that only made Blix more furious.

'My dear child. I am already in Hell. That is rather the point. But my foot shall slide in time, I have no doubt. If it is you that finally sends me on my way, I bow to you now.' He doffed his top hat in faux civility.

'Bastard!'

'But you attack me with such vigour! I am nonplussed. I understand why she hates me,' the magician continued, looking at Blix, who was now rocking with repressed anger. 'What have I ever done to you?'

'YOU KILLED MY MOTHER!' Kit screamed. Then she put her hand to her mouth, shocked by what she'd said, shocked that the magician had goaded her to reveal so much about herself so easily, to reveal something so important.

Dragonville's eyes glittered in the firelight.

'Oh, that. Yes. I set her on fire and watched as she burned to death. But, you know, all things must pass from this mortal realm. This way or that way, what does it matter? If it means anything to you I didn't wish her ill and she didn't suffer, particularly. I'm not a monster.'

'Why?' The word broke under the weight of Kit's pain and emerged in a choking half-sob.

'It was necessary for my purpose. Her death has contributed, in a small way, to the prosecution of a great and noble cause. My experiment was most successful. I published, to some modest acclaim I may say. And that led to a course of action which brought me here. Quite the irony.'

'Why, damn you!'

'You know what happens when your kind die. I wanted to see it.'

Kit inhaled sharply. 'Don't,' she said, looking hurriedly at Blix.

Dragonville smiled. 'Secrets, *kitsune?* If I have learned anything in my long life, it's that there are no secrets. Someone always knows. Perhaps I will keep yours for now. It will soon be moot. Everything is known eventually. Like the meaning of this young man's Writing, for example.'

Constant choked out as much of a question as his desperate state allowed.

'How... could...' he managed.

'How could I know about your hidden prophecy, guarded by warrior monks on a magic-proof mountain for thousands of years on a different planet to my own?' Dragonville finished, chuckling a little. 'My goodness, you Shambhalhai are very backward. I read about it. In a book. One of your Recognising monks liked to talk, someone wrote it down. Quite prosaic, really. People are people, wherever they are. There are no secrets.'

Constant's eyes rolled upward in his head, then refocused on Dragonville, a look of utter anguish suffusing his face.

'... murderer... brothers...'

'Indeed,' said the magician, acquiescing to the charge with a slight bow. 'Not myself. One has people for such things. But the point was made, no? The fire goes out.'

'... nev... r...'

'I think yes. Don't trouble yourself so, dear boy. It doesn't matter.'

'I've had enough of this,' said Blix suddenly. She tried to stand but her legs wouldn't work properly. She settled for eyeballing Dragonville. 'No one wants you here. Fuck off back where you came from. The only reason you're not dead is because you're not really here.'

Blix was by now heartily sick of the magician's laugh. He absolutely roared at her remark, to the point where he had to turn away for a moment to recover himself.

'I assure you young lady, that is not the reason I am not dead.' He wiped a tear of mirth from his eye. 'Ah, me.'

He took a pocket watch from his waistcoat and glanced at it. 'I will take my leave now. I'll collect my property once our business is concluded.'

'You won't... open...' said Constant, each word a ferocious act of will. 'I'll... destroy... first.'

'My dear boy,' Dragonville began, but Kit talked over him.

'And I'll never give up. An eye for an eye, Dragonville. Burning for burning.'

'As you wish. When death takes you, don't say you weren't warned.' He looked at Blix, sizing her up. 'And you, young lady? Do you have anything stirring and dramatic to say?'

'You have my sister,' said Blix simply. The fury and pain were suddenly gone, as though her body had paused for breath before howling once more. She felt drained and strangely hollowed out. 'I want her back.'

'Quite so. And who would not? I expect you'll meet again, by and by. You may find she is a changed woman. Echmoth is not gentle. It is a matter for regret. I rather liked her.'

'Don't dare say you're sorry!'

'Then I won't. I'm not, in fact. I do find though that it's often terribly upsetting when people discover how little they matter. I am not a cruel man, unless that is necessary. Are there words that would soften that blow for you? You have but to say them, and I will repeat them as though I mean it.' The eyes twinkled once more.

'Piss off, you smirking cockbite.'

'Goodness me. Well, perhaps some advice then. Young lady, you are new to this magic lark. I perceive that you have recently received an unwelcome gift, shall we say. Consequence of using werewolves, messy and profligate creatures. Anyway, if you insist on continuing this hopping and popping from world to world, all footloose and fancy-free, there is something you should always establish as soon as you arrive.' He paused expectantly.

Blix's couldn't help herself.

'What's that, then?'

'How many moons there are. Cheerio,' he added, and vanished.

Blix looked confused. 'How many... Wait, what?'

'Oh no,' said Kit. 'Blix, the sky!'

Over the crest of the distant headland, in a different quarter of the sky, a second moon was rising.

It was a full moon.

'My God,' said Blix.

She felt a sudden wetness between her legs. She reached down, and stared in astonishment at the crimson staining her hand.

'I'm bleeding,' she said.

'I'm so sorry,' said Kit.

Pain beyond understanding splintered Blix's mind. She fell back, screaming, thrashing violently against the earth. The bones in her legs snapped of their own accord, twisted, extended, and reformed anew. Black claws burst through her nails, curling wickedly. Then she was on fire, every inch of her skin burning like molten metal had been poured onto her flesh. She clawed at her clothes with new strength; they tore away easily and with them came her skin, sloughing away like blood-soaked paper. Beneath it was a second skin, hairy, bloody, waiting to be revealed.

Kit backed away from her, horrified, putting herself between Blix and the boy. Somehow in the depths of her suffering Blix saw this and found her voice.

'Take him through the gate!' she screamed. 'I'll kill him! I'll kill you!' She buckled and screamed again as her spine cracked.

'No...' croaked Constant feebly.

'Ah! Leave a fragment! I'll follow when-'

Whatever else she might have said was cut off when her jaw shattered and pushed forward, shaping itself instantly into a muzzle. Long fangs pushed her own teeth out. Blix's screaming became deeper; as she screamed the screams became howls.

'No,' whispered Constant. 'Must... stay... all for... nothing... they win...'

'Goddamn mother of… fuck!' spat Kit. She gaped helplessly, transfixed by the horror Blix's body was inflicting on itself. Her eyes went between girl and the boy and the stone circle in the distant darkness. Then, as Blix continued to change, a calm came over Kit as she made a decision, and knew her purpose. Now determined, Kit strode up to Constant and hopped up next to him. The look he gave her could have melted stone.

'Don't... kill... not... her fault...'

'Shut up. This is going to hurt like hell. Trust me, kid.'

She gently pushed the little bottle of snake oil between his lips and upended it. The last drops of liquid dribbled into his mouth. Then she pulled out her knife and smoothly rapped the edge against the base of the bottle, which flew off smartly leaving a tube of glass behind. Then she yanked on the noose under Constant's chin, loosening it momentarily. The boy gasped instinctively and in the same moment Kit pushed the broken bottle hard into his throat, down into his windpipe, releasing the noose as she did so. The rope tightened instantly as Constant struggled, holding the bottle in his throat. He gagged horribly and twisted as his terrified mind rejected the intrusion.

'Don't panic. Don't panic. Breathe. Breathe deeply. A whiff will do you good. Say your words. Say them kid, say them again and again and again.' Kit met his eye. 'This won't take weight. It won't last forever. You're on your own. I hope you don't die.'

The howling stopped.

Where the woman had fallen a different creature now arose, made new from the annihilation of Blix's body, unrecognisable as her former self. Taller than she, and far more muscular, the female werewolf rose unsteadily to its feet, fur covered in blood from head to toe, looking at the world with new eyes at the moment of its birth.

Kit jumped down and began stripping off her clothes.

'Damned if I'm gonna ruin my shirt again,' she muttered, as she pulled it over her head. 'And these pants cost two dollars!'

The werewolf hadn't moved, and didn't seem to have noticed her. Its gaze was fixed on the wound in Constant's side. The drop of snake oil had tried to heal it, but the spear was still there and it had opened again almost immediately. Blood drenched Constant's side. The werewolf licked its lips. Uncertainly, it took its first step.

'Hi-hi-hi! Over here! Look at me!' Kit danced sideways, waving her shirt wildly above her head, struggling out of the rest of her clothes as she did so.

The werewolf transferred its attention to her.

'That's it, follow me! You want some? Come on, over here!'

The werewolf took another step, steadier now, in Kit's direction. It took another.

'That's it! Oh Jesus, look kindly, I hope this works. Come on, you damn wol-'

Kit stopped suddenly. She stopped dancing around and stared at the creature. Then she spoke, not to the werewolf, but to the woman inside her.

'I'm sorry you have to see this. I hoped you never would. But I'm also sorry I didn't tell you. We shouldn't have secrets. I want to tell you everything.'

The werewolf took another step.

'You think you love me. You don't know what that is yet. But I am inclined to help you find out. Yes, I am. Remember that. I hope you come back.' Kit swallowed hard. 'I hope I come back. Come, now. Dance with me.'

The werewolf lunged. As it did so Kit jumped into the air. In less than a breath the woman was gone and in her place a grey fox floated in the sky, aglow with its own light, its streaming fur touched with silver, shining like ice under a winter moon. Behind it flew not one but nine tails, each thick, white-tipped brush shivering with excitement. Long ears twitched with a curious joy; the vixen darted away from the werewolf's crude charge, then raced back to stop a little way beyond it, further away from the hanging tree.

The werewolf jumped again but the fox was too high. It howled in frustration; in return the fox yipped almost playfully, sporting through the air, swinging to one side or another, swooping and turning and swirling in front of the werewolf, always close to the beast, never within range of the teeth or the claws, never attacking or biting and slowly, so slowly, leading the monster that had been Blix Summerland away from Constant.

And as the fox moved away from the firelight the frost-fire glow surrounding it grew brighter, silver-bright, brighter than the moon in the sky above. As it did so a curious change came over the blood-drenched werewolf. It ceased howling and clawing at the magical creature. The rage and hunger drained away. It gazed at the fox with a strange adoration and when the fox moved, the werewolf moved with it, enraptured by the light of the gambolling spirit it followed.

The werewolf and the nine-tailed fox danced together into the darkness. As they went further, the fox's ghost glow became a will-o-the-wisp in the distance, then a bursting bright spark, then a star-white mote drifting through the sky, a point of light alone in all creation.

Then it was gone.

Constant dreamed.

'Now we are alone,' said the boy. 'And look at you. I think we may have made a very serious mistake.'

Another voice spoke in Constant's mind, which he alone heard.

You're not alone. I have a plan.

Chapter Thirty-Five: The Well of Urd

In my dream, I stand in a field of red poppies. The field turns to waterland as it approaches a river. Unicorns drink and sport in the water margin, rubbing their long whorled horns together affectionately. The sun shines in a rich blue sky, making water and unicorn alike sparkle. The boy stands with me. I recognise him.

'Here we are again,' said the boy.

'Again?'

'Don't you remember? We were here when you died. Before they brought you back.'

'I don't remember.' The landscape felt so real to Constant it was difficult to believe it was all in his head. 'This is... earlier? Or yesterday? I've lost track of time. We stood on the hill and watched gryphons attack these unicorns. Why are we here?'

'It's beautiful,' said the boy. 'You said this moment was the most beautiful you'd ever seen. You think it's a good place to die.'

'Am I dying, then? Really this time?' Constant was surprised how unmoved he was by that thought. The calm the words brought to him seemed to have followed him to this place in his mind.

'It looks like it. You were right about the gorgon blood, obviously, and in other circumstances I think you would have made it. But, of course...'

The boy lifted his hands slightly in a nonchalant what-can-you-do-eh kind of shrug.

'Blix.'

'Yes, a bit unfortunate, her turning into a werewolf just as you needed her and the other one to keep you alive. That magician was awfully smug about it, I thought. "How many moons there are" indeed. Very self-satisfied.'

'He knew about you,' Constant said. 'He saw you in me.'

'Yes, that was a bit concerning,' said the boy, and Constant didn't even need to hear the tension in the boy's terse, studied response to recognise the deep understatement in his words. 'Twice in two days that's happened. Something which should be impossible,' he added, slightly bitterly.

'Two days for us. The first one was really four thousand years ago.'

The scene shifted; they were back in the stable watching the hooded magician talk to the child who would become the first Constant. Now that he'd seen Belmont Dragonville it was obvious that the hooded man was someone else. Before the memory could play out again the stable dissolved away and they were back in the field of poppies.

'How are you doing that?' asked the boy. 'These are my memories. You obliterated yours. You're not supposed to be able to do that.'

'I don't know. I don't suppose it matters, since I'm dying.'

I know. And I'm not going to let you die.

The voice of Darcen Ysir sounded softly inside Constant's mind. Calm, reassuring, but also curiously affectless, as if what he said mattered little to him.

Now would be an excellent time to tell me your plan, Constant thought. But Ysir did not reply.

'I don't suppose it does,' the boy was saying, oblivious to the other voice. 'I'm very sorry.'

Constant watched a unicorn foal gambol through the flowers. It was the same one which had approached Blix, the one which had been killed in the first gryphon attack and carried off into the skies. A life ended in an instant, alive only in his memory.

'Am I really dying?' he said again.

'I'm afraid so. You aren't aware of time? Some has passed. It was a clever idea of the *kitsune* to shove the gorgon blood bottle down your throat, and it kept you alive for longer than you would have lived otherwise, but it just wasn't enough. Hey, at least we know what kind of creature she is now. Mystery solved. Not that it matters to you, but it was playing on my mind.'

'She's a fox.'

'A nine-tailed fox. I must say my money was on her being another werewolf, given her previous association. Werewolf boyfriend,' he added, seeing that Constant didn't understand.

'Won't they save me?' Constant asked, a little plaintively.

'I'm afraid not,' said the boy. 'The girl will be a wolf until dawn. But even if they started back now they wouldn't make it in time.'

'Will it be soon?'

The boy smiled sadly. 'It will be now, Constant. I'm keeping you alive to say goodbye. Soon I'll leave you and join the girl. She's special. Like you.'

'What if she dies when she changes back?'

'Then I will be alone again, in hell,' said the boy soberly. 'And I must hope that a light shines for me somewhere on this world, for I do not know how to find it. But I think she will live. She has the strength. You thought that.'

'You could keep me alive longer,' said Constant suddenly, as a memory popped into his mind. 'You said you kept me alive in the mountains. I should have died of exposure.'

As he remembered it the moment appeared in front of him. Constant saw himself crouching under the overhanging bank of the tiny mountain stream, fighting not to fall asleep and failing at it.

'I look so hurt,' he said, surprising himself with the words. 'I wasn't injured when I fled the Anvil.'

'There are other wounds than those the flesh bears,' the boy said quietly.

They watched the seated boy shiver, nod off, and jerk back awake suddenly. Constant remembered he had dreamed of being Darcen Ysir.

'I imagine there are,' he said. 'You did keep me alive, though.'

'That was cold. This is death.'

The scene changed again; they were back among the unicorns.

The boy opened his mouth to say something, paused, and for the first time looked genuinely unhappy.

'I wish I could, Constant,' he said. 'I do. You matter to me. But I can't.'

'I don't want to join the memories,' said Constant, in a small voice. The boy gave him a sad little smile.

'I'm sorry, Constant. That's what happens. Part of you dies. Part of you remains. That's just the way it is.'

Suddenly Ysir was back, raging in Constant's mind. *He is lying. That is not what happens. That will never happen to you. It is an abomination. I will not allow it.*

If you have a plan Ysir, now is absolutely the time, thought Constant fervently.

It is time. While its guard is down. Take us to the sparrow. Take us to when he was sick.

Then they were on the Anvil, in the apartment of the Great Father, where a boy lay in Constant's bed, dying.

Large parts of his legs had turned black, and there was a foul smell of gangrene. The rest of his flesh was covered with ugly red pustules, which clumped together, swollen like toad flesh, glistening unpleasantly in the firelight. His eyes were open but gazed listlessly into nothing, clouded with a mottled white film. Monks busied themselves sponging his flesh, their faces covered with linen masks, their arms clad in long leather gauntlets. Some of them had the same pustules as the dying child; all of them looked frightened.

The *dybbuk* cringed away from the awful sight, and as he did so, Constant felt the scene he was observing as a flash of memory. A memory of fear, and sadness, and disgust.

'Thirty-six,' said the boy miserably. 'Why have you brought us here? I don't want to be here. I don't want you to see this.' He paused, and then said, 'Why can't I make us leave? What are you doing, Constant?'

Don't tell him about me. Think about the sparrow. Think about the thing the monster has kept from you, that I now see clearly.

'I don't know,' Constant replied truthfully. 'There was a memory...'

He opened himself to the life of the dying youth. Remembered, as he had before, his joyful days as a little boy on the island with his father, his recognition by the monks and then, afterward, coming to the Anvil, a child who loved his father now become Great Father of the Faith. And then, a cough. Just a cough, going around, as these things do where people live and work. And then -

'You're keeping him alive,' said Constant flatly. 'The thing you just said you wouldn't do for me, you did for him.'

'It's not like that,' the boy objected, but Constant interrupted him before he could get any further.

'Yes, it is. That's exactly what it's like.' He moved closer to the child, his memory, himself. He could hear the pathetic rattling in his lungs, the long gaps between breaths. More than that now, he could feel them, remember them. 'You're holding him. He should have died... days ago? Weeks? You won't let him.'

'I don't want to talk about it. And he's dying. You're dead.'

'I don't think I'm dead. You'd have left if I was. I'm not holding you.' He watched his predecessor with a mixture of sorrow and compassion, knowing this had all happened long in the past, thousands of years before he was born, but still wishing he could take a cloth from one of the monks and bathe the boy's brow. To give him solace before the wheel turned for him.

'You're... keeping him going? Yes. You could keep me going.'

'I can't,' said the boy, in an anguished whisper. 'I can't.'

Constant searched his memory some more. Whatever barrier had prevented him from remembering this moment was now completely gone. 'And you keep him going for... Great Fathers, almost six months.'

'I can't. Please.'

Ysir's voice insinuated itself into Constant's thoughts once more.

Now take us to the frustrated one. The one who wanted to leave. Take us to his worst moment. It won't let you remember, but I *remember.*

They were in the Sanctum, in the heights of the Monastery. A fierce storm whipped stinging rain across the open platform; the Flame Eternal sputtered and spat, but burned on.

Backed against the chest-high balustrade which bordered the Sanctum on three sides, Palden Ngapoi, Constant the Thirty-Second, wild-eyed and soaked to the skin, held off three other monks with the silver sword now called Sorcha. He looked older than when last Constant had dreamed of him, but not much. One of the monks was Brother Jamyang, who held out his hands placatingly, inching forward when the blade was elsewhere, ducking away when it swung back toward him.

'Great Father, please hear me,' he said, his gentle voice straining to be heard over the storm. 'Please listen. You are not well.'

'WHAT'S HAPPENING TO ME?' screamed Ngapoi, scraping his free hand across his scalp hard enough to draw blood.

'Great Father, please listen,' Jamyang tried again. 'There was a plant, in the last delivery, there by mistake. It has something in it which makes men fear. Makes them see things that are not there. Seven brothers are afflicted, like you. It will pass. Brother Laurin has a potion which eases it, come to the infirmary, please.'

'YOU'RE LYING!' screeched Ngapoi, swinging the blade wildly. The brothers scattered, skidding across the flagstones away from the sword. Jamyang ducked but held his ground.

'Great Father, please.'

'JAMYANG! I WANT JAMYANG! GET AWAY FROM ME MONSTER! WHAT ARE YOU? HELP ME!'

'Great Father,' began Jamyang, but got no further. Ngapoi, crazed and foaming at the mouth, flailed the weapon at his tutor, lurching forward at the same time. Jamyang moved, but not fast enough. The silvered edge cut deeply into his right shoulder and continued down across his chest as Ngapoi pulled the sword away. Brother Jamyang gave a short, sharp scream and went down, blood pumping from his suddenly useless arm.

Ngapoi didn't seem to see the wounded man. Instead he swung the blade up and back at imaginary demons above him, cursing vilely. Then he dropped the sword and clutched his head in his hands. He shouted something unintelligible and started climbing the balustrade. As one the monks cried out 'No!' but their cries were not heard.

'I HAVE TO LEAVE!' he screamed. 'I HAVE TO LEAVE, I HAVE TO LEAVE, I HAVE TO LEAVE!'

The young man leapt high and up and over, out into the sky, out into oblivion.

And now we see, said Ysir.

As Ngapoi cleared the lip of the rail he was hurled backward, seemingly plucked out of the air by some invisible hand and tossed back onto the hard stone. He landed heavily, hit his head hard on the flags, skidded to a halt, and lay still.

Brother Jamyang wailed as if it was him who had fallen and, careless of his wound, scrambled across to the unconscious boy. He cradled him in his one good arm, rocking him back and forth and crying inconsolably. And as he lay there, Constant felt the memory of weight upon his chest, and somehow felt the spread of rust-red tendrils across Palden Ngapoi's torso, a spider's web of magic.

'What am I seeing?' he said, unsure for a moment which of the voices in his head he was asking the question of.

'I had no choice,' said the boy looking as though he would rather be anywhere else. 'He would have...'

'Died,' Constant finished, as the boy trailed off. 'He would have died. Like I am dying.'

'It's not the same,' the boy said, refusing to meet Constant's eyes.

'No, it's not,' Constant agreed. 'It's worse. You took control and you did magic through him to save his life. The magic left its mark. I can't see it under his robe, but I remember it now. You hid it from us.'

'These aren't your memories,' muttered the boy. 'Stop using them. It's not fair.'

'Oh well. My apologies, of course. I wouldn't want to be unfair.'

The boy looked up nastily. 'Sarcasm doesn't suit you. You're normally so earnest. When did you learn to do that?'

'Recently.' Constant watched as the monks gently lifted his still stunned antecedent and carried him out of the storm. 'Did he survive? And Jamyang?'

'Yes. Jamyang never used the arm again, but they both lived until their proper time. It brought them closer together.'

'I am pleased. So, you used magic to stop that Constant from killing himself. But you won't lift a finger for me.'

'I keep telling you, it's not the same,' the boy said, somehow sounding truculent and anguished at the same time.

Nearly there. Now take us to me. The moment of my death.

They were back in the Great Father's apartment. Constant knew without knowing that it was many hundreds of years later than their previous visit. A different set of monks hovered at the bedside of a dying ancient. The old man was shrunken and emaciated compared to the warrior Constant both remembered and felt beside him in his mind. The old Ysir still clung on though. Every now and then he took a ragged breath, only to gasp it out again almost immediately.

I thought I was fighting, said the Ysir in Constant's mind. *Fighting until my last breath. But it was a lie. He was holding me. Stretching my life beyond my time. For years.*

'Fifty-eight again?' The boy said. 'We've seen this. He was just old. Let's go somewhere else. He was just old,' he said again, as though trying to convince himself of something, never mind convincing Constant.

That's not true. Confront him.

'That's not true,' Constant repeated. He tried to form the thought that Ysir was pushing him toward, which had a shape in his mind now but was still just out of reach. 'You made him stay,' he tried, a little tentatively. 'Yes. All of them? Yes. It wasn't about keeping them alive. You... you needed them to stay.'

'No.'

'Yes, that's right, because, you live inside us, and when we die you leave and go to the next Constant, but...'

'No!'

'... but you couldn't leave, because -'

'Because there was no one else!' the boy shouted. Suddenly he was raging, an anger suffused with fear so powerful that Constant stepped backward without meaning to. For a moment, he thought the boy might really hit him.

'Yes, all right! Are you happy now?' the boy said savagely. 'There was no-one special! I would have been cast out, into the agony. I couldn't live like that again, I couldn't, I couldn't! I would have had to go into a monk and I couldn't, I just couldn't! I couldn't destroy another mind. I told you Constant, being you has changed me. So, I waited. I gave them my energy. I spent myself to keep them going after their time, to stop them dying, so I didn't become a murderer again. Kept them until I saw the light in the darkness. The Constant, shining for me. Then I let them go. That isn't wrong. That isn't wrong.'

The emotion drained out of him with his last words. He stood staring at his feet, avoiding Constant's eyes.

'But you won't keep me,' Constant said.

'You're dead, Constant. The girl is special. She's still alive. I can go to her.'

'I'm not dead,' Constant insisted, knowing it was true without knowing how. 'Something remains. You're still holding me. Hold me until she comes.'

Something dark entered the boy's tone. Although he still sounded like the boy Constant had come to know, the way he spoke made Constant think of the wretched half-things the boy had shown him; it was a voice which called up the real *dybbuk* behind the facade he presented.

'You don't understand,' he said. 'This is what they do. The others. They keep the dead alive. It costs them nothing. They don't hold them. They rot. This will cost me everything. You can't understand.'

Press, thought Ysir. *Press on its weakness.*

No, thought Constant.

It was as if time stood still. Constant, the boy, Ysir - the only voices in this false world of memory and mind, all were silent.

No, Constant thought again. *That is just more coercion. That is not the way. It's not* my *way. I have to learn.*

Constant...

No. I am the path that I walk as I am he that walks it, yet I can choose the path I walk. I do not compel others to walk with me.

Constant!

I will tell him the truth.

'It should cost you,' Constant said slowly. 'You've done terrible things. There has been no justice. You haven't been punished. You've paid no man price. What is the word the All-men use? No *weregild.* You aren't even penitent, not really, you keep doing it - yes, you don't kill anymore,' he continued as the boy tried to interject, 'but is what you do any better? You... enslaved me, really. Made me live my life to your will.'

The scene changed once more. They were back on the Anvil, standing in front of the red gates, as Brother Simon took the infant Constant for the first time, and Recognised him.

'You took me from my mother's arms,' Constant said.

'You'd have died with her,' said the boy quietly. 'Died when the werewolves came.'

'Would they have come? I don't know. If so, that would have been my time. This is not my time. The prophet saw that.'

They watched Simon cradle the infant with a gentleness which went beyond love, but included it as well.

'I forgive you,' Constant said, so unaffectedly that the boy gasped with astonishment. 'That is unconditional. I mean it. Whether you save me or not. Your soul is your own. Know that you are loved. But what life do you want to live, now? For all the lives you took. The first, the woman, and all those in between. How will you live for them?'

The boy gaped awkwardly, and said nothing, but tears streamed freely down his cheeks. And although Constant knew they were not real tears, because the boy was not real and nothing he was seeing was really happening, he knew that they were real enough.

They were back where they'd started, among the wild poppies. Constant knelt in front of the boy and lowered himself into a half bow, his arms wide in supplication; the prayer pose of the Night Prayer, in which he opened himself to the immanent universe.

'I am ready to live or die,' he said. 'I want to live. Hold me in your arms.'

After a lifetime, or perhaps just a heartbeat, the boy spoke, his voice thick with emotion.

'Not unto my death. You can't ask that.'

'I don't ask that. Hold me until you have to let go.'

Another lifetime, another heartbeat.

'There is no guarantee. You might still die.'

'I accept that.'

Two hearts, beating. Two, or seventy, or hundreds, or just one. And then:

'I will. Yes, I will. But you won't like it, Constant. You won't. It will cost you too. Even if you live it will cost you a lot. Are you sure you want this?'

The scene changed once more. They were back in the Great Father's apartment again, where the five-year-old Constant sat with the man he thought of as his father, eating breakfast and talking.

'You have to be who you are,' Brother Simon said. 'You don't have to let it rule you.'

'I hope you're right,' the young Constant replied.

'I hope so too,' Simon said. 'Hope carries us when we cannot lift ourselves. Have hope. And faith. Faith carries us when hope fails.'

Then Constant and the *dybbuk* were back among the poppies. Constant lowered his head.

'I know my own mind,' he said.

The boy stared at him, the depths of his gaze unfathomable.

'Remember I warned you,' he said.

Constant said no more.

Well done, Constant. You bent him to your will like a master.

That's not what I did. I meant it. I forgive him. I am ready to live or die.

Now it was Ysir's turn to be silent, but only for a moment.

Oh, Constant. You are too innocent to live in this world. But I will free us. I will. Yes, I will.

Chapter Thirty-Six: The Wolf Age

There was nothing but pain. No thought but pain. The pain of shredded flesh, a breaking agony, like acid corroding the soul of his heart. Unrelenting, electric in its intensity. It consumed him even as it made him anew.

New lungs, piled obscenely with the other shreds of offal in his divided body, sucked down ragged gulps of air through the gaping wound. It was enough. Oxygen sputtered through his blood and into his brain. He wanted to scream - wanted to do nothing but scream forever - but his throat remained torn. His body bucked and writhed as the wolf magic knitted new flesh and bone. Slowly, so slowly, the half became whole, and as it did the First of Wolves remembered himself. Who he was. How he had been killed. The hate he felt, that burnt through him more fiercely than the pain. And when he could scream again he did not do so, knowing it would only summon the cyclops. He endured, and grew, and was remade, fur as grey as stone covering his trembling flesh.

When the pain receded the First of Wolves arose and returned to the gate. He had no sense of how much time had passed. Days, certainly. The corpses of his pack were not fresh.

He noted without emotion the silver wounds that kept his pack dead. Wolves died. These had died with honour. He took a moment to appreciate the clever trap he had walked into. Clever, but foolish. *What if the cyclops had not come? I would be standing over their corpses now. They were lucky. They have been lucky before. Luck is not to be underestimated. Or perhaps it is magic.*

'It does not matter,' he said aloud. 'I will have my blood.'

Then he saw himself, the half of his body which had been left behind. The First of Wolves had received terrible wounds in the past, but nothing like this. More terrible than the wounds was the sight of his own face. He wondered briefly how his body had known which side of him to regrow from. If the silver had not destroyed this half of him, would it have regrown instead? Or as well, would there have been two of him? To be living and at the same time dead was wrong. He felt wrong.

Wolves do not feel like this. Why am I different? Why am I like this? Wolves do not ask why. Wolves only follow, and act. Only the Wolfmaker is like me. What sets us apart? Questions with no answers.

He took up the torn pouch. The magic things were not there. But the things which mattered were. The hair from his dead mate. The hair from his dead cub.

My cub was not like me. He would not have felt my death as I feel his.

With this thought the rage returned. 'I will follow,' he said aloud. But the gem was gone. So was the lens, and the buzzing rock that tormented his ears. No key to open the gate, no eye to see, no guide to follow their path.

I am a wolf. In this at least I am a wolf. I will follow. I will hunt. The moon will lead me.

The First of Wolves knew how magic worked. You said the words with enough strength and what you wanted, happened. But without power there was a price, a terrible price, to be paid in suffering. The First of Wolves knew why Dragonville smelled of rust.

I know what I can endure. I have the strength.

Aloud he said, 'Elysium. *Come and see.'*

The land crumbled into rust. The First of Wolves screamed, and kept screaming, and was gone.

Continued in

Fox Silver

About the Author

David McLean was born in London, grew up in North-East England, and now lives in London again, with his wife and son. The Wolf in the Blood is his first novel. It is the first in a series.

Visit

https://sites.google.com/swordsaintpress.co.uk/thewolfintheblood

for book and series information and exclusive content.

Acknowledgements and Thanks

This book began life as a commentary on the tropes of fantasy. I got over that and most of it got cut, but some still remains. Who doesn't like a giant waterfall or desert world, after all?

Primarily it is about consent, and choice, and how these concepts are handled in worlds where magic exists, and what it says about how we think about them in the real* world. Related to that, it is also about memory, and its role in our sense of self, and what it means when it goes away. I don't think these are original ideas (claims of originality in fantastic literature made later than the *Epic of Gilgamesh* should be treated with caution); nonetheless, that's the idea.

All books are made of other books. I would specifically like to acknowledge books which became references, over the long gestation and writing period of this novel.

J.A. Coleman's *Dictionary of Mythology;* Julian Cope's *Modern Antiquarian* and *Megalithic European,* and his albums; Jorge Luis Borges' *The Book of Imaginary Beings* and *Labyrinths;* Jennifer Westwood and Jaqueline Simpson's *The Lore of the Land;* Jonathon Green's *Cassell's Dictionary of Slang; Bede's Ecclesiastical History of the World;* Michael Largo's *Big Bad Book of Beasts*; Robert Graves' *The Greek Myths;* Caspar Henderson's *Book of Barely Imagined Beings;* Norman Davies' *Vanished Kingdoms: The history of half-forgotten Europe;* Carl Jung's *The Red Book;* Richard Cohen's *By The Sword.* If I have omitted any this is unintentional, and I'll correct it the future. You should buy these books.

My thanks to the friends and family who offered the use of their eyeballs to read through the book: My wife, Fiona Colley; Wai-Ming Lee; Iain Huntington; Greg Hobbs.

This book is dedicated to Fiona and Tommy.

How This Book Was Written

This book was written almost entirely with my right thumb (I estimate about 95%). I wrote it and largely edited it on a series of iPhones, starting on a 4 and finishing on a 7. I used Google Docs and Drive to write it in.

It took over five years to finish the first draft. Most of this time was spent not writing; I stopped writing almost completely for almost a year in the middle. This is the first in a series; I will write faster.

This book is published in beta. This means I almost certainly haven't found all the typos. Also, I may rewrite in future editions, especially if Big Publishing offers me money. I think you're probably safe on this point, but, no refunds.

You can do this too.

D.M.

London, September 2018

Printed in Great Britain
by Amazon

67878060R00296